'Beautifully captures what it means to find both meaning and refuge in community ... This book is a gift'

NICOLE CHUNG, author of *All You Can Ever Know*

'Min Jin Lee is phenomenally the real thing ... I read huge swaths of this book with my heart in my throat and found myself cheering'

JACQUELINE WOODSON, author of *Red At The Bone*

'A profound and moving meditation on the question of what it means to live a meaningful life ... confirms what has long been true: Min Jin Lee is one of the best writers of our time'

CLINT SMITH, author of *How the Word Is Passed*

'After 600 pages, how could I want more? And yet I did, and that is the magic of Min Jin Lee'

TAHMIMA ANAM, author of *Uprising*

'A timeless and universal story of people dreaming and striving for a better life ... Lee is a writer in full command of her craft'

CHARLES YU, author of *Interior Chinatown*

'Magnificent – a deep education from a master storyteller ... A work of grace and beauty that unspools one thread at a time, much like life itself'

MATTHEW DESMOND, author of *Evicted*

'Yearning and forbearance, grace and devastation, course through these pages ... Lee has written a novel that both speaks to the world and illuminates Korean history and culture'

IMANI PERRY, author of *Black in Blues*

Also by Min Jin Lee

Free Food for Millionaires

Pachinko

AMERICAN HAGWON

MIN JIN LEE

4th ESTATE • *London*

4th Estate
An imprint of HarperCollinsPublishers
1 London Bridge Street
London SE1 9GF

4thestate.co.uk

HarperCollinsPublishers
Macken House, 39/40 Mayor Street Upper
Dublin 1, D01 C9W8, Ireland

First published in Great Britain in 2026 by 4th Estate
First published in the US in 2026 by Grand Central Publishing

1

Print book interior design by Taylor Navis

A catalogue record for this book is available from the British Library

ISBN 978-0-00-882390-0 (Hardback)
ISBN 978-0-00-882391-7 (Trade paperback)

Set in ITC New Baskerville Std
Printed and bound in the UK using 100% renewable electricity at CPI Group (UK) Ltd

MIX
Paper | Supporting responsible forestry
FSC® C013604
FSC www.fsc.org

To my teachers and students,
in whose debt I remain

Contents

BOOK I

March 1992–January 1995

The paradox of education is this—that as one begins to become conscious one begins to examine the society in which one is being educated.

—James Baldwin

1

Return

Gaepo-dong, Seoul, South Korea
March 1992

The rules of engagement have changed already.

Within a month of their arrival from Australia, Mrs. Helen Koh found her family a suitable apartment in a good school district in Seoul. The middle-class neighborhood of Gaepo was not as nice as the one where her sister, Sonya, lived, but it had to suffice. After paying key money for the two-year lease, a painful sum that consumed the bulk of the family's savings, and replacing the most urgent things before the shipping container from Sydney could be delivered, Helen accepted that there just wasn't room in the budget for any place better.

Their rental house in Campsie, a suburb of Sydney, had four bedrooms, a den, and a generous backyard for cookouts. Their Seoul apartment, on the third floor of a five-year-old building put up quickly by mediocre developers, had three small bedrooms, a decent-size living room, and two baths. The largest bedroom went to the two boys, Bo and DH; Helen and her husband, John, occupied the medium-size bedroom; and the tiny one near the foyer was for Mido, the child Helen worried about the most.

From the outset of their marriage, John had put his sensible wife in charge of the household finances. Helen's thrift and good judgment allowed him to focus on his career. For almost two decades, on Monday mornings, Helen had given John a weekly allowance for his carfare, meals, and pocket money; then it was her job to make do with the remainder of his salary for their tithes, living expenses, and retirement savings, if any, and in that order. A former math major at Seoul National University, John preferred problems he could solve on paper, and family life had far too many unknown variables.

Raising three children was costly, and when they were still young, Helen began working as a retail sales associate to supplement John's steady income, which was inadequate for their mounting needs. John's work had taken the Koh family to Paramus, Seoul, and Sydney. In each city, Helen's supervisors recognized her talent as a reliable salesperson.

For each of the three Koh children, Helen kept a spiral notebook, and on the back flap, she pasted a manila envelope where she tucked away cash for their school fees, clothing, and sundries. This year's envelopes were lighter than usual because the children had needed many new things upon their return to Korea. In addition to school uniforms, Bo and DH required larger sneakers, thicker winter coats, and stacks of study guides. Mido, the youngest, had not grown as much as her brothers, so her wardrobe would serve another year; however, in Sydney, she had needed to see learning specialists, which had wiped out her portion of the savings.

Mido was thirteen years old and in the first year of the local middle school. She was short and slight for her age, and often mistaken for a much younger child. Like her father, Mido had small, round eyes that formed an endearing expression when she smiled. And like him, she had perfect vision and didn't need to wear eyeglasses, which Bo had required since he was a toddler. Mido wore her dark hair parted in the middle in two thick braids, which suited her pale, unremarkable demeanor.

Although Mido could speak well enough, she seemed almost incapable of doing so at school, church, or anywhere else outside the home. With her family she spoke as needed, and around her father, Mido was especially at ease. On Saturday evenings, after Mido finished her homework and household chores, the two of them watched music variety programs on television, smiling and laughing in a wordless cocoon.

All the children were born in Paramus, New Jersey, when John worked at a Japanese trading company in New York City and reported to Taehun Shin, who had been one year his senior at university. Shin had been like a brother to John throughout school, military service in the elite KATUSA unit where their English-language skills only improved, and at both the Japanese and Korean trading companies, which had allowed the men's families to live overseas as subsidized expatriates. The Koh family had lived in New Jersey for seven years, Seoul for three, then Sydney for almost six, prior to their return to Seoul one month before the start of this school term.

Throughout her childhood, Mido's teachers had asked Helen to come in to discuss her daughter's excessively quiet manner. At her preschool in Paramus, and in the first years of school in Seoul, Mido barely spoke with the other children and was left out of friendships. At her primary school in Sydney, the teachers had hinted at learning issues, despite her high marks. They'd encouraged her to talk more in class, advocate for herself, and work better in groups.

Helen saw herself as a modern, educated parent, and she wanted to help her youngest child. She took time off from work and visited a learning specialist, a speech therapist, and an occupational therapist. The doctors in Sydney pronounced Mido normal, more or less. A reputable pediatrician said there was nothing medically wrong with the girl's hearing or vocal cords. The child psychologist believed that Mido's shyness was cultural, and all the moving around might have confused her. Asian children, the school counselor had observed, were often less talkative.

Mido's father, a high-functioning introvert who managed the natural resources department at a multinational trading company, dismissed such simplistic nonsense. Not all Koreans were quiet. His own family had been filled with loud people. At the slightest provocation or encouragement, his mother, father, and elder brother would shout and argue their well-articulated opinions. To be left alone, John had retreated into his studies, excelling at math and foreign languages. As an adult, he did not ask for much in life. He enjoyed listening to music and being in the presence of his wife and three children.

John wanted to comfort his dear Helen, who was clearly troubled that their daughter did not have friends. Throughout her own childhood, Helen, like her elder sister, was a natural leader—engaging, kind, and deliberate in her goals and methods, articulate in both Korean and English. In college, she had served as vice president of an English poetry society and secretary of a music appreciation group. Helen took her daughter's difficulties personally.

John felt less anxious about his daughter's prospects. Mido was a seventh grader who read at a college level. The other children did not appreciate her, he reasoned. When ready, she would speak up, make friends, and find the work she was meant to do. She would grow out of this social reticence. Helen, a devout woman, prayed he was right. Maybe Mido would be more outgoing if her self-assured brothers didn't crowd her with their larger personalities, or if the Koh family hadn't moved across the world every few years.

John Koh wanted things to be equal for his sons and daughter but recognized their innate personality differences. Above all, he wanted to protect his daughter's peace of mind. All this poking around and extra attention couldn't be good for her. If you looked hard enough, you could always find something wrong. The world was too noisy. It was fine for Mido to be her own way, to seek privacy and solitude.

As might be expected of a child who read a great deal and hardly talked, Mido received admirable grades; however, on her report cards, her teachers often commented, "Mido is a fine student and a good girl. What is concerning is her lack of social relationships."

Helen was accustomed to her sons' strong school performance and popularity. Bo was a standout student, the teachers' perennial favorite, and DH was an exceptional soccer player. Helen was the sort who needed to fix things, and she wanted to know what she could do to bolster her daughter's self-esteem. Mido didn't have to be school president, the prettiest, or the top student; Helen simply wanted her child to be included.

Although Helen had not wanted to return to Seoul, preferring to raise the children abroad to enlarge their opportunities, there was some consolation: Mido's shyness seemed almost commonplace in Korea. A child could be quieter here.

❧

The middle school was six blocks from the main shopping street and less than a ten-minute walk from the Kohs' apartment. The four-story cinder-block building with a slate roof, whitewashed and with a dark-blue trim, housed numerous classrooms, a spacious auditorium, two music rooms, and a new gymnasium. There was a well-maintained field for the three grades of boys and girls. Mido did not attend the coveted middle school in Gangnam, which sent the greatest number of students to the desirable specialized public high schools in the city, but her school was far from the worst.

In Mido's homeroom class, there were forty-six students. Mr. Na, the homeroom teacher who also taught mathematics, assigned Mido to sit in the second row.

Seated directly behind her was an attractive child with dark, large eyes. A formidable student, Yun Kim was also known for being a brilliant sprinter and a fine keyboard player. Each year, her homeroom teacher selected her as the classroom president because her peers listened to her. In the morning, Yun's mother French-braided her only child's shoulder-length raven hair, and although all the girls wore matching uniforms, Yun stood out by wearing American sneakers.

As classroom president, Yun was expected to help Mido, the new student from Australia, assimilate. On the first day of school, it was Yun who told Mido where to put her lunch box, where and when to change into her sports uniform, and what clubs she could join, as well as where all the meeting rooms were located. Mido did as instructed, not bothering Yun with any unnecessary questions, and as usual, she kept to herself. Ever an attentive child, Mido was able to pick up from observation whatever she needed to know.

To make up for her silence around the other girls, Mido smiled often, her eyes curving along her round, pink cheeks. Most adults liked her sweet face, but her classmates would not have considered her as pretty as Yun, whose symmetrical features were often commented upon with great admiration. Mido's lack of distinguishing physical charms did not bother her; if anything, she was relieved not to be noticed.

On the third day of school, shortly before lunch recess, Mr. Na called on Bora Kang to solve a math problem. On the bulletin board by the front door, the teachers posted weekly exam scores, and more often than not, Bora's name was at the top of the lists.

Bora, a serious girl who wore a different-colored headband each day, marched to the board, solved the problem neatly, wiped the chalk dust from her right hand, and returned to her seat in the last row by the window. She tucked her navy pleated skirt beneath her bottom before sitting, then smoothed the front of her skirt to cover the tops of her thighs.

Mido checked Bora's answer on the chalkboard against her worksheet. There was an error. Mido should not have multiplied the numerator. She rubbed the worn-down ear of her blue-and-white puppy eraser against the pencil markings and started again.

Mr. Na called out, "Koh Mido," and she looked up from her paper and smiled at her teacher.

"Number three," he said, pointing to the board.

Mido swallowed and approached the chalkboard gingerly, bringing her worksheet with her. She copied her answer on the board with great care.

"Incorrect," he said, shaking his head in disappointment. Out of consideration for her recent arrival in the country, he had assigned her a relatively simple problem.

Mido bit the inside of her lip, then checked her solution against the way Bora had solved the previous question. She had made the same computation error as before by multiplying the numerator. Using quick strokes of the chalkboard eraser, Mido wiped off her wrong answer, smudging the edge of her blue sweater sleeve, to begin again.

"Who told you that you could do that?"

Startled by Mr. Na's stern tone, Mido froze.

"How can you learn if you do not recognize, admit, and explain your mistake? It does no one any good if you do not point out your error. You erased the error, so now no one can learn from what you did wrong. Erasing it is like covering a weakness. It's lying. It's cowardice and selfish."

Mr. Na had been a college basketball player and became a sports radio announcer in Daegu after graduation. When he couldn't support his family by working at a local radio station doing a job he adored, he had labored hard to become a middle school mathematics teacher for his second career, eventually landing in the capital city with his wife and two children. Female teachers and administrators admired the handsome former athlete, and the male teachers looked up to him for his discipline and dunking skills.

"Koh Mido," Mr. Na said in his rich tenor voice. "Did you hear my question? How can you learn if you do not admit and then explain your error?"

Perplexed, Mido glanced at him, then lowered her gaze just as quickly, having no idea what he wanted her to do now. Was she supposed to write back in her mistake? Tears filled her eyes.

Crying never moved Mr. Na. It only made things worse. If girls were to succeed in the world, he believed, they had to be more stoic. As a father, he was as tough on his daughter as he was on his son. Life was full of terrible disappointment and cruelty, and he didn't see the pedagogical purpose of coddling these middle-class girls, who had no idea how easy they had it compared to his generation and the ones before it.

The teacher crossed his arms and frowned. He didn't like her face—the features were too soft and little, and her head was not yet in proportion to her small body. Mr. Na preferred girls to be bright like a new coin, visually engaging as the loveliest of flowers and with the vitality of youth in their movements. No doubt this girl was an unmotivated, overindulged child from a rich family that had lived overseas. He ascribed her puny size to her being a picky eater.

"Go stand by my desk."

Mido approached the teacher's large wooden desk near the windowed door. Across the hall, uniformed boys and girls lined up in size order against the tile-bordered wall. She wished she could bolt through the classroom door and hide in a bathroom stall until her heart stopped pounding so fiercely.

"Hold out your hands," Mr. Na said.

Incomprehension clouded her shining eyes.

"Like this." Mr. Na held out his large, strong ballplayer's hands, pale palms facing upward.

Mido crinkled her brow and imitated him. Her palms were three colors, more white and pink in the center and bluish around the thumbs and fingers. She had never given much thought to her body, least of all her own tiny hands.

From his pencil cup, Mr. Na withdrew his brass ruler, one of the classroom supplies he'd bought with his first paycheck as a teacher.

He raised his right hand and struck her open palms with the heavy ruler.

"One," he said quietly.

Mido grimaced, stunned by the sharp pain.

The class pitied Mido. She'd had no warning. No one had told her that this was something that happened. The only way to avoid this shame was by getting the answer right, or if the teacher had an understanding with your mother. Things could be different if your father was an important person.

As a class leader, Yun felt especially guilty for not having mentioned Mr. Na's golden ruler, which left red welts across a child's soft palms.

Tears flowed down Mido's cheeks, and she regulated her breath the way Dr. Ryan had taught her to whenever she was afraid. Everyone was watching her get punished, but she had to keep breathing. The gentle, gray-haired doctor from Sydney had told her that when she felt fear or worry, Mido had to keep inhaling and exhaling. *It will be fine,* he'd said. *Breathe.*

"Two," Mr. Na said calmly, then raised the metric ruler with a flourish and swung down.

"Three."

The class heard the final smack of the metal hitting skin, and the girl stood in her place without a murmur. The children knew this was the last time.

Three strikes for the third problem.

Mido wiped her cheeks with the back of her left hand. Only after Mr. Na tilted his chin toward her desk did she bow to the teacher and return to her seat.

"Students, lunchtime," Mr. Na said, his voice elegant and reasonable. He left the room.

❧

Yun retrieved her lunch box and Mido's from the shelves next to where the textbooks were stored. She placed them both on her desk. The other students opened their sacks and fabric-tied parcels, transforming their homeroom into a noisy dining hall.

"Follow me," Yun said.

The girls walked down the long hallway, and Yun pulled Mido into the washroom.

"I hate him," Yun whispered. "A real son of a bitch," she said, savoring the forbidden salt of the insult, and smiled at Mido, revealing her matching dimples.

Mido blinked back tears. She had gotten the problem wrong, so she was at fault. But no one had ever hit her before. Not at home or school.

Yun opened the water faucet.

"You'll feel better after you wash your face. Go ahead," Yun said, and Mido obeyed. From her pocket, Yun retrieved a clean white handkerchief.

"Dry your face. You can't pay attention to that fool."

Mido had never heard any girl talk like this. Even her brothers didn't use these words. At her school in Sydney, you could be sent to the principal's office for name-calling. In their homeroom, Yun was an ideal and well-spoken student. In the washroom, she was someone else. Even her pretty face seemed less placid, her teeth clenched, her jaw firm, and in her anger, the cords of her thin neck had become more visible.

Yun examined Mido's hands. There were pink stripes across the meat of her palms.

"Most of the teachers here are pretty nice and never hit us, but I'd heard about Mr. Na from the older students. I'm sorry I didn't tell you." Yun let out a short laugh. "My mother says it's my fault when the teacher hits me. My father says it's good for me to get the shit kicked out of me by the teacher because then I'll study harder."

Mido couldn't imagine her parents thinking hitting was necessary.

Yun stared hard at Mido's face, trying to read any meaning behind her dark eyes. Since school started, the new girl had barely spoken beyond faint murmurs of assent for roll call. Somehow Mido's silence had not troubled Yun. In a way, she felt more drawn to the new student. Mido made Yun feel useful, which she liked.

"But I disagree with them," Yun added. "I don't study harder because the teachers could hit me. I don't usually get hit, but I don't want to watch anyone else get in trouble, either. I just hate the teachers who do this. There must be other ways to make your point." She shrugged. "Anyway, save yourself some trouble at home, and don't tell your parents what happened today."

Yun glanced in the metal mirror, then looked away as quickly as if the pretty girl in the reflection were a surprise to her.

"Just imagine if you had messed up problem ten." Yun raised both her hands, splaying all ten fingers. "Ten smacks." She giggled.

"Mr. Na doesn't know anything. He won't teach you, but he expects you to get the right answers. If you get something wrong, he'll hit you again and again. I heard that when he gets really fired up, he can use the broomstick on your legs. The ruler's not so bad, I guess. Two years ago, I heard he hit a boy so hard that he bled on the back of his calves. Even his mom came in to complain. Not that it did any good."

With an imaginary broom handle, Yun's wiry arms made dramatic swinging motions below Mido's knees. She shivered, realizing then that the joke was more scary than funny, and she looked down at her clean white leather sneakers.

Yun turned serious. "Mido, are you bad at math? I don't want you to feel worse, but that problem wasn't the toughest one of the group today."

Mido shook her head no. In Sydney, she'd received perfect grades in mathematics. But here the math was far more advanced, forcing her to read and reread the textbook every night. Homework took more time. Her brothers, too, had complained about it. Bedtime kept getting pushed back because of the difficulty of the school assignments.

"Maybe you have to change your hagwon," Yun said.

Mido looked at her blankly.

Yun leaned against the long communal sink.

"When's your birthday?" She turned to Mido. "Mine's October ninth. I'm short, and everyone thinks I'm the youngest, but I'm not. You're not tall, either. Are you older than me?"

Mido shrugged.

"When? When is your birthday?" Suddenly Yun felt entitled to an answer.

At last, Mido replied, "October first."

Yun tapped Mido's shoulder with her bony fist.

"*Yaah!* You do talk. I knew you did."

Mido looked confused, unable to comprehend why everyone cared so much about speaking all the time.

"Eight days' difference is nothing. We're almost twins. We could have been in the hospital at the same time." Yun grasped Mido's left hand.

"Let's go eat. My mother put sausages and dumplings in my lunch box today, and I have a box of Pepero. I'll give you some. You know what? You should go to Eagle Academy with me. For English, I have Sean Teacher. I study math with Henry Teacher. They're from America. Henry Teacher went to MIT. That's a better school than Harvard for math and science. I'll get my mother to call your mother. My parents want me to go to college in America, so I go to this special hagwon run by Americans. I mean, they're Korean but not really. They're *gyopo*." Yun paused. "I guess like you. Anyway."

Mido followed Yun at a respectful distance, taking care not to step on the girl's shadow. The classroom president walked with purpose down the wide, yellow-linoleum-covered hallway flanked by rows of classrooms. At their desk, as they ate their lunches, Yun chatted to the quiet girl, who nodded and smiled. Her new friend had everything figured out for them, and Mido felt grateful to be in her care.

2

Envelopes

No one had expected Mido's teacher to make a home visit.

The living room was furnished with five gray metal folding chairs and two laminate conference tables, one serving as the children's desk and the other as the dining table. The rental apartment still lacked rugs, paintings, and books. It took no time at all for Helen to sweep the bare floors each morning. For the time being, the children slept in sleeping bags, and Helen and John on bedding from Helen's older sister, Sonya. Except for clothing and toiletries, Sonya had loaned them everything, as she had done years before. There was no reason to buy expensive mattresses or pots and pans when their own household things would arrive in two months. It was like camping, Helen told her family, and the children had not complained.

Helen was filling out the application papers for a part-time sales position at the Lotte duty-free store. It was a job that would enable her to get home in time to prepare dinner and help the children with their homework. Helen didn't care much for luxury handbags or expensive face creams; however, having sold enough products in so many places to all different kinds of customers, she had learned to appreciate better-made goods, and understood the value of an expensive and rare gift. Here in Seoul, as a Korean citizen with strong English-language skills, she could work at the nicest places. If she could get thirty or forty hours a week with commissions, she would be able to send the children to a good hagwon and save.

The buzzer sounded, and when Helen answered the intercom, to her surprise, it was Mr. Na. Helen put away her application forms in a blue pocket folder.

The teacher bowed as he entered the apartment and removed his black leather shoes, resoled again, not too long ago. Mr. Na had brush-polished and buffed his penny loafers to a high sheen. He prided himself on his neat appearance.

He was a few years younger than Helen and several inches taller than John. No visible gray hairs. Mr. Na's clear complexion was tanned from morning runs. He was trim, with white teeth that evidenced his distaste for cigarettes and coffee. He wore a gold wedding ring and an affordable Japanese watch, a gray woolen sweater vest over a crisp dress shirt and necktie, and dark slacks.

There was no sofa, so Mr. Na sat down on one of the folding chairs at the children's table and placed his briefcase on the empty seat between him and Helen. He was disappointed by the drab building and the room without proper furnishings. He'd hoped that Mido's family had more means. No servant had opened the door or offered tea. A commemorative mug from a large downtown church, half full of cold milky coffee, rested by a blue folder. The mother was in her house clothes, a white cotton T-shirt and a pair of boys' navy jogging pants. She sat down across the table from him.

Mr. Na cleared his throat. "Thank you for seeing me today. I wanted to stop by and say hello. I was told that you had just arrived from Australia. I understand that your daughter was never educated here."

"Well, Mido went to kindergarten and first grade in Seoul, but my husband's work took us overseas again. I've tried to keep up the children's Korean through books and cassette tapes. Mido is the youngest. She has a brother at your school and the oldest goes to the high school across town."

The teacher knew the school. His cousin had been turned down for a job there.

"In Sydney, the children went to a Korean-language school at the church on Saturdays, but I'm not sure how much they learned. I was working." Her voice trailed off. Helen didn't know what he thought of mothers like her. Nervous, she was talking too much.

Having lived abroad, she didn't always know what to say when she returned home. Things were constantly changing, especially language and schooling, and often, even strangers had an opinion about her parenting. Natives would correct her when she made a mistake and smile like they'd won something, as if to say, *You might have lived somewhere else but you're not so special,* and Helen didn't know how to make the Koreans who had stayed put feel better. Some of them felt left behind and disadvantaged by those who had lived elsewhere, when in reality, Helen felt lost herself.

"This is a nice apartment," he said. "How many bedrooms do you have?"

"Three. It isn't very big," she replied. "We are still waiting for our furniture." The apartment felt even shabbier in his presence. "May I get you something to drink? We have coffee."

"I don't drink coffee."

Helen tried to remember if there was any tea in the nearly empty pantry.

"I live about two hours from here," he volunteered. "I take the train almost four hours a day round-trip for my job. It must be wonderful to live so close to the school."

Helen looked down, embarrassed by what she'd said. He must have thought she was boasting. A teacher had never visited her home before.

"Let me get you some tea. I have some delicious biscuits from Australia." Helen went to the kitchen and found cold barley tea in the refrigerator.

The open kitchen faced out to the living room, and in his sight, Helen put together a tray: two glasses of barley tea and sweets she'd been saving for her husband. She laid out the offerings in front of the teacher.

"Is Mido doing okay?" she asked, thinking it was better to be direct in these situations.

His mouth twisted a bit to the left like he was thinking.

"Her math skills are behind the other children's. I can help her with extra lessons in the morning or after school."

"How very kind of you. Thank you so much."

"I do this for my students, although it is not easy for me. My commute is rather long. I eat most of my meals in the classroom, and I get home late. I almost never see my own children during the week. Only on Sundays."

Helen touched her forehead, and her right hand hid the worry in her eyes for a moment.

"A teacher's work is so difficult. How old are your children?" she asked.

"I have two. One is studying for her high school entrance exams now. She's a hard worker. Like your daughter, she is quiet. The younger one, the boy, is a year behind her. He, too, studies a great deal. It's his dream to go to America and attend a great university there."

"That would be wonderful," she said, having heard some version of this from nearly everyone she knew. The top schools were too competitive in Korea, with never enough spots.

"The cost would be impossible, however. I have to take care of my family and make sure they have a bright future, but it's tough. My parents worked on a farm. I'm a luckless country boy, but I studied and became a middle school teacher. I am honored to be a member of a noble profession, but it's not possible to take care of your family on a teacher's salary alone. My children have to eat, go to hagwon, and I'm the eldest son. There are also my aging parents to consider."

He coughed to clear his throat and glanced at the mother's troubled expression.

"Do you think Mido will need a great deal of extra instruction? I don't want to make work for you. I mean, my husband can help her, perhaps. He's not bad at math."

The teacher frowned, too polite to contradict her. If the child's father knew math well, then why did his daughter fall short on such basic problems, which her classmates could readily solve?

"Mido will need help with her Korean subjects also. Her language has suffered, which is understandable. If she wants to go to high school and college here, she has a lot of work ahead of her. I can do my part while she's in my class. But your child is trailing far behind the others."

Helen felt sick inside. For a second, she thought he was smiling.

Mr. Na tasted a biscuit. He'd never had a lemon sandwich cookie before, and it was delicious. Having made his point, he waited for the information to sink in. He checked the view from the window and saw the tops of older ginkgo trees and the rows of newer apartment buildings sprouting from the sidewalk. The broad pane of glass had been cleaned only the day before, and it sparkled, reflecting the crisp March-afternoon sun. He thought it would be wonderful to live in such a spacious apartment, one filled with natural light, where his daughter and son could each have a room. This woman had complained about the size of the apartment, and her ingratitude enraged him.

The teacher undid the latches of his battered leather briefcase, raised the flap, and kept it open.

"May I use your restroom? I'd like to wash my hands." He glanced at the briefcase, then met her eyes.

Helen pursed her lips, got up, and pointed in the direction of the bathroom the children shared, which she had just cleaned that morning.

While he was out of the room, Helen took the remaining won notes from the manila envelope in Mido's notebook and counted them. It was not nearly enough, so she took the rest from Bo's and DH's stashes and put the cash in one of the new envelopes she kept in her folder. In her elegant hand, Helen wrote: "Thank you, Na Teacher, for all your fine and valuable work. With profound gratitude for your sacrifices. Cho Hejin (Mido-umma)."

The toilet flushed, then the faucet ran. He would use the bar of soap, then dry his hands on a towel hanging off a nail. Helen tucked the envelope in his open briefcase, leaving a sharp white corner visible so it wouldn't be missed when he returned, and it wasn't.

✤

Every night, John went to bed at ten o'clock. His work exhausted him, and to focus the next day, he had to sleep at least seven and a half hours. In the morning, John rose at six. As ever, he remained calm and methodical in his outlook. At work and church, everyone admired his evenness.

John lay on the floor beneath the thick coverlet in his blue pajamas, his head resting on one of his sister-in-law's pillows. The children were still doing their homework in the living room, and Helen was not ready for bed, but she wanted to talk to him alone. She shut the door, then sat cross-legged beside him. Careful to whisper, she told her husband about Mr. Na's visit.

"What else could you have done? Teachers have to eat, too, so they do these shameful things," John said with his eyes closed.

Korea was still comparatively poor and had a growing middle class, but the government had never funded its schools well. They knew that. Even when John was a boy, parents had to hand over these envelopes; the parent-teacher associations had to raise money for building repairs, classroom renovations, mimeograph machines, musical instruments, and audiovisual equipment; and teachers had to charge parents for every little thing. His worst memories were of having to ask his mother, who had labored in a factory, for money to buy sheets of special paper that his principal bullied the students to purchase, to cover fees for fuel costs for the school furnace, and to pay special charges from coaches for sports events. Money. Always, they had needed more money.

During her brief life, his mother, a young widow who had managed to graduate from middle school, had worked at a garment factory, accepting as many shifts as possible to support her younger siblings and parents, then later her own boys. There was rarely anything left over from her wages after the bills were paid. Even now, John could recall the anguish on her small brown face when there wasn't enough money for tuition, uniforms, and fees for both John and his brother. His older brother, who had never liked school, had dropped out against their mother's wishes and worked first at the garment factory where their mother worked, then later as a truck driver, when he began to earn a solid income. John's mother died from what had started out as a tooth infection, and not long after, John's older brother died during his military service in unexplained circumstances, which his friends attributed to a superior's cruelty. John met Helen soon after, during his university days: She was his only remaining family.

Helen sat on the floor, hugging her legs, and even though she said nothing else, John knew his wife was worried about the children and money.

"Maybe I could get another job," he said, opening his eyes. "Put on a cap and drive a taxi on the weekends." He sounded serious.

"No, no. You're forty-five years old and a manager at a good company. How can you get a second job?" Helen shook her head. "That would look bad. I should be able to get this job at Lotte." She smoothed the coverlet over his shoulders. "Everything will be okay. The Lord provides."

"My wife. You could have married the son of a wealthy family but, like a dope, you married a poor math student."

"And you could have married a rich girl instead of the second daughter of two foolish cardplayers."

John opened his eyes, and they laughed. This was their joke—the comedy of their love. Each had failed to marry up in the world when there had been a chance.

"I put my life and our children into your capable hands," John said, closing his eyes again. Sleep pulled him in, and he struggled to stay awake for her.

Helen felt sorry. John was doing everything possible to support their family, and it felt unfair that a hardworking man like this could not sleep in peace. She shouldn't have mentioned Mr. Na's visit. Helen prayed silently over her husband's resting head: *Lord, protect my good husband's rest.*

Overseas, the expenses had been easier. The company subsidized housing and the children's tuition, and the teachers didn't expect extra payments. For Christmas, Helen had given teachers in Paramus and Sydney flowering bulbs she'd potted herself; sometimes a box of Belgian chocolates or a bottle of cognac. Certain schools would allow families to chip in a nominal sum to make up a small year-end cash gift. Helen was competent at making calls and chasing down payments so a teacher could have something extra for her Christmas budget.

In the living room, the boys sat at the table doing their homework. Bo was focused on a Korean history assignment, and DH was finishing his math problems. Mido lay on the floor filling out a science worksheet. They wouldn't go to bed until one, at least, and Helen would stay up with them.

"Who wants night *ramyeon*?" she asked, and the boys cheered loudly. Helen shushed them, her index finger across her lips. She pointed to the closed bedroom door.

"*Appa*'s sleeping. He's had a long day."

The children had eaten dinner earlier, but they were always hungry when studying. In the kitchen, Helen filled the aluminum pot with water and set it on the stove to boil. When she was growing up, her parents would be at the neighbors' playing cards in the evenings, and her sister, Sonya, had been the one to fix her and their little brother noodles when they were all studying.

Helen rummaged in the refrigerator to find three eggs to round out their meal.

3
Work

Two months ago, Taehun Shin had phoned John in Sydney and said it was time to come home.

Shin was his superior, a director of Han River Industrials & Trading, a subsidiary of the Han River Group. He was also John's oldest friend, an elder brother of sorts. Graduates of the same university, they had risen together in the ranks, albeit with Shin, a more canny individual, several steps ahead yet always willing to carry John along.

Right out of college, through a KATUSA connection who knew of Shin's exceptional language skills in both English and Japanese, Shin found work in the trading division of Endo K.K., a multinational Japanese conglomerate. He moved to New Jersey in the mid-seventies and brought along his elegant bride Miran, who went by Mary in the new country. A few months later, Shin hired John, and Helen, who had always wanted to live in the United States, was eager to move to Paramus. John and Helen loved living in Bergen County with its wide roads, big homes, enormous shops that never ran out of anything, and verdant foliage. John liked to drive, and Helen took to their quiet life in the suburbs.

However, when Shin didn't get a promotion he felt he deserved after closing a major deal, he figured out how to get hired by the Han River Group when the Korean conglomerate needed to grow its steel trading business for Han River Industrials & Trading, and he took John with him to the new job.

The two couples, the Shins and the Kohs, who each now had three young, American-born children, returned to Seoul. When HRG opened an office in Sydney, it was Shin, by then a director, who put up John for the senior manager position, allowing the Koh family to live as expats in Australia. Shin's ambition and charisma made up for John's discomfort with office politics, and John's sobriety and diligence supported Shin's grander visions. They made a strong working team, but they were never equals. So when Shin told him to pack up yet again, John did, and the family returned to Seoul within a month.

The school year in Sydney had just started; however, Helen understood that the start of the Korean school year would be more important even if it required the children to repeat a grade. She knew better than to ask for another year in Australia. Shin was not a man to change his mind, and the abrupt nature of the request had already stunned both of them. The children spoke English fluently, and if they had enough supplemental tutoring for their Korean subjects, Helen thought they could attend university in Korea, though it might prove difficult for them to catch up with their counterparts. If it were up to Helen, she would have remained in Sydney or returned to America, but John said that there was nothing they could do about it.

From the beginning of their relationship, Shin had appreciated John's integrity and his even temperament. Shin was clear in his professional goals and muddy in his private life; he was aware that a responsible person like John shored him up. John was dependable, easy to work with, and precise. Superiors and subordinates liked him. Above all, he was neither too ambitious nor threatening, which pleased Shin and his superiors. It was not in John's nature to belittle or betray his boss or team.

Han River Industrials & Trading—HRI—the most profitable division of the Han River Group, teemed with sharks, killer whales, and piranhas, and in such dark waters, a dolphin who could do reliable tricks was valuable. Above all, loyalty was essential to Shin, a man of great ambition, and he demanded it from his subordinates. In return, Shin offered anyone on his team the necessary protection from other predators.

Shin had his reasons for calling John back to Seoul. True, he needed an effective manager for his fast-growing team. Also, one of the new hires, a young woman, had gotten big ideas, and Shin needed her to understand how things worked. He hoped that John's steady and sober presence would help contain her unrealistic expectations.

❧

In the first week of John's return, Shin invited John's new team members to dinner: They'd just successfully completed the training program for the metals division and would now report to John.

It was Thursday evening, and after a pork barbecue meal, the large group walked to an upscale *noraebang* to sing. No one had begged off, because they were all curious about John Koh, who was held in such high esteem by Shin, the big boss.

It didn't take many drinks to make anyone sing. Three of the younger men grabbed the microphones to sing "I Know," a recently released hip-hop song. Two of the female trainees picked up the tambourines and tapped them against their hips. Strobe lights came on and the stage vibrated. More than a dozen Han River employees removed their jackets and transformed into vivacious performers.

Goaded into a song, the guest of honor had to get up onstage. John had anticipated this and sang the first of his standards: "Can't Buy Me Love." If that went over well and the crowds demanded, he had "Yesterday" and "Let It Be" at the ready. No one ever complained about a Beatles song, especially since John's pronunciation and vocal range were impressive. He had a decent singing voice and didn't mind going to noraebangs in general, but his wife disliked the drinking that happened before and after.

John turned red when he drank and had never enjoyed the feeling. Mostly he felt like sleeping after one beer, so he had developed a set of tricks to avoid drinking without being noticed. Depending on the lighting and location, he could spill, spit out, or hide the numerous shots offered. Invariably he was the senior person who helped the others get home and ended up returning home late himself, when he was the one who needed regular sleep the most. Late nights with coworkers were another reason Helen preferred family life overseas. Here, drinking, entertaining, and spending late evenings for work were too often expected.

John sat next to Shin at his table, filled with the most senior men and the loveliest of the female trainees. Miss Danbi Jung sat beside the director, and John observed as she slyly stroked Shin's upper thigh, her thin white fingers grazing the pleat of his suit trouser pocket. John looked away.

He knew Shin's wife, Mary, well. Shin and Mary had three sons. Two of them now attended Lawrenceville, and the youngest went to a public middle school in Bergen County. Mary and the boys returned home to Seoul only during summer breaks. Mary had been scouted for the Miss Korea pageant and was a graduate of Ewha, where she'd been called Beautiful Angel for being both pretty and saintly. At Ewha, Helen was two years her junior, and in Paramus, the two women had been expat wives and young mothers together, helping to raise each other's children.

The waiter came by to refresh their drink orders, and Shin ordered a costly platter of fruit for each of the three tables. Whiskey flowed, and the ladies laughed louder with each additional pour and song.

Shin turned to John.

"Don't you think Miss Jung has the loveliest mouth?"

John reached for his water glass and smiled politely.

"*Ppo-ppo*," Shin said to Miss Jung, the way a grandfather might speak to a toddler, and the young woman pouted and kissed the director's cheek. She inched her right hand toward the director's left pocket and kept her hand there.

Noticing John wince, Danbi rose from her seat.

"Let me sing you a song, Director Shin."

Shin clapped like a child.

Danbi Jung wore an ivory-colored silk blouse tucked into a dark midi skirt. The clothes were modest, almost plain, but her body was so extraordinary that there was something obscene in her sensual appeal. The outline of her old-fashioned brassiere was visible through the scrim of pale silk. The men were transfixed by the way Danbi held the microphone between her hands as if she were praying to it. She opened her rosy mouth to sing.

She had selected an old Nam Jin song, "Love Me Once Again," which was curious. She would have been maybe two years old when the song came out. Danbi had just turned twenty-four, and it was a love song that her mother used to hum whenever she was happy. Could she have known that the director and anyone in his generation might be vulnerable to such a nostalgic choice? The gorgeous young woman had picked a song that reminded a middle-aged man that in his youth he had been vital, leaving him defenseless in his reverie.

From the adoring way she looked at Shin, John understood that she was infatuated, and that Shin was besotted. She might be the reason Shin had brought him and his family back to Seoul. He needed John to rescue him from the siren, tie him to a mast, but John wasn't sure if such a thing was possible now.

❧

The next morning, Shin pulled John away from his desk to get a coffee.

Taehun Shin had a distinctive profile: a sharp nose with a high bridge, a clear brow, and a full head of dark, wavy hair. Each day without fail, he did his calisthenics, and unlike John, no matter how much he'd drunk the night before, his work performance was never visibly affected. At forty-six, Shin felt stronger and more mentally fit than when he'd done his military service. He wasn't as fast as he used to be, but he felt that he could do anything, and could always work more effectively than his peers.

Once they were in the lobby, they walked briskly toward the front of the building.

"She's different," the director said.

John nodded.

"Smart. Top ten in her class at Korea University."

"I reviewed her last report. It stood out from the other trainees. Strong analytical skills and writing."

"It's easier when they're dumb. Normally I choose the pretty ones without much sense, but this girl—" Shin exhaled. "I don't want her to make trouble."

"I think she could. I don't know why I say that, but—" John stopped himself.

Shin was nodding as if he was in a mess already. John let Shin pass through the revolving door ahead of him.

Once outside, Shin lit a cigarette, cupping his left hand over the match flame to block the wintry breeze. He inhaled deeply, then exhaled through his nostrils. John said nothing else.

"She could make trouble because I allow her liberties, which I shouldn't," Shin said.

John had to agree. More often than not, a man knew when he could no longer manage his affairs.

❧

The café was empty, and Shin selected a table in the corner. He made what looked like a peace sign to the server, who recognized him, and the young man went to the kitchen to fix two brewed coffees.

"She is twenty-four," Shin said.

"Yes. I looked at her file." John tried not to sound disapproving. Long ago, he had stopped saying anything to Shin about the other women. From Helen, John knew that Mary knew about them. These were private matters between a husband and a wife, and Shin almost never brought up the women he slept with, but Danbi's age must be bothering him, too.

"Can you speak to her?" Shin asked.

"I don't understand."

"Ask her to resign. I can help her get another job, but I want you to get rid of her. I can't do it. I tried."

John looked puzzled. "Wouldn't she suspect?"

"Probably. She's very clever. But there's a chance she might just think that you don't like her. I can handle it after. After you fire her."

Shin's head was muddled, full of images of the night before—her pink mouth, her breasts shaped like persimmons, the curve of her ass.

"I can't be alone with her at the office. She pushes me around."

John frowned. He had never heard Shin say such things before.

"How do you want me to fire her? For what reason? She just finished a difficult training program. Miss Jung has the right to have this job. Wasn't she hired because of her qualifications?"

"Of course. But I can get her another job."

"Can you end this? End this relationship?" John asked.

"Do you think I haven't tried? I can't. I've even thought of leaving my family for her."

John looked down at the steaming coffee cup, which he had no recollection of being served.

"Give her an assignment she cannot fulfill. Come up with something. Wait a few weeks. Let her fail publicly in front of the team. Be cold to her. She thinks you don't like her."

John put his hands around the coffee cup but didn't drink from it.

"Brother," John blurted out loud. At the office, he usually addressed him as Director Shin, but they were alone.

"Yaah—try to understand. Your brother is in trouble. I told her you didn't like her, that you were a Christian and you wouldn't approve. That you don't look at women the way most men—"

"Brother—" John stared into Shin's eyes. He had never seen him look this way before, frightened and disorderly. He started to protest, but Shin was undeterred.

"Put her on the coking coal projections. The demand numbers on that are a mess. Make her figure out the requirements, too. You can hammer out the details. Don't give her all the information she needs. Mix up the number from Illawarra and Peak Downs, or keep something back that would have been obvious later."

"How could she possibly manage that alone? That would be hard for even my best people to run the models, and if she worked with someone else, any senior guy would know that they'd need more information about the coking coal suppliers, and—"

Shin interrupted him. "I'm asking you for a favor. Please. Make up something. Others have to see how she can't manage and that you won't play favorites. People trust you, and you'd be justified in dismissing her."

Shin drank his coffee.

"She will be fine. I will take care of this afterward. I know someone at Tiger Trading & Mining who needs someone like her, and I'm sure Miss Jung would be promoted there much faster than here. This can all work out." Shin smiled at John. "Everyone happy," he said in English. "Win-win."

John looked up from his coffee cup, wanting Shin to withdraw the request, knowing that he'd never do so.

"It's better for everyone this way. If she's gone, I will be able to keep doing my job. We need me to have this job, right?" He paused meaningfully. "I promise, she won't get hurt."

❧

After work, Danbi was waiting for him at the hotel.

When Shin entered the room, she was sitting at the edge of the bed, an open magazine on her lap, wearing what she'd worn at the office—a white blouse buttoned up to the neck, a navy crewneck sweater, and a pleated navy wool skirt. She had removed her high-heeled shoes by the door. Her camel coat and purse lay on the desk.

"My director is here. Your Danbi is unhappy." She looked as if she might cry as she put aside the magazine and remained still, allowing him to undress her. She raised her arms, and he pulled the sweater over her head.

Shin unbuttoned her blouse and slid the straps of her brassiere off her shoulders.

"Tell me," he said. "I will listen."

"You smell wonderful. I like this aftershave." With both hands, she pulled his head down to her breasts and breathed in the scent of his hair. She kissed his upper cheekbone and left ear.

Shin could not control himself. There had been dozens of girls, so many that he'd lost count, but this one was aggressive and made him do things, made him feel lost in her. The relationship was entirely sexual, but he felt alive in a way that he did not feel elsewhere in his life.

Danbi put her tongue on him and teased. She smacked his bottom, and when he was surprised by the pain, she pleased him.

"I want you to fire him," she said, barely stopping what she was doing with her hands and mouth. She stared at him, looking hurt and hungry. "You have to fire him. Please."

"Who?"

"Manager Koh. He gave me an assignment that no one can do. No one."

"I can't do that," he said, shaking his head, eyes closed.

She pushed him down hard on the bed, then mounted him.

"He hates me," she said.

Her fingers pressed against his backside, and he gasped.

4

Shimcheong

Helen wore a charcoal-gray suit that her sister, Sonya, had ordered for her many years ago from a wonderful dressmaker in Itaewon, which still fit her mostly, though after three children, Helen could no longer close the last button at the waist. Sonya had the fine wool fabric imported from England and ordered a matching suit for herself, though she now wore even more fashionable and elegant things, since she could afford to buy whatever she liked.

Sonya, a natural beauty with a striking figure, was the best-dressed woman in any room. Like Helen, Sonya had studied English, and she had also taken many classes in art history. Her sense of proportion and design was far more cultivated than most people's. In their childhood, none of the three Cho siblings—Sonya, Helen, and their younger brother, Kenny—had traveled, or seen much of man-made beauty, yet all three had been graced with a good eye for form, color, and aesthetic balance.

Helen carried a new handbag made by a respected Australian maker that wasn't exported. The black leather bag had been a farewell gift from her store manager in Sydney. Her high-heeled pumps complemented the bag and suit.

Kingdom Presbyterian Church in Gangnam was known for its influential and wealthy congregation, and Sonya and her husband, Yong-gil, served as elders. On Thursday afternoons, Sonya hosted a well-attended fellowship group at her home in the Hyundai apartment complex. The group was so popular that there was never any room for newcomers. Helen was, of course, an exception.

Sonya, Helen, and Kenny, who now lived in Sydney with his family, had been raised in Catholic churches by softhearted saints who pitied the three children of two inveterate gamblers. Without charity, none of the three would have been able to get a proper education. That said, it would not be accurate to say that the church had provided abundantly, because the siblings had lived at subsistence level, each requiring several part-time jobs to finish their education. They still remembered their sharp hunger and the gnawing shame of lacking what others took for granted.

When Sonya Cho graduated from Ewha, her first full-time job was with a small real estate company owned by Chairman Hong-gyun Mun, an elder at Kingdom Presbyterian, a former real estate broker who had successfully invested in choice real estate in Seoul. Chairman Mun took a strong interest in Sonya. The childless businessman and his wife had adopted Mun's late brother's son, Yong-gil, the brightest of all his nephews and nieces, to train as the successor to his real estate business. Chairman Mun encouraged Sonya to marry Yong-gil, thereby making his secretary his daughter-in-law. When Chairman Mun's wife fell ill, Sonya, who no longer worked at the company, nursed her until she passed away.

It was easy to spot Sonya, her eyes closed in prayer, seated between her husband, Yong-gil, and his uncle, Chairman Mun, in the second row of the enormous sanctuary. Sonya's two high school–aged boys sat in the row behind them, their heads bowed, pretending to read the church bulletin. They were saving the empty pew on the other side for Helen and her family.

The Koh family sat down quietly, and Helen tapped her nephew Seung-man's shoulder. He smiled brightly at his aunt, uncle, and cousins. Seated beside him was his younger brother, Jiman, who was in his first year of high school. Jiman and his cousin Bo were in the same grade.

When Sonya finished praying, she walked over to Helen's seat. There were still a few minutes before services began, and the seated congregants observed the Cho sisters, having heard about Helen's return to Seoul.

Sonya wore a light-beige suit, much like Helen's, but cut closer to her slim figure and made of double-faced cashmere. A thick rope of rare Tahitian pearls circled her neck, and large pearls adorned her small ears. She was only three years older than Helen. Though her face was unlined and her hair still naturally dark, she had the air of someone even older. In the way Sonya carried herself, even as a little child, she had always seemed more mature and self-possessed than anyone her own age.

Her husband, Yong-gil, read the church bulletin with half-hearted interest, while Chairman Mun's eyes tracked Sonya as she returned to her seat. Calmer in her presence, he did not like her far from his side. Chairman Mun doted on Sonya and preferred her company over anyone else's, including that of his nephew and his grandnephews, Seungman and Jiman, whom he had named himself.

The church, attended by nearly three thousand parishioners over two services, remained popular through the years because of its famed minister, Pastor Kim, who gave stirring sermons connecting popular culture with the Gospel. After each service, the church recorded his teachings on cassette tapes so the parishioners could listen to them again, and the cassettes themselves were in such great demand that they were sold at a nominal cost rather than given out for free as in other churches.

An unusually tall man in his fifties with an angular, olive-skinned face, Pastor Kim was more jovial than sober. He was perfectly bilingual, having studied in America, with a doctorate from Princeton Theological Seminary. His principal job was to write and deliver the sermons that had become so popular that a team of pastors had been hired to protect Kim's time to read and write. It was difficult for ordinary members to reach Pastor Kim about mundane matters; however, Chairman Mun had been able to get him to officiate the marriage of Sonya and his nephew Yong-gil. Each December, Sonya invited Pastor Kim to her fellowship group, and he would come over for the Christmas catered lunch and pray for the women.

This morning, Pastor Kim preached about idolatry, and he quoted from Leviticus:

" 'Do not give any of your children to be sacrificed to Molech, for you must not profane the name of your God. I am the LORD.'

"With school starting this month, I have been thinking of my cherished flock and how best to serve you," he began.

"A woman in ancient times was without value unless she bore a child—preferably a son. Sound familiar?" Kim raised his thick left eyebrow. He enjoyed teasing his parishioners. Out of habit, he pushed his tortoiseshell eyeglasses higher on the bridge of his prominent nose.

"As you know, when the Israelites entered the promised land, God told His people that they should not follow the profane practices of the people who lived there. But what did the Israelites do? Some offered their daughters and sons to Molech, the fire god. No doubt some of you may be tempted to offer up your disobedient teenager who refuses to study."

The parents chuckled, and even the younger people in the audience reluctantly smiled. The pastor was hard not to like.

"Molech required more and more daughters and sons. Just imagine a continuous stream of children being burned alive to appease some local deity." The pastor grew serious again. "Children being murdered by their own parents. Imagine that.

"Now, is this just an evil practice from ancient times committed by ignorant spiritual ancestors in a faraway place called Canaan? I think not. From our own country, we have Shimcheong, the folklore legend of the virtuous daughter who trades her life for three hundred bags of rice so her blind father might regain his sight. A child's sacrifice in exchange for a miracle."

The pastor stared hard at his congregation, then broke into a grin.

"Cross-culturally and throughout time, we have had reprehensible practices to appease the idols we created and propped up from our own minds and hands. So are we still barbaric, or are we more civilized? Which gods do we bow down to today? To what gods do we sacrifice our children? To which gods do we sacrifice our most prized ideals—and why?"

John Koh's three children paid attention. Helen's dark-brown eyes studied Pastor Kim's gestures. The parishioners followed along with the minister's sermon and mentally catalogued their man-made gods and their own costly sacrifices. White-gloved ushers stood in the back of the cavernous room, looking somber.

"For what? For what do we give up everything? What do you love more than your child? What do you love more than God?" he asked. "Brothers and sisters in Christ, I implore you to remember the true Lord, our God in Heaven, who despised child sacrifice." Pastor Kim then closed in prayer.

Mido bowed her head and clasped her hands. Not for a second would her parents ever do something so horrible as to sacrifice her brothers or her to Molech. Her parents had never pressured her, Bo, or DH to get good grades; nevertheless, in Sydney, Bo had often been near the top of the class. He was upset that it felt impossible to excel here. Mido disliked the constant talk of pushy mothers and fathers because that had never been her experience. There were always some kids in the class who complained about their parents, but for the most part, Mido did not believe that parents here loved an idol of achievement more than their children. She didn't know to whom the pastor was directing his accusations.

❧

Helen didn't want to go to coffee hour, but Sonya insisted.

"Come on. I have to talk to some of the women in our fellowship group, and you should say hello before the next meeting. You set yourself apart far too much, and you can't do that anymore. Your children need you to be involved," her sister chided.

The smell of coffee wafted in from the fellowship hall. Small children chased each other, fueled by the platters of cookies and apple juice, and parents let their toddlers wander, feeling secure in the basement of the vast church.

Mido remained by her mother's side while her brothers talked to their cousins. The four boys had been close when the Kohs lived in Seoul, and over the years, there had been little opportunity for them to see each other. They still read *manwha* and wanted to go to a comic book store like old times after lunch, but there wasn't enough room in their weekend schedules. Seungman and Jiman had tutors coming over, and Bo and DH had mountains of homework to finish back home.

The two brothers-in-law conversed politely. They got along well enough, though Sonya's husband, Yong-gil, didn't talk much to people he hadn't grown up with, and he didn't have any interest in John, who could be more quiet than most. Streams of expensively dressed women paid homage to Sonya. Chairman Mun spoke to Pastor Kim about the church's latest fundraising campaign for the homeless men who gathered around Seoul Station. Soon after lunch, the family would disperse to their separate lives.

"Koh Mido!"

Yun ran to Mido, her eyes open wide in surprise.

Neither Helen nor Sonya had expected anyone to call out to Mido.

Sonya broke away from the women from her fellowship group to inspect the pretty girl talking to her shy niece. The two girls were smiling at each other, and the sisters were mystified and delighted.

Sonya approached the girl with the French-braided hair and American sneakers.

"Are you a school friend of Mido's?"

"Hello." Yun bowed. "We are in the same homeroom. We're friends at school," she said, bowing slightly again.

Mido grinned, smiling with her whole face, and Helen felt a rush of relief.

"Oh, how nice," Sonya said, turning to Helen, who was always worried about her daughter. "Now you are friends at church, too." She touched the top of Yun's glossy head, then patted her shoulder.

Yun's mother, Nari, had been observing her daughter, and she drew closer to the cluster of women gathered around the famed elder Sonya Cho, who was married to Chairman Mun's nephew Yong-gil. Everyone at church knew the prominent family by sight, but Nari had never spoken to Sonya or anyone connected to them.

Nari felt suddenly self-conscious about her clothing. Her red bouclé dress with the dramatic black sequin flowers along the hem had seemed stylish that morning but now seemed garish in contrast to the tailored gray and beige suits of the Cho sisters. Sonya was reputed to be a kind and gracious person, but at church, she was always surrounded by a wall of the most beautiful and popular women—mostly Ewha graduates with well-off husbands who worked for conglomerates and had also gone to elite universities.

Nari bowed to the sisters and placed her hands on her daughter's shoulders to direct her away from the group.

"Yun-ah, we should go. The driver is waiting for us outside," Nari said quietly, feeling awkward. Her shoulder-length hair fell in loose, permed waves. She was over a decade younger than the sisters and had not gone to college, having barely finished high school. Nari brushed her hair away from her face with her hands.

"Umma, can Mido come to our house for lunch? We can do homework together. Can you tell Mido's mother about the hagwon?"

The Cho sisters smiled expectantly at the girl's mother, curious about which hagwon.

"Oh, Eagle Academy. It's a small one—some Korean Americans founded it about five or six years ago. Are you looking for a hagwon for Mido? I don't know if they're taking new students. There's a long waitlist."

"Oh? Eagle?" Sonya turned ever so slightly to create a barrier between her and the rest of the fellowship women, who were now talking among themselves. They had no idea who Nari was. "I've heard they have a good English program."

"Yes," Nari said. "Everything is taught in English, and they also have a math teacher from MIT who Yun loves. Henry Teacher." Nari found herself wanting the sisters to like her. "Have you heard of MIT? I mean, of course you have—" Nari still had her hand on her daughter's shoulder.

Helen didn't know what to do. She had never needed to get tutors for her children, but all three were overwhelmed by the volume and rate of learning at their new schools.

"Mido, we're supposed to have lunch at your aunt's house today, and then homework."

Nari understood that her child's invitation was being rejected, and she pulled Yun back.

"Yun, let's go." She bowed slightly, smiled, then turned to walk away.

"Goodbye, then," Yun said, bowing. She walked behind her mother, whose pace quickened.

Sonya nudged her sister.

"Are you crazy? Your kids need to start at Eagle Academy right away. I heard that it's really good, and that mother can help you."

"I don't know," Helen replied. "It's expensive."

"Who cares what it costs? You have to pay whatever they ask," Sonya whispered. "Your kids are behind. I know you might send the children to America for school, but you might also be sending them to college here, and these school grades matter when they apply. How in the world will they catch up without hagwons? You just got that job at Lotte. Even if you have to borrow the money, you have to get them a spot."

"But—" Helen exhaled. She didn't want her sister to lend her any more money. Helen wished John would rescue her from this conversation, but he was listening to Yong-gil, who was droning on about a new development project.

"Hejin-ah." Sonya addressed Helen by her Korean name. "Go to that nice mother and tell her that Mido would love to go to her house for lunch. And get all three of your children into Eagle Academy. Don't be a fool. Your primary responsibility is to take care of your children's education. You can't be like our mother, who didn't give a damn if we grew up in a pigsty," Sonya said, upset at the memory of how the three of them had struggled to have shelter, food, and, of course, education. They had begged strangers to pity them, and Sonya would never let that happen to anyone in her family while she was still breathing.

❧

"Yun-umma," Helen called out, walking as quickly as she could to catch up to Yun's mother, whose name she didn't know. The woman could be a deacon or elder, yet Helen had no idea, so she addressed her as the child's mother, hoping not to cause offense. Mido ran behind her mother. Yun turned and pulled on her mother's red sleeve.

"Mido! Are you coming home with us?"

Mido glanced at her mother, who nodded.

"You can use my books. I have a photocopier at home, so we can use the worksheets together," Yun said, knowing her mother would never disagree.

"Yun-umma, are you sure it would be all right and not an imposition?" Helen paused. "We just returned from living overseas, and I don't really know how things work here. Please forgive me if I'm saying the wrong thing. Everything changes so fast. It would be wonderful if you could introduce our Mido and maybe my sons to the hagwon you mentioned. I would be so grateful."

Nari tilted her head. The woman had seemed standoffish and quiet, but she could tell that she was sincere. Nari and her husband, Joonho, bristled at even the slightest affronts from rich, educated people. Her parents had been poor, and she had grown up in the country, hundreds of kilometers away from Seoul. Though she and Joonho had lots of money now, it was hard sometimes, even at church, to talk to people who had gone to fancy colleges and rarely mixed with others. She and Joonho co-owned three convenience stores and two buildings with a partner. They were simple people, she knew that much, but she didn't think college people were better than they were. Nari took pride in the fact that her daughter, Yun, was one of the top-ranked students in her middle school and in the school district.

"If you like, I can try to reach Dr. Tom Song, the president of Eagle Academy," Nari offered. "And we'd be glad to have Mido come over to study. You can pick her up tonight, or if my husband's driver is available, he can bring her home. After they finish their schoolwork, I'll give them their meals."

"Oh, that's not necessary. You're being so kind even to host her. I'll come by later myself and pick her up. I'll need your number or address, though."

With both hands, Nari handed Helen her business card with her home address and number. The card read "Director of White Tree K.K.," the name of the holding company of their three convenience stores. Nari didn't do anything as its director, but it gave her pleasure to be able to hand anyone a card of her own.

Helen didn't have her business card from the duty-free store yet, and even so, it would have only said "Associate."

The women bowed to each other, not knowing if they would be friends or simply fellow mothers.

5

Eagle Academy

Eagle Academy was not a bad place to work. The teachers were well compensated and the children motivated. With only ten students per class, everyone was able to practice writing, listening, and speaking as well as solving difficult math and science problems. The parents who paid dearly for after-school and weekend lessons in the Daechi-dong hagwon witnessed notable progress—not a guaranteed outcome for a reputable hagwon even in Gangnam. Eagle Academy's reputation had spread, traveling to even Apgujeong, where Sonya lived.

With long waiting lists, there was almost never any room for new students who were not siblings of graduates. Sonya's two boys were already enrolled at the best tutoring center near the Hyundai Apartments and performed at the tops of their classes, so she hadn't seen a need to change anything. If there were any issues, however, Sonya would have barreled through any closed doors for her sons with all the resources she could muster. And so she told Helen to push her way into this famed hagwon only blocks from their house.

Tom Song, the American owner of Eagle Academy, had put up the Sheetrock himself. He and his Korean wife, Clara, had painted each wall and ceiling of the two-floor space, which they had rented from Tom's former Cornell classmate Renee Cha.

Tom and Clara had divided the two-hundred-square-meter space into six classrooms, one common area, and two professional offices. Inspirational posters featuring inventors, presidents, and writers papered the corridors. Everywhere you looked, Tesla, Edison, the three Roosevelts—Theodore, Franklin, and Eleanor—and the likes of Shakespeare, Locke, and Montaigne and their most celebrated quotations encouraged young minds to persist and excel. From the corner of a stairwell, a poster of Helen Keller exhorted: "We can do anything we want to do if we stick to it long enough." Teenagers challenged Keller's idea: Effort didn't cut it. They were too short for professional basketball or modeling, or lacked the singing voice to become an idol. Tom would answer with Oscar Wilde, who was up there with Mark Twain for a snappy retort: "Life is never fair, and perhaps it is a good thing for most of us that it is not."

Clara was undeterred by mocking adolescent shrugs and eye rolls. She framed a color photograph of Nelson Mandela with the quotation "Education is the most powerful weapon which you can use to change the world." Though Tom was not religious, Clara was, and she tacked up Bible quotations about love and forgiveness and, of course, the well-known verses from Saint Paul instructing the runner to run his race swiftly and to put on the armor of God. She knew the book of Proverbs cold. Her favorite: "Wisdom is the principal thing; therefore get wisdom: and with all thy getting get understanding."

In five years, without any advertising, Eagle had become the most in-demand hagwon in the area. Its students outperformed their peers, but more importantly, they wanted to study there.

The informational meeting with the Koh children was more or less a courtesy. Clara, who had always liked Nari and her daughter, Yun, had explained to them that there was no space at the hagwon. However, she and Tom would be willing to interview the Koh children for the waitlist in case an opening came up. One of the teachers had to assess Tom's friend's son anyway, so it wouldn't be a problem to have the Koh children assessed at the same time.

In Tom's crowded office, its white walls lined with waist-high bookshelves stocked with study guides as well as Tom's framed diplomas from Cornell and Teachers College, the owners greeted the three teenagers and their mother. The Koh children and Helen took their seats on the two sofas separated by a low coffee table, and Tom and Clara sat on upholstered armchairs opposite each other. Tom thanked the family for coming in.

"Yun insists that Mido just has to be in her classes. I think she's said the same to all her teachers," Tom said, smiling at Mido.

"Mido, do you prefer to speak in English or Korean?" Clara asked in English.

Mido and her brothers were surprised, not having thought they had a choice here. She hesitated, then answered, "English, please."

"Bo?" Tom faced the oldest child.

"English is easier for all of us," Bo answered.

"Yep. Same," DH said with a slight Australian accent, which he had been learning to dial down.

Seeing the children fidget in their seats, Tom felt sorry for them and realized he should not have taken the meeting. Even accepting Peter Son, his friend Renee Cha's only child, had required shuffling the classrooms to keep the roster at ten per class. There was no way Tom couldn't accept Peter, whose mother was not just a close college friend but also owned the building. If it hadn't been for Renee, Tom and Clara wouldn't have been able to start Eagle. Peter was already in the next room, talking with Sean Teacher, waiting for the assessment to begin. Clara touched her left ear and looked at Tom, a signal that he should hasten the consultation since this meeting didn't count and there was much left to do today.

Tom glanced at Mido, and the little girl said nothing. Clara grew concerned.

Tom was born in Hawaii, then his father's work in the military had taken them to Texas, Alabama, South Carolina, and Missouri. There were advantages to moving around, but having done so much of it himself, Tom knew what it was like. For a kid, relocating every few years had been a series of setting up tents, taking them down, then putting them up again, with no one ever asking how he felt about it, or warning him about what would happen. Not everyone was built for such a life. An itinerant childhood had perhaps made his older sister and him hardy, but the instability had been difficult on their younger sister and mother, who had not done as well. His father was a good man, but he had demanded order and sacrifice and expected his family to act as if nothing had happened even though the world had shifted with each new home.

"How are you finding it here? It's not easy, is it?" Tom asked. "How many places have you lived?"

"They were born in New Jersey, and they've lived in Paramus, Seoul, Sydney, and now we are back." Helen smiled.

Clara raised her eyebrows.

"My goodness," Tom said, and studied the children's faces. He had worked with children for a long time. After getting his doctorate, he'd taught social studies at public and private schools. He worked in admissions at three schools, including Harvard-Westlake and Phillips Andover. In Los Angeles, he was set up on a blind date with Clara, an international student who was studying at USC, and they fell in love. She followed him from Los Angeles to Andover, but she wanted to live in Seoul to be with her family, and he wanted to try something new.

"It must have been difficult for you, too," Clara said to Helen.

Helen shook her head. It had been harder for the children to leave each time, learn the rules of a new teacher and a new sports team and the codes of each schoolyard, then leave again when the company said to go. However, she was grateful that they could always be together. And that the children were healthy.

Tom and Clara observed that Mido had hardly made a sound.

Clara smiled. "Mido?"

Helen leaned in. "She's shy."

The boys stared meaningfully at their sister, feeling protective yet recognizing that this interview mattered. Earlier that week, Helen had prepared them for this. They wore their Sunday clothes.

"It's okay to be shy," Tom said, and smiled at her.

Mido held her breath. They were watching her, and she swallowed.

"I'd like to study with Yun here. I know I have a lot to learn in Korea." Mido took a breath. "I'm a hard worker. I promise to do all my Eagle hagwon homework. Yun told me there is a lot."

Clara and Tom laughed, and Helen closed her eyes and exhaled almost silently. Both Bo and DH smiled, trying not to make a big deal of their sister's comprehensive answer.

Helen handed Clara a folder, and she continued to speak in English, which felt strange, but it allowed her to be less formal and less aware of her status. She was a supplicant, although she was the elder. Helen believed in her children and didn't want to sell them as if they were a pair of expensive shoes or an article of designer clothing.

"I brought their report cards from Sydney. They've done well. I don't think their recent grades on quizzes and tests here reflect their abilities," she said.

Clara stood and faced the children.

"We have assessments for all three of you. Come with me. I'll let Dr. Song speak with your mother." She smiled.

The children followed Clara to the next room.

❧

Tom watched them walk out, and Clara closed the door softly behind her.

"Your children are great."

Helen smiled, not knowing what else to say as his face grew sober.

"You see, the problem is that I have a waitlist for new students, and even if the assessments showed that they were an ideal fit for Eagle, I want you to know that it's highly unlikely"—he corrected himself—"no, it's actually impossible, for us to accept them even if something changed with our enrollment, because you're not looking for one spot but three. There are parents who have been waiting for more than two years for a space to open. It's really my fault for accepting this meeting, and I blame myself. I would not want to mislead you. If you would rather that the children not take the assessment, I do understand—"

This was the hardest part of success—the need to say no often. On occasion, a parent thought he was negotiating and offered more money, which was refused. If that didn't work, the ones who were used to getting their way would reach out to a more prominent parent, but the more they tried, the more awkward the situation grew. Tom, a liberal American who had written his doctoral dissertation on education reformers, repudiated status performance of any kind. The irony of him owning a private tutoring center was not lost on him; but the longer he did this, the more he believed that he could make a difference by being a useful educator. The children here needed his care and protection, in some ways, much more than those back in the States.

Helen folded her hands in her lap.

"They won't mind the assessment. At least you'll have their results. In case—" Helen looked up, trying again. Sonya had said Helen couldn't give up until she heard the word "no" at least three times.

"How about just Mido? She's such a good student, and it would mean so much—"

"The assessment isn't long. I suppose there is no harm—" he interrupted, not wanting to hear her plea. It was difficult for him to say no; Clara was the tougher one.

"They've moved around so much, and Bo and DH may take the Suneung and apply to colleges here. Of course, their grades have to be good, too. DH wants to study in America, but it might be hard—"

Helen felt overwhelmed by the number of rungs on the ladder, and, as usual, each child would need different things. Abroad, their education had seemed more manageable, and she hadn't felt so powerless and alone.

Tom picked up the family education forms Helen had filled out earlier. He scanned them as she watched.

"Do the boys want to go to SNU like their father?"

"Well, that's like wanting to go to the moon, I think." She laughed. "Especially for children who have lived overseas. The children haven't talked about the specifics yet. I suppose we will have to do that soon."

Helen focused on the blue paper folder, which had held her job application only a few weeks before.

"Bo, the eldest, is an excellent student, and I know he's determined. He likes living in Korea and may decide to stay here. For a career, the alumni networks are important." She shrugged. "I don't know for certain, but of my three children, I think he could do well here. I'm not sure about Seoul National, though. I mean, no one gets in there anymore—"

Tom smiled. Each year, Eagle sent three or four students to SNU, Korea University, and Yonsei. The wealthier students from international schools often chose to apply to the more selective American universities, which Tom could almost always manage. Many Eagle students had been accepted to the Ivies.

"The most selective schools here will take some of our students, but it will absolutely be more challenging for your children to apply to Korean universities. They are American born? If Bo goes to high school here, he would have difficulty applying as an international student. It makes more sense to send them to the US for college if possible."

Helen bit her lower lip.

"And DH? Where does he want to go?"

"He just wants to play soccer." Helen laughed. She felt most comfortable around her affable middle child. "I mean, he's a great student, but he'd rather be in Sydney, I think, playing on his team."

"Is his soccer very good?"

"Oh yes. He's a striker. He was midfield but switched. He's also such a fast runner that he could play winger if needed. Two coaches said he could almost go professional. I'm sure they're exaggerating. That's not likely, of course. Kids get injured, and I don't like it when the ball hits his head."

"Could DH go to a boarding school in the US? I know coaches at some very good high schools, who would consider a strong player."

"DH is not just an athlete. He's bright. He doesn't have the recall facility and discipline of his older brother, but he's a good student." Helen was determined not to let DH rely solely on his athletic skills to get the education he needed.

Tom glanced at DH's records. The boy had almost perfect marks and a long list of soccer accomplishments, but Tom was also impressed by the fact that he had been voted captain of his school and club teams.

"I can make some calls. It's only April, and school will start in September in the United States. If he's as good as you say, I think this could be a great opportunity for him." Tom didn't tell Helen that he had served as an assistant soccer coach at Andover when he worked in admissions. The thought of a great high school soccer player having to grind it out in Seoul trying to get into a Korean university depressed him.

"I would be grateful to you if you could help my children in any way. I don't know if Bo or Mido could live far from home, but DH has the social skills. Everyone likes him. When he gets a job, I think he will be a great success." She paused. "I'm bragging now. Please excuse me." Helen tapped her mouth twice with her left hand. Mary, Shin's wife, was sending two sons to Lawrenceville, so Helen had looked into the cost at one point, and it would have been impossible to send all three. With just one, though, they might be able to manage if she worked more hours, or if Sonya could help.

"Your youngest—"

Helen prepared herself, and Tom spoke up, seeing her anxious expression.

"Mido is quiet. I can sense that it took a lot for her to say what she did today, but she can speak well and persuasively."

"Oh." Helen covered her mouth, this time in surprise, realizing that Tom hadn't been fooled. He had seen through Mido's brave performance in the meeting.

"I don't mind when a child is quiet, but it makes life harder for her in some ways. I have a younger sister like Mido. Artistic. Private. Perhaps sensitive."

Helen felt grateful to Tom for seeing her children. Whenever a teacher felt hopeful for a child, the parent could not help feeling less alone. Hope felt like a rare gift.

She had wanted them to be accepted because Sonya had said an excellent hagwon was everything, but now she wanted her children to learn from this man who seemed to see them for who they were, even in such a brief time. But they had not yet spoken about money.

"The fees," she said.

"Ah, yes. Of course." Tom handed her a yellow folder, which included a chart outlining the courses taught. Students were required to attend every term, including during holidays and breaks. There was one fee for everything: The price was breathtaking. Her entire salary would barely cover the cost to send all three children. She would have to make top commissions for this to work.

Helen inhaled. John would think the cost was preposterous, but she wanted this, suddenly, more than anything else.

"Since you don't have enough spots, would it be possible for them to just study the Korean subjects and mathematics? Since they already know English so well. Perhaps pay only two-thirds of the fees. I don't mean to—"

Tom stopped her. "It doesn't work that way. I try not to make a kind of itemized option because students need to learn in a comprehensive way. There's English in math if there are word problems, for example, and there's Korean in English if the student reads about a subject in Korean but discusses it in English. My instructors are bilingual, but they conduct their classes in English. I try to integrate a curriculum that's organic to develop critical thinking. Our hagwon is more like an experimental school in America. I wanted to create my own school there, but my wife and I ended up doing so here."

Tom knew he should be wrapping up this conversation to go help Clara, but he was warming to his subject.

"You see, a capable child who is sufficiently motivated can memorize and take practice exams. You don't need us for that. I'm hoping to help these young people become more independent and thoughtful so they can solve problems, not just predict or be familiar with them. Solve problems not just in school but in life."

Mothers loved their children and wanted their growth, but they also wanted their children to get the best results. They wanted their money's worth. However, Tom had seen firsthand too many students who went to the finest schools in the States and Korea. He had learned a valuable principle of education: Academic performance outcomes could never be the priority. Sometimes excellent students flopped in college or in life. Good testing results were often a natural by-product of strong learning and strategic problem solving. Over and over again, Tom had observed that learning was never linear. If the students weren't adaptive, ethical, and resilient, the education might have been pointless.

What Tom knew and felt, he could defend well, so Helen could not help but want more for her children.

6

Interview

Among the eight instructors who worked full-time at Eagle Academy, Sean Morgan was the mothers' favorite, and the instructor the students talked about most at home.

Sean Teacher said this. Sean Teacher said that. Sean Teacher wore funny hats during a lesson to illustrate figures of speech. He wrote them personalized notes on monogrammed stationery and took them on field trips to musicals and museums. He taught math and English, which was an unusual combination, and he and another popular instructor, Henry Teacher, hosted a culture club to discuss films and novels they considered masterpieces.

Except for his glasses, Sean resembled the actor Sidney Poitier, and unlike the other teachers, who dressed casually, he always wore a beautiful suit and tie to the hagwon, regardless of the season or occasion. A summa cum laude graduate of Yale, he had studied physics and European history, then gone for graduate studies at MIT. He left the doctoral program within a year because it wasn't for him. After loafing for a few months back home in Philadelphia, he found a job teaching calculus at Collegiate, a boys' school in Manhattan, then fell in love with Mark, a Korean American banker visiting New York from Seoul. Sean followed Mark to a new country and found that he liked their life in the fast-changing city, traveling in Asia whenever he and Mark could get away.

Sean had been a Whiffenpoof, and if the students were very good, he would sing "Danny Boy," and even the other instructors would stop everything to listen. Everyone was a little in love with Sean, and he was the highest-paid instructor at Eagle Academy. He worked hard to earn his high salary by forsaking everything except for work and his boyfriend.

When Clara Song brought the Koh children to Sean's classroom, Sean was talking to Peter Son, a prospective student at Eagle who had recently arrived from England and was the only child of the landlord, Renee Cha.

Sean waved them in and pointed to the seats in the front row. The Koh siblings stared at Peter, and Peter smiled but didn't say anything.

"Did Peter start?" Clara asked Sean.

"We were waiting for you. How are you feeling, Peter?" Sean asked.

Peter shrugged. His jet lag had passed, but he still felt tired. He perked up when he saw the other three kids. The two boys were almost identical, except that one was taller and the other wore glasses. They had longer hair than most guys from Seoul. The girl wore her dark hair in two braids. They were dressed nicely. Peter touched his dyed-blond hair, cut close to his scalp.

"That's my team!" DH shouted, pointing at Peter. "I always wanted one of those. Where did you get that? I never saw one here."

Peter looked down at his Arsenal Football Club jersey. He had drawers full of them.

"Wait! What? Is that number nine? That's my player. Oh, man! Is Alan Smith your guy? I'm a striker!" DH rushed to Peter for a high five, and Bo shook his head. Mido had not seen DH this excited in a while.

"Hey." Peter slapped DH's right hand. "Yeah, Arsenal is my team," he said with a British accent.

"Well, that's settled," Sean said, smiling. "How about some assessments, and then you fellows can talk soccer." He handed each of them a different assessment packet.

"All in, this should take about an hour. I'll call out at the thirty-minute mark when you should switch between the two sections, and when I call time, you'll put down your pencils."

The students picked up their pencils and opened their assessment packets.

Sean gathered his own papers and checked his watch. He had just finished interviewing Peter, who would head to Andover in a few months. In the meantime, his mother wanted him to study at the hagwon. He was a strong student and quite capable but not a happy kid. For two years, he had been studying at King's College School, a boys' school outside of Central London, but had not liked it much. Since his mother had to work in Seoul, Peter had boarded with Korean homestay guardians in New Malden and commuted to Wimbledon each day. Although he could manage the schoolwork and sports, it had been difficult for him to make friends. When a few boys on his soccer team teased him and didn't include him on the crucial plays, Peter ran away to London. He had tried to see Suede perform but couldn't get into the venue, so he had roamed the streets and ended up frequenting the British Museum. He went missing for almost three days. His mother, Renee Cha, a divorced heiress of a midtier conglomerate, got on a plane. She phoned the credit card company, and, following his charges at cafés in Bloomsbury and the bookshop at the British Museum, eventually she found him in front of the Rosetta Stone, his favorite thing to see in London. It had been their designated meeting spot when Peter first started to roam the museum by himself. "Oh, Peter," she'd said, relieved, and held him. Later, she sorted out the mess at school.

In Seoul, she brought him to speak with her college classmate Tom Song, who suggested sending him to school in America.

Peter applied to five boarding schools and was accepted to Andover, Hotchkiss, and Lawrenceville. Renee preferred Andover since Tom knew the administration well and could guide them in the process. Peter just wanted to leave King's, where he didn't fit in. It had been embarrassing to tell his mother that he hadn't made close friends in two years. He hadn't gone into detail about what his teammates had done, which wasn't anything serious, but their joking and exclusion had made him miserable. The homestay guardians were decent people but insufficiently interested in him.

An hour passed in no time, and the students put down their pencils.

The Koh children looked horrified.

"That bad, huh?" Sean said to DH, who shook his head like he was disgusted.

"Brutal. Well, I guess we're not getting in." DH tried to sound as if he didn't care, and reached across to pat his sister on the back. "Sorry, Mido. Your brother is dumb as rocks."

Bo shook his head, too. "I can't believe I'm saying this, but I think I might be stupid in this country."

Peter laughed at their joking, then frowned, seeing that Mido was crying.

"Oh, what's the matter, sweetheart?" Sean went to her desk to pick up her assessment. She hadn't finished the math section. "Oh, I see. That's okay." He smiled at her. "I wouldn't have been able to do all of this at your age. We have to make the assessment like this because some students here are several grades ahead. Unnecessarily, I might add."

Sean picked up her brothers' papers, and it was the same. The three had finished the English section without making any mistakes, but neither DH nor Mido had been able to finish the math sections. Bo had answered everything, but there were errors in the proofs toward the end.

Sean picked up Peter's assessment, and everything was completed with only a few mistakes.

"This is why I hate proctoring," he said out loud. "Everything is fine, folks. Take a deep breath, Mido. C'mon." Sean inhaled dramatically and exhaled. He had done some yoga in New York, and when he tutored, he taught his students meditation techniques.

Mido copied his breathing. It was easier to settle down in the presence of her brothers. The other boy seemed fine, confident in his performance on the test.

"I'll take a careful look at these, okay?" Sean said.

The instructor couldn't go over anything specific because each had taken a different assessment, but Sean had wanted to gauge their individual level of ability and how they would manage tough examination situations. Beyond the substance of an examination, much of a child's competence was informed by his psychological well-being, and consequently, he had to build them up to face anxiety-provoking scenarios. This was why meditation was not unhelpful.

Testing conditions had to include irritation, disturbances, structural and random interference. Sean believed there should be conflict and anxiety in testing as in life. After a while, his Eagle students could handle any testing environment or circumstance: coughing, gum cracking, truck sounds, ambulance sirens, breakups, unrequited crushes, unfair proctors who couldn't tell time, and even strange odors. Once he brought in a container of blue cheese to make his Korean students adapt to an unfamiliar scent.

It was hard to explain to his friends from college or grad school what he was doing in Seoul besides living with his soulmate. His friends in America thought hagwons were institutions of child abuse, stealing time away from play, athletic endeavors, social lives, and daydreaming. He had heard all the arguments. It was true that private tutoring could reproduce the upper middle class at the expense of the poor or middle class and perpetuate social inequality. His American friends and former colleagues believed that taken to the extreme, private tutoring made children dependent on more hand-holding. There was some merit to this, he thought.

Before becoming a hagwon instructor, Sean would have agreed with them without blinking, but not anymore. Now he knew too many children to break down the world into reductive categories of "rich kids are bad," "poor kids are needy," and "middle-class kids are normal"—none of that reasoning would suffice in the face of real children who had individual personalities and learning styles. His dataset was too large and varied. He could no longer operate in generalities.

In America or Europe, most students would never go to another school after a full day of regular school, but it was par for the course here. Few students skipped hagwon. There were certainly students who didn't want to attend hagwons, but there were more who sought refuge in them. The students at Eagle didn't want to go home. They liked it here. Eagle was a haven away from intrusive parents and school bullies, and a place where they could ask questions and learn at their own pace. It was true that the Eagle students did better in school, but it was also true that the Eagle students were mentally stronger because they felt they had room to look foolish and someone caring to guide them in case they couldn't ask their teachers. What was cruel, Sean believed, was that every child could not have such needed attention. However, it didn't make sense to him to get rid of something good because not everyone could have it.

The Koh children were obviously bright. They spoke English with Australian accents and were native Korean speakers. The parents must have worked on it. Hearing the four students speak English and Korean made Sean miss living in New York, where it was possible to hear a jumble of different languages and accents. Every year, he thought about going back, but Mark wasn't ready, and Sean would not leave without him.

Sean smiled at Mido.

"I might have flunked out in Korea at your age. I'm not being modest. I'm brilliant at math. The way they teach math here would decimate most children in America. It's sort of absurd." He laughed. "I mean, it's doable because obviously, many of the kids can do it here, China, Japan, Taiwan, Singapore, and elsewhere, but it's just not the focus in the West. Especially in the States. But it doesn't mean that American kids can't do it. You have the necessary aptitude. However, this material at your grade level is just unfamiliar. Remember that unfamiliar is not the same as impossible, or even difficult."

This was a speech Sean had to give often, especially to bright students, who could be discouraged when they didn't do something well quickly.

Mido tilted her head. She'd never heard a teacher talking like this.

"I really tried," she offered. "I'm sorry." Mido found herself crying again.

"Oh, dear." Sean exhaled. "It's not important, Mido. This is an assessment. These papers don't show anything really except for what you have learned so far. If you have done the work you were asked to do, and if you don't know something new, then it isn't your fault. What you choose not to learn is certainly your responsibility, but it's also our responsibility as teachers to explain things, to share what we know. Right? How can I teach you what I know unless I know what you need? That's why we have assessments." He trained his large, amber-colored eyes on the girl's teary face.

Embarrassed, Mido smiled and sat up straight.

"Yun said Eagle doesn't have a lot of room, and she hasn't seen any new families here. Especially anyone with bad marks," she said.

Bo exchanged a glance with DH. This was more than what Mido usually said to strangers.

"I wanted to study here with Yun," she added.

"Ah, yes. Yun Kim is your friend. Right." Sean touched his forehead as if to jog his memory. "She told me, and Dr. Song mentioned that, too. Did you know that her name in my class is Yvonne?"

Mido shook her head.

"Yun's Western name was between Yvonne and Yvette. She picked Yvonne." He smiled at Mido. "Do you want another name?"

She shook her head again, unable to imagine another one. The two brothers shook their heads, too. All of them had been asked this many times before.

"Cool," Sean said. "Bo, DH, and Mido." He paused. "Yeah, your names are easy to say and spell. Lots of people get my name wrong: They say 'Seen' instead of 'Shawn.' "

"We're really Bo-hun, Dae-hun, and Mido," Bo said. "In Paramus, my kindergarten teacher started calling me Bo, and it stuck. Even my parents call me Bo."

"DH is short for Dae-hun, but I used to play baseball, and my coach used to say DH was for 'designated hitter,' " DH added.

Peter looked up. "Nice."

"Soccer is my game, but when I can, I do track and field and baseball," DH said, and glanced at Peter, who nodded in approval. "So, Sean Teacher, I'm the jock." DH pointed to himself. "Bo is the brains. Mido is our baby sister who is just awesome. She can put up with anything and has the best attitude." DH patted his sister on the back gently, relieved that she wasn't crying anymore.

An only child, Peter felt wistful at how clear DH sounded about who they were in relation to each other. He didn't know which category he would fit into, and no one had ever said it like that. He was good at school and sports, and he'd devoted countless hours to improving his guitar skills, but at King's, he hadn't been able to figure out the others and get into a group. The kids there were different from his classmates at Seoul Foreign School, where he had gone before, and even there, he hadn't quite fit in.

Sean pointed to Peter while looking at DH.

"Peter is a soccer player, too. Winger, right?"

"Yes, sir."

"Peter is going to Andover in Massachusetts in the fall."

"Wow," DH exclaimed. "So cool."

"Have you thought of applying?" Sean asked.

DH rubbed his thumb and index finger together and raised his eyebrows.

"Takes a lot of dough." Of the three of them, he spent the most because of soccer—for uniforms, cleats, and travel matches—and he couldn't imagine asking for even more money to go to school in America.

"But you'd go if you could be admitted?" Sean asked.

"Sure. Who wouldn't? I could play a different sport each season and not study for the Suneung. Man, that would be amazing. Dude"—DH turned to Peter—"you are so lucky."

Peter shrugged, not having thought of himself that way. It had always been understood that he would attend university in America as his parents had. His father had gone to Princeton and his mother Cornell.

Sean looked thoughtful. He gathered the assessments into a neat stack, then picked up his red pen.

The Koh children and Peter looked around, not knowing what would happen next.

"Any questions?" Sean asked.

The teenagers shook their heads.

"Listen, I need to take a careful look at these. Go on, get out of here. Your mothers are waiting for you."

Sean winked at them.

Each of the students thanked him in turn.

"The pleasure was mine. And I hope to see you again, Bo, DH, Mido, and Peter."

❧

After Sean graded the assessments, he told Tom and Clara to accept the Koh kids.

"There's no room at the inn," Tom said.

"They would be excellent for discussions in class. I can make them sort of like teaching assistants. The little one needs more confidence. I can work on that," Sean said.

"There would be major complaints if the waiting list parents found out," Clara said.

"Peter is only here until the fall before he heads to the States, so there will be room for at least someone in DH's grade," Sean said. "It's a shame, though."

Clara looked at him quizzically.

"DH would be better off going to boarding school in the States."

"I don't think they can afford it," Clara said.

"I can talk to Peter's mother," Tom said, who knew Renee was worried about Peter's troubles at King's. There was little Renee wouldn't do to help her son adjust at school, even if it meant funding a possible companion. "If Peter went to Andover with a kid like DH, he might be better off. They're both soccer players, and DH seems like the kind of kid who'd be much happier studying in the US."

Sean gave a thumbs-up. "OK, Dr. Song, do your behind-the-scenes prime ministering. No matter what, my vote is for all three of them to be accepted. It would be good for the existing students to have these native speakers, and I don't know why, but I think these kids need this."

Clara made a face, worried.

Tom considered his star teacher's evaluation. Sean was never wrong.

7

Absence

Summer 1993

For Mido and Yun, the second year of middle school was a major improvement, because they had a new homeroom teacher. No one missed Mr. Na. Their eighth-grade homeroom teacher, Mrs. Lim, also taught them Korean.

Mido and Yun spent a good deal of time discussing Mrs. Lim's personal life, which no one knew much about. They wanted to one day imitate her bohemian style—collarless white blouses, dark V-neck sweaters, and a rotation of pencil skirts worn with dark tights and black loafers. They were classically tailored clothes that Mrs. Lim had bought as an undergraduate at Ewha and that she could not yet afford to replace since she and her husband, a fellow teacher, were saving for a larger place to live for when they started a family.

Mido and Yun admired Mrs. Lim's ability to discuss writers of classic literature with a kind of ease and familiarity. Almost nothing ever ruffled her, and even if a student didn't know an answer, she had a way of making the student feel fine about it. She inspired them to do all the reading and led them in animated discussions about ancient poems and stories, which they had to know well for future standardized exams.

That morning, Mrs. Lim's hair was worn in loose waves, making the young, slim woman appear even more glamorous than usual. Mido was curious as to what Yun would think about Mrs. Lim's new style, and was disappointed to see that her friend's desk was vacant again. For three days, Yun had not been in class. Twice she'd phoned Yun's house, and no one had picked up.

The Koh family had now been in Seoul for about a year and a half. Mido liked middle school. She had Yun, and, not having had a friend before,

Mido realized how much better things could be with one. Even Mr. Na's class had become manageable, because Yun had advised her about how to act, and Mido had become a more capable student: observant, prepared, and better able to recognize patterns. Her classes at Eagle Academy helped her to keep up with the top students, who had been tutored since kindergarten. The two girls had decided that with a teacher like Mrs. Lim, school could be a wonderful place, and it did not seem terrible that her brothers were so occupied with their own lives that neither had time for her.

In his second year of high school, Bo studied night and day. It was a testament to Bo's remarkable efforts and the tutors at Eagle Academy that Bo had the necessary grades and high class rank to qualify for Yonsei University's entrance exams. He could not test for Seoul National, which was reserved for the very top students, but his rank was close enough that his advisors thought even a school like Yonsei might be possible, especially if he applied for sociology, which was a subject Bo wanted to study.

Bo couldn't sleep much. There was no time for that. In the evenings, when he worked, Mido studied as well, but she could never stay awake as long as he could. Helen did her best to stay up with Bo, but even she had to turn in because she had her job the next day and had to prepare breakfast for the family.

Home wasn't the same without DH, who was now heading into his sophomore year at Andover. The family believed that a private foundation that Eagle Academy had a relationship with had given him a merit scholarship, allowing him to go to Andover only four months after the Koh family had returned to Seoul. He had repeated freshman year at boarding school with Peter Son, the boy he had met at Eagle Academy. Fast friends, DH and Peter planned to bunk together for their second year, and both played on the varsity soccer team.

After another day without Yun at school, Mido walked to Eagle by herself. It was difficult to concentrate at hagwon because she was worried about her friend. Even Sean Teacher's jokes seemed less funny without Yun laughing with her.

As class ended, the students trickled out, and Sean handed Mido her graded assignments.

"You did a terrific job. Again." Sean smiled as he returned his pencils to their case.

Mido smiled briefly, thanked him, then turned to leave.

"You're sad about Yun."

Mido looked at him blankly.

"It won't be the same without her."

"Hmm?"

"She's moving to California. I just heard from Dr. Song. Isn't that why you have the long face, my young friend?" Sean asked, soon realizing his faux pas. From her stunned expression, he figured out that she hadn't known.

"You're upset," Sean said. "Oh my." He got up and closed the door.

Mido tried to be calm. There was no way for her to explain what this would mean. They were supposed to have a birthday party together in October. She had never had something like that before, a friend and one born within a week of her. Everyone liked Yun, and she had chosen Mido to have lunch with and go to hagwon with. In church, they always sat together. Now her friend was moving to America, thousands of miles away, and Mido did not believe she could have another friend. No one like Yun. In her time in Seoul, Mido had not made another friend. There had been no need. She had the best friend a person could have at the whole school.

Mido swallowed, blinking back tears. She picked up her bag and bowed to her teacher.

"You can't go yet. Here." He handed her a packet of tissues. "Listen. I know. It's hard to make friends, right?"

She turned away from his concerned expression, and then the tears started again.

Sean looked at the little face and the childish braids. He patted her back the way he had seen her brothers do. The girl was devastated, and he had never seen her this emotional.

"She's your best friend."

"Best friend," Mido repeated, wiping her face.

Sean covered his mouth, wanting to cry himself. He knew what it was like to feel this way. Even though he'd had many friends growing up, not everyone had known about him being gay. In college, he was out and had friends, but it wasn't until he fell in love with Mark that he felt he had someone who could read his thoughts and be with him in silence. He handed her another tissue.

"I'm sorry, Mido. Life can be painful. I can tell you that things will get better, and I want you to believe me. But I know you still suffer right now, and no one will understand exactly how you feel. I'm sorry I broke the news to you in such a careless way. I should have checked. How can I help?"

Mido shook her head, feeling bad for him. It wasn't his fault. In a way, she was relieved that Yun wasn't in a hospital.

"Is she already gone?" Mido asked, unable to believe that her friend would move without saying goodbye. But Mido had left Paramus and Sydney without much notice or fanfare, never thinking that anyone could care about her absence.

Sean waved his hand no. "I don't think she's gone yet. I was just told she wouldn't be coming in while they prepare to move."

Mido was clutching her schoolbag close to her chest. Jane Teacher would have started her lessons. Hagwon was expensive, and her parents had to sacrifice so Bo and she could attend. It would be wrong to sit here and feel sorry for herself. She bowed to Sean Teacher and rushed to her next class.

♣

In the morning, Mido got up earlier than usual and went to Yun's house.

She walked the eight blocks down the main shopping thoroughfare, then took a sharp left. Past the furniture store, konditorei, and vegetable market, there was a cluster of high-rises, where Yun lived in Tower 6.

On the second buzzer ring, Yun's mother, Nari, opened the door.

"Mido, what brings you here? It's so early. Are you all right?"

Mido burst into tears, relieved that they hadn't left yet.

"Oh, Mido, what's the matter?" Nari tapped her forehead. "Oh, of course. You heard. Come. Come inside."

Mido removed her shoes and put on the pair of red house slippers she wore at Yun's house. Nari had bought them just for her because she'd wanted Mido to visit often.

Nari guided the girl to the gilt-edged sofa. Mido breathed in the scents of Yun's house—a mixture of food aromas and Yun's father's lime-scented cologne. From floor to ceiling, the living room wall was mirrored, and if you stood in the hallway with a closet door open, you could see seven or eight images of yourself. Nari wore a pink cotton apron over her burgundy wool dress, its hem trimmed in fur. Somehow, in this living room designed like a miniature palace, Nari's extravagant clothes made sense.

"Yun is upset, too. She's in her room resting. I was going to phone your mother next week." Nari wrapped her head with her hands. "When I was her age, I would have been thrilled to live in America. I don't know how I raised such a brat. No doubt it's all my fault. I thought she would go there for school. I mean later. For college. She's in there sleeping. She was crying all night."

Mido wanted to defend her friend. Yun was the most generous and brave person she had ever known. She was the furthest thing from a brat.

"Mido, you should go to school. You don't want to be late. Mrs. Lim will not like it." Nari stood up.

"May I talk to Yun?"

"Have you had breakfast? I have some bread. I can put jam on it and wrap it for you."

Nari looked exhausted. She wore no makeup, and her dyed-auburn hair was gathered loosely with a fabric tie. Mido had never seen Yun's mother without black eyeliner and dark-pink lipstick.

"Be a good girl, Mido. You should go to school. I will tell Yun that you came for her."

Mido looked up at her again, unable to ask further. She tried to smile at the tired mother, suddenly feeling sorry for her. From all their moves, Mido knew that her mother had worked even harder than her father to organize everything.

"She is resting, Mido."

In the foyer, Mido put on her shoes. She opened the front door but turned when she heard her friend's voice.

"Is she gone?" Yun stepped out of her bedroom, her face red, bruised and swollen.

"Yun!"

Yun's hair was loose around her shoulders. She was still in her long flannel nightgown. Shocked, Mido covered her mouth. She didn't know how her face had become like that.

Nari opened the front door.

"You'd better go, dear. You can see Yun next week. She will return to school."

"Yes, ma'am." Mido tried to have courage, and smiled at her friend. "If you want me to bring your homework, I can do that." She wanted to stay longer, but Mrs. Lim would notice her lateness. Mido wanted to tell Yun about their homeroom teacher's new wavy hairstyle and how lunch had been so dull without her, but it seemed wrong to whine about such things when her friend had been hiding in her room like that. Someone had hit her, and Mido remembered what Yun had said the time Mr. Na struck her with a ruler, that Yun's parents thought teachers should punish a disobedient child.

"I missed you," Mido blurted out, and waved goodbye.

For the first time, Yun was the one who didn't speak.

❧

After church services, Helen heard about Yun's family from Sonya. Yun's father's business partner had sold their three convenience stores without his knowledge and signed promissory notes, pledging their buildings as the asset. The partner was nowhere to be found, and Yun's father was suddenly near ruin. He had family in Orange County, and they planned on moving to California in August.

Helen didn't understand how this could happen.

"The partner was Yun's father's best friend from high school. He was in charge of the money because he had the initial investment capital, while Yun's father was the one who did the work, but apparently they bought the buildings together. The partner had a gambling problem, and he borrowed money from banks and some bad people. After he sold everything, he left the remaining debts and then ran away. Yun's father has no idea where he went."

Helen leaned in closer, not wanting to be disturbed by the other women who wanted to speak with her sister. They stood below the staircase near the church auditorium, with Helen's back against the crowds to keep Sonya for herself.

"Do you know these people?" Helen asked.

"Yun's family? Of course not," Sonya said, surprised. "I never even spoke to Yun's mother until Mido became friends with the child." She caught herself sounding haughty and felt ashamed. It seemed uncharitable. "Yun's mother seems like a very nice woman. My husband and the Chairman were talking about the scandal during dinner last week, and I didn't realize who they were talking about until he mentioned the stores, and it occurred to me that it must be Mido's friend's family."

Helen wasn't sure what to say. It must be terrible for Yun's family, yet selfishly, she felt disappointed that Mido's only friend was moving away.

"Apparently they lost everything and have just enough money left to get to California. His sister could sponsor their immigration. The partner stuck them with tax problems, too, and the company that bought the stores had all the legal documents in place, so there's nothing Yun's father can do. The Chairman said the whole matter is sordid and you can't trust weak people with addiction problems."

The two sisters understood. Their parents had routinely gambled and fled, leaving them behind whenever they became a burden. When the parents returned home, Sonya, Helen, and Kenny knew their mounting debts would continue to plague the family.

"The Chairman said the scandal was featured in the major business paper, so all the other papers carried the story. Anyway, now they have to go to America. Can you imagine starting again at their age? I don't think they can speak English. That poor woman."

"Yun's mother has always been so nice to Mido. I was grateful for that," Helen said. "Mido is heartbroken."

"Are you sending her to Sydney during vacation?"

"Yes," Helen said. "Kenny called last week. The children are so excited, and Mido can go to Lily's school. She got permission."

"I like Lily. She's always thinking. Kenny is lucky to have her," Sonya said. The sisters had not known what to think when their younger brother Kenny migrated to Australia on his own, then married a White Australian girl, but things had worked out well for him there, and Lily had turned out to be a wonderful sister-in-law. She was devoted to Kenny and their four children. She worked in the bursar's office at a girls' school.

"Have you seen Yun's mother at services? I looked for them. Yun usually sits with Mido, but she wasn't in their pew this morning."

"She can't show her face, I think," Sonya said.

The sisters said nothing else, understanding how things could get that way.

❧

On Monday evening, Helen picked up a jam roll cake at a bakery near the Lotte Hotel. Mido had told her that this was Yun's favorite.

Nari was home alone. She accepted the cake and smiled, ushering Helen into the living room.

"Mido was here the other day."

"Oh?"

"Yes, she came by to check on Yun. I thought that was nice." Nari offered Helen tea.

"I'm sorry to drop by without any notice. I won't be long. I have to get home and make dinner. I just heard you're going away, and I was sad to hear it. Mido has never had a friend like your daughter before. Yun is very special. I wanted to thank you for always welcoming her to your home."

Helen didn't want to say any more. Seeing Nari's anguished face, Helen reached for the woman's hands and held them for a moment, then let go.

Their daughters were friends, but Helen and Nari moved in different circles. Nari tried to keep herself from crying.

"I don't want to go to America, but it's hard to stay here. My husband thinks it will be good for Yun. There's only three of us, so we'll stay at my sister-in-law's in Orange County. I don't speak English. Not like you. You're so smart. I have an empty gourd for a head. I just know how to spend money, and if I had been a better wife, then maybe—" Nari could not continue speaking and clamped her mouth shut. She fidgeted with the tissue box on the mirrored coffee table.

Helen looked away, feeling terrible for the woman. She knew what it was like to decamp and move somewhere else, though of course it was different when your husband still had a job.

"You're going to be fine. I've moved a great deal over the years, and each time, it was difficult, but I focus on my children and husband. Within each country, we moved several times, too. Sometimes more than once in a year because apartments cost too much, and we had to watch expenses. I wish life could be easier."

"Yun is not herself. She was elected the head of the class again this year, and I think she could have done so well here. We thought she could go to university in America one day, but not like this. In an American high school, she's going to be last at everything."

"No, no. You can't think like that. Children are good at adapting. I worry more about you." Helen laughed. "But I know you'll be able to manage. You'll see."

"I didn't know you were so nice."

Helen raised her eyebrows.

"You and your sister are so smart and went to good schools. I'm just a country girl who married a bumpkin. Yun's father made a lot of money, then he lost it all. It was that terrible man." Nari's mouth grew firm. "I can't talk about it. I hope he burns in hell." She had surprised herself and looked up. "I'm sorry. I shouldn't say such things. No matter what, I must not hate my enemies, right?"

Helen nodded, trying to understand. She had never been in this situation before. Her father had taught her not to judge people if you could help it. You never knew what they were going through. Perhaps he needed to say this since he was a gambler who drank and never kept a job. He had not wanted her judgment.

"My father and mother never had much, and whenever they did, they would throw it away. For nothing. They never planned for next week. It was always for today. They played cards." Helen shrugged. They were long dead, and she wasn't angry with them anymore. This was something she and Sonya never discussed with others.

"I didn't know."

"It's shameful to discuss. But my sister and me, you have the wrong idea. We had nothing growing up except our parents' debts and messes, and no one thought our family was any good. But we still got through school, and we're fine. The church helped us when our parents would abandon us. They died young such a long time ago, when we were young students. Anyway—"

Helen paused, not wanting to talk about the past.

"Yun-umma, you are going to be okay. You're healthy and strong. I've heard California is a wonderful place. You'll make money again. More than anything, Yun is a bright and beautiful girl, with such a big heart. Mido wasn't herself until she met Yun. I'm here because your daughter does you credit."

Nari wiped her face with a tissue. The mascara had run, smudging the hollows of her large eyes. She looked lovelier in a way. Helen had righted a piece that had fallen out of place in the past week, just by telling her something about her life.

"I heard you're not leaving until the end of the summer. During break, I was going to send Mido to Sydney, and I wonder if maybe Yun would like to go. Improve her English. My brother works for Qantas, so we'll take care of the tickets, and it won't cost anything once the girls are there. They can go to school where my sister-in-law works. My brother Kenny has four lovely children. Their break is different from ours. Would you like that?"

Nari looked hopeful. "I can pay for the plane ticket."

"No, no. That's not necessary. My brother gets extra ones that he never uses. His wife, Lily, was born in Australia and works at a nice private school. She loves Mido and needs help with the children. They're very young, and one is a newborn. There's an au pair, but they can use all the hands they can get. Mido loves to go to their house. She talks the most when she's with little ones."

Nari covered her face with her hands.

"This means so much to me. Thank you. My husband has been so angry. He's not himself anymore. And there's so much to do. While Yun is gone, I can get ready for our move. Her English will improve, too, right?"

"Of course," Helen said, smiling.

Briefly the two mothers held hands again, then Helen rose from her seat.

"I will call with the dates and schedules," Helen said.

In the elevator, Helen smoothed her hair, her back reed-straight.

The polite security guard in the parking lot bowed as she left the building, and she smiled at him, recalling that as a girl who'd had to plead with nuns for a small bag of barley, she would have been grateful if her father had worked a steady job like his and just come home each night.

8

Winter in Sydney

Sydney, Australia
July 1993

Helen phoned her brother and sister-in-law in Sydney. Right away, they agreed that both girls should come stay with them for their break. Sonya and Helen's younger brother, who went by Kenny rather than Kyung-jin, arranged for the airline tickets, and his Aussie wife, Lily, received permission for both girls to attend the school where she worked as visiting exchange students.

Lily Hughes Cho had not intended to fall in love with a Korean man, but she did, and Kenny turned out to be an ideal husband and father to their four children: Henry, eight; fraternal twins Jonathan and Neil, five; and the seventeen-month-old baby, Donna.

Lily, a laconic, no-nonsense mechanic's daughter, met Kenny at a TAFE school for accounting and bookkeeping. Tired of horny boys from Campsie who wanted to spend their lives watching footy and playing darts, the ambitious brunette had been drawn to the international student who wore a clean, pressed white shirt to class each day and took his coursework seriously. They both earned their certificates, and Qantas hired Kenny straightaway. After a number of promotions, he worked at the main offices in Mascot as a senior manager in the accounting department, while Lily did the bookkeeping in the bursar's office at Erickson Ladies' College, a girls' school in Epping. The pair worked hard, lived below their means, and raised their children with the help of a rotating cast of au pairs.

Mido and Yun arrived in Sydney in July, excited for their new adventure. Quickly they settled into their new routines: helping Lily with the children and attending Erickson, a pleasant single-sex school, where math and science were almost easy compared to the classes at their public school in Seoul.

Lily and Kenny's Epping home was a spacious, ranch-style house with four bedrooms and three baths. The dwelling was modest, but its interiors were well maintained because Kenny was handy. Through TAFE courses, he had picked up some knowledge of carpentry, plumbing, electricity, and even heating and air-conditioning, saving money on repairs. There was plenty of room for everyone, and a small suite for Iris, the current au pair. The children shared two large bedrooms, and Mido and Yun slept on cots in the den, which also served as a playroom. A sturdy sectional sofa anchored the living room, and it was upholstered in a brown plaid tweed, which wouldn't show dirt or spilled juice.

Learning from how-to books, Kenny had built two sets of monastery tables and benches—one for the children to do their schoolwork on in the living room and another for family meals in the sun-filled, open kitchen.

Each morning Lily left a stack of clean bowls and spoons, a pot of porridge, a tin of sultanas, a gallon jug of milk, and a box of Weet-Bix on the dining table, then headed to work. Kenny, Iris, and the children fixed their own breakfasts. Lily finished her workday before Kenny, so she cooked their simple dinners, and it was Kenny's job to wash up and help with the children's bedtime.

The girls didn't miss their lives in Seoul. There was no need to go to hagwon because schoolwork wasn't impossible. With some effort and focused attention, the girls were able to do their studies without extra help. For the first time, Mido did better in her coursework than Yun. With time to spare, the girls read English-language novels, watched television game shows with the family, and learned to bake. Within only a week of school in Australia, Yun's English improved: It was as if the words and phrases needed the right context and setting to make sense and come alive.

On a Sunday afternoon, after the family returned from church, the girls went straight to the kitchen and rooted in the pantry to find the ingredients for chocolate chip Anzac biscuits. For once, the kitchen was quiet. Kenny was in the backyard with the boys, and Lily was doing the wash. Iris had taken the baby to the park for air.

Yun loved learning a new recipe. In just two weeks, she had figured out how to bake a chocolate cake, currant scones, and Anzac biscuits. The baking pleased the children because Lily rarely bought sugary treats but did not mind the homemade goods.

"We have the main ingredients, but maybe we can get some chocolate chips at the store. I have the money Umma sent," Yun said, feeling inspired, before her expression dimmed. "Oh, never mind." In her last letter from home, her mother said that she should be careful with her spending, and never to borrow. Before her father lost the business, with bottomless pocket money, Yun had never thought about what things cost. If anything, she had been the one to buy yogurt drinks for her classmates, or lend money without expecting repayment. Her mother habitually bought too much of everything and was always giving things away. Yun felt bad for being stingy about the chocolate chips, which she knew the other children would like.

Mido sensed that Yun was thinking about the cost of the chocolate, which would certainly be a few dollars.

"I have money, too. You always pay. It's my turn."

Yun looked ashamed and Mido wanted to take it back, having hurt her friend's pride.

"Uncle Kenny doesn't like chips in his Anzacs," Mido said. "There's enough ingredients to make dozens of large ones. Let's start now."

Yun stayed silent, wiping down the counter with a sponge.

"Your dad will get a good job," Mido said.

"Appa is older now. It will be harder," Yun said without looking up from her work, repeating what her mother had said.

Yun washed the last frying pan, and Mido dried the plates and returned them to the cupboard.

On Monday afternoon, Iris picked up the girls from school, then drove them to the boys' school, where she asked the girls to get Henry while she remained in the car with the twins and the baby, who was fussing. In no time, they spotted Henry bolting from the gates. He ran into Mido's arms and hugged her. Then, remembering himself, he pulled away slightly, glancing around in case his classmates had seen him.

"We brought you something," Yun said with a smile, removing a large biscuit from her plastic lunch container and holding it up high.

Like a puppy, Henry jumped at it. "Yes!"

"Hey, Henry Cho!" An older boy patted Henry on the back.

"Hey, Tek!" The boy's black hair was cut short on the sides and kept longer in the front. His uniform navy blazer was unbuttoned, and a rep tie hung askew across his tall and lanky frame. His dark eyes were playful, like he was game for anything.

"Your sisters?" he asked.

Mido caught herself staring, then looked away.

"Nah, mate. Mido's my cousin, and Yun's her friend. They're visiting us from Korea." Henry pointed at Yun. "And she's about to go live in America."

The boy said this with a mouthful of biscuit, and with awe. Thanks to his father's job at Qantas, Henry had been on an airplane several times, but he had never gone as far as the United States, a place as mythic as any in a storybook. It was Henry's dearest wish to go to Disneyland, which was located somewhere in a place called Anaheim, California. He had looked it up in the encyclopedia.

"Have you been to Disneyland, Tek?" Henry asked him.

"Nope. Haven't ever been to America," Tek said. He glanced at Yun, impressed that this girl would go somewhere so far away. "Hey, Henry, what's that you're eating?"

"Anzacs. The best." Henry snapped off a large corner for Tek, who popped it whole into his mouth.

"Oh, these are really good. I always get the homemade ones at the bake sale. Store-bought is not the same," he said. "These are good because they're not completely crunchy. The middle's still chewy. Key factor." Tek concentrated and pronounced: "Buttery. The coconut ratio is amazing. Mom never bakes. I didn't know Koreans baked."

Mido felt happy that this boy liked their baking, while Yun thought he was dumb to think that Koreans didn't bake just because his own mother didn't. That was poor logic, Yun reasoned.

"I'm Korean, too," Tek said to the girls, hoping they'd say something. "Can't speak it much, though." He shrugged. "I'm going to pick it up when I go to uni."

Yun furrowed her brow, unable to understand how overseas Koreans didn't speak the language.

"Henry is my little brother here. He was assigned to me a while back. We're still buddies. A school tradition," Tek explained. "The older boys at Queen's are supposed to be role models for the little ones, you see. Teach them how to study, behave, and do sports. I guess you're not so little now." Tek mussed up Henry's hair.

"Tek's in Year 11. He watches out for me," Henry said proudly. "Hey, Tek, you want more biscuits?"

"You have more, mate?" Tek brightened.

"We have them at home. Come over. We can do homework and eat 'em with milk," Henry said. "We have lots more, right?"

Mido nodded, not knowing if it was okay to invite Tek to the house, although there were neighborhood children over all the time.

"Race you!" Henry shouted, and started running to the parking lot. Tek counted five-four-three-two-one, then flew down the road and cleared well ahead of Henry, who did his best to keep up with Tek's long strides.

❧

At home, Henry brought out the large tin of biscuits from the pantry, and Tek ate five Anzacs and drank two large glasses of milk with ice.

"Homework time, Henry. C'mon, mate. Let's get serious. We are scholars. We must earn our biscuits."

Tek pulled out his books and did his work with great concentration. He finished his English assignment in less than an hour, then began his problem set. Henry imitated the boy almost twice his size and did his work quietly. While they worked, Yun and Mido did their assignments.

"Break," Henry announced before going to the washroom.

"Hey, Yun," Tek said, "you excited about going to America?"

She shrugged and continued with her English grammar exercises.

"What's school like? In Korea," Tek asked the girls, and Yun didn't reply. It was odd because normally she wasn't afraid to talk with anyone. Mido pulled out crisps from the pantry and poured them into a thin wooden salad bowl.

"School there is hard," Mido said.

Tek smiled at Mido, wanting her to talk. He didn't know many girls, since he went to a boys' school.

Mido slid the bowl of crisps toward him, noticing that his dark eyelashes were much longer than hers. Like her brothers, he had nice clear skin and a straight nose, but he was much taller than they were, and he slouched when seated.

"I had a difficult time adjusting when we moved back from Sydney to Seoul. Yun helped me a lot," Mido said.

Yun smiled. "Mido is smart, but our teacher last year, Mr. Na, was not good. Mrs. Lim, our teacher this year, is good," she said slowly, feeling awkward speaking in English to a Korean boy.

Tek smiled. At last, he had gotten them to say something.

"There are no Koreans at the Queen's School, except for me and Henry. He's half Korean but you know he's a Cho—"

Henry had returned to his spot next to the older boy and elbowed him jokingly as if they were the same age, and continued with his astronomy worksheet. He felt proud that he had brought a cool guy like Tek to the house.

"Tek doesn't have brothers or sisters," Henry said. "Isn't that weird?" he remarked to Mido, who made a reproving face.

"Yun is an only child," Mido said. "That's not weird. Her parents just chose to have one."

"You are?" Tek said, delighted. "I guess you get everything, too."

Yun continued to read her grammar book.

"I have two brothers," Mido said to Tek.

"Nice." Tek said it like he meant it, then reached for more crisps.

❧

In the evening, the girls washed up for bed and collapsed on their cots. It had been a long day, filled with school, kids, then a guest, who had ended up staying for dinner and talking to Kenny and Lily about Queen's and all the Year 11 teachers.

"You like him," Yun whispered.

"Yeah, he's nice," Mido said before realizing that Yun had meant romantically.

"Mido has a boyfriend," Yun teased, pulling her blue camp blanket all the way up to her chin.

"We're too young to have boyfriends," Mido said.

"Well, he's at least a year older than we are. Boys do lots of things earlier than girls. You have to be careful or else you can get pregnant. My mother said you have to avoid boys until after college." Yun didn't understand what her mother meant by this. It was just better not to talk to them or give them any encouragement, she'd said.

"Pregnant?" Mido tapped Yun's arm.

"You like him." Yun laughed. "You were talking a lot. For you. Many, many words."

Mido blushed. She didn't know how to explain that it was easier to speak when Yun was with her. There were occasions when she wanted to talk more, and she was also in Australia, where she could speak English. Then it occurred to her that soon, they wouldn't be together anymore, and Mido forgot about Tek. In a few weeks, the girls would leave Sydney, and Yun would go to California, and the color and warmth Yun brought to her life would be gone.

9
Games

Seoul

"She did all the work. She's not bad at her job," John said, finding himself defending the young woman he was supposed to fire. Danbi Jung made him uncomfortable; however, he had to admit that she pulled off assignments that employees with her experience should not have been able to manage.

"You haven't given her something she could not do," Shin said, knowing it would be difficult for John to be unfair. "I saw the projects you gave her. They were doable."

"Not by someone who's been out of the training program for only a year. I don't think I could have done them at her level."

"I'm having a hard time." Shin put down his tumbler of whiskey, and the ice cubes clinked in the amber liquid. "I know I told you to lay off for a while, because I thought she understood the terms, but you were supposed to make her want to quit or else find cause for her to be fired—" He broke off, unable to confess to his friend that Danbi wanted him to leave his wife. None of the women he had slept with would have dared to ask for something so unreasonable.

They were in the bar at the Chosun Hotel, and John didn't feel like drinking anymore. It was only nine o'clock, but for him, it was late. If Shin weren't his oldest friend, John would have left, without making excuses. He was tired. Not for a moment would he have listened to this nonsense from anyone else.

Shin wanted to keep his girlfriend, family, and job. He had no plans to break it off with Danbi, and felt that he could still control the situation: She simply had to quit or get fired. Competent and attractive, Danbi could get another entry-level job. That said, HRI was the most prestigious trading company in Korea, and she had wanted to work there ever since she'd heard of it. Shin could get her another position, even a better-paying one, but any other company would be several rungs lower than where she had already climbed.

After John gave Danbi two additional assignments, both seemingly impossible, Danbi told her lover again to fire John for being an unreasonable manager. Regardless, Shin instructed John to assign her more difficult projects to show that he did not play favorites. But no matter the level of challenge or volume of work, somehow Danbi completed her tasks. Her work improved at a notable rate, and she grew even more competent than the members of her training group. It didn't hurt that the midlevel and senior members of the team figured out that she was Shin's mistress and understood it would be in their best interest to help her out.

Company dinners became unbearable for John. It was like being in the presence of teenagers, with their public displays of affection. Danbi made no secret of her feelings for Shin, and the middle-aged director did not mind his subordinates admiring his sexual prowess with the gorgeous young woman.

John had not told Helen about Danbi; she would hate to know that her friend Mary was being betrayed like this.

"Is it possible for you to give her up?" John asked, still hoping for reason to prevail. Mary was a good mother to their three boys, and though she had tolerated mistresses, refusing to ever consider divorce, Danbi Jung was a different sort. She was the kind of mistress who needed to become a wife.

Shin took another sip of his drink and ignored the question.

"Can you write poor reviews for her work performance? Then she can't get promoted. Also, give her an assignment that even the senior guys can't do. Something where she has to make an error. Make her give a presentation where the others can see that she got it all wrong. Change the data if you need to. I promise I'll take care of it. You won't get in trouble. I know I'm asking you for a big favor. Please."

"I should get home. You know me. I have to sleep early."

Shin nodded. Danbi was waiting for him in a hotel room upstairs.

❧

Helen had eaten alone. The apartment was empty of children. Bo was at the hagwon studying for his Yonsei entrance exam and wouldn't be home until late. DH was at soccer camp in Vermont, and Mido was in Sydney. To save money, the plan was to move to a much smaller rental as soon as the lease ended. The private scholarship that the owner of Eagle Academy had arranged for DH took care of most of his tuition at Andover, but there had been unexpected costs like soccer camps, plane tickets, and meals and gifts when he stayed with friends, or at Mary's during breaks when he couldn't return to Seoul. Helen didn't like the idea of her son not having enough pocket money or receiving free meals from others. DH had offered to get a part-time job, but Helen and John had forbidden it. He was too young, they said. Whenever she could, Helen picked up extra shifts at the store to boost her sales commissions.

When John came home, Helen was standing by the kitchen counter, picking through dried black beans in a large stainless steel bowl.

"Did you have dinner?"

"Yes," he said, glancing around the empty living room where the children used to do their homework. "It's quiet without the kids."

Helen placed her hand on his shoulder.

"Are you okay? Did you drink? Do you want water?"

"I didn't drink much. Just sleepy." He smiled to reassure her and went to his room for the night.

Helen soaked the black beans and finished prepping side dishes. She wished she could phone DH. He had left a message on the answering machine to say hello. "Everything is good here. I miss you, Mommy, and I bet you want to see me," he'd said, laughing. In less than a minute, he had gotten off the expensive overseas call. She wanted to hear more from her second child—the one who was always cheerful and made her feel calm—but there was no way to reach him except a call to the camp offices for an emergency, and this wasn't that. DH had been right, she did want to see him. She loved her children equally, but it was DH who paid attention to her moods and knew how to make her smile. If he hadn't been doing so well at Andover, then he would have returned to Seoul, but his academic reports were far superior to his reports from Seoul and Sydney. The practices at the soccer camp were difficult, he'd said, but even there, DH was flourishing.

❧

It was seven in the morning in Burlington, and DH had already showered and dressed. Chilly, he pulled on a UVM sweatshirt.

His eyes half-open, Peter Son remained in bed, still groggy with sleep.

"Dude, you want breakfast? I'm starving. I'm going to have five eggs with bacon and cheese. Chef Brenda said I can have as many eggs as I want in my omelet." DH grinned like he'd won a prize.

"You're her favorite. I get it," Peter groaned, throwing the covers over his head.

"Who doesn't love Chef Brenda? She's the greatest." DH got on well with the summer college kitchen staff, but especially with the seventy-two-year-old white-haired head cook, who wore a black hairnet and a spotless white uniform and laughed at DH's knock-knock jokes. She always gave him extra bacon.

Peter closed his eyes. He shouldn't have been surprised by how quickly DH learned people's names at camp and found something to like in everyone; he was the same at Andover. Peter was known as DH's friend, not the other way around, and he was relieved to have an ally who was kind of like an ambassador.

"Hey, get up, sleepyhead." DH stood over him and smiled. "Good morning."

"Yes," Peter said, and sat up. "Why are we doing this again?" He picked up his guitar by his bed and started to play "Should I Stay or Should I Go."

"You should go, go, go," DH said. "We are doing this again so we don't get our asses kicked this season. Also, you gotta look sharp today. Remember? The college coaches are coming by again to scout this afternoon."

"Right, right." Peter headed to the showers. "Go. Go. Go."

❧

At morning practice, as Peter sprinted to the goal line during a drill, the head coach blew his whistle and called him off the field. His mother was here.

At the office, Peter found her chatting and laughing with Larry, the physical trainer.

Renee Cha was wearing a sleeveless white linen sundress, with a navy silk cardigan slung loosely over her pale shoulders. In the summers, she always wore white linen, and if she needed a sweater or jacket, they were only in khaki or navy. In fall and winter, she wore tailored suits made from fine flannel or tweeds in gray, navy, or camel. She wore pale blue or tea green for spring. She never wore diamonds.

Peter's mother, a striking and confident woman, looked like no other mother. She was divorced from Peter's father, Byron Son, who had remarried when Peter was in primary school and lived in Hong Kong with his new family. Renee had no interest in marrying again. Like her oldest brother and cousins, Renee was a director for her grandfather's family company, which manufactured tires and other automobile parts.

Peter greeted his mother with a long hug. He was relieved to see her. Peter was wearing his blue Andover jersey, which should have been washed, but as usual, he was behind on laundry.

"Oh, my goodness. Excuse me." Renee turned apologetically to Larry. "My beautiful child smells awful."

"All the boys stink," Larry said, winking at Peter. "Have a good visit. Lovely to meet you, Mrs. Son." The trainer left them alone in the waiting area of the office. The camp secretary continued to deal with the bills and didn't pay them any mind.

"I've been divorced from your father for over a decade. Why do people still call me Mrs. Son?" Renee muttered. Women in Korea retained their surnames after marriage, so unlike divorced women in the West, Renee never even had to change back her name. She sank into the brown leather sofa and patted it, inviting Peter to join her.

"How are you?" He was used to her unannounced appearances, and, in many ways, appreciated them. She seemed to be able to intuit whenever he needed rest or comfort.

"I missed you. I wanted to take you and DH out to dinner after practice. I got permission already. I even found a Korean restaurant if you want to go. The driver can take us." Renee pointed to the parking lot, where her chauffeur waited in a black sedan.

"Also, I brought you clean uniforms and clothes." She raised an eyebrow. "Are you ever going to do your laundry?"

"Thank you, Mother. I promise I'll do it, but it'll be nice to have some fresh supplies," Peter said in his most posh British accent, relieved he could avoid laundry for a few more days. Trying to find a machine felt impossible whenever there was time to do the wash, and he was always tired after practice, so it was hard to stay awake when the machines were more readily available.

"How much longer is practice?" Renee asked. "Can't we just leave?"

"It's a big day, we can't just leave," Peter told her. "There are scouts coming to watch us, from colleges."

Renee raised her right eyebrow.

"Any school would be lucky to have you," she said. "My son is the best."

"Thank you for your confidence, Mother," Peter answered. "I better get back."

❧

The boys cleaned up and wore fresh clothes to meet Renee, and they didn't go to the Korean restaurant, which was almost an hour away. The boys were too hungry, and there was a bistro downtown, which apparently had excellent steaks.

DH glanced at the menu and tried to conceal his shock at the high prices, though he should have been used to it by now. Renee would never allow him to pay for his meal, but he felt guilty that the entrées were so expensive. His mother had taught him to always order the least costly items and never to order drinks, with their high margins, when he was someone's guest, so he ordered the spaghetti marinara, which was $14.99, and no appetizer. He drank ice water.

Peter ordered a French onion soup, the rib eye steak, and a baked potato. When Renee passed the bread basket to them, DH took a large onion roll. Peter grabbed a Parker House roll and slathered butter on it, and Renee asked the waiter to refill the basket. She ordered the Dover sole, two servings of meatballs, two large salads, an extra rib eye steak, and two large baked potatoes with all the trimmings. She asked for a chilled pitcher of whole milk.

When the food arrived, she said she wasn't hungry, and the boys ate the appetizers, entrées, and salads, while she picked at her Dover sole.

"How were the scouts?" she asked DH.

"The Yale coach said he was interested," he answered between bites. He wanted to be polite, but as usual when Renee took them out, it was hard not to focus on the excellent food, far better than his daily fare at the dorm.

"How wonderful," she said, and turned quizzically to Peter.

"The Yale coach said I'd be a good walk-on."

Renee smiled broadly and clasped her delicate hands. "Are you going to the same college?" she asked. "I hope so! That would be brilliant."

"The counselor said that if I got into Yale, I could look into a financial aid package," DH began, reaching for another meatball. His parents had said that they'd find the money and not to worry about it; however, he understood that he had far outspent his siblings.

Renee was looking thoughtful. "It would be great if the two of you could go to college together after such a great experience at Andover. DH, if you took care of Peter, I wouldn't need to worry about him so much."

"Hey, I take care of him, too," Peter protested. He turned to DH and raised his milk glass, and the boys clinked before drinking.

Renee would have spent double what she was paying for DH's tuition at Andover if it meant that her son would thrive. Her friend Tom Song had hatched the scheme to send DH to Andover with Peter, and it had worked out far better than expected. Unlike at King's College School, where Peter had been lonesome and withdrawn, her son seemed happier than he'd ever been because the boys were best friends and teammates.

DH had no idea of the source of his private, anonymous scholarship. Peter didn't know, either. Tom Song had told DH's parents that the hagwon had a connection to a private foundation that helped exceptional scholar-athletes study abroad. If DH could go to college with Peter, Renee would gladly pick up all the costs, but she couldn't say that. She would tell Tom, and he would help with the administration of the scholarship. She tried not to let herself anticipate too far ahead, but that her formerly alienated and melancholy son could flourish at an Ivy League school in the company of his best friend was almost too wonderful to imagine.

"Any nice girls here?" Renee asked.

"DH likes this hot blonde from school, and now they're summer pen pals." Peter grinned at DH.

"Yo." DH shook his head, embarrassed, though he didn't really mind.

"Virginia Cooper, right?" Renee said.

"How do you know her name?" Peter asked, though he should have expected it. His mother had an unbelievable facility with names.

"Oh, DH mentioned her the last time we spoke."

Virginia Cooper, a year younger than the boys, had been writing letters to DH from Nantucket, and their friendship had been intensifying because he was a regular correspondent. Peter had a crush on Virginia's classmate Eliza Ying, a pretty brunette, but that had fizzled during summer break, and Peter wasn't too concerned about it. He'd already had sex on his sixteenth birthday, but nothing had come of it except for the ensuing awkwardness. DH hadn't been with a girl yet. He said he liked the idea of a girlfriend at Andover, but he wanted to focus on getting into college first.

"Do you want to go to Yale?" Renee asked DH.

"The soccer at Harvard is supposed to be a little better, but I don't know if I want to go to a school just for that. I think I want to study English, and I like what I've read about Yale's program. I still have a lot to figure out," he admitted. DH smiled at his friend's mother, who was always interested in how he was doing. Suddenly he missed his own mother, who wrote him short, brisk letters reminding him to eat good food and take his multivitamins. Without fail, she enclosed a $10 or $20 bill in the envelope for him to buy pizza, and he wondered when she found the time to get the currency changed.

10
Power

It was late in the afternoon, and the office lunch crowd had long since cleared out. The restaurant was nearly empty. John and Shin sat silently at their usual table, two bowls of short rib soup between them.

"The risk team told her that the numbers on her Australia report made no sense," Shin said, straightening his necktie, though it looked fine.

In the past month, John had warned the senior men on the team that she wasn't allowed to ask for their help. They must not do her work for her.

"I didn't tell her about the mines in Queensland, which affected the overall coking numbers," John said.

Shin looked relieved. "Can you do it today? She's already upset, and these things are best done quickly."

John put down his metal spoon. He didn't feel like finishing.

"She now has a few weak performance reviews, but I thought maybe I could get her to redo the report and submit it to risk again. Still get it wrong. Establish her incompetence. Have another department's support."

John felt sick, unable to believe that he was doing this to the poor young woman. He had reasoned that the worse she performed in front of others, the more justified it would be to terminate her. He needed more evidence to build his case.

"No, no," Shin said. "Now is the best time. After you fire her, I'll get her something else. I can take care of this. I have a friend in Busan who has already agreed to hire her. I will see her, just far less often." Shin didn't plan to go cold turkey; he would taper off.

"You think she'll go to Busan?"

"If she's fired, then the new position in Busan would mean no gaps in her employment. It's a slight promotion, actually, and she knows she can't get a promotion this year. She can take a week off before starting there.

This weekend I'm taking her to Hakone. She loves *onsen.* Should cheer her up." Shin seemed confident that the mess he'd created could be tidied.

John wanted this to end. He didn't want to keep giving Danbi increasingly difficult tasks and, worse, making her doubt herself. No matter the circumstances, a firing was never easy.

"Couldn't you tell her to quit? That she can work in Busan without getting fired? Just get her to switch jobs."

Shin smiled uneasily. He had already tried. Danbi would not budge. She wouldn't leave him and a prestigious job. She had come from a quiet farming village, and to her, everything but Seoul was a backwater. If not the capital, she wanted to live in New York or Los Angeles. More than once, she had asked him to take her to the United States, preferring the West Coast since his wife and children were in New Jersey. She had a wealthy cousin in California.

"Today," Shin said. "Please."

❧

John arranged for Danbi Jung to meet him in the glass-walled conference room by the bank of elevators. He got there ahead of her and waited, reading her thick file. This was the usual room where employees received their reviews, promotions, and terminations. As usual, the Venetian blinds were half lowered for privacy, but the slats were not fully closed. The smoky glass door was polished and open. Seated at a conference table that could accommodate a dozen people, he felt very alone.

John believed he was a reasonably honest man. Over the course of his life, he had witnessed many unfair things, which had troubled him. When necessary, he had turned a blind eye. When he had a duty to report, he had done so, but not always. In school, you weren't supposed to snitch. In the military, you protected your fellow soldiers. In the office, you took care of your people, trying to discern what had to be done for the greater good versus what a company needed to do to survive. It would have been preferable if one didn't have to do this sort of ethics calculus, but being an adult was never easy, and being wise required some sacrifices, if only to simplify the moral equation. As his career progressed, and he'd come to understand what was required to get ahead, John had given up a measure of professional ambition and sacrificed opportunities. He had done his best to forgo any ill-gotten gains. He loved his wife and children, and protecting them had become his primary goal.

Over the years, clients had offered him money to get discounts from the company. Suppliers had offered him kickbacks to be selected for lucrative deals. John never accepted money he hadn't earned, and what seemed difficult for most people was easy for him. The act of refusal had to be done carefully, so as not to insult the one who had made the offer. Each time he did it, that muscle of refusal grew stronger. By now, those with shady intentions knew better than to approach him for preferential treatment, and went to his colleagues or superiors instead.

John Koh's squeaky-cleanness might have been one of the many reasons he was sent abroad and kept there even as a young man. Controlling greed protected a company from catastrophe. Employees who took a packet of cash and turned the other way while favored suppliers or clients did shoddy business created dangerous situations for the manufacturer, distributor, supplier, trading partner, and end user. Both John and his boss Shin believed that financial greed was a market inefficiency.

Shin's only vice was women, and he admired that John had a professional conscience and did his work well. A colleague could drink too much, gamble, or have secrets that made him vulnerable. Weaknesses caused problems, but they also created bonds. Shin expected John to lie for him about the mistresses.

Every Sunday, John Koh went to church with his family, and he paid careful attention to the sermons. He believed that a wise man must regularly cultivate his morality and faith, no differently from reading the news to be informed, learning more about his profession, and exercising regularly. A preacher in Sydney had once shared a German theologian's definition of wisdom: competence with regard to the complex realities of life.

John wanted to be wise like that. It was one thing to refuse sin for oneself, but he wanted to be competent even when facing the sins of others.

Ministers preached against sin. There were many kinds. However, he noticed that ministers rarely dwelled on avoiding bad business practices. In college, he had attended a Bible study group at SNU, where a young woman who studied economics noted that the Bible instructed merchants to use standardized measurements and avoid cheating. A faithful person was supposed to be honest in trade, she had insisted, quoting chapters and verses to prove her point. Of all the sermons John had sat through, not a single pastor had ever talked about the evils of lying in business.

In reality, for John, the big sins had been easy enough to avoid. He and

Shin had only worked for large companies, which often had the power to control prices and markets. Coking coal, iron ore, steel, and fuel were always needed, and powerful traders could find trading relationships and keep the business going. Mostly they had been able to keep their hands clean. Unlike goods, people were harder to control, because human beings were irrational.

There was a phone in the center of the conference table. John felt a sudden urge to pick up the receiver and call his wife. Helen would know what to do. She would tell him not to do this.

If John did not fire Danbi, Shin would not fire him. However, Shin would view the failure as insubordination and a kind of betrayal. John knew that Shin was embarrassed to have asked for this favor. John was letting his morals, or perhaps cowardice, get in the way. Loyalty had always been the strongest bond between the two men. If Danbi stayed at HRI, John realized that it was Shin who would lose his job. If Shin was gone, John would not get automatically promoted. He would become another mark—an easy target for the tougher men in the company.

With Shin gone, if John was pushed out, he didn't know where to go. He was too senior to make a lateral move, yet not senior enough to insulate himself from internal politics.

John had never done anything like this before. No one had ever asked him, and if anyone but Shin had, he would have refused. He felt like quitting, but that seemed impetuous. There would be no job for a man his age in a company as good as HRI. John could visualize the risks like they were bars of a graph, and the highest bar of risk to his career would be disobedience to his boss.

Danbi knocked on the door, entered, and sat opposite him.

John tried to smile, but she stared frostily across the table.

"Your coking ore numbers were wrong," John said. "You missed the mines in the northeastern region."

"I didn't know about them. No one told me to include that."

"I did tell you," John said, immediately regretting his words.

"No, no." She shook her head, exasperated. "You didn't."

"You should have asked for more clarification," he said, knowing this was unfair.

"I took careful notes when you gave me the assignment. That's like asking me to ask you if there were more factors, when you were the one providing all the factors. How can you—?" Danbi stopped herself. "I have been trying to understand the project, but the scope is enormous. There are variables that are virtually incalculable and unknowable. These projects you give me remind me of theoretical math problems from university. In fact, those were easier."

Danbi covered her mouth with her hands as if to stop herself from speaking. She dropped her hands in her lap and sat up straight in her seat. She was wearing a simple peach-colored silk blouse and a gray wool flannel skirt.

"I'd hoped that you would have made greater progress by now," he said, wanting to stop this performance.

"You gave me two weeks, and this Australia project could have taken a month even if I had all the Queensland numbers. I don't understand why—"

"Miss Jung, you are clearly a bright young person, but perhaps this is not the kind of work you should be doing."

"I don't understand."

"Well, part of what I do is to evaluate the needs of my team and department, and I don't think this is the right place for you. I hope you understand. Human Resources will be reaching out with a package. I think—"

Her mouth fell open.

"I'm trying my best. The assignment was impossible! There have been so many absurdly difficult projects. All of which I completed. How could you do this? You wouldn't want to be treated this way—"

John stared mutely at the glass door behind her chair. She was not wrong.

"I'll provide a strong reference, and I think there are others who can help you as well, to find another position elsewhere. I hope you can understand—"

"No, I don't understand. I was doing very well before you got here."

John furrowed his brow. He was the kind of manager who could tolerate dissent, but even he was surprised by her bold insistence, especially since she would need his reference in the future. He had fired other people before, but never like this. Normally the person left the office understandably upset, but no one had ever shouted at him.

"You don't like me," Danbi whispered. "You're jealous of my relationship with the director."

"What?" John's head snapped back.

"You know we're in love, and you're judging us. I know his wife and your wife are friends. But he loves me, and he wants to take care of me. I'm a good employee, and you're trying to kick me out. I'm going to tell him to fire you. You'll see. I'm not going anywhere. You won't get away with this."

Danbi got up from her seat and marched resolutely to his side of the conference table. She breathed in deeply and stared at him.

John pulled away from his chair, unable to look away from her. The ripeness of her youth was overwhelming, reminding him of sex, peaches—and rage.

"You're attracted to me." Her voice was quiet now, her eyes narrowed. "I know you are, and you want to punish me for it."

John felt his pulse race. "I don't know what you're talking about. You didn't do an assignment properly. I have no choice but to let you go. Please return to your seat."

"Men like you just want girls like me to spread our legs and throw us away when you're done. You think I don't know that? I was one of the best math students at Korea University. The only woman who could keep up with the men. That assignment you gave me could not be done. If I were you, I'd be preparing to leave your office, Manager Koh."

John looked past the glass walls. No one walked by.

Danbi moved closer to him, standing over his chair. He could smell the jasmine of her perfume.

"You want this," she said.

John moved his chair back and remained seated.

Danbi gripped his right hand and placed it on the neckline of her peach blouse. Her hand clasped over his, she ripped open her blouse and screamed.

"Get away from me! Help me! Save me!"

She pushed up her skirt as if it were the most ordinary thing in the world and sat on the table, her legs straddling his thighs, exposing her underwear and stockings.

John tried to move away, but she clamped her calves around his thighs. She pushed aside her brassiere to expose her left breast. The pink aureole looked like a target. Helen was the only woman he had ever seen naked. He broke away from her forcefully.

"Help!" she cried again while staring at him steadily. With her left hand, she smeared her mouth to mess up her lipstick, then threw herself on the floor.

Colleagues rushed in the door.

"I didn't do anything. She's crazy—" He pointed at Danbi, who was now sobbing. "She's crazy! She attacked herself when I fired her—"

An accountant, a middle-aged man and the father of two college-age girls, removed his jacket to cover Danbi's nakedness.

"Manager Koh, I don't think this is right," he said.

"I didn't do this. She's making this up. I tried to fire her, and she—"

Shin moved through the crowd and looked at John with understanding. Danbi continued to cry, whimpering now as if she were being tormented by the memory. John shook his head in disbelief, unable to comprehend what had just happened to him.

❧

Almost no one believed her because everyone knew John Koh was incapable of such a thing. Danbi Jung was disliked by the women at the office and by most men on her team. However, what everyone had witnessed was unquestionably compromising. It was hard to imagine a woman revealing herself like that at the office. Human Resources, Legal, and Auditing were called in to investigate that afternoon. They interviewed John and Danbi separately. Shin supported John, but it didn't make things go away. John was put on leave without pay. It wasn't clear for how long.

John went home to an empty apartment. He sat in his living room, dumbstruck.

He didn't know how much time had passed when the doorbell rang. Shin stood in the doorway until John wordlessly stood aside to let him in, without offering him slippers or anything to drink.

"Is your wife here?"

"She's at work."

"I didn't know Danbi could do something like that."

"I can't believe she would lie and accuse me of something so horrible. I would never ever—"

"I know you wouldn't."

"I need my job—" John broke off, unable to imagine his family's future, now at risk due to his friend's insane folly.

Shin spoke quietly. "She is threatening to press criminal charges against you, which would be far worse than losing your job."

"But I didn't do it. If I tell the truth, then—"

"If you tell the truth, then I will lose my job, too, and then who will help you get something else? Do you see the predicament we're in—"

"You were behind this. I didn't do anything wrong—" John paused because he had done something wrong. He had been asked to lie, and he had lied.

"You asked me to fire her because you knew she was dangerous. She said you two are in love. You're a married man with three boys. Brother, you should come to your senses."

It felt easier for John to warn Shin than to think of himself. He had no idea what to tell Helen when she came home.

Shin looked at him helplessly. "I love her. I do. She's crazy, but I don't know how to make it stop. I can't lose her."

"If you want to go to hell with a woman like that—"

"She's not what you think. She comes from a terrible family. Sometimes it's like watching a trapped animal trying to survive—"

"That may be, but I know when a person cannot be trusted."

Shin fidgeted with his mother-of-pearl cuff links.

"What will you do when she turns against you?" John asked.

"At work? Against me?" Shin glared at him. No one could understand his relationship with Danbi. She could not live without him, she had said again and again. Never would she hurt him, she'd said.

"Yes. She'd do the same thing to you if she has to."

"She can't accuse two men of rape. No one would believe that."

John understood then that Shin had already considered this outcome.

"She could call your wife."

"She already has."

"And?" John closed his eyes, knowing Mary. She would do nothing to stop him. She would pray for Shin's soul and likely Danbi's as well. She would pray to find forgiveness. She would pray for her children. She would not divorce him because he would be even more lost without her. This was something Helen had explained to him once, and the logic of it would make little sense to anyone who did not believe in God the way Mary did.

"She said this will pass. It always passes."

"Will it? Will you make Miss Jung go away?"

"Don't worry about me," Shin said. "I will take care of this. I have to—"

John covered his face with his hands and took a breath.

"I listened to you. Somehow I justified her being fired because she would create disharmony. Isn't that ridiculous? Not once did I think that this could—" John couldn't say any more.

"I appreciate what you did. I will never forget this."

"How will I take care of my family?"

"I'll find a solution. I'm talking to everyone I know to find you another position."

"I'm not getting paid until I go back to work."

"Danbi said she won't press charges against you or the company, as long as you quit."

"Resign?"

Shin said nothing.

"I have three children I have to educate. I have to save for their weddings and my retirement. Helen can't work forever, and HRI makes us retire when we're sixty-two. Shin, I have to work. There are people who depend on me. Bo is studying for Yonsei now, and DH is at Andover. And Mido—" John covered his mouth with his left hand.

Shin held up an HRI duffel bag he had brought with him. He laid it beside John.

"It's a year's salary."

"No. I want my job. Give that to Danbi. I want to keep my job. I deserve it. At my age, where am I to go? Can you imagine if I leave like this? People will think I might have done this terrible, terrible thing. How?"

"Don't you think I've tried? She intends to stay."

"She's holding you by your penis." John blurted out the first thing that came to his mind. Suddenly he remembered the coldness of her stare. "She is a twisted person."

"I never intended for you to get hurt," Shin insisted, but John was unmoved. "Let me see what I can do. Give me some time. We have to keep this out of the papers. I'll do my best to persuade her to drop the accusation. I am sorry."

John did not get up from his seat to show him out.

11
Disgrace

John hadn't visited this part of Myeong-dong in years, not since college when he'd worked weekends at a record shop on the corner of a narrow street, next to a clothing store owned by a sharp-tongued widow who disliked almost everyone. In the evenings, John would put the outdoor sale bins back into the record shop, then help close up her store. At the end of the season, she gave him nice sweaters and trousers she'd set aside in his size that she claimed hadn't sold. Both places had vanished long ago. Pretty much the only familiar things were the street signs and sewer covers. Lately he'd had more time, and whenever he walked through parts of Seoul where he'd been before, he found that even the width of the roads had changed, and if it weren't for a significant landmark that had been preserved, he would've gotten lost, no different from a tourist.

With some luck, he located the brick structure behind the cathedral, whose tall spire cast a blurry shadow over the low-slung buildings on the street.

John stepped off the elevator on the sixth floor and paused at the tax preparer's office, shifting his weight from one foot to the other. There was no one else in the whitewashed hallway. Standing in front of the blue-painted metal door, John stared at the company name on the brass sign screwed into the wall. Judging by the size of the suite, he estimated maybe five or six employees.

He tucked in his shirt and straightened his tie and jacket. He'd dressed as he always did for work, in a tropical-weight wool suit with a French silk necktie. Only a month ago, he had managed a team of twenty-one people for HRI, which he'd joined right after leaving Endo K.K. In Sydney, he'd managed ten employees. He had worked at two global conglomerates. At SNU, he had been third in his class in his major. At forty-six, he was starting again, and looking for a temporary job.

The internal investigation had been fruitless. HRI still wanted him to resign, refusing to pay him. Not knowing what to do, John had done nothing. Only Helen knew. They could not tell the children. John did not want to use the money Shin had left; he'd asked Helen to store the duffel bag somewhere safe in the apartment.

John knocked on the door, and a woman's high-pitched voice answered, "Yes?"

The office was warm and smelled like food. It was lunchtime, and it seemed strange to him that the employees were eating at their desks while working. No one did that at HRI, where there was a well-run cafeteria for everyone, and often, he and his peers went out to one of a number of local restaurants for a proper midday meal.

Here men wearing white shirts and rayon neckties occupied the eight large desks piled high with documents. Two desks remained empty. The employees looked up briefly, then returned to work. The lone young woman, who functioned as the receptionist, sat behind the desk closest to the door.

Tiny and pale with a pointy chin, the receptionist wore her short hair parted on the side with the longer piece pinned back with a rhinestone-encrusted barrette, like a schoolgirl. She wore a frilly white blouse, and a brown cardigan hung over her bony shoulders. She was nibbling on a large fried pastry; seeing John, she put it down by her tea mug and patted her mouth with a tissue.

"Hello?" she said, more a question than a greeting.

"Excuse me. I didn't realize it was lunchtime," John said, embarrassed.

"Is anyone expecting you?" She checked to see if the owner had noticed. Seated in the back, the boss was still on a phone call. The side of his desk faced the only window in the office.

"My name is Koh Yohan," John said. "I saw the advertisement for the tax preparer position. I thought I'd drop off the résumé myself."

Puzzled, the woman tried to smile. He was nearly her father's age. The position was for a trainee.

"I had an appointment in the area," John volunteered, seeing her confusion. He handed her his résumé in a folder. "Is there an application that I could fill out?"

It had been over twenty years since he'd last looked for work. His mouth felt papery.

Unsure, the woman touched her sparkling barrette with her left index finger.

"Wait, please. I'll go ask the owner."

When she got up, she was even smaller than she had appeared behind the desk. Her standing height matched the height of the seated man in the back. The owner was now off the call, and he looked up from his uneaten lunch and shrugged. For a moment, he studied John. It took him no time to figure out that the poor bastard with the fancy suit had been sacked from a big company that had no use for him. There were legions of men like this. The owner had no use for leftovers, so he whispered to the receptionist, and she returned to the front of the office.

"The position has already been filled, sir. Thank you for stopping by."

❧

John walked toward the cathedral and did not enter it. Rather, he went to the courtyard, where people were gathered in clusters. He found an empty bench.

Not long after his brother died, John had converted. His college friends were Presbyterian, so he had gone to Protestant services with them. It was all he knew. Helen had grown up Roman Catholic. When her parents would abandon her and her siblings on their gambling sprees, the children had received help from neighborhood churches. An American priest had even given her the name of a saint, and she preferred it over Hejin. Saint Helen was supposed to be Greek, and John had long planned to take her to Greece one day, after the children finished school and were married. He wondered if that would ever be possible now.

John decided to walk for a while. There was little else for him to do that day. At home, he could tidy the house, though it wasn't dirty. When she returned, Helen would cook dinner, and Bo wouldn't get back from the hagwon till late.

The wide shopping streets bustled with people rushing, haggling, selling—and it occurred to him that everyone was occupied and needed to be somewhere. The small woman in the tax preparer's office had pitied him. He saw it in her face. That gentle smile, which she had meant as a kindness, had affected him. He had given that same look to others. Pity and sympathy had to be doled out with greater consideration, he realized. John walked a little faster, wanting to leave that moment behind him.

Lately he had come to understand that he had done it all wrong. He had not saved enough. He had not built other relationships besides the ones at HRI. He didn't have any interests except for work and his family. There had never been enough time for hobbies. Had he known that something like this could happen, he might have lived differently, but could he have imagined such a thing? That a woman could be so cruel and his friend so thoughtless and out of control? Why had he listened to Shin? John had trusted him with his family's well-being.

Two weeks before, Shin had come by the apartment again and said that he was still trying to fix things. If John told the company everything, then they would both lose their jobs, because the company would argue that John should have reported Shin's scheme to fire Danbi from the start. To blame Danbi alone would require evidence, and John had none. It was his word against hers. Shin had not yet left her.

John was not a violent man, but he had wanted to hit Shin, so instead he'd asked him to leave.

When John was a boy, he had read a *manhwa* about "hubris," a word from Greece, like Helen's name. Icarus, Achilles, Odysseus—all of them had hubris, and the gods had to punish them for it.

Because John had done everything as well and as honorably as he could, he had believed that he did not need to develop other skills, and that he would be protected by his education and achievements. He had only worked for two important companies, and he knew no one personally who had been fired without cause.

Two classmates had lost positions at big companies. Neither found work in an equivalent place; however, both were okay because they had come from prosperous families, and there was enough money to wait things out until something at least halfway decent could appear. They each got another turn.

His own parents and brother were long gone, and if they had lived to see this, they would likely not have had any advice or help to give. For John, the man who knew how to survive best and whom he had leaned on was the very man who had brought him disgrace.

❧

After dinner, Helen asked John to go to the mart to get eggs. As soon as he left, she phoned Australia.

Lily picked up, and she and Kenny took the call in their bedroom, closing the door behind them.

Kenny held the receiver between them, and Lily sat at the edge of the bed, half expecting one of the children to interrupt at any moment. Lily tucked loose threads from the fraying bedspread into the seam of the ribbon binding and smoothed the fabric with both hands. Lily leaned toward her husband's ear, and she could hear her sister-in-law's quavering voice. Helen spoke in English.

"It's been almost a month, and he's been looking. Just in case things don't work out at HRI. We're thinking of leaving Seoul." Helen was embarrassed to be talking about her husband's situation. "He doesn't get interviews. His old friends from school hardly remember him. The school connections have dried up. We were away for too long." She didn't mention the part about his age and seniority, which was obvious to them.

"I can't even imagine," Kenny said. He could not believe this was happening to his brother-in-law. "What else can he do?"

"Kyungjin-ah."

"Hmm?" His sister usually called him Kenny.

"What do you think of us going back to Australia?"

"How?" Kenny blurted out. "I mean, great. We'd love to have you. Does he want to do the same thing here?"

"He'd take what he had before, which would be a step down."

"Can he get that job?"

"I don't think so. Do you know if Qantas is hiring?" Helen held her breath as if she could bottle up the worries inside her and keep them from escaping. It was wrong to trouble her younger brother, but she didn't know what else to do. Already she had asked Sonya, who had offered money, but there was apparently no job at Chairman Mun's company, where her husband was president.

Kenny faced Lily, who frowned with concern.

"Right after you told me, I checked. Nothing. You could get a travel visa, maybe, and try to find something here, but—" He shook his head. It just meant immigration trouble later.

She heard the elevator chime and checked the wall clock. Helen spoke faster.

"Maybe he could do something different?" Helen had been afraid to say this because if she said it out loud, their problems would grow more real somehow.

Lily took the receiver from Kenny.

"Sweetie. Oh, sweetie." Lily was a tough girl from Campsie, but she was soft with her tribe. "I can only imagine how hard it must be for you right now with the kids being everywhere. I will keep Mido here forever if you let me. Yun is amazing, too."

Helen wiped her eyes. When they heard, Sonya and Kenny had been immediately pragmatic, but not gentle. Right away, her siblings had come up with practical solutions. There was never any time for sadness or griping. Lily's tender voice softened Helen's stoic resolve.

"I've been thinking. Of course we want you here. But before you start at zero, I think you have to do one more thing."

Helen waited. Lily was wiser in some ways than her brother.

"You have to talk to Shin's wife. Call her and tell her to fix it."

"Mary?"

"She will know how. She's your friend. Right now, she still has the chance to save your family from the situation you're in. That asshole Shin will drag this on. Call his wife and tell her what's going on. I've had enough of this guy jerking you around. It's bullshit. Tell Mary to clean it up. It's not her fault, but it's still her mess, too."

Helen looked at the wall and envisioned her sister-in-law's pretty oval face, the radial laugh lines around her kind hazel eyes.

"Oh, darling. I'm so sorry this is happening." Lily paused. "Listen, you're not making a request. You're telling her that she gets to fix this." Lily felt it was fair for Shin's wife to share the burden.

"I can't. It would upset John. She's done so much for DH, letting him stay with them during so many school breaks. Mary is even DH's emergency contact at Andover."

Lily ignored this. "You must tell her. She's your friend."

"Mary is suffering, too."

"Her husband is ruining your family's life. She's in Korea now, right? Time is not on your side. Call her now, and if she doesn't answer, then go to her house. Show up at her beauty salon. Go to her church. Make a scene. Stop being polite. You can't feed and educate your kids in Korea on your salary alone, love. If you don't call her, I will," Lily said. "Try me."

Helen didn't know anyone like Lily.

"When does she return to New Jersey?" Lily asked.

"She's here. For another week, I think. I'm not sure."

"Get off the phone now and call her."

Lily smiled at her husband and passed back the handset.

❧

They arranged to meet at Lucky Girls, a tearoom near Ewha that had been around since their school days. Mary was early and waiting for Helen. She had already ordered tea and cake.

"I'm glad to see you," Mary said. Sympathy pooled in her large eyes. She wore an old black linen jacket, which Helen remembered her buying on sale at B. Altman. A classic beauty, Shin's wife looked chic—gray wisps framed her dark bobbed hair. She wore pale lipstick and no other makeup.

"It's nice to see you, too, Sister."

"I've been thinking about this all night. I couldn't sleep. My husband said he was working on it, but I don't think—" Mary looked away.

It occurred to Helen that this might be their last conversation.

"Your husband," Mary sighed. "Such a fine person. I'm so sorry. I know he didn't do anything with that girl. I am ashamed of my husband's behavior. It's inexcusable. If you hadn't told me, I don't know when he would have. No, I think he might never have told me. I knew about her because she phoned." Mary paused to collect herself. "But I didn't know what she did to Koh Yohan. I apologize. I apologize."

Helen sat silently for a moment, then said simply:

"My husband needs a job."

"Of course he does," Mary said, indignant. Last night, her husband had not come home, and if he had, she thought she might have killed him then herself. They spoke in the morning when he finally returned to change his clothes for work, and he promised to fix it, but she didn't believe him.

Helen sighed. "My husband can't find anything else. Nothing like Han River Industrials & Trading. None of his friends called him back once he said he's looking for work. Apparently he can't work for that Japanese company because they are still upset that our husbands became competitors. Every day, John cleans the house, goes to the grocery store, and sits and says nothing. He doesn't complain. We haven't told the children. Bo knows something is wrong but doesn't know what to—" Helen took a sip of water. "Mido will be home soon, and I'm so grateful that DH is still in Vermont. And thank you for letting him come to your house during breaks. I can never repay you for all the things you've done for him."

"He's like my son, too. And the boys love him. Everyone adores DH," Mary said.

"I'm working full-time now, but I can't support our family on what I make. We have to change apartments." Helen blinked back tears. "I don't want to burden you."

Mary shook her head.

"My husband is weak. I should never have married him. My father was right. He said Shin Taehun was self-centered. I'm glad my parents didn't live to see any of this. If I wasn't Catholic..." Mary looked up at the ceiling as if she could stare at God's face, then closed her eyes. "That woman called me, and she was awful. I've heard from many of his girlfriends, but there's something different with her. She told me they're soulmates. She actually used that word. But I can't be angry with her. There's no point. My husband invited her into his bed. My father helped us, you know. Taehun had nothing except his degree. We bought that house in New Jersey with money from my father. Taehun sends us money for the kids' school, but I still work because it isn't enough. Anyway. I wanted to see you today because I already made the call."

Helen wiped her eyes with a thin paper napkin.

"I called Kang Joonah and she fixed it. It's not as good a job as the one your husband had."

"You called the wife of Vice-Chairman Han?"

Mary nodded. "I told her what happened."

Joonah had been in the same Ewha class as Helen, and she married a grandson of the founder of HRG. Helen knew Joonah only from a distance, but Mary and Joonah had grown up in Seongbuk-dong and attended schools together. They were members of the same church. Joonah had never liked Mary's husband—a boy not from their world—but there had been a consensus among the girls at Ewha that Shin was one of the most attractive undergraduates at SNU, and he had seduced the beautiful and well-off Mary, who had known nothing whatsoever about men.

"Joonah talked to her husband, who already heard about the incident."

Helen stared at Mary, uncomprehending.

"So this is Joonah's husband's solution," Mary continued. "You and John move back to Sydney. He will have a job, but your husband can't have contact with that woman. The job is for a team leader, but it's a much smaller team than he had before. The vice-chair will call your husband tomorrow.

HRG doesn't want to lose our husbands. They have specific skills the company apparently needs."

Mary pulled out more napkins from the dispenser and handed them to Helen.

"I want you to keep the money that my husband gave you. It's not enough for what we've done to your family. Joonah doesn't know if there will be a subsidy for housing or schools because the new job is not as senior," Mary said. "I'm hoping that somehow, the money can cover at least the move."

"I don't know what to say. I am grateful to you, Sister."

Mary reached over and took Helen's hands into hers. She bowed her head, her forehead touching their hands, and without saying a word, Helen understood that Mary was praying for them.

Helen knew that her husband would accept the post in Sydney. They had been back in Seoul for seventeen months.

12

Cho Sisters

January 1995

Even as an infant, Helen and John's firstborn had a calm temperament and an accommodating disposition, as if he appreciated what it meant to be a *jangnam* with the attendant privileges and responsibilities of primogeniture. Bo never seemed to let the burdens of being the eldest child overwhelm him. He exerted himself in the classroom and on the sports field, he got along well with his peers. A nice-looking and thoughtful young man, Bo was a blessing and a relief to his busy parents.

Often, Helen's friends asked: How did she raise her son? Was there a method to rearing such a fine student and good boy? The credit, however, belonged neither to Helen nor to John. Bo came that way, she would say.

Bo's mother could admit this truth not because she was modest, but rather, the experience of having more than one child in the same household amply demonstrated to any self-aware parent that each child was entirely unique. Eventually every small human—even flesh of one's flesh, which should have provided some illusion of predictability—asserted his individuality, no matter how much a parent tried to control, shape, or design his formation.

As educated and earnest middle-class parents, Helen and John had provided more than the basics, and certainly more than they had been given as children of poor parents. Parenting was a haphazard experiment for even the best-intentioned humans, and Helen and John observed Bo, DH, and Mido with profound fascination, as only parents can. Each child was immutably distinct from the others.

When Helen read a sad story in the news about a child who had gone astray, rarely did she assign blame to the parents. Life had taught her that the debate between nature and nurture was almost moot: Excellent parents sometimes had badly behaved children, and careless parents could have admirably performing progeny. The bond between a human and her child was binding, yet it had to be loosened. A mother had to love, and a child had to grow up. The results were often out of one's hands.

In America, Bo was almost nineteen years old, but his Korean age was nearly twenty since the year in the mother's womb was counted. Girls admired his glossy chestnut-colored hair, olive complexion, and large brown eyes. He spoke English like a native, making him an exotic curiosity at a public high school in Gangnam, and he studied from morning till night, almost not needing to sleep. Most remarkably, Bo had maintained an impressive grade point average in the second stanine nationally, allowing him to apply to Yonsei University. The school did not think he could test for Seoul National, his father's alma mater, which was fine by him. Bo preferred Yonsei's old-fashioned campus and admired its alumni. His cousin Jiman was admitted to Korea University, the school of his father and brother Seungman.

There was a precocious beauty named Ara Yang in his homeroom class whom he liked, and who adored him. Once she showed up at his hagwon and invited him to her house to study, and right there in her bedroom, she proposed sex. Stunned, grateful, and naturally tempted, Bo was still able to control himself and demurred. He made a deal with her. After they were accepted into college, they would make love. Whenever he masturbated, he fantasized about the twin possibility of the college of his dreams and the tantalizing promise of sex with Ara.

When Bo failed to be admitted to Yonsei University, he broke up with her. Ara had been accepted to Sungkyunkwan University, but the only daughter of two preoccupied college professors told Bo that she would be happy to wait for him as he prepared to take the Yonsei exam again. Almost everyone took these exams more than once, especially for schools as hard as Yonsei, she'd said, trying her best to encourage him. Bo, guilt ridden at the heavy expense of his failure, told her firmly that he would not hold her back. To make the situation even clearer, he told her that they should not even be friends.

Bo took the national college exam in November 1994, which was called the 1995 Suneung. In addition, Bo had to take the *bongosa*, a school-specific admissions exam, and although the bongosa devastated many students, Bo thought that, for him, the Yonsei-specific exam had gone well enough.

The bongosa essay question he could never forget was "Describe the difference between digital and analog."

For his answer, Bo wrote that a digital clock stated a moment in time whereas an analog clock revealed the process of time.

As soon as they finished the Yonsei bongosa, Bo and his classmates rushed back to their Yonsei exam hagwon, which was different from Eagle Academy, his hagwon for his high school studies. The bongosa hagwon tutor had been more or less flying blind because there were almost no prior tests from which to teach. Each student, fresh from having taken the exam, was asked to recall the test questions, and three tutors recorded the questions and typed out their speculated answers. Bo's tutor said his digital versus analog answer was terrific. Not that it mattered.

Bo's Suneung score was what kept him out. With 200 being the perfect score for the 1995 Suneung, he received 153, a strong score but not invulnerable. Predictably, with his focus on studying for the college exams, his high school grade point average had fallen to the lower end of the second stanine, so he was no longer in the top 4 percent nationally.

Bo wanted to take the exams again. Helen did not know what to do. The Suneung was offered only once a year, in November. She had to consider their housing, Bo's hagwon fees for another year, and the family's stretched expenses spread across Seoul, Sydney, and the United States with DH. If he had done well and been admitted to Yonsei, she would have left for Sydney, where she would have earned far more at the Emporium.

❧

Sonya's apartment complex in Apgujeong was comprised of many separate towers. Helen entered the elevator in Sonya's building and pushed the button. She finger-combed her hair, tucking the loose wisps behind her ears. That morning, she'd noticed two more gray hairs sprouting from her side part. No doubt her sister would comment on it. There wasn't enough time to get to the salon, and for each week Helen could hold off on getting her cut and color, she could put aside more for the children's school and hagwon fees. With John and Mido now settled in Sydney, Helen was still able to work full-time at the duty-free shop, and whenever the manager had extra shifts, Helen raised her hand.

When the elevator opened on Sonya's floor, a uniformed maid stood waiting at the apartment's front door. Sonya's home was larger than most houses in Seoul—comprised of both apartments on the tenth floor of

Building 11. Three generations lived in the two units separated by a small hallway. Sonya spent her days taking care of the household, Chairman Mun, her husband, Yong-gil, and their two sons. She managed a sizable staff: a formidable housekeeper, two maids, a cook, and a driver.

A maid guided Helen to Sonya's home office, where her sister was busy reviewing the household accounts. Chairman Mun was at the health club with his physical trainer and afterward was scheduled to have lunch with high school classmates, which made this the ideal time for Helen to drop by. The Chairman did not like to have guests.

Sonya's office was the size of Helen's living room. A large square of southern light flooded the elegant room. Behind the modern oak desk was a sofa upholstered in green mohair wool where Sonya read in the evenings. Stacks of art books covered a low hand-carved Korean pine table. Tall branches of persimmons filled an enormous cobalt-blue fishbowl on a rosewood pedestal.

The maid remained at the door while Helen took a seat on the sofa, and Sonya frowned.

"I can't believe you're going to leave. Again. You've barely been in the country," Sonya said, too exasperated to bother with pleasantries. She asked the maid for tea, and the young woman bowed before closing the door.

"Is she new?" Helen pointed toward the door.

"Just the niece of the cook," Sonya said, then regretted sounding so dismissive. "She is part-time. I don't really need her, but the cook asked me. She's recently divorced. There are two little kids."

Helen understood. Everyone asked her older sister for help, and Sonya had a hard time saying no.

"Did John find a house in Sydney?"

"They're still at Kenny's."

"Still?" Sonya raised an eyebrow.

"Well, Kenny and Lily said it's fine, and Mido is helping with the kids. John is always working and hasn't had time to look."

"Are you okay with money?" Sonya asked bluntly.

"It's tough," Helen admitted. "We returned the money to Shin. John couldn't accept it," Helen said.

"What?" Sonya raised her hands. "Why? Your husband got a demotion and that... that woman ruined his reputation in Seoul. If I didn't believe in God, I would slap her."

Helen didn't want to talk about Danbi anymore. She drew a breath. "Bo didn't get in."

"Oh no!" Sonya exclaimed. "Was he close? I bet he was close. Bo is very smart. The hardest-working boy. I shouldn't have favorites, but he is the best. Nicer than my sons," Sonya said, then smiled. "Then are you going to stay another year so—"

"I can't stay. The apartment lease is ending, and we need that deposit back so we can get a place in Sydney. We can't keep relying on Kenny and Lily. Bo missed that test by just a few points, and the counselors said that this year's Suneung was a nightmare."

Helen folded her arms and closed her eyes, unable to forget what her son had said after the test results came out.

Umma, I want to take it again. I failed you and Appa. I'm sorry.

She told him he hadn't done anything wrong. He had never failed them, but Bo could not be consoled. Her oldest child did not cry or waste more words. He was certain that if he had studied harder, he would have passed. Acceptance was within his grasp. Three points, maybe four? All this expense and time would not have been squandered. How could she say no to a child who wanted to study harder? Helen could not. For her son, passing that test was his redemption.

The boy's apology continued to press down on his mother's brain like a tiny ball of tungsten, a deceptively heavy metal she had once held in her palm in a chemistry class.

Of course, the aunt felt terrible for her nephew. Sonya's younger son, Jiman, had just been accepted to Korea University. Like his older brother, he hadn't been allowed to apply to Seoul National. His academic record was strong but not the best in his high school, so he had tested for KU and been accepted as an economics major, which had delighted the Chairman and Sonya's husband.

"It doesn't make sense for me to stay here and lease a smaller place," Helen said. "DH is doing well at Andover. We're maintaining three households. I must be out of my mind."

Sonya understood. Helen's growing expenses were unsustainable, and how would she ever save for the children's weddings and her own retirement?

"Sister, I was wondering, I know the Chairman wouldn't like it, but do you think Bo could stay here to take the test again? He'd be at the hagwon most of the time and wouldn't be underfoot. I know it's a big—"

Sonya had been afraid of this. The Chairman had already warned her and said it just wasn't possible. She felt unable to refuse her little sister but unable to say yes, either, because this was not her house. With her head bowed down, Sonya sat, not saying a word.

"Never mind," Helen said. She understood that her sister couldn't ask. "I was thinking of renting a room for him. I can't decide if he should stay at a boardinghouse or a *gosiwon*."

"I've heard that boardinghouses can be terrible about meals," Sonya said, wanting to be helpful. "The newer gosiwon can be nicer," she said. "The rooms are small but some of them are well run. I can help you with that. I am sorry about this. You know that if the Chairman and my husband weren't so against—"

The Chairman felt strongly about allowing anyone outside the immediate family to stay overnight. He had never liked Sonya's family. For her sake, he tolerated them.

"We'll be fine," Helen said, feeling foolish.

"I can help you with the cost," Sonya assured her. "Find the best gosiwon for him, right next to the hagwon. The boardinghouses are often far away, and you don't want him to waste time commuting. Just pick the best one, and I'll take care of it. I'll check in on him often. I promise."

Sonya paused. "You look tired," Sonya said. "The sweater is pretty, but the lilac color highlights the gray in your hair. You look older than me! Get an appointment and get your roots done. I'm a mean older sister, aren't I? But who else is going to tell you to take care of your looks?"

Helen touched her head. Her sister was picking on her because she felt bad. Sonya had married a man from a wealthy family but had quickly learned that none of their money was hers. This vast home she took great care of did not belong to her. Sonya nagged or teased only two people in the world: Kenny and her. With everyone else, Sonya was detached, her behavior unimpeachable. To everyone else, her sister appeared flawless.

"I promise to get my color done," Helen said.

"How is Mido?"

"School is easier for her there, of course. Mido and DH could never do what Bo is trying to do. And they would never want to."

Sonya crossed her arms and tilted her head slightly.

"Why is Bo doing this? It makes no sense. He should be studying in America."

"He likes being here. He feels closer to the people. He was even thinking of trying to get into military service," Helen said, mystified.

"Has my favorite nephew lost his mind? My sons would be overjoyed if they didn't have to go through this. Well, actually, Seungman is looking forward to military service, but Jiman, not so much." Sonya made a face, because her younger one wasn't the tough kind. He would likely be picked on, and it worried her. Though the Chairman said it would be good for them to serve. *It will make them into men.*

"It's crazy enough that Bo wants to take the test again and live in Korea. Do not allow him to give up his American citizenship to do service. I will not allow that," Sonya said sternly.

Helen nodded.

Sonya glanced at the clock.

"Listen, let's have something to eat now. The Chairman will be back soon."

It always felt to Helen as if the rooms were filled with listening devices and Sonya's de facto father-in-law could hear her. The Chairman controlled every decision and expense in the household, and Sonya did everything she could to please him.

Helen brushed her hand across the mohair wool fabric that covered the sofa.

"Umma used to love this color so much."

"Yes. She had a dress this exact shade," Sonya exclaimed.

"I wish she could have seen this sofa. This beautiful home," Helen said, admiring the view of the river.

Sonya considered what it would have meant for their profligate parents to see the splendor of this place, how well her sons were doing, and how far she had traveled from their squalid childhood. She missed them.

BOOK II

November 1996–March 1999

It is in playing, and only in playing, that the individual discovers the self.

—Donald W. Winnicott

1
Letters

Los Angeles, California
November 9, 1996

My Mido,

Yaah, I miss you.

The photographs are wonderful but not the same. I sound ungrateful. Sorry.

Thank you for sending them in your last letter.

Seeing the pictures, I wished to be back in Sydney. I know I was there only briefly and gosh, over three years ago, but for me, it felt like a pretty dream during a terrible time. You reminded me again how much I loved my few weeks there.

The twins are enormous! And the baby. Wow. Is she starting preschool? That sweet white dress. I hope I can have a little girl one day, or four of them like in Little Women. You can be their aunt. And Henry. He's as handsome as a drama star.

I hope Henry got the Disneyland postcard I sent from our senior trip. I should've gotten him the Mickey Mouse hat with his name stitched on it, but I wasn't sure how to send it without the mouse ears getting crushed. Tell Henry that if he comes to Los Angeles, I promise to take him. It was so much bigger than I imagined and more expensive, but worth it. No one could believe that it was my first time.

I'm ashamed to admit this, but back home, I used to feel a little better about myself because our family had plenty of money. No one could ever make me feel inferior because my mother would take me to all the fancy places and buy me things no one else had, but here,

I don't know any of the cool things and haven't been anywhere interesting. A White girl in my freshman writing seminar said she was a debutante in Atlanta, which she'd hated, and I had to look that up because I didn't know what it meant. There were some kids in my high school whose families belonged to country clubs, but I don't think it's the same thing. A lot of the wealthier students at UCLA have traveled to Europe. I'm a country bumpkin here.

Maybe one day, you'll come to America, and we'll go to places like San Francisco, New York City, or Washington, DC. I'd love to go to a Broadway musical and walk through Times Square.

I should mention that you look pretty and happy with your boyfriend.

Tek seems more serious in the picture than I remember him. Then again, that time he came over with Henry, after he ate almost all the Anzac cookies, he studied and got all his schoolwork done, which I admired. I'm glad he likes uni and is taking Korean classes. I wouldn't want you to marry a Korean who can't speak it at all. I wish I didn't have an accent, but I can speak both languages now. I can even get by at work with my high school Spanish. If I could, I'd like to learn more languages.

Oh, remember to be careful with Tek, if you know what I mean. Ha ha.

My mother has also been nagging me about being cautious because I have big news.

Are you ready?

Like you, now I have a boyfriend, and he's not a boy. He is old, and he wants to marry me. Ever since I met Lion Han, I liked him but I never thought I had a chance. He is 23, so five years older than we are.

So, is that four years older than your Tek? He reminds me of a 1,000-year-old turtle who's been walking the earth forever. If you meet him, you'll understand what I mean. He looks nothing like a turtle or a lion, but there's something about the way he is so wise and purposeful. Everyone at church calls him the Oracle of Orange County.

Naturally, since he's older, my mother is worried that I'll get pregnant. Lion said he could wait for as long as I wanted, but I don't know how long I want to wait. Your friend Yun is still a virgin but I'm now in college, and between us, most of my friends from school and church have done all the things. Yet I haven't, so naturally, I'm curious. Ha ha.

He wanted to be a musician, and his father cut off his tuition, so he put himself through Princeton by tutoring. He owns a hagwon in Cypress with employees. I know you will like him.

Let me tell you about my classes at UCLA.

Here goes: Communications, Psychology, Spanish, and Writing. Writing and Spanish are requirements for me to graduate and the classes are small. Comms and Psych are huge, and I have section leaders, who are graduate students. The classes are not boring. I much prefer college to high school.

You know what, though? I think I'm still tired from high school. College is great, and UCLA has a beautiful campus but I don't live in the dorms, so I have a long drive home to Cypress five days a week. Traffic is the only part about California I hate. I'm getting to be a great driver, though. I can't graduate in three years like Lion did, but I'm going to try to pick a major early and focus, so I don't waste time. I need to pick something. I was thinking maybe Business Economics? I'm not that interested in business, though, but the math won't be too bad.

Where do I study?

I do my work at the school library here, or at Lion's hagwon office, which is quiet and I get to see him when he's free. Also, he can help me with schoolwork. He's good at editing my papers.

Nothing has changed at home. My father is still having a hard time. Same as usual. He's still angry at his former partner, and he hates working at Shrimp Castle and wants us to go to São Paolo, where his younger cousin lives. My mother doesn't like his cousin. She said she's not moving again unless it's back to Korea. I can't imagine going to Brazil and starting over again at eighteen. I guess I'd learn Portuguese. Both of them agree that UCLA is good for me, so even if they went, I would get to stay and finish my degree.

Here's my jansori list. Nagging is love.

Take your vitamins.

Make sure you get enough sleep.

Buy yourself a treat once in a while, it's okay to buy yourself a lip gloss or a nice sweater.

Enjoy your last few days of high school. I think you're graduating soon, then you have those HSC exams, right? You're going to get into a great uni. I know it.

If you can, after you finish your HSCs, please consider taking the SATs, 3 SAT IIs, and apply to UCLA and a few American colleges. Your school will have sample study guides in the library. I had some problems with the reading comprehension section, but the math was fine. You will do great on both sections.

College here is expensive and out-of-state students pay more, but Lion said for some schools, it's worth taking out loans. I live at home so I don't have to pay for room and board. The community colleges here are also excellent, and after two years, you can transfer to schools like UCLA and Berkeley. A lot of my classmates went to Cal State schools, which are great, too. Can you tell that I want you to move here?

As soon as I have enough saved, I'll send you a ticket. Lion wants me to concentrate on school, so he doesn't want me to work at Shrimp Castle as much, but business is getting better, and my parents need help. If I worked at Lion's hagwon, I'd make more per hour, though.

My mother's English has improved. Dad works in the kitchen so he doesn't get much chance to talk with customers. They both say hello to your parents and brothers.

Send me a long, detailed letter soon.

Love,
Yun

❧

She had filled up two blue aerograms with her tiny handwriting and marked the letters "Vol. 1" and "Vol. 2." In them, she had done her best to sound cheery, focusing on the good news.

On Saturday night, Yun's father, Joonho, smoked a cigarette in the alley behind Shrimp Castle. After stubbing it out, he picked up the cigarette butt from the ground, closed the back door, and tossed the butt into the plastic-lined garbage can in the kitchen. The new helper, Rafael, had needed to leave early, so Joonho had to clean up the kitchen by himself. Joonho changed into his rubber boots and mixed disinfectant into the wash bucket.

Joonho's wife, Nari, had already locked the front door and settled the cash receipts and was busy tidying up the bathrooms.

Joonho, dressed in a white short-sleeved cook's shirt, navy drawstring polyester trousers, and rubber boots, scrubbed the tiled kitchen floor before hosing it down.

Yun had driven from Cypress to Garden Grove to pick up her parents. In the parking lot, she waited for them in the car while she did her Spanish homework. In some ways, Yun liked the sound of Spanish more than English. She'd always had good high school Spanish teachers, and *Profesora* Martinez at UCLA was her favorite teacher.

When her father opened the front passenger door, Yun looked up from her language workbook. Joonho slid into his seat, reclined his head, and shut his eyes.

In the back, Nari buckled her seat belt.

"What did we make today?" Joonho asked his wife. Yun knew he'd be hoping for a big number. From the kitchen, he could estimate how many entrées and sandwiches they'd sold, but it was the front-of-store sodas and iced teas that could make a big difference in their profit margins.

Yun started the car, feeling sorry for her father, whose clothes reeked of fishy oil. His uniforms were harder to wash than her mother's.

"A little over nine fifty," Nari answered. It was not a good take for a Saturday, and they still had to get over the middle-of-the-month hump and earn enough money for the rent, utilities, supplies, and insurance, and Lenny's and Rafael's salaries. They could keep what was left after everyone else got paid. The promissory note they'd signed was getting paid off at a regular clip but not fast enough for Nari, who worried about Yun's tuition.

When they were already on the freeway, Joonho suddenly said, "We have to go back."

"What?" Nari said.

"I forgot to lock the back door. I closed it but didn't turn the knob. I had a cigarette—"

"This is the second time in two months. Do I have to do everything? Your head is still in Seoul. Or you're fantasizing about Brazil like you're a young man. You're almost forty," Nari shouted. "Your daughter has to pick us up because we have only one car. She studies, works hard, and never hangs around with her friends. My little girl shouldn't have to do this. I can't believe that you forgot again—"

Nari's complexion was gray from exhaustion, her eyes bloodshot. In Seoul, she had almost never yelled at Joonho, but here, as she worked beside him each day at the shop, she understood that he was no longer the same confident young man she had known as a teenager. He used to call her his princess.

"It's okay. It's okay," Yun said calmly. "I don't mind. Really."

Joonho said nothing. He leaned against the headrest and stared at the dark-blue interior of the Volvo.

With traffic, it took another forty minutes to get back to the shop, and it was true. Joonho had forgotten to lock the back door, but nothing had happened to Shrimp Castle.

"No harm, no foul," Yun muttered under her breath as she secured the dead bolt, repeating a thing that her boyfriend liked to say. She could not imagine telling Lion what had happened, though she felt certain that he would not judge them.

❧

Back home, everyone was too tired to cook, so Yun reheated the leftover pizza from the night before while Nari and Joonho washed up and put on clean clothes. Since Yun had the car most days, Nari hadn't had time to pick up groceries. Joonho didn't like American takeout and refused to eat fried chicken or fish. The only non-Asian delivery food that he could tolerate was pizza, so whenever they ordered any, they ordered a spare box for the following night.

Eating had become a chore. Joonho had grown thinner each year, unrecognizable as the brawny man who used to go to a boxing gym in his spare time. Here he was all loose skin, bones, and sighs held back.

Wearing his dark sweatpants and a clean T-shirt, Joonho sat down at the dining table, his head resting in his hands.

"Yun-ah, can you get your father a beer?"

She brought him a cold Heineken with a beer glass from the cupboard.

"Don't have more than one," Nari reminded him. "Last night you drank seven bottles and threw up before going to bed. I can't live like this."

Yun stared at her mother, willing her privately to stop nagging him. Of course, her mother was not wrong, but they both knew he would not listen.

She put a slice of pizza on her plate and reached for a paper napkin.

"I need to finish my homework," she said. Yun wasn't hungry, but she didn't want her mother to remind her to eat and start another argument about nothing.

"I should never have married you," Nari said to her husband.

Joonho got up from his seat, opened the apartment door, and walked out.

He didn't return until Sunday night and didn't offer an explanation of where he'd been.

On Monday morning, he went to work, and Nari said nothing.

2

Suneung

Sydney
December 17, 1996

Dear Yun,

I think I read your sentence about your boyfriend wanting to marry you at least three times.

You've never been the boy-crazy type, so this Lion Han must be a special person. I need to figure out a way to get to California to see you and meet this Oracle of Orange County. No need to send me a ticket because Uncle Kenny still works at Qantas. I've been saving my babysitting and tutoring money for uni fees, and I'm skipping Schoolies, so I might have enough to get to you soon.

You are not allowed to get married before I meet him.

I can't imagine getting married myself. I like Tek, but I don't really understand all this talk of love. I enjoy hanging out with him. But it's strange to think about marriage, which sounds so permanent. There's so much left of life, right?

I'm looking forward to going to uni. Now that I'll probably go to the University of Sydney, I'm wondering if we'll always live here. My parents don't talk about it anymore.

I've been worried all day, and it's calming me to write to you. My older brother Bo hasn't called with his Suneung results. He's failed twice already. My parents think he might have failed his third time. They keep trying his pager.

He must be ashamed. Of course, he shouldn't be. I can't even imagine how hard that exam is. This year, they got rid of the bongosa, which is the school-specific exam for Yonsei, then made the Suneung longer and more difficult. Everyone at church was talking about the changes because there was a greater number of questions, without more time given.

DH said test writers in Korea are sadists. The SATs are supposedly gentle compared to the Suneung, so I looked at some of the questions, and he's right. He feels even guiltier than I do for being at Yale. He just finished his finals and said college wasn't as hard as Andover.

The reality is that both of us are stupid compared to Bo, and yet, both of us have gotten into good colleges. I find out for certain soon, but I'm pretty sure I got into Sydney. The HSCs went fine, and my TER will come out any minute, and then my offer will be official. I sound like I'm boasting. I'm sorry. It's just not as difficult as Korea or as complex as the States. Here, it's my school grades, ranking, and how many applicants want a specific course. I didn't choose Law or Medicine, so it's easier to get in.

Unlike you, I'm no good at sports. I'm no class president or yearbook editor. I'll never be popular. I'm okay with all of this. However, it turns out that I can ace standardized exams in my sleep. As long as they're in English.

Because you told me to, I found a study guide with old SATs at the school library, and I took three of them, and each time, I got perfect scores in the verbal section and only two or three wrong in math. The third time I took it, I got everything right. I'm a freak. DH agreed.

Feeling smart, I tried a couple of the Suneung exam questions, and I almost died! I don't know how Bo could even understand most of those Korean vocabulary words. My Korean is respectable, but the Korean literature questions were impossible. I had no idea what they were talking about. Even my mother was stumped a few times, and she studied English and Korean literature at Ewha. My father was able to do the math questions, but he said that they were written in a weird way to trick the kids. Why?

When I showed Tek the SATs, he thought they were manageable, too. He got into the law course at University of Sydney, so his TER was excellent, but he found the SAT math a bit odd. He refused to do a whole test with me. "What's the point?" he asked, and he's not wrong. So unlike me, who finds taking a standardized test relaxing, my boyfriend is normal.

I wish I could see Bo. I hope he is okay. Bo is the most responsible of the three of us. It isn't like him not to call after we try his pager. DH tried his pager, too, but he didn't reply.

I know we agreed not to exchange presents for Christmas, but I don't have to listen to you. You're not supposed to enclose money in the post, but my mother sends DH a twenty-dollar bill for pizza in her cards to him, and they've never gotten stolen or lost. I don't think you can get much for forty dollars, but maybe you can find a pretty top on sale or go to the movies and get a burger. You're not allowed to save it. I thought if I got you something here, then I'd end up spending more on postage. Yes, I'm still practical. So, please do something silly. Just for yourself. Promise me.

When I read your letters, I can hear your voice. Write.

Love,
Mido

❧

Bo took the 1997 Suneung on Wednesday, November 13, 1996. It was his third try.

On the Tuesday before the Suneung, Seoul was cloudy and cold. By the middle of the day, it got warmer, about nine degrees Celsius, and Bo jotted it down in his pocket-size diary.

After his last hagwon class ended, he got on a mostly empty subway car to the Yonsei campus and sat in a seat near the back. Cold, he tried to warm himself by tucking his blue woolen scarf into his faded black parka.

"If you want to be a Yonsei student, you have to behave like one," Kim Teacher, his hagwon instructor, had told him. "Go to the cafés where Yonsei students have their snacks, read the books they read, and inhabit the peace of mind of being an admitted student. Visualize. Draw the picture in your mind."

Kim Teacher had graduated from Seoul National University—the same school as Bo's father—having studied law. A Suneung wizard and a legend for having gotten one of the top scores of the country for his year, he charged an extraordinary fee to be a Suneung tutor, which Bo's aunt Sonya paid. As a bachelor not yet forty years old, Kim Teacher earned more than several lawyers and judges combined and already owned two commercial buildings in Hongdae. It was rumored that he didn't have to work anymore for money, and it was clear that he enjoyed teaching. His specialty was retakers, the ones who had not passed on their first or second tries.

Kim Teacher was convinced that Bo would pass this time. His practice scores were in the safety zone, so he focused on preparing Bo's mental game. He advised Bo to go to the campus at least once a week to be in the mindset of a Yonsei student. After the last class ended, Bo heeded his teacher's advice and went to the popular two-story café near Sinchon station, frequented by Yonsei and Ewha students.

At a corner table near the window, Bo picked up a discarded copy of a Yonsei literary magazine and read it while having his tea. All around him, young men and women huddled together, warming their cold hands on hot coffee cups. Attractive girls in bold-patterned sweaters and denim trousers discussed politics in hushed tones, ignoring the boys sniffing around them.

Bo tried to imagine himself as one of the young men writing in their notebooks or doing their assigned reading. A young woman with short permanent-waved hair resembled Isul, his friend studying for the civil service exam at the gosiwon. She was reading *The Stranger* in French. Bo hadn't had time to read a novel since summers in high school, when he used to read classic European and American novels in English.

He'd always imagined working and living in Korea, but he also wanted to be the kind of Korean who knew more about the world—through books, film, and history.

In less than twenty-four hours, he would take the Suneung again, and since last November, he had done little except for study for this exam, sleep, and eat. He felt good about it and ready to put it behind him. He had failed the Suneung exam in his last year of high school and the second time after high school graduation, and he hoped tomorrow's Suneung would be his last one. This was his third November in a row dedicated to the annual college entrance exam.

After Bo finished his tea he walked through the main part of the campus, which was decorated with banners for student elections. Cheerful undergraduates rushed to their classes or exited lecture halls, relieved that a period had ended. It couldn't have been that all the students were happy, but everyone appeared calmer than he felt inside.

Kim Teacher had assured him that this time would be his last. Bo's practice scores were solid, and it had made sense for him to skip the extra practice session tonight, where he would've unnecessarily absorbed the anxious feelings of the other exam retakers.

Earlier that morning, after class ended, Kim Teacher had asked him to remain a bit longer. When the other students were gone, his teacher gestured to Bo to approach his desk.

Bo stood awkwardly while the teacher remained seated, his long brown face tilted in deep thought. The teacher was unusually tall, with broad shoulders and a square jawline. Even when he smiled, he looked more like a curious detective or a former professional athlete than a once-stellar student from a strawberry farm in Goseong who had decided to earn more money as a celebrated hagwon teacher rather than become a prosecutor or judge.

"You will do very well," Kim Teacher pronounced. He handed Bo a paper box filled with the customary taffy. "Make the score stick! This is the best *yeot* in Seoul. Not everyone can get this."

Bo smiled his thanks.

"One more thing," Kim Teacher said, digging into his vest pocket to pull out a 500-won coin.

"Take this with you tomorrow. It's a good-luck charm from your old teacher. When you get nervous, just touch it. Remember, you're not alone. Think of the millions and millions of students who have taken difficult exams before you. Now you're part of this group of strugglers. It is good to be examined. A young person should learn and be tested so he can retain knowledge."

Surprised, Bo stared at the coin in his palm. He wouldn't have pegged his teacher as superstitious.

"My hagwon teacher gave me a coin when I took my test. I passed and got into SNU for the hardest course. A farm boy got a top score!" he said, laughing. "So here I am, training you to take an exam, giving you a coin, and wishing you luck."

Bo bowed and thanked him.

"How are you feeling?" The instructor prided himself on checking in with his students. He felt that his personal approach was the reason his students got their best scores and shook off their past failures.

Bo grinned, staring at the pale-blue walls of the large classroom.

"I'm well, Teacher. I believe I've prepared as much as I could."

"You will have fine luck, too. You deserve it."

"I guess I haven't had much luck before."

"Sometimes it isn't just preparation. There's timing, circumstances, and personality. You have good habits, and you did the work, Bo. You're hardworking and a good person. Go easy on yourself. Make sure you go to sleep early tonight. Tell yourself that the exam is just another practice test. You'll be fine."

At the café, several tables had cleared out, and Bo was alone in his corner. He put aside the literary magazine for the next person who might want something to read. When he went to the cashier to pay the bill, he could feel the worn edge of the 500-won coin in his coat pocket. He took the train home and stopped at the grocery store near the gosiwon to pick up supplies for dinner.

❧

Sonya had selected the best gosiwon near Bo's hagwon, and it rarely had a vacancy because it was so well maintained. Regardless, it was still a pay-by-the-week lodging, filled with transient students, day workers, and ghostly figures who came and went, and, of course, it was nothing like home. The kitchen for the residents was a modest-size rectangular room. There were three rice cookers and three electric kettles on a long white counter by a deep sink and a dish rack. Everyone was required to wash their own dishes.

Bo found Isul at the communal table, her eyes closed and her head propped up on a Grade 7 civil service study guide. An aluminum ramyeon pot with rounded handles simmered on the stove. Isul wore her usual indoor clothes: black sweatpants, gray sweatshirt, white ankle socks with black-and-white plastic slippers. She was bone thin and tiny, and although she was four years Bo's senior, she looked like a primary school girl wearing her older brother's clothes. Severely nearsighted, Isul wore eyeglasses with thick plastic lenses that obscured her lovely small eyes.

Bo had met Isul in the communal kitchen on his first day at the gosiwon. Within a week, she made a point of sitting him down to tell him that he was nothing like the other residents.

"You're not a loser like most of us. You'll have a bright future. Keep studying."

She had already graduated from Pusan National with good marks but hadn't been able to get any office jobs. Dejected by the process of applying for any more white-collar jobs, she had taken a break for a few months to work as a barmaid at a restaurant owned by her aunt, who had borrowed money just so Isul could study in Seoul for civil service exams. Isul had failed twice already. On the first try, she got to the interview stage but had gotten a severe cold and lost her voice.

Isul's windowless room was one of the smallest in the three-story gosiwon, and she had to share a bathroom on the women's floor. She teased Bo for being a rich kid because, though his room was also small—about six square meters—at least he had his own bathroom and a transom window that opened, allowing him to get fresh air from the lobby windows. Isul and Bo had made a wager that whoever passed on the third try would buy the other a beef barbecue dinner.

Every day they ate at least one meal together in the third-floor kitchen, where they could have as much rice, kimchi, and ramyeon as they wanted, all supplied by the gosiwon. With the allowance that his parents sent, Bo bought eggs, sausages, tofu, and tins of *jjajang* tuna, and he shared his groceries with her, though she ate so little that her intake was hardly noticeable. Whenever her aunt sent her fish or *banchan* from home, she shared it with him. She called him her little brother.

The ramyeon in the pot burbled over, and Bo hurried to the stove to turn off the gas.

"Sister! It's done, right?"

Isul didn't open her eyes, and he nudged her shoulder gently, feeling the sharp edge of her shoulder blade beneath the thick sweatshirt.

He saw that she was sleeping soundly, having forgotten to take off her eyeglasses. As he removed them from her small face with both hands, Isul still didn't wake up.

Big Uncle, a middle-aged security guard at a downtown bank, peeked into the kitchen. A longtime resident and a kind of mayor of the gosiwon, he favored Isul and Bo. After his elderly father died six years ago, Big Uncle had moved into one of the back rooms with a bathroom and never seen the point of finding a bigger place of his own. He preferred the bustle of the gosiwon to the idea of living alone and took great care to remember the birthdays of residents and staff. On a birthday, he'd buy a red bean bun from his favorite bakery and leave it in the kitchen with the person's name and a smiley face in a heart drawn neatly on the paper bag.

"Our little Isul looks tired," Big Uncle said. "Maybe we can get Manager

Hwang to open her room, so she can sleep properly. Her neck is going to hurt if she sleeps that way," he said, clucking his tongue. "Manager Hwang is at the store now. He'll be back in half an hour or so."

"Sister, Sister." Bo jostled Isul's shoulder but got no response. He spotted the familiar green lanyard with her room key in her sweatpants pocket. He turned to Big Uncle. "Maybe we can take her ourselves. She must weigh forty kilos, if that."

Big Uncle bent over her chair and scooped up the young woman in his arms like an infant.

"She weighs less than a small sack of rice," he said with concern.

They both checked that she was breathing.

Taking her key, Bo walked ahead of him to open Isul's room. Having never seen the inside of her room before, he was startled by how small it was, easily half the size of his.

She had almost no possessions. The white walls were bare and the A4 paper–size patch of floor immaculate. On the clothing rack, which was less than half a meter long, hung a navy woolen winter coat, a black interview suit, one white dress shirt, and the Burberry scarf that Isul's aunt had sent last Christmas. Every centimeter of her desk was covered with heavy piles of test guides and notebooks. Her bed was made and covered with a thick red-and-green checkered blanket. On the pillow was an open box of cold medicine from the corner drugstore. Eight of the capsules had been removed from the tabbed aluminum sheet.

❧

At the hospital, the doctor pumped her stomach and gave her fluids. She would be fine, the nurse told them.

Big Uncle had to meet someone and asked Bo to stay with her until her aunt could come from Busan.

When she woke a few hours later, Bo was struggling to stay awake in a chair next to her bed. Isul looked startled.

"Bo, what am I doing here?"

"You troublemaker," he said, relieved that she was back to normal.

"Where are my glasses?"

Bo picked them up from the bedside table and handed them to her.

"Did you take all eight pills?"

"What pills?"

"The cold medicine."

"I don't think so. I took two at first, then they didn't work, so I took two more. Some last night."

"You dummy," he said. "You need to take a child's dosage, and you probably didn't eat. I can't believe you have a college education and still don't understand basic chemistry." He looked at her sternly but started to laugh.

"Watch it. I'm still your elder," she said, smiling weakly.

"How do you feel?"

"I have a cold. And my throat hurts."

"They pumped your stomach. They thought you tried to—"

Isul raised her hand briefly from the bed as if to stop him from speaking, then let it drop. "Bo, I'm so tired. Let me sleep. I just want to stop feeling so tired and sick. I keep getting these colds, and it makes it hard to study. My poor aunt. She wants me to work in an office. I better get well soon."

Bo watched her fall asleep. After Isul's aunt finally arrived, he left her a note, promising to return the next day.

❧

It was four in the morning when he returned to his room, and he closed his eyes for a couple of hours, washed, and remembered to pack what he needed for the test, including his exam ticket, his identification, sharps, marker pens, a packet of tissues, and the hard peppermint candies he liked. He tossed the box of taffy into his backpack.

As soon as the proctor allowed them to open the exam booklet, Bo plowed through the questions. After the first section, he had a short break, and that was when he felt dizzy, the exhaustion hitting him all at once. He had taken his seat at 8:10 a.m. and the exam would end at 5:20 p.m. There would be another short break and an hour for lunch, and it was during the breaks that he felt nauseated.

His head felt heavy and hot, and Bo could not keep his eyes open. He was sick. When he reached the literature section, he couldn't puzzle out the meanings of the questions. He stared at the reading passages, trying to make sense of the sentences. The shorter questions were more confusing than the longer ones. He reached into his trouser pocket and fumbled with the 500-won coin.

He turned to the next literature passage: excerpts from ancient poems, and he was supposed to select a verse that most resembled the style of the poems. The indecipherable words began to swim in his mind.

What had made him think that he could go to Yonsei at all? He had been born in New Jersey, had grown up in Sydney as well as Seoul, and he was sitting in a room filled with students who had been living, breathing, and eating this once-a-year exam since they were in primary school. This year, the bongosa exam had been eliminated, so this test was everything. Bo opened his eyes as wide as he could, doing his best to wake himself up from his stupor. His mind didn't go blank; rather, all the what-ifs multiplied like exponents and crowded his mind, disabling him from being able to envision anything else.

The night before, Big Uncle and he had rushed Isul to an emergency room. The doctors had treated her as if she had overdosed intentionally since they had seen this sort of thing far too often. In his former high school, Bo knew of at least two suicides and multiple attempts.

Bo stared at all the questions left unanswered. Another year spent in preparation.

The proctor told the students to stop, and Bo put down his marker pen.

He walked out alone, leaving behind the examinees who'd gathered to discuss the hardest questions. They complained loudly about the passage comparing the old Korean poems, and Bo chuckled briefly in recognition. He had not been the only one to get it wrong.

At the train station, a beggar slept soundly on a bench. Easily over eighty, the man had a deeply furrowed brow, yet the lower half of his face was oddly cherubic—plump jowls and a small pink mouth, almost smiling. A threadbare coat was draped over his chest and arms like a blanket. By his left hand and cane were a polished brass bowl and a laminated sign: "Blind from birth and abandoned by my mother. I ask for mercy. I wish you good fortune."

Bo placed the coin in the man's bowl.

3

Transit

Bo's hagwon teacher paged him twice, but Bo did not call him back.

The results came out right before Christmas. Alone, the young man read his scores on the slip of paper and sat down on the bed in his rented room. That year, the scoring had changed from a top score of 200 to one of 400, and the newspapers reported that this test had slaughtered hordes of top students. The top scorer had hit 373. Bo had not cleared 300. He felt as if he couldn't breathe. He didn't know how long he sat in his room, but eventually Bo walked out of the gosiwon and applied for a job.

With his high school degree and good manners, he got a job right away at the nicer mart a block from the gosiwon. Working full-time as a cashier and stocking shelves, Bo felt productive. The mart manager, a thirty-two-year-old man from Daejeon, admired Bo, who was punctual, responsible, and honest. When other employees came late or didn't show up, Bo picked up extra hours. One evening, the manager mentioned in passing that he had graduated from a college no one in Seoul recognized and hadn't been able to get office work no matter how hard he'd tried. He didn't see the point of the years and years of hagwon payments and countless job applications, all to end up at this mart, but the degree, matted and custom-framed, had made his late parents proud. The manager's cheerful wife, who was a head taller than he, also worked at the mart. They did not plan on having any children.

Bo's parents offered him a ticket to Sydney, but he asked for time to consider his options. Moreover, he asked Helen and John not to send any money until he knew what he was doing. With his own earnings, he was able to keep living at the gosiwon. At the end of the workday, a mart employee could purchase discounted meals, and often, the manager and his wife saved him the best of the expired goods, which were still perfectly good to eat.

Between Bo's mother and father, it was Helen who took Bo's news harder. She had trouble sleeping and focusing at work. Even as she completed everything she had to do—work, family meal preparation, housecleaning—even as DH and Mido were doing well in their studies, Helen's mind dwelled on her disappointed son in Korea. It was difficult to imagine her brightest child selling cigarettes and beer and sweeping the sidewalk. Hearing that the manager and his wife were being kind to him gave her little comfort.

Born to careless parents who often ran away from creditors and gambling debts, Helen and her siblings had grown up on their wits, dependent on the charity of the church and pitying neighbors and doing jobs that were forced on children.

One summer, when the girls were in primary school and Kenny was still a toddler, her parents had disappeared, and she and Sonya had packed sneakers in boxes for the owner of a small factory, who gave them food but almost no pay; during another school break, Helen had washed towels and cleaned the facilities of a public bath. In middle school, Kenny had mopped floors and broken down crates at a nearby dry goods store. All three of them had plucked chicken feathers and scaled fish at a wet market, when they could even get the work. When Helen was pregnant, the memory alone of slippery chicken carcasses had made her unable to even look at a bowl of chicken soup.

If Helen didn't have to keep her well-paying job at the department store, she would have flown back to Seoul to get him. Her husband asked her to be patient.

"Bo will figure it out. He's the most sensible of the three," John said.

Helen called Sonya anyway.

❧

When Sonya met Bo at the *tonkatsu* restaurant, she wore a simple camel-colored dress and didn't carry one of her expensive handbags. Bo arrived on time and took a seat across from her. He looked remorseful, as if he deserved to be reprimanded.

"I ordered your favorite set and a cola with ice," Sonya said, smiling.

"Thank you, Aunt."

The young man in front of her had just turned twenty-one, but Bo was still a boy. Like her sons, her nephew was the size of a man, but despite his clean-shaven face and the rising Adam's apple of his thin, corded neck, Sonya could still see the childlike innocent expression behind his eyeglasses.

"I'm sorry for all the trouble I've caused you. The tutor you found me was very good. It isn't his fault."

"What are you talking about? I think you're amazing, Bo. I imagine this feels awful right now, but this could be providence," she said. "I believe this needed to happen. Your aunt is over fifty years old, and this is what I've learned. Sometimes the things you wanted most and still don't get are terrible things you've been delivered from."

Bo looked up, his mouth opened a little.

"It's still upsetting. I understand." She paused, sensing he might resist her next proposal.

"I talked to an admissions counselor about you, and she said that you should go to America."

Bo's expression darkened. "Aunt, I can't give up. I should take it again. I already spent three years on this, and my scores were really high in my practice exams, and on the first two. I was just tired, so I thought this job would be a kind of break. I don't even have to learn that much more for the next Suneung. I just have to wait another year."

"Your mother said something about a girl that you were helping the night before. Is she your special friend?"

"Oh, no." Bo shook his head, understanding her meaning. "She's like my elder sister at the gosiwon. She got sick, and we had to take her to the hospital. It's not like that."

"Is she well now?"

"Oh, I think so. She's studying to take her civil service exam."

The boy was too nice for his own good, she thought. Sonya's husband thought it was crazy that he wanted to live in Korea when he had US citizenship.

"So you're not staying in the gosiwon because of her, then." Sonya looked at her nephew carefully, the way she did when she spoke with her sons, checking for even the smallest of telltale facial expressions. Bo shook his head again, and she decided to believe him.

"The admissions counselor had an idea, and I think it can also help your parents."

The server placed the tonkatsu sets on the table and left them.

They bowed their heads and prayed silently, then she gestured for him to eat.

"Bo, this admissions counselor is famous. She is the best in Seoul and she has a plan, which apparently she's used many times with her students who can get visas. You move to California and go to a community college for two years. After you establish residency, then the cost will be almost nothing. You can pay for it by doing part-time jobs if you like working so much. If you do well, and I know you will, you can transfer to a California State school, or one of the University of California schools, or any four-year school. You could transfer to an Ivy if you wanted to." She detected her nephew's resistance and felt herself trying to sell him on the idea. "The rich schools give financial aid. Just think, you don't have to do military service since you're an American citizen, and Bo, you can start again. I know you will flourish. It's not your fault that—"

She stopped herself. The boy was clearly upset, but trying not to show it.

Bo felt worse. She must think he couldn't pass, yet he could not defend himself because the evidence against him was irrefutable. He had failed. Three times. None of the context mattered, only the results. He chewed the fried pork but tasted nothing.

"I've spoken with your parents. They think this is a good idea."

"Aunt, I can pass. I know this has been a terrible burden, so I thought I'd save the money from this job and try to do it alone—"

"Bo. Listen to me. I know you can pass, too, but what for? Is it worth it? Do you really want to live here, or did you just want to know that you got into Yonsei University? If you really wanted to live here, you could have chosen an easier school to get into, isn't that right? There were dramatic changes in the past few Suneungs—first the Yonsei bongosa, which they didn't have before, then they get rid of the bongosa, and all those extra questions in this recent one. Almost all of the children of my friends didn't get good results. It's not their fault. This unpredictable system of testing just to weed children out is unfair, and I don't know why you have to bear it any longer."

Bo said nothing. He had believed in his plan, and in a few sharp, well-reasoned words, his aunt had pierced his logic and purpose.

"I don't know anyone in California. Where would I live?"

"Mido has that church friend, Yun, from middle school, and her boyfriend, Lion Han, said you could work for him."

Bo looked confused.

"Yun's boyfriend owns a hagwon in Orange County, and he needs a van driver and a math tutor. You can live with him, he said. You can go to school and work part-time."

"How would I get there?"

"Uncle Kenny will get you a ticket to Sydney, and then, after you see your parents, you can go to Los Angeles." Sonya held her breath. This plan had been in the works for over a week, and if Bo agreed, she felt it could be the ideal situation.

"I guess no one thinks I can get into Yonsei."

"You're wrong," she said, impatient and unwilling to indulge his self-pity. "You want proof that you can get in. I get that you feel embarrassed. That's normal."

Bo put down his fork and knife and wiped his mouth with the paper napkin.

"I know you can get admitted. There were some tough breaks, and I'm positive that if you keep taking it, you will pass. I read that this Korean-language section for the 1997 Suneung was the hardest one in the history of this stupid exam. How were we supposed to know that? Your friend got sick and had to go to the hospital. You did the right thing."

Sonya lowered her chin and composed herself. It was on her to convince him. Her sister was beside herself with worry. In Sydney, Helen was working every possible shift at the department store. To economize, the family had moved into a two-bedroom rental above a garage in Strathfield South. They had to send money to DH at Yale and also support Mido at the University of Sydney. Mido couldn't qualify for HECS because she wasn't an Australian citizen.

No one wanted to tell Bo how much his attempts were costing them, but he knew. Of course he knew. He was the oldest of three children, just as she was. The oldest needed to know what had to be done for the family.

"If you go to California and study there, you won't be vulnerable to all these exam and admissions changes. You won't keep delaying your life year after year to prove something that everyone already knows you can do. I know you want to be Korean and work and live here. But my husband said the men in some companies could resent you for getting to skip military service. None of this is your fault. Life is terribly unfair, but we have to—"

From his disheartened expression, it was evident that Bo had already thought of these things, and Sonya took another breath, not wanting to say any more.

"I spoke to Kim Teacher. You're the best retaker student he's ever had. All of us believe in you, Bo. We don't believe in this exam."

He stared at his barely touched plate.

"We don't believe in the Korean education system. Do you understand?"

"I won't blame Korea," he said.

"Eat your food," she said as kindly as she could.

After he finished, he told her he'd think about it.

❧

Two days later, he ran into Isul in the kitchen. She was drinking her first coffee of the morning and looked chipper.

"Thank you for the toast bread and strawberry jam, little brother."

Isul was referring to the day-old baked goods and expired jams he'd brought back the night before. The gosiwon residents were delighted to supplement their rations with Bo's regular food bonuses. No one paid any attention to the expiration dates. More than one of them had joked, "If only the mart could give us expired soju." She slid the plate of toast toward him.

Bo nodded thanks but didn't say anything. He poured boiling water over the powdered coffee in the bottom of his mug and watched the water bloom into coffee.

"My parents want me to go to America."

"Go," Isul said. "I'm glad somebody is making sense. Yaah—you better go. I'll kill you if you don't go." Isul raised her fist over his head, grinning.

On seeing his expression, she put her fist down.

"You don't want to go? Why?"

"You too?" He shook his head. "I want to take it again."

"Forget Yonsei. You can pass next time. I'm positive. I would bet my eye surgery savings on that. And when you pass, so what? Have you seen how hard it is to get a good job here? You don't have any connections, right? Does your rich aunt know any conglomerates that are hiring?"

"I spent three years," he whispered.

"Big deal. Go. Listen to your parents. I wish I had smart parents." Isul smiled to soften the blow of her words. "You speak English perfectly, you have US citizenship, and you're a genius. You're better at math than any hagwon teacher I have ever had. Except for your nearsightedness, which you should get fixed, by the way, you are a nice-looking young guy. Go to America. Forget this hell. If I had your choices, I would've been gone a long time ago. You foreign-born Koreans are all messed up. You think you have to prove something. Prove you're Korean. C'mon. There's no test for that.

There are Koreans who are born here who hate being Korean. Hey, maybe that's being Korean!" She laughed, then grew serious.

"Forget Australia, too. A friend of mine went there, and she's doing just a little better than here, but everyone wants to go to the US. You can. Do you need money for the ticket? I don't have much, but for my little brother, I would give you some of my eye surgery money—" Isul still felt terrible that he had not slept the night before his Suneung on account of her. He swore it wasn't her fault, but she couldn't help feeling guilty.

"My uncle works at Qantas. We can get cheaper tickets."

"Wow. If you weren't such a nice little brother, I would not like you. You have it made. What are you upset about?"

"I failed the Suneung three times. I'm twenty-two years old." It occurred to him that in the US, he would be his American age of twenty-one, and it sounded much younger, though he was still the same person. "Three times."

"So damn what? I failed my exam two times. By the time I get a job, if I get a job, I will be an old lady with thicker eyeglasses. But you know what? Your gosiwon sister will pass this son of a bitch civil service job test, ace the interview, and I'm going to get my nearsightedness corrected. I'm not so bad-looking, and I'm going to have some fun. I'll have tall, good-looking boyfriends who like short women, and one day, I'm going to buy my aunt a little building back home. It's not expensive like Seoul." She put her twig-like arms on her hips. "This is my plan. I believe it is a good plan. Every day, I work to make my plans into reality."

"You will definitely pass. I'm positive you will," Bo said.

"Go. You go to America. That's a better plan. But first, you better go to work." Isul gestured to the kitchen wall clock, then picked up her free toast and jam.

Bo laughed.

"I better go."

Isul winked, and when he left the kitchen, she imagined the big gosiwon without him, which was depressing. She made herself another coffee and opened her study guide.

4

Sydney University Dramatic Society

Sydney
July/August 1997

As a first-year university student, Mido had no problems with the written coursework. Just as in high school, she found writing research papers and taking exams manageable and often engaging. She had selected the education course, specifically at the primary level rather than secondary, because Mido felt comfortable with small children.

Tek was in his third year, studying commerce and law. After classes, meetings, and work, the two undergraduates met at his rental apartment, which he shared with old friends.

One Friday afternoon, they made love in the empty rental, fixed scrambled eggs with baked beans and toast in the common kitchen, then returned to Tek's room to do their schoolwork.

Mido was seated upright on the bed to do her reading, using two pillows as her lap desk. Tek was at his desk, which was pushed up against the long wall. Before starting his assignment, he remembered.

"How did your presentation go?"

Mido inhaled. Everyone in her primary school survey course had to give a brief oral presentation about their research paper, and it had been abysmal. It was a quarter of her grade.

"That good?"

She looked at him, her expression full of worry, and sighed.

"When I talk to my tutoring students, even in a group of four or five, I feel fine. I explain the concepts, ask them questions, and teach what's needed. I must be doing okay because the kids are doing well, and I get referrals since their marks improve a lot."

Mido collapsed into her open book, burying her head in the comforter.

Tek tried his best to understand her situation. He had debated since Year 9, but even before that, he had been able to handle anyone who interrupted, shouted down, or fought a point to death. At his boys' school, arguing had been a kind of sport, and he'd have qualified as a varsity athlete of talking. Nothing thrilled him more than persuading a thoughtful opponent. If the opponent was an ass, Tek enjoyed taking him down even more. He loathed bullshitters—people who just liked arguing or talking to get attention. The better he got at debate, the more he became aware of the power and responsibilities found in the gifts of logic, rhetoric, and argument.

As a skilled debater, he felt more strongly than most that speaking and listening should be meaningful. If he had to expound on the matter, he would say that the highest aim of debate was to reveal truth and knowledge among well-intentioned minds. The mark of a great debater was to be truthful in the structure of an argument. An assertion based on verifiable evidence, clean logic, and fair execution of delivery should triumph over a weaker point.

One of the things Tek admired about Mido was how she spoke: Her words were essential. There was nothing unnecessary in her thoughts. Whatever she said felt true and valuable. It upset Tek, who had been around so many loudmouths, to think that Mido's ideas could be lost or diminished because she didn't know how to deliver them well enough to others.

His parents, both professors at the University of New South Wales, had taught their only son that almost any subject could be learned competently by a student of average ability. Tek's parents had graduated from Korea University and received doctorates at the University of Sydney, where they had met and married. Tek's father was a political scientist who specialized in East Asia, and his mother was a well-regarded economist. Despite their own educations and professions, they believed fervently that a child should never be forced to study. That said, they had provided a number of opportunities for Tek to explore diverse fields of interest in academics, sports, and extracurricular activities. Both prided themselves on never pushing a child to excel. Rather, they taught Tek about the need for intelligent schedules and delayed gratification and the value of consistent, high-quality work.

Tek's father argued that Koreans back home had the wrong ideas about education.

"All that memorization, rule following, and class ranking. Foolish business," Professor Do would mutter.

His wife, Professor Yoon, who went by her family name, would add, "Such willful disregard of the child's personality and abilities. No wonder the country is in such a mess."

It wasn't that they idealized the Australian education system; however, they thought it was preferable to the one they had experienced and had remained in Sydney in the hopes that their Australian-born son would get a proper Western education. They had not stressed learning Korean. Tek understood the language but did not speak it well.

Professors Do and Yoon liked Mido, but noticed how quiet she was.

"Is she like that with you, my chatty son?" Professor Yoon asked.

"She's not like that around me when we're alone," Tek said. "She's brilliant, actually."

Even though most university students lived at home, his parents had encouraged Tek to live in an apartment with classmates so he could gradually experience being an adult. As an added bonus, Professor Yoon was relieved not to have to think of her son's meal preparation—labor she had never enjoyed as a mother. Early on in her career, she had published a paper on the social utility of housework and the opportunity costs of women's labor in South Korea, which was still cited widely. Professor Yoon loathed grocery shopping and cooking, and thankfully, her husband would have eaten a fried egg and Marmite sandwich for dinner every night of his life without complaint.

It was Professor Yoon's idea for Mido to join SUDS. If Mido and her son were to marry and have children, Professor Yoon knew that the mother would need not only to speak to her own children but also to advocate for them in varying situations—in schools, at hospitals, and at social events. And of course, Mido would need strong, effective oral communication skills at whatever work she chose to do.

"My students who know how to perform onstage are not always extroverts," Professor Yoon advised her son. "Introverts can learn skills like improvisation, telling jokes, and public speaking. I don't like talking, but I can give lectures to hundreds," she said without any false humility, and Tek realized this was true. His mother and father were not loquacious people. They seemed most happy reading and writing in their shared home office.

It irritated him a little that his mother was correct. He had to admit, however, that being around performers would be good for Mido. As a general rule, Tek was not impressed with the intellects of actors and singers, but many of his friends were performers. Fun and attractive, they were invited to better parties. Actors and singers tended to be more sympathetic than debaters. He would rather have a beer with a mate who was an actor than a debater, who could be exhausting.

In bed, Mido was sitting up again, reading. Even when she was frowning, he thought she was pretty, not in a conventional way.

She wore almost no makeup ever and dressed plainly. Mido had little interest in fashion or shopping and wore what her mother bought her. She rotated her outfits, made up of simple skirts and dresses, wool sweaters in solid colors, and pressed white shirts bought from the boys' section. Recently her friend Yun had sent her a pair of Levi's jeans, which she wore often.

Her skin was bright and clear, and she'd kept the same style haircut since they'd met as teenagers, a neat pageboy that grazed her small unpierced ears. Unlike Tek, she had no trouble sleeping, and she usually appeared well rested and imperturbable.

While his four roommates shared two large bedrooms, Tek had his own room and a queen-size mattress, where both he and Mido had lost their virginity at the start of her school year. They liked studying in his room because it was the quietest part of the house and no one bothered them when the door was closed, thinking they were having sex.

"Mido."

She looked up from her textbook and smiled at him.

"Professor Yoon had an idea."

"Your mother?"

"She mentioned that some of her students learn how to present by taking a theater class or joining a dramatic society."

"Acting?" Mido raised her eyebrows. "Me?"

"A couple of mates run the Dramatic Society. I'll find out more about it if you want. I can go with you if you're nervous—"

Mido scrunched her nose like a puppy and said nothing.

"They do improvisation exercises. I've seen them. Hilarious and liberating, I think," he said.

"Improvisation?"

"You get a prompt—like 'Two goldfish fighting for the same taxi'—and then make stuff up. Act the part. It's usually brief. Anyway, actors do loads of these exercises to loosen up. I think it's good to try these sorts of things. Low stakes, and you get to practice performing. If you think about it, a presentation is a performance," Tek said. Noticing that she did not protest, he turned back to his work. "I'll find out when the next general meeting is."

Two weeks later, Mido had more or less attached herself to the Sydney University Dramatic Society. She became a SUDS person, which felt like being in a joyful cult. She did not act, sing, direct, sew costumes, work sound, do lighting, or know how to make sets. But she liked working in the ticket booth, hanging up posters, and organizing props for performances. None of these activities interfered with her schoolwork or her part-time job as a math tutor. Mido went to all the rehearsals, and she observed how performers behaved. It felt impossible for her to get onstage, but when she wasn't busy, she sat in the back of the theater, a bundle of programs in her hands, and she admired the courage of the performers.

❧

In her first semester, not once did she improvise or do acting exercises, and no one seemed interested in making her do anything she didn't want to do. What she had not anticipated was the inspiration she'd feel to write a one-act play. She showed her second attempt at a one-act to Trevor Kimball, a well-liked student director, and he offered to pitch it at the next general meeting. When the members took a vote, Mido's *Desde/Mona/Rockstar*, written in not-too-terrible iambic pentameter, was selected.

The Cellar Theatre was showing its age. The black paint needed attention, the floors were shabby, and one of the stage lights was permanently broken. No one bothered to scrape off the old gum beneath the benches.

Despite its drab atmosphere, the black box theater of the Sydney University Dramatic Society couldn't help but light up with the youthful beauty and spirit of the vibrant cast and crew.

On Tuesday night, at the second rehearsal of *Desde/Mona/Rockstar*, Mido sat in the front row and took notes, while the two gorgeous leads flirted.

Cynthia Hendrin, a lissome, dark-haired third-year from Brisbane, who was playing Mona, had already memorized her lines and was busy refining her character's air guitar and head-tossing gestures. She batted her mascaraed lashes at the handsome Harry Chang, who was playing Otto, the prosperous and jealous head of a record label. As usual, they were in the midst of some private joke, which Mido could not hear from her seat. Everyone knew they were screwing, and in a way, it was lovely to watch their erotic charge.

The director, Trevor Kimball, a third-year, raised both his hands like an aircraft marshaller and pointed at the actors, giving his cue for the scene to begin.

Cynthia recited the lines with her characteristic verve, but there was something off in her delivery.

Trevor cocked his head. The director, sensitive to and respectful of Cynthia's prickly nature, gave her notes. He started by admiring her performance, then suggested that perhaps she should slow it down and consider what Mona would be feeling at that moment. Wouldn't she be more sensitive to what Otto had just told her—that he could not bear to see his beloved talent switch record labels and work with a despised competitor?

Cynthia tried it again, and this time the performance felt even colder, more precise, each phrase inflicting a sharp, brutal wound. Her tone was angry. Hearing her give the speech surprised Mido, who had written the words herself.

"Um." Mido raised her left hand lightly, her fingers fluttering a bit from nerves. She'd never been interested in directing but felt that she should intervene.

"May I?" Mido said, even surprising herself.

Cynthia smiled. "Please do. I'd love to hear how you had intended it."

Mido spoke Mona's lines from memory:

"I must leave, Otto. Yes, I'm in your debt.

I get that, however, I need to go.

Without you being in charge, there's more in me.

There's more music for me . . . for me . . . to make."

She paused for a beat between "me" and "to make" to emphasize Mona's hesitation about leaving Otto's label but also her recognition that she needed to leave to make room for her own art.

"I wish you'd get how difficult this is.

But our love, Otto, is unchanged.

My devotion to you remains the same.

No, no. Actually, it only grows.

Our love... my love... for you. Hey... hey, Otto.

Why can't you see that? Why can't you see me?" Mido lowered her voice.

"Yes!" the director shouted, springing up from his seat. "Exactly! It must be quieter and full of worry. She's scared of his reaction. Right?"

Trevor turned to the crowd, who'd been absorbed by Mido's performance.

In fact, the cast and the dozen members present were astonished by Mido's rendition of the title character, and, perhaps, that she'd said anything at all when normally Mido said next to nothing. She usually smiled and got along and did the necessary work.

Harry crossed his arms and stared again at the first-year playwright, whom he had never really noticed before. She was a small, plain Asian girl, and not at all his type. He liked sexy green-eyed girls like Cynthia, with her long legs, perky tits, and tiny waist. Cynthia was the kind of knockout that every man and woman could not help but notice. She sizzled just by crossing her ankles.

Harry felt startled by little Mido. He could not remember ever having heard the playwright's actual voice. It hadn't mattered because SUDS didn't need another actor, and writers could be lousy speakers. Mido was a small, quiet person who had written a solid one-act with a decent premise.

"Can you read a bit more with Harry?" Trevor asked, for a moment ignoring Cynthia, who seemed more curious than threatened. It wasn't really possible to upstage Cynthia at SUDS. Whenever she was in a play, the performances were guaranteed to sell out.

Harry continued to read as Otto, and Mido picked up where she had left off, not needing to scan the pages.

OTTO

You can't mean to leave me again, Mona.

MONA

Why can't you see that I want my work?

OTTO

I'm a rich man, and I can make you rich.

MONA

You and I can keep our love separate. It'll be best if I record elsewhere.

Harry was about to read Otto's next line, and Trevor raised his right hand to stop him.

"Let's try now with Cynthia," the director said. "Make it softer, Cynthia darling. We'll lean in more if you're quieter."

The rehearsal improved, and Cynthia, an acting whiz, took the notes well and did exactly what was needed for the first scene in the one-act.

When the rehearsal ended, Trevor held Mido back.

"Mate, your play's good, and you can act."

Mido laughed.

"No. I've no interest in acting. I don't even know if I'll write more plays. But I learned something tonight. It's easier to speak when I write my own words."

Trevor didn't understand, but it didn't matter. Mido couldn't imagine how to explain something she'd been struggling with for most of her life. It had never occurred to her before that writing could make talking easier because writing could direct her thoughts and prepare her for when she'd eventually need to say something.

✤

Mido closed the theater door and climbed the concrete steps to wait outside for Tek to arrive in his old green Ford. From her bag, Mido pulled out her needles and yarn. She was knitting a cardigan for her mother and working on the buttonholes. When she heard the familiar honk, Mido raised her head and waved, then put away her unfinished cardigan before easing into the passenger seat.

"How was rehearsal?" Tek asked, leaning closer to give her a kiss.

"I feel like I understand the play better. That's weird to say, but somehow, I inhabited the words this time. The director said he wants to see more of my plays." Mido shook her head. "He said I can act."

"Yeah?" Tek smiled. "Very cool. I'm glad he's got sense as a director."

"I mean, I don't have the right look to be an actor, but—"

"My girlfriend's lovely," Tek said, glancing at her with a smile before checking his mirrors to reenter traffic.

Mido buckled her seat belt. Uncharacteristically, she pulled down the dashboard mirror and studied her face. She winced a little, disappointed by her pale reflection, seeing her round unblinking eyes and the unremarkable nose. There was nothing wrong with her appearance. She looked friendly and nice. During Year 12, right before final exams, she'd once overheard Franky Alcott, a swimmer at her high school, say to a teammate, "Mido's fine, but she won't win Miss Australia."

Mido would never have thought to enter any beauty pageant, but hearing a popular athlete's offhand assessment of her looks was hard to forget. Often, Tek told her that she was attractive, and she would just shrug, remembering what the swimmer, whom she barely knew, had said to another faceless boy in their class. She examined herself in the mirror so rarely that it was possible for her to forget she had a face at all.

"Well, I didn't join SUDS to be an actor, you know that. I can't do this for a living. There's no money in experimental theater."

"Hey, you shouldn't say that." Tek sounded serious and reproving. "You've only been at it for a semester, but you've been so engaged. Lately it's just school, work, and SUDS."

"Well, I have to be realistic. I'm going to teach when I graduate. Be a grown-up. Make a good income."

"After graduation, you can live with me. Focus on your playwriting. Or acting. Maybe we can have kids."

Mido smiled at the possibility of children. She wanted at least two.

"My mum always worked. When Dad was fired, she was the only one making money. I'll never forget that."

"Your dad was fired?" Tek laughed briefly.

"In Seoul. A few years ago. He has a job now." Her father was still a manager at the HRI Sydney offices, but Bo had explained that their father had a lesser-paying job.

Tek waited for her to continue.

"Mum used to keep these envelopes where she'd save money for each of us. There was always a budget. If she didn't work, there'd be no money for extras for my brothers and me. For tuition overseas and tutoring fees. I wouldn't want you to have all that pressure. Doesn't seem fair."

"There's always pressure, with a paying job or not. If you stayed at home and wrote plays and took care of the kids, then I could make money. I'm going to be a barrister and make loads of it. You watch."

"As a teacher, I'll take care of kids and get paid to do it. Like your parents."

"My parents are university professors. It's different. They make a lot more than a primary school teacher."

Mido said nothing, staring through the windshield at the road ahead.

"You should focus on this play. Finish what you started," Tek said, thinking it would be cool if his wife was a playwright.

5

Financial Crisis

Established in 1865, Josiah Crawford's Emporium had its beginnings as a dry goods store, selling cotton fabrics, silks, velvets, ribbons, millinery, gloves, then later cosmetics, perfumes, and imported pottery and ceramics to a prospering middle class in Sydney. After the Second World War, in fits and starts, then gradually, the store expanded from a two-thousand-square-foot shop to fifty thousand square feet of retail space in the most fashionable part of the Harbour City, carrying the finest collections of brand-name merchandise in Australia. Its handbag and leather goods department rivaled the toniest boutiques of London, New York, and Paris, and the Emporium was the exclusive purveyor of the latest luxury goods from Europe. In the mid-1970s, the Crawford family sold the legacy brand to Winchester Hall, an upstart gourmet food purveyor, which put a stunning food court in the basement level and ran the retail business with effective corporate fiscal controls.

Starting in the late eighties, Crawford's best customers were not Australians, but the most stylish Japanese and Korean tourists, who loved the curated selections of the store's famed retail buyers.

Helen had worked at Crawford's for three years when the family moved to Seoul in 1992. When she returned in 1995, she was immediately rehired as a senior sales associate, focusing on high-end Korean-speaking customers.

In the imported handbags and small leather goods department, she was one of six salespeople, three of whom were Asians—two Japanese and Helen, the Korean. In the past decade, the Asian sales associates had brought in the highest sales commissions. Their overseas customers were decisive and unstinting in their luxury purchases. At the height of the bubble in Japan, when a businessman had to buy gifts for his wife or girlfriend, or both, he'd hand over an itemized list and salespeople would wrap up the purchases, with the appropriate labels denoting the respective recipients.

The financial crisis began midsummer in Thailand, then toppled like dominos cascading across Indonesia and South Korea, followed by Malaysia, Laos, and the Philippines. The countries had borrowed in US dollars, and when their local currencies depreciated, their governments and corporations couldn't pay their debts. The failure to protect against currency fluctuations and the ensuing panic, among other factors, caused the terrible devastation.

John explained it to Helen like this:

"Just imagine: You're a Korean worker who gets paid in Korean won. You ask a friend who's going to New York to buy a watch for $1,000 on your behalf. She agrees to buy it, and you agree to pay her back in US dollars within a year with five percent interest. In your mind, you think you will owe $1,050.

"In November 1996, that $1,050 watch cost 840,000 Korean won.

"In November 1997, that same $1,050 watch cost 1,048,950 Korean won.

"Now you have to cough up the difference of over 200,000 won or $188. For the Korean, your watch just became twenty-five percent more expensive.

"Imagine running a razor-thin-margin business that's growing rapidly and needs to borrow like crazy to survive, and out of nowhere the cost of your debt goes up almost five times. Of course, you'd no idea that the Korean won would depreciate at that rate and that the dollar would become that much stronger. Your salary hasn't risen at a comparable rate, nor your investments. You can't pay her back. Simple."

Helen had not borrowed any money, and she hadn't purchased any imported watches or designer handbags. As ever, she lived far below her means. Every Australian dollar she earned went toward her children's costly overseas educations.

Bo was in Orange County, California, driving a van and tutoring. In less than a year, he'd meet his California residency requirements, which would reduce his tuition costs and enable him to enroll at Fullerton College. DH was in his second year at Yale, majoring in economics. Although he'd received a private scholarship, it didn't cover his books, allowance, or travel. Mido wasn't eligible for HECS, a government loan program for Australian citizens. It had always been a struggle to keep up with the children's education costs, but after November, the Korean tourists vanished and with them her commissions, making her budget unbearable.

Of course, Helen knew of wealthy women who had significant cash reserves for exquisite bags, French silk scarves, Japanese skin creams, and Italian designer clothes, but fear shut tight their purses. The high heels worn by her best clients no longer clicked across the gleaming marble floors of Crawford's. In the food court, she'd spot them, but now they averted their gazes to focus on their cake and flat whites. Helen stood sentry behind the counter anyway, waiting for the clients to return.

In the first week of December, the store's general manager called Helen's manager, Scott. Three heads, the GM demanded.

When Helen got the call to appear in Scott's office, she sensed what she was about to hear. "I don't know what to say. I'm so sorry, but Crawford's has to let you go. I apologize, Helen. You know that I think you're a terrific salesperson. The business has changed so much. The finance people upstairs refuse to carry a loss. I hate them." Scott was a fair-minded person, and she felt upset for him.

"Things might improve over Christmas," Helen said. "I'm trying to develop a new client base with the locals."

"Yes, but you know how our team works. Our local clients have long-established relationships with Jenny, Clarissa, and Richard. You, Akemi, and Sara have taken a big hit. Sadly, you've taken the worst of it. I know it's not your fault."

"I can try to work just on commissions. Give up my salary if that helps."

"That's very kind, but Crawford's wouldn't let you do that. I'm sorry, Helen. There will be a severance of two months' salary. I thought maybe if you looked for a position now, during the holidays, it might be a bit easier than looking in January. I called a friend at DJ's, but he said they were okay with seasonal people for now. Everyone's nervous about the economy."

"I can even wrap presents—"

"It doesn't pay anything." Scott exhaled, not knowing what else to say. He had to make two more of these speeches after Helen left his office.

"You can count on me for an exemplary reference. I'm hoping that this crisis in Asia will pass soon, and I can phone you in a few months and beg you to return. I promise you'll be the first person I call." Scott's brow furrowed with concern.

She knew this was hard for him. Scott had always been kind to her when so many other Australians had been unfeeling. He had hired her all those years ago, not minding her accent, and arguing that it would be a good idea to have a native Korean speaker on his team.

"Thank you, Scott. You've always been a good boss."

"I'm not the boss. If I was really the boss, I wouldn't be doing this right now. I'm a midlevel chump."

Helen laughed.

"You're okay, though, right? Your husband still has a good job. Of my six salespeople, I thought you'd be the safest." When drawing up the list, Scott had considered that Akemi was divorced and had two children. She was fourth place in commissions, but she was also the sole provider, so he had decided to save her job. He'd ended up cutting Helen, Sara, and Clarissa, because they were married.

He handed her the envelope from Human Resources, and she accepted it.

❧

A week later, John's boss flew in from Seoul.

Taehun Shin had hardly aged. His hair had a few more streaks of silver, but he dyed it well enough that it looked natural. Shin could pass for forty. He brought his mistress, Danbi, who'd become a team leader at HRI. She'd never been to Sydney before.

Shin's wife, Mary, still lived in their house in New Jersey while their middle son attended Fordham University. Their older son was in his second year of law school at NYU, and the youngest was taking time off before college. The boys commuted to school to save money. Mary worked at a popular florist's in Englewood and didn't mix with the women at her church. Her sons didn't know about Danbi. Shin visited his family once a year.

Shin paid for most of the upkeep of both households, but since Mary and the boys almost never returned to Seoul now, he leased a studio in a high-rise in Apgujeong. During the week, Danbi slept at Shin's apartment. She still kept a tiny apartment near the office.

On the flight to Sydney, Danbi had not slept much, so when they reached the hotel, she showered and fell asleep right away. Shin had trouble sleeping. In the morning, he had to fire John's division. HRG was shutting down most of its business in Australia.

They were staying at a decent hotel, but it was not as nice as the one Danbi would have preferred. However, she was in a good mood because Shin had allowed her to accompany him to Australia.

In the middle of the night, Danbi woke up. She removed her nightgown and unbuttoned his pajama bottoms. Aroused, Shin woke up.

"Give me a minute. I need to go to the toilet."

"Shower, please," she said.

He grunted yes. One of the reasons he'd brought her was that Danbi acted like a whore in hotels, and he had missed this. When stressed, Shin needed to have sex more often, and she wanted it even more than he did.

Shin showered, toweled off, and returned to bed.

Danbi got on her knees and started licking him.

He held out, then said, "Get on top. Hurry."

Taking her time, she turned on the lights, and he could see the fullness of her beautiful young body.

Danbi stuck out her pink tongue and continued to lick. In a flash, she mounted him and buried his face between her breasts.

Shin could not resist, and he closed his eyes.

"You have to get rid of her," she said.

Shin felt close.

"Just finish," he said.

"No," she said, laughing, and dismounted.

"What?" Shin pulled her down, got on top of her, and continued.

She stopped smiling and tried pushing him off.

"You son of a bitch, I control this." She smiled again.

Danbi tried to pull away, but he was stronger.

Shin slapped her bottom hard.

"Fine. Just try to finish," she said.

He'd never hit her before, and suddenly he felt more foolish than sorry. They played these rough games, and sometimes Danbi could be cruel in her teasing. He was more afraid of her than he let on. Usually he let her get her way, but it felt different this time.

She climaxed, then, when he was done, she separated from him.

"You're getting fired," she said.

Shin stared at her, confused.

"You're here to fire most of the Sydney office, but when you return, you'll be fired. Then I'm all you'll have left. I love you, so I'll care for you always, but you'll have nothing without me. Get rid of your wife."

Shin sat up in the bed, not comprehending what she'd just said.

"Vice-Chairman Han told me."

"Why would he tell you?"

"He did."

"Are you fucking him?"

"No," she lied. It had been a closed-door office blow job with her top off and nothing else. They hadn't even had a meal together, although the vice-chairman had offered dinner afterward. She had declined, but she intended to reach out to him again for investment advice.

"I love you, Shin Taehun. You're my whole life. You'll be my husband."

Shin stared at this beautiful girl who looked like an angel but had the heart and mind of a beast. It was hard to believe that she might sleep with that rich shithead with the comb-over. He told himself she wouldn't.

"The vice-chairman is firing me and keeping you there because he wants you for himself. Your plan was stupid. Of course he'll get rid of me now. What have you done?" Shin placed his hand on his forehead as if to still his mind.

Every minute with this woman had been insane and wrong, yet she compelled him toward her. His wife, Mary, was good and wise, but he had no interest in sleeping with the mother of his three sons. He was going to get fired, and no one was hiring in Korea.

"I'm not staying at HRI without you. We're going to California. My cousin lives there and he is going to help us. I have money. Get rid of that woman and sell that house in New Jersey. You can split the proceeds. Then you're going to marry me. I want to have a child. Two months ago—"

Shin turned, his throat feeling dry.

"I stopped taking the pill. I'm not pregnant now. Make me," she said.

He got out of bed to find water.

❧

In the morning, Shin went to the Sydney offices. The secretary offered coffee, but he declined.

In the fourth-floor conference room, he spoke to each employee on the list individually. In his career, Shin had fired numerous people. It wasn't hard anymore.

At last, when John Koh entered the room, Shin got up from his seat and went to shake his friend's hand.

Shin was wearing a suit and tie, and John remembered that he had left his jacket hanging on the back of his chair. What he wore didn't matter. He was getting fired.

"Have you been well? It's been a while," John said.

"I'm getting laid off, too," Shin said.

"I understand," John said.

"What will you do?" Shin asked.

"I don't know. Helen wants us to go to California. Bo's there now." He paused. "It's hard to imagine starting again somewhere else," he admitted.

"Life doesn't give you the choices you like," Shin said. "The IMF deal is going to shut down the markets for a while. If I had a lot of money, I'd buy up everything because assets are going to get cheap."

John smiled in spite of himself. Shin was always looking for a good trade. After she was let go, Helen had mentioned California again. She wanted them to be with Bo, and John had been thinking about it. What would he do there? There were no jobs for him with Korean companies overseas, and no jobs for him in Korea, where everyone in his family was gone. What was holding him to Korea?

"Maybe we can work together in the United States again," Shin said.

John smiled. "I think my wife has other ideas. Maybe opening a small business."

"I'm still with Miss Jung. She wants me to divorce Mary and marry her."

John opened his eyes wide, incredulous, then shook his head. He had expected things between them to have ended by now.

"She's not so terrible. I mean, what she did to you was not fair, I realize. She was afraid. When Danbi is afraid, she attacks."

"Brother," John said, "pay attention to your house. I don't normally give you advice, but your wife is a fine woman. Maybe she can forgive you. A woman can sometimes put aside her pride better than a man. I've met Jung Danbi. It cannot be wise to share a whole life with a person like that."

Shin did not reply.

6
Economy

January 1998

After washing the breakfast dishes, John went to take a shower, and in the bathroom he found Helen leaning over the sink, massaging hair dye into her scalp.

She wore a beige plastic smock over one of DH's baseball T-shirts and his blue sweatpants from middle school. Helen smoothed a wide-toothed comb over her wet hair. Drops of brown dye dribbled down her smock.

"In less than an hour, I will have darker hair again," she said.

John looked in the bathroom mirror, their middle-aged faces reflecting back at them. The couple stood in the white-tiled rental bathroom, each wondering how old they really looked to others.

"Should I do this, too?" He picked up the box of hair dye, never having given much thought to his appearance. John touched his graying part. In April he'd turn fifty-one. It had not occurred to him that he'd be sending out résumés again.

He had time now to read the newspapers in English and Korean, closely following the IMF bailout and how the financial crisis was playing out back home. If it hadn't been for the IMF's strict austerity measures, companies wouldn't have needed such drastic restructuring and wholesale layoffs. Some economists argued that at times, strong medicines could kill a sick patient.

As a manager, he knew that more than ever, HRI needed to keep the Sydney office open, but no one asked him. The top guys wanted to save their jobs, and it was cheaper to cut those who couldn't complain.

Every night, John and Helen discussed going to California. If he couldn't get another job here with a visa, they had to find another way. No matter what, they couldn't afford to stay in this two-bedroom apartment on Helen's salary.

Helen put on a shower cap and left the bathroom so John could shower. In the kitchen, she put rice in the cooker and set the timer, then prepped the night's dinner. When she got home from work, she'd finish the cooking. In thirty-five minutes, she had to rinse out the dye and catch the bus to Mrs. Silars.

❧

Helen was grateful to have work. Her manager, Scott Cudahy, had remembered Mrs. Silars, a former client who could no longer care for herself, and with Helen's language skills and strong references, she'd been hired right away, even though she'd never been a home health aide before.

She had been out of a job for only a week, and working an eight-hour shift as an aide paid the same as her base salary at Crawford's. When there were two shifts, Helen could make up for some of the lost commissions. Mr. Silars, a retired banker, paid her in cash, and as soon as she got her envelope, Helen deposited the sum in the bank. Mido's second-year tuition was due in two weeks.

Helen and John's prestigious degrees from Korea meant little to nothing in Australia. Their white-collar peers in Sydney were executives at Korean companies, or service professionals with their own offices—doctors, lawyers, accountants—who had skills neither Helen nor John possessed.

Right after John lost his position, Helen went to a real estate agent to find a cheaper apartment, but they couldn't move until their current lease terminated in March. John's work visa would expire in a few months.

They had $8,000 Australian in their bank account, and with it, they had to cover Mido's tuition, expenses for DH at Yale, and their own costs.

For now, Bo was the only one who didn't need money. Lion—Yun's boyfriend—had hired him at Exodus Academy and charged him only $200 a month to live in the furnished rooms above Lion's garage. From his earnings as a van driver and math tutor, he was able to save for his college tuition and pay off the used Subaru he'd bought.

Helen's new job was not easy. But she didn't mind caring for Mrs. Silars, a Korean woman who had married a wealthy Australian banker. One of three aides who worked around the clock, Helen had the day shift, when Mrs. Silars had the most energy.

Mrs. Silars had been one of her better clients at Crawford's before the onset of Alzheimer's in her mid-seventies. The former art director of a fashion magazine, she'd been a stylish, vivacious woman with short raven hair and a bright, flawless complexion, one who always kept up with the latest trends even after her retirement.

In all the years Helen had worked at Crawford's, Mrs. Silars would buy a new handbag each season. She wore her trademark carmine-red lipstick, one-piece silk shirtdresses in solid colors, and low-heeled shoes. Mr. Silars bought her exquisite jewelry each year on their wedding anniversary. Not long after her illness began, she lost all interest in her clothing, bags, and gold and diamond jewelry.

Now she spent most mornings seated in her crewelwork-covered wing chair in her bedroom, dressed in a gray zip-front tracksuit, white ankle socks, and white running sneakers. If any of the nurses tried to vary her clothing, Mrs. Silars would scream.

In complete contrast to her former self, she was no longer tidy, elegant, or trim. If allowed, she would eat seven or eight meals a day. None of her old clothes would ever fit her again, and since they were too small for her, her daughter Annabelle had given them away. The other two aides, Korean migrant women, cooked, cleaned, and laundered the numerous sets of gray sweatsuits so she could wear them in rotation.

Mr. Silars was a kind man who loved his wife, and he accepted that she was more or less gone, replaced by a person who could not recognize him. The most challenging thing for him and for Annabelle was that Mrs. Silars now spoke only in Korean, her native language, a language neither Mr. Silars nor Annabelle understood, requiring a translator for everything, especially doctor visits.

When the weather was good, Helen took Mrs. Silars to nearby Hyde Park. She liked to sit on the grass near the large fig trees and have a chicken salad sandwich and a decaffeinated coffee with cream and three sugar cubes.

That morning, when she got to Mrs. Silars's house, Helen realized that in her rush to dry her hair and clean up the mess in the bathroom from the dye job, she'd forgotten her house keys. She phoned Mido and arranged to have her bring the keys to Hyde Park, since later that day Mido had a tutoring job near the Harbour.

It was a sunny and clear day, not quite hot but summery. The park breezes felt gentle. Helen guided Mrs. Silars to the shaded spot near her favorite fig tree with the tall, cavernous roots, which came up from the ground like triangular screens, creating deep pockets of space between the roots.

"Hello, Tree Teacher," Mrs. Silars whispered to the tall fig.

Helen spread a picnic blanket on the ground and unpacked the sandwich and coffee thermos. Helen hoped that Mrs. Silars would be calm today. The aide Helen had just relieved had reported that she didn't have a good night. If she was receptive, Helen would read to her. After the book, Mrs. Silars would get three biscuits and more coffee.

"Would you like to have your lunch now?"

Mrs. Silars lay down to stare up at the fig leaves. They looked like large green paw prints.

"Are you tired?" Helen asked, and Mrs. Silars didn't answer.

Helen scanned the park but didn't see Mido. She unwrapped the sandwich and placed it on the paper plate, then poured coffee into the short metal mug. Mrs. Silars liked to count out the three sugar cubes, so Helen left the sugar tin by the thermos.

"Your picnic is ready," Helen said, and Mrs. Silars sprang up like a child and reached for the sugar tin.

"One, two, three," she counted in Korean, and dropped the cubes into her coffee.

Helen smiled and watched her eat the sandwich.

As she was finishing it, she looked up and noticed Mido approaching.

"Here's my daughter," Helen said.

Mrs. Silars stared at Mido, who smiled at them.

"Who's that?" Mrs. Silars asked.

"My daughter. She's my youngest child. Remember, I have three children," Helen said.

"No," Mrs. Silars said defiantly.

Mido bowed deeply to Mrs. Silars and greeted her formally in Korean.

"Get away from me," Mrs. Silars screamed. "Get away!"

Mido looked confused.

"Should I go?" Mido asked in Korean. She looked as afraid as Mrs. Silars, who was now crouching behind Helen.

"This is my daughter, Mrs. Silars," Helen repeated slowly in Korean.

Mido smiled again and turned to her mother, "Here are the keys. I don't want to interrupt your work." Mido moved back a little.

Mrs. Silars picked up the mug and threw it at Mido. The coffee splashed across her shirt, and Mido could feel the lukewarm liquid on her chest and stomach.

"Mrs. Silars, Mrs. Silars. That's not nice," Helen said, then turned to Mido. "You should go home and change. She's tired and upset. I'll call you later."

Mrs. Silars slapped Helen's back.

Mido was alarmed but didn't know what to do.

"It doesn't hurt," Helen said. "You should go."

Mrs. Silars crumpled into herself and began crying, and Helen did her best to console her.

"Everything will be all right. Everything will be all right," Helen said to Mrs. Silars. "I can read to you now if you like. I'm sorry. I left my keys and my daughter brought them. Everything is okay now."

Mrs. Silars picked up her sandwich, and Helen retrieved the book from the picnic bag. Her daughter's figure grew smaller as she walked farther away.

❧

Mido went to Tek's house to change. It was easier than going back home.

"You're here?" Mido said, seeing the lamplight in his room.

"I wasn't expecting you," Tek said. "What happened?" He pointed to her stained white shirt.

"Coffee. I have to head back to the Harbour. I have two tutoring appointments tonight. Is there anything to eat here? I have about an hour. So sorry to bother you."

Tek got up from his desk. "We can make eggs. I have some pasta from last night. Oh, hey, did you choose your classes for next semester?"

Mido paused on her way to the kitchen. She'd been avoiding this conversation.

"My parents are thinking of moving to California."

"Not going back to Seoul?"

"There's less work there. What did your mum say about the IMF thing? Any insight?"

"Yes, Professor Yoon said it's very bad and the short-term pain will only get worse."

"I see."

Mido grabbed a T-shirt from her small pile of things in Tek's closet and changed. Tek tried to embrace her, but she pulled away. "There's no time."

"We can make time," he said, smiling.

"Later," she said. "I'll come back later. I have to eat and get to work."

Tek took her by the hand, and they went to the kitchen. He started to pull things out from the refrigerator. Mido took a deep breath.

"Tek," she said, "I'm going to go with them. Drop out of school for now. I'll finish my degree in California."

"What?" Tek put down the frying pan and turned.

"This is the right thing. It'll be better for us in California."

"That's crazy. You can't quit uni. You're doing great here!"

"I'm paying full tuition, working nonstop, and my parents can't afford to live here. Soon they won't have a visa."

"You can stay, though."

"I have to go with them. Even if they told me to stay, I'd go."

"What about—" Tek looked hurt.

"We'll be fine," she said. "They have to get settled. I'll do what Bo's doing. Work, then study." She hadn't actually thought this through, but as she was saying it, the plan grew clearer in her mind, making sense. No matter how hard her mother worked, they were still not getting by. If they didn't need to pay her tuition for uni, then there'd be more money.

"I never thought something like this could happen to me. I never thought of myself as poor. Isn't that funny? We always had more than enough for everything, I thought." Mido blinked hard, then opened her eyes. "But we don't. My folks are scared. I can tell. Because they're getting older."

"They're not old," Tek insisted. "And what about your plays? *Desde/Mona/Rockstar* was great, Mido. Everyone said so, right?"

"I have to be realistic. Plays aren't going to put me through school or get me a job."

"And . . . ?" He pointed at his chest.

Mido didn't know what to say.

"I can't stay here. My family needs me."

"You can stay with me. Why can't you live here? You take up no space."

"No, I could never do that. Depend on someone else."

"I'm not 'someone else.'" He wondered if they should get married, but that seemed insane, even to him. She was only nineteen, and he was about to turn twenty-one. His parents would never allow it, either, and he still depended on them for everything. He'd never had a paying job.

"When you came back to Sydney, I thought it was a sign," he said.

Mido tried to remember the first time they'd met. She and Yun had gone to pick up her cousin Henry at Queen's School. Tek had run into them by chance. He was a boy who liked homemade Anzac biscuits. When Tek heard from Henry that Mido was starting school in Sydney and not returning to Seoul, he invited her and Henry to see a movie. Somehow he'd become her closest friend and then later her boyfriend and lover.

She would go to California with her parents. Being a playwright seemed impossible, and now that her parents needed money, Mido could not believe she'd spent all that time caring about things that couldn't give them security. Even White Australians couldn't make a living writing in iambic pentameter, how could a migrant like her do so?

If she finished her degree in primary education, she still wouldn't make enough to take care of her family. Mido's white shirt with the coffee stain lay on the dining table, reminding her of Mrs. Silars, who could not control herself, and her earnest mother, who could not control their family's minor economy.

"I better go to work," Mido said, sad yet suddenly clear about what she had to do. "I'll call you later."

"You didn't eat."

"Later," she said.

"Mido, everything will be okay with us."

Wanting to believe him, she agreed.

7
Property

Unlike Helen, who'd married for love, Sonya Cho had refused to give up her marriage prospects for romance. Since childhood, Sonya had been clear-eyed and pragmatic. She was beautiful, capable, and motivated to excel. At school and work, she had outperformed everyone.

Neither an optimist nor a pessimist, by living in the present with great concentration on what was most important, Sonya had become a gifted adapter and a brilliant problem solver.

Only a few years after she finished Ewha Womans University, her contemporaries believed Sonya had won at life by becoming the handpicked bride of the heir of her employer, Chairman Mun, the owner of some of the costliest real estate in Seoul. Starting out as a small-time real estate broker, the Chairman had purchased abandoned factory buildings one by one and fixed them up. With foresight and luck, he'd acquired dozens of others, developing them into a wildly impressive real estate portfolio. He was reputed to be an honest landlord, unwilling to overcharge desperate tenants while never suffering liars.

Yong-gil, Chairman Mun's chosen nephew, was a hard worker. Not only was he smart about people and diabolical in business, he loved his successful uncle like a father. Yong-gil's late father and the Chairman had the same father but different mothers. As the boy of a luckless father, who died early of a stroke, and a cruel mother, Yong-gil had understood early that his savvy uncle was his only ticket out of the average life of a salaryman—the best that a person like him could achieve without family money and significant connections.

Yong-gil did not want a mediocre life. He wanted power and extraordinary wealth that would protect him and his family for generations.

Chairman Mun chose Sonya for him, and Yong-gil obeyed. He would've preferred a girl from a higher class of people. However, there was an advantage in marrying someone from an inferior background: Her people could never look down on him.

Sonya's ne'er-do-well parents had been gamblers who left debts wherever they lived. Her mother, a coarse, illiterate woman who loved to smoke cigarettes and play go-stop, had done odd jobs, working more frequently than her husband, who died in his mid-thirties from exposure after a night spent drinking.

At age thirty-six, when Sonya was in high school, her mother collapsed at a market from a coronary, leaving all three children in the care of a neighbor who made life so difficult that the orphans had to figure things out for themselves.

The Cho sisters applied themselves at school, and with the guidance of a few upright public school teachers and a collection of priests and nuns, they ended up graduating from an excellent women's college, then married. With a letter of introduction from a priest, Kenny migrated to Australia, where he settled and flourished. The Cho siblings almost never spoke of their parents or their childhood.

Chairman Mun had watched his late half brother's son Yong-gil grow up and recognized his unstinting ambition and relentless work ethic. What his nephew needed was not a high society beauty who would waste time and money on things that did not matter, but rather a diligent and ethical girl from an unimportant family like his favorite secretary, Sonya, who was also an exquisite beauty.

Her undisciplined parents had given her no money, security, or pedigree, but she had been born with a face and body that would rival any Miss Korea's. Men used to gape at his secretary, who remained loyal, appropriate, and virtuous. Sonya's refusal to flirt or acknowledge their romantic and sexual advances impressed the Chairman.

Tycoons asked him privately, "Does Miss Cho have a boyfriend?" and the Chairman would deflect any requests for an introduction. Wealthy men, by nature more persistent than poor ones, tried anyway. "Miss Cho, would you make some time for me so I can buy you something delicious?" the bold ones asked, as if the woman could not afford to eat, when for a secretary she was paid handsomely. Always, Sonya declined.

"If anyone bothers you, please let me know," the Chairman said, and she'd always handled it without any fuss.

The nephew, a canny negotiator, understood that marrying the girl that his uncle had selected would be to his benefit. Obedience in such an important decision in a man's life would demonstrate the requisite filial piety that even most sons would not practice. Moreover, with Sonya's impoverished background and lack of protectors, Yong-gil would be free to do what he liked, so he bought a proper one-carat diamond and proposed to her as expected.

After two dinners and a day trip to the seaside, Yong-gil asked, "Miss Cho, would you be my wife?"

Sonya accepted him.

The Chairman and his wife threw the couple an intimate reception at the Chosun Hotel and gave them a honeymoon in Rome. Sonya was a virgin when she married the Chairman's nephew, which pleased her husband.

Yong-gil worked six days a week. He came home late at night if he came home at all. Sonya understood this arrangement from the beginning. After she gave birth to their two sons, she cared for the Chairman's ailing wife, and after she passed, Sonya became the lady of the house.

The IMF Crisis affected the Chairman's holdings inasmuch as the corporate rental income was diminished; however, because he didn't have much debt, his company fared far better than most.

The morning after Sonya learned that Helen and John had lost their jobs, Sonya bathed, did her makeup elegantly, and dressed in a cream-colored dress that the Chairman had selected for her. She wore a thick rope of white South Sea pearls, which she had inherited from the Chairman's wife, around her smooth, pale neck.

Sonya knocked on the main door of the Chairman's suite of rooms, which combined his home office, living area, and bedroom.

"Chairman, may I come in?"

Chairman Mun was seated on the built-in sofa by the large window overlooking the Han River, reading a newspaper. He had a broad forehead, a strong brow, and large brown eyes; he always reminded Sonya of a retired statesman. The Chairman had a habit of staring at people, and his approval and disapproval came quickly.

At home, he wore charcoal-gray wool flannel trousers and a white dress shirt, a gray necktie, and a black cardigan vest. He was sixty-three but looked a decade younger. His hair was graying well, and unlike his peers, he refused to dye it.

Seeing her, he removed his reading glasses, the better to scan the plea behind her eyes.

"I arranged your lunch today. It will be served in the dining room. I thought you might like duck."

He sensed she needed something. The girl was clever and knew he didn't like to be asked for anything, so she always began with an offer, or the announcement of a task performed.

"Do you want to come sit by me? Tell me how you are."

She bowed her head.

"Come."

Sonya made sure the door was closed.

"You're wearing the dress I bought you."

"Yes."

"This dress. Let me think. That was from when we stopped at Shinsegae after the lawyers."

"Yes. Thank you again." Sonya's lower lip trembled, and out of habit, she touched the fine cashmere fabric along her hip with her right hand.

"It's your sister, isn't it?"

"They have to move."

He exhaled.

"Where will they go?"

"My sister thinks America. California. Their eldest son, Bo-hun, is there. It's too difficult to return here. There's no work for my brother-in-law, I think."

"This is a terrible time. It'll be better for them there. No one there seems affected by it. Some Americans are here already, buying things up. The dollar's strong. They're going to pick up bargains."

Sonya swallowed. She knew he knew. He always knew.

"They don't have money to immigrate," the Chairman said.

She touched her flat stomach, smoothing out a fold in the fabric.

He studied her waist. He liked that she was trim even after giving birth to two large boys. He didn't like her to be too thin, but he liked that she paid attention to her form. It embarrassed him that he had imagined her undressed.

"How is the new physical therapist?" she asked, wanting to change the subject from her sister. "I ordered more of the salts and pads she recommended."

"She has bad breath. Otherwise, she's perfectly fine. Tell her to brush her teeth and tongue."

Sonya hadn't noticed. The therapist had come highly recommended, and she didn't want to offend her.

The Chairman put down his newspaper.

"I'll give them the money."

"I'll ask them to pay it back," she said. "They'll need time, though."

"I'm not the IMF. Your sister has to educate and marry off three children. I doubt they even have a house or much savings for their retirement. This money won't affect me."

Sonya tried to keep from crying.

"I'm so grateful to you for your generosity. I know it's not the first time."

"I doubt it'll be the last. However, it hasn't been frequent, and I know that they're working very hard. Sometimes life isn't fair. It's harder for poor people to get to the next steps. It's hard for people in this country. I've been lucky."

Sonya admired the Chairman. He could be tough and blunt, yet he was never mean or stingy with his money.

She covered her mouth, and the Chairman reached for her free hand.

"There's no need to cry. It will be fine. I have the dollars, so it will be possible to move them. I'll talk with Yong-gil."

He felt aroused and powerful.

She was only growing more beautiful to him, and he couldn't help but want to please her. As his workload lessened, he had more time. Often she accompanied him to meetings, and on the way, he'd make them stop at expensive stores. The more she resisted, the more he wanted to buy her things.

The Chairman liked to dress her, and it pleased him when she tried on exquisite clothing at boutiques. Salespeople couldn't figure out at first who she was to him. She was too mature to be his daughter, and soon it became clear when they spoke that they were not a couple, yet they seemed intimate.

Sonya wore her diamond engagement ring and wedding band, but she had also inherited the jewelry of the Chairman's late wife. He wanted Sonya to enjoy them. The precious ornaments made her elegant bearing more regal, and even more alluring to a wealthy and elegant man. The gold, rare pearls, and paper-white diamonds brightened her clear, unlined skin and made her look more valued and esteemed by the man who must have bought them for her.

He did not buy her jewelry, thinking it too intimate. However, last Christmas, the Chairman had bought Sonya a one-of-a-kind sheared mink coat from France, which had surprised even Yong-gil. It was an exceptional coat, and Sonya was embarrassed by the cost. She couldn't imagine wearing it outside, but the Chairman insisted. Although it wouldn't be possible, if she sold the mink, she knew it could pay most of her sister's bills for the year.

For Sonya, family and God were everything. Each morning, Sonya prayed for her family—Helen, Kenny, and their families, Yong-gil, and her sons, Seungman and Jiman—and she prayed to God for forgiveness for loving the Chairman more than her own husband. It couldn't be helped, she thought, since she'd met the Chairman first, and he had rescued her from every privation and humiliation, and now he was being gracious to her sister, too.

⁂

A month after Helen had settled in California with the money Sonya sent her, a young woman came to see Sonya in her office.

She was even younger than the others, tall and striking; she wore more makeup than needed. She would've been prettier without all that eyeshadow and mascara. She wore a maroon dress. Her long legs appeared shapely, even with her feet in house slippers.

"How may I help you?" Sonya asked.

"I am involved with your husband," the woman said.

"What is your name?" Sonya asked.

"Noh Jayoon."

"May I ask what you need?"

"We are in love," Jayoon said.

"I see. Does my husband know that you're here? Shall we phone him?" Sonya reached for her desk phone.

Jayoon's eyes widened but she held her ground. "He doesn't know, but I know he wants a divorce. He said you don't have relations anymore."

"Is that right?" Sonya considered the girl's small oval face. Her hair was shoulder-length and dyed caramel blond. Her light-brown lipstick worked well with the pale hair. Her nails were painted neatly in a color to match her lips.

Now Jayoon looked embarrassed, perhaps having imagined some sort of conflict or at least a wife's indignation.

"Would you like some coffee, or tea? I can ask my housekeeper to bring us some. Have you eaten?"

She shook her head no, not understanding what was happening. The wife seemed genuinely concerned about her welfare.

"No thank you. I'm fine."

"Well, let's just phone my husband. It'd be easier than if I called his uncle, the Chairman. There's no need to get anyone in trouble, I think." Sonya spoke calmly and slowly, measuring her tone and words. She hoped the girl would stop her.

"You don't love him, do you?" Jayoon blurted out. "If you did, you'd be jealous."

"Is that what love is to you?" Sonya tilted her head slightly and looked out the window, admiring the blue and green colors of the river. A large black ship carrying cargo freight was off in the distance. She wondered where it would go.

"I love Mun Yong-gil," Jayoon said.

Sonya understood why she had to say his name like that rather than say, *I love your husband*, which would sound wrong to even her own ears. Sonya wouldn't question the genuineness of the girl's feelings. It took enormous courage or some other urgent emotion for her to come to the house like this. Yong-gil would've lied to her to get her to sleep with him. No doubt there had been many words exchanged, some true but most not.

"Are you pregnant?"

Jayoon shook her head no.

"That's fortunate for you."

"I'm not the first, am I?" Jayoon said, realizing then why the wife's reactions had been bled of all feelings.

"No. You're not the first to come to this house. You will not be the last."

"So you do not have relations with him, then?"

"How would you feel being asked that question by your husband's latest mistress?" Sonya asked.

Jayoon said nothing.

"I suppose you think that if I divorced my husband, then all this would be yours. This dress that I'm wearing, the pearls on my neck, this beautiful green sofa I'm sitting on—the view outside my office window. I suppose you think this would be yours."

The young woman had not thought that far, but it made sense. *If I wasn't married, then I'd marry you tomorrow,* Yong-gil had said to her not once, but many times.

"He told you that he would make you his wife, did he?"

She nodded, feeling tricked.

"I see."

"Why can't you divorce him? It's obvious you don't love him."

"One day you'll understand how love works. How a mature woman's love is different. You see, I love my family. I love my husband. I love my sons. I love the Chairman. I love my brother and sister. I'm a Christian, so I guess I should say you are my neighbor, so I love you."

Jayoon shook her head in disbelief.

"Even if you were my enemy, I am called to love you." Sonya said it dryly, because she was talking to a child, and she was tired of being upset, humiliated, and angry at her husband's poor behavior. "Do you work at a bar?"

"It's a club."

"Do you work at a club?"

"Yes," she said.

"My husband works at a club. This is our club. This is our bar. He works. I work. We work for someone. My husband doesn't have the power to give any of this to you. He is an employee. Like I am."

Sonya looked at her hands and folded them in her lap. The first time a girl showed up at the house, she had been far more disturbed, but Sonya prided herself on her self-control. Even then, she had tried to remember that she had two wonderful sons, and she was loyal to the Chairman, who was a great man, and she would never embarrass anyone, including her husband.

"I think you should call him," Sonya said. "You can use my office if you like. I can step outside. Would you like that?"

Jayoon stared at her.

"I've done this before. You can imagine what happens. Can't you?"

Jayoon shook her head slowly.

"Do you know how to play go-stop?"

"Yes," Jayoon said.

"In the game of your beautiful young life, you still hold most of the good cards. Make a wise decision on how you play your hand. Throw away the useless cards. Never get attached to any one card. Remember the game."

"I don't understand," Jayoon said.

"He will never see you again. He will change bars. Or clubs. He will talk to your employer, and you will lose your position. That is what usually happens, because you see, my husband is an important client at these clubs, and your employer cares more about money than you. There was no love. Are you the useless card or is he? Is he the valuable card, or are you? It's up to you to decide."

With the back of her hand, the young woman wiped her eyes and, for a moment, looked as if she had just woken up. Sonya handed her a box of tissues.

8

Solace

Los Angeles

Dear Mido,

What a mess we're in, you and me. It's not a contest, but I don't know who's doing worse. It's almost laughable.

Your parents lost their jobs, and my father has now left us to go to Brazil. I've no idea what this will mean for my mother and me. Mom says she'd go back to Korea if she could. I want to stay here. Dad's older sister who sponsored our family for our green cards won't return Mom's calls. So it's only Mom and me. Aunt blames Mom for letting Dad leave and says we're ungrateful. Mom said she resents how well I'm doing. In high school, her son Jimmy got involved in a gang, then went to jail for stealing a car and drug possession. I don't see how me going to UCLA has anything to do with Jimmy's problems. Anyway, thanks to Aunt, we got our green cards right away, but we still need to get our citizenship.

Lion's sister Sarah, the immigration lawyer, said we can file soon. She can't file for Dad because he's not here, and if he doesn't return, he's messing up his continuous residency requirement. I can't believe he's gone.

Dad said he'd rather die than work a day longer at Shrimp Castle. He didn't go to work for a whole week, saying he had a terrible headache. It turned out he was preparing to leave for Brazil.

He didn't sneak off, though. At the end of the week, we had a family discussion, sort of. He talked, and Mom cried a lot and yelled.

"I'm never going to São Paolo. If you can't wake up from your fantasy, that's too bad. I'm going to stay in California until Yun finishes school. We have a lease, we own a business, and I'm not starting again. Go. Go, chase your dream."

Mom thought at first that there might be another woman, but I don't think so. She watches too much television. Dad pleaded with us.

"Yun-ah, there might be some luck left in my life. My cousin thinks there might be. Every morning when I walk into that kitchen, the smell of the oil makes me want to throw up. A man cannot be chained to that stove. I owned three stores and two buildings. If it wasn't for that son of a bitch who took everything—"

You can just imagine how that went. Anyway. I should've told you all along how terrible things were, but I was embarrassed. Dad was thinking of going back to Seoul, but then the IMF happened. In America, no one cares about the crisis, but most of the Koreans in California are paying attention to it, of course. Many of the UCLA students from Korea are having to drop out because their parents back home can't afford to send money anymore, the dollar being too strong.

I'm complaining too much. I'm sorry. You and Lion are the only ones who know what's going on. Mom won't tell anyone that Dad left. Anytime anyone asks at church or at the store, she just says he went to visit his family in Brazil, which is sort of true.

My mother thinks he'll return. Just like in the dramas. He's going to make a fortune and somehow come back and rescue us. I hope she's right. I used to think my parents knew everything, but I don't think they do. I used to think they were so wise. How do you live a wise life, I wonder. Mido, do you doubt your parents, too? They're more educated than mine are. I wonder if that makes a difference.

I cannot imagine what you and your parents must have been going through. I'm sorry you have to move again, but I'm really happy that you're coming here. Finally, we'll have a reunion before five years have passed.

Bo has been so great. Lion says your brother is a wonderful teacher. He works really hard, and the students at Exodus love him. He's making a decent salary now, but he lives like a monk. I have never seen a person work like that. Your parents should be proud of him. Lion knows that Bo intends to go to college, so he's trying to figure out a way to help him, too. He's sad that Bo will move out once you get here, but of course, he understands.

Lion's brother Ray has already reached out to our landlord and found an available unit in my building.

The unit is not big, but Bo said that it fits the budget. He said once things get better, you'd get a bigger unit. He has everything figured out. You and I have never lived in the same place before, so that will be fun.

I'm sending you my heart, my dearest friend. Finally, I will see you in a month.

Yours,
Yun

❧

The remodeled church basement of Gospel Presbyterian was a cavernous multipurpose room with high ceilings. The enormous space was used for coffee hour, church meals, and assemblies. In the back of the room, facing the north side of the highway, was a highly varnished platform stage with six steps on each side.

Yun felt happiest on that sturdy wooden stage. She enjoyed going to school and helping out at Shrimp Castle, but she loved Wednesday praise team rehearsals and service on Sundays. Back in Seoul, she had disliked piano practice and her teacher, whose clothes had smelled of cigarettes and mothballs. But if she ever ran into Mr. Kong again, she would thank him because she had turned out to be a skilled pianist, able to play almost anything on the Yamaha keyboard.

After Wednesday-evening practice, Yun tidied her sheet music and prepared to leave. She didn't want to go home, where her mother, Nari, would be watching her rented drama videos. If Nari wasn't in the middle of a drama series, she would be talking back to the television screen while the Korean news aired.

When Yun's family first moved to Orange County, her parents had been stunned by the immense difficulties of their new life. Her father, Joonho, was angry all the time, and her mother was morose, disappointed by how far they had fallen in the world. Now her father had taken half their savings, bought a one-way ticket, and left for a country that seemed as unreal to her as the moon. He'd asked Yun to understand that this would save his life, and in a way, she believed him.

"You can visit me," he'd said at the airport. Yun had driven him there. Nari had gone to work.

"I'll write to you, but you know I'm not much of a writer. Thank you for being such a good daughter," he'd said. "You and your mother deserve better than an idiot like me who lost everything. Your father will work hard in Brazil. Maybe it'll be easier for a man alone."

"Appa, I think I understand," Yun said, and wished him the best.

He sent a postcard, and then they did not hear from him for a very long time.

❧

At church, more than anywhere else, Yun felt lighter and more capable. Surrounded by other Koreans, she felt like the middle school classroom president again. When the person she liked best at church, the praise team leader, Lion Han, asked her to be his girlfriend, Yun felt like life in America might turn out okay for her, though it had not for her parents. She enjoyed college, and she was in love.

When rehearsal ended and everyone else cleared out, Yun stayed back and waited for Lion, who would drive her home. Everyone knew they were a couple, but in the church building, they still felt shy around each other.

"Want an ice cream?" Lion asked.

They headed to his car.

❧

At Blinky's, Yun selected a vanilla soft serve and sat down on the red stool and faced the plate glass wall in front of the asphalt-paved parking lot. Almost every car was parked neatly inside the painted white lines. Lion brought their cones over, and as she ate hers, he put his arm around her shoulder and studied her face, lit up by the pink glow of the neon sign of the ice cream shop.

"You're getting prettier."

She smiled.

"It's not easy dating you," she said. "I'm doing my best to keep up my appearance so no one feels sorry for you, dating such a plain girl."

Lion laughed. His physical beauty had been commented upon throughout his life. With dark eyebrows, mahogany-brown eyes, a clean jawline, and a straight nose, he had what most Koreans considered an ideal face. He was just shy of six feet tall, with the wide shoulders of a tennis player. Even Yun's mother, Nari, said Lion was nice-looking enough to be a film actor.

If not for his strict upbringing in a long line of pastors and missionaries on his mother's side, he might've been more vain. When anyone mentioned his looks, Lion would frown and change the subject.

Yun was an attractive girl, almost as striking as her boyfriend. Lion's girlfriend in college, another Korean girl, a brilliant chemistry major and fairly ordinary in appearance, had ended up breaking up with him, and one of the reasons she cited was the frustration she felt when everyone made it seem as if she was the lucky one to date such a deity. Lion had learned that some parity in physical and intellectual gifts might make for a more harmonious relationship.

"How's the ice cream?" she asked, still staring at the rows of neatly parked cars. One filthy gray car was parked askew.

"It's fine," he said. "But I've been dying to tell you my news. I found a bigger space!"

"Really?"

"I signed the lease. Exodus now has a larger home. I went with Bo today, and he liked it, too."

Yun tapped her cone to his like she was making a toast.

"How many rooms now?"

"Seven. Lobby, office, and five classrooms. I plan on hiring three more tutors at least. I'm already too busy."

"And light? Is there more light?" This was something he'd wanted, believing that children needed to be in a brighter space with natural light.

He smiled before becoming suddenly serious. He put what was left of his cone on a napkin on the counter and shifted to face her fully.

"What are you looking at?"

"That gray car." She pointed to the Honda Accord. "I want my car to be clean. I want it to be parked within the white lines."

Lion patted her back. She was upset about her father leaving.

"I spoke with my sister, Sarah, about your citizenship application."

"What?"

"I took Bo to see my sister for his parents' immigration issues, and when Sarah was talking about Bo sponsoring his parents, it occurred to me that you have to apply soon."

"My mom said she could go back to Seoul. Her brothers are there."

"How about you?"

"I'm staying. I'm going to become a citizen. Your sister said I need five continuous years of residency. I want to become a citizen, go to college, and move out."

"You can live with me. I mean, after we get married," Lion said.

"What?" They'd never discussed marriage seriously before.

"You're worried," he said.

"I'm fine."

"You're comparing yourself to a beat-up car that looks abandoned," he said, smiling and looking hopeful. "You have your green card. In less than a year, you can file papers to become a citizen. You can do it with your mom if she wants, or alone. You can move out if you want. Your dad is living his life, and so is your mom. I became financially independent in college. But you don't have to be alone. We can get married."

Yun tried to understand what he was saying.

"I love you, and you love me. I was going to ask you after your graduation, but why not now? Why not?"

She didn't know what to say. "Why not?" was one of Lion's favorite phrases. He thought the world was too unquestioning, and often he would ask in his polite, thoughtful way, *Why not?* His students loved it when he'd say this. The two words had the power to make resistance disappear.

"Sarah got married early, too. Your mother can come live with us. Bo is moving out."

Yun ate some ice cream and thought about it.

"I'm a native-born citizen, and I can provide for you. Sarah said if you're married to a US citizen, then the continuous time requirement is shorter. More importantly, I love you, and I'd be so grateful if you became my wife."

Yun looked at him. She was nineteen years old and about to finish her second year in college.

"When?" she asked.

"Soon. Whenever you like," he said, never having thought about a wedding before. He'd never thought about marriage at all until he started dating Yun, and then he had known she was the one for him right away. It occurred to him that perhaps he should've mentioned that before talking to her about immigration law.

"You would do this for me?" she asked. Her eyes looked enormous with concern.

"You would be doing this for me," he answered. "We're going to have a wonderful life, Yun. You're marrying a struggling songwriter and successful hagwon owner. How fun is that? You're my person. I know this."

"Really?"

"Really. Now finish your ice cream," he said. "You have to eat more."

"Why not?" she said with a smile.

❧

To save on the electric bill, Nari rarely turned on the overhead lights. The dark living room was illuminated only by a table lamp with a beige pleated shade and the blue-and-red glow of the television set Nari was watching when Yun came home from church.

Yun hung up her raincoat in the closet, placed her tote bag on the chair by the door, and removed her sneakers.

"Did you have dinner?" Nari asked. Her legs were raised on her husband's recliner and covered with a red fleece blanket.

Yun nodded, although she had only eaten ice cream.

"How was Castle today?" she asked.

"The new cook started. I don't know how long he'll last."

"Oh?" Yun looked up.

"He's complaining already. He wants more money."

"I can work on Saturday if that helps."

"What about your midterms?"

"I can still be there," she said. "Oh, Lion rented a bigger space today."

"For the hagwon?"

"Yes."

"Can't he do something else? He's still young."

"What's wrong with the hagwon?"

"Yun-ah, the boy went to Princeton. He's smart and comes from a nice family. Can't he go to law school? His sister is a successful lawyer, right? And his brother has that nice real estate business."

"Not everyone wants to be a lawyer. He's a musician."

"But he can't be a successful musician here. Maybe as a classical musician. Does he play the piano, or violin? I don't know a single Korean American who's on the radio. Every day at Shrimp Castle, I have the radio playing, and I've been paying attention to the singers, and everyone is American."

"Lion was born here."

"All the American singers are White or Black. No Koreans."

Nari didn't want to argue with her daughter, but she couldn't stop thinking about the young man's far-fetched goals. If things became serious between them, she didn't want her only child to be with a man who was disappointed, who had failed at his dreams.

"It's not like in Korea, where there are so many pop singers."

Yun didn't say anything. Even Lion had said that Asians from here didn't get record deals. But things would change, he said. Yun believed him.

"You can make a nice living as a lawyer," Nari said. "How will you have a big house and give things to your children?"

"He has a house. I'm not telling him what to do. He's doing well as a hagwon owner, too. He doesn't depend on anyone."

"You can be a lawyer, then, and in law school, you can meet someone else with more ambition," Nari said. "My daughter would be a great lawyer. You're excellent at talking. Even when you were a little girl, the teachers would always choose you to lead the assemblies and classroom. I'm always so proud of you. And you even got into UCLA after being in America for only a few years. You know how to fight for yourself. You learned how to argue."

"I don't argue with you, Umma," Yun said. "To you, I lose," she said, smiling. "You should've gone to law school."

With her father gone, the apartment felt messier and more cramped. He had been the one who threw out the old newspapers and grocery bags. He would never leave a dirty dish in the sink. Exhausted and sad, her mother worked six days a week and watched dramas in her remaining waking hours. No one cooked anymore or bothered to order food. There were empty soda cans and peanut butter jars on the counter and expired food in the refrigerator. Yun didn't want to live here anymore.

She imagined living in a nice house with a grassy backyard. There would be sunlight streaming through floor-to-ceiling windows. In her mind, there was an upstairs, from where she could hear children laughing. Having grown up as an only child, she wished for a large family. Lion had two siblings, and what she liked best about his family was how the three got along. Lion seemed stronger even when he was alone because somewhere else he had backup. You could feel the presence of his brother and sister when you were with him. He had extra knowledge, relationships, and experiences because he had been raised with a team.

"Lion wants to get married."

"He's not stable yet," Nari said, frowning.

Yun was surprised. "I thought you liked him." She'd figured her mother would be more worried about her age or that she hadn't finished college yet.

"Lion is a nice boy," Nari admitted. But she still wanted someone better for her daughter—a kind of prince who would take Yun away from their two-bedroom rental, its lobby smelling of roach spray. The prince would be a warmhearted, noble person from a distinguished family and would be kind to her and her husband. He would never look down on them.

"You don't have to marry a Korean," Nari said. "You have time to get married. I'm not like the ignorant Koreans who insist that their daughters marry a Korean man. If you bring home a yellow-haired man with blue eyes who is worthy of your heart—"

"Umma." Yun stared hard at her mother. "Lion is a good man. He is already doing well."

"Do you have a lot of homework?" Nari asked. She tended to change the subject when she ran out of arguments.

"Just some reading and a problem set. It's almost done."

"Are you looking forward to Mido coming soon?"

Yun nodded and smiled.

Nari stood up and left the blanket crumpled on the recliner. Joonho would have folded it, but he was in Brazil.

"Going to sleep now," she said, and patted her daughter's shoulder.

❧

At her desk, Yun opened her finance textbook and continued to work on her assignment.

Her mother was wrong about Lion. There was no need for him to be a lawyer. About music she couldn't be sure. There was so much they didn't understand about that world. Yun believed that he was incredibly talented. There were no guarantees in the arts, but someone had to do well. Everyone liked music. *Why not,* he'd say, *why not me?*

Lion didn't want to be a pastor or a lawyer or work in finance. He didn't want to work in real estate like his brother, Ray. Lion had created this life because he wanted to write music and play in a band. He needed at least three hours a day for his music and an hour to exercise. It was Lion's plan to have a top-performing hagwon with the best tutors and the strongest students. Later he'd replicate his model in other locations, he said. Through tutoring, he had found a way to be financially independent, do work that he enjoyed, and pursue his music.

His business model was simple: He paid the highest salaries and bonuses to the most gifted teachers in Orange County. Already his small tutoring business had shown a net profit of $175,000. Now there was no way for Lion to have more students, tutors, and profit unless he had more space.

Yun didn't tell her mother what he had earned last year, because it wasn't her information to share. He made more money than lawyers his age. Lion wanted her to run the office for him so he could focus on growing the business. He was impatient for its success. They would have a beautiful life with a good purpose, he'd said. Too many American kids weren't even getting a basic education, and Lion thought he could provide better ways for the students to study and become capable learners. *I want kids to* like *learning*, he said. Yun respected the way he lived.

She finished her problem set and put it aside. From her church tote bag, she took out the sheet music. From beneath her bed, she retrieved her small Casio keyboard, and she propped it up on her lap. Without turning it on, she tapped "Blessed Be the Lord" and sang quietly.

9

Self-Determination

Orange County, California

"Are you sure you don't want a dress and a party?"

"I do not want a dress or a party."

At the traffic light on North Brookhurst, Lion turned to look at her.

"You can change your mind."

Yun shook her head. There was no way she'd allow her mother or Lion to incur such an expense. Besides, they didn't have the money. Weddings were wasteful, she reasoned. The marriage was what mattered. A dress worn for a day could cost thousands of dollars, which made no sense.

They were driving to Anaheim. Lion was wearing his dark-blue suit and a gray tie, and Yun wore a white cap-sleeved shift trimmed in buttercup yellow and high-heeled sandals without stockings. The dress and shoes were new, and both could be worn again.

"What will we tell our children?" he asked.

"When are we having children?" Yun asked. "And how many?"

"My father used to say he wanted 'Quality Five.'"

"Huh?"

"Five kids of high quality. For example, you could have ten kids, but only five make the cut. His grandparents had a pig farm. Statistically speaking, he said, not every member of the litter makes it, and some are of an inferior grade. I know. Crazy."

"Wow, he doesn't seem like that when you talk to him," she said. "All three of you are the best quality, right?" She laughed.

"No idea. None of us will cure cancer or win an Olympic medal," Lion admitted cheerfully, looking straight ahead, thinking of his parents, who he hoped would understand their decision. His mother liked Yun.

"We have no federal prosecutors, either. At first, they weren't thrilled about Sarah becoming an immigration lawyer, but now she helps all their friends. And Ray's doing well in real estate, owns several buildings. For my parents, owning buildings is also considered successful."

Yun worried about what his parents would think of her father heading to São Paolo to try his luck and her mother operating Shrimp Castle by herself. And, of course, about today. They weren't happy about Lion's hagwon expansion or his playing music, but at this point, what could they do?

Lion's mother would say, *A parent always loses to the child.*

❧

The sun-filled annex chapel, used for the smallest of church services and funerals, was empty. Wide beams of light from the clerestory windows divided the oak-paneled room with diagonal stripes.

It felt odd to be at church on a Tuesday morning. The vast parking lot of the Anaheim megachurch—managed on Sunday mornings by volunteer traffic guards wearing yellow safety vests over their suit jackets, directing the lines of vehicles around orange cones—had almost no cars.

The young couple held hands and sat in the front pew, waiting for Sam Yi, the youth pastor, and his wife Andrea Kim.

"Ah, there are the lovebirds!" Andrea shouted, rushing past her husband, who walked more calmly.

The bright, tiny Korean woman with waist-length blond hair was a favorite with the younger congregants. She was a junior partner at Price Waterhouse, and for Lion and Yun, she had taken the morning off to serve as a witness and photographer. Everyone adored her husband, the thoughtful and brainy youth pastor. Sam, a reserved transplant from the Bay Area, was someone everyone trusted with their secrets, and people felt comfortable around the couple, who were well-matched opposites.

"Our baby Yun is marrying Lion, the Oracle of Orange County," Andrea whispered dramatically, although there was no one else in the chapel, "in a secret wedding ceremony. This is the most romantic event of the year."

Looking serious, Andrea adjusted the viewfinder. The camera had a large lens with a petal-shaped hood, and it obscured her small face. "I am now the photographer. Ignore me," she said, and began snapping pictures.

Yun smiled. If she couldn't have Mido with her, at least she'd have Andrea.

Lion and Yun took their places at the altar, and in less than fifteen minutes, Sam married them, keeping his homily the length of a decent benediction.

After Lion kissed and embraced Yun, Sam blessed them again.

"Normally I advise against these sorts of private weddings, but I respect your wishes and understand," Sam said. "You're both sort of grown up."

"Lion would never rush into anything," Andrea said. "So, do you kids feel different?"

"Yes," Lion said. "I feel different. I'm the happiest I've ever been."

Yun was beaming.

"I was twenty when I got married," Andrea said. "But I was pregnant." She laughed. "Then it turned out to be a false alarm."

"I didn't know that," Yun said, mildly shocked. "But you have the girls." She tried to do the math in her head but wasn't sure when Andrea and Sam had married. Their three girls were already in high school.

"Yup, I got really pregnant with Susie, our first, right after we got married. I trapped him, Yun," she said, laughing again.

Sam shook his head to deny this. Marriage had been his idea. He couldn't imagine living one day without her.

Still holding the camera, Andrea wrapped her thin brown arms around her husband's waist. She was a head shorter than he was.

"Not as gorgeous as your Lion, but my Sam has always been a catch. I think every girl in the English service is in love with either my husband or yours."

Yun blinked, realizing that Andrea was referring to Lion as her husband.

"Can we buy you lunch?" Sam asked, and Lion smiled.

"Another time. Maybe next week. We'll take you," Lion said.

"When will you tell your parents? Both of you?" Sam asked, pausing before saying, "Secrets are not good."

"I've always done what I wanted," Lion said. "Besides, my folks like Yun a lot, so that helps. It'll be okay. Just think of all the money we saved them." He smiled, having figured it all out. "We would've gotten married after Yun's graduation anyway."

"And you?" Andrea pointed her camera toward Yun. "Your mom and dad?"

Yun glanced at the stained glass window depicting the Transfiguration above the pulpit.

"My father went to Brazil. No one at church knows about him being gone. My mother will be sad about the wedding because, well, you know. She wanted something huge, but I know she'll understand. I figured it's best if we just did it, then told them after. This is what I want for my life."

"You're an only child, right?" Andrea asked, adjusting the lens.

Yun nodded.

"We could have another wedding later," Lion said. "Something massive. In the main sanctuary, and invite every Korean in Southern California. Why not?"

Yun smiled, and Andrea snapped another picture.

"Today was beautiful. It was just right. Thank you for making the time," Yun said.

"Where are you going now?" Sam asked.

"Believe it or not, we're going back to the hagwon because I have to meet a friend of Bo's younger brother who's applying for one of our tutor positions. Then I'm taking my wife away somewhere." Lion raised his eyebrows with a grin.

⁂

Peter Son was waiting with Bo at Exodus. As usual, Lion's office was free of any clutter. Lion did not leave papers about. At the end of the day, his desk was clear. No half-empty coffee mugs or water tumblers topped the pristine glass coffee table.

Floor-to-ceiling shelves lined two of the walls, stocked with multiple test guides and reference books about education and child-rearing.

On the walls, there were no diplomas. Rather, Lion had framed and hung black-and-white yearbook pages, photos of high school students from various schools taken after the Korean War that he'd found in an old bookshop on a summer trip to Seoul when he was in college. Hundreds of boys and girls in dark uniforms and well-pressed white shirts stared out from the gray and sepia images. Rows and rows of clear-eyed students—their young faces fresh and sober—peered into the camera. Lion often thought about them and what might have happened in their lives. A number of them could still be alive, and they could be anywhere in the world, or back in Korea.

When Lion entered his office, Bo and Peter got up from the long sofa along the wall.

"You're wearing a suit," Bo remarked, forgetting to introduce Peter. "You don't even wear one on Sundays."

"I got married today," Lion said, smiling.

"To Yun Kim?" Bo blurted out.

"The very same," Lion said, not mentioning that Yun was waiting for him in the conference room, doing her psychology homework.

Bo was clearly surprised but remembered.

"This is Peter Son, my brother DH's best friend."

Lion grinned at the young man, who wore a Chuck Berry T-shirt beneath a black cotton work jacket, blue jeans, and sneakers. His hair was shaved close to the scalp along the sides and back, with long platinum-blond fringes covering his pale forehead. Peter had three piercings in his left ear.

Lion pointed to the image of Chuck Berry playing an electric guitar: "The Father of Rock and Roll."

"Yep," Peter said.

"His Gibson ES is the coolest—"

"Gibson ES-355," Peter corrected him with a small smile.

"Peter Son is a musician," Bo added. "And a math wizard."

"Ah. You might need a job, then." Lion rubbed his hands. "And I need a math wizard. How do you feel about middle school and high school kids?"

Peter smiled. "I prefer kids over adults."

"Same," Lion said with conviction. "We're a mess, but the kids, they're awesome. You look like a kid yourself, though. How old are you?"

"Twenty-one. You?"

"Twenty-four. I guess we're sort of big kids. Though I am the oldest in this room," Lion said with mock gravity. Bo had just turned twenty-two.

Dramatically, Bo bowed to Lion, and Peter followed. Everyone laughed.

"Congratulations, man," Peter said. "I'm sorry to bother you on your wedding day."

"Oh, you're not a bother. Are you kidding me? Bo told me that you're here just for the day, and I'm desperate for good math teachers—"

"No, no. Our wires must have crossed. Apologies. I'm staying in Irvine for now, and I was coming in to Cypress to see Bo just for the day. If I'd known today was your—"

Lion waved this off. "What do you play?"

"Bass and guitar. I write some songs. I was playing in New Haven and some in New York. Then I decided to follow this girl here and apply as a transfer student to Pomona, against the better advice of his brother." With his thumb, Peter gestured to Bo, referring to DH. "But Cesca, the actor, I mean this girl, broke me in two, and now she's gone. And I just don't feel like going back to old New Haven."

"Sounds like you're writing a song," Lion said, looking at him sympathetically. "How much school do you have left?"

"Less than two years. Maybe a year plus. I've always taken extra classes."

"You didn't like Yale?"

"It's fine. I was on the soccer team with DH. We've played since Andover. In my freshman year, I blew out my knee pretty badly, and I couldn't play anymore. So I ended up taking a lot more classes to fill the time. I could probably graduate in a year and a half. Then I met this girl, I mean woman, and, well, she dumped me. Anyway, maybe it's all a sign. I should focus on my music. Get over Cesca."

"I like your candor," Lion said.

"Life's too short to tell lies," Peter said.

"So if you get into Pomona, you're going to quit Yale?" Lion asked.

"Why not?" Peter said.

Lion laughed. "Best answer. Your folks okay with this?"

Peter shrugged. Finishing a degree was better than dropping out altogether. He didn't see much point to college.

"It's just my mom and me. She's not like most people."

Peter couldn't imagine returning to Connecticut, which had seemed even grayer and colder than Andover. After losing soccer, he'd felt lost. DH was always at practice or away at games, and Peter didn't begrudge him that. Falling in love with Cesca had been far better than soccer, and now that feeling was gone, too.

Pomona, a small liberal arts college, had been the solution suggested by his former hagwon teacher, Tom Song. Peter's mother said she'd support transferring as long as it made Peter happier. She owned a house in Irvine she rarely used, and California was closer to Seoul than Connecticut. Peter's father, who had graduated from Princeton, would be furious at Peter for throwing away a Yale degree, but Renee didn't care what her ex-husband thought.

Bo had not known this detail about transferring colleges until now. DH had said that Peter might need to do something like tutor math just to get out of the house while he took the semester off and got over a girl. Maybe work the summer, too. Peter's mother was worried sick because her son wasn't leaving his place or picking up the phone. She'd been calling DH and Bo, asking if Bo could check in on him more regularly.

It had been Bo's idea for Lion to hire him for Exodus, since it would give Peter something to do, and the hours were flexible, so Peter could work on his music. Renee said she just wanted her son to rest and be happy.

She was also grateful that the girlfriend was gone. DH and Renee had not liked her. Cesca was certifiably gorgeous, but wild and unpredictable. Cesca had enjoyed seducing the attractive college musician from Korea with the posh British accent who knew a lot about the Premier League.

After they'd been dating for five months, Cesca got a good feature role that took her to Toronto, and she phoned him from location to tell him that she was in love with a cameraman.

"You're far too young for me anyway," she'd said kindly, and that was when she finally admitted her real age. Thirty-four. Peter's first love had been over a decade older than he.

Lion and Peter discussed music and guitars, and Bo tuned out because he couldn't follow. What was important was that this meeting was working out, and he could call DH afterward and reassure him that Peter seemed better, and that his mother in Korea didn't have to worry.

Bo raised his hand to get Lion's attention.

"Hey, Lion, I already showed Peter the lesson plans and practice exams, and he knows what to do."

"And this is why I owe you, man," Lion replied.

Everything at Exodus had gotten better after Bo's arrival. Soon, Bo would be starting classes at Fullerton College, and the hagwon would need more math tutors, and now Peter was here.

❧

On their ride to the hotel in Laguna Niguel, Lion talked excitedly about Peter Son, who could start as a math tutor as early as tomorrow.

"I don't know how long he'll last at the hagwon, but I have a good feeling about him. Also, he plays bass. Maybe he can join the band."

"Does he go to church?" Yun asked.

"Not the praise band. The Zekes."

"Oh, right!" Lion's band had lost its bass player several months earlier, and though it'd been easy enough to find occasional bass players, none of them had stuck around. No one had fit in the right way.

"Wife," he said.

"Husband," she answered.

"If Peter is Bo's younger brother DH's best friend, you must know him?"

"No," Yun said. "Mido has mentioned him, but I've never met the guy."

"He wants to transfer to Pomona."

"Really? Not UCLA or USC?"

"Nope. Wants a small school, I guess."

The red Honda Civic moved smoothly along the highway. There wasn't as much traffic on the 405 as they'd anticipated. As they approached the hotel driveway, Yun felt strange inside and didn't say much.

They checked in without any luggage, but no one minded. Yun was glad she was wearing her gold wedding band.

Lion opened the door of their hotel room and prevented her from walking in. He picked her up to carry her over the threshold.

"I saw this on a television show, so I thought I'd try it," he said, then kissed her while she was in his arms and put her down gently. "I don't think Koreans do this, though."

Yun laughed. "I think it's American." She went to the enormous window to admire the view of the shining blue ocean.

On a tray were a small strawberry cream cake, a plate of fruit, and a bottle of champagne and two flutes.

"You don't drink," she said.

"I know. Again, I thought we should do something traditional."

"Champagne is not Korean, and this looks expensive," she said, looking concerned.

"I can't handle soju or makgeolli, and certainly not on an empty stomach," Lion said, picking up the champagne bottle, and he removed the wire casing over the cork. "I saw someone do this at a party once." With a firm grip, he twisted off the cork in one shot, and it made a pleasant sound.

"Do you have ID?" he asked.

"No."

Lion filled the glasses only halfway.

"We can have just a sip. I'm nervous," he said.

This was why Yun liked him. He didn't pretend to be cool. She was nervous, too.

In college, he'd had sex before, but he and Yun had not slept together. They had agreed that this was the right way—to marry first, and that this afternoon would be their first time. Yun was a virgin, and this was what she had wanted to do today. They would not spend the night, but they would remain for the afternoon and early evening before going back home.

Tonight they would go speak with her mother.

"This room looks fancy," Yun said, grateful that Lion had picked such a beautiful hotel and had made the effort with the cake and champagne. "Can we afford this?"

"Yes, absolutely. When things get easier with Exodus and staffing, we will go on a real honeymoon. I want to take you to London. To the Ritz Hotel," Lion said. "I went there for afternoon tea once when I was in college, and I'm going to take you there. I think you would like it. You can have as many cucumber sandwiches as you like. Scones, too."

"Cucumbers in sandwiches?"

"You'll like them." Lion handed her a glass, then raised his.

"To my wife, Yun."

"I'm glad we got married," she said.

"You okay?" he asked, not understanding why she was crying.

"Yes," and she kissed him.

They had never done anything like this. When they made out, it was usually in his car or at the Exodus office after everyone was gone. Once, on a beach at night, they got dangerously close. Usually they stopped right before sex, keeping on some clothing. Before things got too difficult for them, Lion would stand back and take deep breaths. There was no reason to stop now.

Quickly they removed their clothing, feeling shy and excited.

Yun had gone to Bloomingdale's to buy a matching ivory-colored brassiere and panties for today, but in their hurry, she took them off before there was a chance for him to notice.

She stood naked before him, her arms folded across her chest. The room was filled with afternoon sunlight, and the curtains were open, but no one could possibly see them.

Lion smiled at her. He was naked, too.

The two young people could hardly talk. Each knew what the other looked like, more or less, from having been to the beach and swimming pools together, but this felt new and wonderful.

"You're so pretty," he said. "I'm very lucky to be with you."

Yun shrugged, feeling sort of proud. She was a runner, and she'd always felt fine about her body in a way that most girls did not. She liked the strength and speed of her legs and the distance they'd carried her.

He put his hands on her shoulders, then stroked her upper arms. Lion kissed her neck and she led him to the bed.

Yun had tried not to think about what it might feel like. When they made out, she'd felt his erection beneath his clothes, but had never seen it.

As if he knew what she was thinking, he kissed her again, and Yun grew aroused, the way she did only when she was with him. They took their time, and when they were done, Yun felt glad they were lovers now. At nineteen years old, she was married and no longer a virgin.

10

Orange County

The unit wasn't a true two-bedroom because the second bedroom didn't have a window. The landlord had put up illegal partitions and a door to what must have once served as part of the kitchen and dining area, then listed it as a two-bedroom for $750. The so-called bedroom would be Mido's, and Bo would sleep in the living room. He kept later hours than everyone else except for DH, the family night owl, who was still in Connecticut.

At only eight hundred square feet, this apartment was the smallest place the family had ever rented, and if DH came home for the summer, Bo thought he would have to return to Lion's garage apartment if the family could figure out the transportation situation. For now, they had only Bo's used Subaru, but if there was any room in the budget, they had to get another car, and Mido needed to learn how to drive on the freeway.

When Bo first arrived in Orange County, he'd tried taking buses to get around, but it was not like Seoul. You needed several extra hours a day to make the buses work. No one they knew took them.

Bo had cleaned and furnished the apartment for his family's arrival. For his parents, he purchased a queen-size mattress set, and for Mido a full-size mattress. For himself, he bought the floor-model sofa bed from a furniture warehouse in Buena Park, which was owned by a deacon at their church, who had given him a discount. Lion loaned the family a collapsible conference table and six folding chairs from the hagwon storage facility.

Yun had driven Bo to the Costco in Garden Grove to buy the most necessary things for the kitchen: waste bins, a dish rack, dishes, bowls, a set of pots and pans, and cutlery. From Sharon Mart, he bought a Japanese rice cooker that Yun's mother, Nari, had recommended.

Every item had to be essential and within budget, and Bo was proud to have managed it, but when his family walked into their new home—sleepless from the long, noisy flight and even more exhausted after an interminable wait for their luggage—he realized that nothing here was beautiful. Through their eyes, he saw how shabby and dismal everything looked. He had forgotten to wash the small windows in the living room.

"You did a nice job," Helen said, doing her best to hide her disappointment. "It must have been difficult to find all these things. Son, you're all grown up: You know how to set up a household."

John patted Bo on the back, and Mido smiled at him. He knew they were just being polite. The kitchen walls, once painted gray, were grimy with grease, no matter how much Bo had scrubbed them with diluted bleach. The baseboards along the walls were cracked, with pieces missing, like a gaping underbite. The linoleum floors, possibly once yellow, were a depressing indeterminate color; there was no sense in buying wall-to-wall carpeting for a rental, he'd reasoned.

It occurred to Bo now that perhaps he should have bought the rugs that the church deacon who owned the warehouse in Buena Park had tried to sell him, but it would've pushed him well over his budget. He'd refrained as much as he could from borrowing on his recently issued credit line.

"Next weekend, I thought I'd paint the apartment white. There wasn't enough time this week," Bo said to his family.

"Are we allowed to do that?" Helen asked with hope in her voice. Over the years, she'd read a number of leases and deposit terms, and renter's alterations were often not permitted.

Mido put her arms around her mother, wanting to make the ugliness disappear somehow. At her high school in Sydney, she had read a British novel about coming down in the world, and though she had understood then what the words meant, she felt them now for her parents, and this grieved her.

"We won't be here long," Mido said, and John and Helen looked at one another, silently resolving to move as soon as possible.

⁂

The first guest to visit the Koh family was Yun's mother, Nari. The morning after their arrival, the doorbell sounded twice, and when John opened the door, Nari was balancing a thick stack of brightly colored floor cushions on top of a flat box of pears and a box of ramyeon. In one hand, she clutched a full shopping bag.

John relieved her of the heavy load, and Nari rushed in, slipping off her kitchen clogs. She bowed quickly to the family, then sat down on the bare floor to pray.

In silence, Helen, John, Bo, and Mido watched her.

Yun's mother had aged visibly in only a few years. Her hair, pulled back with a banana-style hair clip, was dyed brown, a shade lighter than her natural color, and the roots along her side part were white.

In Seoul, Nari's nails had always been vermilion, but here they were clipped short and unvarnished. She wore the tan-and-brown uniform shirt for Shrimp Castle and matching brown polyester slacks, which smelled lightly of frying oil.

Her mumbled prayer ended in a few minutes, and Nari rose to her feet. Helen approached her, and Nari took Helen's hands in hers. She looked around the almost bare living room.

"It's small, isn't it? Our apartment is the same, and I may try to get into a smaller one. Yun moved in with her husband after the wedding."

"Congratulations," Helen and John said at the same time. "Your son-in-law is wonderful. We met him last night when he picked us up. Yun looks very happy."

Nari smiled weakly. When Yun and Lion came to tell her about eloping, Nari had been upset, but it didn't change anything. They would've gotten married later anyway, Lion had explained, and it did make some sense to do it now for Yun to be independent. Marrying an American could help Yun get citizenship faster, and Lion was a good young man. Nari knew Yun had wanted to move out and had always felt sorry that her daughter couldn't live in a dorm like many of her classmates from high school.

Later, when they were alone, Nari asked her daughter if she had eloped because Joonho had gone to Brazil, and Yun said she didn't think so. Yun insisted that she loved Lion and that she was ready to be his wife.

"She's not pregnant," Nari said, as if this explanation were needed. "Yun is going to finish UCLA. Lion is a kind boy. He thought of being a minister, but he changed his mind. He wants to be a songwriter. He sings well. He put himself through Princeton in only three years. Now he's a hagwon director. He earns good money." She shrugged. "But it's a waste of such a good education."

Helen smiled. "Lion seems like a wonderful young man, and he is fortunate because Yun is the best."

Nari shook her head, unable to accept praise for her child, though it felt nice to hear it.

"My husband is in Brazil. I think Yun told you. I have to get to work now."

"Are you running the store all by yourself?" John asked her.

"I just hired a nice student. Part-time. Alex is a good boy and very strong, but he can only work fifteen to twenty hours. I still have Lenny, who helped my husband, but he can't work more than thirty-five hours. The new cook quit after a week. Koreans won't work this job, and Americans can't work like us," she said.

"I don't understand," John said.

"Labor laws. Lion said I'd need at least two workers to replace my husband." She sighed. "I better get back."

"It was nice of you to stop by. Thank you for all these things. What is this?" Helen pointed to the shopping bag.

"Roach traps and steel wool."

"Roaches?" Mido turned to Bo.

"I haven't seen any," he said.

"They come out at night. You've only had one night. Put out the traps in all the cupboards, and if you see any mice, then you have to plug up the holes with steel wool. They're usually behind the refrigerator or beneath the sink. I should've given this to Yun last night when she picked you up, but I forgot, and I got home late from church."

Helen rubbed her arms. Mido knew her mother was scared.

"You're so kind to think of this. I don't like mice," Helen said, trying to sound natural. "I remember them from when I was a child. They were always in the house. Getting into everything."

Bo was mortified. It had never occurred to him that where Yun and Nari lived, there could be bugs and rodents. When he was renting Lion's garage apartment, he had never even seen a mosquito inside, which reminded him to check the living room windows: There were no mosquito screens, either. He'd never considered bugs.

If Lion's brother, Ray, hadn't mentioned the air conditioners, he wouldn't have known to check if they worked or not. In the kitchen, there was no dishwasher, but his parents rarely used it even when there was one. The refrigerator worked, and he had to buy a small microwave. The coin-operated washing machines were in the basement.

"Are there many mice?" Bo asked Yun's mother.

"Oh, once you plug up the holes with steel wool, they'll move on to the next place. They live in the walls. You can hear them at night," Nari said. "I don't have them inside my apartment anymore. But we did the first month or so. No matter how clean you are, these buildings that you share with people have problems."

John stooped over the shopping bag and pulled out the roach traps. He separated the individual traps from the large packet.

"I better go," Nari said. "I'll bring you some large pots and pans tonight. For soup."

"Oh, we're going to the store soon. That's okay," Helen said. "You've already done so much."

"We'll see each other on Sunday, then. I'm so glad you're here, especially since Yun moved out. That bad girl," Nari said, smiling, and then she grew serious. "It's terrible being poor here, but you'll work hard, and things will get better. When we first got here, my sister-in-law rented us a spare bedroom from another family. She had no space. We were trying to save for a down payment for the store. It's not easy, but we have strong bodies and even stronger minds," Nari said, looking at Mido and Bo. "Remember that we are very strong people and we are good learners. I wasn't the best at school, but life is also a school, isn't it? Living can sharpen us."

Nari had a plain way of speaking that Helen understood. She wasn't putting them down. She was trying her best to protect the people she claimed, and Nari was claiming her family. Helen felt grateful.

Both Nari and Helen had grown up with very little, and though they'd seen far better times, they wouldn't complain now. This was no time for self-pity. Their children had lived for most of their lives with money, but they had lived without for far longer. Helen didn't like mice. Growing up, there had often been rodents where she and her siblings lived. She could remember mice running across her feet when she went to the bathroom at night, and how if she screamed, no one would come to make them go away.

Nari went to the door and slipped on her clogs. Mido bowed deeply to her.

Nari patted Mido's shoulder. She'd been worried about her daughter's best friend, who'd left Australia without finishing her degree, and she looked at the girl with great affection.

"Things will get better. You have nice, educated parents. They're going to figure things out that I don't know how to do. They speak English so well!"

Nari opened the front door as if she were leaving her own house, and the family bowed to her as she left. The apartment felt quiet again, and Helen got on her knees to straighten out the shoes by the front door. John glanced at his wife's white cotton socks, their soles already black from the dirty floors.

❧

Bo found parking for the van not too far from the main entrance. When his family couldn't contain their shock at the gargantuan scale of the store, he burst out laughing.

"Welcome to Costco," Bo said.

"I read about this store, but it's even bigger than I imagined," Helen said.

"We don't have a lot of time. I have to drop you off, return the van, and get back to work."

Mido pulled out the list of things they needed.

The store was cold, and Mido rubbed her hands. Helen and John had worn fleece vests, but Mido wore only a T-shirt, so Bo gave her his blue Exodus Academy windbreaker, which had the word "DRIVER" written on the back.

"If we want to get a television, they have some on sale," Bo said.

"We can wait on that, but we'll need to buy a phone and an answering machine today," Helen said. "We need to find jobs and can't miss messages."

Along the way to electronics, they picked up jars of instant coffee, boxes of tea, and laundry detergent and tucked them away in the giant cart.

Bo moved quickly while his family continued to marvel at the store. They passed rows and rows of goods, and Helen picked up two boxes of water glasses and coffee mugs.

She tried not to think of all the beautiful dishes she'd given away to her friends at church. If she had been living in Seoul, she would've been able to leave them with Sonya, but it hadn't made sense to ship them to her, either.

Helen had crisscrossed the world with her possessions, but always the container shipments had been paid for by John's employers, and when she looked into the cost of shipping their things herself, she'd realized that they couldn't possibly afford it.

"Here." Bo held up a box containing a white Panasonic phone with a built-in answering machine.

Alarmed at the price, Helen scanned the lower shelves for a cheaper model.

"I think this is the best one," Bo said. "I have a job, Umma. I can get it for you."

"No, no. I'll buy it," Helen said, plucking it from his hands. "There's another kind here. Besides, it's a better color," she said. The one she'd selected was a third of the price at $49. "It's black, so it won't get dirty."

John looked over the Panasonic phones and found an even more expensive one that was also black.

"No, we'll get this one," John said. "This is black, too."

Helen said nothing, pushing the cart toward the pots and pans, and Mido walked beside her.

Behind them, John asked his son, "Bo, where is Shrimp Castle?"

"It's not far. We're already in Garden Grove."

"Can you take us there after this? I'd like to see it. Do you have time?"

Bo checked his watch.

"What do you think Shrimp Castle can pay?" John asked.

"Lion said they'd have paid someone $900 a week, but they're only paying Alex $350 because he arrives exactly at eleven and leaves at three p.m. and takes a half-hour lunch break, which is making Yun's mother crazy. That's why they can't afford two men. The other guy, Lenny, who's always worked there, gets $500 a week."

After they packed up the car with their purchases, Bo drove them to Shrimp Castle, and John went inside while the family waited in the van.

❧

The front door bell tinkled when John entered, and Nari turned.

"Hello! What are you doing here?"

"May I see your kitchen?" John asked.

Nari couldn't understand but brought him back to where Lenny was washing the cabbages.

"Where's Alex?" John asked.

"He'll be here soon. If he shows up."

Before leaving the kitchen, John turned to Lenny to say goodbye, then went to the cashier station, where he could speak privately with Nari.

"There's enough space," John said.

"Huh?"

"You could have all three of us in the kitchen. I can work for $550 a week in cash. If either of your guys quits, then I'll do his work and make his salary."

"You can't do this work," Nari said out loud, then turned to see if Lenny could hear them, not that he could understand Korean.

"I worked in kitchens when I was in high school and college, and I'm still strong. I can't work on the books, because it will affect our green card application. Lion's sister, Sarah, already explained all this to us. In a few months, we have to adjust our status, and Bo will sponsor us since he has a job. In the meantime, my wife and I have to find work that pays in cash."

Nari wasn't sure how to respond.

"I can start today," John said. "I just need to change my clothes."

"Have you asked your wife?"

John smiled, knowing that Helen wouldn't like it.

"A man with your education should not be in the kitchen frying shrimp and making fish sandwiches. Do you know how terrible you can smell? Your hair, your skin, it gets into your pores. I think my husband went to Brazil just so he could get that smell out of his nose."

"I'm sure your husband had good reason to do what he did. You don't know what a man is thinking until you've walked in his shoes. I have a good reason, too, for wanting this job."

"I don't know," Nari said, because she really didn't.

"I have a request, though. I will work as hard as possible, but I'd appreciate it if you could drive me to and from the apartment, and I will pay for part of the gas until we get a car. My wife will be looking for work, and it would be ideal if she could find work on this shopping strip so she can commute with us," John said.

"I can ask Mrs. Chung. She's always looking for someone at her store," Nari said, though a frown flashed across her face, and John picked up on it.

"What's she like?" he asked.

"Picky," Nari said.

John wanted to spare his wife another trial.

"But she's not a dishonest person, and she's an alumna of your wife's school. Ewha. Don't people have to be nicer to you if you went to the same college?"

"It depends," John said.

For once, Nari felt hopeful, believing that Mrs. Chung would give Helen a job and that with John's help, she could pay off the promissory note on Shrimp Castle on time. She knew her husband expected her to lose the business and join him in São Paolo, and Nari wanted to surprise him.

Things had been so difficult, and suddenly a path was cleared.

11
Mall

The next morning, Helen and John met Nari in the carport below their building. Nari drove a dark-red Volvo, which her husband had insisted on buying. Every time she placed her dishpan hands on the leather steering wheel, she calculated that the Volvo's monthly payments would have allowed the family to have two used Corollas.

"You look nice," Nari said.

Helen and John bowed their heads to greet Nari.

For her interview, Helen was wearing a white blouse with a Peter Pan collar, a straight navy skirt, and navy leather pumps with a low stacked heel. John wore Nari's husband's old uniform, which had his surname, Kim, embroidered on it. As it turned out, the men wore the same size. Nari had offered to order John his own uniform, but he'd declined, saying his mother had been a Kim.

From the front passenger seat, Helen kept glancing over at her husband, who'd said little all morning. He didn't seem troubled but appeared more withdrawn than usual. Neither had talked much about John starting work at Shrimp Castle.

When Helen and the children had seemed surprised by his decision, John said, "I won't run into anyone I know. I have to get a job. I checked the classifieds, and it would be hard to make almost $600 a week in cash right away. If that part-time student, Alex, leaves after the summer, then I can make $900 a week. We need to pay the green card lawyer and save for a bigger place."

John looked out the back-seat window, unable to recall the last time a woman had driven him anywhere. He could tell Nari was a good driver.

"Was it hard getting a license?" Helen asked Nari.

"I drove in Seoul, so I wasn't worried about the driving, but I had no confidence about speaking to the driving test examiner in English. My husband understands English better than me, so he was fine. I couldn't believe we passed on our first try. I was so afraid. You can't do anything without a car here." Nari remembered how happy and proud they had been—their first victory in the new country.

When her husband had wanted to buy an almost-new Volvo rather than a used Toyota, she hadn't put up a fuss because he'd said, *When we drive to church, we drive in something nice.*

When they'd had money in Korea, Joonho would let her buy anything she wanted. *My beautiful Nari should have the nicest things money can buy.* No matter how much a face cream from Japan cost, Joonho would say, *If my wife wants it, she must have it.* Both of them had grown up with so little, and during their years of plenty, Joonho wanted to give her and Yun every single thing, even if they did not need it. Joonho didn't want them to be the kind of rich people who, having once been poor, still felt poor inside.

"I can drive, but I still get nervous in traffic. Driving in Paramus seems much easier than here," Helen said.

"I'm a great driver. I've never been the one for academics, but I have excellent hand-eye coordination. My daughter is an athlete because of me, not my husband," Nari said with pride in her voice.

"We really appreciate you taking us," Helen said, and when she turned around this time, her husband's eyes were closed.

♣

The shopping mall in Garden Grove was a massive rectangle with dozens of businesses along its four sides, as well as within the four square islets set in the black asphalt ocean of the parking lot, which opened out to the boulevards along the lengths of the mall. The largest building, a multistory branch of a Korean bank with a hip-and-gable roof, was set in the center like a curious pagoda ornament.

Shrimp Castle was one of the seven stores in the southern subdivision of the mall, and it did brisk business because there were no other shops that sold fried foods. The mall was a kind of Korean neighborhood, filled with people who would never have crossed paths in their previous lives back home.

Nari's store was fifteen hundred square feet separated into a dining area, a kitchen, a storage room with a little desk and file cabinet, and two restrooms. The white-tiled open kitchen, about three hundred square feet, faced out to the dining area. There were sixteen tables that could be moved around to seat thirty-two customers. Nari suggested that Helen have a seat at a table far from the kitchen while she waited for her interview.

Nari handed John a disposable hairnet, a new baseball cap, and a fresh white apron. From the supply closet, she pulled out her husband's black, knee-high rubber boots for spray washing the kitchen floor each night.

"These might work, too," she said, being mindful not to cause offense by offering something used to her daughter's friend's father. Nari would've bought him a new pair, but there hadn't been enough time.

John thanked her. He put on the hairnet and tied the apron over his uniform as if he'd been doing this for years.

When Lenny arrived, the two men went into the kitchen, and John pulled out a small notepad to write down whatever Lenny taught him so he wouldn't have to ask twice.

Nari fixed instant coffee for them and distributed the ham and egg sandwiches she'd made at home earlier in the morning. She asked John to say grace, and afterward they ate their breakfast quietly before starting work.

From industrial-size containers of tartar sauce, vinegar, and ketchup, Nari prepared individual portions in plastic containers for takeout customers. When Helen tried to help, Nari told her not this time.

"You can't get your clothes messy, especially today," Nari said sternly. "I already told Mrs. Chung about you, and she's expecting a high-class salesperson almost like herself. I'm so worried that you might smell even a little like frying oil."

Suddenly Nari got up and opened the front door to let fresh air in. From behind the cash register, she withdrew her prized bottle of Chanel No. 5, a gift from Yun last Christmas.

"Just in case. You can use this," Nari said.

❧

At ten minutes to ten, Nari walked Helen to the Emporium, which was only five stores down from Shrimp Castle. Helen smiled at the name: It was a world away from Crawford's Emporium, where she'd worked in Sydney for so many years.

The lights were on, and Nari pushed the door open.

"Good morning, Elder Chung," Nari said, bowing. "I brought you my friend, Helen Cho. She's the wife of John Koh, who is now working at my store."

Seated like a dowager on her low stool, Mrs. Chung gestured for them to come in, but Nari sent Helen in alone.

"I have to get back and help Mr. Koh. It's his first day," Nari said, then, to Helen, "Come back when you're done. It's just there," she said, pointing in the direction of Shrimp Castle like a concerned mother leaving a small child at a new school.

"I'll be fine. Thank you so much for everything," Helen said, and watched Nari return to her store.

Mrs. Chung was decades older than Helen, but it was difficult to tell how many from her appearance. She had to be over seventy; however, in a certain light, her hair professionally colored and with her forehead and neck unlined, she could look far younger.

The Emporium's owner wore a black bouclé jacket with gold threading that matched her skirt and a long rope of pearls with large mabe pearl and diamond earrings.

The shop was twice the size of Shrimp Castle and crammed with costly inventory. On one wall were floor-to-ceiling shelves filled with suitcases, bags, and briefcases; on another was a stock of thick satin-covered quilts, pillows, and embroidered bedding from a famed maker in Seoul; and in the glass display cases were imported Swiss watches as well as gold and diamond jewelry. On the sales floor were several racks of high-end suits from Italy and France for men and women. Crystal vases and porcelain dishes from France, England, and Ireland covered every available surface. Security cameras hung from each corner of the ceiling.

The store was neither beautiful nor elegant. Mrs. Chung had not spent any money on the interior design; however, even Helen was impressed by the variety and quality of the imported goods from Europe, Japan, and Korea. The stores might look dissimilar, but Mrs. Chung's luxury merchandise could also have been found at Crawford's Emporium.

"Would you like to be called Mrs. Cho or Mrs. Koh?" the owner asked.

"It's a pleasure to meet you." Helen bowed formally. "For here and Australia, people address me by my husband's last name, Koh, especially at my children's schools. You're also welcome to call me Hejin, or Helen. Sometimes I think Americans are right to be simpler with first names and dispense with titles."

"Well, yes, but we are Koreans in America," Mrs. Chung said. "I will call you Mrs. Koh, because we just met. Please sit."

Mrs. Chung had been sitting on a low-backed stool behind the counter, and now she got up and wheeled the stool to face the leather armchair kept for guests.

"Thank you for speaking with me," Helen said. She pulled out a résumé and handed it to Mrs. Chung with both hands. "The first page is in English, and the second is in Korean."

Mrs. Chung read it carefully.

"You've worked in sales for a long time."

"Yes." Helen continued to speak in formal Korean.

"I was told you don't have your green card. That you might be getting it soon."

"All three of our children were born in New Jersey when my husband worked in New York. We've always had proper work documentation through my husband's companies. I have a Social Security number from back then. Our son Bo will be able to sponsor us, but it will take some time."

Mrs. Chung paused in reading to study Helen's pleasant face.

"You went to Ewha," Mrs. Chung said. "Yun's mother told me. It's my college, too." She checked the résumé. "You majored in English."

Helen smiled, having loved Ewha, but she didn't think it was the right time to ask what Mrs. Chung had studied.

"I can't pay any more than $450. It's six days a week. I close on Sundays so I can go to church. Do you go to church?"

"Yes, we will be going to Gospel Presbyterian in Anaheim. Our son said it's nice, and that's where Yun's mother goes, too."

"I am an elder there," Mrs. Chung said proudly.

"I should call you Elder Chung, then."

"Yes, you may." Mrs. Chung shifted on her stool. "How old are your children?"

"In America, Bo-hun is twenty-two, Dae-hun is twenty, and my youngest, Mido, is nineteen. My middle one is at Yale, but my oldest and youngest still need to go to college. We moved around so much—"

Mrs. Chung nodded with understanding.

"The weekly salary for six days' work is $450," Mrs. Chung said. The thought of getting this poised and well-educated woman to work for her was appealing. She regretted having hired young women who talked too much, or brought her their complicated personal problems, then ended up quitting. Mrs. Chung just wanted someone to stay on and take the work seriously.

Helen took a breath. "I've always received a base salary and commission. I'd be happy to work for $300 a week and take a ten percent commission of the retail price, if that would be okay with you."

Mrs. Chung appeared surprised by Helen's counteroffer.

"I haven't given you the job yet."

"I'll make more money for you. I am good at what I do."

Mrs. Chung laughed, more than a little pleased by her fellow alumna.

"I don't know," Mrs. Chung said. "It's not personal. I've hired many people, and they often disappoint me."

"We can try it for a month, if you like. I'm able to keep track of sales and can make it simple for you," Helen said, unwilling to give up her commissions. It was really the only way she could make more money.

Mrs. Chung looked doubtful. She wanted to hire Helen but didn't like the idea of sharing profits.

"Let's try your way just for today. What do you think?" Mrs. Chung asked.

Helen asked to study the floor inventory and checked price tags. She asked Mrs. Chung about her markup structure and how much room she had for discounts, because here, the customers expected to negotiate.

Mrs. Chung was not disappointed. Helen had a wonderful manner with customers. She greeted them politely, observed them without being intrusive, and knew precisely when to be helpful. Without much context, she was still able to discern which customers sought attention, which required deference, and which needed to be left alone to browse. Some customers wanted privacy to imagine themselves with the desired good—whether it was a pair of Italian shoes, a rare handbag, or a cashmere coat. However, she knew that she could not disappear. Helen was able to anticipate the needs of her customer. Above all, she knew never to judge the worth of a customer based on her appearance.

Where she excelled uniquely was in honoring her customer without being subservient since aspirational goods, which were what Mrs. Chung sold, required a knowledgeable salesperson who wasn't off-putting and yet was also the kind of person whose approval customers sought. Helen was like your kindest, most tasteful ally, who would tell you the truth and never let you get in trouble. Customers felt comfortable asking Helen questions about how to put on a diamond necklace with a tricky clasp, how to tie a large silk scarf as a cummerbund, or what kind of watch one bought for a lawyer son-in-law.

Of the Korean shopping malls in Orange County, Mrs. Chung's store had the highest-priced luxury retail inventory, and though her customers were Koreans who had once shopped in fine department stores in Seoul or Busan, they still felt uncomfortable walking into an equivalent American department store or boutique. More importantly, they had little time to drive over to the fancy mall, which could take half a day from work on a Saturday, and certainly never during the week, when they worked from dawn till dusk.

The Emporium opened to the public at 10:00 a.m., and for a Thursday morning, business was not bad, with a fairly steady stream of customers and some decent sales. Around lunchtime, Mrs. Ku, who managed the video store across the shopping mall, came in.

Mrs. Chung said hello and returned to her newspaper. She was on cordial terms with the video store owner but didn't know Mrs. Ku well enough to chat.

Helen had been wiping down the counters with a glass cleaner; she put away her dust cloths and bowed her head to greet the customer.

Although it was warm outside, Mrs. Ku wore a long-sleeved cotton jersey shirt, elastic-waist pants, and a woolen vest, all in shades of blue. Her hair was gray. She was in her late fifties but seemed older. Her skin was papery and mottled, and she appeared a bit intimidated and anxious.

"How may I help you?" Helen asked.

"You must be new," Mrs. Ku said shyly. "I haven't seen you before."

"Yes, my family and I moved here recently."

"From where? Did you find a place to live?" Mrs. Ku asked, wanting to help the newcomer.

"Yes, thank you, we've just arrived from Australia," Helen said. "Is there anything you need today?" She knew that a person like this didn't come into the Emporium unless she had to buy something specific.

"My son is getting married," Mrs. Ku said. Her voice was quiet but proud.

Hearing this, Mrs. Chung looked up from her newspaper.

"What wonderful news. Do you like the bride?" Helen asked.

"Yes. Yes, so much. She's a dental hygienist. I think she'll take good care of my son. She's a hard worker."

Helen smiled.

"My son bought her a ring already, but I wanted to get her something myself. She's a very attractive girl. She cares about how she looks. Not like me." Mrs. Ku laughed, looking down at her white sneakers from Costco. "But she's not vain. I'm not trying to say that. I'm so lucky. I'm not trying to brag. I'm so sorry."

Mrs. Ku blushed. She was a woman who wasn't used to speaking about her recent good fortune.

"What do you think she'd like?" Helen asked. She was too tactful to ask her directly about her budget.

Mrs. Chung pretended to read her newspaper, but she was paying attention.

"I thought maybe a necklace or earrings. Diamonds or pearls maybe. I've got some money I have been saving for her."

"Do you have to get presents for her family, too?" Helen asked.

"My son said they'd prefer cash."

Helen nodded.

"But I want to give her something. From me. I don't want her to think I'm not happy about it, because I am so grateful. He's my only one, you see." Mrs. Ku could hardly say this last bit. She wanted her daughter-in-law to like her, want to visit now and then, not feel pressured but want to see her, even though their apartment was small and not very nice.

"I have something that's beautiful," Helen told her, and guided her to the jewelry counter, where she took out a tray of earrings.

"What do you think of these?" Helen pointed to a pair of pearl and diamond earrings. "Very suitable for a young woman, and not old-fashioned. Or maybe these diamond studs." Helen showed her the small ones first, which were not inexpensive.

Mrs. Ku tucked her lower lip inside her mouth like she was afraid. She had never bought jewelry before.

"The pearl and diamond ones are $1,500. And the diamond studs are $3,000. We have larger sizes, but maybe they might be too old-looking for her. This is a high-quality diamond. We have the papers if you want to take a look, and if she wants to insure them with her ring."

"Her ears are pierced." Mrs. Ku touched her own lobes, which were not.

"The earring backs have a safety feature so she won't lose them," Helen said, showing her how it worked.

Mrs. Ku swallowed. "Is it possible to have some sort of discount? I'm sorry to ask."

Helen looked over to Mrs. Chung, who lifted her chin slightly in approval.

"If you have the price in cash, then we can take off ten percent."

Mrs. Ku looked relieved.

"The diamonds, please. I'll bring the cash tomorrow. Will that be okay? I work right down there. At Star Video."

"I've never been there, but my friend who owns Shrimp Castle already mentioned it." Helen smiled.

"Do you know Yun's mother?" Mrs. Ku asked excitedly.

"Yes. I've known her and her daughter for a long time," Helen said, smiling.

"She's my best customer. She borrows a bag of videos at least twice a week. She knows everything about dramas. Do you watch them?"

"I don't know much about them, but I like some of them," Helen said.

"What kind do you like?" Suddenly Mrs. Ku sounded confident and serious.

"Oh, the historical ones and sometimes the love stories," Helen said. "But truly, I don't know many of them. I'm always working, so I—"

"Well, please come and see me," Mrs. Ku said, "if you ever want to borrow videos. Though I guess you can watch them with Yun's mother, too. That would save money." Her smile disappeared as she realized she might've lost a customer.

"I think she's far ahead of me in every show, but I promise, when I start watching dramas, I will only go to your store," Helen said, then gathered the earrings and put them in a black velvet box.

"I will wrap them for you now, and you can pick them up tomorrow anytime."

After Mrs. Ku walked out of the store, Helen calculated that after the 10 percent discount, the $3,000 earrings would cost $2,700, so her own sales commission would be $270. The wholesale price of the earrings had been $1,500, so Mrs. Chung would still net $930 minus her overhead.

When Helen had worked in Sydney and Seoul for large luxury stores where she almost never met the owners, she had not given much thought to store rent, taxes, utilities, garbage removal, storage, workmen's compensation, health care, insurance, and all the other variables in running a small business, but working here alongside the owner and Matty, the stock person, was teaching her that they had to survive together. Everyone had to eat. Mrs. Ku had paid a hefty retail premium, but she left the store happy.

When the day ended, Helen walked over to Shrimp Castle, where there was a line of customers. Helen put on an apron hanging on the hook behind the counter, but Nari waved her away.

"You should sit down. We're fine. Only five more orders."

Helen looked around. The drink refrigerator needed restocking, so she went to find sodas in the storage room. Then she found the mop and pail and started on the bathrooms.

After the last customer left, Nari went to the front door and locked it. She turned on the red neon "Closed" sign.

In the kitchen, John was scrubbing the stainless area around the fryer. Lenny had already finished his section and left for the night.

Helen stood by the kitchen doorway.

"How was business?"

"Busy. We sold a lot of fish sandwiches but even more shrimp baskets. Yun's mother had to call the supplier to bring another shipment for tomorrow morning instead of Monday."

"I had a good day, too," she said. "I got a nice job."

"Mrs. Chung called Nari a few hours ago to tell us. You were busy with customers."

"You must be tired," Helen said, seeing his expression. His hair was matted down with sweat and oil beneath the net.

"Shin Taehun came by," he said without looking up.

"What?"

"He came by to talk with the big Realtor across the lot, and they came in to buy sandwiches. He saw me in the kitchen."

Helen couldn't speak.

"He and Danbi just moved here."

"What about Mary?"

"She's still in New Jersey. She won't give him a divorce." He paused. "That woman is pregnant."

Helen shook her head in dismay. "You can't meet him anymore."

"I didn't look for him. He found me. Look at me."

The crisp white apron from the morning was spotted with oil and soapy disinfectant. John wore Nari's husband's black rubber boots. His jaw firm, John continued to wipe down the long metal counter.

"He was wearing a suit. He's going to sell insurance and annuities, he said. Wanted to know if I needed a job."

Helen checked his face.

"I said no. I have a good job," he said, removing his hairnet and wiping his brow with the back of his hand.

"Ah, there's my nice-looking boyfriend," she said, pointing to his face.

John grinned and went to the sink to rinse out the cloths.

12
Lost and Found

March 12, 1999

Dear Tek,

I'm writing to you from the Exodus staff lounge. It's about the size of my new classroom and where we also store everything.

Right now by the door, there are six cases of juice boxes, a dozen tubs of pretzel sticks, and several pallets of toilet paper and paper towels which need to be put away.

I'll get to it right after I finish writing this.

Before you frown, no, it's not officially my job to organize the supplies, but I do as much as I can to save Yun and Lion the trouble. Everyone here pitches in. Even the parents help out when things break down or we need something special.

There's an extra-long conference table near the back wall of the lounge, and a dozen chairs for teachers to prepare for classes and grade homework. This is also where I eat two meals a day. There's a refrigerator, coffee machines, two microwaves, an industrial-size sink, and a dishwasher. Yun keeps a basket stocked with granola bars, cup noodles, and crisps.

When the door's closed, the room feels like my sanctuary. I finished preparing for my class early today, so I thought I'd write. My letters have been infrequent. Forgive me.

For lunch, I'm eating a chicken salad sandwich that I brought from home with a bag of crisps from here. Every time I have a sandwich, I think of you layering yours with pickle slices or jalapeño peppers. It would make me laugh when you'd take a bite and bits of pickle or peppers fell out of the sides, making a mess. You'd smile like you were pleased. I don't know if you do this in front of anyone else, or if you just did it to make me laugh. I never got a chance to ask you. I hope you're having good lunches.

Last month was my one-year anniversary at Exodus, and Lion gave me a nice raise. Also, he's letting me teach one of the boot camp classes for specialized high school admissions tests, which will start tomorrow. I'll make an extra $1,500 per session, and if that goes okay, I might get to do a couple of those per semester. Bo taught those already, and he said I'll be just fine.

My new afternoon class is going well. I have twenty-seven middle school students five days a week. The work isn't difficult. The kids do their school homework, and I help them when they're lost, and of course, I give them hagwon assignments and check their progress. A lot of quizzes, but I try to have games and treats, too. On Fridays after they finish their homework and assessments, sometimes I take them to the park for relay races and frisbee.

Last year my kindergartners were so young, it felt more like babysitting. I thought middle school kids would be tougher, but they're not all that different. These kids are a little more serious, and they listen to me, which is a relief. But they're like nutty puppies. It's hard to get upset with them because they're adorable, but I have to pay attention to all the relationships. The girls have built their own worlds upon worlds, and the boys are still daft and goofy, which makes them a little easier. There's one boy who looks like he could be my cousin Henry's twin. Most of my students are ethnically Korean. In my Saturday boot camp classes, I'll have a few kids who are ethnically Chinese and South Asian.

When I have my middle schoolers during the week, I can still see my former students who are now in first and second grade. There's a plexiglass partition separating my room from theirs.

I feel proud of them. Is that silly? It's as if I'm the only one who taught them to put away their things in their cubbies, wash hands, and wait quietly for snacks before worksheets and story time. During breaks, they knock on the plexiglass and wave at me. My middle schoolers are sweet, too, but they're awkward and funny around each other like little adults. I remember being self-conscious around that age. How did we ever survive all this, I wonder.

Bo's taking two classes at Fullerton College, but he's still driving the hagwon van and tutoring a few high school kids. Sometimes I go with him to take kids home when the parents can't make pickup, and I make sure they get into their apartments while Bo stays in the van. Often, there's no one home. Even though my mother always worked, she was usually home to meet us at 2:30 p.m. Also, I had my brothers.

I imagine the parents have no choice. When the kids whose parents can't pick them up live in my apartment complex, I just let them stay in our place until someone gets them.

If the kids weren't here at Exodus, nearly all of my students would be home alone in their apartments until an older sibling or grown-up gets home. Not everyone lives with their parents, I've learned that too, so I try not to assume that the adult is the kid's mother or father.

In my middle school class, only one or two of them fool around and give me trouble, but if I give the kids the right book to read and let them use the beanbags, they settle down eventually. I had no idea what kind of power a juice box, an extra pretzel rod, and some attention would have over even an eleven-year-old.

Sometimes, the kids are so quiet I get to learn more test prep materials. I've started working through the GREs, GMATs and LSATs just to see if I can. They're all manageable. I like figuring out how the questions work. They're like complex, long puzzles. I realize I'm not normal.

I know you want me to go back to Sydney and finish uni. You write that in every one of your letters. Your last letter was almost shout-y about it. Maybe that's why I took so long to write back. Either you don't understand, or I haven't been clear as to why I can't return now.

I don't know about college. I mean, of course, it would be a good thing to get a degree, but I always wanted to teach young kids, and now I am teaching. I earn more money at the hagwon than I would teaching at a public or private school. Most tutors don't get health insurance or other benefits, but Lion gave me health and dental because I started out as an administrative assistant, and I still do a lot of that work. I guess I work maybe sixty hours a week.

For the first time, my family needs me. I've always needed them, but now, they need me. To work. I don't mind. Really. I feel useful. I don't know how to make you understand more than that. Also, it's not forever, right?

Bo's earning as much as he can while he's starting school. DH has only one and a half more years left at Yale. My salary helps the family, and if I can get some private tutoring jobs, then I can set aside money for me. I don't want you to worry.

The good news: Bo can pay in-state tuition because he's been here long enough, and he's considered financially independent from our parents. That's also how he's able to sponsor their immigration. The plan is to send him to school first, get our parents' green cards, and I'll keep working to help out.

Everything is expensive here. I looked into the community colleges, but because I'm not a resident yet, I'd have to pay out-of-state tuition. I'll be an in-state resident soon, but the reality is that even if I can afford to pay for my credits, when I'm at school, I'm not earning money. Opportunity cost. Oh! I forgot to tell you. I got a California driver's license. Ta-da! However, I'm terrified of driving on the freeway.

Tek, I'm lucky to have this job. I like the kids so much. They're not stressful like adults.

I miss you, and I'm sorry I didn't write sooner.

Love,
Mido

❧

She wrote letters, and he called now and then, even though it was prohibitively expensive. Sydney was nineteen hours ahead, so he'd phone for a few minutes before his day started and when it was her early afternoon.

"What's your Monday like?" she asked when he phoned her after church.

"It's good. Working for Judge Alcott is preferable to classes. School feels boring these days. Anyway, he's kind of a genius. How's your Sunday?" he asked.

"Fine. Did you go to church yesterday?"

"No, I had to finish up some research."

Tek walked over to his wall unit, where there was a photograph of them in front of the Opera House.

"Housemates okay?" She tried to sound cheerful. It was good to hear his voice, even though he sounded tired.

"Everyone's fine," he said. "Mido . . . I thought you'd be back by now."

"Oh," she said quietly, not wanting to start this again.

"I'm working," she said. "I wrote you."

"I know, I know. How were services?"

"The sermon was about self-control."

They laughed.

"You're strong on that," he said.

"Not when it comes to ice cream or cake."

"I miss you, buddy," he said.

"Easter?"

"That's why I called. It's not looking good."

"Work or school?"

"Both," he said.

"You can't control these things. I get it." She had no right to ask him to change anything for her when she was the one who'd left.

"One of the clerks got sacked, so I'm beavering away on his behalf. Judge Alcott is looking for someone else, but he really needs me. My last few classes aren't hard, but there's still exams. I'm sorry, buddy."

Mido nodded as if he could see her from 7,500 miles away. He had planned on coming for Easter, his first trip to America, but this was an important year for his budding career as a solicitor. They would likely not see each other for the remainder of the year.

❧

At Exodus Academy, Lion told everyone that hiring Peter Son had been one of the best decisions he'd ever made.

After Pomona accepted Peter as a transfer student from Yale, the philosophy major arranged to take classes only on Tuesdays, Wednesdays, and Thursdays, leaving him free to work at Exodus on Saturdays and Sundays. During the week, he stayed in his single dorm room on campus, and on the weekends, he slept at his house in Irvine. On Friday and Saturday nights, he played bass in Lion's band.

His commuting life formed a triangle whose three points were Cypress,

Claremont, and Irvine. He enjoyed driving his unwashed blue Volkswagen Passat. It was easy to forget that he was only a junior in college.

At Exodus, he taught both verbal and math, which was rare. In general, teachers had a preference, and although Peter taught math mostly because there was a greater need for skilled math tutors, if a verbal instructor went missing, he could teach it just as well.

As a musician, he was also a natural performer. One-on-one, Peter could be reserved, more willing to listen than chat. However, as onstage, in front of a class, he brought an infectious, engaging energy. In primary school, he had learned to play the guitar and bass from a private music teacher, and whenever he sang, he surprised everyone, especially girls. He liked performing and could teach difficult subjects with a learner's enthusiasm and a singer's charisma. Naturally, the students thought he was cool.

Lion didn't know why exactly Peter had left Yale for Pomona, or why he needed to work so many hours. He didn't seem interested in money. Nevertheless, he took every class or gig Lion offered, so when he wasn't in school or playing bass, he was at Exodus. Neither Lion nor Yun knew of his plans, and Bo couldn't figure them out, either. Bo had gotten to know him only because of his brother, DH, who said Peter preferred not to talk about his family. Peter got along well with his mother, Renee, but had no intention of moving back to Seoul for work. He wanted to be a rock star, he'd say, as if joking, and live in the States no matter what.

Lion preferred to hire actors, visual artists, musicians, filmmakers, and writers, and not just because they could accommodate flexible schedules. For one thing, students responded well when creative adults taught them the subjects and tests they dreaded. People in the arts also tended to stay on longer at hagwons for the steady income they provided, a ballast to the uncertainties of the artistic life.

Lion had been composing, writing lyrics, and performing his own music for eight years, and so far he hadn't found traction. Now and then he thought of touring, but he preferred being at home with Yun. He was beginning to accept that he was a competent but unremarkable musician who loved being in a band. And he was proud of his hagwon, pleased that he helped kids do well in school and provided dozens of well-paying jobs at his flourishing tutoring center. He still played music several times a week and had a standing gig at least once a month at Rascals, a steak house in Newport Beach. It was starting to feel like enough to him.

On Saturday morning, when Mido started teaching her specialized high school entrance exam boot camp, her new classroom was next to Peter's SAT boot camp filled with high school juniors and seniors. In the past year, she hadn't seen him as much because she worked during the week and on weekends helped out at home and church.

After the boot camps ended, they had to attend the general staff meeting led by Lion and Yun. At the end of the meeting, it was customary for the teachers to bring up any special issues, and Mido raised her hand.

"I haven't seen Ginny Noh in a week, and when I phoned the guardian, Mrs. Chiu, I didn't hear back," she said.

"Maybe she's ill," Yun suggested.

"I thought we could check in on her," Mido said. "Her guardian lives near Garden Grove."

Peter looked up. "I'm heading to Irvine, so I'm not far from where she lives. Do you want me to go?"

"Do you think I could go with you?" Mido asked him. "It might be odd if you went and Ginny didn't recognize you."

"Sure. Let's do that." Peter got up from his seat, and Mido followed him.

❧

In the car, Mido put on her seat belt. She smelled cigarettes but had never seen Peter smoke at the hagwon.

"I smell cigarettes," she said, switching to Korean. At Exodus, she almost never spoke Korean, but alone in the car with Peter, it felt normal.

"Busted. Only while driving, and I try not to do it too much. My ex used to get on me to quit, and I'm now down to maybe one or two in the evening when I want to feel more alert."

"I didn't know that about you."

"Not much to know," he said in English.

"My brother said you're a good musician."

Mido stopped speaking in Korean. It was as if she'd opened a door, then he'd closed it.

"DH?" he asked, wondering how that would've come up.

"Yes." Mido didn't want him to think they'd been talking about him. Peter could be voluble when teaching yet so cryptic around others. She noticed that when Bo or Lion talked, Peter was included but he didn't say as much. "Yun said you're playing in Lion's band. You're a bass player, right?"

Peter smiled. "That's right. You should come out when Lion and I play next time at Rascals."

"Okay."

"You're supposed to be a playwright?"

It was her turn to be surprised. "How did you know?"

"Bo. He said you were in a drama society in Sydney. Do you want to act? This is the right place."

"Oh, I'm not an actor. I joined SUDS, that's the drama society at uni, because I wanted to learn how to talk better. I'm fine with little kids, but—"

"But peers are harder," he said like he understood.

"Yes, exactly. The drama society helped a bit with that, and I ended up writing a few plays, too. I still write a little bit, but I can't imagine doing that for real. No one does that."

"Actually, I think a lot of people do that here."

"Well, I admire people who can, but it's not for me. Though I did like what happened when I finished a scene."

"What's that?"

"People made sense. I started to imagine what everyone else was feeling in a conflict, for example. Writing a scene would force me to think not just about one character, but everyone in that scene and even people offstage. Not sure if that makes sense," she said.

"No, I get it. I do. Are you going to keep writing plays? You don't have to go to school for that, right? Or do you?"

"It's hard to imagine doing anything like that now."

"Well, I'm not going to encourage you."

Mido faced him and laughed.

"Why is that?"

"It doesn't matter if you're a good or even great writer. I wouldn't want you to suffer," Peter said. "Art feels impossible."

"Thank you. For not wanting me to suffer," she said, laughing again. "Now I just want to work, and maybe later, I'll finish school," she said, realizing then that he hadn't asked her what her plans were, and she didn't know if she'd said too much. He was trying to respect her privacy, and she felt like he was teaching her to respect his.

"What's this kid like?" Peter asked.

"Ginny? She's one of my favorites. Her parents live in Busan, and they sent her here by herself two years ago."

"That's crazy," he said. "When she was nine?"

"She boards with a guardian."

Peter made a face. "My folks sent me overseas when I was fairly young. I've experienced homestay guardians."

"What's that like?"

"When it's bad, it's like a Dickens novel. The guardians eat good food and the kids get frozen pizzas and cup ramyeon, and there's never enough to eat. I met one kid who boarded at a giant house in Englewood Cliffs. He slept on a dirty mattress on the floor with the other homestay kids, and the guardian family lived like royalty on the second floor. They put a lock on the fridge and pantries. His dean at the private school had to come rescue him."

Mido stared at him, hoping that Ginny wasn't going through something like that.

"Did that happen to you?"

"I had enough to eat because my mother could pay, but the experience was weird. I wouldn't do it to a nine-year-old." His mother had believed that a Western education would be superior to one in Korea, and her work required her to be in Seoul, forcing him to board overseas. His father thought it was important for a boy to be tough. Peter had always been close to his mother, even more so after the divorce, and his father didn't want him to be a mama's boy.

"I heard that you went to Aunt Mary's—I mean Mrs. Shin's house with DH during breaks. Is that because you didn't like your homestay?"

"They were fine."

"And the ones in the UK?"

"When I was in England, I had a good host in New Malden. Mrs. Oh was kind and tried to make sure I was okay. She was a great cook and would bake me scones on Sundays. Her British husband was a bit of a cold fish. I cried once about something, and he said I should buck up.

"Then they moved and I got another family. Very proud people. A woman who went to my mother's primary school. Mrs. Lee would tell me that she didn't need to take my mother's money but she did not want to harm their friendship. I had no idea what she was talking about. I did well in school, but I had regular problems with some of the other students. I was one of the only minority kids, and if I hadn't been an athlete, it would've been worse. Some of the kids were shits, and I didn't think I could tell Mrs. Lee what was going on. When I got older, I tried to run away."

"Where?"

Mido realized that he was signaling to enter the 405, which had five lanes in each direction. Although she'd gotten her license, she hadn't yet tackled this particular freeway, always teeming with traffic. "Oh. You need to pay attention. Sorry," she said quietly, embarrassed by her keen interest.

Peter merged smoothly. "All good."

"You ran away?"

"Yes. That's how I ended up in Seoul. My mother had to come get me because I refused to go to school. I went to London to listen to this punk band I liked but couldn't get admitted into the club. Naturally. So I slept here and there and hung out in Waterloo station. I had a credit card, so I didn't starve or anything. I walked around Bloomsbury a lot. Eventually my mother found me at the British Museum. I just kept returning to the Rosetta Stone, because that's where we always met. I knew she'd find me. Renee always knows where I am. Anyway, that's how I ended up at Andover with DH."

"Renee?"

"I'm allowed to call her that. It's a joke. I mean, it's actually her name, but anyway." Peter smiled.

"I remember meeting you. At Eagle Academy," Mido said. "I didn't know you didn't like England."

"I like England very much. It's one of my favorite places in the whole world. I'm a musician only because that little island has produced some of the greatest bands."

"But you didn't like school there."

"No, when I think about it, I realize that I liked the school a lot. I learned loads. I just didn't know how to deal with some of the kids. I could've stuck it out, but it was hard. I was alone. My mother couldn't visit often. She was working in Seoul. Also, I didn't want to worry her."

Mido didn't want to ask about his father, but he'd read her thoughts.

"My dad lives in Hong Kong. I don't know him. I mean, I know him, but we're not in touch. He's not interested in me, and I'm not interested in him."

Not knowing what to say, she blurted out, "You're a good driver. I don't know how to drive on the freeway."

"Practice. Now we have to merge onto the 605 to get to Garden Grove," he said. "Driving in California is next level. You might start smoking if you have to drive as much as I do." He laughed.

"Is that why you offered to go to Ginny's, so you could smoke?" she teased him, still thinking about how Peter had grown up.

"Garden Grove is on the way to Irvine," he said, and turned on the tape player. They listened to Talk Talk, and the car filled with a happy, familiar sound.

Then Peter said quietly, "I was worried that Ginny's guardian might be a bad person."

❧

It took a few minutes for someone to come to the door, and Peter made a face like he didn't like that. When the person inside asked who it was, Mido introduced herself as Ginny's hagwon teacher, and the door opened right away.

"Ginny is not feeling well," the woman said in Korean. She was in her late sixties, wearing a beige-and-black plaid sweater with dark slacks and blue house slippers. She didn't invite them inside.

"You must be Mrs. Chiu, Ginny's guardian. I brought these packets for her. Ginny likes to do them. Of all my students, she completes her work the fastest and always asks for more." Mido smiled. "I feel certain she'll get into Oxford Academy. She's very bright. I hope you'll tell her parents how hard she works."

The woman smiled briefly, then turned quizzically to Peter, who hadn't introduced himself. He looked serious and had a nice face, but she didn't approve of his bleached hair and piercings.

"I'm also a teacher at Exodus. Can we say hello to Ginny, please?"

"She's not well. It's late. I'll tell her you stopped by."

"Will she be able to return to class next week?" he asked.

"I don't know," Mrs. Chiu said. "Her mother is late on payments."

"You've paid up for the month," Mido said.

"Yes, because I'm never late with payments. But I advance the fees for the students who stay here. Ginny's mother is late to pay me."

"Is she okay?" Peter asked.

"IMF. That's the excuse every parent is giving now for being late."

"It's not the child's fault," Peter said. His voice was sterner than usual. "The won is worth a fraction of what it used to be compared to the dollar."

"I still have to pay everyone in dollars, though," Mrs. Chiu countered. "The groceries, utilities, taxes, hagwon, and the mortgage." She gestured with her hands toward the roof as if she needed to demonstrate the concept of shelter to the two young idealists on her doorstep.

"You're not sending Ginny to the hagwon because her mother is late with her payment to you?" Peter couldn't hide his irritation, his voice tremulous, and Mido placed her hand on his back to calm him.

"I'm sure you must be in a difficult situation," Mido said. "Both my parents lost their jobs because of the IMF Crisis."

The woman nodded with a modicum of empathy. She resented Peter's tone. She'd heard of Miss Mido from Ginny, who loved going to hagwon.

"She's actually not feeling well, and it's late. You don't have to believe me," Mrs. Chiu said to Peter. "Thank you for stopping by. I'll give the packets to Ginny." The guardian dipped her head ever so slightly, more a nod than a bow, then shut the door.

❧

"So how old are you again?" Peter asked.

"Twenty."

They walked back to his car, feeling defeated.

"What do you remember about being in middle school?" he asked, not expecting a real answer. He was still thinking of the little girl.

"I was living in Seoul. We'd just returned from Sydney. The first day of school, my math teacher, Mr. Na, hit me with a brass ruler. Yun saved me."

"She fought the teacher?"

"No. She became my friend. I didn't have any friends in Sydney."

"Yun is great," he said.

"I'd fall on a sword for her."

"I wish Ginny had that kind of person," he said, opening the passenger door for Mido.

13

Rescue

On the following Saturday, the boot camps resumed. When Ginny walked into class and smiled at her, Mido felt relief. The little girl looked fine. Her pretty oval face was sunbrowned, her hair held back by a thin black plastic headband. Ginny sat in her usual seat at the front table near Mido's desk and nibbled on one of the pretzel rods Mido had put out for the students before class.

"Take a few minutes to settle in. Have your snacks, and we'll go over the practice exams."

Mido tapped Ginny's shoulder and took her to the hallway.

"How are you, Ginny? I'm so glad to see you."

Ginny's eyes filled with tears. No one here ever looked at her like that. She missed her father, who always took her side.

Mido told Ginny to wait and popped her head into Peter's room next door, asking him to keep an eye on her class. "I need to talk with Ginny for a few minutes in the lounge," she told him.

In the empty lounge, Mido gave Ginny a glass of water and motioned for her to take a seat on the couch. She put a hand gently on the girl's shoulder.

"What's the matter, Ginny?"

Mido passed her a tissue.

"My parents can't pay Mrs. Chiu, but they don't think I should come home because I'm doing well here, and they can't afford the plane ticket. My mother says that she will make more calls, but we don't have family here—"

"What did your guardian say?"

"I can't stay for free. She says she's sorry, but she can't afford to do that. Each bed has to be used for a paying student."

"I see."

"She's paid for the hagwon through the month, so I'm allowed to finish out the next two weeks, she said. But my parents owe her a lot of money."

"I'm glad you told me. What a grown-up you have to be now," Mido said, feeling awful. "These are big things for even adults to think about. I admire you."

Ginny reached for another tissue.

"Miss Mido, thank you for bringing the worksheets. I finished them. I have them in my bag for you to check later," Ginny said, trying to steady her breathing.

"I know you did the work. You're a wonderful young person, Ginny."

"Where will I go, Miss Mido?"

"I'm sure your parents will let us know."

"Will I have to go to foster care?"

"What? No, no." Mido shook her head, but she didn't actually know what would happen to the child.

"I want to stay here. I want to go to UCSF and become a doctor."

Mido laughed in surprise. Her middle school students occasionally said things like this, but it never felt normal to hear. How did someone so young know about foster care, or UCSF?

"I promised my grandmother that I'd become a heart doctor. She has a weak heart that has irregular beats."

Mido patted the girl's shoulder.

"If anyone could become a heart doctor, I think you could."

"Dad lost his job and everything. Our house and the car. They had to move back to Busan, where my grandmother lives. Mom said the school near Grandmother is not good enough for me. My little brother is too young, so it doesn't matter for him. She wants him to come here, too, because he was also born here, but he was so young that he had to go back with them. But I wanted to stay, so my mother found Mrs. Chiu for me."

"You were born here?"

"Yes."

"Your Korean is so good."

"We only speak Korean at home. We lived here, then moved back. Mother said all their extra money was spent on me so I could be in California."

Mido didn't understand why a parent would tell a child this.

"Your father lost his job because of the economy. The IMF Crisis is not your fault. Your parents sent you to school here because they wanted you to be educated in America."

"We owe Mrs. Chiu money, and she's always talking about it."

Her eyes shining, Ginny stared at the refrigerator, still trying to calm her breathing, unable to face her teacher. She was eleven years old and perceptive enough to understand that she was alone in this country and the adults didn't know what to do with her.

"Miss Mido, where did you go to college?"

"I started at University of Sydney. In Australia, but I couldn't finish because I moved here with my family."

"Are you going back? To Australia?"

"It's unclear." Mido patted Ginny's back. "Let's wipe your face and return to class. Everything will work out."

❧

At the end of the day, after the kids left, Mido tidied up the classroom.

Peter knocked on the doorframe and entered.

"She came back?"

"Ginny?"

He sat down near the snack table and opened a new tub of pretzels.

"I think I must have eaten a thousand pretzel rods since I started here. I never ate a single one before. Not in England, Andover, or Yale. I had no idea how many of these I could eat. Have you ever had one with the chocolate and caramel on them?"

Mido shook her head no. "Ginny's parents can't pay the guardian fees. The guardian is going to kick her out because she needs to rent out the room. I can't believe an eleven-year-old has to deal with this shit."

"Are you cursing? There could be children here." Peter glanced around dramatically.

Yun and Lion passed by the classroom.

"Hey, is this cocktail hour?" Lion asked. "What are people drinking?"

Peter smiled. "I didn't find any beer in the faculty lounge fridge, but let me know if there's a secret stash anywhere. I'll never tell the boss."

❧

At the pizzeria next door, Lion ordered pitchers of soda and beer for the table and a sausage pie. The Coke came out first, and Lion poured everyone a glass.

"You're saying that Ginny doesn't have a place to stay? She's eleven!" Dismayed, Yun looked at Lion expectantly.

He shook his head at her unasked question. "We can't just take a student into our house, Yun."

"I have an extra room in my place," Peter said, "but I can't take in a little girl who's not my family. That looks bad. Right?" Peter glanced at the women.

"Peter, that would not work. We have to do something, though," Yun said.

Lion puffed out his cheeks and exhaled.

"It's not like a stray cat. She's an eleven-year-old human. We can't just take in children who have no place to go."

"You can't take in every child, I guess, but that guardian is scary, Lion," Peter argued. "I met the lady. I wouldn't want to stay with anyone calling my parents debtors."

"I can help out with taking care of her," Mido said.

"Lion, we have to take her, or at least get her a ticket home, right?" Yun said, her head tilted to the side, and Lion covered his eyes.

❧

At Communion, the ones who took the bread and wine proceeded down the center aisle to receive the sacrament from the ministers. Held once a month at Gospel Presbyterian, Communion Sunday was a parade of congregants—for some, a slow march of bowed heads in private contemplation; for others, a full strut in glorious peacock mode, heads tall, bodies draped in vivid colors. Many wore their best clothes, but there were as many who abhorred fancy dress or luxury clothing, eschewing excessive consumption.

When Shin and Danbi marched to the head of the Communion line, Shin was noticeable in a sharp navy suit and a silver-striped necktie, and Danbi in a tight-fitting white skirt suit with nude-colored heels.

It was the first time Helen saw the woman who had caused her family so much grief. Her husband had described her, but Danbi's beauty still took her by surprise. John had not said that she was gorgeous, but she was.

When the service ended, Helen and John left the narthex as quickly as they could.

Bo and Mido followed, not understanding why their parents were in such a rush to exit. Normally they lingered to talk with friends, and they often caught up with Lion, Yun, and Nari.

"Aren't we having lunch at the Patio?" Mido asked. "I was going to see Yun."

"We have to go home," John said firmly.

They still only had one car, and as usual, Bo had driven.

"Okay, let's go," Bo said, shrugging.

As they went to the parking lot, the family could hear Shin calling out to John.

Shin and Danbi walked briskly to catch up to the Koh family in the parking lot.

Ignoring Shin, John and Helen continued to the car, and Bo and Mido kept pace with their parents, uncertain as to what they should do. Before that horrible business with Danbi, of course, they would have greeted Shin, who had been like an uncle to them, yet Bo and Mido knew enough to say nothing.

It was no use trying to avoid them. As they neared Bo's car, Danbi appeared, a wide smile on her face as if nothing had happened in the intervening years since she'd last seen John in that Seoul conference room.

"It's been a long time," she said.

John and Helen didn't respond.

"We wanted to know if you could have lunch today," Danbi said. "We could eat here, or go somewhere much nicer." She turned to the children. "Of course, you're invited, too, unless you have something else to do."

Bo and Mido bowed their heads, no differently than they would have with any of their parents' friends. Danbi was not much older than they were, and Bo's first thought was of Shin's wife, Mary, who had always been so kind to them.

John turned to the car, and Bo opened the front passenger door.

Helen looked directly at Danbi. "Please leave us alone."

John got in the car, grateful that Helen had said this because Danbi was not a person he could manage.

"We just took the sacraments," Danbi said. "I wanted to say I'm sorry. I'd hoped you would accept my apology," she said to John, now facing forward in the passenger seat, unable to meet her gaze.

"I said I wanted to apologize," Danbi said again, her tone businesslike and crisp.

John faced her. "Why now? You've had years to do this."

"It's a small community here in Orange County, and this is the best church. I thought we should clear the air. Let the past be the past. There's no need to keep avoiding each other," she said, her attractive face calm and full of light.

Helen glared at her, astonished at the audacity. "You ruined my husband's career and hurt our family."

"Your husband tried to ruin me. What choice did I have?" Danbi replied. "I had to save my career, and my man."

John turned to Shin. "Please leave us alone. I don't have any good feelings left of us. Let me at least have peace." He smiled sadly. "You don't mean any of this apology. We cannot go back to what we were. It is broken."

The rest of his family began to settle into the car, but Danbi held open the driver's-side door before Bo could close it.

"You're supposed to be Christians," she said. "You're supposed to forgive. I already forgave you for what you did to me. I think you should grow up."

"Bo, start driving," John said.

Shin took Danbi's hand.

"Let them alone. You tried." Shin led her away.

❧

Back in the apartment, Helen put a pot of water on the stove to boil. There was rice already in the cooker, so she took some cold ingredients and rolled up gimbap. It was the fastest thing she could think of. Although she couldn't imagine eating, she needed to do something to feed them, so she made four rolls anyway. When the water was heated, she added soybean paste, dried seaweed, and tofu to make soup.

Mido set the table and they sat together. They bowed their heads in a quick, silent prayer.

"I'm being tested," John said. "I don't think I can go to that church anymore."

Helen covered her mouth with her right hand the way she did when she was thinking of something to say.

"Why are they following me?" John asked. "Why can't they stop?"

Mido had never seen her father this agitated, and it worried her.

"We could find another church," Bo said.

"They'll find us again," Helen said. "We cannot run away."

Mido touched her head, remembering.

"I was supposed to talk with Yun and Lion. I better call them."

"Have you told Yun and Lion about that woman?" Helen asked her daughter.

"No, no. I have to talk with her about Ginny."

"Who?" Bo asked.

"She's one of my students. She's in my regular class and the boot camp for the specialized high school exam."

"Is she okay?" Helen asked.

"Her parents owe the homestay guardian money, but they want Ginny to stay in America." Mido surveyed their small apartment. There was no room for another person. "She's only eleven and definitely our brightest student."

"What will happen to her?" Bo asked, picking up his soup spoon.

"Not sure," Mido replied. For the first time in her life, she wished that she were a wealthy and powerful person. It had seemed wrong to want this for her own family since they had each other and were able to find jobs. This period in their lives was a temporary setback. Eventually things would work out for them, but Ginny was eleven, and she was alone. "I wish—" she started to say, and saw her father's crestfallen expression. She knew he felt the same way.

"Everyone has troubles," John said. "Even little children."

14
Debtors

In the church parking lot, Shin had watched his friend's face turn sickly white. He could not forget the surprised looks of Bo and Mido, whom he had known since they were born.

Shin had tried to dissuade Danbi from this absurd lunch plan; he knew Helen and John would never accept the invitation. Yet no matter what Shin said about a man he had known for almost three decades, Danbi was certain that John would be civil, that he might even be open to a reconciliation. She had to try, she'd said.

In a way, Danbi was correct, because Helen and John had not made a scene. They did not raise their voices; if anything, John became more passive, retreating into the privacy of his car. Shin knew that look, that bloodless expression, belonging to a man who was fighting with all his might to pull his punches, the strain of drawing down his own power.

Shin was afraid.

He should not have left his marriage and three sons.

It had begun with flirtation with an intoxicating young woman, then a romantic affair. He'd had those before, almost too many to count. Mary had overlooked them. She had not maligned him to their sons, who did not know about Danbi until Mary had no choice but to tell them.

Shin had done everything he could to extricate himself from this woman, but she would not let him go. He had used his best friend, hoping that wise John could clean up this mess. The wish to be free from Danbi was inevitable because like with all affairs, eventually fun transformed into the grim reality of rights and responsibilities. Shin had sworn vows to his wife and made promises to his girlfriend, and Danbi did not see the difference between the words spoken, the agreements made, or the identities of the parties. Now there was a baby with Danbi, an innocent.

Danbi's wishes and fears could not easily be dismissed. For her, Shin had sacrificed his wife, his sons, and his closest friend.

After church, when Shin and Danbi returned to their house, the baby was asleep. The housekeeper had put her down for a nap and was cooking in the kitchen. Danbi went to speak with her.

In the bedroom, Shin removed his necktie and hung up his suit, changing into khakis and a white golf shirt. At fifty-three, he had kept himself trim and attractive. He still had a thick head of hair, which Danbi liked. Since he was a boy, he'd been vain, and now his enduring good looks almost embarrassed him. In high school, the popular girls used to call him the lodestone and themselves its mere metal shavings. By midlife, he had squandered his pull and felt like a cheap horseshoe magnet stuck to a factory anvil, affixed to a mass with a hold far greater than he could ever manage to be free of.

Shin sat down on the love seat. From his mind, he could not dislodge John's forlorn expression—the shame, repulsion, and despair.

Danbi had pored over the Gospel Presbyterian church members' guide to find clients for their insurance agency. While creating spreadsheets for potential client outreach, she had learned that John and his family had recently become members. There were other large churches in Orange County, but Danbi wanted to settle at this one because her American-born cousin Frank Lim and his pretty Korean wife, Bina, who owned a large insurance agency, were elders there.

"You know John Koh and Helen Cho?" Bina had once asked Danbi. "They arrived not too long ago, but they're a well-regarded family. Helen's sister, Sonya Cho, is an elder at that big church in Gangnam and the daughter-in-law of the Mun real estate family. I heard John and Helen lost everything during the IMF, but everyone at church likes them. The wife has very good taste and works at Mrs. Chung's."

Danbi listened to her wealthy cousin's wife prattle on about John and Helen, and nothing Shin could say reassured her that they would not gossip about them. She needed to make things right with John and Helen if she was to do well here.

It was possible to repair this relationship, Danbi told Shin. She was even willing to apologize.

They could not wed because he was not yet divorced; however, Danbi had told everyone they were married. She wore a large emerald-cut diamond ring, which Bina had admired, and addressed Shin as her husband. Danbi wanted to make sure that Helen and John never told anyone about Mary or Shin's three sons.

Danbi entered the room, and Shin looked up without saying a word.

"Are you upset with me?" she asked, closing the door behind her. She unbuttoned her jacket, then stripped off her blouse, dropping it to the ground. She pulled down the shade behind him and removed her brassiere and panties.

Shin closed his eyes. "Why did you have to do that to them? I don't understand you."

"I'm not making trouble. I'm trying to fix things. For us. Our family."

She climbed onto his lap and pressed her breast on his mouth.

Shin pulled back. He picked her up in his arms and laid her on the bed. "Get dressed."

Danbi turned over.

"You can punish me," she said, glancing at him like she was frightened. "Maybe that's what I need. Punishment."

Shin returned to the love seat and sat down, his hands cradling his heavy head. This was what they did.

She shaped the world's needs and values through the machinery of her reasoning, and when he disagreed, she offered her body in ways that were shocking, even to him.

For her, there were no taboos. In the beginning, he'd been dazzled by her seeming innocence. But she was not a virgin as she had first implied, then later neither affirmed nor denied. There was little she hadn't done, and there was nothing she wouldn't do.

A man who needed to have sex often, Shin found her exhilarating, as if he'd discovered some sort of fountain of youth in her body; then, later, sex with her became a compulsion.

Many times he'd gone to room salons and slept with other girls, to check if he could forget her and replace her with some nameless body, but he found that he couldn't. No one was like her. Before Danbi, he would have said a lay is a lay. Pussy was fungible.

It was not. Even this request for punishment. He was furious, yet he felt aroused. His dick refused to listen to his brain's command: *Cast her out.*

Danbi sat up and rose from the bed to approach him. Getting on her knees, she removed his pants, then turned around to slap her own bottom hard, then bent over. She slapped herself again and again until she reddened. Shin took her hands in his to make her stop. He obeyed.

When it was over, Danbi showered, then returned wearing a white gauze sundress, unrecognizable as the woman who'd been hitting herself less than an hour before.

Shin was still seated, half dressed, neither understanding nor accepting how he had done this again. What he felt was hatred for his own weakness, and the hatred seeped further and further into him. For a long time, he'd thought it was a kind of self-loathing for his lack of discipline, and now this shame felt as fierce as violence. He wanted to hurt her, but he was afraid, too.

"I'm going to check on the baby. She'll be ready for her bottle," she said, approaching him.

Like a gentle mother, Danbi gathered his head in her cool hands and smoothed his hair. She turned and went to the door. For a moment, she stood still.

"We have to stay at Gospel Presbyterian, and your friend is not leaving, either. This church is important for our business, and our little family will be respected here.

"I forgave you and that man for trying to get me fired. Your friend is supposed to forgive me if he believes that he was forgiven by God. Isn't that how this religion works?"

There was nothing Shin could say.

⁂

All weekend, Lion and Yun discussed the possibility of taking Ginny into their home. Everything would change, Lion argued, and Yun couldn't disagree, but she also thought it made sense since there was more than enough room in their new house. They had no plans to have children anytime soon, and Ginny had nowhere to go. Finally, as she'd known he would, Lion agreed with Yun, and at nine o'clock on Sunday night, they phoned Ginny's parents in Busan.

"Your daughter is a wonderful student, and we're happy she attends our hagwon," Yun said.

Ginny's mother started to cry. "We owe you money, and as soon as we find work, I promise to send it. I promise you. I promise."

Yun tried to interrupt, but Ginny's mother continued.

"It's just that if she comes back here, we don't know how she can return. The school in my mother-in-law's neighborhood is not good. Ginny has always been such a bright child, and Oxford Academy is supposed to be great—"

"There's been a misunderstanding," Yun broke in. "My husband and I are not calling about money. In fact, we're proposing a solution. The guardian needs to rent her room, so we could let her stay here. At our house. We don't have any children, and we have a bedroom for her."

Ginny's mother grew quiet. She didn't understand why these hagwon owners would do this for a stranger.

"There wouldn't be a fee. She can stay as long as she needs until you want her to come home. We want to support good students," Yun said.

"I've been praying for a miracle." The mother burst into tears again and sobbed.

Lion frowned. Although he was so religious that as a little boy he had wanted to be a pastor, he disliked references to miracles, angels, and "the Lord's will" even more than the flintiest of atheists.

"Ginny is a delight," he said. "Her teacher—"

"Miss Mido," the mother said. "My daughter mentions her all the time. Was this Miss Mido's idea?"

"Yes, it was Miss Mido's idea. She would have taken Ginny into her house, but she doesn't have the room."

"My husband and I would be grateful if you could take Ginny in until things are a bit better for us here. We would be in your debt, of course. Every cent would be repaid."

"Ginny has been studying to go to Oxford Academy, which as you know is an excellent new public school that starts in the seventh grade," Yun said. "It doesn't cost anything to go there, but she has to take a test, and there is an application process, which we know how to handle."

"If she's accepted, then we have to find a way for her to go." Ginny's mother sounded worried all over again. "We have no friends or relatives in Orange County."

"Why don't we face that situation when we get to it? Do we have your permission for Ginny to come live with us?" Yun asked her.

The mother gladly agreed, promised to call the guardian, and thanked Yun and Lion again before ending the call.

❧

The homestay guardian told Lion that she felt swindled. Mrs. Chiu stood at the entrance of her house in her brown house slippers and didn't ask him in.

"The parents owe me last year's fees, and with every call the mother promised to pay it. They've already gone through the deposit. Thank God I made them pay that before I took the child in." The woman stared at Lion like he was an idiot. "Why would you take this problem on?"

Lion glanced at the living room behind the woman to make sure there were no children around. He couldn't imagine having to hear this sort of talk all the time.

"You've heard from Ginny's mother? That she's given us permission?"

"Yes, she must have called right after speaking with your wife," she said. "Ginny is at school now."

"Good, good. I'm here to pick up her things, and she'll be coming to Exodus this afternoon anyway. My wife and I will take her home tonight from the hagwon."

"Why do you want to take her?"

"My wife thinks—" Lion stopped himself from saying that Yun thought it was the only correct choice, not wanting Mrs. Chiu to feel judged. "We understand that you need to house another boarder."

"I'm not a bad person," Mrs. Chiu said. "I'm retired, and this is my only source of income. My husband died of leukemia, and my daughter is in graduate school in Boston. I paid for everything for Ginny, believing that her parents would pay me back. Now they owe me $6,000. I don't charge a high fee to care for these children. That's why I have all these problems. If I only took in the really rich kids, then this sort of haggling, owing, and delays wouldn't happen. I'm dealing with middle-class children of parents who have company jobs, who have no business sending their kids to the United States. I felt sorry for them, and I didn't charge enough to have any cushion for me."

The woman was clearly frustrated.

"$6,000 is an enormous sum of money for me. I turned down several students so Ginny could keep that room. I've given her everything that I'd promised her parents. What would you do if your hagwon students didn't pay you?"

Lion nodded sympathetically, having had his share of bounced checks and nonpayments, but the parents almost always found a way to make good. The hagwon fees for Exodus were not high for Orange County, and the Koreans here hadn't lost their jobs from the IMF Crisis. Moreover, working parents couldn't afford to lose their child's spot because there was no other nice place for the kids to go at these lower rates.

Mrs. Chiu stood aside to let Lion in. "You can take her things. I've already packed them. Ginny is a good girl. She studies and behaves herself." She shook her head in disgust. "But I can't believe how terrible that mother is. She lied and lied. I'm not a rich woman. Look!" She gestured to the modest living room with its old brown furniture and threadbare carpets. Nevertheless, the town house was well maintained, tidy and free of any visible dust.

Lion removed his sneakers and went upstairs, where there were three bedrooms and two shared bathrooms. The primary bedroom was being used by three boarding students, and the second bedroom was used by two brothers who attended Fullerton. The smallest room was Ginny's. Mrs. Chiu slept in the laundry room by the garage. Lion carried down a large vinyl suitcase and a blue plastic milk crate full of books.

"Is this all?" Lion asked.

"There's a CD player on the desk. That's hers. Last night, she tried to give it to me for the debts, but I cannot accept it. What use do I have for a CD player?" She shook her head in exasperation. "I made her three meals a day and packed her snacks. When she got good grades, I would get her pizza. I noticed that she needed underwear and socks, and I bought them for her."

Mrs. Chiu felt cheated, not just because of the debts, but because she had been a decent person, a good Christian woman. She never overcharged any of her boarders. There was always food in the cupboard, and she protected her female boarders vigilantly, like they were her own daughters. "Just because I accept money to care for children doesn't make me greedy," she said defensively.

"Mrs. Chiu, you have been more than generous with Ginny. Her good report card and fine personality must have a lot to do with your excellent care and guardianship. Thank you for caring for her."

Lion withdrew his wallet, where he kept two extra blank checks. He took out a pen and wrote out the guardian's name and the full sum.

Mrs. Chiu didn't understand.

"You were owed this money," he said.

"You don't even know these people."

"Well, I know you now," he said, smiling at her as he folded the check into the guardian's warm hands.

BOOK III

October 1999–January 2001

Liminality is the realm of primitive hypothesis, where there is freedom to juggle with the factors of existence.

—Victor Turner

1
Maslow

October 1999

Bo wanted to be cautious.

In the spring, he enrolled at Fullerton College and took two classes while still working at Exodus fifty hours a week. The math classes were far too easy for him.

When he received A's in Calculus II and Discrete Mathematics, he made an appointment with Mr. Gonzalez, a soft-spoken counselor in the Transfer Alliance Program, whom the students called TAP Guy.

A month into his first fall semester, Bo showed Mr. Gonzalez a draft of his course selections for the next year and a half.

"You did all this yourself?" Mr. Gonzalez asked, impressed.

"My friend Lion helped me think it through," Bo said. "I created the spreadsheet and chose the classes."

"So how's this semester going?"

"Good so far."

"Favorite class?"

"Psychology 101," Bo said, adding, "Honors Focus."

"Ah, you have Dr. Wilson. She's great. Once you have her for Honors Focus, you might get converted."

"How so?"

"She might make you want to be a psych major. She's that good."

"Do you become a psychologist then?"

"You can do lots of things with a psych degree, but you'd have to get an advanced degree to become a clinical psychologist. You can ask Dr. Wilson all about that. We're getting ahead of ourselves.

"For now, if you stay on the honors track, there's a lot of upside: smaller class sizes, meeting serious students like yourself, and most of your credits can transfer over to a school like UCLA," Mr. Gonzalez said, snapping his fingers. Self-conscious about getting too excited about his work, TAP Guy lifted his wire-framed eyeglasses, which had slid down a bit from the bridge of his button nose.

"That's where you said you want to aim, right? UCLA? My alma mater."

Bo shrugged. Lion had already explained that he could get his associate degree in two years and then transfer to a four-year institution like UCLA to get his BA.

"I need to stay in Southern California," Bo said. "Do you think I could get in? To UCLA?"

"Yeah, definitely. But man, you need to work a little less. Not your schoolwork, but your paid work. Fifty hours is a lot. Even if it isn't mentally taxing for a brainy dude like you, it's still a lot of time. You still need to sleep and eat. Can you afford to work less hours?" Most students at Fullerton had to work. "You got a kid or something?"

"Me?" Bo looked startled, then laughed. "Oh, no. I don't have any kids. I help my family. We just moved apartments, and the rent's gone up."

"Right. I get you. Same," the counselor said, nodding. "Life. Family. It's expensive." Mr. Gonzalez shook his head, feeling sorry for Bo. He, too, had worked since high school to help his mom and younger brothers.

❧

Bo did his problem sets in the van while waiting for the kids. At Exodus, before teaching, he'd finish his homework in the lounge, and if that was crowded, Lion let him use his office. At home, when everyone went to sleep, Bo did his studying at the kitchen table. The family had recently bought a television and a VCR from Costco, but after dinner, no one watched anything, and the house was kept quiet so Bo could do his schoolwork. It was all work, school, and, on Sundays, church, but he felt like the family was making progress.

Just last month, when a family moved out of the building to try their luck in Atlanta, the Kohs had moved into the vacated three-bedroom apartment on a lower floor, which had an extra bath and an additional bedroom with a window for Bo and DH when he visited. The unit cost an extra $400, but with four people working, the rent was manageable, and now they would have a houseguest. Sonya was arriving, and she'd stay in Mido's room. Bo was picking her up at the airport after Psych 101.

This fall, there were twenty-six students enrolled in Intro Psychology

101 (Honors Focus), taught by Dr. Rhoda Wilson, a forty-eight-year-old mother of two, who had earned her PhD in Psychology at UCLA in her late thirties, after putting her husband through law school. The professor was highly regarded for her pioneering scholarship on anxiety and immigrants from the West Indies.

The daughter of immigrants from Jamaica and Saint Kitts, she had grown up in Altadena and started at Cal State Long Beach, then transferred to UCLA. It had been her idea for Bo to meet with Mr. Gonzalez.

On campus, Professor Wilson was famous for her unbelievable recall. She could learn the class roster on the first day and somehow remember your name years later. Attractive, friendly, and able to pass for mid-thirties, she was used to older male students flirting with her during office hours; however, when a student lingered too long and tried to make a move, she'd tilt her head and say with a smile, "C'mon now, really? That's how you want to get an A? No, thank you, dear."

Attendance was part of the grade, but even if it weren't, Bo couldn't imagine missing Professor Wilson's class. Before Fullerton College, he had known almost nothing about psychology, and he had never expected to like the subject this much.

"Definitely take Intro Psych. It'll help you understand Americans, who are not like Koreans," Lion had advised him, and whenever Bo did the reading from the used Myers Fifth Edition, which had cost almost $40, he found that he enjoyed it even more than his eighteenth-century British literature class, which he loved, and certainly far more than Multivariable Calculus, which he could handle fine since he'd done so much math in Seoul.

As he settled into life at Fullerton and Exodus, he thought about his years spent studying for the Suneung. Having failed three times to hit the target score for Yonsei, Bo had felt stupid and ashamed. Looking back, he couldn't understand why it had been so important to him. His aunt Sonya had argued that if he wanted to remain in Korea and be more Korean, he could apply to another school with easier requirements, but he hadn't.

Bo had bet everything on one school, one of the toughest in the country, for which there was an entrance exam given only once a year. Now that he earned a living teaching college entrance exams that were given several times a year, he wondered why the Suneung for schools like Yonsei, SNU, and Korea University was offered only once each November, when the nation held its collective breath for the exam's duration.

Almost never did Bo talk about his years studying for Yonsei, but even as he grew more optimistic about his life in America, he could not forget his stubborn quest. More than anything, he hoped that he'd never make such a mistake again with his time, his choices, and his life.

Once he had tabulated the cost his family had borne for his three tries, and the number humbled him. Of course, Bo wanted to make it up to them.

Psychology appealed to him. In Seoul, he'd selected sociology largely because his high school counselor said that if he wanted to get into Yonsei, a sociology concentration would be easier for admission than, say, law or medicine. As for psychology, he had once believed that it was the study of people who were not well mentally, and the idea of it had scared him.

In class, no one seemed unwell. Professor Wilson was easily one of the most joyous adults he'd ever met, and her class was fun. The class was full of interesting people who asked intelligent questions he'd never considered. Students didn't talk as much in his other classes, but here, his fellow classmates surprised him at each meeting.

Every time he did the reading, he thought of more people he'd encountered in his life. He wanted to know more about his own life and started to remember how he had grown up in Paramus, Sydney, Seoul, and now Southern California.

In addition to chapter 7 of Myers, the reading for today's class was Abraham Maslow's "A Theory of Human Motivation," a research paper from the 1940s, which was supposed to be important. Professor Wilson put up a poster of a five-layered pyramid symbolizing the different levels of human motivation.

"Maslow himself never depicted his theory using the pyramid image. Others did that. However, I think the image is helpful," the professor said, and looked across the room, not expecting anyone to agree or disagree on that point. She had a tendency to offer a thought, let the statement linger in the air, then move on.

The students shuffled in their seats, took notes on loose-leaf paper or in cheap notebooks not much different from the paper they'd used in middle school or high school. Bo copied the diagram, certain that the material would appear on the midterm.

"Initially Maslow argued that human beings had five stages of needs: At the base level are physiological needs—air, water, food, shelter; then above that is the need for feelings of safety—the wish to be free from violence but also insecurity. For example, even the need for insurance would fall under the need for safety because that feels like protection from harm to one's body or property. Above physiological and safety needs is our need for love and belonging. Human beings are social creatures, and we crave love and community.

"Above physiological, safety, and love needs, we have our need for esteem—both self-esteem and esteem from others. For example, if you are a football player and achieve a touchdown, you may feel good about yourself, and the crowds may respect your achievement. The touchdown can do both things.

"Finally, the top of the pyramid is self-actualization, when a human being fulfills his potential. Maslow later revised the five and added more over the years, but today, we'll focus on the original paper."

The class wrote down the five.

"The four bottom levels of the pyramid—physiological, safety, love, and esteem—are called 'deficiency needs,' because when we feel deprived of them, we need them even more. Say you're freezing cold: Your need for warmth only increases. You are motivated to find a sweater, a bowl of soup, or better heaters."

The students wrote down Dr. Wilson's examples.

"The fifth stage of self-actualization is called a 'being need,' because it's a need to be a fully developed person. After one's basic needs are being met, and, of course, there are fluctuations and a wish to maintain these levels, a person will wish to seek her fullest expression of who she is."

She looked out to the assembled students. "In the paper, how does Maslow define 'self-actualization'?"

A young woman in the front row, wavy brown hair and large earrings, raised her hand and read from Maslow's paper:

" 'Even if all these needs are satisfied, we may still often (if not always) expect that a new discontent and restlessness will soon develop, unless the individual is doing what he is fitted for. A musician must make music, an artist must paint, a poet must write, if he is to be ultimately happy. What a man *can* be, he *must* be. This need we may call self-actualization.' "

"Thank you, Priscilla," Professor Wilson said, then continued.

"Now, what's interesting is that if your needs for self-fulfillment and growth are being met, you may have motivation to keep growing. As you grow toward your full self, you'll keep expanding your human capacity.

"Maslow argued that a human being could wish to seek her maximum potential. However, it would be difficult to seek self-actualization if your basic needs, such as housing, warmth, food, love, and esteem, are not met. Although there are counterexamples, of course. One can be a prisoner who writes beautiful music, so he has little public esteem, but he is still growing in his human potential, so it is important not to think of it only as a sequence. There are many people who may never seek to become self-actualized."

Bo took notes and thought of his family and how they had gone backward to meeting their most basic needs, but their motivation to rise had not yet flagged.

When Bo didn't get into Yonsei on his first try, he broke up with his girlfriend Ara, who had been accepted to SKKU, her first-choice school. She'd insisted on being with him, but he broke it off, saying that she'd be better off without him. He hadn't wanted her pity.

Now it occurred to him that in terms of Maslow's theories, he might have valued self-esteem even more than love. He had lacked self-esteem, and, feeling ashamed, he hadn't thought he deserved a girl like her. His need for esteem might have distorted what was in plain sight. Ara had been kind, smart, and lovely. By now, she'd be finishing up SKKU, and he'd only just started school again.

Remembering her didn't make him feel worse, and he didn't want to go out with her again; he liked knowing that he could try to figure out things like Maslow's hierarchy. If anything, he wished he could ask Professor Wilson about Ara and his three tries, but he couldn't imagine having so much nerve.

After each class, he felt a bit of darkness lifting away from him, even though he hadn't realized it had been there, and he felt lighter inside.

As he walked out of the class, Professor Wilson called out to him.

"Bo, you haven't been to office hours lately. Why is that?" she asked.

"I'm sorry. Is that a requirement? I thought it was for extra help."

"It's not required, but almost everyone in this class comes now and then, and you should, too. Mr. Gonzalez called me."

Bo didn't know what to say.

"You're not in trouble. He just said that you had questions about psychology and studying it possibly at UCLA, and I'd be glad to talk to you about it. Just stop by sometime." She picked up her book bag, and they walked out of the classroom toward the quad.

"Can you want esteem more than love?" Bo surprised himself by asking her. It felt safer to ask in private.

"Of course. Maslow argued that it wasn't a matter of consecutive stages, and it wasn't a kind of rule that one must have achieved or acquired love before getting esteem."

"Is that a life worth having?" Bo asked. "A life with esteem but no love?"

Professor Wilson smiled.

"Well, personally, I don't think so, but I suppose one can protest and reason that he doesn't need love, perhaps, at that time in his life? I doubt it, though, don't you?"

Bo nodded, still thinking of Ara.

"I'd rather have love than esteem, but I can't imagine not seeking self-actualization," she said. "There are so many kinds of love, too. I value the love of my family of origin, friends, as well as my husband and children. Human beings need love, I think."

Priscilla, the student from class, caught up with them in the quad.

"Professor Wilson, I have so many questions."

Wilson smiled. "Yes, Priscilla. Do you know Bo?"

"Hey," she said to Bo with a passing glance, then turned to the professor, her enormous silver hoops skimming her shoulders.

"Maybe I'm meant to be an actor, which I think is self-actualization," the pretty freshman said, "but how about if I never get a role and die?"

Wilson looked perplexed.

"Why so grim? Were the other needs met? Why acting? Not enough details here. But regardless of the outcome—I think in your case, you think it's getting a role—what we need to value is your pursuit of growth as an actor and, more importantly, as a human. It's the outcome orientation that I question."

As Professor Wilson fielded Priscilla's follow-up questions, Bo looked around the quad where they stood. Asbestos was being removed from the library, and the school had set up a massive tent for a temporary library. The low-slung buildings appeared serviceable and modest. The Fullerton campus had none of the grandeur of Yonsei's neo-Gothic edifices or the stunning architecture and beautifully landscaped greenery of UCLA, and again, Bo had to remind himself to care less about esteem and prestige. He was at Fullerton now, and so far, what he was learning from his classes and instructors was transforming everything inside of him, he thought for the better.

Was it again his vain wish for esteem that made him compare the campuses? Weren't the schools entirely different in their histories and purposes? More than anything, Yonsei didn't want him, and here, his professor had even asked him to come by to speak with her because she was interested in him. Wasn't it good for a school to be getting rid of asbestos? Perhaps a better library would be built later.

On his first day, someone had told him that the film director James Cameron had gone to Fullerton College, and he had made *Titanic*, a film Bo had watched twice. Again he wondered, What did it matter if a legendary filmmaker had walked along the same quad, or if he never had? It didn't matter, or it shouldn't.

What mattered was that Bo was here now, and he wanted to learn more in his classes rather than just preparing to get into UCLA, the next step in his education. He had learned all this from reading a twenty-six-page paper a person had written over fifty years ago.

"I think Maslow would argue that the pursuit of being an actor has great value in self-actualization. The process matters, I think," Bo said to Priscilla, and Professor Wilson agreed.

Bo checked his watch and excused himself to get to the airport.

❧

Although the new apartment was larger than their first, it still felt crowded. They were saving to buy a two-family town house, but it seemed almost impossible to gather a down payment. Bo made about $40,000 from his driving and tutoring. Fullerton tuition was less than $1,000 for the year because he was in-state. Sometimes his textbooks were more expensive than his classes, because Bo preferred to buy them, and Lion said he must. Reading and annotating the actual text itself, Lion said, was far superior to simply reading a library book.

Since Bo was sponsoring his parents' residency, he had to show a sufficient income, but lately Mido had been earning more as an administrative assistant and tutor. He couldn't qualify for a mortgage yet.

The plan was for him to graduate and get a higher-paying job; then they could get a mortgage in his name. For a while, the family savings account was building steadily, but during the summer, Helen had a persistent stomach virus, and she missed two weeks of work. The medical bills were paid in cash, wiping out a portion of their savings.

Sonya didn't know any of this when she arrived at her sister's house.

Bo put her bag in Mido's room and brought her a glass of cold barley tea. He showed her the clean towels his mother had left on the bed for her.

"If you'd like to wash up, the bathroom is over there," Bo said. He remembered the size of his aunt's palatial home in Apgujeong, and he wondered if she could be comfortable here.

"Where will Mido sleep?" she asked.

"She's sleeping in the living room. I used to sleep in the living room in our old place, but I have a lot of schoolwork, and she offered hers. We always knew Mido was the nice one." Bo smiled. "Is the room okay?"

"It's very nice," Sonya said, removing her jacket and laying it on the sofa.

Right away, she went to the kitchen. Rice was kept in the cupboard below the sink, and the refrigerator was filled with tofu and vegetables. Helen kept a clean and well-stocked kitchen.

"I'm going to fix dinner," Sonya said. She pulled out two $20 bills from her purse and handed them to Bo.

"Can you go to the store and get two whole chickens? Is that enough money?"

"I have money," he said.

She frowned at him, no differently than when he was a little boy. There was no need for her to remind him that she was his elder even though she was a guest, and it did not seem right that a guest should pay for groceries and cook dinner, especially on her first night visiting. Bo worried what his mother would say.

"Aunt, I think Umma is going to make dinner, or she'll bring something home."

"Be a good nephew and go to the store now. Your mother will be tired when she gets home. I've been sitting on a plane for a long time. Business class. It will be good for me to be useful. My sister has to rest and eat."

Bo went to the store.

Sonya put on the red apron hanging on a nail near the kitchen door and rolled up her sleeves. After soaking the rice, she began preparing the spinach.

2

Plans

With varying work and sleep schedules among five people, there was usually someone in the apartment. On Sunday afternoon, the Cho sisters finally got a few hours alone.

The women were seated in the living room. Perched on the corner of the new L-shaped sectional, recently bought for Sonya's visit, the older sister nursed a cup of Earl Grey, while the younger one sat cross-legged on the floor, hemming a new pair of khakis for her son.

Uncomfortable, Helen set aside her sewing work to stretch out her legs and touch her toes.

Sonya remarked, "You're still so flexible."

Helen smiled. Sitting up, she winced and rubbed her stomach.

"You didn't eat much. Are you hungry?" Sonya asked.

"No. I can't digest well at night. I had too much coffee this afternoon. I have to cut down. We drink Taster's in the morning, and I switched to Sanka for my second cup, but a nurse I know from church said all coffee has too much acid. Even decaf." Helen took up her sewing again.

"Drink barley tea," Sonya said.

"Is Mido's room okay?" Helen asked, rethreading the needle. She cut the gray thread from the spool with her teeth, then made a neat knot.

"Use scissors," Sonya said.

"Ah, there she is. My nagging older sister. Gosh, I missed you."

"You could lose your nice teeth," Sonya said. "You wouldn't be as pretty without teeth."

Helen smiled like a little child, exposing her straight teeth, feeling content to be with her big sister.

"Remember that room in Haebangchon after that time Father disappeared?" Sonya said.

Helen almost shivered at the recollection. A distant older cousin had rented a place for them in a shantytown at the bottom of Namsan.

"That wasn't even a room, was it? I don't know how we slept there. That horrible woman who owned it was so mean to Mother."

Sonya's chin dipped, breaking up her lovely profile and straight posture. Abruptly, she looked up and exhaled at the memory of the landlord who'd push their mother around and call them peasants. After the cousin paid the first month, he refused to help any more. They were late with the rent until their mother got the cleaning job at the bathhouse.

"She smelled like mildew."

"Right!" Sonya slapped her own thigh with recognition. "She wore that awful yellow sweater with the brown elbow patches. Ugh, I hated that room. And that man who rented the room next to ours. He was always trying to touch us."

Helen had tried to forget. There was a handsy neighbor who'd leave the outhouse door ajar, and if she or Sonya opened it by accident, he'd try to pull her in. Once, when he attempted this with Mother, she picked up a pebble and threw it at his head.

"If it wasn't for school and church, I think I would have died when we lived there," Helen said. There had been so many neighborhoods like that growing up, and it was a wonder that the three of them had survived at all.

After school and on weekends, the three children would go anywhere else because there was nothing and no one for them at home, and they learned quickly that if they were studying or doing odd jobs, strangers didn't bother them. They studied in the back pews of churches, in any empty classroom or auditorium, and Sonya and Helen would take their baby brother Kenny to the park along the river when the weather was warm enough and teach him whatever they were learning, and of course, whenever they could, they'd find part-time jobs. Helen and Kenny would give their earnings to Sonya, who'd hide the money from their parents, who would certainly squander it on cards or soju.

After Sonya was accepted to Ewha, she helped Helen get in, and a priest from St. Francis found a way to help Kenny go to Sydney. He swore never to let the soles of his feet touch Korean ground again.

"Mother shouldn't have drunk so much," Sonya said.

"Father, too," Helen said. She looked up at her sister, whose gaze was fixed on the empty space below the television stand on wheels.

"I miss them sometimes, though," Helen said. "They died so young, and you know they weren't all bad. Even that landlady could be nice. When she had extra cakes, she'd give us some. Remember?"

Sonya smiled. The nuns and priests had taught them never to forget a kindness, especially from an unkind person.

"I'm thinking of buying a business here," Sonya said.

"What?" Helen stuck her needle into the unfinished hem and looked at her sister. "Why? Why would you do that?"

"I think it might be a good idea for me to have something here."

"You don't have to work," Helen said. "I don't understand. Did the IMF hurt your husband's business? I thought the Chairman owned his buildings and land outright."

"They're fine. It's just that I have some dollars, and I thought I'd buy a business. Do something useful, and one day, maybe I can earn a living. The lawyer said that I can get a visa if I invest in a business and create jobs. I was thinking of something not too difficult. I mean, I can still work hard, but something manageable with regular hours. I think a business like Mrs. Chung's requires too much costly inventory. No restaurants. Too much work. Shrimp Castle has good hours, but it's very hard work." Sonya couldn't imagine the smell of oil on her clothes. In the apartment, even though Helen did the wash four or five times a week, it was impossible to escape the smell of frying oil from John's uniforms.

"I heard that car washes can make a lot of money. Or coin-operated laundry machines. Again, that's still a lot of people to manage. Maybe your kids can help me run it," Sonya said.

"Are you getting a divorce?" Helen studied her sister's calm expression. "Your sons live in Korea. I know they're grown men, but I never knew you wanted to live in Los Angeles. I don't understand."

"My sons are fine. They'll work at the company. They love their father. I still need to care for the Chairman—"

"Why would you?"

"He's getting messy."

"The Chairman?"

"No. My husband. He's always fooled around with hostesses, and he used to be more discreet. Respectful, I thought. I know he didn't want to marry me." Sonya shrugged. "I don't care anymore. Being here with you—that's what matters. I feel like there's so much to do. You need my help still."

Helen smiled. It was true. She needed her older sister, and it was hard to live like this. Every day she would think about how Sonya would have approached a person or a problem.

"But your sons? How about them?"

"If I leave Yong-gil without divorcing, I think they'll be okay. A few of my friends live abroad while their husbands live in Korea."

"Your sons have always wanted to work with their father."

"Yes, that's true, and they're genuinely interested in the business," she said, sounding a little sad. "If they took my side, they'd lose their positions. They have no interest in living in America anyway. Korea is the only place for them."

Helen felt a weight of sadness descend upon her. Her sister had raised two ideal heirs, trained to take over the Chairman's business, but it had cost her something greater than she could name.

"They're better off without me. I think they'll understand when they get older. It's just—" Sonya couldn't say the words to Helen, when it appeared as if she had everything. It seemed wrong to talk about humiliation and pride in front of her sister, who was working so hard to start again in a new country when she was fifty. What nagged at her inside was this feeling of wondering what it was all for. Though, of course, she had done good things. She had raised her siblings, cared for her husband, her sons, the Chairman, and even his late wife. Sonya had served the poor at her church and taken care of the women in her fellowship group for over two decades. She knew she hadn't wasted any of her time. But these recent visits from the hostesses—had there been four or five now? She couldn't remember how many exactly—exposed the fractured core of the life she'd crafted with such care.

And so she had drafted an escape plan: Go to Los Angeles to check on her sister. Helen's fiftieth birthday had been a good excuse. She had spoken to a lawyer, who had told her how to get an investment visa. She thought that her husband might help her with the money. She wasn't sure the Chairman would understand. He would feel betrayed.

In this small brick building in a California suburb, Sonya had felt hopeful and well for the first time in years. No one knew who she was here. She felt younger and more alive. Even at fifty-three.

"So you don't want to go back?"

"No." As soon as Sonya said this, she realized that it was true. She could not go back to the way things were. The idea of running that house again while being so disrespected by her husband felt impossible. Of course, her husband knew her feelings. He cared, but not enough to change. She would miss her sons terribly and the Chairman, too.

"If I go back to Seoul, I feel like I'll die," Sonya said. She got up and went to Mido's room, returning with her carry-on bag. She laid it on the coffee table, opened the hidden bottom of the trunk, and lifted the silk scarves hiding the stacks and stacks of $100 bills she'd taken from her husband's safe without his knowing. "I need to speak to a lawyer and deposit this money into a bank account."

❧

At four o'clock, Shrimp Castle was almost empty of customers. John was in the kitchen preparing fish fillets for the next day when Nari said there was a call for him from his second son. John wiped his hands on his apron and rushed to the counter, worried that something bad might have happened.

"Dad?"

"DH, are you all right?"

"I'm good, Dad. I wanted to let you know that I'm thinking about applying to law school. I got a good LSAT score, and my advisor thinks it's not a bad idea."

"Oh, that's nice, right?" John felt proud and hopeful suddenly. It was as if he were a young man again and applying to law school himself. "When I was a boy, I thought about becoming a prosecutor, but I knew I couldn't get into the law program at SNU. I stuck to math because, well, I'm very good at it." John wiped his hands on his apron and looked down at his black rubber kitchen clogs. The only time he used math now was when he divided the fish into uniform pieces or weights. "I think it would be wonderful for you to study law. So proud of you," he said, but something struck him. "Your voice. You don't sound happy."

"That's why I called, Dad. I'm worried about the cost. I can take out loans if I get in. I heard they're easy for law students."

"Don't worry about money. We have money. You study. I'll work as many hours as I need if that means that you kids can—" John exhaled and sat down on the stool by the cash register. In the back of the restaurant, Nari was folding paper takeout boxes while watching a drama on the VCR television set anchored to the ceiling. He felt a swell of relief at knowing that DH was embarking on a far different path from the one he'd somehow taken.

"Where will you apply?"

"All the top ones and a few safeties. If I don't get in, I'll look for jobs in California."

"Did you tell Mommy?"

"I wanted to ask you first. I know she's going to say the same thing. I just felt bad because I've spent the most. I can't ask the foundation for any more money. Dr. Song said it was only through undergrad. I still don't know how to even thank whoever paid for Andover and Yale. You and Mom still paid tens of thousands of dollars, and Bo is putting himself through school and sponsoring you guys. Mido is pulling a paycheck. I should do more. I don't know how I became the student in the family. I'm the dummy." DH laughed.

"No child of mine is a dummy," John said. "You call Mommy and tell her that I told you not to worry about graduate school. If you want to study, we will find the money. Okay, DH?"

DH exhaled. "I'll start on the essays, then. These applications are really long."

"How much do the applications cost? Tell us and we'll send you the money right away," John said.

After they got off the phone, John felt lighter. He went into the kitchen and counted the number of fillets he had left to prepare. The kitchen felt brighter and cleaner than he remembered. Even the smell of oil had lifted somehow.

Buoyant, John hadn't realized how much he needed something good to happen, to remind him of a time when the future seemed unrestricted by limits and unfairness. Things had been so up and down that he had started to believe that nothing truly good would happen to them anymore.

Money—something they had once rarely discussed at home—had been present in every decision ever since he was fired from HRI, and even though he and Helen worked all the time, they could not seem to return to how things had been. There had been nicer neighborhoods, excellent public schools with fine teachers and facilities, and special occasions when they could eat at a restaurant without looking at the price per item.

It wasn't as if DH had been accepted to law school or become a prosecutor. John had no idea if being a lawyer was easy or hard in America. What mattered now was that his children, even his middle son who had preferred sports to school, wanted to keep climbing the steep hills, so he couldn't give up. John would carry them as far as his body let him.

❧

When the last student was picked up, Mido started cleaning up her classroom. Peter's students were older and tidier, so all he had to do was turn out the lights, and he came to help. While she collected the test materials and the geometry diagrams, Peter straightened the rows of desks, then started on the blackboard.

"Have you heard from DH?" Mido asked. Her brother and Peter spoke regularly. Peter didn't seem to pay attention to the cost of long-distance calls. "I miss him."

"I spoke to him last night, as a matter of fact."

"And?"

"He's applying to law schools now. He did really well on the LSATs. That's our boy."

"What? I can't believe he didn't tell me."

"I found out last night. He didn't want anyone to know until he got his scores back. He said the logic section gave him a bit of trouble, but he'd practiced on a bunch of old tests," Peter said.

"Yeah, that logic section is weird. I don't understand how that's related to law."

"I could never be a lawyer," Peter said. "Sounds dreadful."

"Tek will be a lawyer soon. At USyd, it's a five-year law program. It's not like going to law school for three years after college in the States. There are some requirements, but basically you become a solicitor when you graduate. But he wants to become a barrister. You know, the lawyers who argue in court? It's like being a litigator in America. Becoming a barrister takes more time than being a solicitor."

"Your boyfriend wants to get paid to argue. In court," Peter said, grunting dismissively.

"Tek's always been a good debater." Mido felt obliged to defend him. "And he's good at arguing. Not with me. I mean, he doesn't argue with me."

"I wouldn't argue with you, either," Peter said with a smile.

Mido picked up her jacket and tote bag to head out.

"You want to get food?" he asked her.

"I should get home. I think my aunt is making dinner."

"Is she a good cook?"

"Yes."

"I'd love to have a home-cooked meal."

"You aren't really Korean, are you?" Mido laughed, admiring how he just said what he wanted.

"Koreans can be straightforward, too, you know. Don't make generalizations," he said.

❧

John, Helen, and Sonya had already eaten, but there was plenty of food left over for Bo, Mido, and Peter. Everyone was happy to see Peter, who served as a kind of stand-in for DH. Peter ate two servings of everything, delighting Sonya, and when he left for his place, the apartment felt quieter.

"If I keep working at the hagwon, I can help DH with his law school tuition," Bo said.

"Aren't you going to apply to transfer to UCLA?" Mido asked him.

"Yes," Bo said. "The Fullerton counselor said I should. I think I'm going to major in psychology."

Sonya clapped. "My nephews will be a prosecutor and a psychologist. Wonderful. So wonderful," she said.

"I think you should start school, too, Mido. Maybe take a few classes at Long Beach or Fullerton, then you can make some progress with your education," Helen said.

John nodded. "Your mom and I will keep working, and we'll help with the tuition. DH said he can take out some student loans."

"I'm going to keep working," Mido said. "With all the private tutoring I'm doing, I'll make almost $70,000 in a year. I can help us buy a house. It makes sense for me to do this, and I really like the kids," she said. "When my brothers are done, they can help with the house, too. I almost don't see why I have to get a degree."

"You have to go to college," Helen protested.

"Your mother is right. You have to go to school, too," John said. "You like school," he said quietly.

Mido spoke to her parents directly. "I'm already teaching students. Here I don't need a degree. I make more than an elementary school teacher in the district."

John looked at his daughter with concern.

Bo jumped in. "*Waaah,* will the family baby send me to school? I don't know if I should be embarrassed or proud."

"Maybe later you can send me. After you and DH are done and we own a house," Mido said firmly.

John and Helen shook their heads, not quite believing what their youngest was saying. Regardless, for a moment, they felt happy, wanting to feel like this decision to come to California had been a good one, and it occurred to Sonya that her sister's family had much more than most.

3

Election

During the offertory, ushers in black suits with white carnations pinned to their lapels passed brass collection plates. Backs straight and alert like soldiers, in lockstep, they waited at the end of each pew before moving on to the next row. Parishioners gave them their envelopes and nodded respectfully in the direction of the ushers.

The Cho sisters were sitting in the balcony. To Helen's left, John was listening to the magnificent baritone solo. Bo and Mido sat in the pew behind them.

Helen felt a nudge from her right and turned to see her sister's dark eyes widening with anger.

"Look." Sonya pointed to the last page of the church bulletin, whispering: "Isn't Shin Taehun your husband's friend? I mean, the man who—" Like a pretty meerkat, she swiveled her slender neck to check if anyone was listening.

"Also, Jung Danbi? She's also nominated? Is he divorced now?"

"Later." Helen mouthed the two syllables in Korean, her chin firm and resolute.

Helen never read the back of the church bulletin, so if her sister hadn't pointed out that Shin and Danbi had been nominated as church deacons, she wouldn't have noticed it. John had been nominated as an elder, and Elder Fred Byun, another SNU alum and a venerated member of the church, had assured John that he had everyone's support. Gospel Presbyterian had no lack of men who wanted to lead; however, what they didn't have enough of, Elder Byun said, was those who wished to serve the Lord humbly.

Elder Fred Byun, the bright middle son of a soybean farmer, came to America in 1966 as a young engineer. Bored of his job at a pharmaceutical company, he founded Taegeuk Bank with his friends and became a fabled first-generation immigrant success. The bank set in the middle of Garden Grove mall was central to the lives of many Koreans in Orange County.

Every Friday, Elder Byun treated himself to the number two fish sandwich special at Shrimp Castle, which came with a side of fries and a can of 7UP. In no time, the chatty bank president had walked up to the kitchen and introduced himself to the new fry cook, John Koh, whose quiet manner and good work reminded him of his father.

Last Christmas, Elder Byun had invited John to the church men's group when they cooked meals for the homeless. John came, worked the food line, then washed the heavy pots without having to be asked. Not long after, Elder Byun brought Elder George Hong, the real estate developer who was married to his niece, to Shrimp Castle for a late lunch. The two powerful elders who controlled the wealthy church's Finance Committee and the multimillion-dollar building fund pulled John out of the kitchen to sit with them to discuss church business.

Both Fred and George were impressed by John's background, his humble acceptance of his downward career trajectory, and his plainspoken honesty. John's competence was self-evident, and having been a very wealthy man for most of his adult life, Fred Byun could spot a man who knew how to serve without being servile. Fred and George decided to make John a member of the Finance Committee.

Every year, there were far more nominations than seats for deacons and elders; however, John was already in. When Fred Byun told John this, John didn't understand how it worked. He told Fred Byun, "I'm honored to have been considered. If I cannot become an elder, I'm fine. Please give the seat to someone else. I trust the Lord will choose wisely," and, of course, Fred and George had laughed at how correct they had been to tap a fair man without political ambition.

In America, John had retreated, hoping no one would notice him. John wanted to be left alone. Each day he went to work with Nari, and on Sunday morning, he put on his coat and tie to attend morning services. When he had any time to himself, he read history books in English, and now and then he watched musical variety shows on Korean television. He liked trot music.

At church, the Koh family kept to themselves. They learned of any important church updates during announcements or later from Lion and Yun. Mrs. Chung, Helen's employer, also an elder, would often share gossip or news at the Emporium.

After services ended, Sonya linked arms with her sister and insisted on having lunch at church.

"I want you to tell me everything. I need to know who is in charge here. How in the world could those terrible people become deacons? It must be prevented," Sonya said quietly, all the while smiling at every parishioner who greeted the exquisite newcomer with the South Sea pearl necklace and enormous diamond solitaire. She wore an ivory summer tweed skirt suit with tan sandals and carried a French leather handbag in a similar color.

"You really want to eat here?" Helen asked. "I mean, the food is fine, but—"

"It's your birthday dinner tonight, so we'll eat light. I just want to understand how you live. Big sister needs to know. I need to see everything."

Helen gathered her family to explain that they'd stay for lunch, for the first time in months. Ever since they had run into Shin and Danbi, Helen and John had done whatever they could to avoid them, even if it meant bolting out of the sanctuary. Bo and Mido followed their parents and aunt toward the Patio.

Their church in Seoul had one large main building and an annex, but Gospel Presbyterian was more like a school campus, with standalone buildings for classrooms, gymnasiums, a theater, and a dining hall. It was expanding still and had raised over $6 million for a state-of-the-art worship and education center. Beneath a wooden portico covered in vines, a large window on the first floor of the old church building opened out to connect the church kitchen with the outdoor cafeteria, which was called the Patio. Any parishioner could buy a meal for a nominal fee, and children ate for free. A rotation of volunteers signed up to cook and serve meals. Dozens of picnic tables were set up in neat rows, half of them shaded from the bright midday sunlight. The second morning service had just ended, and many parishioners had already eaten, while others were just starting to line up.

At the Patio, Mrs. Chung spotted Helen and waved her over. She was sitting with her friend Mrs. Kwon, also an elder, and her son Marcus.

Helen introduced her sister.

"You also went to Ewha," Mrs. Chung said. "Mrs. Kwon went to Ewha as well."

The four alumnae smiled and bowed to each other. They were connected, having shared three different eras at a school—six thousand miles away—founded by a White American Methodist woman. Mrs. Chung was the eldest, but Mrs. Kwon was not far behind.

"We have room here," Mrs. Chung said kindly. "Please sit down."

John pushed two picnic tables together and then joined Mido and Bo in the line for food, while Helen and Sonya remained at the table.

Gospel Presbyterian Church was immense. There were over eleven thousand registered members and three services held each Sunday, not including the English service. Mrs. Chung introduced Elder Kwon's son Marcus Yim as a world-famous doctor who lived in Newport Beach in a mansion by the bay. Marcus was a pleasant-looking man in his late thirties with short, cropped hair and round eyeglasses.

Sonya was accustomed to people trying to impress her, and she knew how to react appropriately without being rude or false.

"How wonderful that your busy son attends church with you," Sonya said.

"He wants me to retire," Mrs. Kwon said, looking annoyed and proud at the same time. "My Marcus and his wife attend another church in Newport Beach, but he comes by once a month to nag me."

"Umma," Marcus said gently, and she smiled at him as she led him in the social dance of a mother's pride.

John, Mido, and Bo returned with five metal cafeteria trays of food and sat alongside Sonya and Helen. Rice, soup, bulgogi, spinach, and radish kimchi.

"Why do you want to retire?" Mrs. Chung asked. "I'll never retire. My grandchildren are all grown up now, and I never see them anyway."

Mrs. Kwon replied, "I don't want to retire. Maybe I should just cut down my hours." She glanced at her son, who looked reprovingly at her.

"Your business is going so well anyway. You have twenty girls now, or thirty?" Mrs. Chung added.

"What kind of business do you have?" Sonya asked.

"A nail salon. It's in Buena Park, near Zion Market. I have twenty-two employees."

"I'd love to stop by during my visit," Sonya said, and all the women turned to admire her pale-pink-manicured hands. "We should go. Hejin, I'll treat you. It's your birthday. Is it open now?" Sonya asked.

Mrs. Kwon looked a bit embarrassed. "Well, I should really close, but some customers prefer to go on Sundays, so yes, it is open, but only until eight p.m."

"Will you be there later?" Sonya asked.

Mrs. Kwon shook her head no. "Tomorrow. I work six days a week. Please come on Monday: It's the Rose Salon. If you can only come today, then I will call the store. You will be my guests, and happy birthday," she said to Helen.

Marcus smiled and patted his petite mother's rounded shoulders.

"My mother must like you, and you must be nice people," he said to Sonya and Helen. "I've seen many patients, but my mother is far better at diagnosing people than I am. I've never known anyone like her. My brothers and I joke that she is a personality radiologist," Marcus said, beaming. "We think that's why she's been so good at business and was able to send all of us to medical school."

John followed Marcus's sudden upturned gaze. A person shaded their view.

Shin appeared before them, his arms hanging by his side, palms open.

"I haven't seen you in a while," Shin said to John, who stayed silent. He could feel Marcus watching them.

"Are you going to the congregation meeting next week?" Shin asked. "I've been nominated to be a deacon," he said. "I saw that you're nominated to be an elder. The Lord is discerning."

John wondered where this new piety came from. Shin had never been religious. He had gone to Mass with Mary and the boys when they were in New Jersey but never in Seoul. John felt that he was in no position to question any man's faith, but Shin's talking about God seemed uncharacteristic.

Marcus nodded at Shin, and Shin bowed to him.

"You're one of Mrs. Kwon's famous doctor sons, isn't that right?" Shin said.

John touched his brow. He couldn't understand how Shin knew all these people when he'd arrived only a little over a year ago.

Helen turned her back to face Sonya, who stared hard at Shin, astonished by his shamelessness. A young woman approached the two joined tables.

"Hello, Dr. Yim, nice to see you again. You were in front of me on the lunch line. Last month, I think." Danbi laughed when he did not seem to recall, then bowed to everyone at the table. Everyone nodded in greeting except for Helen and Sonya. John stared over Helen's head in the direction of the cafeteria window as if he weren't sitting there at all.

Shin and Danbi tried to make conversation with Marcus and Mrs. Kwon, but Marcus, having noticed how quiet John and Helen had become, grew quieter himself.

Shin tried to leave the table, but Danbi asked for a minute.

"Dr. Yim," she said.

"Yes," Marcus replied.

"My cousin, Elder Frank Lim, mentioned you," Danbi said. "You have a practice in Irvine, don't you? I've been meaning to get my husband to see you, but your schedule is always full."

All Helen could think of was Mary and their three sons. Were Shin and Danbi married now? Shin didn't wear a wedding ring, but Danbi wore a large diamond engagement ring and a diamond wedding band.

"I know men should have their prostate checked at my husband's age," Danbi said.

"You should call the office again and tell them that you go to my mother's church."

"I already did," Danbi said, touching her collarbone with her right hand as if to draw his gaze toward the swell of her bosom beneath her yellow silk dress.

Like watching a magic trick, Helen noticed that Marcus's eyes tracked her right wrist, resting on her breasts.

"Is there another number?" she asked, opening her pink mouth slightly.

"I don't have a card on me," Marcus answered. "What is your husband's name?"

"Shin Taehun," Danbi said, now touching the milky exposed skin below her collarbone.

His eyes followed her hand as if she were training him like a dog, holding up a biscuit in the air. Danbi smiled.

"I'll call your office and mention our meeting today. Will you remember me?" she asked.

Marcus tried to look serious, unable to keep his pale face from coloring.

Mrs. Kwon pulled at her son's elbow, forcing him to face her and end the conversation with Danbi.

"We have to get our food," Danbi said, then turned to Shin. "Maybe you can get ours. Is there room here for us?" Nobody knew how to respond.

Sonya rose from the table and approached Danbi.

"Excuse us. I'll only be a minute," she said, taking Danbi's left arm gently and guiding her toward the shaded area on the other side of the Patio.

❧

As they walked away, Marcus turned to his mother, surprised. Heesung Kwon got along with everyone. She was the sort of person who would've asked him to make room, but she had said nothing.

With Danbi and Shin out of earshot, Mrs. Kwon said to the table, "Those people are snakes. You must avoid them and their family."

"Mother," Marcus said. "Why do you say that?"

"That woman is dangerous, and her uncle was a loan shark in Namdaemun Market. Her cousin Frank is honest, but even he said there is something off about her. We can feel charity for our fellow Christians, but we must never be stupid about assessing character. 'Be as shrewd as snakes and as innocent as doves.' "

"Amen," Mrs. Chung said.

Marcus looked puzzled. "She only wanted me to see her husband for a checkup. Men have to get their prostates checked. Also, is it fair to blame her for her uncle?"

"There are other doctors. You can't see him," Mrs. Kwon said. "You can help other people, but not them. They're the kind who will do something terrible, then sue you. I know. I know from experience."

❧

On the AstroTurf-covered deck area, the two women stood out, Sonya in her ivory-colored suit and Danbi in yellow silk. Spotting an empty picnic table under the awning, Sonya asked Danbi to sit.

"This won't take long," Sonya said.

Danbi smiled politely. She didn't understand who this person was, but she'd been sitting next to important church members as well as the Koh family.

"I'm the sister-in-law of Koh Yohan. I've wondered about you," Sonya said quietly.

Danbi bowed her head and raised it quickly. She knew enough about battle not to show fear.

"Forgive me for being so direct, but I don't have much time. I don't live here. I live in Seoul and will not be here next weekend. I wanted to speak with you briefly."

Danbi stared at the woman's beautiful face. She was striking in every way, elegant in an almost otherworldly sense—her skin, hair, nails, and exquisite suit. Even her handbag was worth thousands of dollars and impossible to buy.

"If I had known what you were planning to do to my sister's husband, I would have made sure that you reconsidered. Sadly, I learned too late." Sonya sighed. "I don't know what motivates a person like you to cause such great harm; however, I know this. You do not wish my family well. My sister's husband is my family. He is my dear brother. What you don't know about me is that I am a relentless woman, severe, harsh, and unforgiving. This is my worst quality as a Christian. I have difficulty with forgiveness. I will continue to pray about it.

"It's my understanding that my brother and sister want to be left alone by you and your—" Sonya hesitated before saying, "Shin Taehun."

"I don't understand your meaning," Danbi said, putting her hands on the table to get up. "I should go."

"Wait. You think I'm just another woman who is angry or protective. No. That would be a mistake. I'm not threatening you. There's no need for that. I am telling you never to speak to my sister or brother-in-law again. Never." Sonya smiled kindly.

Danbi touched her throat reflexively as if she were guarding herself. She checked her surroundings; everyone at John's table was looking in her direction.

"You're moving your hand toward your chest. It's the reflexive behavior of a novice seducer to think every person would fall for this. A habit is sometimes a lazy thing, which one must address. I don't care about your tits. I'm not some stupid man who thinks only with his dick. I'll never believe that you—you of all people—are a damsel in distress. Women are not fooled.

"I'm telling you that you will regret it if you do not stay away from my family. I know who you are. I know who your cousin is, and where your mother lives. I know where you live. I will hold this grudge forever. Here is some wisdom: Let life tutor you. Learn quickly where danger lies. I am danger. Have a good day. I shall not keep you."

Sonya smoothed out her skirt and rose elegantly from the bench. She looked directly at Danbi to give her a moment to respond, and when she could not, Sonya smiled and returned to her family.

4
Presents

Sonya had rented a private oak-paneled room at a French restaurant in Newport Beach. When she guided Helen and John inside, the seven people waiting for them shouted, “Surprise!”

Helen covered her face with her hands.

“Mommy!” DH shouted, laughing. “Oh, don’t cry.” The tall college senior sprinted over to hug his astonished mother.

Bo laughed and said to Peter, “The favorite has arrived.”

Yun and Lion laughed for having kept the secret so well. Nari clapped her hands together like a happy child. It had been a long time since she’d been to such an elegant place, and it was her first time being invited to a surprise birthday party.

The long table was covered with white linen, and Sonya had requested pink dahlias and beeswax tapers in pewter candlesticks. An antique Provençal chandelier with jewel-colored glass apples, grapes, and pears hung from the center of the high beamed ceiling, diffusing red, green, and gold across the pale cloth and silver flatware. At the head of the table, a large cake covered in buttercream dahlias rested on a green majolica pedestal.

Sonya had told Helen that tonight was a dinner for the family at a nice restaurant she’d heard about from a friend back home who knew Orange County well. She’d kept DH’s arrival a secret.

“Yaah.” Helen tapped her son’s chest. “What are you doing here? You’re supposed to come home for Christmas. How did you get a ticket?” Helen asked, realizing the answer as soon as she asked the question. Her sister, of course. She cradled his lean brown face in her hands. “So thin.”

“We’re not even going to pretend that they care as much about us,” John joked to Bo and Mido. Bo turned to Peter. “Glad you could make it.”

Helen looked up, remembering herself, and wiped her face.

"Sit, sit," Helen said to everyone, and she took the seat between DH and Sonya.

"How did you get here?" she asked DH. "Are you missing school?"

"It's October break, and Aunt sent me a ticket. I'm going to stay at Peter's. I know the inn is crowded right now. I'll come visit every night, though. Aunt and I figured it all out. Pretty clever, huh?" DH embraced Helen again. "My mommy," he said happily, and because he was a head taller than she was, it was funny to hear him sound like a little boy.

More than his brother or sister, DH had always been affectionate like a small child, and in a way, because he was so open and caring, everyone loved him best.

DH stood up from his seat and greeted everyone. He hugged Mido and held on to her for a long time. "My shy baby sister. All grown up and pretty. Peter said you're a big earner now."

Mido hit his arm affectionately and glanced at Peter, who grinned, happy to be at the table with everyone.

John looked across the table at his wife. More than anything, Helen had wanted to have her whole family with her tonight. It was hard to believe they were together like this. This felt like their old life, the special meals, the relaxed joyfulness, and all of them safe. He had forgotten what it was like not to feel dread and worry about how they would get by. Helen looked light enough to float above them.

♣

After cake and presents, everyone headed back to Cypress, except for DH, who went to Irvine with Peter.

At the house, it was late, but DH wanted coffee, and Peter made a pot.

"If I drink that, I'll be high," Peter said. "You drink coffee, and I'll have a cigarette."

They sat on the deck by the pool.

"This place is really nice," DH said. "Has my family seen it?"

Peter shook his head.

"It's going to freak them out a little. I haven't told them about your situation."

"What situation?"

"You're loaded."

"Oh," Peter said. "I'm not loaded. My mother has money. It's not mine."

"I spoke with Tom Song. From Eagle Academy."

"Oh? Why?"

"I'm graduating, and I wanted to tell him thanks for the scholarship."

"You always had good manners, dude."

DH swallowed his black coffee. He had put a few ice cubes in it so it wouldn't be hot.

"This weather is sick."

"Right?" Peter said. "That's why I couldn't go back."

"Seriously?"

"Well, I guess I could have gone back. But I was too messed up after everything with that girl, I mean woman. She was thirty-four years old."

"Damn," DH said. "I always forget that part. She looked younger."

"Anyway, after Cesca dumped me by phone from Toronto, I felt like quitting school. Tom Song told my mother that Pomona would be better than not finishing my degree."

"Did you jump the gun? Like, if you had waited a year, would you have returned to Yale?" DH asked, thinking that his friend wouldn't have wanted to graduate later.

"I don't know. I just don't know what the point of this college degree is anyway. Pomona is nice. The classes are basically the same as Yale, but smaller. I mean, the work is fine. I don't really know anyone there. I just work all the time at Exodus, do my schoolwork, and play music with Lion."

"You didn't answer the question."

"Oh. No, I don't think I would have returned. I was in a pretty dark place, just stuck in my apartment, until you sent me to Bo and Lion. Once again, DH to the rescue." Peter raised his cigarette to him. DH raised his coffee mug.

"Happy to oblige. Listen, man."

"Hmm?"

"I learned something from Tom Song. In our call."

Peter turned. DH's face was lit by the deck lights. His mother was right, he had lost weight. Even his legs looked thinner.

"What's that?"

"Your mother has been paying for my tuition."

"Oh, that."

"You knew?"

"Yeah. She told me my senior year at Andover. Asked me if it was okay if she paid for Yale."

"I have to pay her back."

"Why?"

"It's weird. Don't you think?"

"No," Peter said. "She has more money than most people, and it makes her happy to give it to folks who work. If you didn't work so hard, she wouldn't give it to you. It's not charity, man. She said that it's the optimum allocation of resources for a better society. Something like that. You know Renee."

"Well, I'm going to pay her back."

"If you want. She'll probably say something like you can pay for some kid's school someday," Peter said, stubbing out the cigarette. "You mad at me?"

"No, of course not. I'm really grateful. Your family changed my life."

"Oh, man. You're always so grateful and nice," Peter said, looking a little disgusted. "This is why everyone likes you so damn much."

DH reached over to give him a side hug, and Peter shook his head and smiled.

"Does Mom know?" Peter asked.

"I'm going to write to her. I want you both to come to graduation. I looked up the dates, and our graduations are only a day apart in May. Not sure if we can pull it off, but I wanted to ask. If you wanted."

Peter went inside to get his guitar, then returned to the deck and started to play "Rosetta," a new song he'd been working on.

"You sound really good," DH said.

"Next week the Zekes are playing. I wish you could come," Peter said. "Lion will also be singing."

"I wish. I head out on Saturday night," DH said. "Haven't heard you in a while. My sister said Lion has a good voice."

"He's really good. It's too bad we can't get booked anywhere except for Rascals," Peter said. It wasn't as if he hadn't known that music would be an uphill climb, but he hadn't realized how hard it would be. "We should be touring, sleeping in a van, and playing anywhere that would have us, but the hagwon is taking off. Also, Lion doesn't want to tour. I'm in no rush."

"How do you like the work?" DH studied his friend's face. Peter's tiniest feelings and expressions fluttered across his large eyes, strong brow, and small mouth. If DH noticed everything, Peter showed everything without necessarily saying it. His friend's transparency was one of the things DH liked best about him. If asked, Peter always told the truth. "Is it fun?"

"I was going crazy just practicing the guitar all the time in the house. I don't want to work in an office or go to school anymore. I mean, I'll definitely graduate in May, but I don't care really. The tutoring suits me. I like the kids a lot. Lion's a good boss, and my hours are good. I get there at two or three and leave at eight. I'm free in the mornings to go running and do music. On weekend nights, we play gigs at Rascals. It's a pretty good life."

Peter's family in Korea was supposed to have a lot of money. DH didn't really know what they did, something about tires. Peter almost never spoke about them. His rich father had remarried and had another set of kids, and his mother was said to be even wealthier than his father's family.

"I tried just doing music and nothing else, and I couldn't handle it. When Cesca was gone, I didn't see the point of leaving the house. We were only together for a few months, but it was an intense thing. At least for me.

"I can see why half the musicians I've met do drugs or drink too much. I never liked drinking, and getting high makes me feel like dying," Peter said.

"Dying?"

"Yup. At Yale, when I was playing soccer, I didn't do drugs."

"I know."

"Well, after my injury, when I'd go to parties—"

"Without me—" DH was trying to look hurt.

"You were at travel games—"

"Ah, yes."

"Anyway, I got stoned a couple of times, and you know, depressives and pot. Not a good combination for me." Peter shrugged.

DH had never even smoked a cigarette. In the States, he'd been offered every kind of drink and drug, and always he passed. He'd joke, pointing to his athletic form—the powerful legs from years of soccer and his hundred daily squats and push-ups even in the offseason—"This is my temple," and most people left him alone.

"Is your sister still dating that Tek guy?" Peter asked suddenly.

"I don't know what's going on with him. She doesn't talk much. I still haven't met him." DH looked at Peter and his mouth made an O. "Hey, my little sister is off-limits."

"Innocent question." Peter laughed.

❧

The next day, on his way to school, Peter dropped DH off at Cypress. Mido was home alone, washing the breakfast dishes.

"What's going on with you and Peter?" he asked her.

"Nothing," Mido said lightly. "He's your best friend."

"You don't want to date Peter."

"I don't want to date Peter," Mido agreed. "I don't want to date anyone."

"How about Tek?"

Mido pursed her lips thoughtfully. She turned off the faucet and removed her yellow rubber gloves. Not knowing what to say, she switched the topic.

"How much are you borrowing for law school?" she asked. "I think Mom and Dad are trying to figure out a budget."

"They can't swing it. They don't even have a second car. I'll be borrowing the maximum, but it's going to be tight. And I still have to get in, right? I just sent off one of the applications. I have six more to do."

"I read that your first-year law school grades are really important."

"Yup, and my summer internships are make or break," DH said. "Unlike you and Bo, I have to study to do well. I can't just waltz into an exam and get a good grade. Your dumb brother has to make a serious effort. It's like training for a sport."

"You've never been dumb. You're doing the best of the three of us. Of the five of us." Mido smiled. "I'm really glad you're applying to law school. It's the only thing that makes Dad smile lately."

"He's not doing well, is he?"

"No."

None of them knew what to do about John.

He'd always been quiet with a steady inner optimism about him. But in the past few years, he had transformed into an almost silent person, often with a blank, private expression, a husk of the man who'd been their father. Each morning John got up and went to Shrimp Castle, and when he returned home, he bathed, put his uniform in the wash, read something, then went to bed.

Even after they got their green cards last month, he didn't look for work anywhere else. He made $1,250 a week, and Nari had given him a $10,000 cash bonus at the end of the year. As a fifty-two-year-old immigrant with a college degree that didn't matter here, John was making more than he could wearing a suit.

For DH, who had not lived with his family since high school, his father's transformation had been far more dramatic. Of course, his father had been pleased to see him, but there was something wrong now, and DH wished he could bring his old father back.

"He didn't want me to come by Shrimp Castle."

"I think he's embarrassed," Mido said. "But you going to law school makes him happy. So thank you," she said. "No pressure, though."

DH shook his head, wanting to cry. When he'd been studying for the LSAT, he'd thought about how much his parents were going through after losing their jobs in Sydney. Thinking of them had made taking dozens of practice tests bearable.

"You and Bo have been working really hard," he said.

"Bo's going to apply to UCLA in a year. He's getting really good grades at Fullerton. And after he graduates from UCLA, I know he's going to get a good job."

"I just need three years, Mido, then I'll start making real money," DH said. This was the plan that he and Bo had drafted. The two Koh brothers would do whatever they could to help get their parents settled and send Mido to school.

"I can pick up more hours at the hagwon. Once Bo goes to UCLA he'll need to reduce his Exodus hours so he can study—soon I'll make more than him. I'm going to send you an allowance when you're in law school. By the time you both graduate, maybe you'll make as much as me," she added.

DH looked at her carefully. He could tell she was serious, and he felt awful thinking that Mido would have to wait that long, and she punched his arm lightly as if she'd read his mind.

"I'm not just doing this for you. There's no need to feel guilty. Lion says I'm the Michael Jordan of verbal SAT tutoring."

"Michael Jordan finished his college degree," DH retorted. "You're the kid sister. We should be taking care of you."

"I'm finally good at something," Mido said, and until she said this part out loud, it had not occurred to her that she had felt this lack. "I'm learning all this on my own. I read the study guides, took the practice exams, and figured it out. The books were in the library or at the hagwon. I learned how to make money from books."

"Mido, are you sure about this?"

"Of course."

"Listen, if you can spot me while I finish school, we can take turns."

Mido patted his shoulder the way Helen used to, and DH closed his eyes.

DH opened his eyes and shook his head, remembering another part of Mido's life.

"What are you going to do about Tek?"

"He wants me to go to Sydney, but I can't. It makes more sense for me to stay here with Mom and Dad."

DH wondered what Tek was like. She didn't seem too upset that she couldn't go back to Sydney. Whenever DH asked about him, Mido would only say that he was nice to her. Everyone in the family was curious about why Mido didn't insist on being with Tek, but it had always been Mido's way not to say much about what she wanted. He'd never expected her to insist on skipping college.

On Saturday, Bo drove Sonya and DH to the airport. The apartment felt emptier without them, but their visit had left an impact: It was as if their presence had reminded everyone to pay attention to their goals, and that they had a mission.

❧

Shortly before Christmas, Yun and Lion asked Mido and Peter to lunch at a Greek restaurant on Orange Avenue. The cheery hostess grabbed four menus and led them to a booth in the back. Lion waved at the owner's wife, whom he'd gone to middle school with. Yun smiled, used to everyone in the neighborhood saying hello to her gregarious husband.

Before they'd even ordered, bowls of lemon chicken soup appeared with baskets of warm flatbread.

"It's always good to eat with you, boss," Peter said. He picked up his spoon, then paused, noticing Lion and Yun bow their heads in prayer. He could never get used to them doing this. Mido didn't when she ate with him, but with Yun and Lion, she also bowed her head to pray silently.

When everyone lifted their heads and opened their eyes, Peter swallowed a spoonful of soup.

Lion announced, "I'm thinking of expanding Exodus and opening another hagwon just for high school kids. In Irvine."

Peter reached for the bread. "Cool. Closer to me."

Mido glanced at Yun, who'd mentioned that the waiting list kept growing, and wondered why they couldn't find a much bigger space in Cypress. Yun had not mentioned Irvine, which was farther away and more expensive.

"I'd like you two to manage it," Lion continued. "I've found the space already, but I need people I trust to manage the business. Mido, you're getting so good at the financials, scheduling, and the general operations, and Peter, you could manage the curriculum. I thought I could start with four teachers, not including you, of course," Lion said, studying Mido's face more carefully than Peter's. She needed the money more than Peter did, but it would require greater changes to her life.

Peter asked, "How many more hours, you think?"

"You'd have to pick Mido up and drive her there and back on the days Bo isn't working. He has to cut down his hours in the fall," Yun said. "I know you're still in your senior year, and I'm not sure of your plans after graduation, but this would be a full-time job, Peter. You'd be working twenty-five to thirty hours there for now as we build out, but it would ultimately be forty to fifty hours. You'd get two days off. I think once we get the place up and running, we could hire another manager to help."

Peter turned to Mido. "What do you think?"

Mido gave him a thumbs-up.

"What about school?" she asked Peter, feeling bad about all the driving. The family still had only one car, and Bo had priority because of school. They were saving for a second car, which would require another parking spot, insurance, and more for gas. Nari still drove John and Helen to Garden Grove, and they'd been able to get by with one. "Can you work so many hours and still graduate? You'd be living on the 405."

"I like driving. Also, I have enough credits to graduate today, probably. I could take two classes on the days I have off. I'll figure it out," he said. "I'll get my degree in May. All good."

Lion pulled out a legal pad from his bag and started writing down some of the things they could do right away. The new hagwon would be called Fortress, he said.

5

Ginny

February 2000

At church, everyone called him the Oracle of Orange County because he was so smart.

When they were still in primary school, Dr. Carl Han, Lion's father, a physics professor at Chapman University, had all three of his children take an IQ test. The results bothered Ray, the eldest, because his was higher than average but much lower than that of Lion—the youngest child. Ray wouldn't disclose his score, but he didn't mind bragging that his younger brother's IQ was 159. All three Han children qualified for Mensa, but none of them joined because their father wanted them to do it—their first collective protest.

Neither Ray nor his sister Sarah spoke Korean, and they were called "bananas" for being white on the inside when they joined Korean social clubs at school. Lion taught himself Korean and could read newspapers and business magazines.

When he skipped three grades in primary school, Korean newspapers wrote about him and his family. The news coverage gave Lion the reputation of being a genius. When he was a little child, grown-ups would ask him tough questions and give him logic problems. Ever helpful, he did them. High school students would try to get him to do their math and science homework when he was nine or ten, and he would teach them how because he was opposed to cheating.

Lion met his wife when she played keyboard for the praise band during English ministry.

"Why did you ask me out?" Yun asked once.

"I'd noticed you one day when you walked into EM service."

"I don't remember that."

"You were still a senior in high school, and I'd just joined the praise team. I saw you. Pow!" He pretended like he'd been punched in the stomach. "Like a gut punch. I just knew. But we didn't talk until you joined the band."

Yun pretended to hit him in the stomach.

"Pow. Pow. Pow. You barely spoke to me. I didn't know you thought I was alive. You waited until I turned eighteen?"

Lion shrugged. "Yes, and thankfully, you were not dating anyone."

"You should've asked me out sooner."

"Yun, if we were meant to be, then nothing could have prevented it," Lion said confidently. "Sometimes it's important to wait. To hope."

❧

On Monday afternoon, Lion went alone to Oxford Academy for Ginny's parent-teacher conference. Yun had a seminar at school she couldn't miss.

"You must be Ginny's homeroom teacher, Ms. Hamilton." Lion smiled at the young woman with short dark hair. She wore a green cardigan with a brown skirt and knee-high boots. "I'm Ginny's guardian. Lion Han."

"I'm Olivia. You own Exodus Academy," she said. "My friends have worked there."

"Oh?" Lion said, startled. "Who?"

"Selina Kim, Sharon Chiu, Aaron Schwartz, Ibraham Suleiman, and there's another one I'm blanking on. I heard you're hiring, too, for the new location in Fortress. That didn't sound right. I'm not looking for a gig."

"Wow, I love those guys. Aaron's still with us. He's our middle school science guy, but he's not allowed to have kids from his school in his hagwon class. Sharon moved when she got married, and Selina may start again with the older kids at Fortress. Ibraham is moving with us to Fortress."

"I know. They told me. They said nice things. Selina said that she worked in other hagwons, and she had not liked that at all."

Lion had heard about many of Selina's experiences. Nearly all hagwon teachers had war stories of teacher abuse, but Selina, a very patient person, had suffered quite a few terrible hagwon owners and mean-spirited parents.

"Let's talk about Ginny," Ms. Hamilton said.

"Yes, please. How is our Ginny doing?"

"She's kind of amazing. An extraordinary reader. Her math and science skills are good, too. She wants to be a doctor. She already has the medical school picked out. A seventh grader!"

"I know. UCSF," Lion said, shrugging. "I kind of wish she wasn't so focused on it already. I mean, it would be great if that's really what she wants, but she feels a lot of pressure."

"From you? Or her parents?"

"Not from Yun and me, I don't think. Her parents don't tell her to be a doctor in so many words, but her mother thinks she's well suited for the work."

"How long has she been living with you and your wife?"

"Since spring. She's so easy. Almost too easy."

"I wish I could meet her parents."

"I could give you their number, but you might need a translator. I know her father can speak enough English. He worked here for a while, so Ginny was born here. But they had to move back, and Ginny wanted to stay. Is there an issue?"

"No," Ms. Hamilton said. "I just wish they could know what a great kid they have. No problems. She has friends, too. She's a really great kid."

Lion smiled and relaxed, suddenly feeling like he could breathe again.

"Is she still in school?" he asked, checking his watch.

"Yes. The kids are in the auditorium doing work during parent-teacher conference day."

"Oh, I'll get her. Thank you, Ms. Hamilton—"

"Olivia—"

"Olivia, thank you. Thank you for taking good care of our Ginny."

❧

In the auditorium, Lion saw Ginny reading with two other girls, and he didn't want to disturb them. A group of seventh-grade boys who had gone to Exodus for years ran over to him. "Mr. Lion!" they shouted, then growled. "King of the Jungle!"

"Hello, boys. Here for Ginny."

"She's over there."

"Yup, I see her. And you are doing your homework? I was told all of you had some work to do."

"Yes, Mr. Lion." They growled again, quieter this time. They shuffled around him awkwardly, feeling younger just being in the presence of a teacher they'd known since kindergarten.

"See you guys," Lion said. Ginny had spotted him and was packing her bag to go.

"You had a terrible report," Lion said to her. "Disappointing, really."

Ginny opened her mouth in dismay.

"Kidding, kiddo. She said you're perfect, which we already knew. So you no longer have to be perfect."

Ginny shook her head. "You're always joking."

"A lot to joke about. Let's get ice cream."

Ginny trailed after him, and they left school to walk toward the mart near Exodus.

"My father said you went to Princeton."

"I did."

"And you skipped grades, so you graduated before you were twenty."

"Yes."

"Can I do that?"

"Why?" Lion stopped walking.

"Well, I could save money."

"What money?"

"Tuition for hagwon, college, and medical school, and all the money you and Miss Yun, I mean Mrs. Yun, are spending on me."

"Gosh. Is that why you think I skipped grades?"

"Well, you skipped grades because you're smart. I don't have your IQ."

Lion laughed. "We don't know your IQ. Yours might be much higher than mine. Also, your IQ doesn't mean you're smart. It's just a dumb number—something about pattern recognition abilities. Who cares? You know what, though? I hope you won't have to skip grades."

"Why? Wouldn't everyone admire me?"

"That's not important," he said. "Never do something or be something just to be admired. Our Ginny is wonderful just the way she is."

They entered the mart and peered into the ice cream freezer near the door. Lion slid open the door. "Pick whatever you want. I'm having strawberry shortcake. Oh, maybe I should have the ice cream sandwich. Hmm." He stared at all the choices.

"Should we get a cone for Yun?"

Ginny nodded.

Lion paid for the ice cream, and they took off the wrappers.

"My mother would get so mad when I ate and walked at the same time."

"Why?" Ginny asked.

"I don't know. Something about how it's not proper. She said beggars do that."

Ginny said nothing, not wanting to disagree with either Lion or his mother, whom she'd never met. For five seconds or so, they bowed their heads and prayed before eating the ice cream, then Lion said out loud, "You know that ice cream came from God, right?"

Ginny smiled. "Definitely."

"You know why I named my hagwon Exodus?"

"Is it a Bible story? There's a chapter in the Bible named Exodus."

"No and yes," he said. "When I was in college, I wanted to be a musician, and my parents stopped paying for my tuition."

"Did they have the money?" Ginny asked, wondering if his parents were like hers.

"Yes. They have money. They just wanted me to have a secure life, so they thought I should be a professor or lawyer or something like that. Being a musician is financially very unstable."

"What did you do? When they stopped paying your tuition?" she asked.

"I started tutoring. I was able to pay my own way, and then I realized that I liked what I was doing. I still play music, but my parents were right, I'd starve to death if it was just playing." He laughed.

"Should I start tutoring?" Ginny asked.

"No. You're just a kid. You are welcome here. Your parents are finding their footing. The crisis has been difficult for many, many people in Korea. It's not their fault, okay? We're fine. There is no need for you to worry. You have us, kiddo."

They sat down on the bench outside the hagwon. The parking lot was mostly empty. The vans wouldn't show up for another hour.

"I wanted to tell you about Exodus because it's a story about freedom, and when my parents cut me off financially, I learned that by knowing things and teaching other people to know things, I had freed myself from doing something I didn't want to do. I wanted to free myself from hierarchies, conventional thinking, and status obsessions," he said. "I don't know if that makes sense to you now, but I wanted you to know that you can do anything, Ginny. I believe in you."

"Isn't Exodus a Bible story?" A religious child, Ginny had learned this story in Sunday school many times, had even acted it out in a church play.

"Well, yes. Moses fought against a bad ruler, freed his people, then entered the wilderness, trusting only in God. He's kind of weird, but I thought he was cool, too. Like you, kiddo."

"I'm weird?"

"No. Mostly cool. I'm weirder. Please don't skip grades unless they make you. I wish I hadn't skipped all those grades. I graduated high school so early and had to do independent study at home for a while because I was too young to go to college. My schoolwork was not difficult, but learning how to deal with people and being so different from everyone was really challenging. I don't want that for you. Okay?"

Ginny frowned.

"Are they still mad at you?"

"My parents?" Lion said, smiling. "No. They were just scared, I guess. They're still scared. I think being a parent means being scared."

"Huh?"

"You can't control kids, and even if you could for a while, you can't control the world around them. So you get scared."

"My father would prefer it if I came home, but my mother wants me to stay here. My father is upset with me, I think."

"Where do you want to be?"

"Here. I'm going to UCSF and I'm going to be a doctor."

"Yes, you've said." He laughed. "You might change your mind. You can."

"No. I won't, but I think my father is angry that he owes you money and can't pay it back."

"Your father is not mad at you, kiddo. And even if he was or they were both furious at you, they would get over it. My parents got over it. Eventually."

Lion got up first and Ginny followed. Their ice creams finished, they entered the hagwon together.

❧

At home, Yun told Ginny that she could watch television before going to bed. Like Yun and her mother, Ginny loved watching rented videos of Korean dramas. It was one of the few things the child allowed herself. When she wrote to her parents, she'd mention the programs she'd seen with Mrs. Yun.

They were watching *Hello Again, My Darling,* and although Yun had already finished the series, Ginny had several episodes left in the video tote bag. When Yun told her that she'd borrowed the new episodes, Ginny dashed to the television room to watch a full episode before bedtime.

Yun picked up the bowl of tangerines and went to the study where Lion was working.

"How's the song?" She handed him a tangerine.

Lion looked up from his book and started peeling the fruit.

"It's not any good. In fact, it's so bad that I'm reading this book on commercial real estate."

He showed her the cover.

"Wow. Seriously?" Yun exclaimed. "Are you okay?"

"You know, this is the best year we ever had for Exodus, and the enrollment at Fortress is unbelievable."

"Yeah. We're going to have to turn kids away, which is kind of sad."

"Well, I talked with my brother, and Ray said I can rent the store three doors down. It's not next door, but it can work. I can separate the older kids from the little ones. Or maybe use the smaller space for an office and the faculty lounge. I can hire three more teachers at this rate."

"And the song?"

"I'll work on it later."

"You sound more excited about renting space."

"Yeah, maybe I should write a song about that." Lion laughed. It bothered him how much his own music was disappointing him. The more he wrote, the more he realized that all of his stuff was fine, but not great. Lately his lyrics embarrassed him and the melodies seemed incomplete, like fragments of songs he'd already heard. Seeing the kids at Exodus made him joyful. He liked being a hagwon person. His parents, on the other hand, didn't like it, and they hoped he was going through a phase. He was young enough to change his mind, they kept reminding him.

"If you want to rent that space, I think that's good," Yun said. "I hate turning kids away."

Lion smiled at her.

"Maybe we can take Ginny somewhere on our next break."

"I worry about that child," Yun said. "She's too grown up."

Lion nodded, grateful that his wife wasn't asking about the music.

6

I'll Stand By You

May 2000

It was easier to speak in the car with both of them looking straight ahead. The round trip from Irvine to Cypress could take over an hour and sometimes two. With Peter driving and Mido in the front passenger seat, they ended up talking a lot. When they weren't, Peter played music. Initially she didn't recognize much of it, which surprised him.

As a boy in England, Peter fell hard for older music—the Clash, the Ramones, and the Sex Pistols—and then the Cure, No Doubt, the Pretenders, Blondie, Nirvana, and Radiohead. In the car, he played Talking Heads, R.E.M., and Peter Gabriel.

Peter would put in a disc, and Mido would pull out the paper liner notes from the clamshell case and follow along. "They're like smart poems," she said, not having thought much about lyrics before, and Peter shrugged. He didn't like explaining lyrics. "I'm more interested in the feelings and the stories within a song," he'd say.

Nearly all of the songs were unfamiliar to her, and gradually she found herself listening to his music when she was alone. Mido approached his favorites the way she'd approach books recommended by friends. When she mentioned to Peter that a lot of what he liked seemed to be sad songs sung by men, he said: "Hang on. Here's one. A female vocalist, and not a song of despair."

Now whenever they drove together, "I'll Stand By You" by the Pretenders was their last song in the car.

It was Friday. To manage the awful commute to Cypress, they'd left Irvine an hour later than usual.

"What? You're going to skip your Pomona graduation?" Mido asked when they got in the car.

"Yes," Peter said.

"Why?"

"Not a big deal."

"But you and your mom are going to DH's graduation at Yale?"

"Yep."

"Why?"

"Because it's a big deal to him, and I'll already have graduated the day before."

"But without going to your ceremony."

"I don't stand on ceremony."

"Ha," Mido said. "This is okay with your mother?"

"Mother Renee is not normal. You haven't met her. She's cool about stuff like this." Peter smiled. "I wanted us to go to DH's. Mine's not important."

"You'll see my parents there, then," she said.

"But you?" Peter frowned. "You're not going?"

Mido shook her head. She and Bo were sitting it out. They couldn't afford the flights and missed wages from skipping work. There was a strong demand for finals tutoring and boot camps that week. DH had understood.

"The Zekes will be playing tomorrow night. Yun is playing keyboard," Peter said. "Spot is on guitar and Will on drums. Lion will sing seven of the songs. I have five. I'll still play bass, of course. Can't imagine singing without holding something."

"How's the music going?"

"It's good," Peter said. "We're the best cover band in Newport Beach." He laughed.

"Is this what you want to do?"

"Don't know," he said. "I'm thinking about working more."

"On music?"

"No. Teaching. I like running Fortress Academy a lot more than I thought I would. The music is, well, it's a side thing."

Over the years, the Zekes had played several decent clubs in Southern California. There had been a few nervous evenings when talent scouts and booking agents were in the audience. However, other bands were picked for more venues but not them. One agent had told Lion and Peter that a band of Asian guys, except for Spot Johnson, their one White guy, who played guitar, wouldn't get any traction.

Of course, there were successful musicians in every country in Asia, but it wasn't like that here. Peter couldn't name a single Asian American rock-and-roll band that ever got played on the radio or booked for larger venues.

Peter drove straight ahead through the dark, open freeway. Blaming his race and ethnicity felt like making excuses, and he hated the way that sounded. It was also true that Lion didn't want to tour, and Peter wasn't sure where to go from here as a vocalist. No one needed another competent bass player, and while Peter liked writing music, he didn't feel like he had all that much to say. Sometimes the lyrics would come in pieces, but the melodies not so much. Everything he wrote sounded depressing.

There were plenty of musicians in Korea whose sound he liked, but he and Lion were more alternative rock grounded in LA, and the rules for them were different, it seemed. They couldn't find a manager, and Lion was busy with the hagwons. Peter didn't have it in him to promote their work, and now there was Fortress to think about.

The last time he was in Seoul, his uncle, his father's older brother, had said, "Men have to face reality. Dreams are just dreams. Wake up."

Now and then as Peter drove, Mido stole glimpses to catch his mood, but he didn't seem to notice her. He appeared more resigned than upset, and she thought she should drop it. It wasn't any of her business.

"It's nice to drive with almost no traffic," he said. "I'm glad we waited to take off."

He paused before speaking again.

"I thought Tek was supposed to visit this summer," he said.

"He was. But work came up." Lately there had been fewer calls, and the intervals between them were growing longer. They were both busy. The calls were expensive. She wanted to support his career, which was flourishing. If Tek wanted to be a barrister one day, he had to work even harder now as a young solicitor, get more legal experience, and build networks to get referrals. Since she left, they had not seen each other once. It had been over two years, but neither ever discussed breaking up.

"What's he like?"

"Only child. Born and raised in Sydney, both parents academics. Speaks Korean better now. He's working as a solicitor with a mind to becoming a barrister, which requires more years of training, an exam, and more legal relationships."

"How long have you been dating?"

"I met him when we were kids, then we started dating my last year in high school, so . . . four years now, but the last two have been long distance. So many questions, Peter."

"So two years really, then, and you don't have the exact number of days?"

Girls he knew from Korea would celebrate the number of days—day one to day one thousand. One girl he'd dated briefly—less than a month—had expected him to remember the dates, and before they broke up, he recalled marking off the boxes on the calendar as if measuring a prison sentence.

Mido laughed. "I don't think that way, sorry."

"Are you going back?" he asked.

"Where?"

"Sydney or Seoul?"

"I could finish my degree in Sydney, I guess, but I can't go back right now."

"Why are you working at the hagwon?" he asked. "You don't fit the profile."

"I didn't know there was one."

"Grad school dropouts, actors, musicians, and teachers who need more money. It's supposed to be a transition job. Not the endgame. No one grows up dreaming of becoming a math tutor."

"I haven't even finished college," she said, her voice breaking. Yun would graduate UCLA at the end of the month, and she had only finished a year.

Peter realized that he'd upset her and felt lousy.

"But you're a standardized test genius."

Mido smiled. "I'm in between things."

"You want to finish college?"

"I like school, but I do wonder if it's always necessary to go to college," she said, almost surprising herself with this admission. "I like learning."

"You don't have to. It shouldn't be assumed that everyone wants to go to college. Half the kids we teach have no idea why they're even trying to get in. If they really thought about it, they wouldn't even go. They probably shouldn't go. Not right away."

"What? You work in a hagwon and teach high school students. We're actively prepping kids for higher education. You're being contrary, Peter." She laughed.

"No, no. I'm not. Not everyone should go to college. Nobody should follow a fucking script. You're smart not to—" He laughed, then saw that she looked shaken, when he'd only been trying to justify her position.

"Peter, I *want* to finish something I started. But what I really want is to learn things, do things. I want to be active."

They stopped at an intersection, and finally he turned. She was lovely, he thought. When Mido was thinking about something, she opened her eyes wide and looked up as if the answer would be written on the sky.

"Why finish, though? What's the point of it?"

"I, I . . ." She faltered, her chin tilted upward, her neck exposed.

"See. You don't know, either, and you're not sixteen years old like our students. You've had time to think about it, and you don't know," he said softly. "I'm saying all this because I respect you, Mido. You have choices." Peter turned off the music so he could hear her better.

"Well, I liked going to school in Sydney. I guess it was expected—going to college, I mean. I'd be okay going to Fullerton or Long Beach, then transferring like my brother. I don't have to go to Yale or Pomona like you and DH. Right now, I'm working to make money. I'm trying to take care of my family."

"I get it."

"No, I'm not sure if you do."

"I didn't mean to—"

"Never mind. We're good. Thanks for driving me home. It's out of your way."

Peter parked the car in front of her building and watched Mido get out. She fumbled with the keys at the glass lobby door until she finally got it to open.

Right before she entered the elevator, Mido turned around and saw that Peter was still parked, watching her get in, making sure that she was okay. Mido waved at him, and he waved back.

Peter turned on the ignition. He felt more resolved, somehow, about his future. He wanted to keep singing and playing bass even if it never amounted to anything, and he wanted to see if he could build out this new hagwon business in Irvine for Lion.

❧

Rascals was a fancy Newport Beach steak house split into two large rooms—in the front, a spacious bar serving a bistro menu with an elevated stage for live performances, and in the back, a grand white-cloth dining room with a full wine list. Its best-selling dishes were steak frites, mussels in white wine, and dry-aged porterhouse with garlic butter.

On Fridays and Saturdays, local bands played to strong crowds. There was karaoke on Thursdays and Sundays. Guests signed up at the bar to sing.

The Zekes' drummer, Will Guo, was also Rascals' owner and manager, a fourth-generation Chinese American whose family owned seven successful restaurants in Orange County. Will had agreed to go into the family business as long as he could have his way designing and managing the steak house and play music on the side. A terrific percussionist, he played piano or drums in three different bands that performed at his restaurant. The deal with his family was that as long as Rascals made money, Will could do as he liked.

Like Lion and Peter, Will didn't have much regular practice time, but the Zekes had a standing gig at least once a month, and when other acts canceled, the band got first dibs. The joke was that they were the house band, playing mostly cover songs and music that Lion had written. Will didn't pay himself, but the Zekes got what all the other bands got: drink tickets, burgers in the kitchen, and $300 a gig, which Lion usually gave to Peter and Spot.

On Saturday night, Lion wanted to open with a ballad that he'd written for Yun years ago but had reworked to have a faster tempo. He'd come to Rascals straight from work, so he was wearing jeans and a black T-shirt from the Gap. He'd taken off the blue button-down because it made him look like a guy holding down an office job rather than a musician. He and Peter had worked out the set for the night, and thankfully, Spot Johnson, their second guitarist, who managed produce at Vons, showed up on time. Will knew the set cold, and Yun had been practicing keyboard the whole week.

The dining room was packed, and Lion felt relaxed. Peter was focused on his bass and did backup on Lion's songs and vice versa. Spot was a fine guitarist but wasn't the kind of guy who believed in practicing too much. He also had two kids, a wife who taught fifth grade, and no time.

Lion opened with his ballad, "Figs," and they played through eleven more songs, covering "One," "Iris," and "I Drove All Night," and the crowd wouldn't let them get offstage. At the end of the set, Peter huddled with the band, and after he nodded, Yun played the intro to "I'll Stand by You," and Peter took the center microphone and sang the intro. The crowd was rapt, and he turned slightly toward the bar, but the lights were too bright for him to make out Mido's face.

When the set ended, they returned to the greenroom to pack up, then met at the bar, where Mido was sitting alone. Spot's wife was at home with their daughters, and Will's wife managed another restaurant on the other side of Newport Beach, so neither had been able to make it. Mido clapped vigorously when she saw the band approach her.

The bartender told Will that there was an issue in the kitchen, so he gave Lion the pay envelope, and after getting his share, Spot guzzled his diet soda and went home to relieve his wife.

"Great night, fellas," Spot said. "And madam." He winked at Yun.

Yun took a bow, holding the sides of her short black dress, which she wore with combat boots.

"You were amazing," Mido said to them.

Peter raised his hand in thanks. "We better head out, too. Another big day tomorrow in Irvine." He turned to Mido. "You need a lift?"

Mido glanced at Yun and Lion. It made more sense for her to head out with them, but she knew they had to get back to Ginny, who was with the housekeeper.

"You sure, Peter?" Yun asked. "We're running late. It is not easy to be a rock star couple with a middle school–aged kid at home."

In Peter's car, Mido put on her seat belt.

"I think I should start giving you gas money, Peter."

"I was thinking the same," he said, laughing. "No need. I'm good."

"You were really great. It's a terrific band. I'd listen to you guys all the time, and I'm not even someone who gets music."

"There's praise in there somewhere. Is that a compliment, when someone who doesn't know music likes your stuff?"

"Oh, I mean I don't know much about alternative rock and the music that you like on KROQ. It's all so new to me. I love that last song, though, the Pretenders song. Did she write it?"

"Chrissie Hynde? She's one of the writers," Peter said. "It's also by Steinberg and Kelly. They wrote a lot of songs you know. 'I Drove All Night,' 'Like a Virgin,' 'True Colors,' 'Look Me in the Heart.' So many. But others recorded them."

"I do know all those songs."

"It seems impossible to write songs like that," Peter said. "The reality is I can't even imagine trying to—" He stopped and signaled before turning.

Mido waited for him to finish his sentence, but he didn't. It grew quiet in the car.

"The better we sound and the less traction we get, the more I think the Zekes is a waste of time."

"When my weird experimental play got put up at SUDS, it was such a cool experience, but I knew I didn't have what it takes. I don't feel like writing plays all the time. I think I wanted to do it to be somebody in that world. At least once."

"And I think I moved to California because I wanted to impress Cesca, who saw me sing at Toad's."

"Toad's?"

"It's a bar in New Haven. Cesca is that woman I moved to California for. We dated for a few months."

"Oh."

"When I'm onstage, and I sing, I can tell when the sound connects. I feel powerful and safe. Also, it's nice to have girls think you're hot."

Mido laughed, remembering how it felt to have him look at her while he sang. Until he sang it, she hadn't realized they had a song.

"You do it for the girls?"

"Got you in the car, didn't I?"

"Peter, it's kind of your job to drive me."

"Yep," he agreed happily.

A few minutes from her building, he put on the Pretenders, and softly, they sang along.

7

Yokshim

It was DH's idea to room with Peter. He'd work at Fortress for the summer before starting Columbia Law School in the fall.

At the first Monday staff meeting with Lion and Yun, he had a proposal.

"College counseling," he said. A big smile crossed his long, handsome face, and he raised his thick eyebrows with enthusiasm. "What do you think?"

Lion and Yun glanced at each other.

"Exodus is on autopilot, right?" DH asked rhetorically. "Fortress has been up for five months, and already you're having to turn kids away and hire more teachers. Why not go after the big-ticket item and help everybody with college applications? These are your kids that you're raising. You know them. You'll know best how to help them with their applications. Let's have everything here: one-stop hagwon for high school students."

Lion looked skeptical. He'd been thinking of college counseling for the Irvine students but hadn't wanted to rush into it.

"We can put our degrees to work," DH said, his excitement undiminished. "Among us, we have Princeton, Yale, Pomona, and UCLA. Mido went to University of Sydney, and Bo will be transferring to UCLA from Fullerton. We're like a California dream team."

"I thought you had to leave for school in August," Mido said, wondering how her brother who'd never worked at a hagwon could show up on the first day of his summer job and tell Lion how to run his business. "Are you going to stay with us until they submit their applications in the fall for early admission and then for regular?"

"No," DH said. "You'll be in charge of that. You're great at admin, and high school seniors are terrible at it."

Peter stared with mixed wonder and admiration at his friend, who could sell sand to people in the desert.

"Hear me out. Two guys I know from Yale were doing this for a lot of money."

Lion and Yun frowned, and Yun made a little disapproving noise. One of their founding principles was making the hagwon accessible to as many students as possible.

"We don't have to charge as much. Mido can teach essays, and you guys can keep doing the test prep. Mido, Peter, and I can help the kids with the application. And Yun can teach a weekend boot camp to the parents and seniors about FAFSA, which is its own kind of trial."

Lion sipped his black coffee.

Finally he said, "Let's try it." He threw out a number. "Six students?"

"Twelve," DH countered. "Twelve at $5,000 per student. Ten applications per student from beginning to end, with revisions and counseling."

"$5,000?" Lion looked shocked.

DH raised his hand. "And each additional application costs another $500. The consultant gets half and the house takes half. This would be a bargain. My friends were charging three times that. They told me that it's market rate. And for your lower-income and middle-income students who'd qualify, the FAFSA boot camp can be a town hall–style lecture with Q and A. It can be open to the public and at no charge as a goodwill gesture."

"Consultant?" Mido asked.

"You," DH said, pointing to her.

"So the consultant gets $2,500 per kid, and Fortress gets $2,500? And you're doing all this work and Fortress provides the space, consultant, and students?" Yun was thinking out loud. "Lion might disagree, but I think the numbers would work for us if we charged $3,500. You'd still get the $2,500, but we'd take $1,000."

"That sounds better," Lion said. "Even $3,500 sounds like a lot."

"You don't have to hire a consultant," DH said. "Or we can also have a general class like the FAFSA lecture for a lot less, but you'd get less individualized attention. We can try hybrid models," DH said. The econ major wrote out pricing and numbers on a legal pad.

"It's not a bad idea," Peter said, exhaling. "Just figure out what's a fair number. Maybe we can take a quarter of the kids on scholarship."

"One full scholarship or two partial scholarships would work. Three would be tough to break even," DH said.

"Oh, DH." Mido hit her brother on the arm.

In less than a week, the college counseling program was filled. Lion selected two students on full scholarship on the condition that no one could ever disclose this fact.

❧

Saturday was the first day of SAT boot camp at Fortress. The tutors had already prepared the rooms for the diagnostic tests, and they sat waiting for Lion to begin the morning meeting, but he'd been continuously interrupted by parents showing up without appointments.

Sixty high school students were scheduled to attend the boot camp. They were supposed to start in an hour, but half a dozen high school juniors had already arrived and were waiting in the testing room, the largest classroom in the building.

Unlike at the Cypress hagwon, everything here was new and matched—the desks, chalkboards, folders, books, coffee makers, and even the enormous copy machines. There were three vending machines in the student lounge, something they'd never had at Cypress. Lion and Yun had financed the new site with profits from the Cypress location and a small HELOC on their home, which they were able to pay off in three months. Despite Yun's efforts to air out the classrooms, the scent of fresh paint and new carpets lingered.

Yun and Mido were checking the class lists in the front office when Mido got a call.

"I'm here," Tek said.

"What?" Mido said, covering her mouth in surprise. She was standing by her desk phone, and Yun looked up from her papers.

Mido mouthed "Tek," and Yun nodded, returning to her work.

"How long will you be at Fortress?" he asked.

"I have to be here until six."

"I'm at the Westin. When can you come by?"

"You said you weren't coming. I can't just leave—"

"I know. I have work, too. I wanted to see you. Take your time. I'm going to go for a run, do some reading, and we can get dinner."

Mido wrote down his address on her memo pad and returned to the empty chair by Yun.

"Tek is here?" Yun asked.

Mido nodded.

"You don't look happy about it."

"I am happy. I'm just surprised."

Yun smiled. "I better go rescue my Lion. Those parents are scary."

❧

Yun knocked on the glass portion of Lion's door. Without hearing a word, just from his posture, she could tell that Lion was trying to reassure someone. Seated on the edge of his office armchair, Lion leaned toward the two parents, his back bent at a sixty-degree angle.

The father was a state judge, a local celebrity in the community because he was the first Korean American prosecutor turned judge in Orange County, and the mother a former Olympic speed skater from South Korea.

Tracking the parents' gaze, Lion looked up and saw his wife. He waved her in, and Yun took the seat nearest him.

"I was just telling Judge Seo and Mrs. Seo—"

"You should call me Melanie," the mother said.

"I was telling them about how the SAT boot camp works."

"The diagnostics and the review classes sound great," Melanie said, "but is it possible for our daughter Catherine to get individual tutoring if she needs it? She's weak in math and may not be able to keep up with the others. All these kids have been going to hagwons forever, and they're super prepared. I don't even know why they're here. Anyway, she's shy and isn't good at advocating for herself."

"Do you think these classes can really change scores?" the judge asked.

"Of course. Scores can change dramatically. Isn't that right?" Melanie looked at Lion and Yun.

"Yes," Lion said. "If the child studies, their scores can change. I've seen extraordinary progress depending on a number of factors: the child's foundational skills, interest in the subject matter, habits, and her ability to withstand testing stressors."

"Stressors?"

"Well, the lower her scores are, the more we can raise them. The score differential toward the higher end is harder to change. You'd be surprised at what's required for a 1400 and a 1600. At those scores, it's not just skills but also confidence, pattern recognition, familiarity, and mental fortitude. Sometimes a hundred-point score difference is about just getting four or five questions correct."

"I don't remember taking the SATs," the judge said. "Isn't that strange? I know I took them, but I can't recall the fuss. Lately it's all we talk about at home."

Melanie shot him a look. "Catherine is worried, and we have to help her. The school is putting a lot of pressure on her."

She turned back to Yun.

"Do you have a child?" Melanie asked her.

Yun shook her head no.

"You're too young, of course," Melanie said.

"We take care of a young student right now. In our home. She's at Oxford Academy."

"Oh, Catherine is at Troy," the judge said. "It's a great school. Oxford is newer, I think. I heard it's very good."

Yun smiled. "We have many students from Troy at our other location in Cypress. It's an academically rigorous school, so it's bound to have a lot of kids talking about exams. Even if you and the judge never said a word about the test, she'd probably hear about it at school all day. If she wants to talk about it, I can listen to her. Get it out of her system if that's possible."

"I took the Suneung, and I remember what it was like." Melanie shivered at the memory. "I had to hit a specific score. You know how it is. Thankfully, it was easier for an athlete. No one expected me to have good grades. When I moved to the States, I went to UC Irvine to finish my degree. It's where I met my husband."

"Let's see how Catherine does on the diagnostic, and if she needs more tutoring, we can figure that out," Lion said.

The parents looked at one another in agreement.

"We came early because we know that not all the kids can be tutored privately, but we'd like Catherine to get first consideration," Melanie said. "We thought it would be fair if we came early, rather than try to pull strings."

"I understand. You were here first. You didn't cut any line." Lion smiled.

❧

The students left at five o'clock, and an hour later, Mido still wasn't able to leave. She had been working without a break, and the phones had been ringing nonstop, it seemed, once word got out about the college admissions counseling. Mido buzzed around the building, tidying up the offices. After straightening up each one, she'd turn out the lights and lock the door. All the tutors were still working in the testing room, reviewing scores:

Each student would get a diagnostic report and a class assignment for the following week. She had to phone Tek and let him know that she'd be late, and when she got to the main office to make the call, she saw him sitting there, chatting with Yun and Lion.

"I was just about to come find you," Yun said, getting up. "Tek just got here. We were surprised, too."

Mido's face grew flushed.

"Hey, stranger." Tek rushed up to embrace her. "Yun and I were having a reunion, and I just met her husband." Tek turned to Lion. "Mate, how did you get that name?"

"I used to carry a stuffed lion around as a little kid. Talk to it, take it to school, and I couldn't be separated from it, so my big brother Ray called me Lion's friend, and eventually, I just became Lion. My real name is James, but no one calls me that. Even my parents call me Lion."

Mido laughed. "I never heard that story." She turned to Tek. "How did you get here?"

"The most expensive taxi ride in the world. I thought I was going to rent a car, and then I realized that I didn't have it in me to brave the roads of Orange County in the dark," he said. "I'm ashamed to admit this as a dude, but I have no sense of direction, and I wasn't even sure about my license working here."

Mido smiled, wondering how to ask Peter to give them a lift back.

"We could take you two," Yun offered. "Tek's hotel is closer to us anyway."

"Oh, okay. Just let me tell Peter."

"Tell me what?" Peter asked, walking into the office. He waved goodbye to the other tutors who were leaving.

"I'm Tek. Mido's fiancé."

Mido looked at him, puzzled. "What?" They were not engaged.

"Peter Son. Math tutor," he said, a slightly confused look on his face.

"I'm going to drive them to Tek's hotel," Lion said to Peter. "You and DH want to come to dinner with us? Yun and I are going to get food. I'm sure these two want to have time alone."

Peter nodded curtly. "I'll get DH and follow your car, then," he said.

❧

In the hotel room, Tek kissed her, and Mido folded herself into his warmth.

"Why did you say you're my fiancé?"

"Because I am, more or less, no?" Tek said. "Do you know how long that bloody flight was?" He smiled. "Every minute was worth it, though. I'm so glad to see you."

He started to remove her clothes, and she wriggled a bit, not feeling ready to make love.

"Aren't you hungry?" she asked.

"I ate lunch late. My schedule's off. I'm sorry—you must be hungry." Tek stopped unbuttoning her shirt.

They became shy then, and Mido bit her lip.

"I'm fine," she said, and began undressing. "I want to shower first. Is that okay?"

"Of course. Why don't I order us some dinner?"

Mido headed to the bathroom and closed the door.

❧

As soon as they got home, Lion, Peter, and DH said hello to Ginny, then ran off to the garage like kids. They wanted to try out a song that had been giving them trouble.

"Thirty minutes. Tops," Lion promised.

Yun didn't mind. Dinner could wait. It was a relief when Lion was working on his music. Though he counseled anxious students and parents with great patience, he was intolerant of self-pity.

Lion was kindhearted and self-controlled, and in the presence of wives who complained about their husbands, Yun didn't know what to say. Among women, sometimes it was good manners to commiserate, but Lion didn't give her sufficient material to file any complaints.

In the four years she'd known him, she'd observed that what made the most dramatic change in Lion's mood was his music. Whether practicing or performing, Lion could transform from levelheaded to rapturous—eyes closed, body fluid in sync with the melody. Seeing him so joyous, Yun wished he could play music and do little else.

Once she had suggested this to him, and he'd pointed to a stack of the envelopes that arrived with regularity in the red-painted mailbox beside their doorbell.

"Bills," he said. "That's my job, too."

They owed money: a mortgage on their home in Sorrento, Yun's student loans, two car loans, homeowner's and car insurance, real estate taxes, rent on two hagwon locations. They also needed to pay dozens of employees on time.

From the kitchen, Yun could hear the guitar and keyboard. They were playing "Flower Girl," a song Lion had written years before—one of her favorites.

Ginny had already eaten dinner with the housekeeper, and now she helped to set the table. She was twelve years old but physically smaller than her classmates. The week before, Yun had cut her hair in a pageboy style with the bangs Ginny preferred, and while it suited her pretty face, it also made her look even younger. Yun was concerned that Ginny wasn't growing as much as the other girls, so she made her favorite dishes—gimbap and hearty Korean stews—while being careful to refrain from commenting on the child's eating.

At the hagwon, mothers of girls talked often of eating disorders, and Yun didn't know what to do because she was neither the mother nor a family friend. Technically Yun was the guardian, but unlike a homestay guardian—a surrogate parent who was paid to house and feed an overseas student—she was more like a host to a houseguest who happened to be a child. It was an odd arrangement, because there was no formal end date, and Yun didn't have the heart to find one. Ginny wasn't any trouble.

Always, Ginny did her best, not wanting to disappoint anyone or need anything.

Yun had heard mothers joke that their husbands could be so irresponsible it felt like having an additional child; she felt as if she were living with two sober adults rather than a husband and a child.

"Ginny, do you want to eat with us? I know you had something, but there's chicken and ribs from Johnson's." Yun pointed at the boxes of takeout. "I was also going to fix a salad."

Ginny shook her head.

"I'm okay. I'm going to finish my homework."

"It's Saturday night. Do you want to watch some television before going to bed?"

Ginny brightened a little.

"I saw the bag of videos," she said hopefully.

Yun smiled. "We have to wait till Sunday. My mother's coming over. I will not allow you to study on Sunday. We are going to watch until our vision goes blurry." Yun laughed.

Ginny smiled. Growing up, she had not watched dramas with her family. Her mother didn't like them. At the homestay guardian's house, she'd never been allowed to watch any since she was supposed to be doing homework. More than anything else in her life in America, Ginny loved to watch rented drama videos with Yun and her mother, Nari.

"Then I'll finish up all my weekend homework. I only have two more worksheets left."

"You always finish," Yun said. "Would you like to phone your parents tonight? They're expecting a call soon, right?"

Ginny had been waiting until she had Yun's permission. In the den, Ginny picked up the phone and dialed. On the first ring, her father picked up.

"Our daughter, have you eaten?"

"Yes, Appa." Ginny closed her eyes and tried to picture her father's morning unshaven face. When she was little, she'd jump into her parents' bed, and his morning beard would scratch her, and she'd burrow herself into her mother's sweet-scented embrace.

In the morning, while he shaved, Ginny would sit on the bath stool to watch him, waiting patiently until he'd dab shaving cream on her nose. Now that they were living at Grandmother's house, she imagined that he'd have to shave in front of the tiny framed mirror in the green-tiled bathroom, which had a red plastic washtub and a corded showerhead instead of a bathtub.

"How was school this week?" he asked.

"One hundred on my social studies test and a one hundred on my science test."

"Our great, praiseworthy daughter," he said. "Appa wishes he could have breakfast with you."

"Is that Ginny?" Her mother came on the line.

"Umma, hello. How is your health? How is Granny? How is my little brother?"

"Everyone is well. Grandma is making breakfast, and Jiho is good. He's been studying a lot, too."

Beneath the friendly conversation, there were things that none of them would mention for fear of causing worry.

When Grandma did piecework for the hairpin factory, little Jiho helped her, getting faster all the time. Umma sold yogurt drinks in the neighborhood, although her knees were giving her trouble. Appa's old blue truck had broken down again and needed a new carburetor, which had wiped out their savings. Grandma had a cough that wouldn't get better, but she refused to go to the doctor.

Ginny couldn't mention that at school, she knew everyone but had no real, close friends and didn't know how to make them.

"Oh, I have to go. Grandma needs me. I miss you, Ginny. I'm praying for you all the time," her mother said.

"Hearing my daughter's voice makes me feel like I had the most delicious meal. I feel full. I won't even need breakfast," Appa said, sniffling a little. "You make us so proud, our beloved daughter. You make us so proud."

Ginny couldn't speak anymore. If she started crying, it would make her parents feel awful.

"I know you are doing everything well, so I won't tell you to do anything else. Please tell Yun Teacher and Lion Teacher thank you again. We're so grateful, Ginny-ya, we're going to pay all these debts. Umma and I are working and saving money by living at Grandma's. You can study hard and not worry."

"Appa, I better go now. This phone call is expensive," she said. "I'll call you next week."

Ginny closed her eyes. Grandma's house usually smelled like camphor liniment, soy sauce, and the coal briquettes they used to heat the *ondol* rooms. When Grandma would hug her, Ginny would breathe in the clean, nutty scent of her hair oil.

After she hung up the phone, her family vanished again for the week. There was no way of knowing when she'd see them again. Ginny wiped her face with the back of her hand, then went to the bathroom to wash. She'd get into her pajamas, finish the worksheets before bed. The adults were eating now, and she wouldn't bother them.

❧

Yun served the salad in bowls and passed the bottle of ranch dressing. Everyone took ribs and chicken from the boxes and began eating.

"Tek was a surprise," Yun said, confused by his appearance. She knew things were awkward between Mido and Tek. Mido had been mentioning him less. Of course, she'd also noticed her friend's growing ease with Peter, but Mido had said nothing about him. Peter was harder to read, but it was obvious that they got along, and she never saw Peter with another girl.

"He told her that he couldn't make the trip. Then he showed up at work. At the new location."

"So do we like him?" DH asked. "So weird they left even before introducing him to her brother. Don't you think he should have met me?"

"Well, I met him when I was in middle school," Yun said, "and he seems sort of the same. Good-natured. Funny."

"Mido said that he had a crush on you then," Peter said.

Lion smiled. "Everyone has a crush on my wife."

"Not me," Peter said.

"Me neither," DH chimed in.

"Okay. Me neither," Lion said, laughing.

Yun threw a balled-up paper napkin at her husband.

"Yes, I think Tek might have had a tiny crush on me, but it passed since I had zero interest in him. He seemed so Australian, not Korean at all. I guess Mido is fine with that since she grew up partly in Australia, but I found his informal behavior strange. Also, his Korean is not great."

"Let's just be honest," Lion said. "You were waiting for a better-looking man, and I happen to be that ideal combination of intelligence, musical creativity, and movie star good looks."

"Indeed." Yun rolled her eyes good-naturedly. "I was waiting just for you."

"Aaaww," DH cooed.

"So... do we like him?" Peter asked this time. "I didn't get a chance to really speak with him."

In terms of looks, Tek was quite attractive—tall, clear-skinned, and fair. He kept his black hair short, and there was something happy and light in his expression. His smile came quickly.

He wasn't like Peter, who always appeared sober, almost too serious. Even when Peter joked, he kept a straight face. Tek was the sort who'd laugh at his own punch line, inviting you to laugh with him.

"I wonder how long he's staying. Apparently his job is really intense," Yun said.

"I thought he seemed pleasant," Lion said. "I mean, for a lawyer. He wasn't full of himself."

"Be fair. How many lawyers do you know?" Yun asked.

"Enough," Lion replied. "I could never be one. Tough job."

Lion habitually gave everyone the benefit of the doubt and a half dozen chances at redemption besides. Yun thought Tek was fine, but couldn't figure out why he hadn't come sooner, or why, though he and Mido weren't formally engaged, he had used the word "fiancé" like it was nothing.

"They're not going to get married," Peter predicted. "I'd put a bet down on it."

"Married?!" DH exclaimed.

"He told me he was her fiancé," Peter said. DH crossed his arms.

"He's fine, but no one is good enough for my Mido," Yun said.

"Fiancé, huh? We'll see about that," DH said. "My baby sister."

8
Danbi

Clutching a pink stuffed rabbit in her arms, Danbi sat in the rocker watching Anna sleep—her chest, its width barely a handspan, rising and falling with each deep breath.

Her daughter's nursery was painted a pale green, because the color was the only thing Danbi had liked about growing up in a farming town.

Born and raised on the outskirts of Sangju, Danbi had loathed almost everything about her rural hometown: the narrow-minded elderly villagers who clucked their tongues and gossiped about her profligate, drunken stepfather; the harsh sun that etched even young mothers with indelible wrinkles and frowns, capturing their too-early disappointments; the cheap nylon clothing saturated in gaudy colors and incongruous prints that covered squat country bodies; and the jet-black-dyed, permanent-waved hair of middle-aged women, including her weak-willed mother, who would not leave a terrible man no matter how much Danbi begged.

Through tremendous efforts at a competitive girls' high school and two Suneung trials, Danbi was accepted into Korea University as a math major and graduated near the top of her class. Always surrounded by men, she had refused countless romantic overtures from peers, graduate students, and young professors, developing the reputation of being an ice virgin. Discreetly, far away from campus and under a different name, she'd dated a series of wealthy married businessmen who gave her money for school.

As soon as she was hired at HRI, Danbi threw away her second pager, broke up with all the older men, and moved to a small apartment closer to her office, where none of them could ever find her.

Contempt for her rural upbringing had made Danbi aspire for more, yet now, over nine thousand miles away, in an elegant nursery in a grand house in Irvine with her two-year-old daughter fast asleep in a toddler bed imported from Italy, she yearned for Sangju's verdant fields, rock terraces that touched the clouds, evergreen mountains thick with ancient trees, and blue-and-white streaked skies edged by water. She missed the plaintive sounds of the people's voices, the rounded Sangju dialect that bore little relationship to Seoul speech, and her umma's sad way of phrasing everything as a question.

Danbi heard Shin's footfalls down the hall. She covered Anna with her pink quilt, kissed her forehead, and left the room, closing the door gently.

"Where were you?" she asked.

Shin didn't answer her question. "I want to take a shower. It's late."

For a moment, Danbi felt afraid, wondering if he could have gone to a room salon. She'd heard of two between Garden Grove and Anaheim. They had sex nearly every day, and she couldn't imagine him needing more.

"Are you upset with me?" she asked.

"No, no."

"Do you want me to scrub your back?"

He shook his head and went to the bedroom and closed the door.

Danbi went to the kitchen. In the refrigerator, she found the ingredients to make a stew, and she heated the short ribs. The housekeeper had already made rice.

The first time she had sex with Shin had been at a motel in Sinchon. He had flirted with her after a work dinner.

"Miss Jung is the smartest and loveliest trainee in the world," he'd said to her at the taxi stand.

So she asked him to take her home, claiming she'd had too much to drink. "I'm afraid of being alone with the driver. Would I be out of your way? Could you be my protector?"

In the taxi, when they passed a motel, she looked at Shin first, then asked the driver to pull in. In the lobby, without any words exchanged, Shin knew exactly why they were there. He asked for the honeymoon suite, which was the most expensive room.

"I've always wanted a grown-up man to be mine," she'd said as he undressed her slowly. She took him to the bathroom, got on her knees, and washed him, not letting him touch her until she was ready.

On the bed, he turned her around and made love to her, and she bled a little, making him think that it was her first time.

With her index finger, she tapped the blood on the sheets.

"Will you take responsibility for me?"

"Of course," he'd said before climaxing.

Danbi knew that the first year of their affair had intoxicated him. With the energy of a twenty-four-year-old woman, she thought of new things and places each week. She bought erotic novels and manhwa to learn what men and women wanted from sex. She didn't like pornographic films, finding them more unhelpful than vulgar. The women were often unappealing and looked artificial.

For her purposes, the images weren't important. She studied the motivations in the novels and manhwa because if she could control a man's motives, she could get what she wanted.

Of course, Danbi had lovers before, but none of them could do enough for her. Money was a commodity that many men possessed, and many young women could extract it from them.

Never before Shin did she want to possess a married man. He wasn't rich, and he was not the most important officer in the company. But he was beautiful and strong. When he talked about his sons, she envied them, and loved him more. He could be old-fashioned about what a man was supposed to do for a woman, and he was tender with her, even when she could be cruel. Always, he forgave her, though she could not understand why. When he was angry with her, she was afraid of losing him.

After Shin's numerous attempts to be free from her, she realized that she even loved his failure to escape.

A year after they met, she went to his apartment and made him dinner and asked him to leave his wife. He ate the meal and they made love.

"It isn't up to me. My wife is Catholic, and she refuses to give me a divorce. I'm responsible for her and our sons." And his answer had not wavered in all the years they had been together.

After Anna was born, he promised never to leave her. Danbi had not realized what it would feel like to be a mother. For Shin, she would have killed a person; but for Anna, she would have died. Everything had changed after she had a baby. Anna was perfect—creamy skin, Shin's large eyes, and Danbi's button nose. Already she could speak well. Her first word had been "cat."

Danbi wanted another child, but Shin said no and got a vasectomy. "In twenty years, when Anna finishes college, I'll be seventy-five. Let's be reasonable."

❧

In her large kitchen with its double-door, stainless steel refrigerator, twin German dishwashers, and six-burner stove, Danbi cooked a meal for Shin and set the table.

His dark, wet hair was combed back, and his tanned profile was still remarkable—the unusual aquiline nose, the sad deep-set eyes and elegant mouth. Shin wore a black polo shirt and khakis. He was barefoot.

"You made dinner?" Shin seemed surprised.

"Yes."

He sat down at the table, having retained the manners of an older generation, vulnerable to a woman pouring him a drink or cooking him a meal. Shin was good at being grateful and liked the roles from another era a woman and a man played.

"Do you want a drink?" she asked.

"No. I'm okay."

She served his dinner and sat opposite him without eating.

"You ate?"

"Yes," she lied, always watching her figure, never allowing herself to weigh more than fifty kilograms.

She poured his water and sat quietly, letting him eat in peace. When he was done, she cleared the dishes.

"Did you call her?"

"No. I told you I wouldn't," he said. "The answer would be the same."

It wasn't as if he hadn't tried. He had sent her a divorce agreement. The house would be hers. Again and again, Mary had refused. Shin couldn't ask anymore.

"I did a bad thing," she began. "I'm sorry."

Shin looked concerned.

"I called him."

"Who?"

"Your eldest son."

"Joey?"

She nodded, her eyes full of fear.

"I told you that's not allowed. There's a line. My sons should be left alone. My life is separate from theirs now, and—"

"But you send them money still. Every month. I've never seen you not send—"

"My wife and sons are still my responsibility. What did you say to my son?"

"I invited him to visit us in California. He has a baby sister now. I invited him and his brothers. This summer. Anytime. If she won't give you a divorce, why can't we be modern? Why can't you see your boys? You have a right to see them."

"I can go to New Jersey."

"Why can't they come here? We have guest rooms."

"Do you know where I was today?"

Now it was her turn to look worried.

"I went to see Koh Yohan. But I couldn't find him."

"Why?"

"I needed to talk to someone. You're making me crazy."

"I'm sorry," Danbi said. Shin closed his eyes, and she knew he was trying to be calm, so she went to him and sat on the dining room floor by his chair and laid her head on his lap. "Forgive me. I was wrong. I won't do it again. I want us to be a good family."

Since moving to California with Danbi, Shin had gone back to New Jersey only once, and it had been an awkward three days. Mary had barely spoken to him, and the boys were still in shock. Joey, in particular, could not contain his disappointment. Luke, the middle son, had walked out of the restaurant before the food came out, and the youngest, Patrick, had sat in his chair and cried, begging his father to return.

"I won't do it again," she promised.

This was how it was between them. He would tell her no, and she would test him until he warned her, and then she would apologize, and he would forgive.

"What did Joey say?" he asked her.

"He won't come here."

"Is that all?"

"He said I was a bad person because I knew that you were married."

Shin dropped his chin to his chest, a gesture of such sorrow that Danbi felt desperate to make things right.

"Do you still want to be friends with Koh Yohan? If you miss him, why don't you hire him? I can't imagine him wanting to work at that fried fish place."

"You think he would work at our insurance agency?" He laughed.

"Yes. He's fifty-three years old. There's no trading company that's hiring a man like him. You know that. We had to create our own business and jobs. He has no choices. All these salarymen—"

"I've already asked him. Months ago. He flat-out refused. And the last time we saw them at church, don't you remember what his sister-in-law Sonya said? You are never supposed to talk with his wife or him again."

Danbi said nothing, having later learned more about Sonya and her husband's family's business from Bina, her cousin's wife, who still kept up with everything back home. No one trifled with Sonya, her husband, Yong-gil, or Chairman Mun.

9

Wedlock

Seoul

In the morning, Sonya accompanied the Chairman to view a large parcel of property in Hongdae—six attached buildings not far from the university. The canny seller, who had come down from the North during the war with his family as a young man, now wanted to retire, and his middle-aged daughter, who lived in America, couldn't manage the properties.

The eighty-year-old seller, wearing a maroon wool vest over a charcoal cardigan and gray corduroys, said he wanted a fair price without fuss, and the Chairman was the first person he'd contacted, knowing his solid reputation in the shaky world of real estate. Mun's handshake was a surety of a clean and open deal.

As he was leaving, the Chairman told the seller that he would send the company team for due diligence, but as far as he was concerned, if the engineer, accountants, and lawyers thought it was what the seller had purported, he would buy it.

Seeing the valuable site lifted the Chairman's mood considerably, and he proposed lunch at the Shilla, which was thirty minutes away.

Without having to ask, the host seated the Chairman and Sonya in the back of the restaurant with a grand view of the mountain.

"I feel like a young man," he said.

"You are not an old man."

"You always speak in such a kind way."

Sonya smiled.

"Did you want to get the buffet or order à la carte?" she asked.

"I feel like eating well today," he said.

The two ordered a bottle of sparkling water to share because the Chairman never drank alcohol in the afternoon.

As they ate their lunch, now and then a person would stop by and bow to either the Chairman or Sonya. Across the main room, they spotted a number of friends, and even the pastor of their church was dining with several businessmen.

"I always forget how busy this hotel is," Sonya said.

"It's good to be around and about with my Sonya."

When the bill came, the Chairman paid it, and they walked out of the restaurant, again greeted by a number of people they knew.

"Would you like to pick up some bread?" he asked as they passed the hotel bakery.

Sonya paused to look over the pastries. Her sons had loved the cream bread as boys, but they were now grown men. She selected a loaf of the milk bread and a twist doughnut for the Chairman. When she looked up to ask if he wanted anything else, Sonya spotted her husband walking hand in hand with a slender beauty toward the elevators.

She was not the same woman who'd visited Sonya two years ago. This one was taller and looked more professional in her beige suit-dress and beige suede heels. They stood in front of the bank of elevators and released their hands only for Yong-gil to press the up button.

The Chairman followed Sonya's gaze and frowned before checking his watch. "It is two o'clock."

He motioned with his right hand toward Yong-gil and the young woman, and Sonya suddenly put her right arm on the Chairman's left shoulder.

"It isn't that I don't care," she said. "I do. But I don't think it's wise to approach them now. I'm sorry you had to see that."

The Chairman looked sad.

"It is hard for me to believe that my nephew could be so thoughtless."

"I would prefer to return home," she said, leaving the tray of bread on the counter.

❧

The car ride home was silent. The Chairman rarely spoke about private matters in front of the chauffeur.

At home, the Chairman asked her to come to his office.

"What would you like to do? This is not the first time, and surely it will not be the last. I know a little about some of them, and so far, there have been no children out of wedlock. I suppose I should be grateful for that."

"You looked so happy after seeing the property and during lunch. It's a pity that your good afternoon was spoiled," Sonya said. It was unusual for her to speak of unpleasant things like this with him. She didn't want her husband to be out of favor with the Chairman, but he had witnessed her humiliation, and for the first time, her husband's philandering struck a different chord within her.

"You married him because I asked it of you," he said. "You trusted me and my choice. I take responsibility for this. I did not know the extent of his weakness. He is an excellent businessman. I suppose all of this was not enough." The Chairman raised his right arm slightly, gesturing to his exquisite home.

"I am not enough," she said.

"That's not true. He is a fool. Young men are fools." The Chairman corrected himself. "He is no longer young. In fact, it is precisely when men are this age that they act most absurdly to prove that they are not old. I thought he would be wiser. My sister-in-law spent a fortune on his education and raised him to be a smart businessman, but she did not raise a good man. I thought too little before choosing him for you. What a waste," he muttered.

Sonya felt miserable. She was a failed wife. She had not been able to keep her husband's interest or esteem. In the middle of the day, he held hands with a woman at a hotel where anyone in their world could have seen them.

Everything about her life in Seoul seemed false. Worse, she had let the Chairman down, after he had rescued her from the fate women from her background usually faced. She'd admired no one as much as the Chairman.

The Chairman was embarrassed by Yong-gil's flaunting of his mistress. Their pastor had been in that dining room only moments before. He could have seen his nephew with the woman. The Chairman had always prided himself on properly assessing the character of his employees, and he had treasured Sonya so much that he had asked her to be his nephew's bride.

The Chairman had already written a will leaving his business to Yong-gil, Sonya, and their two sons, whose births he'd awaited in the hospital just the same as Yong-gil. He had named the boys himself.

"I took his dollars," Sonya said, looking up. "From his bedroom safe. He knows it was me. Only I have his passcode. I deposited the money already in an account in California. It was $250,000. I don't know where he got it, and I didn't ask. I took it as my compensation. For all the terrible, terrible conversations I'd had over the years." For a moment, she could hear her own self-pity, and she stopped speaking and looked at her manicured nails.

"It wasn't enough," he said. "A million wouldn't cover it. Not $10 million."

Sonya laughed, and she covered her face with her hands.

"I'm glad you can still laugh."

"Would it be possible to get a million dollars?"

"What?"

"From him."

"Why?"

Sonya couldn't believe the words had come out of her mouth, but when she'd said it, she'd realized that this was what she needed.

"I spoke to a lawyer. I can get an investor visa for America if I invest in a business and create new jobs. She said I'd need a million."

"I'll take it out of his share of the business. I can do that. It's my money to give."

"Really?"

"Yes," he said, feeling pleased. "You never ask me for anything. You can have two. It's easier for me to give you money from his share of the estate than to kill him for hurting your feelings."

She laughed again.

"But why do you need a visa? Did you really want to leave?"

Sonya didn't say anything.

"I need you here," he said. "Even if my stupid nephew—" The Chairman stopped himself. "And the boys need you."

"They're twenty-five and twenty-three," she said, shaking her head, not believing how old they'd become.

"They're fine sons," he said. "You're a good mother. They're better men than their own father."

Neither of them wanted dinner, so Sonya and the Chairman stayed in the den and watched a documentary about a man who had climbed some of the highest mountains around the world.

The housekeeper and cook came by to tell Sonya they were leaving for the night. At ten o'clock, Yong-gil wasn't home yet. What would the Chairman say? she wondered. She was afraid to ask him. It was hard not to think about her husband in a room at the Shilla with that tall beauty in the beige dress.

Whenever mistresses had visited her, it had been during the day, and the conversation had taken place in her office at home. Almost never did she think about the woman and her husband making love. It had been many years since she had been with him, but since he was the only man she had ever slept with, everything she knew about lovemaking was related to Yong-gil. Sometimes she blamed herself for not being sexually attractive or skilled enough to keep him interested in her.

Seeing Yong-gil at the elevator banks holding the woman's hand had made all the prior conversations feel different. Her husband had looked happy and in love. Perhaps he was proud to be with a young, beautiful, and elegant woman in daylight at a luxurious hotel. Perhaps every man knew what they would do, and he had indeed felt young again, drunk on the wine of other men's admiration.

"Do you think I'm attractive?" she asked the Chairman. "I'm sorry. I can't believe—"

"I think you are the most beautiful woman I have ever met," he said. The Chairman put his index and middle fingers lightly between her eyebrows and smoothed out the ridges.

Sonya sat beside the Chairman and watched the clock, wondering if Yong-gil would appear before eleven. If he didn't come home in thirty minutes, he would sleep out and join them in the morning for breakfast. Yong-gil had been more lax recently about his evening schedule.

"He won't be home tonight," the Chairman said. "You should go to sleep."

Sonya went to her room. After she bathed and changed, she went to bed but couldn't sleep. She rose and went to the kitchen.

She got her glass of water and saw that the Chairman was still awake in his room.

"You're not sleeping," she said. She wore a bathrobe over her pajamas.

"Come in and sit down. Talk to me," he said. "I'm worried about you."

Sonya entered his room. He was seated in his reading chair by the large window with an open newspaper on his lap.

"Will you give the American business to your sister and her husband?" he asked.

"I thought if I lived there, then I could be useful. I'm not useful here. They could also work for me. To get the visa, I have to create jobs. I met a woman who owns a nail salon that's really successful. I looked at the numbers. It's impressive. I would be able to pay you back in a few years."

"You've thought it all out. You are leaving me. When I haven't done anything wrong." The Chairman smiled.

"My sister needs me more, I think."

"No. I need you more, Sonya. You and the boys are all I have in this world. I'm sixty-five years old, and all the money and buildings are nothing without you."

Sonya pulled the white robe tightly across her body as if she were cold.

"Is the air-conditioning too strong?"

She shook her head, and then she got up and went to close his door.

Sonya opened her robe and unbuttoned her pajama top. The Chairman looked at her body, then her face.

She moved closer to him and placed his hands on her breasts. He was still seated and dumbstruck at what she was doing. He kept his hands lightly on her, breathing quietly, not speaking.

"It would not be right—" she said, and as she stirred as if waking from her own spell, he pulled her closer to him.

"You're everything that's good in my life," he said, removing her white robe, and she stepped out of her clothes. He followed her to his bed.

Like young lovers, fumbling and shy, without any extra words, they remembered what they were supposed to do, and, submerged in a deep dream, they found each other.

10
Debate

Orange County

They made love, and it was good like before.

Mido buttoned up her cocoa-brown cardigan over her indigo sundress and sat on the armchair. On the bed, Tek was still wearing his blue cotton boxers.

The room wasn't big, but there was a desk for work and beside it a single-cup coffee machine on a mini refrigerator. The window overlooked the tarred roof of the building next door and the half-empty hotel parking lot. It was dark outside, but it was possible to make out the tall palm trees alongside the streetlights.

"I can't stay over," she said.

Tek had assumed that she would, and he began debating with her, which she never enjoyed.

"You're almost twenty-two years old. Your parents can't possibly think that you're a virgin."

Mido didn't know what they thought, never having discussed it with them.

Tek pulled on a blue sweater and a pair of jeans. He stood barefoot on the tan carpet, hands on his hips, ready to argue.

"Your parents would understand. It defies logic that I'd fly all this way and we would not see each other as much as we could. Be reasonable, Mido," he said, then closed his argument: "Deceit breaks bonds. Truth builds trust."

He took her hands into his.

Mido remained seated and looked up at him.

"Tek, my parents expect me back home."

"This isn't a play," he said.

Mido looked at her bare feet. Had she known that he was coming, she would've given herself a pedicure. She tucked her coarse heels beneath the armchair.

"Are you writing out a part for me? Am I the handsome romantic lead? Or the villain? The young lawyer from Australia who travels 7,500 miles to Los Angeles to rescue the budding playwright or to kidnap the sacrificial heroine?" He wagged his eyebrows, trying to make her laugh.

This was Tek. He knew the old Mido—what she had once cared about. In her bedroom, she had not yet unpacked the small stack of plays and writing books that she'd allowed herself to bring to California. In a battered footlocker, she'd stored away her secondhand copy of Lajos Egri's *The Art of Dramatic Writing*, which she'd read cover to cover three times, and treasured books from childhood that Bo, DH, and she had read together. Until now, she had forgotten about the trunk.

In Sydney, she'd seen nearly every new play, musical, and film. Here, only an hour's drive from Hollywood, a place that made movies for the world, she had not watched a single American film. It had been easy to forget what had once given her immense joy because there was always so much work to do at the hagwon. If she had any free time, she'd go to Yun's to eat takeout and watch rented videos of dramas that sometimes had sixty episodes, which she'd never done in Seoul or Sydney, since her parents didn't like television then. She'd sit in Yun's living room with her and occasionally her mother, Nari, and Ginny, not knowing which episode she'd happened to drop in on, not that it mattered, because she was just there to be with people who gave her strength. They could have been eating a pizza, talking about their lives, or baking a cake. She enjoyed watching their rapt faces and listening to the Korean being spoken. It didn't seem to matter how similar the romantic plots were, no matter which era; the stories seemed to comfort Yun and her mother in their predictability.

It was in Mido's nature to keep from mentioning the number of times the same plot devices would occur: A man would give a back hug to a woman cooking or cleaning in the kitchen; a man would grasp a woman's forearm to keep her from walking away; a woman would trip and fall into a man's arms, teaching them to look into each other's eyes and feel the power of an accidental embrace; lovers would never kiss until the second or third episode from the final one. She knew Tek would mock the stories—amnesia, evil mothers-in-law, fated reunions, finale weddings, the way everyone good got a happy ending.

In Seoul and Sydney, Mido's family had watched Korean news occasionally, but here, if Bo wasn't studying, her parents might watch a Korean documentary or the latest drama on a Korean channel. They were living in America, but it didn't feel like it. They spoke more Korean in Orange County than they had in Sydney.

Mido didn't know how to explain any of this to Tek—so bright-eyed in his hopeful expression. He had asked to say hello to her parents, but she had put it off.

He was staying in California for a week, and she'd told him that it would be best for him to see her parents after church, when they could all go out to a restaurant for a meal. She didn't want to bring him home. They had met him a number of times in Sydney, and liked him, but everything was different now.

He would have been startled to see how they lived. Her father fried fish, and her mother sold imported face cream and handbags in a makeshift Korean department store that looked like a warehouse.

At least the new hagwon in Irvine was smart-looking and new, unlike the one in Cypress—three one-story storefronts capped together like uneven teeth to accommodate over a hundred children of salesclerks, line cooks, nurses, schoolteachers, mechanics, and shopkeepers.

Only three years ago, Mido had been a first-year student at the University of Sydney with a play chosen to be staged and performed at the Cellar Theatre by the oldest student theater group in Australia. That part of her life seemed, even to her, to have belonged to another person.

Before Tek arrived, she had been feeling proud that she was helping to pay the rent and contribute to the savings account for their house down payment. The hotel room felt too cold, and she hugged her arms. Mido didn't want to feel embarrassed about her family's place in the world, but she was.

Tek sat on the floor by her feet. He picked up her right foot and massaged it, and she pulled it away gently, not wanting him to feel the rough heel.

"It tickles," she lied.

"Are you writing at all?"

She didn't know how to answer him. He didn't mean to be hurtful, but she felt awful.

"Why did you come?" she asked.

"What? Because I missed you. I thought you'd be glad to see me."

"You said you had work. I wasn't expecting you. I would've planned something—"

"In record time, I finished the PLT and found a new place to live. For the next five or six years, I'll be working like a crazy person at the firm, then start the bar training course so I can read at the best chambers. It's madness how much I have left to do before I become a serious barrister, but I fixed it so I could come right away—" Tek looked hurt, and Mido felt worse.

"I'm sorry. I'm glad you're here."

"You could come back with me. I know all the answers you're going to give already, but I wanted to hear it from you. In person. That's why I came. I make decent money now, not as much as I'll earn as a barrister, but I can cover our costs. Without my parents paying for everything."

"I can't go back."

"You could go back with me if you wanted. This is your life, Mido. Finish uni. Get your degree. You can live with me. I can pay the tuition. I have savings. I have a plan. Stephen Jackson is the best in complex commercial litigation in all of New South Wales—a legend—and he said after my bar training course, I can read at his chambers. His floor has some of the best barristers in Sydney. I've been so busy because I was setting things up for us. Before I turn thirty, I could really be on my own, and I'll get referrals from my firm and from the others on the floor. I'll be arguing really interesting cases. There's not a lot of money now, but there will be loads later. Stephen said that he's never seen a person so young who can argue tactically as well as me.

"If we live simply at first, maybe we can send some money to your folks later. I know they're hard up right now and you're worried about them."

"They're fine," she said, getting up. "I have to go."

"Why are you pissed? Just stay and discuss it. Tell me why I'm wrong. I'm capable of admitting that I'm wrong, but tell me why."

Mido stared at the door, its polished brass knob, and she wanted to go home. She didn't want to explain that she had to help her brothers finish school, that she was thinking of maybe not going back at all. If she kept her salary as the manager of Fortress and increased her tutoring, she could make almost six figures, and she could help her parents get a house and stop paying rent. There had been immigration lawyer bills, car payments, insurance, furniture, rent deposits. What she had not realized as a child was that every day you're alive costs money. If she stopped earning, then someone in her family had to earn more and defer their goals, or put them aside altogether.

"Mido, your parents are good people. They can't possibly expect you to sacrifice your future."

"My folks didn't ask me and don't expect it. This is my decision. My salary is meaningful to our family right now."

"I can help you."

"I don't think that's right."

"I can't move to Los Angeles, Mido. I can't practice law here like in Sydney. I'd have to start all over again, go to law school here, and I've already finished my PLT and have a job at a great firm. I've laid out the course to become a barrister. Do you know how hard this is? There are very few solicitors who are Korean in Sydney and less than a handful of barristers. I've even learned enough business Korean to speak with my firm's Korean corporate clients. My achievements mean something back home—"

"I didn't ask you to live here."

Tek looked pained. "Why, why don't you ask me?"

"I couldn't ask you to start again." She looked pleadingly at him. "And you are meant to be in Sydney, Tek. You love Australia."

"I do. I was born and raised there, and I've worked toward this since I started debate in middle school. This is all I want to do: become a great barrister. And I want to be with you. I don't think you have a better counterargument because I know you want to be with me."

Tek stood up and opened the refrigerator. He took out a bottle of water and drank it. "You didn't ask me to come. You've never asked me to come. This trip was my idea originally, and when I thought I couldn't make it, not once did you put up a fight. And now that I'm here, I know you're happy. Then why can't you come?"

Mido was silent.

"Why didn't you tell me to come here?" he asked quietly.

"I felt bad about the costs."

"It's not like I'm rich now, but what's the point of having any money if I can't see you? What's the point of us dating if we never see each other? It's been two years."

Mido covered her mouth with her hands.

"I'd be happy to marry you," Tek said.

There was that faithful resurgence of confidence. This was how Tek worked. He would push his case, and when it felt hopeless, he'd come up with something else. He couldn't lose. And somehow, this didn't sound like a proposal. He'd be happy to marry her, he said. It was a declaration of love, but it wasn't a request.

"I can't get married. I haven't finished college."

"Are we back to square one, babe? I've submitted a plan. Sydney. I pay all the costs. You. Me. Couple. Happy. What do you say?"

"I'm grateful that you came all this way, but I can't go back to Australia now. My family—"

He shook his head and inhaled. From his expression, she could tell he was thinking of the next argument.

"Can't you stay tonight?"

He'd gone back to the first.

"I told you. My folks."

"It's always about your family. Always. For fuck's sake, I flew all day and night to see you. Remember me? The love of your life? You're my best mate, Mido. I need you to come back."

Mido didn't want to repeat herself, so she said nothing.

Tek wasn't having it. He grimaced and clasped his hands together.

If she stayed with him, her parents would worry, then think poorly of him. But there was the bigger problem: Their outlooks and values were no longer aligned.

Tek was a Korean born in Australia and had grown up only among other Australians. He had visited Korea once. He was an only child of two successful professors. Tek's parents were sophisticated intellectuals. They had never expressed any preference for the race of the woman Tek married and had told her so, which she'd found strange because their opinion was unsolicited. His mother knew they were sleeping together because Tek had told her.

She had never told her parents that she wasn't a virgin. Her parents wouldn't approve, but they wouldn't have said anything.

If she stayed over, she'd be communicating something more than the fact that she was sleeping with her boyfriend. She'd be telling her parents that she didn't care what they thought, and perhaps that was the greater offense.

"They won't like it," she said at last.

"Fine." Tek's face hardened as she gathered her things to leave.

Outside the lobby, there were two taxis waiting for customers. Tek handed her five $20 bills for the fare, which embarrassed her. He opened the car door.

"I'll see you tomorrow morning, then?"

"I have to work tomorrow, but I'll try to get out early."

"Can I come to the hagwon? In the morning? I can work there rather than in my hotel room."

Mido pursed her lips, not knowing what to say. She glanced at the taxi driver, whose hands grasped the steering wheel.

Closing the taxi door, Tek said to the driver, "I need a few minutes, mate."

The driver raised the window to give them privacy.

"I'll stay in the offices where you and Yun work and see you during your breaks. If there's a desk, I can get my work done."

"Wouldn't you be more comfortable working here?"

"No. I would be more comfortable working in Sydney, Mido. Should I just get on a plane tomorrow?"

"I didn't mean that, Tek. I'm sorry. You can't get mad at me when I didn't know you were coming."

Tek turned from her and closed his eyes in frustration. Mido had never seen him so angry.

"Are we still dating?" he asked, raising his left hand as if he were arguing a point with the opposing counsel. "Seriously."

"Okay. Okay. I'll ask Yun and Lion to pick you up tomorrow. We'll go to the dawn services at eight in the morning, then head out to Irvine. I haven't even mentioned to my parents that you want to say hello. I was thinking that maybe after work ends, maybe we could all go out, but my parents get so tired on Sunday nights. I have to go to hagwon after church. I'm in charge of all these kids. Weekends are the busiest at Fortress, and I'm off only on Wednesdays. Do you want to go to church with us?" Mido was exasperated. He had no idea how hard it was for her to move her schedule around. "I don't have a car, Tek, I can't just—"

"No. Just forget it. Forget tomorrow."

Mido touched his forearm, making him turn to her.

"You're right. I won't get out until late tomorrow, but if you come to Fortress, then I can see you during lunch and whenever the kids are taking tests. I might be running around, but if it's quiet, I'll get more time with you. After church, we'll come by. I'll phone when we head to the hotel."

"Okay." Tek closed his eyes and exhaled. "I'm sorry, Mido. You're right. I took you by surprise. By coming." He opened the taxi door, and Mido got inside. He closed the door and, out of habit, knocked on the roof of the car as if for luck.

"Tomorrow, Mido," Tek said.

The driver put his taxi into gear, and Mido turned around in the back seat. Tek stood in place and watched them drive away, willing her to change her mind.

11
Fortress Teachers

Fortress Academy took up the second and third floors of Building E at the Blue Gate office complex. Ever the optimist, Lion had negotiated an option to rent out two additional floors in the same building at the first availability. The high-end commercial complex was owned by Joel Bu, the second son of a wealthy landowner in Hawaii. Joel was friendly with Lion's older brother, Ray, and had given him a favorable lease.

Lion and Yun had designed the office section of their second hagwon with great care. There was a large office for the directors and a smaller one for Mido, the business manager. As at Cypress, the walls were lined with shelves filled with books on education, psychology, parenting, self-improvement, and college admissions, as well as every kind of test guide.

Lion and Peter managed the teachers and curricula, and Mido took care of all the administrative functions. She was in charge of enrollment, scheduling, practice tests, updating study guides, inventory management, and payroll. Both Peter and Mido taught boot camps, tutored privately, and managed the pilot program for college counseling with DH, who had a month left before law school. There were six regular tutors, six part-time tutors, including Bo, and three college counselors.

When Tek arrived at Fortress, Mido let him use her office, and he started his work immediately. As usual, he could focus wherever, regardless of any number of distractions. Mido did not have this ability to tune out everyone around her. He claimed that his foam earplugs did half the work, but when she tried them, her focus was only marginally improved.

It was Sunday, when teachers reviewed the practice tests from the day before. The students were separated according to their verbal or math score ranges, but the class roster was not fixed. Each week, students could be moved from one class to another.

Seated in an armchair opposite Mido's desk, Tek read his files while she reviewed student score reports. Just as with her kindergarteners and middle school students, Mido wanted to get to know each of the Fortress students.

Throughout her years in school, Mido could not recall ever having a teacher care about her in a personal way. She had witnessed many other students being chosen by an instructor—clear favorites who had been marked as gifted or special—but long ago, Mido had accepted that she would never be one of those students. She was too quiet, shy, and plain.

A student like her could not stand out in a large classroom of thirty or forty students, or in a lecture hall of hundreds. It wasn't the teacher's fault. They were busy trying to teach the material and manage a large class. Now that she had been in front of the classroom herself, she was beginning to appreciate just how impossible the job must have been for her teachers.

The only instructor Mido recalled paying careful attention to her was Sean Teacher at the hagwon in Seoul. He didn't seem to have a favorite, but in the classroom of ten or eleven students, he listened to her and seemed to genuinely care. She felt like he liked her the way she was, and perhaps because he thought she was okay, she wanted to learn more about whatever he knew.

After Tek finished his last page, he removed his earplugs and looked up. Mido was taking notes on a yellow legal pad.

"What are you working on?" he asked.

"I'm putting together the list of kids who requested private tutoring. Demand exceeds supply. Peter thinks we should create study groups. Then we don't need to hire more teachers—keep costs down for everyone, and, most importantly, keep the kids more motivated."

Tek looked doubtful, never having been a fan of hagwons or private tutoring.

"Will you be leading a group?"

Mido nodded.

"Really? You haven't taken the SAT here, right?"

"Actually, I have taken it."

"And?"

"I did well enough to teach it. To get hired here, all the tutors have to show their results. In verbal, I got a perfect score."

"And for math?"

"I did quite well, thank you."

She didn't mention that she'd scored in the ninety-ninth percentile. "I could apply to UCLA or Berkeley, or I guess any other university in the States. But getting in is another thing altogether. There are many more factors here than just the standardized tests and grades."

Mido checked the digital clock on the wall. It was already one thirty. "The kids are breaking for lunch."

"What are we eating?" Tek jumped up and rubbed his stomach. "Hungry."

"There are lunch boxes for the faculty in the lounge. Do you want to eat here? I can bring you one, or we can join the others."

"I think we should eat here, no?"

❧

They fed the students at Fortress SAT boot camp. Mido had ordered enough gimbap and cutlet sandwiches for everyone. With only a forty-five-minute break for lunch, the kids ate in their classrooms, but the tutors could eat anywhere.

In the faculty lounge, as Mido was collecting two lunch boxes and two bottles of water, Peter walked in.

"Hey," he said, pointing to her lunch boxes. "Is one for me?"

"Oh, here." She handed him one.

"You want to eat here?" he asked. They usually ate together.

"Tek's here. In my office."

"Your fiancé is following you to work now?" Peter laughed.

"He's not my fiancé. He was kidding."

"Didn't sound that way."

Mido punched his left shoulder lightly, and Peter winced dramatically, pretending to fall backward.

"Why do Korean girls hit?"

"Why do Korean guys need to be hit?"

Peter laughed. She used to be so quiet; now she snapped back at him.

"He's not here for long and wanted to hang out today."

"You're hiding your boyfriend in your office? Do your students know?" Peter grinned. "Should I tell them?"

"You better not, Peter Son."

"Got it. Well, then." Peter sat down at the empty table opposite the food and opened his lunch box.

"How was class?" she asked.

"Highly motivated bunch," he said. "No joke."

"I gave you and my brother the top scorers because they need help on the hardest problems."

"Thank you." He liked being the musician who could make precalculus look easy.

"There's a very long list of kids who want math tutoring. How many do you want?"

"I can do six."

"Can you do sixteen? I was thinking of trying out that group thing. There would be four groups of three."

Peter laughed. "I'm glad you teach verbal."

Mido tapped her mouth. "I mean four groups of four." She pretended to punch his shoulder and tapped him with her fist.

"Wait, you get the math wrong, and I get hit? How is that fair?"

They both turned when they heard the knock on the heavy glass door of the faculty lounge.

Tek waved at her, then entered.

"Here you are."

Peter leaned in and whispered, "Doesn't give you much breathing room, does he?"

Ignoring him, Mido picked up another lunch box.

Peter picked up his food and followed.

"May I join you? So we can keep chatting about the small groups?"

Just then, DH and Bo arrived. They would want to eat with them, too.

"All right," she said.

❧

The five of them moved to the director's office for more space. They had less than half an hour before Peter, DH, and Bo returned to their classrooms. Mido wouldn't teach until later, when the kids switched to verbal.

Tek didn't seem to mind that the others had joined them, which was a relief to Mido. Occasionally Peter spoke to Bo in Korean, and though they knew each other well, Peter still used honorifics and addressed Bo as Brother, because he was a year older. As DH's best friend, through a kind of social transitivity, Peter had become Bo's younger brother, too. Recently Bo had given up the van driving to take more classes at Fullerton and increased his weekend tutoring, which made more money and gave him more time for his schoolwork. Now that DH was here, creating the college counseling program and teaching math, Mido was working with both her brothers and Peter. She enjoyed their company and knew she'd be sad when DH left for school.

Tek had a lot of questions about college admissions and standardized tests. He didn't understand why there were so many factors in college admissions.

"Why should it matter if a person can throw a ball?" Tek asked.

"I wouldn't have gotten into Yale unless I played soccer," DH said, taking a bite of his chicken sandwich. He was already on his second lunch box. "I got a likely letter way before most of my peers at Andover."

"With all due respect, mate, why should soccer matter to your admission status at a top university?" Tek asked.

"Athletes are as valuable to a school community as someone who does well in math," Peter offered. "I was a walk-on for Yale soccer, and it was a tip for me to get in." He studied Tek's profile, realizing that Tek was likely considered better-looking to women than he was. "What was your thing outside of school?"

"I was a national debating champion," Tek answered. "It's quite academic, though. Debate. I wouldn't have been able to do law or become a barrister one day without that early training. I think it's terrible for society that we overvalue athletes. Sports are fine, but they don't help society. Only a few athletes can have jobs doing it, and so many boys lose their minds over it."

"Is my sister's boyfriend putting down soccer?" DH turned to Peter, aghast.

DH had met Tek for the first time earlier in the morning, but hadn't spent any time with him. Bo knew him a little better since they'd met when Bo was in Sydney. Bo felt sorry for Tek; it couldn't be easy to face two older brothers and Peter, who loved watching soccer almost as much as he loved playing music.

Peter switched to Korean with Bo.

"Brother, would you like another sandwich? I'm going to grab another one."

Bo shook his head no. Mido handed Peter half of her sandwich.

"I'm good," she said, and Peter thanked her.

Tek glanced at Bo and Peter.

"How many students does this hagwon have?" Tek asked in English. His Korean had improved dramatically at school, but it would not have occurred to him to speak it with these guys.

Peter replied in English, "A hundred and twenty now, but there's a waiting list. We could have two hundred if we wanted, but I'd have to hire more tutors. As it is, I had to pull Brother out of semiretirement. I hope I'm not going to affect your grades this semester."

Bo was taking two extra classes this summer and working on a psychology research project. He would apply to UCLA in the fall. He studied, worked, and slept. At church, several college girls had tried flirting with him, but Bo refused to notice. He was determined to transfer and eventually get into grad school.

Tek looked around the office. "This place looks like a serious business." He stretched his arms and put his feet up on the coffee table, the soles of Tek's shoes facing Bo.

Bo glanced at Tek's feet and frowned.

Peter cocked his head in surprise, never having seen a Korean put his feet up on a table, especially in front of an elder.

"This place is clearly a moneymaker, mates," Tek said, and he meant it as a compliment.

DH unwrapped the remaining half of his tonkatsu sandwich. He was trying not to deduct points. In his mind, everyone started with a hundred, and they could keep that score or go down. Earlier, he had met Tek in Mido's office only briefly, and though he wasn't an old-fashioned person, having spent most of his life in the States and Australia, even he'd been put off by Tek's breezy casualness.

Bo could be far more accepting of people and would never look for an offense. He would argue that Tek, an Australian-born Korean, wouldn't necessarily know proper Korean etiquette. DH wasn't just offended by the athlete comments, which questioned the merit of his college acceptance; it also surprised him that Tek wasn't recognizing his subordinate status in the room.

Tek was younger than Bo by a year and Peter by a few weeks, which shouldn't have mattered but sort of did, and DH was almost a year younger than Tek, but he was still Mido's older brother, which meant something, too. Tek had committed the social sin of being too familiar. The national debating champion had failed a test without having recognized its existence.

It wasn't that Tek couldn't sense that the guys didn't like him. He knew something was off. He was perplexed and checked Mido's face. The guys were annoyed, but he had no idea why. He had gone to an all-boys school for most of his life and would have thought that he understood men, but Tek had not been around enough Korean guys.

Mido looked at his shoes, which were still on the coffee table. Tek followed her gaze and removed his feet and sat up straight, unable to believe that a bunch of young men could get so worked up about something so minor.

Tek said to Peter and DH, "I heard you two went to high school and college together?"

"I transferred to Pomona my junior year. Graduated in May." Peter put his right hand through his buzz cut. He missed the long fringe, but this was much easier to maintain with just clippers.

"Was Yale difficult?" Tek asked.

DH shook his head, looking annoyed. "No, it wasn't difficult for him. Peter's a fucking genius. He was too smart for us knuckleheads on the soccer team. He just wanted more sunshine and smaller classes."

Peter didn't say anything. He got up from his seat and tucked his black T-shirt into his jeans.

"I heard you're a musician," Tek said, pointing to Peter's head. "Cool hair."

"Yep," he answered. "We better get back to our students." Peter closed his empty lunch box and tossed it into the wastebasket.

Unlike his musician friends, Peter didn't hate professional types. His own family had money, and he was required only to finish college and stay out of trouble, which he had done. That said, from Tek's tone and manner, Peter could sense Tek didn't think much of hagwons or those who worked in them.

Bo picked up his lunch box and water bottle. "Time's up."

"Let's go back to class." As if on cue, Peter and DH followed Bo. Mido got up as well, and Tek was not entirely unaware that he might have lost their good opinion.

12

Bonds

On Monday morning, when Peter drove up to her building, Mido was already waiting outside.

"Where's the fiancé?"

"Peter."

"Kidding. Are we picking him up?"

"No."

Peter had more questions. She wasn't staying over at his hotel, so he figured she was either the kind of girl who didn't sleep with her boyfriend at all or the kind who didn't let her parents know that she was sleeping with her boyfriend.

He didn't want to think about her with Tek, who didn't seem terrible but didn't seem right for Mido. Last night, when they went to get pizza, DH, Bo, and he had talked about the boyfriend. As usual, Peter had said little, so finally DH asked Peter what he thought of Tek.

"He's a suit but doesn't think he's a suit," Peter said.

"Not a fan," DH muttered. "My sister is wasted on him. Too full of himself. Doesn't he know how hard athletes work? If he said 'mate' one more time, I was going to—"

"You say 'mate,' too," Bo teased. "We used to say 'mate' all the time. We just stopped because we moved away. Now you say 'dude' or 'bro'—" He laughed. "He's a perfectly good person. We should trust Mido. She would never date a guy who wasn't decent. We probably made him nervous. My issue is that if she stays with him, she'll have to move."

"Dad would be devastated. She's his favorite," DH said.

"She could do worse," Bo said. "He's clearly smart and a hard worker. Already a lawyer and working to become a barrister. Apparently he's going to do his bar course, then read for some important barrister. Has the chambers figured out and everything. It's impressive. I hadn't done anything like that at his age. You have to give him credit."

"You're right. You're right," DH said grudgingly, and turned to Peter. "My brother is the noble one in the family."

"Yes, I've noticed," Peter said, smiling.

"Thanks, man," DH said. "I mean—*mate.* Have more pizza."

❧

In less than a year, Peter had gotten closer with both Bo and Mido, and it had also occurred to him when Tek showed up that Mido could go back to Australia with him. It made sense for her to do so, since she had to finish college, and she'd already started at the University of Sydney. Her parents had received their green cards earlier in the year, so he figured the family was more stable now.

"Are you going back with him?" Peter asked her straight-out.

"No."

"Does he want you to go back?"

"Yes."

"I heard from Lion you were going to do more tutoring."

"Yup."

"Are you upset or something?"

"No."

"You fight with Tek?"

"Nope."

"Are you going to speak in sentences sometime during this ride to Irvine? I am your nice driver, after all."

Mido laughed and faced him.

Peter looked straight ahead. He wore a black Ramones T-shirt and jeans, looking far younger than his age. She liked the shape of his rounded scalp.

"You don't dye your hair anymore," she said.

"It's also not long anymore." He patted his head.

"When I met you in Seoul, your hair was sort of blond. Then when you started working here, you had it bleached white almost."

"Yup."

"Why did you stop dyeing it?"

"Felt like a stereotype of a musician."

"You're not a stereotype. Of anything."

"Thank you. I think that might be the nicest thing you've ever said to me."

"Oh. Hang on. I can think of more. You're a good teacher. The kids think you're a cool genius. Their scores go up like crazy after you work with them. And most importantly, my brothers adore you."

"Wow. Am I dead? Is this a eulogy?"

"I thought I was always nice to you."

"Yeah, but you don't say nice things to me. I mean, you don't not say nice things. Never mind. You just don't talk as much as other girls."

"I'm not a stereotype, either."

They laughed.

When they got to Fortress, Mido unlocked the doors of the hagwon and turned on the lights. She liked the airy design of the facility and how there was a space for everything. Unlike the hagwon in Cypress, with its ad hoc add-ons, the Irvine site was seamless and clean. Everything was new and attractive, and Mido felt proud to work there.

Peter went to his office to review files and test results, and Mido made a pot of coffee in the kitchen. She carried two mugs of coffee and placed one on his desk.

"Thank you." Peter raised his mug to toast her.

"No problem."

"I guess I could make coffee, too." Peter looked a little guilty.

"It's not a big deal. I'm a college dropout doing admin and tutoring. I know my place." She winked.

"I'll make it tomorrow."

"You drove. We're even."

"I think you got the better trade," he said, and Mido agreed.

❧

The meetings with the parents went quickly. Mothers acted like they didn't care about where their kids were going to college yet were visibly anxious about their children's practice test scores.

Mrs. Kim, Mrs. Cho, Mrs. Im, Mrs. Eom, and the two Mrs. Lees—each of them was distinct in appearance, manner, and personality, but it was as if they had studied the same script.

Often the mothers wanted to know how their child had done relative to the others, and Peter evaded answering because it didn't matter. Over and over, he reassured them throughout the meeting that if the child followed the Fortress plan, most weaknesses could be resolved.

For each student, Mido had already written a detailed individual report and proposed plan of action. The parents liked the reports, and no one objected to the fees that Yun had implemented for individual and group tutoring. Yun had read an article about a famous Koreatown hagwon in Manhattan owned by a former doctor, where the tutors and consultants could charge anywhere from $100 to $300 an hour. Yun had created lower pricing models for Irvine, but they were considerably higher than the ones for Cypress, because it was more difficult to find teachers for the upper-level subjects the high school students here required.

The judge's wife, Melanie Seo, the Olympic medalist, was the last parent Peter and Mido had to meet that day.

Catherine Seo was another pretty teenager from Orange County. She was tanned, with large round eyes with dark lashes, and during her diagnostic exam, she'd had a nervous habit of dabbing her lips with clear lip gloss. Her black hair was streaked blond, giving her a cool LA girl look. On both Saturday and Sunday, she'd worn a black miniskirt with combat boots and an oversize sweatshirt that dwarfed her tiny frame. One would not have guessed that her father was an important judge. Her mother had the squat, muscular frame of a speed skater, but Catherine was built more like her rail-thin father.

Mrs. Seo entered, her face glum. "We had asked Lion Teacher for Catherine to get priority for private math tutoring. As we expected, she didn't do very well."

"Actually, Mrs. Seo, she didn't do badly. She's a bit weak on geometry, but that's teachable."

The mother looked doubtful.

"Also, the longer word problems need some attention," Mido added.

"Yes. I saw that. She got several of them wrong," the mother said as if to bolster her argument for private tutoring.

"I think she'd benefit from group study," Peter said.

"No, no. I think she'd be more likely to admit she doesn't know things if she is working with a tutor one-on-one."

"No," Peter said firmly. "I disagree. I don't think your daughter is like that. I could tutor Catherine privately; however, I think she might be more motivated in a smaller group. Kids like to see other kids solve problems, and my students support each other."

Melanie Seo was not persuaded, and turned to Mido.

"Well, if anything, I think Catherine might need more help in verbal. Especially on reading comprehension," Mido said.

"I was also surprised by that," she said, visibly irritated by her daughter's lower-than-expected score.

"Again, I think a small group would be better for Catherine. I'll be teaching that cohort. If Catherine doesn't improve in two weeks in either math or verbal, we'd be happy to get her private tutoring. It costs less to be in a small group rather than one-on-one."

"The cost doesn't matter," Mrs. Seo snapped. "We all know you have to pay up for the best coaching."

Peter exhaled, having heard this before.

"I believe Catherine will get better results from the smaller group if she could see her peers as teammates in this process, rather than as an individual race," Peter said.

"I disagree," Mrs. Seo said.

Surprised, Mido looked up from her notes.

"Why is that?" Peter asked.

"Ultimately, my daughter will be competing with these kids to get into her first-choice college. The best schools cannot take that many kids. What is the point of them becoming friends when in fact, they are each other's rivals?" she said. "They're not teammates. It's a pretty idea, but be realistic."

Mido was about to speak when Peter broke in: "It's true there are limited seats; however, the race is long, and your daughter would benefit personally from both the best teaching and the community to stay the course. I hope you will respect that."

The mother's jaw appeared immovable. She resented these American Koreans. They had no idea how hard life was, that sometimes true competitors had no choice but to be loners.

"Two weeks. We'll try it your way for two weeks."

The tutors bowed as Catherine's mother walked out.

✤

When Mido finally reached Tek's hotel, he was at the hotel gym. She was almost an hour late. He had left her a key at the front desk.

She sat down in the armchair and pulled out her files, and he walked in, a white towel around his neck.

"I'm sorry," she said. "Work."

"Keep at it. I'm taking a shower," he said. "Then dinner."

When Tek came out of the shower, he was wearing a robe, his hair still wet. He held her tight, and Mido felt good to be with him.

After lovemaking and then a quick dinner at a nearby Spanish restaurant, she returned to the hotel with him.

Tek rummaged through his knapsack and pulled out a box.

Mido didn't have to open it to know what it was.

"Babe, should I get on a knee?"

"No, Tek. No."

"You didn't even see the ring. It's one whole carat." He smiled and opened the box himself to show her the setting. Mido admired it, then closed the box.

"Tek," she said gently. "I need to be here, and you need to be there."

Tek's eyes widened in dismay. "You want to live here and work as an office manager who didn't finish college? Come on, Mido. Why would you throw your life away? Your parents can't possibly expect you to do this. It's not fair. I can speak to them. I can convince them that I can take care of you."

"No, Tek. I don't want that."

"Okay. We can discuss this later."

Mido sighed. "I have to go home. We're not breaking up. That's not what just happened, right? But I can't get married and move to Sydney."

"We can get engaged."

"I can't do that."

"Then we're breaking up?"

"No. Why does it have to be in your time frame?"

"Why does it have to be your location?" he asked.

"It would be wrong to take the ring," she said. "I—"

"I have to return to Sydney. My firm gave me the week, but a big matter came up, and it would be a good opportunity for me to start with the team that—"

"I thought you were going to see my folks and stay the rest of the week."

"I'm changing my ticket, Mido. My work is there. You can keep thinking about my offer. I want you to come to Sydney. I can always send you a ticket."

Mido sat down in the armchair, not knowing what to do. He had taken her by surprise again: first the visit; second the ring; and now the change of flights. She was exhausted and felt angry suddenly.

"Will you leave early?" she asked. "Is this because I can't go with you?"

"Not can't. Won't."

Tek looked in her eyes. She wouldn't change her mind, and he was upset that he had done this all wrong. He could not back down now.

"There are tickets for flights tomorrow. I checked."

"Got it."

"Are you playing hardball with me, Mido?"

"No, you are. I don't even know how to play."

"Fine. Do you need money for the taxi?"

"No, I'm fine. Let me know when you arrive in Sydney."

13
Austerity

October 2000

October was almost over. Bo had started his second year at Fullerton; DH was in his first year of law school at Columbia; and Mido worked as an office manager, college counselor, and tutor at Fortress. John and Helen worked six days a week at the mall in Garden Grove, encouraged by their children's efforts and progress. Already they had managed to save $11,000 for a down payment for a house. They still had only one car, but no one complained.

It was a Saturday night, so the last customer of the day was also the last customer of the week. Helen had already shown Deacon Sobin Ha all the suitcases they carried at the Emporium. Finally the deacon settled on a model, but she wanted a red one to match another bag she'd bought years ago at Mrs. Chung's.

Sobin Ha was not quite forty years old. She wore her dark hair very short, which complemented her lovely oval face. Born and raised in Seoul, she had moved to California at age seventeen to attend UC Irvine and graduated as a chemistry major. A devout Christian, she'd once considered missionary work but didn't like it when she tried it for a year in Bangkok.

Her family came from a great deal of money, and Sobin's father was a successful real estate developer. Sobin's husband, George Hong, a popular elder at Gospel Presbyterian, worked for her father. Her maternal uncle, Elder Fred Byun, was the founding president and chairman of Taegeuk Bank in Garden Grove, and when Sobin shopped, she patronized Mrs. Chung's Emporium, since Mrs. Chung was one of her uncle's oldest customers.

Like her own frugal mother, Sobin refused to spend extra on personal items like clothing, handbags, shoes, and luggage, which were quickly depreciating assets. She'd been taught that status markers were indicative of social insecurity and the downfall of many Koreans.

A person of a good breeding lives in the best neighborhood, owns his own home, attains the best education, and never carries any debt. There's no need to show off. Your address and résumé are everything, her mother had taught her. Sobin did not agree with everything her conservative mother believed; however, she never bought designer clothes or bags or drove an expensive car.

Sobin and her husband, George, owned a $5 million house with a forty-foot-long pool in North Tustin, where they hosted church gatherings twice a year. Each day, she wore a four-and-a-half-carat, emerald-cut, flawless, colorless diamond ring—a tenth-anniversary gift from George. They drove only used Honda Accords and tithed more than 20 percent of their income. They had four children, two girls and two boys, who attended private schools.

Sobin wanted a red suitcase. Of this model and make, Mrs. Chung stocked only black and navy. Helen had made the mistake of telling Sobin that it was manufactured in red but they just didn't carry it.

"Couldn't it be ordered?" Sobin asked, looking hopeful.

Helen smiled and shook her head.

There was no way Mrs. Chung would order six red bags, the minimum number the wholesaler required of each color. If Mrs. Chung had her way, they'd no longer sell bags like this one, which took up a great deal of inventory space and had such modest margins. The collapsible suitcase with swivel wheels cost $200 retail, and there were nine in stock—six black and three navy. The wholesale price was $100, and Mrs. Chung had marked it up by another $100. Helen would make $20 on this sale.

Almost half an hour ago, Mrs. Chung had already closed up the register and wanted Helen to wrap up. No doubt Sobin would buy a bag, but she would not be rushed.

"I prefer the navy, but my husband George doesn't like the color blue. He loves red," Sobin said, opening and closing every zipper. She prided herself on never having been cheated on a purchase, not even as a girl at a no-name stall in Namdaemun with the canniest of hawkers.

"I can't understand why anyone would buy a black suitcase when everyone has one. It's confusing when you go to baggage claim and every bag looks exactly the same. Sometimes my husband will pull out the wrong one from the carousel, and another person gets angry, and it's nobody's fault. Isn't that right?"

Sobin chattered on in Korean as if no one else had ever made the same remarks to Helen before. She had a wide-eyed innocence about her, and if Helen weren't tired and it weren't so late in the evening, she would not have minded any of this.

Helen smiled and kept her breath even. She was exhausted. In the past few months, it had been increasingly difficult for her to sleep and keep her food down. Her neck felt warm all the time, and at night, she perspired, which she'd never done before. Sonya said she'd had similar menopause symptoms, especially the difficulty sleeping. Helen also had stomach pains and had been taking antacids, and even though she didn't eat much and avoided spicy meals, her stomach looked bloated.

Sobin rolled the navy bag to and fro in front of the mirrored wall. Trim and clean-cut, she wore a simple white T-shirt, jeans, and white tennis sneakers.

"Are you taking a trip?" Helen said, and when Mrs. Chung glanced in her direction, she immediately regretted having asked.

"I'm going home to a wedding. We have to bring so many things. It's my older cousin's son."

It was late, and this was no time for small talk. Mrs. Chung kept checking her watch. She liked Sobin Ha enough but disliked how little she spent. In her experience, very wealthy people could be terribly cheap in places like hers. They could throw money around in fancier establishments, but with Koreans, they would haggle down to the last nickel. She wished Sobin would shop elsewhere. That said, Sobin Ha was the niece of her banker, Fred Byun, and her husband, George Hong, was a fellow elder at the church.

"The wedding is in two weeks," Sobin said, checking the wheels below the bag with great care. "I can't miss it."

"Congratulations," Helen said.

"My cousin's son is marrying a pediatrician. They met in college. The bride's father's a surgeon and so is the girl's brother. Some families have all the brains."

Helen pressed her hand against her abdomen. The dull pain had returned. It came and went. This afternoon she had eaten only a quarter of her ham and cheese sandwich, which Mrs. Chung had ordered her for lunch.

"Are you all right?" Sobin looked up from the bag and examined Helen's face, from her neck to her forehead.

"Your coloring isn't good. Your eyes look a little yellow." The deacon leaned in and whispered, "Have you been to the doctor? Maybe you should get a liver function test. You're perspiring. Are you warm?"

Helen removed her left hand from her abdomen, touched her brow, then placed both hands on the counter as if to steady herself.

From across the shop, Mrs. Chung glanced at the two women, who were whispering.

"I'm fine," Helen said.

One of the hallmarks of a high-level service worker was that she never drew attention to her own needs. Whether it was at a store in a Garden Grove shopping mall or the finest department store in Sydney, Helen wanted to present competence and fine service. Then she had a thought.

Helen turned and rooted around in the glass cabinet behind her. She pulled out an attractive red canvas luggage tag from the bottom drawer.

"If you put this tag on a black bag, then your husband can get the color he wants, and you'll be able to tell that it is your bag."

Sobin smiled.

"Is the tag included?"

"It's $20, but I'd be happy to include it as a gift," Helen said, smiling through her discomfort.

Mrs. Chung nodded. The wholesale price for the luggage tag was $7, and she wanted to go home.

"Oh, no. I could never accept that," Sobin said, fingering the modern-looking tag, which she liked. It was exactly the right color. "Oh, I know. I'll accept this one as a gift and buy another red tag for my bag at home."

Helen smiled and began to write up the purchase on her sales pad.

❧

The lights were still on at Shrimp Castle, but the shop was closed. Helen knocked on the glass door, and Nari let her in. John was still cleaning the range.

"You look tired," Nari said.

"Yes, it's been a long week. I want to get home and take a bath."

"He's almost done," Nari said, peering into the kitchen. "I feel so bad at how hard he works. What a smart man, and what he has to do now."

Helen didn't know what to say. Her husband had done nothing but work hard all his life, and now he was frying seafood and cleaning an oil-splattered range six days a week. There might be white-collar jobs that would consider him, even at his age, but the starting pay would be less than half of what he made here. Already Nari had increased his salary to $1,300 a week.

"I don't know what I would have done if you two hadn't come and saved me. After my husband went to Brazil, I thought I'd die."

Helen shook her head, leaning on the chair near her. "No, no. We're grateful to you. You and Yun have helped us so much," she said. Then, suddenly, the pain in her abdomen grew more intense.

"Are you okay?" Nari said. "Sit down, sit down."

Helen exhaled. Beside her was a table with four chairs, and she slumped into the chair closest to her and put her head on her forearm.

❧

When Bo returned to the apartment around ten o'clock, no one was home. It wasn't like his parents not to be there on a Saturday night. Once every few months, John and Helen might go out to eat, but they would come home first to wash up, and his father's uniform was missing from the laundry basket.

He called Fortress and Peter answered. He and Mido were about to head back.

Bo went to his room and took out his seminar assignment. He had photocopied the assigned pages at the library because the textbook was so expensive, and he hadn't been able to purchase a used copy. As he read, he underlined the important concepts so he could create an outline of them later, but, worried about his parents, he couldn't focus.

Half an hour passed, and Bo wasn't sure what to do. He phoned Yun's mother, Nari, and got no answer. When he phoned Yun to see if she'd heard from her mother, she hadn't.

When the phone rang, it was Peter, who was at the gas station, filling up.

"Mido is asleep, but she asked me to call to see if her parents were home."

"Not yet. It's odd. They should have been home a while ago. It's not like them."

"Okay, I'm not far from you. I'll bring Mido home. Maybe it's nothing," Peter said.

Bo hung up and went to the kitchen to make coffee. As he waited for the water to boil, he put a teaspoon of instant coffee into his mug. Silently he prayed, *Help, God. Let them be okay. Please.*

❧

Mido woke up when Peter got back into the car.

"Can I help pay for the gas?" she asked, even though he never let her.

"I called your brother, and your parents still aren't home."

"What?" Mido rubbed her eyes. "Where's the pay phone?"

Peter pointed.

"I'm going to call Yun."

"Do you want to wait until you get home? It's only ten minutes from here."

Mido agreed, and when they reached her house, she invited him up.

Bo was drinking coffee and sitting in the living room without a book in front of him.

"You haven't heard anything?" Mido asked.

"No," Bo said. "It's so strange. I can't reach Yun's mother, either."

Straight after taking off her shoes, Mido went to the phone and called Yun, and as they were talking, she paused when the call waiting beeped.

"Hang on. There's a call," Mido said, picking up.

Bo and Peter saw Mido's eyes widening. "I'll be right there," she said in Korean.

14
Wives

Helen never returned to the Emporium.

After the rotation of emergency room doctors and nurses, a succession of specialists followed. First there was an ultrasound, then a scan, which revealed a large mass on the pancreas, and that the cancer had already spread to Helen's liver and bones.

The doctors were kind and respectful. They listed the ailments she'd been experiencing without her ever mentioning them: back pain, bloating, cramps, weight loss, fever, vomiting, constipation, dark urine, and inability to eat. She said yes to most of them.

How did you bear it? they asked.

How you must have been suffering, they said.

No, they did not know how she'd gotten this.

No, no, no. Of course it was not her fault.

Yes, we will do everything possible to relieve you of your pain.

Hospital clergy stopped by to pray with them, and a nice social worker who spoke Korean gave them some phone numbers. While she was hospitalized, Mido, Bo, and Peter took turns staying with John, who had to miss work.

Helen and John did not have health insurance. Everyone in their household earned an income above the poverty level, and Helen and John had just finished their immigration paperwork and received their green cards. They were on track to get their citizenship. They would not qualify for Medicaid because they made too much money. Bo and Mido told them not to worry. They had jobs and credit cards.

Doctors offered treatments without much enthusiasm. Helen received a stent to improve her bile flow. Over the course of a month, her condition deteriorated so rapidly that the doctors recommended palliative care. They laid out her options. Helen wanted to be at home. She made everyone promise not to tell DH until Thanksgiving, when he came home. "It's his first year in law school," Helen pleaded. "I have to tell him myself. When he's home."

❧

Bo picked him up from the airport, and as soon as they walked through the front door, DH shouted, "What's the matter with Mommy?"

Helen was resting on the sofa with an aluminum cane by her side. Her skin dark gray and her body nearly skeletal, she was watching the Korean news with her eyes half-open while Mido set the table. Over her yellow flannel nightgown, she wore DH's Andover sweatshirt.

Removing his shoes and dropping his coat on the floor, DH rushed toward her.

"Stop. You should wash your hands," Mido said, and pointed to the kitchen sink.

DH scrubbed his hands with soap, and, his hands still wet, he went to his mother. Helen opened her eyes and smiled when she saw him leaning over her, his wide shoulders and tall frame towering over her shrunken one.

"Ah, my Dae-hun is home. Mommy is so happy to see you. I waited." She touched his wavy hair and mussed it up playfully. "Didn't I do a good job waiting for you? I missed you so much."

DH glanced at Bo and Mido, both weeping silently.

"How could you not tell me?" DH said, bursting into tears as Helen explained. "Oh, Mommy. Oh, Mommy. Not you. Please, not you. Please."

❧

DH wanted to take a leave of absence, but Helen said absolutely not. In exchange, even though it was expensive, she asked him to phone her for a few minutes every day.

When DH argued that he couldn't study because he'd be worrying about her, Helen told him that people usually die without warning, and in a way, this was far better because every call mattered, and she would have more peace of mind if he was in school. If things were really awful, she promised he could come home right away. It would make her happy if he did well in his first semester at Columbia.

"I want you to stay on track. Bo is doing his very best to finish Fullerton while working so hard, and he will get his four-year degree soon. Both of you and Daddy will make sure that Mido gets her turn at school, right?" Helen looked at her sons while smiling at Mido, who did her best to smile, not wanting to disagree or upset her mother. "Mido earns more money than all of us now. Isn't that amazing? Oh, my children."

"I can stay home and help," DH said. "Drive you to the doctor and run errands."

"I'll ask God for another Christmas, when you can come home. Maybe I will get another Christmas."

"Ask God for another summer, because I'll get an internship in Los Angeles."

"Deal," Helen said, smiling weakly before closing her eyes.

❧

Each morning, Nari drove John to Shrimp Castle.

He could not afford to stay home. The hospital bills continued to arrive, and though a social worker had connected them with an organization that assisted immigrants, John could not see how they could ever pay all the bills.

The mailbox filled him with dread. Bo and Mido told him not to worry. The three of them were paying for everything in installments. Every credit card they had was spent up to its limit. Just when it looked like the total amount of debt was $36,000, suddenly another bill would arrive for a scan and a doctor's visit from weeks ago, and it would be for a few thousand dollars. The pain medication always had to be paid for.

Like a faithful ox pulling a plow, John worked silently each day. Nari made sure that he ate breakfast and lunch. She raised his salary to $1,400 a week, which was the best she could do while she paid off the promissory note for the store. Yun, having graduated, now worked full-time at Exodus as the CFO. With her salary, she was helping her mother with the rent and utilities.

❧

On the Monday following Thanksgiving weekend, Taehun Shin dropped by while John was hosing down the kitchen floor.

The shop was closed but, recognizing the deacon, Nari let him in. She bowed to him and pointed to the kitchen.

"You should stand back because the water might get on your nice clothes," she warned Shin. Nari knew there was something wrong between the men, but no one had told her about what Danbi Jung had done to John Koh. Helen had never mentioned that Shin wasn't divorced from Mary, or that Danbi wasn't his young wife. Nari just knew the men had once worked together and that they were not close.

"Knock, knock," Shin said, tapping on the counter.

"What are you doing here?" John asked sharply. He was tired.

Taehun Shin wore a clean white dress shirt with a crimson silk necktie and navy suit trousers. He'd left his suit jacket in the car, not wanting to show off; however, his well-tailored clothes were costly and looked so.

"I heard about Helen. I wanted to see you. If there is anything I can do, you should know that I'm here. I always thought Helen was a kind person. An elegant woman and a good mother."

"She's not dead, you son of a bitch. Get out. Can't you see that I'm working?" John flung his sponge on the ground, missing the boots he wore when he sprayed down the tiled floor. What was the point? he wondered, wiping his forearm across his forehead. The smell of bleach water on his gloves overpowered him and stung his eyes, making him blink back tears.

Shin stood there, feeling the weight of the man's sadness. He'd known John for almost three decades and had never seen him like this.

The back door of the kitchen opened and Ernie, the new helper, walked in, having finished his cigarette.

"Boss," Ernie said, "I'll finish up if you want to go home."

"Thanks, Ernie," he said, picking up the sponge, then removing his wet apron and gloves.

❧

Shin offered to drive him home, but John refused.

"Oh, that would help me," Nari said. "I have to wait until Ernie is done, then I can head straight to Yun and Lion's place, and you can get home faster." She knew he was worried about Helen.

John sighed and followed Shin to the parking lot. He drove a new white Mercedes sedan. Shin and Danbi had opened their insurance agency, and many of the newer parishioners from their church bought their policies there. They'd quickly made a success of it.

"I know you're angry with me," Shin began, "but the church asked me to come by. Do you want to get a drink? I can buy you dinner."

"We are never going to drink together again," John said.

"Do you know how many hundreds, no, thousands of meals you and I've shared? You are one hard-hearted bastard," Shin said, pulling out of the parking spot.

John leaned against the headrest, feeling the weight of the day worsen. He was in Shin's expensive car because he didn't have one of his own. Bo was driving their only car to and from work and school. He closed his eyes.

"You're tired. If you don't want dinner, you can sleep. There's going to be traffic, so you can rest."

"Why did you come again? I told you to never show up."

Shin didn't answer. At an intersection, he stopped the car and turned around to take out an envelope from the pocket of his suit jacket, which was hanging on a hook above the back passenger-side door.

"I wanted to give you this. You must have a lot of bills."

"I don't want anything from you. I'd rather fry shrimp for the rest of my life."

Shin exhaled, having anticipated as much.

"It's not from me, you bastard. It's from the deacons' fund. The church wanted to give it to your family. Helen's not working, and I don't know about your insurance situation, so—"

"Why didn't the pastor give it to us? He was at the house the other day."

"The deacon fund is different. Yaah—don't be so difficult. If you want me to ask another deacon to bring it to you so you don't have to accept anything from me, I can do that. Don't be such a prick. Your wife is—"

"Shut up. Shut up."

"I was wrong for what I did back in Korea, but I also helped you out a bunch of times. You've been mad at me, and I'm not saying you don't have a right to be, but I've said I was sorry a hundred times. I *am* sorry."

John looked straight ahead. It didn't seem fair to have to forgive him, too, on top of everything else. If Helen died, then he would have been forced to lose almost everything in his life—his parents and brother, his career, his only friend, and his treasured wife. Shin could not possibly understand how cruel it was to make him sit in this car, scented by some car freshener that smelled like vanilla candy. Shin missed him, and that was why he had come, but not forgiving him had been the only thing John could hold on to that had allowed him to keep his dignity. Now Shin wanted that as well.

It occurred to him that he hadn't been in a car with Taehun Shin since they were in Seoul.

"This morning I was thinking of when we got snowed in that time in western Alberta," Shin said, laughing.

John remembered that long drive from Calgary to Hinton. They'd gotten a flat tire and the snow had started and wouldn't stop.

"I thought we were going to freeze to death. I didn't want to die trying to visit some coal mines," Shin said, smiling.

John recalled how beautiful it had been in that car, the snow falling, falling. The hush of the powdery white flakes descending upon them, and the whole world remembering to be still.

"You brought those sandwiches and chocolate bars. Koh Yohan. Always prepared."

They had stopped driving and sat in the darkened road until the snowplows arrived. The men had eaten their ham sandwiches, then the Hershey bars. Shin had told funny stories from their days at KATUSA, and John had laughed in the warm car, unafraid because the two men were together.

"Are the children okay?" Shin asked.

"Are yours?" John had always liked the boys. Joey was responsible, Luke was studious, and Patrick was like a comedian. John could remember little Patrick doing funny dances. Mary had done a good job raising them.

"The boys don't speak to me anymore. They took their mother's side. I can't blame them."

John shook his head. Nothing could have made him give up his children, and if they gave him up, John did not think he could bear it. In the kitchen at Shrimp Castle, he had hung a plastic-covered photograph of his family taken in Sydney years ago, which always made him smile.

"I have a little girl now. With Danbi. Her name is Anna."

"I saw her at church. How old is she?"

"Almost three. Girls are different than boys. I think she owns me." Shin laughed.

John knew what he meant. He loved his sons, of course, but Mido was different. He didn't know if that was because she was a daughter or if it was because she was Mido, but if she asked him, he would have fought a war for her.

"My little girl talks all the time and has so many questions. When my sons were small, they were kind and sweet, but none of them was as affectionate as my little Anna. She's smart like her mother, but of course, unlike her, innocent."

John said nothing and let the silence fill the car. He would not say anything about that woman. This was something that he and Helen had agreed upon, to never speak of her. The only people who knew about Danbi were Helen's sister and brother.

"I tried to leave Danbi a few times, but she threatened to kill herself and Anna if I did."

"Crazy woman," John blurted out.

Shin exhaled. "I've never met anyone as crazy as the woman I am living with. Every day is a kind of new hell. I am being punished for all that I have done to my family. I am being punished for what I did to you. It would be easier for me to die now. If I could die instead of your wife, it would be justice," Shin said. "If I could have my way, I would ask for that. I am so sorry. You have always been a friend to me, and I was wrong. I was weak."

Shin was looking straight ahead, his right hand on the steering wheel and his left covering his mouth as if to suppress a scream. John recognized that expression.

When they had been in the army, a soldier would be picked on and on occasion hit by a superior-ranking soldier or just someone stronger. When a man was being beaten and didn't know when it would end, he looked like Shin did now, as if he knew it would be worse to let the pain out. At first, when a soldier got yelled at, smacked, punched, or kicked, naturally there'd be some fear, but when it didn't let up, there was a kind of horror, not just from the pain that would surely come but also from the thought that there might be no end to the beating and more might come the next day and the days to follow.

Shin got off the freeway and drove toward Cypress.

"There's a restaurant down that street," John said.

15
Fruit

Most evenings, Sonya sat in the den with the Chairman as he read his business periodicals and books. In the morning, he read three newspapers, and at night, he caught up on real estate journals and business books in translation. He had not attended college, and from reading and public lectures, he had taught himself finance, accounting, capital markets investing, and business theories. The Chairman kept tidy notebooks, summarizing the key points of everything he studied.

Sonya was crocheting a red cardigan for Helen's Christmas present. The torso complete, she was working on the arms. By November, she had already finished her sons' matching blue sweaters. Now and then, the Chairman would look up from his papers, remove his reading glasses, and admire her handiwork.

After the household staff went home, and if her husband, Yong-gil, had not returned for the night, they would go to his room.

A virgin before marriage, Sonya had only been with Yong-gil. After the birth of their second son, her husband had been less and less interested in going to her bed. They'd always slept in separate rooms, because he came home late frequently and she was a light sleeper. A dressing room and bath connected Sonya's bedroom with her husband's.

The Chairman's bedroom was on the opposite side of Sonya's, so when she slept in his, she'd lock the door to the dressing room and the main door to her bedroom; however, her husband never tried to open her doors.

Except for when the boys were home, visiting from their military service, the Chairman asked her to sleep in his room.

In his bed, she called him by his name, Hong-gyun. Elsewhere, she addressed him as the Chairman, no differently from when he had hired her out of college.

Hong-gyun was sixty-five years old, and she was fifty-four. Like her, he had not had many lovers, and like her, after his wife got sick, he had been abstinent. Neither had made love for almost two decades. There had been numerous opportunities for him to find women to bed; however, the idea of being with someone he neither admired nor loved repulsed him. If he could, he would have made Sonya his wife.

He liked watching her undress, and asked her to remove her clothes slowly the way she had done the first time she came to his room in her nightgown and robe. They had been lovers for a little over four months, and it was as if time had passed backward. The years seemed to fall away.

From the beginning, she had fought her unyielding infatuation with her married employer, not wanting to feel the guilt and shame. When the Chairman asked her to marry his nephew, it had felt like a gift. She had initially imagined falling deeply in love with Yong-gil, but he was never enamored with her; at best, he was grateful for their two sons and respected how she did not make a fuss about his affairs. The marriage was a kind of professional relationship.

Long ago, she'd accepted that she would never be loved as a woman, and had taken consolation in the love and admiration of her sons, her friends, and the Chairman. She knew this kind of love and esteem were far better than what most people could expect. When Sonya prayed to God, she prayed for the well-being of her family, her friends, and even her enemies, but it had never occurred to her to petition for love.

The Chairman excited her, and she loved being with him. Although she had always been fastidious about her appearance, she took even greater care with her bathing and dress to please him. The Chairman was besotted with her.

"You make me feel like I'm thirty," he said.

They were in bed, about to go to sleep. Sonya thought she should return to her room, but again, he didn't want her to go.

"I'll get up early and wake you. Before the housekeeper gets here—" he promised, kissing her neck and shoulders. They'd made love several hours earlier and had been listening to music together in bed, but as she was about to close her eyes, his hands reached for her breasts and hips, and Sonya yielded to the growing pressure of his cock.

Sonya could not believe this part of her life. The Chairman loved her, and she him, and this interval felt like a burst of pure joy after decades of duty.

Still, she knew it was wrong. Despite the guilt, she justified this because she had raised her siblings, taken care of her husband and sons, and nursed the Chairman's wife. This unexpected love had made her realize how little she knew herself, and how unhappy she'd been.

They did not speak directly about her marriage.

"Would you make sure that he never enters your room?" the Chairman asked her more than once. "Can you keep that closet door locked in the evening always? I cannot bear the idea of him going to your—"

"We haven't been together since Jiman was two or three—" Sonya could hardly recall. Perhaps it was when her younger son was in preschool. Like an incubus, late at night, when she was asleep, Yong-gil had come to her room to make love to her, then vanished, never to return.

For years, she'd wondered how she'd failed to keep her husband's sexual attention. After menopause, she reasoned that he wanted the flesh of much younger women, and there was little she could do.

Her friends had surgery, difficult procedures, and regular costly treatments, and some looked unbelievably young, fresh, and beautiful; Sonya had resisted this. She swam, did yoga and Pilates, and stayed out of the sun.

She had the ordinary vanity of an intelligent woman who had been beautiful from birth. For now, she felt lovely enough for a woman in her fifties. She had resolved long ago that she could never compete for her husband's sexual attention with knowledgeable young women from hostess bars, and there had been both resignation and dignity. Awakened by a midlife love affair, Sonya looked in the mirror more often, and she did not dislike what she saw.

Within fourteen weeks, the Chairman and Sonya had tried various positions and oral sex, which was new for her. They had bathed together, and once they met at a hotel suite to try Viagra, a joke present from a former high school classmate of the Chairman's that he had never thought to actually use. The experiment had been painful for her and uncomfortable for him. For days, they laughed at the memory of this seemingly endless erection.

After almost never having any sex, they had it so frequently that Sonya had to get antibiotics for a tract infection and learn about lubrication. Like teenagers, they made love more than once a day, and on occasion, they would meet in the middle of the day at beautiful hotel rooms in Seoul. They became inseparable.

Often the Chairman bought her presents—a diamond pendant, a long South Sea pearl necklace, more exquisite clothing, and jewel-colored silk lingerie.

One Sunday he made a reservation at a hotel not far from their apartment and gave her a key. After church, they separated publicly, then met an hour later in the room.

He was already there waiting when she arrived.

"I don't know if the hotel manager noticed me," she said.

"It doesn't matter," he said, smoothing the hair away from her brow. He felt the need to touch her, and this wasn't possible outside of a hotel room or his bedroom. They never went to her room. "I almost don't care anymore about getting caught."

Neither knew what would happen if they grew more careless. They were more worried about her sons than Yong-gil.

During church service, as usual, Sonya had sat between her husband and the Chairman, and even the scent of the Chairman's vetiver and woodsy aftershave reminded her of their intense lovemaking. She was eager to meet him at the hotel room after church, and she felt ashamed of her weakness. However, after services, without blinking, she lied to Yong-gil, saying that she couldn't have lunch with him because she was meeting a friend from college. The Chairman had left them already, giving some excuse himself.

For the first time in years, Sonya wasn't angry at her husband. If anything, she found him almost pleasant. He was a hardworking executive who took good care of the Chairman's company. She enjoyed their polite interactions. They never fought. If they discussed anything, it was the company or their sons.

In the room, she immediately stripped off her clothes, and he led her to the bed, where he took her from behind. With both hands, he held on to her breasts, then, when she was about to climax, he lay down, and she climbed on top of him.

"I need you," he said, and she murmured the same.

They lay in each other's arms, and when room service arrived, she hid in the bathroom so he could let the server in.

Naked and seated on the ledge of the cold marble bath, she saw herself in the mirrored wall. Her face was glowing, and her pink nipples were flushed and raw.

He knocked on the door to let her know that it was safe for her to come out.

"Would it be possible for me to divorce him?" she asked, standing before him, her forearms covering her small, lovely breasts. "Is there a way for us to be together as husband and wife?"

How could this be wrong when she was so in love with a man she'd known even before her husband? she wondered.

In his white terry cloth hotel robe, the Chairman was seated on the sofa by the window. He'd found her appealing the first time she entered his office, and he had told himself to be appropriate and distant. It was she who had reached for him first, coming to his room, and now she was proposing.

"Aren't you cold?"

She shook her head no. "Do you want me to put a robe on?"

"No."

Sonya went to bed and drew the covers over her shoulders and waited for him to come to her.

"There's no need for anything to change," he said. "I promise not to ask too much of you. I am a man, and you are a woman. Yong-gil is not my son, but he is my dead brother's child. You and your sons will have everything I have one day."

She opened her mouth to say something, but he shook his head. The conversation was over.

❧

When they returned home in the evening, Yong-gil was out. The household staff had left for the day. There was a voicemail from her brother-in-law.

"Sister, I am so sorry to leave this message—" John's voice was broken and strange.

Sonya glanced at the Chairman, and he remained with her.

"My wife is very ill. She didn't want you to know. But." He hesitated. "I think you should come to California and see her. I don't think there's much time. If you could call me—"

Sonya phoned Helen's house, and John picked up. Helen couldn't get on the phone because of the morphine. "On the next flight," Sonya promised.

During the call, the Chairman had been sitting beside her.

"Let me call my secretary. He'll put you on the next flight."

"This is my fault. I'm being punished. Every day I was happy, I worried that something terrible would happen to the boys, and for them, I prayed for mercy. If something bad happened to me, then I'd deserve it." Sonya clasped her hands. "But Helen—"

"I don't think the Lord works that way."

"I'm being punished. I should be punished."

"Then shouldn't Yong-gil have been punished for all of his affairs?" he asked.

"He was, though. I no longer love him. His affairs never gave me the right to dishonor my vows, though."

The Chairman grew serious.

"Hwang, an old friend of mine who is living mostly in New Jersey, wants to buy a building in Seoul for his son. I've made arrangements for you."

"What?" Sonya looked at him.

"That business visa you wanted, to buy a business. If I buy Hwang his building in won, he can get you the dollars right away. He's already in the States, so the cash transfer will be easier. You can buy that business and whatever else you need. I've already spoken to the lawyers. I thought I'd get you that money when you went to California, but this trip came up sooner than planned."

Sonya understood. He would not allow a divorce with Yong-gil for the scandal it would spark, but he'd give her the money she needed.

"I know you're worried about them. Take good care of your sister, but after—" He stopped himself from saying what was inevitable.

"I will be waiting for you here."

Sonya headed to her room to pack.

♣

When Sonya arrived in Cypress, she didn't allow herself a visible reaction to Helen's jaundiced and gaunt frame. Her sister's face was all bone and angles, her eyes yellow and their sockets hollow; gray skin stretched across a sharp jawline.

The morning after she arrived, Sonya rented a collapsible wheelchair and a large hospital bed, which she placed in the living room alongside a twin bed for herself. She hired hospice nurses to administer pain medication and to care for Helen around the clock.

Sonya took charge of the kitchen and cooked meals for Helen and the family. When she wasn't with Helen, she was on the phone with medical experts in her extraordinary network. Now and then she would leave the house to meet business sellers, immigration and estate lawyers, and real estate brokers. The household seemed to shift, and it hummed along as if a competent general had arrived with reserves for a devastated squad of soldiers.

Even when it was eighty degrees outside, Helen was often cold. Most days, she lay on the living room sofa beneath a comforter and a fleece throw, writing in one of her three notebooks whenever she had any energy. She slept a great deal, and when she was awake, she didn't talk much. The house was crowded with people, but it was mostly quiet. As before, John went to work six days a week. On Sunday mornings, everyone went to church while a nurse stayed with Helen, and they returned home unless they were working.

Now and then, Helen would wake and be clear and talkative. She worried about debts.

"How will we pay for all this?" Helen asked John, pointing to the rented hospital things and the team of hospice nurses.

"No more talk about money," Sonya said. "I have plenty."

John showed her the envelope from the deacons' fund, which he had been meaning to deposit.

"Shin Taehun came by."

Sonya looked surprised. "What?"

"It's from the church," he said. "The bills will get paid."

"How much is it?" Helen asked, clenching her brow. The stony gray-brown skin stretched across her forehead.

"It'll take care of the bills," John said, avoiding her question. $5,000 wouldn't come close to covering the growing pile of bills, but Helen didn't need to know that. "Shin Taehun said this is from the deacons at the church, and if we have more needs, we can ask for help."

Sonya looked stern. "No more talk of bills. You focus on getting well." She turned to Helen. "My little girl, haven't we solved every money problem we've ever had? Every single one. We were no better than paupers, and somehow, you and I paid college tuitions and didn't starve. You rest."

"I don't want to have these debts between your husband's family and us."

"And I don't want to talk about money anymore. What can I do if I don't have you?" Sonya turned her face away and took a deep breath. "You have to trust me. I can be trusted, right?" she said calmly, stroking Helen's warm head. Sonya brushed away the wisps of baby hair that continued to grow. "I will protect you."

In the morning, her head and body heavy and dull from morphine, Helen shook her head no when Sonya tried to feed her porridge.

"I want to eat grapes," Helen said as if she were in a dream. "Isn't that the oddest thing? All day yesterday, I was thinking of those purple grapes from Mr. Jo's market."

"You mean the mart near the bakery behind the elementary school?"

"Yes, that's the one," Helen said. "I always wanted to eat those grapes again. Buy a box of them and eat the whole thing."

"We got caught, didn't we?" Sonya laughed, recalling the time she stole a bunch when Mr. Jo wasn't looking. Kenny had begged and begged, and finally, Sonya took some and walked away. "Mr. Jo was so angry."

"Mother caned you with that back scratcher, but you didn't cry once," Helen said.

Sonya had brought her sister and brother the purple grapes wrapped in white paper. They had never tasted grapes before. In an alley, the three children had eaten the fruit, seeds, skins, and all, their fingers and faces stained a deep purple.

"I can get Bo to drive me to the store."

"No, no. Don't bother him. He's writing a final paper."

"Our children are better than we are," Sonya said. On her last call home, her elder son, Seungman, had told her to take as much time as she needed in California. "I don't deserve my sons."

"What a thing to say." Helen patted her sister's hand. "My sister deserves all the good things in this world."

16

Instructions for the Living

Within two weeks of Sonya's return to Orange County, by mastering the church networks and through introductions from important friends back home, she was able to find a real estate broker, a property inspector, a banker, real estate and immigration lawyers, insurance agents, private nurses, and a new three-bedroom house with a garage and driveway in Cypress. Before Christmas, the Koh family closed on the house.

The lawyer advised Sonya to protect the property interest of the children in the event that her brother-in-law remarried. "Surely your sister will want to make sure that her children own the house and can never be evicted if they continue to make payments," he said.

So the deed was held in the children's names, and although the Kohs' individual incomes were not ideal, in the aggregate, they made enough that several lenders were more than willing to give them a mortgage, and the borrowers were John, Bo, and Mido, since DH had law school loans and no income until he started his summer internship. Sonya gave each member of the family money separately to avoid gift taxes, and together, the family was able to put down 25 percent on a $225,000 house. The monthly loan payments, HOA fees, and real property taxes came to a little more than their rent.

The house was not grand, but it was a new construction by a reputable builder, one of ten in a row of town houses, painted white with pale-gray trim. It was located in the center of town and close to an excellent public school, and the broker had predicted that the property value would only increase. Sonya had visited almost two dozen houses, and the one on Candlestick Lane was everything they desired and in their price range.

Two days before Christmas, Sonya pushed Helen in her collapsible wheelchair across the threshold.

Bundled in a quilt and scarves, Helen looked up at her sister and said quietly, "I never thought we could own our place in America so soon. Thank you."

Lately, John said even less than usual, but he was grateful that Helen was comfortable. As long as he was able to work, he was determined to make good on the loan. He promised Helen that he'd repay her sister's family, and she believed he would.

Helen refused to go to hospice. There was little point to it now. The nurses were wonderful, and, ever watchful, Sonya never seemed to sleep.

Sonya had the maid's room by the kitchen. The boys shared the large bedroom, which had a bathroom with a shower, and Mido got her own room beside the master bedroom.

Helen didn't want to miss anything whenever she was awake, so the rented hospital bed was placed in the living room. John slept alone in the master bedroom, but when he wasn't asleep, he remained by Helen's bedside to read to her and do chores. He washed and folded laundry so well that he joked that if Shrimp Castle shut down, he had another career waiting for him.

As soon as his fall semester ended, DH arranged to have a shorter study period and to take his 1L exams early. He flew home as soon as he could and never left his mother's side. Only he could get her to eat porridge or have sips of water when things got worse. When Helen slept, he read casebooks to prepare for his second semester. Helen wanted him to return to New York when classes began, and he told her he would but didn't mean it, having already gotten permission from the dean if things turned for the worse.

"I want you to be my secretary," she said one morning.

The house was empty. The morning nurse had just left, and the second nurse was running late. Bo and Mido were tutoring at Irvine, John was at Shrimp Castle in Garden Grove, and Sonya was at a meeting with a lawyer in Buena Park.

DH removed his blue hooded sweatshirt and tossed it on the sofa. From the hallway closet, he retrieved three heavy knapsacks. Helen had saved each of their JanSport knapsacks from middle school when they had become too worn out to carry any longer. Bo's was black, DH's navy, and Mido's green. Inside each bag was the notebook Helen kept for that child.

"Can you get me my jewelry box?"

"Why, Mommy?"

Helen just smiled, and DH went upstairs to fetch the lacquered Korean jewelry box, no bigger than two cigar boxes.

"Open." She gestured with her jaw.

"Find the pearl necklace and put that in Mido's bag."

DH opened the silk drawstring bag and placed the pearl necklace in Mido's knapsack.

"The diamond engagement ring. That's for Bo. He'll get married first, I think."

"Definitely," DH said. "I'm not getting married anytime soon."

He pulled out the diamond and platinum engagement ring in its velvet box. The diamond was a third of a carat but set in a way that made it look a bit bigger.

"Your daddy used every bit of his savings to buy me that ring."

DH admired it. Even he knew it couldn't have cost very much. He tucked the box into the black knapsack for Bo.

"The Swiss watch. It's fourteen-karat gold. That's for your wife," Helen said, admiring the small watch face on the thin brown leather band, which she'd bought as a replacement when she was still working in Sydney. "Your daddy bought that for me the first time he went to New York. I don't know if your wife will like it, but she'll know it is from me."

"I don't even have a girlfriend," DH pointed out. He'd had two in college, and neither had worked out. In law school, he had decided to avoid all such entanglements until he was settled with a job.

"You will have a wonderful wife," Helen said. "I will pray for that in heaven. I will be watching over you."

"No, no," he said. "Please don't go." DH bowed his head, unable to look at her, and when he opened his eyes, he saw that she had fallen asleep.

❧

When Sonya returned from her meeting to relieve DH, she went to the powder room to wash her hands, then sent him to his room to get some rest.

"Sister," Helen said, her voice soft. Sonya rushed to her side.

"Do you need the bedpan?"

Helen shook her head. "Sit, please," she said.

Sonya sat on the twin bed beside Helen's. There had been no time to buy more furniture than whatever they'd had in the apartment, and John had pleaded with Sonya not to spend any more money. There were no rugs on the floor or pictures on the walls, and again, they were starting all over without any additional decorations or furnishings. The first floor, which functioned as both a living and a dining area, was furnished with a long sofa, dining table, and television. Helen's hospital bed and Sonya's bed were set up beside the dining table.

"I don't feel well," Helen said. "I don't want to worry the children anymore. Before Bo and Mido come home, I want to talk to you."

Sonya patted her sister's thin arm, covering her up to her shoulder with the blanket.

"I know you've been unhappy with things at home. You always say you're fine, but I know things have been difficult. I worry that no one will take care of you, my sister, the one who takes care of everyone. I'm sorry to have been such a burden to you. You've always—"

"Hush, you should rest."

"Will you call Kenny for me? I want to talk to him. Just in case."

Sonya dialed their brother, who had already booked a flight.

Kenny recognized her voice and started crying.

"I'll be there on Monday. Please wait for me."

"I wish I could see your face, Kenny, but I'm afraid that I might not be here."

"I'm going to try to change my ticket for tomorrow. I don't care if I get fired," he said.

"No, no. You have to take care of your family."

"*Noona.*"

"Don't cry, dear Kenny. I wanted to hear your voice because I'm so tired. Everything hurts. I'm trying not to complain. Our big sister is working every single minute to take care of everyone. It would be easier for me if I could go."

Sonya shook her head back and forth, unable to speak.

"If I'm not here when you get here, will you do something for me?"

"Don't say that. Noona, please don't say that. Please."

"Will you make sure that our sister is okay? When I'm gone, you have to check in on her and see if she is okay. Umma and Appa were never able to do much for us, so it's just us, right?"

"Please. Please don't—"

"Kenny, I'm so proud of you. You made a good life for you and your beautiful children. When we were in Sydney, you took such good care of us. I'm sorry for not taking better care of you."

"Noona, I promise to do everything I can. I promise. Please wait for me."

Helen handed the phone to Sonya.

"Kenny, I better let her rest. I'll call you tomorrow."

Sonya put down the receiver and turned to chide Helen but saw that her sister was asleep again, her breathing steady.

❧

Late that evening, when everyone was home, the family gathered around Helen. John was seated on the sofa, and the children sat on the wooden dining chairs arranged by the bed. Sonya sat on the edge of the bed and massaged Helen's calves.

Propped up with three pillows, Helen admired her family. All day, she'd been thinking of what she wanted to say, and she worried she could never get through it all.

Ever since the trip to the emergency room and the first scan, her odyssey had taken another turn, mocking all her well-organized plans. Nevertheless, her boys were getting their education, and after they were done, Mido would return to school and get hers, too.

She felt terrible for her husband, but in her time here, she'd found that she admired him far more than when he had graduated from Seoul National and gotten a good job right away. He had been mistreated, but he was still a good man. A minister had told them at their wedding service that in a marriage, your spouse should make you grow closer to God, and John had done this. He had tried to see the better nature in a person, and he had done this whenever she couldn't.

"When the Lord calls for me—" She began to cough and couldn't finish.

DH was the first to take his mother's hand.

"Thank you for being our mother."

Bo and Mido sat silently, grateful that DH could say this for them.

John smiled. "Our baby lawyer, DH, is speaking for us."

"It hurts when I laugh," Helen said.

Mido couldn't speak. She had never seen a person die, and she could not have imagined that the person who always seemed tireless could transform into this shadowy frame before her eyes. She was near her mother's feet, and she held them in her hands.

"Children," Helen said. "I will miss your graduations, your weddings, and the births of your children. I will not be here to take care of your wonderful father, who has been my guardian angel. But I want you to know that in heaven, your mother will ask the Lord to protect you and watch over you every single day. Maybe the Lord will take pity on me for missing so many valuable things with you that He will have to listen to me. I don't know why I have to go, but I believe God is fair."

Bo got up from his seat and put his arms around her.

"Bless us, Umma."

Helen reached for her children.

"I will ask God. I will argue with Him. I will ask the Lord for satisfaction for cutting short my life. The Bible says that God likes a wise servant, so I will plead for him to take my life in exchange for the protection of my family."

Sonya stroked her sister's wasted legs while John and the children held her body.

Helen faded and fell asleep again, her breath uneven. No one wanted to leave her side for fear that they'd miss her, but John told everyone to go to bed. He would keep watch.

17

Sunday After

The seller's broker had recommended installing blackout shades for the master bedroom, but there'd been no time for that. The bedroom faced east, and on Sunday morning, the enormous California sun flooded the room with a glorious, incandescent light.

After the family had come home from the burial the previous evening, John had showered and gone straight to bed. Having slept deeply, he wasn't tired, but he didn't want to rise.

As usual, the pillow next to him lay untouched, and for a moment, he thought Helen was asleep downstairs in the living room in the rented hospital bed.

But her body was resting in a plot at Westminster. Church services were in a few hours. Before bed, he'd hung up his black suit and tie on the hook by the master bath. He wouldn't have to dress in his Shrimp Castle uniform this morning.

Helen Hejin Cho
October 10, 1949–December 29, 2000
Beloved Wife, Mother, Sister

The funeral director had asked for an inscription, saying the headstone would take months to fabricate and install. If there was anything the family wanted to add, please let him know, he'd said. Fifty-one years old. What could he add?

There was no one he'd ever loved more than Helen, and there'd be no one else.

A week ago, she'd said to him, "You are my dearest friend. Please be well and take care of our children. If the Lord will allow it, I'll do everything, everything I can to watch over you."

John believed in God and Helen. He didn't feel at peace, however. He was angry. If he could, he would have lodged a complaint against heaven that his angel had been taken from him too soon. What could he add to the headstone? "Stolen." "Cheated." "Denied." They'd deserved many more years together. His sole consolation was that she was out of pain. That was all.

He rose, shook out the comforter, and smoothed it over the queen-size mattress.

❧

In the kitchen, Sonya was drinking coffee. The children were still asleep.

"Would you like breakfast? You didn't eat yesterday."

Sonya's large brown eyes were still swollen. Helen's blue apron covered her black dress with a white collar. She wore no jewelry except for a thin gold wedding band.

John poured himself a cup of coffee and sat down.

"Sister, I'm so grateful to you for having been here. For all of us. I know how much it meant to my wife. She looked up to you more than anyone else."

Sonya shook her head and waved her hands in denial, wanting him to stop. She couldn't cry anymore or bear to think of Helen's goodness, which she had always wanted to protect. She swallowed and sat down at the table.

"I'll close on Mrs. Kwon's nail salon next week. Everything happened sooner than expected. She'll run it for six more months and train the new manager." She looked at John. "I need to ask you for something."

"Anything."

"Would you manage the nail salon? It's a profitable business and the financials are good, but there's a lot to do. When I first heard about Mrs. Kwon's business, I'd imagined that Helen and I could run it together one day."

"What? Why would you—"

He paused when Sonya looked away, not wanting to answer.

"After the closing, I need to return to Seoul, but I'll be back."

John shook his head. "You have to get back to your family. You've already given up so much for us."

"I don't think I can live in Seoul much longer."

"What about your family?"

"I don't want to live the way I do anymore. I'll speak to my sons."

John didn't understand. Helen had said that Sonya wasn't happy with her husband, but it wasn't like her to complain.

"After the closing, I'd like you to take over and be trained by Mrs. Kwon, and I'll return as soon as I can. I thought of asking Bo or Mido, but I thought you might like this work. Also, I can pay you more than what you make at Shrimp Castle."

Sonya studied his face. She knew it would be difficult for him to leave Shrimp Castle, not because he enjoyed the work, but because he'd feel loyal to Nari, who had helped them from the beginning. Being a manager at Rose Salon would be complicated, but easier than frying fish, lifting boxes, and cleaning a kitchen six days a week. He'd oversee at least two dozen nail technicians and mind the financials.

"I thought if you became my partner, then we can split the net receipts in half. It's a solid business with an excellent location in Buena Park, and even after taxes, I think you could make a weekly salary of $1,800. At the end of the year, we can see how things are. The accountant said we can do a quarterly profit sharing and a year-end bonus, but to keep the salary at a lower level."

John held his coffee mug with his dry brown hands. When he worked in an office, they had been smooth and well cared for. After almost three years at Shrimp Castle, his hands and forearms were covered in oil splatter burns. In the first few months, he'd cut his left index finger with a cleaver, requiring stitches and a tetanus shot. He raised his battered, scarred hands, fingers splayed out, for Sonya to see. She smiled weakly, understanding.

"I've never been inside a nail salon."

"You'd never fried fish, either."

It was hard for John to imagine working at a nail salon, where people decorated their hands and had their feet scrubbed by others. Of course he could do the job, but he worried about what would happen to Yun's mother, who depended on him. Nari was a soft woman who had become nervous from the disappointments of life, and she had helped his family. At a cost to herself, Nari had given him a generous salary in cash, but this offer he had to accept. Sonya had never asked him for anything. More than anyone else, he was in her debt.

"Do you need time?"

"I'll tell Yun's mother today. She'll need to find a replacement right away. Do you think I can have two weeks?"

❧

At church, the Koh family sat in their usual pew, aware of Helen's absence. Sonya was there, as well as DH, who was often away at school. After services, they went downstairs to the Patio for lunch, and many of the same people they'd seen the day before at the funeral came by to say hello.

A few mothers with college-age daughters inspected DH. They knew he'd gone to Yale as a soccer player and was now a 1L at Columbia. Though mournful and considerate, the mothers still could not seem to control themselves. Already two had stopped by and asked about DH, and Sonya had diverted them, saying that her nephew had no time for girlfriends because of the demands of law school. The women bowed to the family and smiled at DH before leaving.

DH frowned, aware that no one was asking about Bo. It would have made more sense to inquire about him since he was older.

"No thanks, man," Bo said to his brother. "I'm fine. Not in the market. I guess this is just what happens to Ivy League lawyers."

DH laughed and turned to his aunt. "Are our cousins getting pressure to marry?"

"Too young, and girls don't want to get married in Korea."

"Even to your sons?" Mido asked. "They're so nice."

"And good-looking," Sonya added with a smile. The Chairman and her husband had strong opinions about whom the boys would marry. The brides had to come from established families, preferably well connected in media and government.

"I'm done," Bo said, picking up his empty tray.

"Can I get a ride to Fortress?" Mido asked.

"Sure. I have a student in the afternoon, but I can go now."

DH raised his hand. "And me?" He sounded plaintive, much younger than usual. It felt like the old days, when the three of them had moved as a unit.

Bo glanced at their father, still eating his bibimbap.

"You kids can go. I'll see you at home. I need to speak with Yun's mother."

"How will you get home?" Bo asked.

"We'll get a ride," Sonya said.

❧

On Sundays, parishioners filled the airy café across the street from Gospel Presbyterian. Along the wall, churchgoers of all ages, some still clutching programs, gathered along the banquettes upholstered in yellow and green vinyl.

In groups of three and four, teenagers from youth assembly sat as far away as they could from the clusters of grandmothers in print dresses. Retirees sat close to each other and nodded with enthusiasm while taking turns telling amusing stories.

Sonya led John and Nari to one of the empty tables in the back. Once seated, John went to buy their coffee. At church, hot drinks were free, so he'd never frequented the café before.

He was relieved that Sonya had wanted to come and talk with Nari as well. His head felt thick and muddled. He knew he wanted to work for his sister-in-law but was worried about how to tell Nari. In the past few years, he had lost some confidence in his own judgment.

Before getting fired from HRI, John had been the sort of man who believed that the world was a reasonable place. He wasn't naive, but he could not have expected a person like Danbi to exist or an old friend like Shin to change so completely.

The server placed John's coffee order on the counter.

"Sir? Sir?" the young woman behind the counter repeated.

"Oh." John remembered himself and paid for the coffee, surprised by how expensive it was.

Nari had already wiped down the table with a napkin, and when John placed the tray down, she smiled gently at him.

"I should have ordered cake. I wasn't thinking," he said.

"I'm not hungry," Sonya said, glancing at Nari, who liked sweets but was always watching her weight.

"No cake," Nari said.

For a while, they spoke about the funeral, which had been well attended. John could not remember it clearly. If it hadn't been for the funeral book and all the condolence cards, he wouldn't have really known who'd come to pay respects. Shin had come—thankfully, alone.

"I'm buying Mrs. Kwon's Rose Salon," Sonya told Nari. "I've asked my brother-in-law to be the manager."

Nari opened her mouth. "Oh, oh," she murmured.

John looked at Nari with concern.

"We're so grateful to you for everything you've done for our family. I don't know how we would've survived," John said. Nari was about to cry, and she covered her mouth with her hands.

"I didn't do anything."

"No, you did so much. My wife and I received so much of your help. I will spend the rest of my life paying back our debts to you and my sister-in-law."

Sonya put a hand on Nari's arm. "I apologize for this inconvenience. I've been asking around to find you another person for Shrimp Castle."

"I can stay for another two weeks if you need, unless you find someone else sooner," John said. He felt terrible. "I don't want to burden you with another problem. If we can find someone right away, I'll still help to train him."

Nari stopped him. "I've wanted to close for some time. After my husband left, Yun and I talked about doing something else. If you hadn't helped us at Castle, I would've been forced to sell much faster. The promissory note is almost paid off now, and I own the business. I have three more years on the lease. I can sell the store. Lion's brother told me I could get a decent price on it. My husband needs the money. He wrote me not long ago, but I didn't know what to do."

"But your store is doing well," Sonya said. "Why would you sell it?"

"My back and knees hurt all the time. I'm too old for this. I'd prefer work where I can sit."

John felt bad for her. He had never wanted his wife to work behind the counter, either. Helen hadn't complained when she was at her sickest, until it was too late. He blamed himself for her needing to work the way she had. If he'd made more money or knew anything about investing, then she wouldn't have had to work so hard. Perhaps she wouldn't have died, he thought.

"Maybe you can work for me, then," Sonya said. "It would be easier work than Shrimp Castle. You don't have to do the nails. You could book appointments and deal with the schedules for the technicians."

"I don't know," Nari said. "I'm not as clever as you and your sister. My English is not as—"

"I'm sure you can learn how to handle appointments. Also, my brother-in-law will be there, too."

"He went to the best college and worked for a big company—"

"Let's not disagree," Sonya said, glancing at John, who looked lost. "You would be helping our family again. I'd worry less if I knew that you and my brother-in-law were managing the salon together."

John smiled gently. He was seven months younger than Sonya but looked much older, having aged years in a matter of months.

18

Independence

January 2001

After the morning meeting ended, the tutors headed to their first-period classrooms while Mido compiled the test materials and Peter lingered in his chair near the whiteboard. He could've gone to his office but took his time jotting down reminders in his spiral notebook, which was filled with song fragments and a growing list of tasks. Sad and exhausted, Mido cradled her head in her left hand, elbow resting on the table. She didn't want to talk about her mother or how nothing made any sense now that she was gone. She wanted to work.

"There's a rising junior if you want another student," Peter said. "A tough cookie, but I think you might click with her."

"Sure," she said indifferently. "Which kid?"

"Susie Yoon."

"Oh, right. The cool customer." Mido raised an eyebrow. "Wasn't she working with Joe for verbal? He's really good."

"Yeah, Joe is terrific, but his nice-guy methods are not working on her. Her mom called me last night. She wants to quit."

"Can't we just let her quit?" Mido didn't believe in making kids do things they didn't want to do.

Peter gave her a hard stare and pointed to his black T-shirt with a heavily made-up image of Robert Smith.

"Remember me? I wanted to be a punk rocker when I was in middle school. I know I sound like some sort of boss person, but you know me by now, Mido—"

Peter thought most kids should be learning how to surf rather than being stuck in an office park all weekend memorizing SAT words they'd likely never use in a sentence or solving math word problems.

He stood up from his chair and mussed up his gelled hair, raising it a good two inches from his scalp. He played air guitar, rocking his hips back and forth, and started to sing "Just Like Heaven."

Mido laughed out loud. "I'm sorry. I shouldn't have said that. To you especially."

"Of course she should quit if she wants to. I don't believe in forcing kids to study here. But her mom called me at almost eleven p.m. last night to plead her case. Apparently they're going through a divorce, and Susie, who was on track for all the fancy college things, decided to throw her academic life to hell to get back at her dad, who went to Wharton and wants her to go there."

"Wharton? That's the business undergrad at UPenn, right?"

Now that she was also a college consultant, Mido had been researching the Ivy League schools that Fortress kids talked about all the time. She'd never visited any of them, so it was hard to understand how they were different from each other. Of course, she'd heard a lot about Yale from DH.

She'd grown up in Australia, so the names confused her, let alone the sheer number, variety, and costs. UPenn was an entirely different college from Penn State, she'd only learned recently. UMass Amherst was distinct from Amherst College, though they were in the same town. There were over a dozen schools in the University of North Carolina system. Higher education in America was nothing like Australia or South Korea—countries with far smaller populations.

"I guess Susie doesn't want to study business?"

"Wharton's a professional school. Not for everyone."

"This is Susie Yoon with the blue hair?"

"Wharton could use a little color," he said, smiling. "Anyway, thank you for taking her on, and I'm going to send her to your office after lunch."

He'd checked the master schedule, and he knew Mido was clear in the afternoon. Peter didn't ask why she'd returned to work so soon after the funeral. Both Yun and Lion had tried to encourage Mido to take more time off, but she had insisted on coming back and taking on her full load. Bo was also teaching his private students and going to school. He'd had to give up the van driving because the hours didn't work, but he taught every weekend.

Fortress now had 150 students—in SAT boot camps, subject test tutoring, subject tutoring, and now college counseling. They had to turn students away. Tutors left other hagwons to work at Fortress because Lion paid the highest salaries, although he didn't charge the highest tuition fees. The owners of competitive Irvine hagwons didn't mind, but Fortress's growth upset the owners of the struggling ones.

✤

Mido had a good-size windowless classroom in the back of the building for private tutoring and college consulting. On two of the walls, she'd put up whiteboards, and on the narrow remaining space beside the glass door, she'd hung up postcards, posters, and drawings of American writers: Toni Morrison, Anne Sexton, F. Scott Fitzgerald, Kurt Vonnegut, John Dos Passos, James Baldwin, Stephen King, John Cheever, Isaac Bashevis Singer, John Steinbeck, Maxine Hong Kingston, and Zora Neale Hurston. She stored copies of their novels and stories on a library cart next to a beanbag chair and reading lamp.

Mido sat at her desk with a legal pad and Susie Yoon's latest SAT practice test results. Her verbal scores were significantly lower than on her initial diagnostic test in September, which made no sense.

The door opened and Susie entered tentatively.

Mido gestured for her to sit in the chair beside her.

"Heard you want to quit."

"Yes."

The girl was fifteen, and besides her blue hair, she had a nose ring and two piercings in her left earlobe.

"What does the rest look like?" Mido pointed to her inked forearm, half hidden beneath the sweatshirt.

Susie pushed up the sleeve to expose a skinny right arm that had a beautiful image of a weeping willow.

"Cool. Did it hurt?"

"Like a motherfucker."

Mido laughed.

"Heard about the divorce."

"Yup."

"Listen. You can quit if you want to. I know I'm supposed to talk you out of it, but I'd rather hear why you want to quit. If you tell me why and convince me, I will persuade your mother myself. I have nothing better to do than to act as your fake free lawyer. You can quit. It will not affect our bottom line. I'll still pull in a great salary. In fact, it would be less work for me."

This time Susie laughed, and Mido felt glad because life was shitty, but it felt bearable if you could still laugh.

"My dad cheated on my mother. He's marrying some West Hollywood bitch with gigantic boobs, and my mother is drinking a lot of wine. They're not acting like Korean parents. I don't give a fuck anymore."

"I see. That is a lot."

"If they act like assholes, I don't see why I have to act like a genius."

"Fair point."

Susie smiled.

"Listen. You can quit. You can blame your parents, who are going through whatever. Frankly, I don't care what the adults are doing, because they're not my students.

"However, I would like you to have many wonderful choices. Fucking up your life right now is not going to help you become liberated from your parents, who are going through some possibly delayed rebellion. Maybe if they had blue hair when they were kids, there might be more peace in your life now. No idea. I'm guessing all this without knowing any of the facts. Regardless, I'm on your side.

"The reality is that the way you can get away from their nuttiness is by doing well at school and going across the country and having them pay for a college education, which they're able to do. Lucky you."

"Where did you go to college?" Susie asked.

"I finished my first year at the University of Sydney, then I came to the US with my family."

"You haven't finished?"

"Nope. Your verbal teacher and college essay specialist is more or less a college dropout, or you can say that I took a pause."

"Cool."

"I can't afford to finish my college education right now."

"You can't get loans?"

Mido wondered if she should bother telling her about how her life had not ended up the way she'd thought it would when she was Susie's age.

"I need to earn money. I'll get to my degree later. The only thing that's relevant for you right now, though, is that you are sitting in a room with a person who not only knows how to get a perfect score on the verbal section of the SATs or most standardized exams, I'm tremendous at teaching high school students how to get one, too. I may not have any other gifts, but on this testing thing, I'm a savant. Look up the word if you don't know what it means. The dictionary is behind you on the shelf. I can and will raise your scores. Joe is also excellent, but you didn't realize that. He's nicer than me. Anyway, his loss is my gain."

Susie was paying attention. When it came to students, it was easier to talk plainly like this. Around adults, Mido spoke as needed, measuring every extra word, but with children and teenagers, she wanted to simply tell them the truth, however long it took.

Susie glanced at her practice test in front of Mido.

"I wasn't even trying for that score."

"I know."

"If I focused—"

"It's not the score, Susie. Respect language. If you respect words, sentences, and meaning, you will have command of one of the greatest gifts of your life. Forget the test. Attain command of the English language."

Mido checked her math scores.

"Do you like your math group?"

"Meh."

"Do you know Catherine Seo? She's also at Troy."

"Blond girl."

"Yeah. You want to join her group? Peter leads it, and they're doing very well."

"Okay."

"Done. Let's turn to this reading comp passage."

Mido sat up straight and gestured to the page.

Susie picked up her pencil and brushed away the blue hair from her eyes.

⁂

Ten days after the funeral, Tek arrived in California. Work had prevented him from traveling to Helen's services. He'd sent an enormous wreath of white chrysanthemums. He called Mido often and, when he missed her, left brief messages on the answering machine. They wrote each other emails instead of letters.

Right after work, Mido went to his hotel, and as soon as she walked into his room and closed the door, she collapsed into his arms. It was as if they had forgotten their disagreements and disappointments.

"I'm so sorry, Mido. This was the soonest I could get away."

Tek's dark hair was longer in front than usual. A while back, he'd mentioned changing his barber. Mido was surprised by how unfamiliar a person could look just from a new haircut. His fine features—the thoughtful sloping eyes and straight nose—became more distinct shaded by his dark hair. He'd lost some weight and his cheekbones were more defined. Tek was more handsome than before.

"Are you hungry?" he asked.

She wasn't. The thought of food made her think of her mother, who always asked about her meals. "You must be tired from the flight."

"No. I'm okay. I was reading this fascinating case. I'm studying it, actually." He gestured to the papers on the hotel desk. "Are you tired?"

They were being polite. The last time they had been in a room at this hotel, almost right away they'd made love as if two people needed to do something to remember each other. Now it felt strange to think of sex.

"How's work?"

"Fine," he said. He was swamped and learning more about the business side of law.

Tek had met Helen only a few times, but he had felt her kindness. From an early age, his mother, Professor Yoon, the famous economist, had drilled it into him that women did paid and unpaid work in and out of the house, but it was all work.

"You're back at the hagwon so soon."

"It's better to keep busy."

"I felt bad I couldn't be here for you."

Mido had understood. In order for this to continue, neither could expect much from the other. This was how they had managed to last.

Tek had no intention of moving to California. It made no sense, and of course, she respected it. There was the stronger argument for her to move to Sydney to finish her degree. But Mido would not leave her family now. Her income was more important than ever.

Hospital bills, mortgage for the new house, insurance, taxes, car payments—all of it required Mido to help out. They no longer had Helen's earnings. Bo had two more years of school, and he wanted to be a psychologist, which would require a doctorate, and that could add another six to eight years. DH would graduate law school in two, and his grades mattered for the jobs he wanted: He couldn't spare the time to work.

"How long can you stay?"

"Two days at best. I should leave tomorrow, but I think I can stay until my original flight."

"You flew two days already."

"I would've been here sooner, Mido."

"I know."

"Come back with me. I'm a working lawyer. You know I have a plan. After I'm called to the bar, I'll become a barrister focusing on commercial litigation. I've already figured out which chambers. I can send money back to your family and put you through school. My offer stands." He folded his arms against his chest. "This can't go on with you being here and me in Sydney."

Mido hugged her knees. His reasoning made sense, and she was so tired.

"You're going to sacrifice your life for your father and brothers? No, Mido. This isn't some Korean fairy tale. This is your life. We've entered the twenty-first century. How's this okay? Your mother wouldn't want this."

"You're right. She wouldn't want me to do this for them, but it's not just for them. I like working at Fortress."

"You can't be serious. You're an office manager and SAT tutor. You're helping kids with college essays when you haven't finished your own degree. You can do any of this in Sydney if you want. They have hagwons there."

"No, no. I don't think you understand. It's not just a job."

Mido felt inadequate to argue with a lawyer and was too worn down to try. How could she ever persuade him? She could not.

"I give up," she said, then saw him grin at the thought of winning. Again he'd misunderstood.

"No, I mean us. I'm not going back."

BOOK IV

January 2003–December 2005

Nothing exerts a stronger psychic effect upon the human environment, and especially upon children, than the life which the parents have not lived.

—Carl Jung

1
The Rose Salon

January 2003

John had never worked with so many women before.

For most of his professional life, he'd worked with men and a few junior women. Although Taehun Shin had preferred including attractive female office workers for drinks after work, John had largely avoided socializing with them one-on-one or in a group. As the father of a daughter, he hoped that no one would treat her unfairly. A man, he knew, could get the wrong idea when a woman was just being polite or kind. His widowed mother had gone through a lot with landlords, bank officers, and shopkeepers, and John took pains to be respectful, even at the risk of being viewed as rude or cold.

The previous owner, Mrs. Kwon, had called all the workers "girls." Sonya, however, insisted that each technician's name tag reflect her preferred status. Everyone was called Miss or Mrs., and the women with church titles, if they wished, were addressed as Deacon or Elder. John preferred the formalities, wanting to keep as much distance as possible between himself and the women. He made sure that he was never alone with anyone anywhere in the shop. The workers found Manager John Koh, as his name tag read, competent and polite but far too quiet.

If he ever needed to talk with a worker in private, he'd schedule the conversation, always accompanied by Nari, in the employee break room, which had a mirrored two-way window as well as security cameras.

The technicians addressed him as Manager John, and those who were also members of Gospel Presbyterian called him Elder Koh. They were curious about Helen and admired the widower's reserve and grief. Several workers had considered pursuing John as a prospective husband, but Nari put them off. "You can try, but there's no point," she'd say. "He's never going to remarry." If a technician or customer tried flirting, John would nod politely and return to his tiny business office, which could barely hold his desk, chair, and filing cabinet.

"Was she pretty?" they'd ask Nari, having met Helen's sister Sonya, the beautiful owner of the salon, who came by the salon several times a year.

"Oh yes," Nari stressed. "She had style, too. Deacon Cho was pretty like her sister, but they looked different. The deacon's face was softer and more olive-toned. When she listened to you, you could tell that she was interpreting you in the best possible way.

"She wasn't tacky. She didn't wear much makeup or bright clothes. Didn't talk so much, like me. Almost never watched television."

Nari loved working at the Rose Salon. Unlike at Shrimp Castle, where she'd worn a long white apron over a brown-and-beige polyester uniform, here Nari could wear her clothes from back home, which still fit her—dresses and skirts in jewel tones—and plenty of eye makeup. Her hands were now always perfectly manicured and painted in the latest colors. There were women to chat with about the latest dramas or the fashionable clothes in the magazines she kept stacked next to the manicure tables. She styled her hair up or down, depending on her mood, and she could wear her fanciest things, including any jewelry she hadn't sold when they needed money. At the salon, with its mirrored walls and chandeliers, it wasn't inappropriate for Nari to wear sequined skirts or fur-trimmed sweaters. For the first time in years, she felt almost attractive again. After only a week at the salon, she told her daughter, "I feel like a girl."

Nari believed that none of the women interested in the widower were on Helen's level. Even though Helen and Sonya came from a poor family, Nari had been struck by how neither seemed intimidated by other educated and wealthy people. Nari didn't know if that unwavering personal dignity came from having gone to an elite college or from what they'd been through and survived. Surely it wasn't just money. Nari had once had a great deal of money, and she hadn't been astute like Helen, or steely and elegant like Sonya.

Nari had a few regrets. She had graduated from high school with decent marks and had once considered becoming a nurse, but she'd gotten pregnant and married. Once she and her husband had money, Nari had seen no point to studying hard to become a nurse or learn English properly, which she now sorely regretted. She missed her husband and wished she'd been better to him. If Joonho ever returned, she vowed to be more patient.

Nari and John continued to work well together. Nari was relieved to sell Shrimp Castle and send money to her husband. Working at the salon was easier on her body. Except for the nail dust and the chemical smells of the polish and remover, Nari thought being a sales manager at Rose Salon was a perfect job.

As the business manager, John minded the books, taxes, licensing requirements, lease management, waste disposal, maintenance, and inventory, and Nari took care of the appointments and workers.

Customers often mistook them for a married couple, and Nari would correct them, saying John was her brother-in-law: easier to explain than the truth.

She was married, and Joonho would always be her husband. He would return.

If her husband wanted a divorce, he would have to come back and ask for one. She'd be sad but give in. Life was too brief to hold grudges, and he had given her many good years and their daughter Yun. Nari had no interest in ever getting married again.

Each morning, John would walk the three blocks to Nari's apartment building and meet her in front of the lobby. They'd go to the parking lot, get into her Volvo, and drive to Rose Salon. In the evening, unless John's kids picked him up, which was rare because they were working or at school, she'd drive them back to her building, and he'd walk back home. They didn't eat dinner together. Each night he'd bow, say thank you for the ride, and wish her good night.

After she parked her car, Nari would rush to her apartment, wash off her makeup and change out of the dress-up clothes, and put on a pair of clean pajamas. In her small kitchen, she'd make herself a bowl of popcorn and watch two rented drama videos and go to bed early. In the morning, she'd make herself a large breakfast of rice, fried eggs, soup, and side dishes.

Her daughter Yun worried about her living alone, but Nari couldn't imagine living with anyone else, unless Joonho decided to return. Nari was still attractive, and at church, the other women deacons who knew about her husband leaving mentioned fixing her up with men seeking a nice, hardworking wife.

"Thank you for thinking of me, but I am still married."

She had no wish to take care of another man. Nari intended to age as well as possible and live quietly. When she wrote to her three brothers that her husband Joonho was gone, none of them advised her to marry again. Two of them asked her to send money for their mother, who was suffering from dementia, so of course, Nari did.

Each month, Nari put aside half of whatever was left of her pay in a retirement savings account. On Sunday afternoons, she drove to South Coast Plaza and window-shopped. Now and then she'd try on a dress or a skirt, but thinking of her eventual retirement, she did her best to refrain from buying anything. It amazed her how much money she'd once spent on clothing, shoes, and bags. Having her husband leave her with a large promissory note to pay off while their daughter was in college had taught her that she should have saved more money.

She saved also for Joonho, who she believed would eventually return, if not for her, then for their daughter. This was what happened in dramas about true love, and Nari believed that their love had been genuine from the start. They'd had troubles, and if both of them had been more self-controlled, they'd still be together.

Her husband was not heroic, but he was a good person. Nari thought about him often. Joonho had made mistakes. Weak and ashamed of how life had turned out, he was trying his luck again in Brazil. After selling the store, she'd sent him money, and on Christmas, he'd called her for the first time in years. She'd been writing him now and then and knew from his cousin's wife that he got the letters. He knew Yun was married.

"How is Yun?" he asked.

"She's happy with her husband."

"I wanted to wish you a merry Christmas," he said quietly. "You've always liked Christmas more than me."

Nari laughed. In Seoul, she'd decorated their home and all their stores and insisted on buying all their employees expensive presents.

"I better go," Joonho said.

"Where are you working?" she asked, wanting details.

"I'm driving a truck, but I found a wholesale fabric store. That money you sent was helpful. I don't have any debts anymore." She heard his voice trembling. "Say hello to Yun. Thanks again. For, you know. Everything. Take care of your health."

❧

On the second anniversary of Helen's death, Sonya returned to Orange County—her fourth trip to the States in the past year.

On Friday evening, when John went to an elders' meeting, Sonya invited Nari to dinner. They went to Horatio's Bar and Grill, a large anchor tenant of the new mall in Buena Park and within walking distance of Rose Salon.

"Business has been going well," Sonya said. "Thank you for working so hard."

"I like the job so much."

"That's a relief," Sonya said.

"I'm surprised, but I don't think I want to go back to Korea."

Sonya didn't want to go back to Seoul, either, and it was strangely consoling to hear another married woman saying the same thing she was thinking.

"My husband left me, and when that happened, I thought I'd die."

"Oh?" Sonya said. "You seem so well. So sturdy."

"I also thought I'd die when we lost all the stores. But I didn't. I didn't die when my husband left."

"Have you heard from him?"

"He called on Christmas."

"He's okay?"

"I don't know. I called his cousin's wife a while ago. That's how I learned that he needed money. She was complaining about how he had debts."

"Have they been paid?"

"I think so. He doesn't live in the boardinghouse anymore. I heard that much."

"What?" Sonya thought of how wealthy they'd once been in Seoul.

"When he got there, he lived in a rented room with some Korean grandmother and her daughters. He doesn't know I know."

"Does it bother you?"

"Yes, but I didn't go there like he wanted. I guess he didn't want to tell me."

"You're a good person. You're always thinking of others. I know that."

"Thank you, Sister. That means so much to me. I've looked up to you and your sister. Your world was so high-class. We couldn't even talk to each other."

Sonya shook her head, though she understood what Nari meant.

"I never thought you'd own a nail salon in America, and that I'd be working for you. I mean, I'm so grateful to be working for you. I mean, you're so rich. You went to Ewha! All your friends are women who went to good colleges who are married to men from good families."

"That doesn't mean anything."

"You're married to an important family, you have two perfect sons who went to Korea University, and I still don't understand why you wanted to buy this business. It doesn't make sense. Unless you bought it for your sister."

Sonya glanced at her untouched plate of food.

"I talk too much. I should shut up." Nari tapped her mouth a few times with her hand.

"I haven't told anyone, but I'd rather be here. If it weren't for my sons—"

"Do you not like your husband?" Nari asked.

Sonya stared at the woman, surprised. Her eyes were warm and curious. It was true that she had never noticed Nari until her child, Yun, walked up to her niece Mido and introduced herself. That moment seemed like a lifetime ago.

They didn't come from such different backgrounds, but after college and marriage, their worlds were far apart, even though they went to the same church. Nari wouldn't have fit in well at Sonya's famous Bible study group. The women would have been polite to her, but none would've sought her friendship.

Even Helen, her only sister, had never asked Sonya the simple question: Do you not like your husband?

Sonya took a deep breath. "I don't like my husband. He sleeps with young women from hostess bars. They call the house. Several have even come to ask me to divorce him. But I'm not a good person, either."

Nari shook her head in dismay. "You are such a fine Christian. You've been so kind and generous to your brother-in-law, all the employees, and me. What are you saying?"

"I don't like my life in Seoul. When I'm there, I feel like I'm dying. That I am in hell. I am sinful."

"Oh my."

"Often I wish I were dead and had no one to take care of. That would make things simpler."

Sonya lowered her chin. She'd never uttered such a terrible thing before but couldn't take it back.

"But your boys—"

"I treasure my sons."

"You're such a good mother."

Sonya smiled weakly. "They'd be better off without me."

"You can't say that."

"I'm tired of living."

Nari took hold of Sonya's right hand.

"Then leave home. Leave your family. It's better to live. If my husband felt this way and that's why he left, and if it saved his life, then I'm glad he's gone. I'd rather he be alive somewhere else than be gone forever."

Sonya covered her mouth with her hands.

"It's not too late," Nari said. "There's still time."

2
Compromise

Sonya's long and frequent absences had taught the Chairman that she might leave forever, and the shrewd businessman decided to change course.

She'd been gone for nearly a month, and it had been more difficult this time, even with the boys home. In May, she'd leave again for her nephews' graduation ceremonies.

"What can I do to stop these frequent trips to California?"

They were in the den. He put down his reading, and she continued to crochet.

"We need you here."

"I am here."

"I don't want you to go so often. And the trips get longer."

"It was not a month."

"Right after your sister passed away, it was almost four months—"

"That was almost two years ago. I had to get my license to transfer ownership."

"You would rather clean a stranger's toenails."

"I told you that I don't have to do any of the work anymore, but I had to learn it for the licensing requirements, and I don't mind doing any of it."

Sonya looked at her hands. Before she left, Miss Hong had given her French tips, cut short, painted in a blush-colored polish. During her early training at Saddleback College, Sonya had liked doing the pedicures, recalling the Bible stories of Jesus washing the feet of his disciples.

"I wish you didn't go so often."

"I have to check on the store. It's an investment, and my family needs me. I promised Helen."

"They're not your family. Your sons are here."

"When I was gone for the licensing, they weren't here. College. Military service. Work. They're young men with their own lives."

"They're home now." He raised his voice.

"Seungman and Jiman are doing well at work with their father. I thought you'd be glad."

"I am glad," he said, pleased by how perfectly his succession plan had worked out. His nephew and grandnephews would take over the company. Neither of the boys was reckless, and like their father, both were ambitious and competent.

Yong-gil still kept mistresses but managed to have them under better control. The Chairman's last warning had been effective. There were to be no more daytime excursions at luxury hotels. There would be no more visits from mistresses to the house with appeals to Sonya.

Sonya picked up her yarn basket.

"It's late. I'm going to sleep. Good night."

"I miss you," he said, looking up at the slim outline of her form beneath the plum-colored cashmere sweater and dark-green skirt. He wanted to touch her skin. "Can you stay with me? The boys are out late."

"We mustn't while they're—"

"I bought the unit downstairs."

"Why? We already own both units on this floor."

"It was up for sale, and I thought the boys might want to live in their own place. They can come up for meals."

"Is that what they want?"

"Who wouldn't want an apartment in Apgujeong?"

"I like them being here. They're not married yet."

"When they marry, I can buy them a bigger place. I've been thinking of getting a house in Hannam-dong. Would you like that?"

Sonya shook her head and closed her eyes.

"Do you want to see it? I got the key last week."

She didn't answer.

"Come." He tried to take her hand but she bowed her head, not looking at him, and followed behind as they walked to the elevator.

❧

The layout of the downstairs apartment was original, and it hadn't been remodeled as much as their two units. The view of the Han River was not dissimilar from the one above. The drapery was worn and faded.

"They left the sofas," she said. "Were they included?"

"Come sit," he said, then kissed her.

Sonya could smell him, the clean scent of starch in his shirt, the vetiver of his aftershave. She leaned into his chest, and he held her.

"You are my woman," he said quietly. "How can you go away? Don't you know that I can't sleep when—"

Sonya raised her arms as he removed her plum-colored sweater over her head. He pushed up her green tweed skirt and reached for her buttocks, and, aroused, Sonya held her breath, unable to resist him. She reached to undress him.

There was a roughness to their sex, which felt different and more powerful in the dark, empty apartment. The heavy sound of their quick breathing seemed louder, and in his arms, she climaxed.

When he was finished, she caught her breath, then pulled away as if waking up to remember herself.

"Where are you going?"

Sonya pulled on her clothes, feeling awful. Again. She had done this again.

"It's wrong. This is something we should not do. I've been wanting to talk with the pastor. Do you think we can do that? Maybe if someone else knew, then we would stop this. I've already lost my sister. If Helen could see me, she would be so disappointed."

"No. It would be foolish to talk to him. He'd never understand. This can't be wrong. And a divorce would merely be a legality."

"Then why can't I get a divorce? It would be terrible, I understand. Terrible. But we wouldn't be sinning against God if we were to marry."

"Are you prepared to deal with the consequences if you were to be my wife? You'd be both mother and great-aunt to Seungman and Jiman, and even if they understood, no one else here would. It would destroy my nephew and my sister-in-law, who has always been good to me. Yong-gil, the one who has cheated on you dozens of times with whores half his age, would be seen as the victim. You'd become a laughingstock, and I'd be a villain."

He didn't even bring up how his company would be tainted by the gossip. That much he could face. He had made the company from nothing, and if he were to lose it, so be it. But he could not imagine hurting his aging sister-in-law, the nephew he had adopted, and those dear boys he had named himself.

"My sister-in-law would never understand."

"My sister, Hejin, is dead. She was punished for my sins."

"I told you already that God doesn't work that way," he said, his voice certain.

"Then surely I'll be punished later. I don't want my children to suffer."

"The scandal would follow your sons forever. Our world here does not forgive or forget. How will they hold up their heads? No one can ever know."

"Their mother is a whore."

He brushed her dark hair away from her brow.

"You could never be that."

"I am your nephew's wife. I was your secretary. I am the daughter of two drunken gamblers. No one will care that I've loved you all my life. None of it will ever matter."

Sonya waited for him to dress. In their lovemaking, her mauve lipstick had been erased and her hair had come undone. She didn't want to run into anyone in the elevator, so they climbed the stairs to go home.

When they returned, no one was home. He asked her to stay with him. "I sleep better when you are beside me."

Sonya went to her bathroom to wash, then changed into her white silk nightgown. Standing in the hall outside her bedroom door, she stared at her heavy doorknob for a few moments, then locked it from the outside before going to him.

❧

For breakfast, the housekeeper served two different meals. The two brothers ate toast with eggs, and the Chairman and Yong-gil were eating rice and grilled fish.

Seungman and Jiman wore dark-gray single-breasted suits. Seungman wore a red-and-navy college rep tie he'd had since high school, and Jiman, the younger son, wore a deep-blue French tie borrowed from his father's closet.

Both young men were tall and slim with thick, chestnut-colored hair, pale complexions, dark eyebrows, and large smiling eyes. Seungman resembled his father with his straight nose, and the younger Jiman looked more like Sonya around the mouth and chin, giving him an almost pretty appearance.

Girls preferred Jiman because Seungman could seem too serious. Neither had any difficulty getting offers of girls' phone numbers when they went to nightclubs with their friends. The young men's fine physical appearances as well as their academic accomplishments fed the vanity of both the Chairman and Yong-gil. Breakfast, the meal the family always shared, was usually a happy occasion, with the brothers teasing each other or their father.

"Jiman has another date tonight," Seungman announced. "I feel sorry for her."

"She will be treated like a queen," Jiman said. "I made a reservation at a cool Italian restaurant in Garosu-gil. I will not be home tonight." He smiled at his mother.

"Yes, you will treat her like a queen until you tire of her. Then you will break her heart like all the others," Seungman said.

The Chairman drank his tea and said nothing, and Yong-gil smiled at his sons.

Neither man pushed the boys toward marriage. The older one was a devout Christian, and he was not against marrying young. He wanted a wife who shared his faith, but his standards were unbelievably high. She had to have the looks of a model, the education of a genius, native English-language ability, and the virtue of a nun.

Jiman, who had loathed his recent military service, wanted to fool around as much as possible with as many girls within reasonable limits. His father had told him three rules: Use condoms for sex; give a generous gift when ending things; and preserve his future by always being better than decent.

More than once at nightclubs, when drunk girls flung themselves on Jiman, his older brother had instructed: No sex with drunk girls. Never. If a sober girl wanted to do things, and if Jiman could not overcome temptation, do everything but intercourse and know that you may not want to marry the girl you sleep with, so be mindful of that. A woman's virtue was something for which he should be prepared to take responsibility.

Seungman was saving himself for his future wife and believed that she should be a virgin, too.

"I guess you don't have a date tonight, Brother," Jiman said. "I can introduce you to someone if you like."

Seungman pretended to hit the back of Jiman's head, and as he swung his arm, he knocked over Jiman's coffee, ruining his brother's shirt and tie.

"Oh, sorry." Seungman laughed.

Jiman shook his head and got up. He was laughing, too.

"Just grab another tie in the closet," Yong-gil said as Jiman walked to his room, removing his jacket. "I guess we'll be late for work."

Seungman wiped up the coffee on Jiman's chair, and Sonya helped him.

"Your brother is so good-natured," she said.

"Yeah, I would have been shouting if he'd done that."

"Well, I guess we can all learn from your younger brother."

"You started all this," Yong-gil said to Seungman.

"I guess I did," Seungman said. "I was just teasing him. Sorry."

"You were just joking," the Chairman said. "None of it matters. Finish your breakfast." He turned to the housekeeper, who had come out of the kitchen with a cloth to clean up the spill. "Bring Jiman more eggs. There's coffee all over his plate."

When Jiman returned with another one of his father's ties, Yong-gil said, "You look better in it than I do."

❧

After Yong-gil and the boys left for the office, the Chairman called Sonya to his office.

"I'm making you a vice president. You'll get a salary, and the salary will be set aside for your retirement. No one can touch the money except you, but you cannot have it until you turn sixty-five."

"That's generous of you."

"Don't you want to know how much your salary is?"

Sonya said nothing.

"It is $150,000 a year. It's more than what you'll ever make owning the nail salon. I spoke to a lawyer, and he can figure out how to transfer some of it to your brother-in-law and your nephews and niece, if you like."

Sonya stared at the bridge outside his picture window. The water was dark green and blue in the bright sunlight of the morning.

"Your sons will get the company as long as they keep doing good work."

Still she stayed silent.

"A woman needs money when she gets older. When I'm gone, you'll be taken care of." The Chairman waited for her to react, then continued.

"Every additional year that I am alive, I will set aside one percent of the stock of my company in an escrow account. The amount given will increase by one percent each additional year. Soon enough, you'll accumulate more stock in my company than my nephew. In the first year, you get one percent, the second year, you get two percent, and so on. In five years, you will already have a total of fifteen percent of the company. If I live long enough, you could control the company. Imagine that."

Sonya blinked.

"Why?"

"I believe my nephew will do right by you after I'm gone, but I won't allow him the opportunity to do something stupid because he can't control himself or recognize what is truly valuable. I know that you would never dispossess him or harm the company. You will preserve and nurture everything for the boys. You will always know what matters."

The Chairman tracked her brown eyes as they stared into the river. She was seeking privacy, and he knew she'd think deeply about what she valued.

❧

In the evening, she ate dinner alone with the Chairman, and afterward, they went to the den. He read on the sofa.

Nothing was amiss in his attire: gray wool necktie, white dress shirt, navy blue V-neck sweater, gray cashmere slacks, and black dress socks. On his feet, leather slippers from England from a maker he favored. At sixty-seven years old, he had remained fit, looking like a man in his early fifties. He was still expanding his business interests and keenly interested in the world. Death was nowhere near him, Sonya thought. He could live twenty-five more years, and she wanted him to live forever.

"Sit closer to me," he said.

Sonya got up from her armchair and sat beside him.

"For your lifetime, you can control the stock and benefit from it; but upon the end of your life, all of it will go to your sons equally."

"This again. I don't know what you expect me to do. It seems crazy."

"The boys are excited to move downstairs, so you can take Seungman's room next to mine. Jiman's can become a closet, and our rooms can be joined."

He framed her face with his hands.

"When you are gone, I cannot stand it."

Sonya looked down, unable to bear his gaze.

"I am here now."

"This is holy and separate from the world," he said, reaching for her mouth, but Sonya knew that wasn't true.

3

Turns

November 2003

As a first-year corporate associate at the white-shoe Los Angeles law firm of Willings & Crane, DH made $98,000 a year. However, with his portion of the shared West Hollywood rent, car payments and insurance, law school loans, credit card bills, and overhead, DH didn't have as much to spare as he'd thought he would. His financial situation embarrassed him.

Of the three Koh children, DH had the smoothest path toward his profession. He'd had full-ride scholarships to Andover and Yale. When DH learned that his benefactor was Renee Cha, he'd felt uncomfortable, but Peter hadn't cared at all.

"Mom has a lot of money. More than you and I can imagine," he'd said. "She's just like that. Mom likes to do secret stuff to support people. Besides, you got me a job and a band. Now I make more than you, and I didn't go to law school. You poor thing," he'd teased.

It was true. Annualized, both Peter and Mido had been earning in the low six figures for the past two years. Unlike DH, Peter lived rent-free in his house in Turtle Rock, and though Mido helped her father with the mortgage and expenses, since she no longer had to send money to DH, she was able to save more toward her own future.

Ever generous, Renee had offered to pay for law school, saying, *You're like my son,* but DH had declined. Once he knew, he couldn't accept any more money. She asked him never to tell his father or mother, and DH had not. He knew it would upset them.

When DH promised to pay it back, Renee had been stern. "I don't want the money. When you're a rich lawyer, please take the best care of your father and mother. If they become rich, then you can give the money to another young person. Okay?" That was classic Renee.

Regardless, DH intended to pay it all back but had no idea how. He also owed Mido money. For three years, his kid sister had sent him $1,500 every month, which had allowed him to only borrow for tuition, and though he earned money in the summers and tutored when he had time, graduate school in Manhattan had been more than he could afford.

He had over $10,000 in credit card debt because he'd had to cover travel back and forth to California, rent deposits, and the down payment for his used Toyota Corolla. There were suits and shoes to buy for work and his share of food and liquor when he went out. He was never not thinking about the cost of things.

When Peter transferred to Pomona, DH realized how often Peter had picked up the tab for pizzas, beer, and even rides to New York. Of course, when Renee wasn't around to visit Peter, there were no town car rides to the city or grand meals at restaurants where she made sure to get everything he wanted but was too shy to order for himself.

DH adored his best friend's mother. When she'd told him that he was like her son, he knew she meant it as a kindness, but in the year and a half that Peter had no longer been living in New Haven, DH had come to understand that day to day, a son lived differently from a scholarship student who was like a son. As a gracious benefactor, she owed him nothing more, and DH would always be grateful to her nonetheless.

DH was not a wasteful person with poor financial habits. Even as a boy, living abroad alone, he'd been thrifty about every cent because there was never enough for the three kids. Helen had sent him extra cash whenever she could, and when he wanted sweets at the commissary or a burger with his teammates at an away game, he had economized. "Not hungry," he'd say when his friends ordered pizza and he would've had to chip in, then he'd make himself ramyeon with the hot pot in his room.

Whatever food the school offered, he ate. He accepted free sneakers that the coach gave him and refused invitations to attend concerts or games that would have required him to pitch in, saying he had to study since he wasn't naturally smart. Almost never did he spend money on things he did not need.

There wasn't enough money to go on dates, but there were always cute girls willing to hang out and watch television in his room. Sometimes the well-off ones didn't understand why he couldn't afford to go to Fort Lauderdale for spring break or Aspen at Christmas.

When Joanna, a girl he was sleeping with during his senior year at Yale, offered to pay for him to go on her family's trip to Saint Bart's, DH had declined, not wanting her father's charity. He wasn't poor. His parents had been upper-middle-class, then middle-class.

Over the years, when girls dropped hints about shopping trips, DH heard them loud and clear, but he thought it would be wrong to buy them shoes or bags when he could barely get any gifts for his own family. He stayed away from the girls with too many expectations.

Once he got the firm job, DH had tried to live at home in Orange County to save money, but the round-trip commute ate into his sleep, so he agreed to pay for a small room in a rented house in West Hollywood with three friends from college and law school.

When he was growing up, there had always been stories of fabled achievers who could ace tests or compete in a tournament on four or five hours of sleep, but having been a scholar-athlete most of his life until law school, DH knew he could not do anything well without at least seven and a half hours. His father, whose sleep schedule could be used to set a watch, had been right. There was no other way. If it were up to him, he'd sleep nine hours, and his work would be done better and faster.

From childhood, DH had accepted that he was fine without being brilliant. At Yale especially, he had met some out-there thinkers and artistic types. DH was ordinary, just intelligent enough, and hardworking. His superpower was that he was able to work steadily and finish what he started. He was always on time.

He had been an excellent soccer player in Australia and in college, but there was no way in the world he'd go pro, and that had become clear his freshman year, when he was just playing at the college level.

What did he want, now that he was a first-year lawyer? DH wanted to be rich. He didn't need to have as much money as Peter's mother's family, sums that seemed incalculable to him; however, this middle child wanted enough money to take care of his family. If one day his son wanted to go on a trip for spring break, he could say okay. If his wife wanted a necklace from some fancy store, fine. If his brother wanted to go to graduate school, no problem.

❧

Mido needed help. It was time to clean up the house.

She asked her brothers to come home on Sunday afternoon after church to clear out Helen's things and go through the unpacked boxes. "I can't do it by myself," she said, and DH and Bo quickly agreed. Their father had Elder Council, then a Finance Committee meeting, which would take the rest of the afternoon.

Bo cooked fried rice with Spam and kimchi, and after lunch, the three of them faced Helen's clothing and shoes, which were in boxes in the garage. After Bo loaded up the car, Mido announced there was more to do.

"Oh, c'mon, Mido. I get no time off ever," DH said. "Can't I just pass out?"

Bo tapped DH on the shoulder. "No whining."

"That's not very sympathetic coming from a psychologist," DH said.

"I'm not a psychologist yet, and I'm probably going into research. I'm not built to listen to people's problems."

"That's so true," DH said, turning to Mido, thinking she'd agree.

Mido put her hands on her hips. To Bo, she said, "In the guest room, there's all your CDs, cassettes, books, and the clothes you've outgrown," and to DH, "The stuff you've shipped from New York. I left both of you alone because you were busy taking a bar exam and working at the lab, but no more nice guy. I want it all cleared out, gentlemen."

"Who are you?" DH asked. "And what have you done to my nice sister?"

Bo laughed. "Let's go, clown. Follow the leader."

Mido smiled.

❧

In the guest room, DH rifled through Bo's boxes. He pulled out Bo's Korean CDs and cassettes, setting aside the ones he wanted to borrow. Bo put on a cassette of trot music, and DH smiled.

"Seriously? You are such an old man," DH said.

"I am," Bo agreed cheerfully. "I'm going to grow a beard like Freud soon."

After two years at Fullerton College, then two more at UCLA as a transfer student, Bo had done something miraculous. In his senior year, he had performed some complicated data tabulation and run models for Dr. Harry Kim, a psychology professor at UCLA, relating to anxiety and depression in aging immigrant communities in LA's Koreatown, and Dr. Kim had listed him as one of three coauthors. A major coup for an undergraduate, it ensured his admission to UCLA's highly competitive doctoral program in developmental psychology.

DH asked, "Brother, how long will it take you to graduate?"

"It's a six-year program, but I might need more time if I want to get my hours for licensing. There are so many steps: coursework, training, and the dissertation. I had no idea it would take this long."

"When do you make money?" DH asked.

"I will never make the kind of money you make. Never."

Mido looked up from her sorting.

"That doesn't matter," she said. "You're going to do important work. You're going to be a doctor."

"What Mido said." Bo smiled and patted her shoulder.

"Did you find an apartment on campus?" she asked.

"I was thinking of staying here. The drive isn't too bad."

"No. You have to get a place. You have to be on campus to teach and do research."

"Rents are way too high—"

"You have to be on campus," Mido said firmly. "That's final."

DH shook his head. "Wow. An alien has snatched your body."

"And you are not going to tutor anymore when you're in school. Just like DH. I'm going to put you through grad school," Mido said. "Your sister is rich now."

"I'm not going to let my baby sister put me through school," Bo protested. "I can work. I made $40,000 last year during my senior year, and that's when I was doing new work for Dr. Kim. If I live on campus, getting to Irvine will be a nightmare. It's better for me to live at home."

DH folded his arms. "She put me through school, and so did you. I'm going to help out, too, and when Mido finally changes her mind about finishing," he continued, ignoring Mido's irritated expression, "we'll send her to college. I can give you five hundred a month. If I get a bonus at the end of the year, I'll add more."

"No," Mido said firmly. Her head down, she folded T-shirts and sweatpants. "You still have school loans and credit card debts. I can do this on my earnings alone. I made $126,000 last year. After you pay off your debts, we'll talk about how you can help." She turned to Bo. "I can send you $1,200 a month for rent and food and $300 for your car expenses."

"That's an awful lot of money, Mido," Bo said. She wouldn't make eye contact as she said these difficult things. However, what she was saying was true. If he kept working at Fortress, Bo's degree would take even longer, and his work would suffer. His advisor had also told him to live on campus.

Mido didn't look up as she organized the old clothes. Sitting cross-legged, she leaned across the floor to push the folded pile of clothing away from her and pulled a messy pile toward her.

"I don't think I'm going to college for a while," she said.

"What?" Bo said. "Why?"

"I just turned twenty-five. Not sure if I see the point of it. It makes more sense for me to keep doing what I'm doing. And last year I made good money: $65,000 from my salary as the manager at Fortress and over sixty from college admissions counseling and SAT boot camps."

"Wow," Bo said. "Lion said you were doing well, but I didn't know. Okay, I'm impressed, but isn't it short-term thinking? Just thinking about how much you're making now?"

"Why, do I have to make more? I heard that some hagwon teachers and college consultants can make high six figures."

"But there's so much more you might want to learn," Bo said, and Mido shrugged.

"Mido. You have to get your degree," DH said. "You have to finish school. Mommy would have wanted that." His voice broke.

The three grew quiet, and after a long pause, Mido spoke.

"Umma would be so happy if she knew you were going to get a PhD." Mido looked up at the ceiling and blinked.

"When I passed the bar, the first person I wanted to call was Mommy," DH said through his tears. From the top of Mido's stack of folded clothes, DH picked up his brother's faded blue sweatshirt from middle school and wiped his face.

Bo put his arm around his shoulder. "I know. I wanted to call her, too. When you passed. Apparently the California bar is hard."

"The toughest," DH said, laughing. "This dummy passed it on the first try."

Bo and Mido laughed.

"I don't know how to be without her," DH said. "I keep reading that notebook she gave me. I was hoping she had written some advice, but she didn't."

"She wrote me a ten-page letter," Bo said.

"What?"

"Kidding," Bo said, and DH pushed him gently with his left foot.

"You're kicking your older brother? The lack of respect!" Bo laughed.

Finally looking at them, Mido said, "Mom wrote that I was her favorite."

"She did not," DH said.

"She did not," Mido said. "We know who that was."

DH started to cry again and buried his face in Bo's old sweatshirt.

"What did she write in your notebook?" DH asked Bo.

"She wrote that I had to make sure Mido finished her degree," Bo answered, eyebrows raised to look more stern.

"No, she wouldn't," Mido said, staring at her brother, uncertain if he was teasing.

"He's kidding, Mido. But Mommy might have if she knew you wouldn't go," DH said, smiling. "So? What did yours say?" He faced Bo.

"Mine was filled with lists of things she had to do for me. Lots of budget stuff. All my report cards were in there, too. I kept thinking there'd be some clues or instructions," Bo said, then grew quieter. "She had such nice handwriting. In English and Korean."

DH exhaled and took another breath. "Same. I couldn't look at it for a long time, and finally, when I read it, it was what you said. Lists of things to do like parent-teacher meetings, the name and model of the cool cleats that I'd wanted for Christmas, and the prices of things I needed for soccer. And, of course, my report cards. There were the worn-out envelopes in the back where she saved money for us."

Mido's notebook had been filled with names of specialists in Sydney, recorded in her mother's remarkable penmanship. Her brothers had not needed all these extra people. She'd given her mother so much more to do, and Mido felt sorry that she hadn't realized any of it until it was too late.

"Everything will get done. Mommy always said this," DH said. "Whenever I'd speak to her from overseas, and I was freaking out about some exam or tournament, she'd say, 'Dae-hun-ah, everything will get done. Commit your plans to the Lord.' Sometimes, when I was really losing it, she'd pray with me. Even though it was such an expensive call."

DH wiped his nose, and Mido looked around for the box of tissues, but there wasn't one in the guest room. Bo was crying, too, and Mido got up to get some from the bathroom. She sat down beside DH and pulled the blue sweatshirt away from his face.

Helen had lived by these words, believing that everything would get done, but everything had not been done because she was gone. There was so much more left to do. The notebooks weren't even full.

"One thing at a time. One person at a time. We will each do our work," Mido said.

The boys looked like their mother more than their father. They had her large dark eyes and the strong nose. Mido alone had gotten her father's full lips. Only Bo was nearsighted and squinted, even with his glasses.

Mido said to Bo, "It's settled. I'm sending you to school, and I can do it for six years. As for my degree, I'll decide then. I went to college in Sydney because it was expected of me. I never once questioned it. But now I'm not sure why I have to go. I'm already a well-regarded, highly paid teacher. College is a nice idea, but if any of us are studying, we're not getting paid. It makes sense for me to earn money. Besides, my education should be my choice."

DH covered his mouth. What he felt was awe. When they were growing up, even their mother, who believed in miracles, would not have guessed that little Mido would be educating her two older brothers.

Bo bowed his head and said nothing, which was his form of assent. He was thinking that with his savings and fellowships, he might be able to relieve her sooner than in six years, but it would be hard.

"How can I let you do this?" Bo asked.

"Easy. You're both now my retirement plans," she said, beaming. "I'm getting the better deal. When you get married, you better tell your wives that you're responsible for me, too." She laughed. "Kidding."

"Our little Mido is impressive," DH said, his chin touching his chest.

Mido said nothing, feeling relieved that she could do something. She liked teaching kids, and she had reason to work harder now. Her brothers would have graduate degrees: a lawyer and a psychologist.

"Hey, how about marriage? You're not getting any younger. When are you going to find a husband?" DH asked.

Bo turned to his younger brother. "Hello. Privacy?"

DH ignored him.

"So, is Tek still out?"

"He's been out for a long time," Bo said.

The brothers checked Mido's face to confirm.

"Didn't he want to marry you?" DH asked. Mido never talked about him anymore. "I would've given my approval if I liked him enough. I mean, after giving him a battery of tests and trials: Go pluck the moon from the sky for my baby sister, slay a modest-sized dragon to be worthy, and find the tooth of a flawless purple unicorn. Though he does get a plus for being Korean, even though he's an Aussie, and Peter said—"

"What did Peter say?" Mido checked DH's bemused expression.

"He said Tek came out again after the funeral, then hasn't in the past two years. That's all."

Mido pursed her lips.

"You still like him?" Bo asked Mido with a little more hesitation in his voice than his brother, who could ask anyone anything and not be put off.

When Mido remained blank-faced, Bo glanced at DH and made a slicing gesture with his hand drawn across his neck.

Undeterred, DH said, "You could go back to Australia and finish school. You liked it there, and if you want to take him back—"

"I want to be here," she said.

DH was watching Mido like a prosecutor. She kept her eyes lowered, unwilling to reveal her thoughts. The brothers knew why she felt compelled to stay. Mido was also keeping their father alive.

"So you're giving up school *and* marriage?" DH asked.

"I like my work. And for the time being, I make more money than either of you."

"Show-off," Bo said, moving near her and giving her shoulders a squeeze. "Hey, I'm proud of you," he said.

"Me, me!" DH shouted, moving even closer to them. "Be proud of me, too!"

"No, not you," Bo said, shaking his head. "Sit down, Counselor."

Mido laughed.

"She didn't write it down, but Mom would have wanted you to take care of yourself, too," Bo told her. "She would have wanted you to get your degree."

"I know," she said.

4
Hagwon Expansion

February 2004

On Friday afternoon, Yun and Mido were in Mido's office, waiting for Lion to drive down from Cypress and for Peter to finish teaching his Advanced SAT Math class. After a quick teachers' meeting, the four of them would head back to Yun and Lion's house. The band had to rehearse, and Mido would hang out with them.

"How's your father?" Yun asked. Having unrolled the yoga mat over the office rug, she was doing her daily sit-ups. "Umma says that Manager John Koh is the most polite and private human being to walk the earth. She's with him six days a week, including a round-trip car ride, and knows almost nothing about him. He could be CIA for all we know."

Mido smiled in recognition. She unknotted the blue cardigan around her neck and pulled it on over her white dress shirt. "Between your mother and me, he's fed and alive. By the time I get home from work, he's reading the newspaper or getting ready for bed. Once or twice a week, he has meetings at church. On Fridays and Saturdays, I get home even later, which makes it hard for me to check on him. I think he has a church Finance Committee meeting tonight? I know he eats whatever I leave in the fridge because there are washed empty containers and dishes on the rack when I get home."

"That's a relief."

On Sunday afternoons and Wednesday nights, Mido prepared rice, entrées, and the side dishes that her father liked and packed them up in glass containers for her father to reheat. On Saturday afternoons, Bo came home to help with the grocery shopping and cleaning. They'd have dinner together, and Bo would stay over. On Sundays, DH joined them at church, and the three of them took their father to lunch.

John was most like his old self at church and on Sundays when the three of them were home. During the week, Mido could see how difficult things still were for him without their mother, but how hard he tried to keep going.

At work, he was determined to show a strong profit each quarter for his sister-in-law's business, even though Sonya never said a word about money. Every month, he made the house mortgage payments and set aside money to pay Sonya back. John kept a ledger and a separate savings account for the down payment, Helen's hospital bills, and the loan to move to the States—a tally of their debts to Sonya and her husband's family. He had promised Helen that he would pay them off.

Working at a nail salon full of women had made him feel conspicuous. Their attention embarrassed him, and John had only grown more formal with everyone, deferring to Nari to deal with any personnel issues.

"How's your mom?" Mido asked, marveling at how many sit-ups Yun could do. She had stopped counting after a hundred. After sit-ups, Yun moved on to push-ups.

"She's good. Every morning when I call her, she says the same thing: 'Thank God, no more Shrimp Castle headaches.' She's never wanted to own a business, so Rose Salon is perfect, where she gets to be the queen without any of the risk. Plus your dad likes doing the numbers, so she's happy not to have that responsibility, either. As long as there are drama videos to rent, she says, she can live in America forever. She doesn't even talk about returning to Seoul anymore."

After ten push-ups, Yun got in position to plank, her willowy frame forming a straight line from the crown of her head to her toes.

"Time me?"

Mido scribbled "5:42 p.m." on a scratch pad. She never wore a watch anymore. With a large wall clock in every room at Fortress, including the bathrooms, it was impossible for anyone to disregard time.

"She misses Appa, but she doesn't miss fighting with him." Yun kept her head parallel to the floor.

"Do you think he'll return?"

"No."

"Really?" Mido knew that Yun's mother thought he would.

"I know. I know. I hope he does, for her sake."

"You don't want him to come back?"

"Of course I want him to, but who knows if he'll stay? We weren't worth sticking around for last time."

Yun's disappointed profile grew stern and her plank form more straight. Without any makeup on her tanned oval face, her long dark hair in a ponytail, Yun still looked like one of Mido's high school students. "His loss. Not mine."

Mido had met Yun's father a number of times but never had a conversation with him beyond polite greetings. He was the opposite of Nari, the chatty mother who was always interested in her daughter's friends.

Joonho was considerably taller than Yun and Nari and well built with powerful arms. He had a striking face, his face usually brown from the sun, and he shared the distinct features of the generations of Kim farmers from Gyeongju: the dark, sloping eyes, which crinkled when he smiled, and the elegant nose.

What Mido couldn't forget about her friend's father was the time he hit Yun in the face, and how she couldn't go to school. He'd never hit her before, Yun told her later, and he'd felt so terrible that he'd stayed away from home for days. He never hit her again, but whenever he was upset with her or Nari, he'd disappear without explanation. This time it was Brazil. Six years. When he was ashamed, he hid. He loved them; he just loved his shame more.

"I'm not mad at him."

"I didn't think you were," Mido said.

"We've had our share of fights, but I know he's a decent person." Her voice started to waver from the strain of her plank pose.

"Time?" Yun said.

"Three minutes."

Yun collapsed on her stomach and exhaled. "Hey, where are these guys?" She glanced at the clock over the door, then pulled herself up and reached into her tote bag for some folders. Exercise over, she was all business once more.

"So, twenty-two more kids signed up for the spring boot camp. Several want private essay counseling, and I think once you meet them, probably all of them will want you. How many can you take?"

"I can handle maybe six to eight more. Maybe ten tops. It depends." Mido shrugged.

"You're everyone's favorite. The mothers are trying to keep you a secret, but they all share your name with their closest friends. As long as their kids are not in the same grade level, that is." Yun laughed. They were continually astonished by what parents were willing to do to give their children an edge over their friends' children.

"Maybe Peter wants a few?" Mido asked. "He's a good writer."

"Peter said he'll take private tutoring for math, but the college admissions stuff makes his skin crawl."

"Yup, I could have predicted that."

"Why does he hate it so much?" Yun asked.

"He hates the competition. For him, the math stuff is worth teaching. All the angling to get your kid into the best schools and paying the extra fees makes him want to hurl. His words."

"Against capitalism and authority. Once a punk, always a punk," Yun said, repeating Lion's assessment of his bandmate. "I can't figure out why he still works here."

"He likes kids and teaching," Mido said. "I asked him if he'd teach at a real school—public or private—but he said never. Peter says, 'A hagwon is only supplemental. Real school is a serious responsibility.' "

❧

Mido rode in Peter's car to Yun and Lion's house.

"I fired Mr. Shim," Peter said.

"What? He just started."

Peter kept his eyes focused on the traffic ahead.

"He was using copies of the SAT tests that you're not supposed to have. He said he had to use them and that we were naive not to. Lion said no way, and he's right."

"When did you fire him?"

"Earlier this morning. I should've called you, but it was very last minute. I figured you didn't want to be involved."

Mido hated firing people, and Peter knew that.

She sighed. "I think everyone has them now. One of the mothers asked why we're not teaching with them."

"What did you say?" Peter signaled before taking a left. The side roads were less busy but darker.

"I said that the kids needed to learn how to do the work. They'll be better off for it. Right?"

"Fucking crazy parents. I'm so tired of this shit."

"Not all of them want their kids to have those tests. I mean, I understand why they'd be upset since so many other kids can study from them at the other hagwons."

"They can go there. Mr. Shim can go. If that's what you got to do to get your kid a perfect score, then fine. I'm not doing it."

"I know you're right," Mido said, "but I understand why everyone's freaked out. They think they're at a disadvantage because the other kids will have seen the exam questions and be able to memorize the answers without solving the questions."

"Listen to you. You sound like Mr. Shim."

"No, no. I just said I understand. These parents are really worried."

"Life's not fair, but it doesn't mean that you teach kids to cheat. What, they're going to keep getting tests ahead of time in college? At work? How can you learn to handle shit you didn't anticipate? We're supposed to give the kids the tools to solve problems. Not give them the answers for specific problems. That makes no fucking sense."

"Hey, hey. I'm not Mr. Shim."

Peter parked along the road.

"I'm sorry I'm yelling. I just had this conversation with Lion earlier, and he said basically what you said, and I lost my shit. I almost quit."

"Huh? You mean Lion didn't agree with you?"

"No. It was his idea to fire him when he found out, but he said we're going to take a hit because our students won't do as well as kids from hagwons that teach from the illegal tests."

"Can we report this?"

"Too hard to prove. Besides, Mr. Shim is just another poor dude who's providing for his family. He's got two little kids and a wife at home. And this is why people hate fucking hagwons. They think we're all cheaters."

"I heard anyone can get the illegal tests."

"Yeah, but they don't come with the answers. Only people like us can create the answer key. You could probably make one up in a few hours."

Mido had liked Mr. Shim. He'd come highly recommended, and it surprised her a little that he'd been so willing to cheat, but lately, the pressure on students and hagwon teachers alike had gotten even worse. It had been easier to work at Exodus with the kindergartners and middle school students. The working parents had just been happy when the kids were safe and their homework was done before pickup time. With some of the high school students in Irvine, there were far higher expectations. Tutoring wasn't enough.

The selective colleges required top scores, beyond-perfect grade point averages, the most demanding classes the respective schools offered, extracurricular activities with leadership positions, letters of recommendation attesting to exceptional qualities, significant publications, nationally important awards, and/or elite and costly sports. A few months back, Mido had met with a high school junior at Fortress who had started a dot-com business selling flashlights during her freshman year in high school, and a boy who had learned C++ and Java so well that he could work as an independent contractor and skip college altogether.

"I like the kids so much," Peter said. "Believe it or not, I do want them to get what they want. But I just can't justify cheating."

"None of us wants that. If we take a hit, we'll get over it," Mido said. "I know you and Lion are right, Peter. In the long run, integrity is what really matters, right?"

The car was parked, yet Peter kept his hands on the steering wheel. He faced her and exhaled.

"How's Tek?"

"What?"

"The lawyer guy from Australia who thought we were losers for working at a hagwon."

"Pardon?"

"Never mind." Peter turned the ignition.

"He didn't think we're losers. He just wanted me to go back to Sydney."

"So why didn't you?"

"I like teaching kids, too."

"That's all?" Peter looked at her again.

"The pay's good."

"I get it." He never wanted to pry.

"You ever see your father?"

"No," he said.

Mido didn't ask any follow-up questions. DH would have asked many more, though he probably knew all the answers.

❧

As soon as the car pulled into Yun and Lion's place, Ginny ran out to meet them. She hugged Mido.

"Did we beat them here?" Mido asked Ginny, stroking her short brown hair. At sixteen, Ginny was almost as tall as Mido, but her bright face with its rounded features and chubby cheeks resembled a middle schooler's, not that of a junior in high school.

"Yes. You won," Ginny said. "Yun Teacher just called. They're leaving Garden Mart. They'll be here in fifteen minutes. I set the table already."

"Did you eat?" Peter asked.

"I had dinner and finished my homework."

"Nice job," he said, smiling. Ginny had become like a baby sister for all four of them.

"Yun Teacher said you'll help me with my college essays," Ginny said, looking up at Mido.

"Did she?" Mido raised an eyebrow.

"Won't you? Are you too busy?" Ginny looked concerned.

"You're my top priority. But you're going to have to really work. My students suffer."

"I've heard," Ginny said, wondering if it could be true that Mido Teacher was called the Surgeon.

"You have to write, write, rewrite and rewrite," Mido said.

"Yes, and somehow you'll like it," Peter said, his arms folded.

"I don't like writing personal essays," Ginny said. "I'm a science and math person."

"You just haven't had the right teacher," Peter said. "The kids say that Mido Teacher will split your skull open and fish around until she finds exactly the right subjects for you, then apparently, she slices open your heart to get all the feelings out. And that's before you start your rewrites. I pity you, Ginny. I do. You have to face the Surgeon."

"I sound scary." Mido smiled. "I like it."

Ginny laughed. "I want to go to Dartmouth now."

"Why?" Peter asked, remembering the guys he knew from Andover who'd gone there. They were smart jocks. Of course, Dartmouth had every sort of student, but from Andover, they took the top scholar-athletes. Ginny couldn't run down the block or throw a ball. "New Hampshire is very far. Kinda remote. And cold!"

"Monica Cho goes there."

Mido didn't recognize the name.

"Is she a Fortress student?"

"No. She went to my high school, graduated last year. Monica went to another hagwon in Cypress—Ivy Leaf Academy."

Peter knew of it. It was supposed to be a good one.

"I saw Monica when she came home for Christmas break, and she told me all about Dartmouth. She said I can visit her, and if I get in, she'll tell me what classes to take and which ones to skip."

"That's how you're going to choose a college?" Peter asked skeptically.

"That's how most of them seem to choose a college. At least when they're being honest," Mido said.

"I have a friend who teaches there," Peter said. "A history professor now. He went to King's, too. He was several years ahead of me. He got his PhD at Yale. I ran into him again when he was a TA in a twentieth-century British history survey course. Smart guy. Published his dissertation on the Reformation, I think."

Mido turned, hearing the wheels of Yun's car crunching across the gravel driveway.

❧

During dinner, Peter brought up Ginny's rationale for applying to Dartmouth, and neither Yun nor Lion was surprised.

"Have you ever asked them about why they want to go to college, or if they even want to go at all?" Lion picked up another piece of gimbap and popped it into his mouth.

Peter taught math for every standardized test, including grad school exams, and did occasional private tutoring for physics and calculus. His students were already mid-to-high-level scorers and liked learning math with him. Most of them tended to get very high scores because he'd teach them how to think like mathematicians.

"Focusing on outcomes doesn't help you learn," Peter said.

"Agreed," Lion said, recalling their earlier conversation that morning about firing Mr. Shim.

"Why is it wrong to think about outcomes?" Yun asked. "I'm not saying I disagree with you—"

"Because then what? What happens after you hit the score? What happens after you get into college? What happens after you get the job? What happens after you meet your goal? Then what?" Peter grew irritated. "I hate that about Koreans. Set the goals. Then set the goals higher. Then higher."

"All Koreans?" Mido asked.

"Well, not all Koreans. Just my father. Never mind."

Peter didn't say "never mind" often. They all knew what it meant.

"Well, how should our kids choose their colleges?" Yun asked.

"We should at least include the question, What is college for?" Peter said, tapping the dining table for emphasis.

"Yeah," Lion shouted, and raised his fist. "What is college for?"

"Seriously," Yun said. "You need that degree to get a good job."

Remembering, she turned to Mido. "Well, you don't need a degree because you're special."

Mido smiled.

"We should take the kids on a tour," Peter said. "A lot of these kids never see the campuses. Their folks either can't or won't take them. They should attend classes. They should know more about these schools. I know we get our students into the fancy schools, but are they doing okay there?" he asked. "Last year, two of them flunked out for doing drugs. One of them locked himself in his room for days and didn't come out because he was playing *GTA*."

They'd heard about John Lee, Seth Kim, and William Chang—kids who had never once caused any problems in high school.

"And one of them is still at home now, right? Brown, Wesleyan, and NYU. Top schools," Peter said.

He remembered Colin, one of Fortress's brightest students, who had graduated from Caltech. He'd been admitted to a hospital for severe clinical depression for over a month. When it happened, Colin's mother had asked Peter to check in on him because he had gotten along especially well with her son. He was now a server at his aunt's coffee bar.

Several students who had graduated with superb records from highly selective schools hadn't been able to find appropriate work and had become discouraged.

"And then there are the kids who can't get jobs for college grads despite their degrees."

"What's wrong with the world that can't employ kids like that?" Yun asked.

Lion crossed his arms. "You can't always get the job you want, right? Several were trying to get jobs in entertainment and media, which is hard for anyone. They had no connections. Eventually they found jobs. Probably not their dream jobs. Isn't that life?"

Yun picked up her chopsticks and put more gimbap on her husband's plate. She knew Lion was upset about it. Their graduates often stopped by the hagwons to say hello. Of the ones who had wanted to work in Hollywood, one now worked at a real estate brokerage and another at an accounting firm.

"The gain from our study is to have become better and wiser by it," Lion quoted Montaigne. His essay "On the Education of Children" was required reading for all employees.

"Maybe we have to teach our students different things about college, not just how to get in but what they should do once they're there," Mido said at last. "We can start with the tour."

5

College Tour

Yun stared at the spreadsheet on her screen, tapping her pencil against the conference table. Seated opposite her, Lion was drafting copy for the Fortress college tour poster. Peter and Mido sat beside Lion.

It had not taken long for Lion, Yun, Mido, and Peter to figure out the itinerary and costs. The Fortress college tour group would fly into Boston, charter a bus, sleep in motels, and fly back home from Philadelphia.

Tufts, Boston University, MIT, Harvard, Boston College, Northeastern, Wellesley, Dartmouth, Williams, Amherst, Yale, Wesleyan, Columbia, NYU, Fordham, Princeton, University of Pennsylvania, Swarthmore, and Haverford—seven nights of lodging and meals plus round-trip flights into and out of LAX for $1,500.

"We won't make a cent from this," Yun said. "We might lose money."

"It'll be a great trip, though," Lion said. "I wish we could go with them."

"We need to be here," she said, and turned to Peter. "Can you and Mido really handle twenty-six kids?"

Peter scratched his head and smiled at Mido.

"Well, the students listen to the Surgeon, and we'll have Ginny, too. She might as well be a teacher."

"This whole trip is for her, really," Lion said, smiling.

"No parents, huh?" Peter asked.

"No parents. No way," Lion said. "They'd be harder to control than two dozen teenagers scrambling to buy Harvard T-shirts at the Coop, then racing for the bus."

"The price for the trip is down to the bone," Yun said, shaking her head. "Is there any room to find some profit in this? How will we pay Peter and Mido for their time?"

"I'm okay," Mido said. "I think this is important."

Lion smiled at her. "Yes. Our students have vague ideas about colleges, and many of them haven't seen a single campus. Most of their parents are too busy to take them across the country, and some will be the first generation to attend colleges in the States. A tour like this could be less intimidating and cost-effective for the families."

"It could also be fun," Peter said.

"But you'll be losing a lot of private tutoring income if you're gone for a week," Yun said, looking worried.

"I'm okay with that," Mido said. "But I shouldn't speak for Peter."

"He's fine with money," Lion said. "We pay him handsomely."

"Handsomely?" Peter cocked his head.

Lion ignored this. "It would be better if the kids actually saw Princeton before applying to it as their top choice, when it's possible that Williams is a much better fit for them. It's just Ivies, Ivies, Ivies. I'm exhausted by these conversations with the parents telling me that their kid *has* to get into an Ivy."

"Husband, you went to Princeton," Yun said, laughing. "Had you even seen it before applying?"

"Yes, because my mother forced my brother, Ray, to take me there. She wanted to make sure that no one would beat me up. I was sixteen when I went to college, and I looked like a tall twelve-year-old. I didn't need to shave until I graduated."

Lion still found it hard to believe that nothing bad had happened to him. Most of his closest relationships had been with his professors, who must have felt sorry for one of the youngest undergraduates at the university. Not a single person had said an unkind thing to him in his three years there; however, he had never felt quite normal, either.

Those years had shaped Lion Han. It was while he was at Princeton that his father cut him off, forcing him to tutor to pay for his tuition.

At school, he had easily grasped the mathematical elegance and mystery of the Fourier series, Dirichlet characters, and Hilbert spaces, and he felt like he had become a man because when his family abandoned him, he could take care of himself and continue to learn.

Not everyone should go to college, but Lion wished that anyone who did could experience the exquisite pleasure of learning for its own sake. Getting a degree merely to get a job could not be the sole purpose of higher education. Lion was about to turn thirty-one, and that was not old, but he had lived long enough to know that one should never be cynical about learning and growth.

Over the years, the more money he made, the less important it had become. If it weren't for Yun's reminders about their overhead, he would have cut in half the tuition bills for the middle-income families at Exodus and forgiven the tuition for all the lower-income kids.

In contrast to Exodus, Fortress never lost money, and its extraordinary profits more than covered Exodus's losses. There were parents who would never be able to pay back the money they owed Exodus, but Lion still allowed their kids to come. The parents had no other childcare, and Lion reasoned that the kids would just get into trouble if they were left home by themselves. He and Yun agreed that they could afford to let 10 percent of the kids attend for free as long as no one else knew about it, especially the children themselves.

For four years, Ginny's parents hadn't paid any tuition or for room and board. Lion and Yun paid for her annual plane ticket to Korea so she could see her family. This year, Ginny had refused the ticket so she could go on the college tour, and when Yun said they could still send her, she would not accept it.

"I want to get into Dartmouth first. Or UCLA. My mother wants me to apply to Yale or Harvard, but I think it would be better if I went somewhere that I chose—"

"You can make up your mind about the college list after you visit some of the schools," Yun said, not wanting to disagree with Ginny's mother, who was a kind woman but single-minded about making her daughter into a doctor. She had initially wanted Ginny to attend UCLA, but with Ginny's exceptional marks and test scores and her high class rank, her mother was feeling more hopeful. Then Ginny was voted yearbook editor, and upon learning that another yearbook editor had been accepted into Yale two years prior, her mother had grown only more ambitious for her child.

Ginny's mother reasoned that being fostered, more or less, by famous Orange County hagwon owners would position Ginny to get into Yale or Harvard. In the five years since its inception, Fortress had sent on average a dozen students to Ivy League schools each year, and its reputation had spread even to Seoul. In the past two years, students had flown in from Korea for the July essay boot camp to work on their applications with Mido.

Finding twenty-six students for the college tour, each paying $1,500, was not a problem. In fact, there was so much demand that mothers asked Lion to create a second tour, and Peter and Mido agreed to take a new group of students a month later. When the students returned, application boot camp would start, and that was another $2,000, which was less than most counselors in the region charged. A bargain, several mothers had said. Yun said they could double the boot camp fee, and parents would pay it. Lion said that wouldn't be right.

❧

When Ginny stepped onto Dartmouth's grassy campus, she felt certain that she should apply. It was unseasonably warm for March, so she removed the blue winter parka she'd borrowed from Yun and stared wide-eyed at the pristine colonial buildings painted white and the Georgian revival brick facades.

As guardians of a responsible child, Yun and Lion had given her latitude and freedom, and Ginny never abused her privileges. If anything, Peter and Mido worried that she was far too mature at sixteen. The other students on the tour followed Ginny's lead as if she had been deputized by Lion himself as a third teacher.

After the group tour led by a student guide from the Admissions Office, Fortress students separated from the others and formed a kind of moving huddle around Mido and Peter as they walked across the Green. They were the only all-ethnically-Korean group of visitors. Some of the other visitors thought they were on a bus tour from overseas and didn't speak English.

"Are you from Japan?" a preppy-looking White boy asked Kate Gwon, Ginny's closest friend.

"No. We're from OC," Kate shot back, irritated. "OC is the acronym for Orange County. That's in Southern California, dude. Near LA, which stands for Los Angeles. Have a nice visit in Hanover." She flicked one of her long dyed-blond braids before showing him her back.

Ginny giggled, then pulled Kate away from the stunned young man. He had been just trying to make conversation with a cute girl who'd reminded him of Sailor Moon.

"I know I could be happy here," she said to Peter, Mido, and Kate while the other students took photographs of each other.

"Really? Why is that?" Peter asked.

"It's so beautiful. There are so many trees that we don't have in Los Angeles. I love this building," Ginny said, admiring Dartmouth Hall.

"Yes, but you're seeing New Hampshire in late March. It's very cold here for most of the school year. I remember being at Andover, which is considerably more south, and wishing for sunshine and better weather so I didn't have to wear a heavy coat. It gets really fucking cold in New England," Peter said, then covered his mouth with both hands when he saw Mido's stern expression. She was always having to remind him not to swear in front of the students, although the students seemed to love it. Lion and Yun never used curse words, and they would have preferred Peter not swear, either.

"Too many trees and mountains for me," said Honey, a fair-skinned girl wearing a baseball hat and sunglasses as if she were a celebrity trying to avoid being recognized. She spoke English with a faint Korean accent. Honey, or Ha-yeon—she answered to both—attended one of the international schools in Seoul. She and six other students had flown in from Seoul just for this tour. "Hanover looks boring. I'd rather be in Boston."

"Don't tell me, you want to go to Harvard," said Charlie, a sophomore from her school.

"No, I don't. Harvard won't take more than one from my school, and my class rank is not top five," she said with certainty. "My mother said I'd be better off applying early to Tufts or Wellesley. She doesn't want to waste my early decision application."

"But you won that international debate thing, though. Man, if you can't get into Harvard, then who goes there?"

"I mean, I'll apply, but I'm not counting on it." Honey put her arm around her best friend, Cindy, who was just happy to be on the trip and had no expectations of getting in anywhere close to the top schools. Charlie snapped their photograph.

❧

After Mido did the room check for the kids at the hotel, she went downstairs to the bar to meet Peter.

"The kids are freaking scary," he said as soon as she sat down.

Mido smiled. "I don't remember knowing so much about schools and my likelihood of getting in or not. I mean, Australia is totally different than here. Nothing is like here. It's madness. Why are so many of these kids from Korea trying to study in the US?"

"Are you serious?" Peter asked, shelling peanuts. He made a pile of the shelled ones on a napkin and set aside the shells in an empty bowl. "This is the globalization strategy."

"Which is what, exactly?"

"Every Korean kid needs to speak English, and ideally, if the parents have any connections, pull, or money, they want their kids to leave Korea and not deal with its education hell."

"I mean, I know that, but still. The kids are so cynical and in many cases, misinformed."

"Well, they're just repeating stuff they heard from their parents, classmates, tutors, relatives, and whatever the media says."

"Did you call your friend Jack?" Mido said.

"Yeah, he's heading over. He couldn't meet the kids. He said it would be a disaster."

Peter raised his hand when he saw his friend walking toward them.

"You're buying, right?" Jack said, giving Peter a hug. He shook Mido's hand.

"Yeah, man. Order whatever you want. On your assistant prof salary, you can't afford the steak here."

"No, I cannot, but I've had everything on the menu here. The History Department pays."

The three of them talked about college admissions, and Mido didn't know if she should excuse herself so the guys could catch up, but Jack kept pulling Mido into the conversation, so she thought it was okay for her to stay.

"What are the students like here?" she asked.

"They're awesome. For the most part, very sophisticated, can handle the work, and a lot of them become consultants, lawyers, or go into finance. No one wants to get a PhD in history. That's only for morons like me."

"Wait, hang on. You have a second book coming out. Religious revivalism, right?"

"You are kind to remember, Sir Peter."

"Sir Peter?" Mido glanced at Jack, wanting more details.

"Yeah, that's what we called him at King's. Even when he was a lad. He was the poshest Asian we had ever seen. His mum would have sent him a valet and cook, but the guardian wouldn't allow it. So Sir Peter had to learn how to make his bed and attend to all sorts of horrid sundry matters. Dreadful. Oh, how he suffered trying to be just upper-middle-class like the rest of us."

"Change topics," Peter said, laughing. His British accent became more pronounced around Jack.

"You have a bit of an Aussie accent," Jack said to Mido.

"Oh, you picked up on that." She covered her mouth. "I thought I got rid of it."

"I never forget a pretty face or fail to distinguish a Commonwealth accent." Jack smiled at her.

"Are you fucking flirting with my colleague? She's too young for you." Peter threw a peanut shell at his friend.

"I'm twenty-five years old," Mido said.

"He's thirtysomething." Peter pointed to Jack.

Mido looked down. "It's late. I better get to my room. Tomorrow starts early. Western Massachusetts. Day four is Amherst and Williams. Nice meeting you, Jack. I'll let you two catch up. See you at breakfast, Peter. I think the bus is at nine a.m."

Jack looked disappointed. "Don't leave me here with this toff."

Peter waved at her. "Good night, colleague."

⁂

In the morning, Peter said that Jack had wanted her number, but he had not given it to him.

"Really? He wants a long-distance relationship with a woman based in Southern California?"

"Not sure if he wants a relationship per se. Jack is a dog. Did you not notice his friendly-mutt qualities?"

"I did sense some of that. He's not my type."

"I know. You like lawyers."

Mido smiled. "Change topics."

"Nicely done," Peter said.

When the kids were on the bus, Peter sat in the back and listened to music on his headphones, while Mido sat in the front reading *A House for Mr. Biswas.*

6

Peter's House

After the last student was picked up from Fortress, Peter and Mido headed to the parking lot, luggage in hand. Peter would take her home.

"Tired?" Mido asked.

"I'm fine. Slept on the flight."

"How's the band?"

"Good. Rehearsal on Thursday."

"Do you still write songs? I was thinking about that one about wasted paper? I didn't catch the name."

" 'Drafts.' It's about writing songs. I've only written six. It's not a lot. I've started dozens but finished only those."

"Yes, 'Drafts.' And that ballad, 'Rosetta.' I thought those were so clever."

"Well, that seems to be my problem."

"Hmm?"

Peter opened the trunk to store their bags.

"I think I'm too clever when I write. Or maybe I want to be seen as clever. When I sing other people's music, I turn to the stuff that's got more feeling, something that I haven't thought about before but feels so true that I wish I could sing it out loud. I want my songs to be smart, of course, but that feeling has to be there," he said, realizing that he'd never admitted this before, not even to Lion.

"Do you like the melody part or writing the lyrics?"

"It's funny, but I think both Lion and I prefer the melody more than the lyrics. It would have been great if he was stronger at one and I was at the other."

"You have a beautiful voice," Mido said.

"Thanks." Peter smiled and looked away.

In the car, she asked him, "I think the tour went well, right?"

"No one died. No one is missing. No one went to jail."

"That's your metric?" she asked.

"Well, no. I'm sure the trip was life-changing for every single child. That's my standard."

"Oh." Mido smiled.

"If the kids had fun, and they got to see differences in the campuses, then I think it was better than nothing. It was a bit of a blur, but they took a lot of photographs and notes," he said. "I'm not sure if the tour helped enough, though. Ginny is convinced that Dartmouth is the school for her. If anything, I was hoping she could feel something was off."

"Why?"

"It's a great school, but what if she doesn't get in?"

"Their loss," Mido said. "Ginny is amazing."

"Yeah, it would be their fucking loss."

"You see what's happened to us? We're like the parents now. We don't want them to be disappointed."

"But they have to be disappointed," he said. "Life has a lot of that. And for many kids, this will be their first major disappointment."

"I think Ginny has had quite a few more letdowns than college admissions. She's been living without her family since middle school. I can't even imagine."

"Yeah," Peter said. "Hey, you hungry?"

"Uh-huh."

"You want to come over?"

"To your place?" Mido tried to sound cool about it.

"I can cook us something. My brain feels noisy. Don't feel like eating alone."

"Seriously?"

"Yeah, and I'll take you home after we eat. No pressure if you're busy."

Mido was curious.

❧

She had never been to Peter's. DH had stayed over a few times, but he'd never described what his place was like. Even something as ordinary as where Peter lived or the kind of apartment he had was somehow off-limits for conversation, so Mido had not pressed it. Always, Peter picked her up in front of her house, and while he'd eaten with her family numerous times, she didn't even know where he lived.

The guard in the security hut waved Peter through, and Mido realized that he didn't live in an apartment at all. He lived in Turtle Rock, a gated community of high-end houses tucked into beautifully landscaped hillsides.

The house was very large and modern with a two-car garage. It was the second house on the hill and had tall cypress trees shading the backyard. Mido spotted the glint of a swimming pool behind the trees. The front garden was well maintained, and the long seamless panes of the glass on the second floor, overlooking the hills, were shiny and clean. In the late-afternoon light, the house cast a blurry shadow across the road.

He pulled into the driveway and pressed a button, which she had never noticed, above his dashboard. The garage door opened and revealed another car, a silver BMW.

"Is that your landlord's?"

"No."

Mido had to stop herself from asking more questions. When she opened the car door, she could smell jasmine and eucalyptus. The evening air felt clean and light.

They entered the house from the garage, stepping into a white-tiled laundry room with a large washer and dryer and a rotary iron. A long hallway connected the laundry room to a vast kitchen with a stainless steel–paneled refrigerator. There were European appliances on the deep marble counters.

She tried to contain her amazement. Peter lived in a magazine spread.

"Do you live here alone?"

Nodding, he pointed to the powder room in the hall. "You can wash up there if you want."

❧

Mido checked her face in the vanity mirror and finger-combed her hair. Her makeup was mostly gone, and she looked more like a kid than the manager of a hagwon. She sniffed the University of Sydney sweatshirt she'd been wearing all day; it smelled like the plane.

In the kitchen, Peter pressed a button on the rice cooker.

"What are we having?"

"Curry rice. In my freezer, there's always frozen Japanese curry." Peter read the digital clock on the rice cooker. "In thirty-eight minutes, we will have dinner."

A foyer connected the kitchen to an enormous living room and dining area. The front double doors were large enough to push a grand piano through. A modern Italian sectional took up a quarter of the glass-walled living room, and near a fireplace, there was a bone-colored leather daybed.

"Okay. I give up. I'm going to ask questions, and you don't have to answer them."

Peter looked as if he were preparing for the firing squad.

"Did you do all this?" she asked, pointing to the well-appointed house. "I'm confused."

He shook his head. "My mother's designer. I know. It's kind of Hollywood. Not my choice." He shrugged. "I couldn't hurt his feelings. If I asked, I guess they could have done it again, but that seemed ridiculous and wasteful."

"This house is big enough for half a dozen people. Maybe a dozen?"

"Yeah." Peter opened the microwave and began to defrost two containers of frozen curry.

"Do you get paid ten times more than I do?"

"I don't think so. I made $150,000 last year. That's probably a bit more than you, but I have more students than you do. I teach two large classes and take private—"

"You do. You have way more students than me. I'm being rude. I'm sorry. This is none of my business."

"My mother comes from a lot of money. Her grandfather started a tire company, and then he created a transport business. Dad comes from money, too. Chemicals. Fertilizer. Anyway. I'm the only child of divorced parents who wants to be a musician and doesn't want to live in Korea. My mom bought this house as an investment and had all this done. I know it's a lot. I'm grateful, but I didn't ask for this."

"That's cool. For you, I mean. I'm happy for you."

She had long ago figured out that Peter was not poor, but because he worked so many hours, she had thought he needed money. However, after what his friend Jack said at Dartmouth about him being posh, she had wondered what he meant by it. Mido had never been to a house in America like this before. There'd been nothing about Peter that suggested he was this wealthy. He drove an old Volkswagen and wore faded rock T-shirts and jeans. His sneakers were less fancy than the ones their Fortress students wore.

Mido tilted her head.

"You do that whenever you have a question," he said.

She righted herself.

"Okay. I don't understand why you don't do music full-time. You don't have to be a hagwon teacher."

"I don't."

"Then why?"

"It gets me out of the house. Work gets me out of my head. I don't want to think about myself all day. When my students figure out how to solve a problem, I guess I feel useful. I don't feel very useful with my music."

Peter opened the refrigerator. The second shelf was stacked with side dishes in Pyrex and stainless steel containers. There were half-gallon containers of milk and pink grapefruit juice and liter bottles of club soda.

He pulled out the side dishes.

She pointed to the kitchen table. "Eat here?"

"Sure."

Mido prepared two place settings. She tilted her head again. They'd been gone for almost eight days, but his refrigerator was stocked with fresh vegetables, drinks, and assorted types of kimchi.

He answered the question without her even asking.

"*Ajumma* comes by twice a week. My mother and I have an agreement."

"An agreement?"

"I pay my bills—food, taxes, utilities, gym, gas. However, my mother has hired a housekeeper to clean, shop, cook, and deal with house stuff. When something breaks, Mrs. Ma handles it. I tried to avoid this but couldn't. The deal makes her calmer."

"Who?"

"My mother. My uncle, her younger brother, persuaded me to let this arrangement continue just to settle her nerves. Until I get married, Mrs. Ma will do all this domestic work."

Mido opened her mouth to speak, then closed it.

"Just say it. DH makes fun of me all the time. Jack spilled the beans, so I figured you might as well see how posh I am." Peter drew air quotes around the word "posh."

"Everything is so nice. Your mother's designer has great taste."

"He tried really hard. Even got me an incredible stereo system. Without having met me, he knew exactly which speakers and amplifier I'd wanted. It's your brother's favorite thing in the house."

"Have Yun and Lion seen this place?"

"Nope."

"They think you're like me? Middle-class?"

"I don't know, but does it matter?" Peter looked at her. "Anyway, if we could keep this quiet, I'd appreciate it."

"That you're rich and your mom hired you a housekeeper?"

"Yes."

"I thought you and Lion are friends."

"Yes, we are friends, but money ruins everything."

"You work really hard at Fortress."

"I always work hard."

"My brother never said anything."

"He knows how I feel about this stuff. Also, it shouldn't matter."

"Do you want to do music full-time?"

"I thought I did, but I couldn't. The isolation made me kind of crazy. That's why DH thought I should work at Exodus. He also wanted me to get to know Bo and you."

"Me?"

"Yeah. He thought we should be friends."

The microwave beeped, and Peter removed the containers and laid them on the table. He gestured to her chair, and she sat down.

"He said we'd get along."

"Tell me about the song you're working on now," she said, not knowing why DH had said this and not knowing how to ask.

"You switched topics."

"Yes."

Peter put a Springsteen record on low, and they talked about colleges and where the kids wanted to go most. After dinner, Mido offered to wash dishes, but he said Mrs. Ma would come in the morning.

He zipped up his navy hoodie and picked up his car keys, and she followed him to the car. Peter would drive her home.

7
Nomination

June 2004

Danbi did not observe the Sabbath.

After Sunday services, there were insurance and small-business seminars to give, youth to mentor, and church meetings. After church ended, often she and Taehun Shin entertained clients.

By the fall of 2001, Shin and Danbi had been elected as elders, and they were now up for reelection for their second term. Elders, if elected, could serve two terms consecutively, but were required to observe a year of rest before serving as elders again if, and only if, they were reelected by the congregation. In the history of Gospel Presbyterian, only Fred Byun, chairman of Taegeuk Bank, had served as an elder for twelve years, and even he, a founding member of the church, had taken a break between the two consecutive terms.

Shin and Danbi were a constant presence at church. They now owned the fourth-largest insurance brokerage in Orange County, with the largest Korean base, and many of their clients attended Gospel Presbyterian. They were active ruling elders sitting on the most important committees. On holidays, Shin led prayers at the popular eleven o'clock service, and Danbi circulated during the various coffee hours. Their work naturally bled into Sundays, and the two spent the day ducking in and out of all three services. Their weekend nanny would pick up Anna after the church sitters were gone and drive her home in the company car.

Although Shin spoke English beautifully, Danbi couldn't seem to speak it, despite ongoing efforts during her six years in America. Her English reading and writing skills were excellent. However, she could not speak it without a heavy accent and grammatical errors, which embarrassed her.

"When you learn to speak a new language, you must look foolish," one

American tutor told her, and she fired him. Danbi refused to make mistakes and lower herself in the eyes of native English speakers. Shin and their employees dealt with the English-only customers. At church, she spoke only her flawless Korean.

Danbi was thirty-six years old. Physically, she had changed only a little in the new country. Still young and alluring, she devoted considerable time and attention to her appearance. Motherhood had forced her to be more thoughtful about her sexual power. With a daughter in school, she realized that she had to get along with at least a few important mothers to learn about the best classes, schools, and teachers, so she befriended the mothers who mattered, refusing to have her child left out.

Anna was six, and she had marvelous tutors. The first grader went to the premier elementary and middle school hagwon for mathematics, reading, and writing in their neighborhood of Woodbridge. On Saturdays, Anna had private lessons for golf and tennis, but it was becoming clear that the child was better at golf. From the golf hagwon, Danbi learned the name of the best children's golf instructor in Southern California.

❧

Although Danbi could have had almost any man, it was Taehun Shin she wanted. Once she realized this, she also understood that if she got him to leave his wife and three sons, he'd have no real money to speak of. No matter how hard she worked at HRI, she'd never be able to earn the kind of capital she'd require for their new life from her salary alone. Danbi had almost no money of her own, so she decided to accrue capital and valuable information, especially when the IMF Crisis occurred and panic set in at every level of the company. She knew better than most that sex relieves tension.

Bonhwa Han, a vice-chairman at HRG, became her mentor. After Shin was fired, Danbi asked the vice-chairman to teach her about investing post–IMF Crisis. At first, they met privately in hotel rooms. He gave her $25,000 US when she playfully teased him about telling his wife. Certain men of significant stature, she had learned, wanted to do things that their wives did not enjoy. Vice-Chairman Han preferred sex outdoors, and after she took care of his specific needs on a penthouse hotel balcony at twilight, she let him know that she required a certain amount of money in American currency.

During another meeting, at a party on a boat in Seoul, they had sex in one of the stalls in the men's bathroom. The following day, he brought her a beautiful purse filled with dollars. Each time, he brought more, and when she refused to meet him again, he raised the offers.

Not once did he get cross with her flirtatious threats and financial requests. If anything, he seemed to respect her more for the increases. However, as he grew more outlandish in his fantasies, Danbi lost interest. She drew the line at recording outdoor sex. Soon he grew possessive, tracking her movements. More than once, he had her followed.

Danbi ended it wisely by introducing him to another young woman who had a far greater appetite for risk and money.

Not long after, she chose the vice-chairman of a telecommunications company. In no time, she learned about his kinks, involving domination and bodily emissions. After a few meetings, she also learned which telecommunications companies would survive the IMF Crisis. Under his tutelage, she took the capital she had received from Mr. Outdoor Sex, bought the stocks, and held them. The masochistic ejaculator had been correct in his stock picks, and if only she'd had more initial capital, she and Shin would have had a far larger nest egg to start their company in California.

Shin never knew of their existence, and in her mind, none of these encounters mattered because they meant nothing to her except for the capital they provided. Danbi had merely raised money for her new venture. She could not help that he was under the false impression that their insurance agency was being backed by her cousin Frank Lim, when in fact, she was the sole owner of the holding company.

She was deeply in love with Shin, and she had allowed him to father a child with her. Much had changed between them over the years; however, she was as attracted to him now as she had been when she first met him right out of college.

Of course, men still wanted to sleep with her. It was obvious from the way clients and strangers behaved. There was a way a man looked at you, handed you his business card, offered to buy a meal, which all led to when he'd plot a way to pass you a hotel room key.

Danbi valued her prowess. Nevertheless, even if she could, she would not exercise her sexual power unless she was willing to pay the price she'd paid before. Before Anna, she had not cared what other women thought of her. Now, as a mother and as a business owner, she put on the frock of church elder to cloak the deep reserves of her power.

So she changed her clothes and makeup. If, as a young single woman, she could have played a sexual ingenue in a pornographic film, now, as a mother of a little girl, she had to play the elegant and cool businesswoman to be an alpha or beta in any women's group. Elegance—a personal quality other women accepted—and raw erotic availability simply could not coexist. Danbi maintained her figure, and beneath her expensive clothes, she wore the lingerie of a prostitute that Taehun Shin could not resist; however, in the presence of other women, she looked chic, costly, and vaguely maternal.

❧

For this Nominating Committee meeting, Danbi had selected an imported black pantsuit cut close to her slender figure, with a long row of pearl buttons and a pair of beige-and-black ballet slippers to highlight her small and narrow feet. Her throat was exposed, and her only jewelry was her emerald-cut diamond ring and channel-set wedding band, which she had purchased herself.

Danbi served as the cohead of the Nominating Committee along with George Hong, the highly esteemed president of a real estate company. Like most men, George, eight years her senior, was attracted to her, and Danbi allowed a bit of joking when they were alone. But she admired his wife, Sobin, whose family owned George's business, so she also made sure to talk about her husband, Taehun Shin, and how he liked to do tae kwon do, which was true.

Seven elders had gathered after the late-morning services. Among the numerous items on the agenda was the election of two elders for this committee. In practice, any elder could be nominated for a seat, but in reality, it was far trickier because so many elders wanted to be on this committee, which allowed greater influence on fast-tracking or blocking a person's ascent in the community.

"We have twenty-one candidates to go through. Fifteen women and five men. I should add that Ryu Seong-tae has been nominated again," George said, without mentioning that Ryu had nominated himself. After several business and tax scandals, Ryu and his wife had been going through different churches in the area trying to sanitize their reputations. After becoming an elder at Gospel by a fairly narrow vote, Ryu now sought even higher status with a seat on the Nominating Committee.

Danbi glanced at the agenda, scanned the list of nominees, and crossed off Ryu. There were at least two Kohs she recognized on the list, including Elder John Koh, who'd been nominated by George's wife, Sobin, who had been a customer of his late wife, Helen, at Mrs. Chung's Emporium.

Over the course of the meeting, the seven elders quickly whittled down the list to three people, and John Koh remained.

"Does John Koh even want to serve?" Danbi asked, even though she knew the answer. No one could be nominated unless they had already agreed to serve if elected. "I mean, really serve. Also, doesn't he roll off in a year and a half, requiring a Sabbath year? I think he must be quite busy in his work. I heard they're expanding."

"That's why I nominated him," Sobin said. "We lost Elder Park because he moved, and we need someone who wants to serve out the remainder of Elder Park's term. He's perfect."

Another elder asked, "What is his work?"

"He manages a nail salon," Danbi said with a polite smile. "He doesn't own it. He runs it."

"I should stay out of it since my wife nominated him, but I think he's managing the business on behalf of his deceased wife's sister, who doesn't live year-round in California," George said. He liked John Koh and felt sorry for the laconic widower.

Elder Christina Bong added, "Elder John Koh is a very thoughtful person. I think he has a business background and went to SNU for math. I really liked his wife, too. Such a wonderful mother. So sad." She paused. "Well, I think it would be wise to have someone who is such a good Christian join us and give counsel. Sometimes these positions go to people who have important jobs. I mean—" She smiled at Danbi and George. "It's possible for a wealthy person to have great faith, but Elder John Koh is known for being self-controlled and thoughtful. The nail salon workers speak very highly of him as someone who is fair about tips and salaries. I'd be happy to second anyone that Elder Sobin Ha would find it in her heart to nominate."

Danbi wrote down her comments, unwilling to look up.

"But Elder Kevin Cho is an outstanding community leader. His law firm has twenty-five associates," Danbi said. "If we have to choose one male and one female elder, then Elder Cho may be a more seasoned leader—"

Elder Christina raised her hand. "Elder Cho is a good man, but he would just be another wealthy partner at a law firm. We have so few male elders who aren't white-collar professionals. Isn't that so? I fear that we will be criticized for favoring the professional class."

"Elder John Koh used to be a manager at the largest trading company in Korea. He graduated from Seoul National University. Without question, he was a member of the professional class. It's not as if he's some uneducated farmer who fell off a tractor after seeing a vision of Jesus," Danbi said, then immediately recognized her error.

The elders stared at her in shock. Elder Sobin Ha covered her mouth and turned to her husband George.

"I think that's not kind," Sobin said. Often she remembered Helen, who had sold her a suitcase and given her a red name tag as a present. She had been so patient with her when she must have been in agonizing pain. Once, Sobin had visited Helen at home. She had been asleep, and Sobin would never forget the woman's altered appearance, ravaged by cancer.

Danbi had been too forceful in her disagreement. Normally she did not show her hand like this. If John Koh was on the committee, then she would have to deal with him. She'd never be able to defeat him. Not once had she forgotten what his sister-in-law Sonya Cho had threatened. Danbi understood how power worked better than most. Sonya was the kind of person who would follow through on her threats.

George spoke up. "At the risk of siding with my wife, I think Elder Christina has made a valuable point. Any elder on the committee should be selected on his character and not just his present socioeconomic status. Perhaps we can place Elder Cho on a short list for another time."

The elders nodded in agreement, and John Koh became a member of the Nominating Committee.

✤

When the meeting ended, George remained behind while his wife went to meet their children, who were still playing basketball with the youth group.

Danbi gathered her papers and said nothing.

"Why don't you like him?" George asked.

"Who?"

"Elder John Koh. I thought he and your husband were old friends."

"Will you discuss the meeting later with your wife?" Danbi opened her eyes wide and smiled at him.

"What?" George looked puzzled. "I suppose we might. Why?"

"Would you tell her that I actually wanted to support John Koh? I don't want her to be upset with me."

"But you were against it. She was here."

"Well, explain it to her. Wouldn't your wife believe your word against the others?"

"I suppose so. I don't understand."

"I'm asking you for a favor, George." Danbi laid her right hand on his left forearm. She parted her lips slightly, and from his expression, she saw that just showing a man a hint of her pink tongue was enough to make him think of her.

"Of course," he replied, and got up. "You supported him all along. I think you just had some doubts about his schedule. That's true, right?"

"Yes," she said, and it occurred to her that Sobin would never like her. Danbi resented this.

"You believe me, don't you?" she asked, pulling him back down to his chair, and he sat, looking nervous.

Danbi recognized that same expression that all men had when she did these things. He was afraid, and she felt aroused.

"How are you, George?"

"It's getting late."

Danbi undid the pearl buttons of her jacket quickly. Beneath it, she'd worn a sleeveless black silk chiffon blouse.

George looked at her breasts, visible through the sheer material.

"What are you doing?" she asked, laughing.

"I should go."

"Have you ever cheated on Sobin?"

It gave her pleasure to say his wife's first name. Danbi wanted to hurt her. She wanted to damage the women who refused to lower their guard and take her in just because she wasn't like them, because she wanted far more than they did. She wanted to crush those who excluded her from entry into their golden circles.

George held his breath. He had been with hostesses in Seoul, but he didn't count that as being unfaithful to his wife, although, of course, it was. Raised as a Christian from birth, he knew that being with any woman who was not his wife was a serious sin, yet he had a rule. He was never with a woman not his wife more than once. He'd always paid good money, which alleviated some of his guilt. If Sobin ever found out, she would divorce him.

He had prayed and trusted that he was forgiven. He had not been with a hostess in years, but he could not answer Danbi without lying, and he did not like to lie.

George didn't answer her.

"Oh, so you have. Naturally you must have. You're a desirable man."

Danbi placed her index finger on his lips to hush him. She opened the door and checked the dark and empty hallway. Danbi locked it and dimmed the lights.

"I need only a few minutes of your time. Give them to me."

George remained silent, and Danbi made herself comfortable on his lap, feeling the rush of his hands moving across her body. She closed her eyes and, as if willed, he stood up, her arms and legs wrapped around his torso, and backed her body into the wall.

8

Teachers

After a tasteless church dinner without any alcohol, Shin arrived home exhausted from the boring conversation punctuated by self-righteous prayers. He shut the front door and rested his head against it in relief.

Danbi rushed to him, fresh and clean, wearing a dress he hadn't seen before, a white strapless sundress. He breathed in her new scent—orange blossoms and mint—and admired her ivory shoulders. He held her tightly, not wanting to talk.

"*Oppa*," she said, her voice throaty and low. "We were in the same building all day and I barely saw you. Did you miss me?" She touched his face, then withdrew her cool hand at the feel of his day's growth of beard.

The housekeeper's car was gone for the night. Their intense lovemaking schedule varied, but without fail, they had rough sex on Sunday evenings. He imagined she had some sort of surprise for him.

He smiled and tousled her hair and headed to the shower.

Shin did his best to anticipate Danbi and to please her because he didn't know how to control her. He had never been afraid of Mary—a beautiful and well-educated woman. She had loved him and given him three sons, and to this day, he felt guilty for having ruined her life. His sole consolation was knowing that Mary was better off without him. They were still married.

There were times when Shin thought of getting on a plane and flying across the country to remain in Englewood, pretending Danbi and their daughter Anna were hazy figures in a dream, but he could not. Already he had harmed his original family, and he thought he should be decent to the new one.

In his military service, Shin had never been the fearful sort. He had not been afraid of his superiors, and they'd admired his cool competence. Shin was astute about men and what they wanted; however, Danbi was not a man, and she was not like most women.

She was unpredictable and far too canny for her own good. If she'd been born a man, Shin believed that Danbi would have been a self-made tycoon or a national leader. He'd never witnessed such determination and ambition. Shin would not cross her, and the wisest thing Mary had done was recognize the terms of their engagement. Mary was too smart to tangle with the likes of a crazy woman, so she kept her distance, yet held her ground.

❧

Danbi was a petite woman: 160 centimeters and forty-nine kilograms. If she weren't so physically striking with exquisite proportions, she might have been overlooked because of her slight stature. Built more like an adolescent girl's with high, full breasts and narrow hips, her tiny girlish body appealed to men who wanted to feel powerful.

In her first year in college, male students dared each other to physically pick her up like a parcel. Every man she'd ever slept with had enjoyed being able to carry her in his arms to a bed, desk, counter, dresser; piggyback; or by straddling her against a wall, so Danbi had forced herself to weigh less so they could feel stronger. Even after having a child, she had starved herself to keep her power.

In the beginning of their affair, Shin had wanted to protect her; however, over the years, she had protected him through her sheer ability to survive. Shin had come to understand that he was merely the figurehead and totem of power. The outside world saw him as the head of the family and their business; however, they were always executing her plans.

After his shower, Shin put on a clean navy polo shirt and khakis and went to the kitchen, where Danbi opened a bottle of beer and poured it into a tall glass.

"Your friend is now on the Nominating Committee."

He took a long swallow of his beer and raised a questioning eyebrow.

"John Koh. Elder Sobin, George Hong's wife, insisted that he was such an admirable person. You'll never believe this, but she wanted him in particular because he works as a manager of a nail salon. Apparently we have too many important people, so we need blue-collar workers."

Shin sighed. He knew John was a decent man who loathed gossip, and although there had been numerous opportunities for John to tell others at church about him and Danbi, John and his late wife had not. He trusted John, and especially after Helen's death, he wished Danbi would leave him be. She was paranoid about John, and no matter what Shin said, Danbi wouldn't let it go.

"Why do you care?" Shin said. "I told you. He's not going to hurt us."

"People like him. Now that he's a widower, women are falling over themselves. Thank God he's poor—they'd lose their minds if he had money."

"You don't have a very high opinion of women."

"Women don't have a high opinion of me."

This was something Shin had witnessed countless times. Danbi had to work much harder to get women to trust her. Able to sense the danger she posed in a way that men could not, women were wary of her. She was envious of anyone who could be accepted without having to try.

"More?" she asked, noticing his empty glass. Danbi liked it when he was a little drunk at night. Alcohol made him talkative.

"I shouldn't. It's affecting my sleep."

Shin placed the glass in the sink.

"You sure?"

Standing in front of the refrigerator, he considered a second beer. He felt good enough and didn't want to feel sleepier. He got down on the floor and did twenty push-ups, a thing he did often. Over the course of a day, he did a hundred push-ups in five sets of twenty. As he was about to do his set of squats, Danbi moved toward him and put her dress over his head, exposing her pale navel and bare hips. She had not worn anything underneath.

He uncovered his head and, lifting her body, he seated her on the counter. She kept talking as he pulled her dress down to her waist, exposing her.

"He can tell someone about us. It was such a long time ago. I was younger and afraid of losing you. I apologized to them. You saw me. But he and his wife refused to greet me. Once I went to the store where she worked, and she wouldn't even look at me. She was a saleswoman and wouldn't try to serve me. Unbelievable."

She leaned back on the counter and pulled his head toward her left breast.

"He can ruin our company."

Shin stopped what he was doing and stroked her hair with his hands as if she were a child. Sometimes this would calm her.

"John Koh doesn't like to talk about people. He doesn't like to talk, period."

"You are my naive oppa. Here, come to me." She sat up on the counter and reached for him. Her nude-polished fingernail traced a straight line from the center of his clavicle down to his belt buckle. Her manicured hand covered his erection, and she held him with both hands. Shin closed his eyes.

He inhaled the scent of her, barely moving, and focused on her light breathing.

She kissed his closed eyelids.

"Today I was very bad," she said, wide-eyed and unblinking in her gaze.

"You fought against John getting nominated?"

"Yes."

"You were afraid," he said, and he pulled her to him.

"I was bad."

"Every day you are bad," he said, smiling. "Every day, every day."

Shin opened his eyes and smiled at her extraordinary open face, upturned pink lips, black pools for eyes, framed by her dark shining hair.

Amused by this game they played, Shin pushed up her skirt over her bone-white thighs, scrunching up the muslin dress on her waist like a thick gauze Band-Aid, covering nothing really. Without any tenderness, he turned his woman around and leaned her over the kitchen counter.

❧

As they'd agreed, on Saturday morning, Elder George waited for her at a parking lot near Hoag Hospital. When he spotted her silver Porsche, he waved at her and pointed to his phone, so she checked hers.

Follow my car, he had texted.

Where are we going?

Near Anaheim.

I have to be back in four hours, she typed, and followed him.

❧

He brought his gym bag to the four-star hotel near Disneyland. The reserved room was expensive, but Danbi said nothing and followed him. She wanted to order room service, and a motel wouldn't have that.

"I could not stop thinking about you," George said, once inside the room. He was embracing her.

"Good morning, Elder Hong," she whispered, taking care not to leave any makeup on his jacket.

"I could leave my marriage," he said.

Danbi pulled back and covered her mouth, peals of laughter escaping her apricot-colored lips. She removed her yellow cardigan, exposing her wide-strapped butter-yellow sundress. Looking up at him, she smiled like an ingenue and pouted. She took his left hand and put it on her belly.

"I haven't had breakfast yet. Can we get eggs and bacon?" She dropped the cardigan on the desk and looked around for a menu.

"I'm serious," he said. "My wife and I haven't had sex in years. Everyone thinks that Sobin and I are an ideal couple, but she never wants me to see her naked or touch her."

"That's a shame. No more talk like this, or be assured that I can never ever see you again, Elder Hong." Danbi opened the curtains wide but left the sheer panels closed. She walked around the room and turned on every lamp and stripped off her clothes slowly, making sure that his eyes never left her hands as they moved across zippers, buckles, and straps.

"Did you want to keep the lights on? I don't mind." She placed her hands on her breasts and moved them toward her abdomen. Bent over the bed, she removed the coverlet and lay across the white sheets, burying her face in the pillow, so he could see her from behind. She raised her bottom a little to tease him.

"Your husband is the luckiest man."

"He is. Let's make rules. Don't talk about him, and we will not talk about her."

"So you don't want to leave him?"

She shot him a warning glance.

"Never."

"Then why? Why are we here?"

"I wanted to own you," she said, laughing again invitingly.

George looked hurt and surprised, and she was charmed.

"My puppy, don't you want to be owned?"

"Are you playing with me?" He looked suddenly furious.

"I'm teasing you, Elder George. You're adorable, and I thought you'd understand that this was for fun. Elder, you and I are sinning in the eyes of the Lord. I want us to be close friends. I need a friend. I think you need one, too. We can be less lonely. Now and then, we should hold each other for warmth when the world is cold."

He looked confused.

"But not too close. Not too often. I shouldn't have agreed to come today, but you asked so nicely, and I've always thought you were fine-looking." She had slept with many men for money or information, and rarely had they been as beautiful as Shin, but George was very attractive. If Danbi had a weakness, it was that she liked fucking too much, and she preferred the men to be handsome.

Danbi got up and approached him, observing his quiet eyes. She looked up at his face with both adoration and amusement. Danbi hung both her slim arms behind his neck and wrapped her legs around him, and George did what every man his strength and size did when she made this move. He lifted her and carried her to the bed, believing he'd won a trophy.

"My darling puppy," she said, removing his khakis and kissing his cock deeply. From her purse, she took out a condom, and she covered him with her hands. "We have to be careful. I'm still young enough to have your baby."

George's eyes focused. His wife Sobin was forty-two, and he remembered that Danbi was maybe thirty-six. He could not control himself, seeing the wildness in her eyes. She wanted this to be difficult. In her flirting, she was pushing him toward the edge.

"I didn't mean to laugh."

He covered her mouth with his to make her shut up, but she pushed him off.

"You cannot leave your marriage. That would make what we're doing so, so much worse." She watched to see his reaction, and she knew he was upset with her.

He wasn't a talker during sex, but she didn't care. He had long, powerful arms and legs much like Shin's, but George was more youthful, and it had been a while since she'd been with a man only a decade older, not needing to worry about a heart attack or stroke.

For fun, she breathed a little louder, noticing that he followed her movements and gestures, so she made more noise, which made him crazy. Normally it was easy to know what a man wanted, and on the thick hotel mattress, she could tell he was fighting for control.

This sex felt different from what they'd done at church because he was no longer surprised by her forwardness. He was still angry with her because she had laughed at him, and he was using the kind of force men used when they thought it was the last time.

When they were done, Danbi said nothing and went to the desk to get the menu. She picked up the phone.

"My husband and I have American breakfast. Yes, two. Toast white. Yes, coffee," she said in English, and listened to the woman repeating her order back to her.

Danbi put on her dress and cardigan and sat with her legs beneath her on the sofa. George was still sulking in bed.

She hated it when men got like this so early on in the relationship.

In the church conference room, they'd barely spoken afterward, and he had tried to kiss her, but she'd begged off and left him, promising to see him another time if he wanted.

She sensed that he had interpreted her rapid departure as a kind of shame or shyness, believing that she had long been in love with him. They had known each other on the Nominating Committee and joked privately often enough. He had been flirting with her, and when she made her move, George had believed that she was as lonely in her marriage as he was in his.

For George, her propositioning had been a kind of confession. It would never occur to him that she was seducing him like a man, or, worse, for a lay.

When the breakfast arrived, she took the cart and closed the door. She wheeled it to the bed, where George was sitting up, his lower body covered by a white sheet.

Danbi picked up a piece of bacon and fed him. He chewed it slowly, still not saying anything. She placed a fried egg on a toast triangle and put it near his lips so he could take a bite.

George shook his head.

"Be a good baby and eat," she said, pleading. "I don't want to eat alone."

Turning to the cart beside the lamp table, George poured her a cup of coffee, then one for himself.

"Thank you," she said, then asked, "How many women have you been with, Elder George?"

He considered his answer and exhaled.

"Three," George said at last. "Danbi-shi," he said, never having addressed her by her first name before. "I misunderstood this. How embarrassing," he said, looking sober.

"Don't be like that, please," she said, and looked at her watch.

George crossed his arms against his wide, muscular chest.

Danbi put aside her plate. Fully dressed, she climbed into the bed beside him and placed her head on his shoulder. George could smell the clean scent of her balsam shampoo and the orange blossom lotion on her skin. She put her hands on him, and he closed his eyes.

"It would mean so much to me if you and I can keep being friends. In secret. I want your protection," she said, glancing up at his jaw and then kissing his chin, nose, and lips.

Slowly, George unfolded his arms.

9

Celebration

October 2, 2005

None of them could remember the last time everyone had eaten together at a Western restaurant, and the mood was joyful. Lion had already ordered, so as soon as they were seated, servers brought out fried calamari and shrimp cocktail. Silver platters of shucked oysters on chipped ice followed. Two waiters brought trays of champagne in glass flutes.

John said a short prayer to bless the food.

"Thank you, Elder Koh." Lion bowed to John, who returned the bow to the younger man, only three years older than Bo.

"Thank you, Elder Han," John said. They laughed.

It had been Lion's idea to host the girls' birthday dinner in a private room at Chip's, the upscale steak house in Irvine. Mido and Yun had been born eight days apart, so they usually had a joint birthday party on the first or second Sunday of October at Yun's house, but this year, Lion had insisted on going out. He made all the plans and invited both families and Peter.

At the long, cloth-covered table decorated with fresh-cut flowers in silver vases, Yun, Nari, Ginny, and Mido were seated on one side. Opposite them were Bo and DH, who had managed to slip out of work that Sunday afternoon, and Peter. John sat at the head of the table and Lion on the opposite end.

John had come straight from a church meeting and wore his best gray suit and a navy silk necktie that Helen had bought for him years ago in Sydney. His graying hair was cut short, and he wore tortoiseshell-framed eyeglasses, which Mido had selected for him, saying they made him look younger and more modern. It would have been difficult for any stranger to know that six days a week, John Koh managed his sister-in-law's nail salon in Buena Park, surrounded by dozens of nail technicians and as many customers.

"Dad looks sharp," DH said to Bo and Peter. "And nice job on the glasses, Mido."

Mido gave a thumbs-up. "He's never needed them before, but I guess he's getting older."

"He looks like an architect," Bo said. "Or maybe a lawyer?"

"Your dad always looks nice," Yun said, and Nari waved her hand in disagreement.

"No, no. Sometimes Bo's father, I mean Elder Koh, looks so tired. But today, in that suit, he's a twin of that actor, Lee Seung-han!" she said, snapping her fingers, pleased with herself for getting it right. "Yes! Exactly like Lee Seung-han in *Trees Without Leaves*."

Nari's encyclopedic recall of shows and actor names was masterful. Her customers, coworkers, and church friends turned to her when they forgot the plot of a drama or which actor played whom. For fun, they'd quiz her and marvel at her knowledge. They called her the Drama *Dosa*. Yun was pretty good for her generation, but no one could beat her mother.

At Yun's puzzled expression, Nari slapped her daughter's upper arm in frustration.

"Yaah, how can you forget that one? It's the one where Lee plays a surgeon from a big hospital in Seoul, but when he goes to a rural hospital to help a medical school classmate, there's a train crash and he gets amnesia. Years later, his wife finds out that he started another life with a woman in a rural beach town. The two women end up becoming friends, but then the second wife gets sick, and the first wife cares for her but the woman dies anyway. Go Jiyon plays the first wife, and she was amazing. I think I cried in every episode." Nari tapped the table for emphasis. "They suffer so much, and the second woman dies only after the surgeon gets his memory back. Too sad, but—"

"Umma, is this when I was in college? I might've been studying for exams."

"No, no. You were in middle school. We saw it in Korea right before we came here. The surgeon forgot that he was a famous doctor—the first in his medical school class and speaks perfect German—and he's working as a fisherman in this rural village, and his second wife, who is played by Hong Haera. So beautiful—"

"Umma." Yun interrupted again, pointing to Lion, who was standing and holding a glass.

"Let's toast first, then we can learn about the surgeon-fisherman who regains his memory," DH said.

Bo grinned. "Lion's so polite, waiting for his mother-in-law to finish the plot summary." Everyone enjoyed teasing Nari, who loved the good-natured attention.

Lion was comfortable speaking in public. As the proprietor of two important hagwons in Orange County, he had to address assemblies of students and parents regularly. He always thought out what he was going to say well before he uttered a word, and he never spoke more than he had to. Now that he was a successful business owner and also the youngest elder at the largest Korean church in Southern California, he thought even more carefully about what he would say because people sought his advice routinely and not only listened to him but often quoted him.

Lion checked to see if everyone had a glass before beginning.

"We are celebrating two important dates in October 1978. On the first of October, our Mido was born, and on the ninth, my wife, Yun, was born. This month, our favorite young women turn twenty-seven. Happy birthday, Mido and Yun." Lion raised his glass, and everyone followed to toast them, but he remained standing and looked expectantly at Yun.

Yun smiled and stood up.

"Lion and I are going to have a baby in twenty-two weeks."

"How could you not tell me, you terrible girl?" Nari said, bursting into tears and embracing Yun's waist. "I thought you had gained a few pounds, but you were pregnant! Umma is so happy!"

Everyone clapped and cheered.

Lion beamed and looked tenderly at Yun. "We wanted to wait until everything was more certain this time."

Throughout the meal and even after the candles were blown out, Nari couldn't stop crying.

"I am blessed. I am blessed. Thank you, Lord. Thank you, Lord," she repeated, and Yun wept with her mother until Lion threatened to sing every U2 song he knew by heart.

❧

When dinner ended, Lion and Yun took Nari and Ginny home, and Bo offered to drive his father home before heading back to Westwood.

In the parking lot, DH turned to Peter.

"Eight ball. Best out of three. Twenty bucks."

"You will lose your hard-earned money, Counselor. You had how many beers?" Peter said, laughing. "Let's go."

Mido followed Bo and their father, but DH stopped her.

"I think you should hang with us."

John waved her toward them. "Go. Go play with DH and Peter."

Mido made a face. "I'm twenty-seven, not seven."

"But you're the killer at pool," DH said. "You can help me beat this guy."

Peter laughed. "Doubtful. Remember, I live with that pool table."

DH turned to Bo. "You want to join after dropping Dad off?"

"Can't. Have to read two books by next Friday and write a paper for a seminar. Plus exams to grade for my intro class. You kids go ahead. Play is important for growth."

Peter saluted Bo, and mockingly, DH bowed deeply from the waist to his older brother. "Good to have a future shrink in the family. Glad to know you are thinking of my mental growth."

"Maybe just growth," Bo said, smiling, and to Mido, "If you hang out with these young men, make sure they don't drink too much. DH doesn't get out of the office very often, who knows what he'll do."

"I will take responsibility for your siblings," Peter said to Bo in Korean. With each other, they had been speaking in English mostly, but in Korean, the teasing sounded more serious in the honorific form.

Bo placed his hands on Mido's shoulders.

"Go ahead. Otherwise it would be three Kohs against one Son." Bo tried to look fierce with Peter but broke into a grin.

"Why am I being bullied by the Koh family?" Peter asked.

"You might as well be a Koh," Bo said.

DH laughed in agreement, woozy and happy. He'd begun drinking beers well before dinner.

Mido handed her bag of presents to Bo, and he packed it in the trunk of his car. John got in the passenger seat and said goodbye, and the three young people bowed their heads in the direction of the car as it drove away.

❧

"I want to watch a movie," DH declared. "I want to play pool, drink more beer, eat tteokbokki, and watch a movie." He was reciting all the things they used to do when he and Peter were college roommates. "And *RedCard.* I want to play *RedCard.*"

"He's drunk," Peter said to Mido. "Your brother only wants to play *RedCard* when he's drunk."

Mido looked confused.

"It's a video game."

When they walked into Peter's house, the living room was immaculate, same as before—almost as if no one lived there. A blue cashmere throw was folded in a tidy square stack just the way Mido remembered from last time.

"Your house is so clean," DH said. "My roommates are disgusting. Nice dudes but appalling housekeepers. Oh, yeah, Mido, I almost forgot. Nick, the one who works at McKinsey, needs a date for a wedding. I promised I'd ask. He saw your picture."

"What?" Peter said. "You're setting up your sister?"

"No, no. He just doesn't have time to find a nice woman to go with, and he can't go stag, or he'll get shit from his frat brothers. He's a good guy. You know Nick Yang."

"You're living with Nick Yang?" Peter said. "From Andover? Did I know that?"

"No. He just got here. Sean was transferred to Dubai, and we needed a fourth. Besides, he's never home. None of us are ever home. All we ever do is fucking work. Beer please. One more makes a six-pack."

Peter handed him an open bottle but didn't take one himself. Mido raised her hand, and he gave her one. She shook her head when he offered her a glass.

"You want to meet him?" DH asked Mido.

"He's okay," Peter said. "No rock star, though."

DH laughed. "He's not bad-looking. I mean not as hot as me, but I'm your brother, so it might be weird to see me that way. But plenty of women do see me that way, I should add."

Mido made a face like she smelled something bad.

"Makes good money, obviously. But has zero time. I think I've seen him maybe once or twice since he moved to LA. I know he's working right this minute. On a Sunday night. I guess I should be working, too, but it's your birthday, and my baby sister should be celebrated." He raised his beer to Mido. "Anyway, let me know, and I'll text Nick Yang right now."

"I don't think so," Mido said. "Not looking for anyone, but thanks."

"Your loss," DH said. "He wants to marry a nice Korean girl. The hot girls at Andover used to fall all over themselves for him, but he was saving himself for his wife. Now he's ended up saving himself for McKinsey."

Peter rolled his eyes.

"Let's play pool," Mido said.

In half an hour, she beat both men twice and picked up $40. DH added one more beer to his total and stumbled upstairs to the guest room to sleep them off. Peter offered to drive Mido home.

In the kitchen, Mido took her jacket and purse from the chair where she'd left them, and she turned around to find Peter standing right behind her.

"Whoa," she said, surprised. "You ready?"

Peter was quiet, as if he was thinking.

"Never mind," he said at last.

"I'm a really good pool player. I know," she said, smiling. He looked so serious that she felt the need to make a joke.

He took a breath.

"May I?" he asked, his face near hers, and Mido nodded.

10
Choice

He didn't know what to say, but perhaps it wasn't necessary, because she liked him.

She had for a while, but he was right to have hesitated. Now it would be weird. In the middle of his spotless kitchen, they continued to make out, Mido dropping her jacket and purse on a chair and Peter his car keys on the table. Slowly he moved her toward the kitchen counter to anchor their bodies.

Mido opened her eyes and saw that he looked happy, and she smiled.

"Do you want to?" he asked, his hands on her waist.

Embarrassed, she couldn't look at his face and turned to the glass patio doors. The blue light of the pool was all she could see, and she felt like going outside. Mido had only been with Tek, and it was a long time ago. A few times he had reached out, but they had agreed not to talk anymore. In January it would be five years since they'd last seen each other. Sydney was a world away.

"Too soon," he said. "I'm sorry."

"No, it's not that."

He kissed her again, and Mido remembered what it was like to do this thing, when you had to breathe only through your nose, the unthinking movements of the face and neck as two heads reached for each other. She liked the way his mouth felt on hers.

It wasn't too soon, because she had known him for so long. Mido couldn't imagine not being with him now. They had spent so much time together. When he teased her, she tapped his shoulder or forearm. In a meeting with a parent or student, they were a pair, almost like a unified voice and mind.

His beautiful hands were stroking her back, and she relaxed into him.

Peter was an attractive man. When he sang, she felt like a fan, and she had to make an effort to act normal around him when he stepped off the stage. Long ago, she'd figured he was off-limits because they worked together. He was her brother's best friend; he was Lion's bandmate; he had become a dear friend to her. What if this ended poorly? she had wondered. Already she had lost Tek because they'd found they didn't know how to only be friends.

When DH offered to set her up with his roommate Nick Yang, Mido had briefly considered it, but even thinking about it had somehow felt like a betrayal of Peter. There was an unspoken agreement: They were together, and had kept that bond unbroken by refusing to acknowledge this attraction. They had kept from touching, holding, and now their hands searched for skin beneath the clothing covering their bodies.

Brushing her hair aside, he kissed her neck lightly, doing something he had wanted to do for a long time. Mido had a graceful neck, always unadorned. Sometimes when she talked, he would stare at the delicate movements of her throat, wanting to kiss it.

"Where?" she asked, and Peter understood her question.

"There's a room in the back. Near the garage."

"Will DH wake up?" she asked.

He shook his head.

"Could he hear us?"

"It's soundproof."

He took her hands and kissed her again.

They'd never held hands before, and oddly, this felt intimate, more than if they had removed their clothes.

He led her to a room and shut its heavy door, creating a calming hush.

Inside were a daybed and two large desks. A piano stood in one corner and beside it, multiple acoustic and electric guitars. The walls were decorated with framed posters of the Cure, the Clash, and Blondie. There was a large gas fireplace.

"Does that work?"

"Yeah." Peter flipped a switch, and blue flames rose above the stack of birch logs. "I almost never use it, but it's nice."

Outside the window, the swimming pool glowed, blue and serene, like a hotel postcard.

"Is this where you write your music?"

"This is my studio." Peter held her waist and kissed her neck. He hadn't been with anyone since Cesca, and he'd almost forgotten how intensely he wanted to be with a woman he cared about. It wasn't clear when he'd started to like Mido, but he'd kept himself from reaching for her so many times, and it was the strangest feeling to have her in his studio. He stopped himself as if waking from a deep dream. "You sure?" he asked.

She nodded.

He unbuttoned her blue long-sleeved dress, which he'd seen her wear numerous times. The fabric was a heavy cotton, worn soft from many washings, and he inhaled the floral scent of her hair and body. Mido pulled his green sweater over his head.

When he fumbled with her brassiere, she unclasped it, and they were both naked.

In a passing moment of clarity, Mido said, "This is kind of crazy. Are we going to be normal tomorrow? At work?"

Switching to Korean, Peter said, "I take full responsibility. Will you?"

⁂

Afterward, Peter made her an omelet, then drove her home. DH was still asleep. There was another guest room in the house, but she wanted to get back for her father. Peter didn't insist, and she felt relieved not having to argue the way she had with Tek about sleeping over. She had never spent the night out with a man. She was twenty-seven years old, and her father must know that she wasn't a virgin, but it didn't seem right to stay out.

In front of her house, they remained in the parked car, not knowing how to say goodbye although they'd see each other in a few hours. The car ride over had been filled with polite talk, and a sweet silence, holding hands.

"The confession," he said in Korean. "I'll make it now."

She laughed. "Seriously?"

"I like you. A lot. I have for quite some time. For several years. Even when you were with that lawyer."

Mido shook her head in disbelief.

"I had no idea. Truly. You could work as a spy."

"Good to know that I am still a man of mystery, not just a failed musician slash math tutor."

He waited for her to say something serious. Their lovemaking had been so erotic and natural, and he would have liked to be with her again, but he'd known he had to bring her home.

"Another thing," he said. "I want to go out with you. I mean, if you want to go out with me. But I don't believe in marriage."

"Is that what you meant by responsibility?" She switched to Korean. "Gosh, what will my brothers say?" She laughed out loud.

"What?" Peter looked concerned.

"I didn't say I wanted to get married, but I think if this is the paradigm you're working from, then perhaps my family can't know that we're together. I mean, for now. The speculation will start right away. They are like regular brothers. I'm pretty certain they're worried about my romantic future."

"DH knows how I feel about marriage," Peter said.

"Not sure if he wants me to date you," she said.

"He definitely doesn't. He told me you're off-limits." Peter laughed. "I guess I didn't listen."

"I don't think I need my brother's permission on who I date."

"So we're dating then?"

"I guess."

"Then today is day one."

"You are Korean." She laughed. "I better go inside."

❧

Getting dressed the next morning, Mido took a little more care than usual with her clothes and makeup. She put on a coral-colored cotton dress with long sleeves, a cherry wool sweater, and white tennis sneakers. Peter picked her up, no differently from any other Monday.

All night she'd thought about Peter and his stated terms for their relationship, and she surprised herself that she might be dating a man who would not marry. After refusing to return to Australia with Tek, she'd wondered if anyone would propose to her again, even though it seemed conventional to care about getting married at all. She hadn't even finished college. After her mother died, it was as if time had stopped. Everything had stopped except for work and family.

None of them knew what to do about the future without Helen. DH dated occasionally, but nothing had stuck. There was a fellow graduate student at UCLA who liked Bo, but he didn't think he could start a serious relationship until he finished his degree. It was as if each of them had agreed to postpone anything that would separate them from the family unit.

Mido had not expected Peter to say he didn't want to marry in the same breath he used to declare his committed interest in her. At this moment in her life, she was okay with dating a man who didn't want to get married, but now that he'd said it, she wanted to understand why.

Mido's first and only lover had wanted to marry her, and though the endless public discussion of her marriage prospects irritated her, it had never occurred to her that she'd date someone who was against it. It felt too awkward to ask, because the act of asking might make it seem she wanted to marry him, no different from all the others in their world who persisted in asking these personal questions.

So pride and shame now kept her from seeking his reasoning, and it wasn't shame about rejection but rather shame about not seeming independent-minded as a modern woman.

They needed coffee. Peter suggested the McDonald's drive-through to pick up breakfast, and she agreed. He knew she liked the hash browns.

Peter ordered the usual for them—two Egg McMuffin sandwiches, three hash browns—two for her—and large coffees. He handed her the bag of food, and Mido unwrapped his breakfast sandwich for him so he could eat while driving. She'd never done this before, blushing at the memory because it was something she would've done for Tek when he drove.

"Thank you," he said, taking a bite, keeping his eyes on the road. "Starving."

Mido drank her coffee and wondered how things would change.

❧

At Fortress, they had meetings all morning with high school parents about college applications and testing, and during meetings, she caught him looking at her. With a two-hour break before more parent meetings and before tutors arrived for afternoon teaching sessions, Peter suggested going out to lunch instead of ordering in.

Instead, Mido locked the front entrance to the hagwon. She led him to the teachers' lounge and closed the door.

He understood and began to kiss her. She removed his clothes, then her own. After they made love, Mido said, "I don't want to get married, either."

"Oh?" Peter looked hurt. "Why?"

"Why what?" He had not even blinked before asking for her reasoning.

"Why don't you want to get married? To me."

Mido wouldn't say. It didn't seem fair for her to have to go first, when she still didn't want to ask him his reasoning. Her pride wouldn't allow it.

"I think we can't tell anyone about this. I don't know how long this can last."

"I don't understand." Peter was upset.

"And I'd like it if we could always be kind to each other. I think we would be anyway," she said. They were dressed now, and she opened the lounge door. He followed her to their offices.

"Are you against marriage?" he asked.

"No. But if you don't want to marry me, I don't want to marry you. I just don't know what this means, though. I suppose we can be together for now. Is this a fling?" she asked, realizing that just asking this made her seem commonplace. A sophisticated person would probably just keep the questions hanging in the air rather than saying them out loud. She didn't feel cool or free.

"I hope it's not a fling," he said. "I made the confession. I said it was day one yesterday. Isn't that the right way to go about this?"

"I can't believe we're talking about this. Let's just, you know, see how it goes," Mido said, feeling mortified.

"It's not what you think. I hesitated as long as I could because I knew that I'd be serious about you. Everyone will expect us to get married if you wanted that, and I would look like an asshole for being against it."

"You're a musician. A rolling stone that gathers no moss, right?" Even to her own ears, she sounded bitter, and Mido wanted to take it back.

"If we got married, then my mother and all three of my uncles would want us to go back to Korea and live there. I can't do that. I can't live in that world. My oldest uncle works for the company, another is a judge, and the youngest is a prosecutor. My mother's family is always in the news because of the size of their business, and my father's family—they have a little less power but they're more well known, so after the divorce, he went to live in Hong Kong just to be left alone. I don't want to live under that level of scrutiny. Here I'm just a struggling musician with a side hustle."

"You've thought this through," she said, fumbling in her dress pocket for her hair tie. The more they talked about this, the more she felt no less conservative than the most ordinary woman at church.

"I suppose they wouldn't approve of my family and me," she said, putting her hair up in a ponytail. Immediately she regretted having blurted this out. It was always better just to be quiet, she thought.

"Except for the college part, my mother and my uncles would think you're fantastic. I don't want you to think they're snobs. They're very understanding, but they care a lot about education. It's everything to them."

Mido didn't know what to say. Was he doubting her ability to go back to school? If so, he wouldn't be the only one. Perhaps others might figure that she was too old to return. If she started part-time, it would take longer than three years, and she couldn't finish before turning thirty.

"Besides, you're going to go back to school anyway. I shouldn't have brought this up."

"Wait, I might not. I might be too old to go back." Giving her age as the reason struck her as dismal and sober, without the radiant glow of sacrifice. She collected her thoughts. "I mean, it's not clear to me that I need to get my degree. For what I do, so far, lacking a degree hasn't held me back. And I don't think you're better than me because you have a college degree."

"Hey, I didn't say that."

"Right." When he'd said his family might judge her poorly for not having finished school, it stung more than she'd thought it would. Clearly he'd considered her CV in relation to his family back in Korea. She knew she could always go back to college, and it hadn't occurred to her that her not having finished college might be seen as something negative in her personal life.

Since her high school students had such extraordinary outcomes, none of the parents at the hagwon ever brought up her lack of a degree. Mido felt sick in a way that she hadn't last night, when everything about their nascent love had been good, thrilling, and possible.

Tek had insisted on her finishing school, but he'd never said that his parents would look down on her if she didn't. Was that why he kept on saying that he'd pay for it? It had been a given for Tek that she'd finish college. Mido pursed her lips tightly.

"I'm sorry. I didn't mean to—"

"No, not at all," she said in English, tinged with her Australian accent, which had been fading in America. "You're just telling me how it is. For people like them. I mean, for people who care about that."

"Hey, I don't care about that. You're brilliant, and I know how smart you are."

"Let me go order lunch. It's my job. It's too late for us to pick something up anyway," she said. There was a binder of menus inside her desk drawer.

In her mind, Mido listed all the reasons she'd had to stop going to school and what she had done with her time. By reading test guides and studying textbooks, without any formal training, Mido had learned to get perfect scores on college entrance exams, fill out college applications, then coach nervous and resentful high school students in a way that got them admirable results and also made the process worthwhile and interesting.

In the time she'd lived in California, Mido had taken everything she'd ever learned in and out of school and figured out how to administer a hagwon, tutor, and counsel applicants. With money she earned, she had sent DH to law school and was helping Bo get his PhD. It seemed particularly cruel to have strangers think less of her when getting a degree and becoming better educated was what she'd enabled countless others to do. It would be pathetic to defend her life, so Mido was unwilling to say any of these things to Peter.

"I'm fine, Peter. We're in agreement. All good."

She excused herself and went to open the main doors.

One by one, tutors arrived, then students and parents with appointments. The two lovers acted no differently than before. At the end of the day, Peter drove her back to his house, and she stayed with him until it was late, and then he drove her home.

11
Exchange

November 2005

Shin & Jung Insurance Agency was not losing money, but its first few years had been far more difficult than expected.

Danbi's cousin Frank Lim, who owned the preeminent property and casualty brokerage in Orange County, had done his best to explain the business to her.

Six years earlier, when Shin and Danbi first got licensed in California to sell casualty and property as well as life policies, Frank had invited them to lunch at his house in Newport Beach.

Frank, eleven years her senior, grated on Danbi. He condescended to her and Shin. And it was unfair, but she also disliked how unappealing he was—his narrow frame, the booming American voice of a know-it-all, and the unfortunate, uneven tadpole eyes. Mostly she envied and resented his perfect English-language skills. His clients were mostly affluent White Americans with special insurance needs for their beachfront properties and large boats. He easily wrote $70 to $80 million in business, taking an average 12 percent in commissions. Like his father, he was tall and had graduated from Berkeley, which she viewed as pluses. He had also grown very rich. Bina, his charming and social wife, wore only designer clothing and had a diamond ring the size of a Charms candy, and she genuinely adored him. As a special favor to his mother, Frank had sponsored Danbi's immigration with a work visa, but he had not required her to work for him.

"Why don't you now really come work for me?" Frank asked that afternoon, as Bina poured iced tea into tall sapphire-blue glasses. They were having lunch on the lanai next to the kidney-shaped swimming pool. "I can get you both set up with desks tomorrow morning if you want."

Danbi smiled at him, hiding her resentment. Frank's mother, Danbi's mother's sister, had pitied their family but had done little to help them. Each Christmas, Danbi's mother prominently displayed Frank and Bina's impressive greeting card and newsy letter, detailing their exotic travels and how well their two daughters were doing. Danbi wanted to tear it up every time she saw it.

Frank would have been fine with her and Shin writing policies for Korean customers, business he had not been interested in previously, but Danbi told him that they ultimately wanted to own their own agency. They had the capital to do so and had taken the trouble and time to study for the necessary licenses.

"For a small agency like ours, should we sell more life policies than casualty?" she asked. "I hear that life policies have the greatest revenues?"

Frank made a face. He made an excellent living, but he had not chosen his insurance products on revenue alone.

"Well, yes and no. There are many exceptions. But life policies can be harder to sell, even for charming you." Noticing her disappointment, Frank explained, "Danbi, if you're really serious about having your own agency without having any insurance experience, which makes no sense to me, you should sell car insurance and homeowner policies, which everyone needs. The profits might be smaller because there's more competition, but slowly you'll grow your business and relationships."

He droned on about trust, learning the business, and starting with less risk, and Shin smiled at Danbi, who was visibly irritated.

When Frank finished talking, Shin spoke up.

"Danbi really wanted her own business, and I'm at the age when I'd like that, too. And we'll need to hire some agents. Do you have any enterprising young people who want to work with Koreans? We're looking at office space near John Wayne Airport, but I hear Buena Park might make more sense."

Frank laughed out loud. "You want to take my people from me? That's confidence for you." He looked at his wife in amusement. "I told you my cousin is ambitious. I guess she wants to eat from my table and take the table. Why not the house?"

"No, no," Danbi said, sounding more girlish. "You misunderstand. My husband has lots of business experience, not specifically in insurance, but—"

"It's fine. I'm going to support you. I promised my mother I would."

Over the course of the meal, Frank broke down the list of things they had to have and do. Danbi pulled out a pad of paper and took notes. Except for the warnings about renting a small, clean space and not having expensive furniture, Danbi and Shin followed his advice. Shin overpaid on hiring bonuses that first year and negotiated commissions with better agents that were not always in the agency's favor, which kept their net profit margins close to 4 percent for several years, which was not ideal.

Also, each month, Shin sent money to his wife and sons. Nothing Danbi said could keep him from doing this.

❧

Danbi wanted more for her life. They still had a substantial mortgage on their four-bedroom house in Irvine. Anna attended a private school in Woodbridge. They leased two German cars. Neither Shin nor Danbi would ever inherit any money. Shin's widowed mother and younger sister no longer even spoke to him since he'd left Mary.

Shin could not divorce his wife. Mary lived in their house in New Jersey, and the boys would inherit it unless she had to spend that money down in her old age. Mary had a full-time job at a florist's, but she didn't earn enough to save for her retirement. Shin sent her $2,000 a month, but that was not enough to cover the mortgage and their sons' education. No matter what Danbi said, it was his plan to one day pay off the Englewood mortgage, if only for his conscience's sake.

Danbi had never been introduced to Mary. When she first started her affair with Shin, she had tracked down his wife, studying her from afar, once even lingering outside their home when Mary and the boys visited Seoul for the summer. She could not help but admire Mary's small, oval face framed by the elegant chignon, the placid beauty and long-suffering manner. Another time, Mary had come by the office, and the women commented on her trim figure and ladylike manner. Finally Danbi called her on the phone, and the conversation lasted less than two minutes. Danbi didn't respect Shin's wife's unwillingness to fight for her husband; however, she admired Mary's willingness to keep her distance. Shin had asked for a divorce, but Mary cited her faith.

Mary focused only on their sons. After seeing Mary, Danbi had said, "She's pretty enough. Why doesn't she get another man? Someone would take her," and Shin had shrugged, knowing he had no right to be jealous. Every time Mary said no to a divorce, a tiny part of him believed that

Mary might forgive him and let him come back home. Despite the proposed terms of the divorce agreement, which Mary had refused to sign, Danbi wanted Mary to sell the house in New Jersey and split the proceeds since the boys were grown. Both Shin and Mary were naturalized citizens, and if Shin were divorced, he could get Danbi citizenship—a point Danbi stressed often.

The two older boys had finished their degrees. The oldest and middle were lawyers, and the youngest was studying to be a nurse. One of the lawyers, the smart and better-looking one, was gay. None would have anything to do with their father. He hadn't been allowed to attend any of the graduations.

On every major issue, Shin lost to Danbi, but he made it plain that he would leave her and Anna if she ever contacted Mary or troubled the boys again.

Danbi needed more money. The people in their circle had a great deal more than they did. At this stage in their lives, their finances were not sufficiently secure. They had a substantial mortgage and credit card debts. She thought they should have a much larger house, with their own pool, not just one on the community grounds. She wore expensive clothes and bought herself designer jewelry, the same as her wealthy clients. For Danbi, Woodbridge, a beautiful community in Irvine, wasn't prestigious enough anymore.

They did not have enough saved for Anna's education and wedding. If Shin ever left her—something a practical woman like Danbi had to consider—then she'd need to have more set aside. She was only thirty-seven years old and attractive enough to make most men do what she wanted, but there would certainly come a time when this power would diminish. Before that eventuality, she had to have reserves.

❧

Danbi's lover George didn't have the kind of cash she wanted. To please her, he taught her how to make real money. Soon Danbi was flipping houses in Garden Grove and Santa Ana.

George had more than enough to pay for expensive hotel afternoons, sexy gifts, and trips. Danbi told Shin that she needed to attend a conference for agency owners, and of course, he let her go. George arranged for a suite at a five-star hotel in Santa Barbara, and as usual, they pretended to be married.

Shin had no idea about George, and he didn't mind her lack of attention. In a way, he was relieved by the slight cooling of her ardor for him.

George's wife, Sobin, was a terrific mother and a leader of their social set. Her father and uncle owned a successful real estate company in Northern California and a fast-growing one in Southern California led by her brother, Tommy. George would never have been able to amass their holdings in Orange County without Sobin's family's support. As the only son, Tommy was the chairman and co-owner of the company, but he did little to no work. George alone had increased his father-in-law's initial capitalization tenfold; however, no one was under any illusion that George, the second son of an office supply store owner, would have been able to become a wealthy man without his well-funded wife.

Only when it came to sex did George resent Sobin. After their fourth child, she lost all interest in it, and for years, they slept in the same bed but never touched. They were like a hand-holding brother and sister. At eleven o'clock, George went to sleep, and Sobin never slept until the early hours of the morning. When the children were at school, she napped.

Also, she was no longer the athletic size two who had once stunned him in a polka-dot bikini on a beach date. She maintained her appearance as a trim, attractive middle-aged woman, but after four children, each of whom she'd breastfed for a year, the occasional yoga, Pilates, and running had not slowed her natural aging. Sobin disliked the idea of plastic surgery or cosmetic dermatology to update her speckled and lined face. "Those perky breasts look so fake," she'd remark with contempt whenever she watched television. George thought plastic surgery shouldn't matter if a person looked and felt better afterward.

Sobin didn't like shopping for clothes, and the athletic, no-nonsense things she'd worn as a young woman now made her look frumpy. More than once, answering the door, she had been mistaken for the help, but she didn't care. George found her appealing enough, and he liked having a wife and mother who was admired by everyone. For thrilling sex and deep conversation, George sought Danbi, who fulfilled those needs.

George had never expected a gorgeous woman like Danbi to seduce him, especially the way she had. Just recalling the experience continued to arouse him. There was something brazen and insane about her, and initially, he had not seen it. He had been with hostesses, and he was smart enough not to get entangled with women who would need to be paid dearly for sex. Women like that came with shadowy figures behind them, and George, believing himself to be clever, had avoided them. He welcomed this married lover who wanted no-strings sex, friendship, and mentorship.

George didn't understand how Taehun Shin could be so clueless and allow a stunning woman like Danbi to remain unsatisfied. George had no idea that she was able to sleep with both men. She needed sex all the time, and George, thinking that women were all like his wife, believed Danbi was sleeping mostly with him, which was not true.

The two lovers rotated among several hotels, but they usually went to the Hyatt in Huntington Beach, got a room with a water view, and never left, not even for food. In the tub, Danbi would bathe him, then they would have sex, order room service, and talk for hours. On most Saturday afternoons, when Anna was at her hagwons, Danbi met him at the Hyatt.

George found that he needed these meetings more and more; he would call her during the week to check if there were any openings in her schedule. It was harder for her to get away then because she worked with Shin, but once, when he was desperate to see her, she met him in a movie theater for an hour to help him get through.

What allowed him to see her more often in public was her growing interest in real estate. Shin did not mind that George was teaching her how to flip houses. This side business was Danbi's alone, they agreed. The money she earned, she said, was for Anna's future.

George showed her the listings, introduced her to the best mortgage brokers, bankers, contractors, painters, plumbers, and electricians, and even an appliance wholesaler. He taught her to buy fixer-uppers for low six figures. Using hard-money loans with their short terms and high interest, she'd spend about $10,000 to fix the house, sell it in two months, and net $50,000 or $60,000 in profit. Any buyer, it seemed, could get a mortgage. She told Shin she made less and socked away the money in a private account. After each closing, Danbi met George at a hotel to celebrate.

George never let her pay for the hotel rooms or food. He was a man, and his pride would never allow it. A year after they became lovers, Danbi mentioned that her birthday was in March. They were in a nice room at the Hilton this time. She was naked and he was still dressed, something he had requested of her. They allowed each other fantasies, and George, who had never had anything like this in his sex life, felt grateful. He learned that the more he wanted her, the more excited she'd get.

"What would you like for your special day?" he asked.

"I want to get my breasts done."

"Don't do that."

"I might need to in the future."

"Not now, though," he said, cupping her round, full breasts. They were luscious and appealing, but George found himself admiring Danbi for thinking ahead. "Don't do it for me. You don't have to change anything."

Her eyes crinkled with pleasure, and she got on her knees. After he finished, she looked up and pouted.

"$20,000. I could put it aside and get it for myself as a gift later. I promise you'll be the first person to see them."

"Not too big, though," he said. "I don't like the ones that look too big."

The next time they met at the Sheraton, he gave her the money in a Gucci purse. He made her promise not to have the surgery until later. She took off her blouse.

"What's that you're wearing?" he asked, pointing to the ivory-colored undergarment that covered her waist and enhanced her bosom.

"It's a corset," she said, then dropped her skirt to show off the matching garters and stockings.

"I don't know why you do this to me," he said, and reached for her and pulled her onto his lap.

Danbi relieved his stress, and he wanted her to have beautiful things. "This is for a new dress," he'd say, putting $1,000 in her pocketbook. In several of his properties in Santa Ana, he received partial rental payments in cash, which reduced their tax bills, and it was easier to put aside a bit of cash for her each week. When he saw her at church, he liked knowing that she was wearing things that he had paid for.

In the past year, they'd taken two weekend trips, pretending to be husband and wife, and he enjoyed the way men looked at him with admiration when she wore a white strapless bikini by the pool. He felt possessive of her and tried not to think of her being with Taehun Shin. At church, he would glance at Shin and wonder how a man could ever let a wife like Danbi out of his sight.

On a trip to San Francisco, in a part of town where they knew no one, she brought up money again. They were dining at the hotel restaurant, which was risky, but Danbi didn't want to eat in their room every night. As they walked back to their suite, she said she wanted to get a bigger house.

"How big?"

"As big as yours."

He laughed.

"How many small houses do I have to sell to get that? And I don't want a mortgage."

"How much do you have saved?"

"Only $300,000."

"Well, you can get a few more little ones and acquire a much bigger one using the smaller ones for collateral. If you sold a whale, you would make a much bigger profit faster."

"Won't it cost a lot to fix a big house?"

"No, you want to get in on a new development. Not a fixer-upper for a starter home. But sell a place that's likely to go up and stay up."

"Everything is rising," Danbi said. "Everything I bought has gone up. If I had more money and time, this is all I would do. I would be so rich," she said. Her laughter sounded like bells, and George kissed her on the mouth.

"How much is your house worth?" she asked.

"Several million," he said. "I haven't had it appraised in a while. I think at least seven or eight?"

"Do you have a mortgage?"

"Sure. Not a lot. We didn't buy it for that much." George didn't mention that it had been a present from his father-in-law.

"So I need more money to buy places and to invest."

"Why do you need such a big house?"

"Why do you?" she asked, and George kissed her again.

"I need more than the house. I also need to care for my mother and my retirement. I won't be poor when I'm middle-aged, and I won't be living with my daughter. My mother is less clear these days, so I need to get more help for her. The agency is doing fine, but we give too much to the agents. I don't make enough to quit working. Maybe if I have a lot, I can just leave my husband." Again Danbi laughed.

A week later, they were meeting at the Sheraton. George got there first, and when he heard the knock on the door, he let her in, excited to share news he knew she'd like.

"There's a new development in Irvine. You can probably make six figures if you flip it. If you put down a little and get loans for the rest. You won't have to deal with fixing this one. It will sell fast."

"Keep talking," she said, and turned around so he could unzip her pink shift dress. She had worn a baby-pink brassiere and panties for him. He spanked her rear lightly.

"If you get in on this new development in Irvine and make a couple of hundred, we can do it again until you become a millionaire," he said.

Danbi faced him. "You'll help me. You always help me."

"Of course," he said, and carried her to the bed.

12
Cool Factor

Turn in the problem sets, please," Bo said as the section ended. One by one, the students passed the work forward. Only two didn't hand them in, which wasn't bad. Alvin had missed class, and no doubt he was still working on it, and Hattie glared at him sullenly, then looked away. She waited until everyone left to approach him.

"I couldn't do it." Hattie sat in the empty chair next to his, and Bo stopped packing his things. A few of his students were talking in the hallway, and the door was ajar.

"Let's hear it, Hattie. You okay?"

Hattie was a junior psych major, a Korean national who had gone to an international school in Seoul. She was normally a strong student, and Bo wanted to give her the benefit of the doubt.

"I had a conflict with a professor about my grade."

"Do you mean in our class? I'm the one who grades Psych 100A."

"No, not this class," she said, touching the back of her neck. Hattie wore a blue UCLA sweatshirt and sweatpants. No makeup, unwashed hair tied up in a ponytail. "I can't tell you his name because you know him."

"Is this about your midterms?"

"Yes. I went to speak to him. He was so rude. I think it's because he got tenure last year."

"What does that have to do with anything?" Bo straightened his glasses and kept from folding his arms. Every time he had office hours, he thought about his body language as a future clinician. He leaned forward and paid careful attention. She was visibly upset. Hattie took her grades seriously.

"He can't get fired now, so if I give him a bad eval it won't even matter. It will be really hard for me to pull this up in my finals. I want to go to medical school, and I have to get all A's."

"No interest in getting a PhD?"

"No way." She stared at him like he was crazy. "There's no money in that. Oh, I'm sorry," she said, laughing. "I mean, some people don't care about money, right? You want to help people."

"Yes," he said, feeling a little embarrassed. He had not disliked Hattie before, and he reminded himself that she was still a kid and didn't know how to talk properly. "Okay, so you want to be a medical doctor, and therefore you need good grades." Bo knew premeds had to have exemplary transcripts. His premed undergraduates were endlessly stressed out. One from another section had killed himself a year before.

"B means I will *be* rejected from a top med school."

"B should stand for 'breathe,'" he said. "Also, I know plenty of students with B's who got into med schools."

Hattie looked him up and down. Bo wore an old white shirt that he had ironed himself last night and faded jeans. She stared at his cheap black sneakers he'd bought from a mart, which even DH had teased him about.

"What grade did you get? On that midterm?"

"B. Only a B-plus or an A-minus would be at all defensible," she said, sounding like a lawyer.

Bo tried to keep his cool. He hated grading, and even worse, he hated arguing about grades.

"I see. What do you think you should do now?"

"I can't fight him anymore. I couldn't even sleep last night, I was so angry. I can't stand the sight of him. He might ruin my chances of being a psychiatrist."

"I don't know if that's true."

"I can't stand these tenured professors. They won't move an inch."

"I suppose the untenured faculty is more amenable," he said, wondering what she must think of a graduate student like him.

Hattie blurted out, "I pay a lot of money to attend UCLA. I'm not in-state. I should get better treatment. His office hours are only an hour once a week."

Hattie thought she was buying her education, like buying a lesson with a private tutor. From her appearances, she didn't seem materialistic. But she was only twenty years old, and probably repeating ideas some adults had said to her.

"Hattie, you might get better outcomes if you focused on the learning. I realize you're under a great deal of stress, and it's obvious how hard you work, but thinking of your teachers as your employees is probably not the best idea. A teacher might feel that you're threatening him with a poor written evaluation. You didn't talk about the eval with your professor, did you?"

Hattie caught herself and covered her mouth. "Oh, I didn't mean to threaten him. I just think that these grades are important, and I need the best ones for medical school. He should want me to do well, right?"

"I'm sure he does," Bo said. "But everyone is human, and it would be hurtful to think that your students don't respect you."

"I don't think he wants me to do well, or anyone for that matter. I think he just wants to prove how smart he is. He's intellectually insecure. The curve in that class is crazy. Only people who are stupid insist on these rigid grading curves. Why can't everyone get an A if they deserve it? In this class, no one might get an A, and now it's too late for me to withdraw."

Hattie appeared so disheartened that though Bo disagreed with her, he didn't want to say anything more.

"Do you have any other B's?"

Hattie got up from her seat, refusing to answer.

"I'll hand in my problem set by the end of the day. I'm sorry I'm late." She bowed reflexively, then left. "My friends are waiting for me."

Bo was still reliving that conversation in his head, muttering to himself, as he unlocked his car door in the campus parking lot.

"You look happy," Priscilla Banks said, laughing. "Not." She was putting her backpack into the trunk of her dusty Nissan.

Bo smiled. They'd gotten to know each other a little during Dr. Wilson's class at Fullerton. She was a year behind him at UCLA, and on the developmental psych track. It was nice to have a friendly face from his Fullerton days at UCLA.

Priscilla was tall and eye-catching. Once an actor, she understood her own presence. In Franz Hall, she stood out because she wore her clothes well and looked more like a well-off humanities grad student than a poor one from social sciences. No one could identify her race or ethnicity exactly, and she seemed to enjoy the guessing. Her skin was medium brown, her long brown hair wavy and usually kept back with a colorful scarf. Today it was shamrock green, which lit up the pale blue green in her eyes. She spoke Spanish well, but wasn't a native speaker, she said.

"You okay?" she asked him.

"I'm fine," he said, settling behind the wheel. "Have a good weekend." He closed the door and turned the key, but the engine wouldn't start. Bo jumped out of the car and waved at Priscilla, who was getting in her car.

"Battery?" she said.

"Yes. Help."

"I can give you a jump," she said calmly.

As they connected the cars, his student Hattie and her friends walked by, staring at the two old cars. Bo drove an eleven-year-old gray Subaru, and Priscilla's car looked far worse. The girls laughed and shook their heads.

"What a day," he said.

"Are they laughing at us?" Priscilla stared back at them. Their tittering ceased as they walked away.

"I hate that girl," Priscilla said.

"What? Why?" Bo was surprised to hear this. Priscilla was usually more upbeat.

"You swear not to tell?"

"Swear."

"Blood oath?"

"Okay. Is there actual blood involved? Or do you mean it metaphorically?"

"Shut up, Fullerton," she said.

Bo laughed.

"That kid Hattie Cho. Can't staaaaand her. Fought with me for every fucking grade. I ended up giving her an A-minus just so she couldn't dispute it."

"What did she deserve?"

"B-plus at best. At best," Priscilla said. "She's just another grade-grubbing Asian kid."

"Watch it, Young Fullerton," he said. "No racism."

Priscilla laughed.

"You know what I mean. She looks dorky and doesn't put on airs, but that kid is rich and thinks we're pieces of shit who work for her."

"Oh." Bo exhaled. "Yes. I think you are correct in your estimation."

"Wait, is she in your class? I should shut the fuck up."

"Yes, as a matter of fact, Hattie is one of my students. That is all I will say."

"I will make a terrible therapist," she said.

"The kid is premed. She's just freaking out. She doesn't mean anything."

"I have White kids, Latino kids, and Black kids who are also grade grubbers," Priscilla said. "I shouldn't have said it like that about her being Asian. Sorry."

"You shouldn't have," he said. "Demerit." Bo smiled.

"I was a grade grubber. How else did I transfer here, then also get into the fucking UCLA psych program?" Priscilla laughed again, and Bo thought she looked beautiful standing in the sunny parking lot, the tall palm trees swaying behind her. "Okay, Fullerton, I have some blood tickets."

"What?"

"I gave blood this morning. They give you movie tickets. I'm a broke grad student who needs to go to the movies. Come with me? My roommate just bailed, and there's a showing in an hour for *Sideways*. It came out a while ago, but I heard it's really good."

Bo hadn't gone to the movies in years; it always felt like an indulgence of time and money he couldn't afford. Now he wanted nothing more than to go with her.

"Okay. I just have to text my sister. I need to be at my job in Irvine by seven. If you give me the ticket, I can buy popcorn, then, right after, I have to push this car and make it to Irvine."

"You live in Irvine?"

"No. I live here. Weyburn." Bo pointed in the direction of his rental.

"Fancy." Priscilla pretended to remove a hat and bowed dramatically.

"It's a studio, and it costs too much, but I walk to classes or use my bicycle. I only keep this car going because I tutor on the weekends and go home on Friday nights. I should find a cheaper place off campus and get roommates, but I'm too old for that. Anyway," he said, and took out his phone.

"How old are you?" she asked.

"I turn thirty in February."

"You look younger," she said, and she waited for him to text Mido that he'd be late.

❧

After the movie ended, Bo ran back to his car to beat the traffic back to Irvine. As he drove, he couldn't shake off his embarrassment. His student Hattie thought his decision to get a PhD was foolish. From the look on her face, his poverty was something to be mocked. He wondered how young people could have learned such terrible ideas about education, money, and hierarchy. She had complained to him, her TA for Statistics for Psychology, a prerequisite for every psych major. In her calculation, he didn't matter.

After each reading, lecture, and assignment, something in him opened up, and Bo believed he was meant to be a clinical psychologist and see patients. Every study, article, and clinical experiment led him to reinterpret his own life, and he felt eager to learn more. He wanted to work with immigrants, and the more he studied, the more he realized that the way most modern Western families functioned would make little sense to diasporic families from Korea, Australia, and the States. If he ever had kids of his own, he wanted to know how to raise them better.

As he studied family structures, he thought of his mother more often than his father, and he regretted having spent so much time in that tiny hotel room in Seoul, trying to get into an impressive college that was different from his father's. When he studied the research on romantic and erotic love in a seminar, he recalled his first love, and, borrowing his cousin's Cyworld log-in, he found Ara without any effort.

In one photo, Ara was at a restaurant in Garosu-gil with a nice-looking young man in a suit, which was enough information for him. In another image, the same man was in his military uniform. Like Hattie, Ara might not respect the degree he wanted. *Why be a psychologist and make less money than a medical doctor?*

Ara might look down on him for having misspent his twenties in a room the size of two coffins. He wanted to give his first girlfriend more credit than that, so he stopped looking at her profile. He diagnosed it for himself as unhealthy.

Today, Priscilla had saved him. She was beautiful and funny. He could not have met her unless he had come all this way, taking the most circuitous path.

Each day, as he walked from Franz Hall to Weyburn, past enormous palm trees beneath the seemingly endless sunlight of Los Angeles, he felt grateful for the end of that college testing period in his life. He would not wish it on his enemies, if he had any. It was self-awareness alone that made him less angry with Hattie. She was a young person with her own rigid thoughts, trapped in her own rented room without windows and doors. Once, he too had lived in that imagined prison. He would never have argued with a teacher for a better grade than he'd received, but he had also given up almost everything for his grades and a test. He was almost thirty years old, and this afternoon he had gone to his first movie since high school.

❧

When he arrived at Fortress, Mido called out to him.

"You have twenty minutes to eat your sandwich," his sister said.

Bo opened the white paper bag she handed him and smiled.

"My favorite."

"For some reason, today I felt like a turkey sandwich, so I got three."

"You ate two?" he asked.

"Oh, I got one for Peter."

Bo had noticed a difference. Something had changed between them. Peter was now attending church, then driving Mido back to Fortress. Then their body language. At the hagwon, the space between them had grown closer. They didn't touch. It wasn't like that. Their father had mentioned that Mido was working too hard and that he was worried. She was coming home later than usual. She'd prepare his meals and leave them in the refrigerator for him to heat up, but often, two or three nights a week, she didn't come home until eleven o'clock.

She was supposed to be at Fortress working, but the hagwon closed at 10:00 p.m. at the latest. There was a strong demand for late-night tutoring, but Lion and Yun had drawn the line at ten o'clock. She could have been doing administrative work, but Bo still had doubts. If Peter was bringing her home, he assumed they had been together.

As an older brother, he didn't know how to broach the subject, and he wasn't sure if it was his place. She was twenty-seven years old—fully grown. Without question, she was more mature than he and DH. She had given up school and Tek. She had worked to earn money to replace their mother's income.

Bo had been observing Mido with Peter at church and at the hagwon to see if they behaved as friends, colleagues, or lovers. If they were dating, he didn't understand why they hadn't told anyone.

Bo got up and checked the glass door. No one was in the hallway.

He turned to face Mido. "Are you seeing him?"

Mido paused, then shook her head.

"Is that a no, you're not seeing him, or a no, you're not talking about it?"

"Oppa, you should eat your dinner."

Bo bit into his sandwich, then opened the bag of chips. DH had told him years ago that Peter came from an important family in Korea with money and connections. He had not specified much, but Bo, who followed the news in Korea more often than DH and Mido, had figured out that Peter's mother was the only daughter from a major conglomerate family, and his father was the second son of another prominent family in business.

"You know about his family, right?"

"No need to know," Mido replied. She opened a bottle of water for him and placed it near his food.

"I like Peter. He's a good guy," Bo said. "DH hasn't mentioned it. I can tell he doesn't know."

Mido glanced up from her pile of test papers. They had been as careful as possible, and Mido knew things were getting serious but had no idea what to do. Peter was clear that he wanted a commitment from her but also clear that he would never marry. She didn't care about getting married, but the hiding was getting awkward. At her age, she felt silly for concealing it.

"It would be hard to marry him, though," Bo said before taking another bite.

Mido pretended to make notes on the student charts. If she asked him why, then it would be an admission that they were seeing each other.

"His family would be upset about you not finishing college. I realize part of this is my fault. If you want me to take out some loans, you can go back to school and get your degree, so no one can say anything about your—"

"Getting a degree from a community college is not going to impress Peter's parents, and besides, he doesn't want to get married." She gave up the pretense. It was a relief not to hide it from Bo any longer. "Doesn't believe in it. Won't move back to Seoul. He wants to stay here to do his music and teach. That's why he doesn't take their money anymore." Mido didn't mention that Peter's mother still paid for the housekeeper, who stocked the refrigerator and cleaned the house.

"I don't want to get married anyway. Are you going to tell?" she asked, sounding younger suddenly.

"I trust you," Bo said, wanting to add that he was there for her, that he'd protect her, do whatever he could to fix things, but she knew all that already. "I went to the movies," he said, changing the subject. "With a woman from my program."

"What?" Mido was delighted. "Tell me."

"Oh, look at the time, I have to teach," he teased. The car ride home would be filled with questions.

13

Hong Gildong

Yun wanted a love story with a happy ending. She blamed her pregnancy for making her sentimental.

From the shopping bag, she pulled out the VHS tapes of episodes six and seven of *The Light and Shadow of Rainfall.*

It was Saturday night, and after fooling around on his guitar for an hour, Lion took his usual seat in the living room on the beige tweed sectional. He picked up his copy of *In Search of Excellence* from the coffee table and removed the pen from where he'd been reading.

Already comfortable in her favorite spot on the deep-pile rug, Yun reached for the VCR remote control.

"Your mom didn't come over?" Lion asked.

"She's seen this many times," Yun said. "She's watching a new show at home on her DVD player. It's a historical drama, and I wasn't in the mood."

"Is this one any good?" he asked, looking doubtful.

"I like it a lot. The male lead is—"

"Don't tell me. Virtuous, handsome, and mildly tolerated. And he won't kiss the female lead until close to the end of the series. Maybe they'll hold hands around the two-thirds mark, or perhaps she'll fall into his arms by accident, sparking romance and not just mutual respect."

"If you're going to make fun of it, I will not give you any of my chips."

"Not making fun. I know this is holy ground for you and your mother. You keep watching. I need to focus and find a quote for my prep talk."

"You haven't done it yet?" Yun was surprised.

The first drafts of Lion's ten-minute lectures were usually finished by Friday morning, revised later in the day, and delivered the following week. He gave the elementary and middle school version to the students at Exodus on Mondays and a high school version to the teenagers at Fortress on the following Fridays.

Lion's prep talks—filled with personal anecdotes, statistics, and inspiring quotations—were legendary and one of the distinguishing hallmarks of their hagwons. Former students remembered them and cited passages to Lion when they returned to visit, and some parents asked for copies to read since their children mentioned them so often at home. They were secular homilies, which most hagwon owners would never bother to write with such care.

"You're usually done by now," she said.

"I was busy helping Mido and Peter on Friday with college app students, so I couldn't get to it."

"They're really jammed with kids."

"Peter's hiring again, but Mido's rightfully choosy, and it's taking a while. She even told me to lighten up on Friday. I thought I was the boss. Guess not." He smiled.

"Mido's never wrong," Yun said. "I'm sure you were too tough. These kids are really anxious."

"I know, I know. When Ginny was going through it last year, I think I got my first gray hairs."

"I still hate Dartmouth," Yun said. None of them could believe it when she didn't get in. It had deferred her, then came the rejection.

"But she loves UCLA, thank God."

"I know she's happy there. But I still think she should have gone to Johns Hopkins or Cornell. It might have been good for her to get a different experience, other than California. We could have paid the difference," Yun said. She balled her fists in frustration. "Oh, I hope she made the right choice."

Lion patted his wife's shoulders gently. "Ginny still wants to be a doctor. There's a long road ahead of her. We should respect her decision. She's a smart kid."

"Yeah, I know. The college apps are just ridiculous. Almost no one is getting into UCLA or Berkeley now. You have to have these crazy good scores, perfect grades, row crew, and be an astronaut. Our students are suffering."

"Yes, they are. As am I," Lion said, staring meaningfully at the potato chips. Yun passed the bowl to him with a napkin.

"Put on your headphones. I'm going to start this now," she said, and hit play on the remote control.

❧

Lion rarely watched television, and Yun had grown up watching everything with her mother. Unlike Nari, Yun preferred mysteries or medical or legal procedurals over melodramas and historical narratives. She could not watch horror of any kind and disliked stories about suicide. Occasionally she watched high school dramas to figure out what young people cared about, but she had not cared for happy romances until she got pregnant. Now the idea of anyone getting hurt was unbearable.

No matter which kinds of dramas she watched, in them, Yun could rely on a neat resolution for almost every character, and fair endings in an unfair world. Also, through dramas, she kept up with the latest slang, and whenever she heard a regional accent from North Gyeongsang-do, she thought of her father, who was from Gyeongju.

When she watched her programs without her mother or Mido, Lion would sit with her, wearing headphones, and read. To give structure to his weekly prep talks, he kept up with the latest translation of classical philosophy, modern advice guides, popular social science literature, psychology of motivation, coaching treatises, and business books.

❧

Lion tapped Yun on her back.

"You know what I noticed about your shows?"

Yun paused the video.

"What's that?" She frowned, wondering how he could make any kind of generalization when he never watched a show from beginning to end. Whenever she brought home a bag of rented videos of some series with dozens of episodes, he'd point out that she could be reading good books instead.

"There's almost always a Hong Gildong character. That's the reason Koreans are so messed up."

"Are you going to complain about dramas again? Also, Koreans are not messed up. You and I are Korean, and we're not messed up."

"Listen," Lion continued, "if people have to have magical powers to be the hero of their lives, then what can ordinary people do?"

"What are you talking about?"

"Hong Gildong, the Korean Robin Hood. I mean, not exactly like Robin

Hood. You know, the maid's son who isn't recognized by his nobleman father, the high-ranking government official, and the mean concubine hates him. But he's got to live at home because he's a kid, and he suffers abuse and neglect. But"—Lion held up a finger, something he did when he was teaching—"the thing that saves Gildong is that he studies super hard, then leaves home to train at a monastery, so the so-called illegitimate son ends up becoming a wise leader and defends the poor."

"Yes, I know the Hong Gildong story. I think every Korean does. I don't get your point."

"There's always an outsider in your dramas who's incredibly gifted and earns his place in the world. Even though he's treated unfairly, he's the deserving heir to the throne or the love of some rich nice girl, because he's virtuous and exceptional. He's always got some extra bizarre abilities. He's never normal. There are female Hong Gildong characters, too, right?"

Yun considered this. Even in the drama she was watching, the heroine was an outcast and a stepchild. Through hard work, the heroine, Jiyon, had become the top cadet in the police academy, and Yun predicted that she'd capture the heart of the romantic lead, Gil-yong, who was superhuman in his ability to memorize police law and had the best marksmanship.

She slapped her head in recognition and irritation. Even the male lead's name, Gil-yong, sounded like Gildong.

Lion wasn't wrong: Many drama plots could be explained by the legend of Hong Gildong.

"I didn't know you were watching my dramas. I thought you were reading," she said, irrationally irritated.

"I am reading. You don't have to pay that close attention to figure out who the leads are and what they want."

"You don't even know what you're saying because you haven't watched everything. Carefully," Yun insisted. Her mother paid attention to every second of a program. She'd go to the bathroom or kitchen only during commercials when they watched a broadcast show, or when the rented video ended. Yun had learned to do the same. Watching the shows, Nari sobbed often, as did Yun. It felt wonderful to cry. The word she had learned in her required writing class in college was "catharsis." When she and her mother wept, they felt a sense of release that they got nowhere else in their lives.

Lion never shed a tear watching a program. Seeing her cry, he would stroke her hair or pat her on the back while he continued to read his books. If his wife and mother-in-law were sobbing together, he'd hand them a box of tissues, or make them tea.

"What bothers me about these programs is that all of it is so unrealistic," he said, not letting up.

"Well, of course it is," she said, exasperated. "It's television. It's not real."

"But at our parent conferences, the parents ask us why their kids aren't doing better. How many times has a dad asked us who's the top student in the class, like his kid needs to have a target? The dad is looking for the Hong Gildong. He wants his kid to be Hong Gildong," Lion said, realizing the genesis of all this madness.

Yun turned off the television.

"I didn't mean for you to stop watching," he said. "There's nothing wrong with the dramas."

"You just said they're ruining Koreans."

"No, I didn't mean that. I just mean they perpetuate these unreasonable expectations of merit and competition."

Yun got up, not wanting to hear another lecture from Lion about the value of education for its own sake. He believed that education should be transformational and not transactional, that it was wrong to want to graduate from a school just for a degree. Of course, what he was saying wasn't wrong. But Yun loved watching dramas, and even if they weren't real, even if their messages weren't always helpful, the emotions she felt watching them were real to her.

Also, when she saw the heroes being good and kind even though the world was unjust, she rooted for the heroes and wanted the villains to be punished. In life, she rooted for her students at the hagwon, wanting them to succeed against all the odds that seemed impossible, too.

At Exodus, the students were often poor kids without sitters whose parents had to work, who had no one to watch them. Some of the parents wanted their kids to do well, but most just wanted their kids to have a safe space to do homework and not be lonely at home. The parents trusted a

Korean place because they couldn't speak English, and there was nowhere else to put their kids.

Yun stared at the dark screen, and it occurred to her that what she couldn't find herself saying, even to her husband, her best friend, was that she missed Korea. She missed ordinary Koreans—the ones on the street, on the trains, in her schools. She missed hearing the language. Her parents had decided to leave without considering her feelings or ever asking if it was okay.

Her father was still in Brazil, of all places in the world, and she wondered if he had learned Portuguese, or if he still spoke with that heavy Gyeongsang-do accent that made him seem like he was from the country when they lived in Seoul. She suddenly wanted to see her father, and Yun started to cry.

Lion looked alarmed and took her in his arms. "I'm sorry, babe. I didn't mean to upset you."

"I know. It's not you. Hormones. I'll watch it later. Besides, I need to get Ginny's room ready for when she comes home tomorrow."

❧

On Ginny's first night back for winter break, Lion was working late at Fortress. Yun and Ginny ate dinner quickly to have more time to trim the tree.

"Hang on, I have something for you," Ginny said. She ran into her bedroom and brought out a shopping bag.

"Aren't I supposed to wait for Christmas?"

"I got my first paycheck."

"What?"

"From my job at school."

"You have a job at school?"

"It's at the library. They're basically paying me to study. I hardly do anything. I'm like a security guard for books."

"I could increase your allowance," Yun said.

"No, no. I want to work. I'm going to send money to my folks."

Yun covered her mouth. "Oh? Are they okay?"

Ginny shrugged. "Same old same old. I don't want to talk about it."

Yun wondered if Ginny was also sending her allowance to her parents.

"Close your eyes and hold out your hands," she said. "I don't have anything for Lion Teacher this time, but I didn't think he'd want this."

When Yun opened her eyes, she saw the shoebox inside the paper bag.

"Sneakers?"

"No. I didn't have any other box, and my roommate had this. Open it."

Inside the box lined with white tissue paper was a Louis Vuitton wallet.

Yun opened her mouth in surprise.

"It's not real. My friend went to Korea, and she got this for me at Itaewon. She said it was the nicest fake. It's a practice gift. One day, when I become a doctor, I'll get you a real one, and a handbag. I just wanted to get you something with my first paycheck. You and Lion Teacher have been so good to me."

"You don't have any extra money."

"You have that canvas wallet that's falling apart. I wanted to get you a real designer wallet, and I will one day."

"I don't need any of that stuff. I don't mind my wallet at all. You know I never buy designer things. I have everything I need. I'm so glad you're doing well in school. You have no idea how grateful we are that you're doing well."

"You don't like it?" Ginny looked concerned. The wallet had cost her $100, which had taken her a whole weekend to earn. A real one cost almost $1,000, her friend had told her.

"No, no, no." Yun shook her head. "This is the nicest wallet I ever had. You can't get me a real one because I have this one now. I'll carry it forever."

"You deserve a real one, Yun Teacher. I wouldn't have anything without you and Lion Teacher. I know my tuition at school is so expensive. I'm going to pay you back."

"Oh, Ginny. You're our blessing. You're our gift from the Lord. I get to share you with your parents," she said, her voice quavering. Everything made her cry.

Yun sat down on the child's bed, clutching the brown-and-beige wallet. She had never wanted designer things. When she was growing up, her mother had yearned for them desperately. When they'd had money, every item in the house was imported or known to be a high-status object. Then, when all the money was gone, everything had turned out to be worth a fraction of what her mother had paid.

Now and then her mother still bought expensive things, and whenever Yun gave her mother extra money, she spent it on designer clothes or accessories to wear to the shop. Yun never chided her mother, because the woman had suffered and had not given up on them. Like a character from a melodrama, her mother still waited for her father to return to her with a good job, an armload of gifts, and a heartfelt apology, and Yun felt fairly certain that this would never come to pass.

Yun looked into her eyes.

"Thank you, my dear, dear Ginny."

The child she had taken in was training to be a supernatural wonder, so she could rescue everyone, and Yun wept for all of them.

14
The Lecture

Lion gave his talk on the legend of Hong Gildong twice—one version for the primary and middle school children at Exodus, and another for the high school students at Fortress. The primary message was "Hong Gildong is a character from a fable, and he cannot serve as our role model."

He told them none of them needed to be like Hong Gildong—a boy with unnatural powers of intellect and skills who tries to save the larger community and earn an honorable station in life.

"Rather," Lion said, "use and nurture the talents you have. Show up and do the best you can on whatever you put your hands to. Be honest and good to yourself and others. Avoid comparisons. Each of you is needed on the team. I like you right now. Just as you are."

The children seemed a bit confused but relieved, too. Lion Teacher always knew their names, said hello to everyone, and looked them in the eye when he spoke to them. They already knew he wanted to lighten their burden.

At Fortress, Jonathan Park, a senior from Troy High School, raised his hand during Q and A.

"My mom said that you have the highest IQ in California, so maybe you don't have to try as hard?" Jonathan said, smiling, and the other children laughed.

"Wise guy." Lion smiled back at him. "To the best of my knowledge, not the highest IQ in California. You are wrong, sir, about something very important. I tried very hard when I was your age, to learn. I still try very hard now, to be the head of this organization, which is only one factor of your education." He was constantly stressing the importance of their regular school teachers, who did nearly all the difficult work five days a week.

"Everything takes an enormous amount of effort for me, but I want to give it that effort. I don't believe IQ measures intelligence. I know for certain that IQ does not measure success in life."

Greg Kim, a senior from Oxford, raised his hand.

"No offense, Lion Teacher, and I ask this out of respect, but what are you not successful at?"

Yun, sitting near the front with Mido and Peter, looked up to observe her husband's face.

Lion's eyes shifted toward the white ceiling, and his jaw grew firm. He paused for a moment before speaking.

"Most people would not call me a successful musician by the world's standards, but I am still a solid musician. I don't think I'll ever win a Grammy, have a national tour, or have one of my songs played on the radio, but that doesn't take away the fact that I still love to play my guitar, write my songs, and sing in a band. I don't want anything out of music other than to play music, so I think I win for me."

Greg frowned, trying to understand. What Lion Teacher had just said sounded like what his basketball coach had been talking about when he said Michael Jordan had a "Love of the Game" clause in his contract that allowed him to play ball anytime he wanted for the love of the game and not just to compete on his NBA team, even though Jordan could risk being injured playing in a pickup game at a park that didn't count for the Chicago Bulls.

Greg wondered if that love of the game was what made Jordan the Hong Gildong of basketball, or if Jordan just had miraculous talent combined with the best work ethic in basketball history. The senior boy wanted to know because he wasn't the best ballplayer on his team or the smartest student in any of his AP classes, and the cute girl he'd asked out at the beginning of the school year had turned him down. Was it possible to think you'd won when no one said you had? What was winning anyway?

Jonathan Park, ever the joker, raised his hand and hugged his study guide.

"So if we love learning, then we can master our SATs?"

Folding his arms, Lion paused meaningfully.

"Possess the right thinking. Only then can you master your art."

Yun turned to Mido, who shrugged.

"Cicero?" Peter asked.

"Master Splinter," Lion answered.

"Who?" Yun asked.

Peter made a face. "You're quoting the rat from the Teenage Mutant Ninja Turtles?"

"Why not?" Lion said.

Peter groaned. Delighted, the children clapped, and Lion took a bow.

After Lion gave the talk, he sat in his office and reviewed his lecture notes and thought about what he'd said to Greg. For his music, Lion had walked away from mathematics and physics—subjects he understood almost intuitively. He had to do the work, but he could almost see the path to the solutions, faster and more easily than most of his peers. Still, it was music that made him feel alive and excited. He was a fine musician and a good vocalist. People told him he had an original sound. That said, the Zekes were just an above-average local cover band that played in a steak house. If that gig disappeared, he'd continue to perform until he couldn't.

Lion would never sign with a label, or record an album, and his music wouldn't hit the Billboard charts. Of course, he had once wanted those things, but he saw that none of it would happen. So far, his hagwons were his albums and his greatest hits, and now he knew he was lucky to have a home with Ginny and Yun, and soon, their child.

⁂

For days, Lion thought about Hong Gildong, how the archetype permeated the mindset of the striving Korean. After church on Sunday, when he spotted Bo on the patio having lunch, he broke down his theory, and Bo listened attentively.

"Of course," Bo mused, "there are other important values in that legend—resistance to unfair authorities and rejecting hierarchy and primogeniture, personal effort, resilience in the face of inequity and abuse, perseverance, generosity toward the oppressed, and individual valor." He shook his head. "Gosh, so many things. I haven't thought about the good parts of that story in a long time—"

"Yes, yes, of course, you're right," Lion said impatiently, "but it's caused a lot of damage."

"Well, yes. Hong Gildong cannot be a role model. Hong Gildong is a fantasy superhero. The need to be endlessly exceptional would destroy the lives of even Olympic gold medalists, because you can't keep winning medals forever."

When Lion met prospective students for either Exodus or Fortress, often the interviews surprised him. About half the children were excessively quiet, nervous, and fearful. The meetings troubled him. It was as if they believed that somehow they'd failed when they hadn't even started at life. How was it possible for an eleven- or thirteen-year-old to think he was dumb?

I'm not as smart as my brother, a kid would say, or *My mom says I get bad grades because I'm lazy.*

Eventually the child shared, *I'm trying. I really am,* or *I'll never be a natural like fill-in-the-blank name of the student with the highest grades in her class.*

Lion didn't blame the schoolteachers or parents. He knew from experience that everyone wanted a child to flourish, but everyone had different ideas about how to make that happen. He worried about the kids. Lion wanted them to learn better so they could feel stronger. He wanted them to be able to solve super problems, not necessarily be super anything.

He finished his coffee and faced Bo.

"All these little kids are walking around feeling like they've disappointed their parents and themselves. I just want to scream. You know, I never had a record deal," Lion said, feeling embarrassed about saying this out loud. He continued anyway. "I still have a meaningful life."

"Exactly!" Bo said. Hearing this admission felt like a gift. He saw now that he was lucky that he hadn't been able to get into Yonsei. He had failed three times. But back then, he could not imagine a life without his dream school.

"Do you know that I still have that blue Yonsei T-shirt in the plastic bag?"

"Where is it?"

"In the back of a drawer. I can't get myself to throw it out, and I can't get myself to wear it."

"It's just a shirt. Yonsei is just a school. It wasn't meant to be," Lion said.

"Still not wearing it," Bo said.

Lion said, "I'll wear it for you."

Bo laughed. "It's yours."

"No, you should wear it, because you earned that shirt more than anyone who ever got into Yonsei on their first try."

Bo grew quiet, remembering that tiny rented room, his friend Isul, Big Uncle, and the kind tutor who had given him a coin for luck. For two years, almost, he had subsisted on ramyeon and cheap rice from a gosiwon kitchen; his Weyburn studio at UCLA seemed like a five-star hotel in comparison. He could not imagine a better life than this one, even with its petty humiliations and the attendant discomforts, because here he had hope.

"What do you think of my Korean superhero theory?"

"I like your theory, man," Bo said.

"I told my students. At Exodus and Fortress."

"And?"

"They looked kind of relieved. But maybe it's going to be forgotten once they go back to school or hear something different at home," Lion said. He tapped his fingers against the patio table.

"I'm glad you told the kids. That's good."

"Thanks," Lion said.

"Now go tell the parents."

"What?"

"Yeah, tell the parents," Bo said. "You should give that same talk to the parents," he repeated. "Get to the root of it."

"Why not? Why not?" Lion repeated.

❧

The new Gospel Presbyterian Learning Center was not even close to being done, so the church let Lion use the big gymnasium on a Thursday night, and he invited parents from both Exodus and Fortress. Of course, members of the church were also allowed to attend.

Over five hundred parents came to hear the famed Oracle of Orange County speak about education. Some of the younger parents didn't even have hagwon-age children, but they'd heard of Fortress's college admissions results. They were preparing to jockey for a better spot on the waiting list.

Tutors from both hagwons stood in the back because they ran out of chairs. Near the church gym doors, Yun and Mido sat behind a folding conference table, checking off registered guests.

Before taking their seats, many parents asked to buy study guides. Not finding any, they walked away, mumbling under their breath at the hagwon owner's business incompetence. They couldn't believe this lecture wasn't for marketing purposes and there was nothing to buy.

Lion had titled his talk "Our Children's Heavy Burden: Education in America." For thirty minutes, Lion spoke about the legend of Hong Gildong and what he perceived to be its impact on students of Korean ethnicity.

Danbi and Shin sat in the second row, one row ahead of George and his wife, Sobin. George never once looked at Danbi and concentrated on forgetting what they had done the day before at the Hilton in Anaheim.

After a bath and lovemaking, he'd told her about a new flip property in Garden Grove and given her the card of a new mortgage banker who had better loan products. For the last property she'd bought to flip, she had been short $100,000, and he had borrowed $100,000 from the church building fund by creating a fake contractor invoice. As soon as she sold it for a premium, he'd returned the $100,000 to the church fund without it being noticed.

During the week, he sent her text messages on her second mobile phone, which he'd bought for her. They played a game where he'd tease her about a valuable lead but wouldn't tell her the details. When they met in the room, she'd cajole until he gave in.

Sex outside of marriage was a sin, but in his mind, what he was doing with Danbi was far worse. He felt committed to Danbi, more than to the mother of his children. He couldn't imagine living with a woman like Danbi, but he didn't want to live without her. All week long, his primary thought was of his mistress and what he could do to please her, and after he saw her, he felt an urge to see her again.

After his talk ended, Lion suggested a fifteen-minute break followed by a Q and A session. It was a polite exit opportunity in case anyone wanted to leave, but very few did. Parents milled around the snack tables in the back of the auditorium, piled high with platters of mart gimbap and grocery store pastries and baskets filled with bags of chips and pretzels. There were coffee, tea, water, and soda on another long table. Everyone in the room had attended school meetings, but this one felt unusual because every parent was ethnically Korean. They knew each other from their children's schools, their neighborhoods, their businesses, and church. The mood in the room felt more convivial than competitive.

Women from church surrounded the popular Sobin Ha, clamoring for her attention, and as Danbi and Shin passed by, they nodded in her direction, but she didn't seem to notice them. Shin bowed to George, who stood by his wife, and George returned the bow, unwilling to even glance at his lover.

15

Q and A

Lion gave the lecture in English, and Mrs. Bu, a woman from church who'd once worked at the UN, helped them out with consecutive translation.

At the end of the fifteen-minute break, Yun rang the wood-handled brass bell, and parents returned to their chairs. Remarkably, only a dozen people had left, and those seated in the back rushed to take the empty chairs in the front. Parents sat patiently, nursing their paper cups of urn coffee while balancing paper plates of gimbap on their knees. The mood in the room grew serious, as if they were sitting for exams. Mido, Yun, and Peter now sat close to the stage and waited for Lion to take questions.

Wearing one of his white button-down shirts that Yun ordered from a catalogue by the stack and blue jeans with his dark-gray running sneakers, Lion looked like an undergraduate. He'd made a concerted effort to look less like a high school musician and had even worn his wire-rimmed eyeglasses instead of contacts.

Since childhood, people had praised Lion for his physical features, and at thirty-two years old—tall, doe-eyed, tanned, and now a successful business owner—he was treated by parents with great deference, which he found alternately discomfiting and normal.

He'd never aspired to what most people wanted—status, money, power—but he understood that the world conditioned his hagwon students to crave these things in excess and to gain them via education. He felt the need to show them another way. Every time he met with his students, he could hear their worry, anxiety, and brokenness. Especially his teenagers. It was as if they'd caught a virus and developed a chronic illness.

Never had he given a lecture in front of five hundred Korean and Korean American parents and had it translated into formal Korean. While Mrs. Bu translated his remarks, Lion had the unusual opportunity to study his audience's faces carefully. He was able to observe his audience react twice to the same message.

What was clear to him was that the parents listened with great intention and understood the substance of what he was saying; however, he could tell that they did not want to believe him.

When Lion opened the floor to questions, a man he didn't recognize raised his hand.

"The gentleman toward the back wearing the red windbreaker." Lion motioned with his right open palm, trying not to point at anyone. He'd grown up in a Korean family and attended Korean church all his life, but now and then he could make an etiquette error in speech or gesture. Often, especially at church, when he was with his fellow elders, he was more deferential than necessary to avoid giving offense. It was too easy to give slights or annoy one's elders unintentionally, and in this room, Lion and the tutors were younger than every single parent, which made him extra careful.

Mido, wearing her old brown cardigan over a blue dress with white Keds, had gotten up from her seat and stationed herself at the left side of the room with the wireless handheld microphone. Tracking Lion's line of vision, she handed the man the mic.

The man in the red windbreaker rose from his seat and covered his mouth with his hand, paused, then removed his hand before speaking. He cleared his throat and took another moment.

"Thank you for your words, Teacher. I'm going to speak Korean if that is okay." The man bowed and the translator nodded. The man paused again, looking worried. "I've heard from other parents that it's more difficult for Asians to be accepted into Ivy League colleges. I read in the Korean newspaper that race is not considered because of prop 200-something in the California public universities, but private schools don't want too many Asians. Is that true? How much better does my child have to be to get into an Ivy League school? My child is not a legacy or an athlete. For example, based on what you're seeing, what scores will be needed for next year?"

Lion had been concerned that this lecture might turn into a college admissions conversation, which he had no interest in. There were numerous qualified hagwon owners and private college counselors who gave those talks regularly. Tonight was not for marketing Fortress. Lion did not want more students, and the more he insisted on limiting enrollment, it seemed, the more parents wanted to send their children to his hagwons.

Lion took a deep breath and smiled.

"I want to thank all of you for attending tonight, and I want to make this clear. I felt entitled to ask you for your very rare free time because I'm concerned about how our students and their peers are doing. Our students at the hagwons—both Exodus and Fortress—enjoy coming to our locations. You can ask them. As you know, I am very fond of your children. I'm grateful for them. However, it's clear to me that they are under too much pressure, and I thought that if all of us could change our mindset, perhaps examine where this pressure is coming from, then perhaps the children could have better lives. I feel certain that they would flourish as well. I'm interested in improving their childhoods, so they can become strong and well-adjusted young adults."

The man scratched his head and sat down. He raised his hand again for a second, then thought better of it and turned to his wife, who pulled down his sleeve to keep him from asking a follow-up.

Sobin and George rolled their eyes. Their eldest two children had been accepted into Cornell and the University of Pennsylvania respectively, but they'd been rejected from other Ivies, where their wealthier White peers had been accepted, although their daughter and son had had far better applicant profiles. Sobin and George had not graduated from Ivy League schools. Sobin had gone to UC Irvine, and George had graduated from Berkeley.

Sobin whispered to her husband, "You'd think that Elder Lion Han would be more forthcoming about what's really going on. Why can't he just admit that Asians have to be much better than everyone else?"

"Leave it alone. He doesn't want to answer it," George said. The guidance counselor at their children's expensive private school had told them that their first two, Cindy and Joe, had a fair shot at the very top schools, and in the end, each had been accepted into at least one Ivy.

Sobin and George's two younger children attended a relatively new private school that catered to mostly wealthy White children and Asians. In their respective grades, there were no Latino or Black children. However, there were enough students in each class whose parents had attended highly selective colleges and universities, and some were known to be very significant donors.

Over time, Sobin and George had learned the mechanics of American college admissions and done as much as they could to boost their children's chances, and even when they knew the system wasn't fair or transparent, each rejection their children had received from the Big Three—Harvard, Yale, and Princeton—had stung, leaving an ugly scar rather than a soft bruise that could heal.

The rejections incensed Sobin and George, who believed that the only unfortunate thing for their beautiful and hardworking children was having been born to parents without an HYP school degree. In his mind, if George had studied harder as a young teenager, then his children could have received HYP offers, especially since they were rich parents.

Knowing now how legacy admissions worked, he would have written big checks each year and dangled even bigger ones if needed. If his older kids had gotten in, he would have donated as much as possible to ensure that the younger ones had their shot. Like her husband, Sobin believed that this was the least a wealthy parent could do without breaking any laws—*What wouldn't a parent do to help their child?* she asked.

For an alumnus, donating generously wasn't bribing. It was entirely legal and desired by the schools since it justified the mounting costs of education, and the generosity of alumni provided financial aid for those who could not pay full freight. Big donations also paid for buildings and important research. Who could argue with that? George and Sobin did not. They would have loved the opportunity to be more generous.

If one of theirs could have attended Harvard, they would have paid tuition for another child. *Buy one, get one free,* George joked to his wife. However, they were not alumni. *To Harvard, Yale, and Princeton, you're a nobody—that's just how it works,* a private college counselor had explained. Unless they were generous billionaires. If they could give, say, eight figures, Harvard might take notice. There were ways to donate significant sums to the schools if you knew someone, but they did not. Besides, to HYP, full tuition for another child was not a significant gift if offered by a nonalum; this was explained to them by people who knew better.

There was no point in arguing about the past, Sobin said. They had two more children who needed to get into Fortress—which never seemed to have open spots—and Sobin had explained to her husband that the two younger ones would need a lot more attention in their essays, because they were not interested in academics. They were good athletes but still wouldn't be recruited by the best schools.

The last thing Sobin and George were going to do was attend this crowded meeting for the most in-demand hagwon in Orange County and offend the owner, Lion Han, who was a do-gooder and idealist.

In the row in front of them, Danbi worried about Anna's chances of getting into Fortress. Of course, she should have known that George and Sobin would attend, but there hadn't been much time to discuss it during her last rendezvous with George. They never had enough time, it seemed. At the thought of him, Danbi sat up straighter, shoulders back, chest out. For her, it was a competition. His wife, Sobin, could not get one of their kids into an HYP, but Danbi felt certain Anna would get into at least Yale or Princeton.

In the past year, almost half the Fortress seniors had been accepted into Ivy League schools and impossible ones like MIT and Stanford, and the majority of them had been offered spots in the most selective schools in the country. Danbi didn't mind admitting that she had the highest ambitions for her child.

Almost eight, Anna could play the "Moonlight Sonata" and read five grades above her level. Once Danbi had been called in and advised to have Anna assessed by a neuropsychologist because, although she was clearly academically gifted, the child had trouble interacting with her peers. "Anna could learn more about social cues," the first-grade teacher had said. "She doesn't get included with the other girls' activities, and clearly Anna would like to have friends."

Danbi thought Mrs. Grace, the hippie primary school teacher at the expensive Montessori school who smiled far too much, was an idiot. Danbi had no friends when she was young, and consequently there'd been no distractions from the horrible culture of little girls and their petty rules of social engagement. Danbi would teach her daughter to excel, and even fight, but in her experience, the most popular children were never the most successful adults. Pleasing everyone was an expensive habit for women. To Danbi, her child didn't have a problem, so she did not bring her to a neuropsychologist.

If a doctor poked around, he would always find a problem. She had read in the Korean newspapers that in America, they gave drugs to children to make them behave. Danbi could not imagine putting chemicals into her own body. She didn't smoke, drink, or take any illegal drugs. Rarely did she swallow an aspirin for a headache.

When she told George what Mrs. Grace had said about Anna, her lover had told her what Sobin had done when their son Harrison was unable to sit still in school. She signed him up for several sports classes until he found basketball, and he made varsity in his sophomore year and loved being on the team. He also liked tennis, but he wasn't ever going to make varsity, so they'd made him focus solely on basketball. Harrison, now a junior in high school, had good grades; his guidance counselor said he'd likely be admitted into a small liberal arts college in New England, thanks in part to his strong basketball skills, but there was no guarantee.

Danbi sat up straight and raised her hand.

She wore an ivory-colored sleeveless dress with a matching cardigan and nude sandals. Around her neck, she wore pearls.

"Elder Jung." Lion bowed. "Do you have a question?"

Danbi stood up, feeling almost nourished by the stares of the men in the room. If it weren't for the fact that she had to get along with more women, she would have dressed differently—more fabric-covered buttons, zippers, and mother-of-pearl snaps—things that made men think of unwrapping her like a gift.

"Elder Han." Danbi bowed and spoke in Korean. "Thank you for your talk. What you said was valuable. We also care very much about our children's happiness."

"Of course," Lion replied in English, "I didn't in any way mean to suggest that parents don't care, or are intentionally hurting their children. There are many sources of pressure: our community, our heritage which prizes education, the schools, their peers, and the colleges themselves. We have to be almost countercultural if we want our children to truly thrive. I called this meeting in the hopes of pointing out that our community, socioeconomic class, culture, and history all seem to demand a kind of unattainable achievement, and it's harming our children. We expect them to do things that we could not have done ourselves."

"But you did," Danbi said. "You finished Princeton in three years. I read about you." She smiled.

Everyone laughed, and Lion bowed his head in defeat.

"But my child is no Oracle of Orange County," she said charmingly in Korean. "However, I'm standing here because I thought the gentleman earlier"—at this point, Danbi turned to the man in the red windbreaker, looked at him, smiled, then bowed slightly, and he returned the smile, his neck reddening with pleasure at her recognition—"I thought his important question should be answered."

"I thought I had answered the question."

"Well, no." Danbi laughed like a flirt, and others laughed with her nervously, taking her side. "You said you wanted to talk about the pressure children feel. However, I want to follow up with the earlier question. Don't the children feel more pressure, not from the myth of Hong Gildong, but rather because they *have* to try harder? Because they have to get better scores than American children?"

"I don't understand your meaning. Our students are American."

"Well, you know what I mean, coming from Korea. Our children are Asian. I've heard the same thing from parents of college-age students, that it's much more difficult for our children to get into the best schools than it is for any other child in America. Apparently it's even harder for South Asian students here, especially if they need financial aid."

"We're not talking about different things. Even if that were true—and I do not think it is—" Lion sighed and started again, realizing that he was angry. "Even if it were true that children of Asian descent have to do better than non-Asian children, the story of Hong Gildong that our generation and previous generations have swallowed will only reinforce the notion that they have no choice but to perform like a superhero because that is what this culture demands. However, as we know, Hong Gildong is not a real person. Our children cannot know everything, create doubles, summon magic, fight better than everyone, and fly through the air.

"This flawed but worthy American project of immigration, reinvention, and multiple chances creates more possibilities, but it requires us to explore different paths in order to have lives of greater purpose."

Frustrated by Lion's idealistic nonsense, Danbi gripped the microphone with both hands and put it close to her mouth. "But many Korean students do get into Ivy League schools. Do those children fly like Hong Gildong? If they do, it's an honest question to ask how our children can also learn to fly so they will be noticed among other children who don't need to fly."

"No. I'm not being clear. I apologize. Each child's acceptance at a college or university is highly individual. If you examined every student who got accepted at Princeton, each application would look different. It isn't like Korea or China, or even Australia, where one of our counselors spent her childhood, where the primary determinant of acceptance or at least a minimum benchmark is a numerical score. Our students who are accepted into Ivy League schools do not fly. We do not teach that. But I'm not here to talk about what we do, I'm here because I wanted to urge us all to think differently, for our children's sakes."

The parents listened carefully, trying to grasp his meaning. It made no sense for a hagwon owner not to take credit for impressive outcomes.

"Our students' achievements have been remarkable, I know that, and for every child that does get into a school of his first choice, there are twenty that do not," Lion insisted. He pushed up his sleeves and took a deep breath. "The point of tonight is that the twenty who do not get in feel terrible about themselves when they shouldn't. They view the college they do get into as a kind of failure or at best a consolation prize, and that is a terrible way to start their higher educational experience, and adulthood."

Danbi opened her mouth to speak again, and Shin touched the side of her hip. "Enough," he whispered. "You have said enough."

"Thank you, Elder Han," she said, handing back the microphone to Mido, who stood waiting near the end of the aisle. Shin smiled at Mido, and she bowed slightly.

❧

"Good evening. My name is Peter Son, and I am the director of Fortress."

The parents sat up straighter and clapped, as if Peter might be able to see their faces and remember who'd smiled at him. They wanted to garner favor for their children.

"Our students at Fortress get excellent results because we have an unfair advantage," he said. "I want to tell you that because it is numerically true that we get an outsized slice of the Ivy League pie for our region. Tonight, by our count, there are five hundred and seventeen parents here." Peter glanced at Yun and Mido, and they nodded, having just given him the number.

"If every one of you had only one child who needed to be admitted to Fortress, we could only take one out of five applicants because we do not accept more than a hundred students per year, and there are only twenty-five students on average for each grade. When we have twenty-five seniors, let's say, spread across several high schools in this large and academically competitive, well-prepared student population, it is very possible for us to help our students get excellent results.

"However, it would be misleading for us to take credit for the fact that our students come from loving families who care immensely about education, for the fact that we have among the most motivated young people, and that the students are willing to do the incredibly difficult work of becoming a desirable applicant while managing their studies, sports, and inner lives."

The parents murmured.

"Your children are asked to sit for an assessment just to be considered for our hagwon. We didn't want to give the exam, but it was easier to explain why a child was not accepted to the families when there was a data point, rather than just saying there is no room. The assessment was a kind of objective measure; however, I want you to know that I would prefer not to do this. I would prefer to have a lottery system, and each year, we argue about this. We feel terrible that we cannot accept every student who wants to study at Fortress."

Peter doubted that this made any of the hopeful parents in the audience feel better, but it was the truth.

"We take some of the best students in Orange County, and in the summers, some of the best students from Seoul have been flying in just for our essay boot camps. So while I believe we may have the strongest teachers and the most effective methods, it shouldn't be a surprise that our hagwon gets among the very best results in California. Now, take that very simple idea and apply it to, let's say Yale, where I spent the first two years of college."

The parents in the audience knew he had gone to Yale, then transferred to Pomona College, but they'd never asked why.

"If Yale has thirteen hundred seats for the class of 2009, and if twenty thousand students apply, then 93.5 percent of the applicants will be unable to attend. These schools want geographic diversity, which means your children are also competing against children from each of the fifty states and every country in the world. Your children come from Orange County, one of the strongest applicant pools in the United States. The 93.5 percent who are not accepted are already from a pool of self-selected accomplished students who felt that acceptance was possible. I've seen extraordinary individuals of every race, class, and background get rejected from these highly selective schools. The admissions committee of each school considers numerous factors in each applicant's evaluation. Fortress gets better results because our students were already selective. Your children may not be considered remarkable in their senior year from the viewpoint of an admissions committee, but they could become remarkable in a more meaningful way later. Children develop at different rates."

The parents shook their heads in irritation, incensed at the suggestion that their children might not be remarkable. They were visibly offended.

Lion moved toward the standing microphone, and Peter stepped aside.

"You're looking at the problem in the wrong way," Lion said gently to the audience as if he were speaking to a math student. No longer did he care if they got upset, but he didn't want Peter to take the heat alone. "If you make your child into the perfect object that these schools want to purchase, then you might make the sale. However, will you get what you want?

"I wish I could tell you how many times I've heard the term 'return on investment' being applied to young humans," Lion said, and his voice broke. Yun, still seated by the stage, inched her chair toward her husband, never having seen him like this. She touched her growing belly, not knowing if she should do something.

Lion spoke into the microphone. "Many of our children, out of the goodness of their hearts and because they love their parents, will do as well as they can. They will try to get that trophy to earn your love or to feel good about themselves, but it will never be enough.

"I've seen wonderful students get accepted into top schools, and once they get in, they break down, no longer understanding why they're there at all. Once the schools have accepted your child, they can only do so much to help him or her flourish. Forget the acceptance rates or the average salaries of majors, I want you to look at attrition rates and the mental health data. If your child is eighteen and over, the schools will not even tell you if your child is not doing well, and it could be too late.

"If your children live in the dorms, they no longer have Mom waking them up, or Grandma making their breakfast, or a hagwon teacher asking about their calculus final. They are on their own. They have gotten into the school, but many of them didn't do it for themselves. What's worse, if they didn't get into the school that they thought they wanted or feel they should have gotten into, they might even feel like they failed you and themselves.

"If you're just focused on what it takes to get in, you have the wrong question, the wrong tests, the wrong child.

"I am pleading with you to consider not the needs of the buyer or the seller. I am pleading with you to remember that your child is a young human being, and that the purpose of an education is to transform his life into who he is meant to be. He needs an education. He needs to learn how to solve problems. She needs to ask good questions and to be critical. She needs to value her judgment. If your children can do those things, they will be able to survive and flourish. No one needs to be a superhero. Our children should not have to save us."

Lion looked at them, arms by his sides.

"There is a crisis in this country and in the country where many of you were born. The crisis is in our education and what it is meant to do. Having a degree from the Big Three or any of the SKY universities will not protect our children from harm. You know of many stories of people who graduated from these schools who did not have a safe and perfect life. I am asking you to consider at least the anecdotal evidence each of you has to disprove the theory that an elite education will create a successful life."

A balding man in the front row handed Lion a clean handkerchief, and Lion wiped his eyes.

The woman in a skirt suit next to him gestured to Mido for the microphone.

"Why can't you just increase the size of your hagwon? I'm sure in this room, there are bankers who'd give you loans to buy bigger buildings and hire more people. Even our church raised $6 million for a new learning center. There's money in our community for our kids—"

Lion smiled.

"Thank you for the handkerchief," he said to the man, then turned to the woman. "If it were just a simple formula of providing test materials and the same training, then we would have done that already. We will keep our hagwon at this size. We just wanted to appeal to you to consider the humanity of your children."

Lion glanced at Peter, and he stepped in front of the microphone as naturally as if they were performing onstage at Rascals.

"The highly selective colleges and universities want to build a class made up of all different types of students, including scholars, class presidents, debaters, athletes, actors, musicians, journalists, and poets, from every place on the planet. However, just because the highly selective school that your child or you may have dreamed of accepts only one student from your child's high school, we cannot treat our students as objects to shape and bring to the market. The market theory is wrong because they're young humans, minors who can't even sign a contract. Their brains aren't even fully formed. As the director of a hagwon, I see how they are suffering under this weight.

"It's not one group's fault. It's that children are being asked to respond to market demands and to believe that life is only about scarcity and musical chairs," Peter said. "This cannot be right."

George stood up and spoke without the microphone.

"The students in Korea work much harder than our kids. They have to go to hagwons almost every day, some starting as early as kindergarten, and not just once a week. Our American kids are just lazy."

Everyone laughed except for the tutors. Lion looked out at the audience, and he shook his head.

BOOK V

January 2006–May 2007

Compressed modernity is a civilizational condition in which economic, political, social, and/or cultural changes occur in an extremely condensed manner with respect to both time and space, and in which the dynamic coexistence of mutually disparate historical and social elements leads to the construction and reconstruction of a highly complex and fluid social system. Compressed modernity can be manifested at various levels of human existence—that is, personhood, family, secondary organizations, urban spaces, societal units (including civil society, nation, etc.), and, not least important, the global society. At each of these levels, compressed modernity necessitates people's lives to be managed intensely, intricately, and flexibly in order to remain normally integrated with the rest of society. Compressed modernity is thereby subjected to a mutual escalation effect among such different levels.

—Chang Kyung-Sup

1
Trades

Seoul
January 2006

For years, Mrs. Im, the housekeeper, had understood the relationship between Sonya and the Chairman. More aunt than servant, Mrs. Im was devoted to her generous employer, who had entered the Mun household as a young bride. As lady of the house, Sonya was nothing like the Chairman's late wife—a capricious daughter of a former cabinet member who could not be gracious to anyone she felt was below her social class.

From the very start, the housekeeper took to Sonya, admiring the young former secretary's fine manners and humble demeanor despite her natural beauty and excellent education. In the ensuing years, Sonya changed little regardless of the rise in her station. If anything, the more she was given, the more she gave away.

Sonya treated everyone fairly and with great consideration, remembering the birthdays, weddings, funerals, and illnesses of those who worked for the family. To be connected to the Chairman's household was to be protected under Sonya's umbrella of concern.

Mrs. Im had never finished high school, but she was more capable than some of the Chairman's brightest employees who'd received MBAs from abroad. She missed nothing, especially the wants and needs of her employers.

With so much warmth between them, the Chairman and Sonya did not seem to be former boss and secretary, nor were they like father-in-law and daughter-in-law. And lacking the casual boredom often induced by the expectation of an eternal bond, they would not be mistaken for husband and wife, either.

In the eyes of a sensitive observer, the two were undeniably lovers, connected by yearning and fear of loss. Exquisite manners and honorific language covered the public interactions between the Chairman and Sonya like a fine silk gauze. At home, it was possible to measure the physical space between them, which was closer than that between Sonya and her husband.

Like his uncle, Yong-gil was a stickler about language, and although he was sufficiently fair to the household staff as well as to his employees, he could be cool and rigid, unable to garner their affection. His business competence shielded him from criticism, and his formal tone kept him at a distance from almost everyone except his sons.

On Friday evening, he came home to change before heading out again. At the door, Mrs. Im greeted him and hung up his raincoat.

"Good evening, Deacon Im."

Yong-gil removed his black cap-toe Oxford dress shoes. She picked up his shoes and returned them to the right shelf in the president's private shoe closet, then withdrew his bespoke leather slippers from the bottom shelf. Mrs. Im knelt on the floor to place the slippers in the appropriate direction for his stocking feet.

"Is everyone home?"

"The Chairman and Madam are here, but the young masters will not be at dinner. Madam said you would not be dining at home—"

"That is correct. I want to shower and change. I have a work dinner."

Mrs. Im, older than the Chairman by a few months, a church deacon of two decades, and mother of three grown children, was not a modern person with liberal moral and romantic sensibilities; however, she knew well what it was like to be married to a philanderer. Mrs. Im was not fooled. The president did not have a work dinner. On Friday evenings, he went to room salons. Over the years, Mrs. Im had met no less than half a dozen of his mistresses who had barged into the house to confront Sonya.

The Chairman's nephew was ungrateful and overly entitled, blind to his true riches. Unlike the uncle, who preferred the self-made individual over those born rich, the nephew, who had grown up in relative privilege, was a playboy who remembered to say please and thank you to his employees but could fire the household driver through his corporate secretary for being a few minutes late. Never did he dole out any punishment himself. Always, he asked his secretary, Mr. Yi, whom everyone called the Sword, to do the distasteful deed.

After Yong-gil was promoted to president of Mun Realty at forty-five years old, bypassing several senior members of the company, rather than being considerate to the executives who had helped to build the successful company, he terminated those who didn't praise the decision. Then he hired his smartest friends from university, shedding anyone whose background and attitude he deemed unsuitable for his vision of the future of Mun Realty.

Unlike the Chairman, who disdained hostess bars and room salons, the president preferred the most selective ones. To the women who worked there, the president was nice-looking, wealthy, and aloof. He wore designer clothes. Naturally they fell in love with him. In hotel rooms, he made beautiful promises, and when the more ambitious girlfriends came to the house to realize their dreams, Mrs. Im was their first point of contact.

In her office, while Sonya met with each young woman, served tea or coffee in fine china, and disabused her of any illusions about her husband, Yong-gil, Mrs. Im chatted with the cook in the kitchen and waited to be called to show the guest out. After she cleared the tea tray, the cook would eat the untouched biscuits and leave the chocolates for Mrs. Im.

The housekeeper was on Sonya's side. For births, deaths, weddings, holidays, and trips, Sonya gave employees an envelope of cash to mark the occasion. When she went to a famed bakery to buy treats for the family, she brought back as many for the staff. Everyone was equal.

Years earlier, even before the boys were born, Sonya discovered Mrs. Im crying in the pantry. When she learned that Mrs. Im's oldest son had a fight at school and had broken another child's arm, requiring payment of his hospital bills and a legal settlement, Sonya advanced her the full amount without telling the Chairman's wife or Mrs. Im's husband, who worked as one of the two family drivers.

Mrs. Im would never tell a soul what she knew about the Chairman and Sonya, including her own husband, because when he drank, he talked too much. Life had been fair enough to Mrs. Im, except for a troublesome husband, who was not all bad, and she found joy in the accomplishments and good lives of her children, each of whom had finished college, been hired for a respectable job, and married a nice person. She was a grandmother of three children, and each day before work, she went to Myeong-dong Cathedral to pray for her family and the Mun household.

As long as her husband did not bring home any diseases and didn't get into any big trouble, Mrs. Im didn't care about the cheating and the drinking. None of it was very serious. Men did foolish things, and he was too old to change. Her son and two daughters took her side always, so if her husband left her for another woman, at least she would have the love of her children and money of her own. More than once, Sonya had told Mrs. Im that if she ever needed a place to live, she could have her pick of the rooms in the servants' quarters.

Although Mrs. Im had been in love with her husband when she married, she had never liked sex very much and couldn't imagine why people carried on the way they did for love. However, even at their advanced age, she felt that men needed it more, and it was better that the Chairman was with Sonya, rather than marrying another woman, which would mean another possible headache for her and the staff, who liked things the way they were.

Yong-gil had finished work early, eaten gukbap near his office, then practiced at the golf range for an hour. He intended to head to Sticks & Stones, but wanted to go home to shower before meeting his friends at the members-only room salon. Yong-gil was smitten with Boram, a new girl, a former beauty contestant and trainee for a girl band. Last weekend, she and another trainee had done an adorable dance number for him and his friends from college who were also CEOs.

A man who loved clothes, Yong-gil didn't want to wear a suit or golf attire to the room salon. On weekends, he wanted to look like a wealthy boyfriend, and he had purchased several new pieces of clothing on a recent business trip to Tokyo. "In that jacket, you look like you're in your thirties," the saleswoman in Ginza had said.

"Would you like something to drink?" Mrs. Im asked. "Tea or a soft drink?"

"No thank you, Deacon Im," he said. "Is the Chairman in his office?"

"I believe so."

"I suppose they will have dinner soon?"

"Madam asked for dinner to be served in an hour and a half."

"Where is my wife?"

"Should I get her for you?" Mrs. Im asked, knowing that the Chairman's bedroom door was closed, and Sonya could be in there with him. Mrs. Im didn't know if the door was locked, but it didn't matter because once a room was closed, she would not disturb anyone.

"Thank you, Deacon Im," he said, before heading to his room. From the closet, he pulled out his new black jacket, a black T-shirt, and a pair of French jeans and laid them on the bed. Cassie, a college girl who worked at another VIP room salon, told him that he looked incredible in his jeans and black ankle boots from Australia.

In front of the closet mirror, he inspected how smart he looked in his pin-striped suit. Before getting in the shower, he decided to greet his uncle. Earlier they had spoken on the phone, but his uncle liked to see him each day and get a brief report on how things were going at the company.

Yong-gil passed his wife's office, its door open, and stuck his head in. The room was empty. He walked into her bedroom, but she wasn't there. He passed the den, then stopped at the Chairman's suite, where the doors were closed. He knocked lightly, then turned the doorknob, which wouldn't budge. Curious, Yong-gil put his ear to the door, and he heard his uncle clear his throat.

"Uncle, are you all right?" Yong-gil asked. "Do you have a cold?"

The Chairman looked over at Sonya and put his finger to his lips. He had just finished undressing her, and she was seated on his bed, quiet, pale, her eyes wide with alarm.

With both hands, the Chairman stroked Sonya's bare shoulders, admiring the elegance of her frail beauty. He felt little anxiety at being discovered by his nephew. In fact, he found himself more aroused. What could his nephew do? The Chairman believed that Yong-gil was a fine businessman but wasn't astute enough to value people correctly. An exceptional businessman knew the true value of his assets and would never part with them.

Yong-gil knocked again, this time more quietly. He took a deep breath, and he could inhale the tuberose of his wife's perfume. She was in there with him.

Sonya was afraid to move. She remained still as if frozen, refusing to breathe, even. The Chairman held her gently by the shoulders, and he didn't answer his nephew's knocks.

The large doors were thick, paneled with Macassar ebony, and their twin brass handles heavy. Only Sonya had the key to the Chairman's suite. Even Mrs. Im didn't have one.

Still standing by the bed, the Chairman moved his hands across Sonya's supple body, and she took a deep, long breath. He didn't care what Yong-gil thought.

Mrs. Im stood at the end of the hallway behind the floral arrangement on the center table in the foyer. She watched him move away from the Chairman's room and return to his room, where he showered and put on his new clothes before heading to Sticks & Stones.

2
Terms

Sticks & Stones, a members-only room salon, occupied the basement and subbasement of a six-story office building in Gangnam. The narrow, unassuming entrance was hardly noticeable to passersby. The white door, located between a bespoke tailor and a jewelry store specializing in men's watches, opened to a short hallway leading to another door and a narrow staircase that went down only to the basement.

Behind a set of oak doors, there was an elegant, paneled reception area, well lit and filled with fresh flowers and candles. The manager greeted President Yong-gil Mun with a deep bow.

"President Mun, your guests are already in the room," said the manager, an elegant thirty-five-year-old woman, her hair in a tight bun and wearing a well-tailored black skirt suit. "We can send Miss Kim Boram in at any time. She has been asking about you."

Yong-gil cocked his head and remembered that he was supposed to meet two of his friends from school, a city government official and a banker. Neither could afford these places, and Yong-gil never minded picking up the tab. Both had done him favors relating to work.

"Can you send Boram and two others for my guests?"

"Of course," the manager said.

After a few drinks, the three men separated, each paired with a hostess. Yong-gil took Boram upstairs to a nice room. He felt like talking. No doubt she would tell him some made-up story about hospital bills, school loans, or a younger brother who wanted to study abroad, expecting Yong-gil to rescue her.

In the room, Boram asked if he would like to take a shower first, and Yong-gil said no.

"Here, sit down," he said.

Boram, a gorgeous twenty-three-year-old from Daegu, appeared confused. A week before, President Mun had been very clear that he wanted to be her lover. He had texted her twice this week suggesting as much. The manager had made a point of making sure that Boram had no other appointments for this Friday evening.

She sat on the edge of the bed, her legs tucked behind her, as if waiting to serve. Her ivory one-piece dress, a copy of a French designer's, flattered her slim figure and long legs.

Boram was a bright young woman. She came from a middle-class family without any tragedy. The mistakes she had made were simple ones: She wanted to be an actress and had spent money on plastic surgery, cosmetic dentistry, acting hagwons, glamorous clothing, and her new life in Seoul, requiring loans from friends, then, later, from disreputable men who charged exorbitant interest rates.

Her family didn't know about the loans, and Boram, able to command a very high fee for flirting and sex, thought this was not the worst way to repay her loans while building her career. In two years, she had been roughed up only twice, and Sticks & Stones was a much better place to work than others. If President Mun or someone like him could support her career development, Boram still believed that she had a shot at becoming a television actor.

"You seem sad," she said.

"You are observant," Yong-gil said.

"Do you want me to sing you a song?"

"No."

"Shall I do a dance? I learned a new routine—"

"No."

"Do you want me to come to you?" she asked.

"Why do you do this?" he asked. Yong-gil could not stop thinking about his wife having sex with his uncle, and he wondered if all women were whores. Nothing could have prepared him for this. True, he had not seen it with his own eyes. It was possible that he was wrong to assume it; however, it would explain the gifts of stock. And there had been costly jewelry, fur coats, then the car. His uncle had bought the very best things for Sonya and granted her every request, even funded her business in California. His wife must have been sleeping with him all this time. How long? he wondered.

She untucked her beautiful legs and stretched them out. Not knowing if he wanted her to be girlish or vulgar, she felt uncertain. It was easier when a man wanted you to take off your clothes.

Boram had been with many men; however, not as many as the other girls she worked with. In a diary, she wrote down the names of all the men and details about them. In two years, she had slept with ninety-two men. Nearly all of them had been remarkably similar. Men wanted flattery, adoration, and for her to appear innocent.

Several had slapped her in the face or spanked her. Only twice, she had been beaten so badly that she had to go to the hospital and miss work for a month. Some men, she learned, liked hitting women, and she had no idea why since she wasn't the sort to provoke them. It was not in her nature to talk back or be rude.

A few of them she had liked. Nearly all were married. The single ones would never date her seriously but sometimes sought her out so they could avoid paying, she figured out eventually. None of them would provide for her, and the manager explained that Boram was not good with scams, as other girls were. *You're very pretty but not clever. You should try to save your money and quit if you really want to be an actor*, another girl had told her.

"What can I do to make you feel less sad?" Boram asked Yong-gil.

"Take off your dress."

Boram did as she was told.

"Take off the rest."

"Yes, President Mun."

The young woman was visually perfect. She was exactly his type—long, slim, dark hair natural, flat-waisted, and pale. He stared at her full breasts, not minding that they were implants. The doctor had done a nice job, he thought.

He removed his trousers and allowed her to put a condom on his erection. Yong-gil knew that even young girls who looked clean carried diseases.

"How can I make you happy?"

Yong-gil frowned, wanting to push her down on the bed. He was not like this normally, but he thought it would be better not to speak because he felt cruel. She was dumb, and he wanted to be with a woman who could talk to him. He wanted an explanation of what was happening at home. Boram couldn't give him that. She couldn't even seduce him properly.

"Mr. President, you're so big," she said.

All the girls said this to him, and Yong-gil didn't know if he was actually big or if this was something that whores said to their johns.

"Don't talk," he said, and pushed her gently on her back.

Yong-gil tried to forget his wife and uncle but couldn't. He recalled his wife's nude body the first time he saw it on their wedding night. Sonya was as beautiful as a goddess. She had been a virgin, and until a few hours ago, he'd believed that she still loved him.

He had cheated on his wife many times, but only with women he'd paid. Sonya was still an extraordinary beauty. Even now, Sonya was prettier than most of these girls. The idea of her in his uncle's bed was disgusting. He felt like killing them both.

"President Mun, you're hurting me," she said, the extreme force of his thrusts painful to her. He held her wrists too tightly.

Quickly he finished and told her to get the fuck out.

❧

Sonya did not come to breakfast. Yong-gil ate alone with his uncle.

"Uncle, can we speak after breakfast?"

"Why can't we speak now?"

Yong-gil glanced at the door separating the dining room from the kitchen, where Mrs. Im and the cook were working. Two maids were cleaning the apartments, and the driver was having his breakfast in the kitchen.

"Where is Sonya?" Yong-gil asked the Chairman, feeling foolish not knowing where his own wife was.

"She had a meeting with a lawyer."

"Why?"

"Something about the nail salon and her green card."

The Chairman got up and headed to his office.

"Do you want to talk there?"

Yong-gil followed him.

❧

The Chairman sat down in the armchair facing the view of the river. Yong-gil closed the doors behind him and sat opposite his uncle.

"Why did you give my wife the stock? Every year her ownership grows. I own only two percent of the company even though I'm the chief executive officer. I work at Mun Realty every single day."

"Every share Sonya receives will ultimately go to the boys. You know that."

"Yes, but every share I have will go to them, too. Why can't you give the shares to them directly?"

"They are too young. They don't know enough about life. They have so much more to learn about how to run the business."

"They are very wise young men," Yong-gil said, defending his sons.

"Yes. So far, it seems that way."

"And me?" Yong-gil asked. "Why not me?"

"I think I haven't taught you everything about life. You have more to learn."

Yong-gil said nothing, wondering if he might be wrong to suspect something untoward between his uncle and his wife. It seemed more absurd the more he thought about it.

"What do I have to learn? What could Sonya possibly know more than me about the business?"

"Where were you last night?" the Chairman asked.

"At a work dinner," Yong-gil said.

"You were at Sticks & Stones."

"Yes."

"It wasn't for work."

"No."

"You were having sex with a prostitute who could come to our house. You could get some room salon girl pregnant, who could make claims upon your property. You could get a filthy disease, which could be passed to Sonya. In all these years, you have brought shame to me and Sonya with your inability to control yourself. I cannot risk my company being exposed to illegitimate heirs or lawsuits from hookers. We've spoken about this. Have we not? When will you learn?"

Yong-gil could say nothing. For once, he'd thought he had the upper hand, but immediately his uncle had made him the fool.

"Your father was unable to control himself with cheap bar girls. Now you. I thought you'd be different. You're a smart businessman, but you leave your family wide open with these indiscretions. You can be blackmailed by any of these women. You're lucky that Sonya has been so patient and wise about how she handles them. Do you know how often you've made your wife, the mother of your sons, cry?"

Yong-gil stared at the wall behind his uncle, trying to control himself.

"She'll own most of the company by the time I die. However, she'll never divorce you, and the company will go to the boys. It should go to the boys equally unless they prove to be unworthy. You will remain president, and when I'm gone, you'll be the chairman. This was my solution to your addiction to whores. You will always be my nephew—that doesn't change."

"She wants to be in California. Why can't I send her there if I make her so miserable?"

"We need her at home. She is the lady of the house."

"Can't you get married again?"

"What?"

"Get a new lady of the house. My wife would rather be in California. Isn't that why she bought that business and obtained a green card?"

"She needs to be here," the Chairman said, seeing the defiance in his nephew's eyes. Then he understood. Yong-gil knew something. "Her job is to take care of her own family. Your job is to take care of the company."

"I am taking care of the company."

"You need to be more careful with those women. So far, you've been lucky."

"I've never fallen for a bar girl scam. I'm not an idiot."

"Only an idiot says he's not an idiot."

"Uncle—"

"You are my brother's son. You are my heir. However, you will be my heir through Sonya and the boys because you've left yourself exposed. This meeting is over."

Yong-gil got up and bowed before heading to work.

❧

In the evening, he went straight to his wife's bedroom without changing out of his work clothes. Sonya was at her dressing table in her nightgown and robe. Getting ready to sleep, she was combing her hair. He was wearing his navy pin-striped suit.

"How are you?" Yong-gil asked.

"Did you have dinner?"

"Yes. I've already eaten. Thank you." He brushed a stray wisp of hair away from her face and moved closer to her. Yong-gil touched the yellow silk chemise robe, and Sonya froze.

"You look pretty in this. I have a beautiful wife," he said to the reflection in the mirror.

"Are you all right? I heard you were upset about the stock."

"I guess he tells you everything."

"I don't understand."

Yong-gil went to the door and locked it.

"I'd like to stay here tonight. Is that fine with you?"

Sonya examined his eyes.

"Have you been drinking?"

"Not a drop." Yong-gil ran his hands across her shoulders. "You feel like my wife."

"Why are you being strange?"

He removed his jacket and loosened his tie. Taking her hand, he placed it on his crotch and smiled like a naughty child. Sonya withdrew her hand as if she'd touched something too hot.

"I don't feel well," she said, doing her best to keep her composure.

"Don't lie to me."

Yong-gil buried his face in her neck. The faint scent of white flowers overwhelmed him. Without a word, he slid the silk robe off her shoulders, and Sonya averted her eyes as he traced the outline of her breasts beneath the yellow nightgown. He pulled her closer to him, unable to see her anxious expression.

She murmured calmly, "I'd rather another—"

"Tonight. I'd rather tonight."

He pulled up her nightgown and moved her against the closet door. When she began to cry, he picked her up and laid her gently on the bed. He sat beside her and stroked her hair and kissed her brow sweetly. She had been like this their first time and had needed to be coaxed. He took off her nightgown, and she closed her eyes.

As he made love to her, he whispered, "My wife. My wife."

3

Possession

The Chairman knocked on her bedroom door.

"Come in."

"Your door was locked last night."

Sonya was sitting in her armchair by the window. Feeling cold, she'd put on her beige cashmere turtleneck twinset and gray woolen slacks. Small gray pearls in her ears. Calm and glorious, the Han River shimmered in the winter-morning sun.

A silver breakfast tray rested on the ottoman. Sonya picked up her coffee cup, not knowing what to say. Her bags were packed and stored in the closet. She had finished her makeup.

"Yong-gil left without eating. I was alone this morning." The Chairman frowned.

"I'm sorry."

"Are you not feeling well? I knocked last night, but there was no answer, so I thought you fell asleep. I waited."

"He locked the door."

The Chairman looked confused.

"He was here last night?"

"I didn't know what to do."

"You let him touch you?"

"I tried to tell him I didn't feel well."

"Why didn't you fight him?"

"I couldn't—"

He raised his right hand and slapped her. The Chairman pulled back in surprise, never having hit a woman before.

Sonya covered her mouth and left cheek where he'd struck her.

"I'm going to California today."

"No, no. You can't go."

"I already bought my ticket."

The Chairman checked the knot of his blue silk necktie and swallowed, feeling sick at the thought of his nephew being with her. Then he saw her. She was holding her face with her hands and crying.

"I'm sorry. I was wrong to hit you. I wasn't thinking. I thought he didn't come by anymore."

"He hadn't. For so many years. Has it been twenty?" All morning she'd been trying to puzzle out what had happened. "I don't know why he did that. It wasn't my idea. Surely—"

"Of course. I'm sorry I—" The Chairman couldn't admit to her that Yong-gil might know.

Sonya knew that he felt awful about hitting her. He shouldn't have, but it didn't hurt. Growing up, she'd been beaten by her parents, employers, and kids at school. To protect her siblings, she'd fought bullies. A number of times, landlords, store owners, and other creditors had taken their shot at the eldest child of debtors.

One landlord's son, a pale gnome of a man who would squeeze her rear end with his stubby hands whenever he passed behind her, had offered to forgive months of overdue rent for sex. "I'd erase all the debts and get you another six months since you're a virgin," he'd said, smiling sweetly. Sonya, who was in college then, ran to the church to beg the nuns and priests for a loan, which she ended up paying back by tutoring.

It was unfair to have someone put their hands on you and try to cause you harm. Mostly they were trying to make her afraid, and Sonya refused. That was the trick, and if you could withstand the physical pain, they couldn't hurt you inside. Even if someone tried to kill you, you could still decide what you thought about it. You could always tell yourself your own story and keep your dignity.

They picked on her, but Sonya was the girl who fought back in her own way, and no one had ever hurt her so badly that she had to go to the hospital. It was only humiliating if she cared about the person who caused her pain or the people who witnessed her shame.

After she started working for the Chairman, no one had ever hit her or even tried to make her feel bad. He had protected her from everything she had endured before. She never thought he would hit her.

His slap was the worst because she adored him. The Chairman was her protector, provider, defender, deliverer, and lover.

When Yong-gil was on top of her last night, she had pretended to be somewhere else, anywhere else. He was her husband, and she could not tell him what she felt for his uncle. As he kept repeating "My wife, my wife," something he had not said since their wedding night, Sonya wondered if her husband wanted to make love to her, or if he was a dog pissing on a spot to mark his territory. She had always belonged to the Chairman. He had told her to marry his nephew, and she had obeyed him, because she owed him everything.

"I have to go now."

"No, you can't leave. If you go, you cannot return."

Sonya turned toward the closet. She pulled out her overcoat and the two large suitcases.

"This was always wrong. I am sorry."

"Sonya, you cannot—"

He embraced her, preventing her from moving.

"I forbid you to go," he whispered.

"Hong-gyun-shi."

Surprised, he looked at her, so rarely did she call him by his name.

"Let me go. Please."

He put his trembling hands on her shoulders, and he thought hard about what he could do.

❧

The flight felt brief because she slept through most of it, and when she woke, she felt grateful for the respite from the worries and sadness that occupied her waking thoughts. Bo was waiting for her at arrivals. He picked up her two large, heavy cases like they were knapsacks and guided her to the car. Sonya felt strangely alert and light. The sun always felt brighter in California.

"Aunt, it's so good to see you."

"You look well," she said, taking his arm.

"Don't I?" He smiled at her.

"You're in love?" she guessed.

"Maybe?"

"What?" Sonya felt suddenly joyful. Helen's first child was happy. "I want to hear more. Is there a wedding coming up?"

"No, no, no!" Bo laughed. "It's only been a few months. I still have to get my doctorate."

"Oh, yes, of course." Sonya smiled. "But you can't blame your aunt for being excited. Tell me about her."

"Her name's Priscilla."

"Like Elvis's wife?"

"Lion said the same thing." Bo grinned. "She's a graduate student in psychology. It's been nice to have a friend in the program. We go to the movies and grade papers together." He did not mention that they were lovers now and he could see himself marrying her. It was too soon, of course, and neither of them was in a rush.

"Now let me focus on my driving," he said. "I have an important passenger in my car."

"Nice excuse," she said. This sounded like the Bo she had known as a child—thoughtful, measured, and quietly confident. Somehow he had returned to himself, and Sonya was grateful. She thought of Helen. More than anything, she wanted her sister to know that her boy was well.

Each morning, after she read her Bible, Sonya prayed for every member of her family, and when she thought of Bo, she could not forget searching for him at his rented rooms when he was studying for his college entrance exams. He had failed to get into Yonsei repeatedly but refused to apply elsewhere. She remembered taking him to eat tonkatsu, worried sick that he might not listen to her plan for him to go to America.

Had the Chairman allowed Bo to stay at the house, would he have passed the exam and remained in Korea? she wondered. What would that life look like? Would it have been a better one? She didn't think so.

Her sons had achieved the scores they needed on their CSATs on their first try, and at every stage of the application process, private coordinators and tutors had guided them to their destination. Bo had had less of that kind of care. He'd lived, studied, and slept in that tiny room at the gosiwon, eating instant food from the mart and attending classes at the hagwons. If he had been at her house without the need to cook, do laundry, or figure out his transportation, Sonya felt certain that he would have gotten in. At least on the second try.

"I still feel terrible that I couldn't take better care of you when you were studying for Yonsei—"

"You took better care of me than my own folks."

"Your parents were in Sydney, and they asked me to—"

"I know they were working. It's not their fault. It was my own stubborn decision to try to get into Yonsei. It's no one's fault but mine."

"I still don't understand why you wanted to go there," she said, laughing.

"I think I picked it because my father had gone to Seoul National, and your sons wanted to go to Korea University, so I applied to Yonsei. The Y in SKY. It isn't a very good reason."

"Really?"

"When I was younger, I used to go to the Yonsei campus, and I'd imagine myself being a student there. I thought if I got in, I'd get one of those Yonsei jackets that men wear, and I thought I might belong in Korea if I had something like that."

Sonya smiled. It was the logic of a child, but it made sense.

Bo didn't mention that he'd bought a bright-blue Yonsei T-shirt, which was still in its cellophane wrapper at the bottom of a drawer. If he'd gotten the score needed for admission, he had promised himself that he could wear it, and if he had been accepted, he would have bought the Yonsei jacket and schoolbag. He would have covered his body with logos. Whenever he saw men wearing the jackets, he'd felt a pang of envy. Those thoughts embarrassed him now.

Sonya turned in her seat and beamed at him proudly. "In a couple of years, you are going to have a PhD. I will call you Dr. Koh. My nephew will have a *baksa*—the first in our family. You will have raised our family in the world. My parents didn't even finish high school."

Bo smiled and continued to drive.

⁂

Sonya's jet lag was always worse on the second day. The day after she arrived, she roused herself enough to go to Rose Salon and sat behind the counter with her brother-in-law. The salon was full of customers, with only one empty chair, and every technician was occupied. It had been almost a year since her last visit.

John got her a large cup of brewed coffee from the café next door instead of the instant kind from the back room. He wanted to do something for her. She didn't touch the blueberry muffin he'd bought for her.

"How is your family?" he asked. "Is the Chairman well?"

Sonya nodded, wondering when she would have to return. Sitting on a plastic folding chair in a strip mall nail salon was preferable to living in a luxury apartment in Apgujeong. She couldn't go back. When her husband had come to her room, it had dawned on her that she could never be okay with this arrangement. The Chairman would not allow her to divorce Yong-gil, and he would not marry her. If she stayed, nothing would change. Every path seemed closed.

If she returned to Seoul, how could she live with the Chairman and Yong-gil? How could she move out and not live with the Chairman? She felt sick missing him. Since her arrival, she would stare at any door in the room and think that soon, he would send for her.

"Your boys? How are Seungman and Jiman?"

"They're both working for the Chairman and report to their father, and I think Seungman might be the president when my husband retires, which won't be anytime soon."

"That makes sense."

"He's the one that pays attention to details. And he likes to be in charge."

John smiled. "You must be so proud of them. They've grown up so nicely."

Sonya picked up the paper bag with the blueberry muffin and held it. In her palm, the bag felt heavy and oily.

The boys had to turn out well. That had been her job: to love her boys and raise two heirs. Sonya had done everything in her power to make sure that their path was secure, and they had been willing to go along. She was grateful for that.

Even with extraordinary sums of money, two educated parents, and every necessary connection, their lives could have gone awry. She had friends in her situation whose kids had suffered—poor decisions, illnesses, sadness. There were hundreds of variables that could have spoiled every good intention and effort. Each morning, Sonya prayed for protection over her family. Thus far the Lord had answered her prayers and favored her children, despite her terrible sins. She felt certain the bill was going to come due. From the moment she started packing the suitcases in Seoul, she had prayed for forgiveness and absolution.

Helen's children would never inherit a company worth hundreds of millions of dollars, yet they were purposeful and upright.

"Are you well?" John asked. She seemed troubled. He wanted to go through the books with her, but she had no interest in talking about the salon, which had been profitable each year. He had been putting aside all the net income in an interest-bearing business account, but she never asked for anything.

"I keep thinking of my sister." Sonya started to cry. "She missed so many things, and I wish I could see her."

John found himself unable to speak. He looked out the glass door. The parking lot was busy with activity, and he imagined driving to Garden Grove to Mrs. Chung's. Behind the counter, Helen would be busy helping a customer. She'd smile at him and tell him to wait. John closed his eyes, and he could see her bright face, how her eyes shone with warmth in the presence of others, how much she cared for her children and him. Her death was his fault, John thought, because he'd made her work so hard. He could never say it, but he believed this.

John picked up the black ledgers.

"Would you like to talk about the books?"

"I'm grateful that you and Yun's mother are running this salon so well."

"What would you like to do with this business? I know you were considering living here when Helen—"

"When Helen was alive, I thought I'd live here because I wanted to be with her as much as I could. I find living difficult without her. Especially now." Sonya said this even though she sensed that it would be unfeeling. No doubt John was missing her more, but he looked healthy enough. Inside, Sonya wanted to die without her. If she were gone, the Chairman and the boys would miss her, but her husband would be fine, she thought. He could remarry a younger, beautiful woman, who would take better care of him than she did.

John opened the books to show her the income column and the clipped stack of bank statements.

"You have a great deal of profit," he said.

She took a deep breath, shook her head briskly as if to erase the dark thoughts inside. "We should expand," she said. "Maybe get another location."

4
Limits

Sonya's broker called the landlord of the Rose Salon space and made an offer. With her savings, Sonya bought the building in Buena Park, and with the profits from Rose Salon, she decided to expand to a second location in Anaheim. DH negotiated the purchase and sale agreements as well as the lease for the new space. After the closing, Sonya took her nephew to lunch at an Italian restaurant in Anaheim that the seller's lawyer recommended. "Calamari, lobster ravioli, braised beef. Can't go wrong," the lawyer said, and asked his assistant to get them an early table.

DH ordered a number of their famed dishes, and the waiter cocked his head at the two thin Koreans, wondering how they'd eat all this food. Sonya shrugged and smiled.

"We'll take home whatever we don't eat," she said, and the waiter left them.

"Nice job today." She switched back to Korean.

"Thank you," he replied in English. He understood everything she said, but his Korean vocabulary was more limited than Bo's or Mido's. He grinned. "I was trying to impress you."

"You did. You are impressive," she said in English.

At the closing, DH had been measured, organized, and clear. The seller's counsel had taken the young lawyer seriously, but in Sonya's mind, DH was still a boy.

"Are you thirty yet?" she asked.

"In America, I'm twenty-eight. I turn twenty-nine in November."

"November second. I flew to New Jersey in December to help your mother with Bo. You were such an easy baby."

Sonya grew quiet thinking of Helen, who had been so grateful that DH ate and slept without any fuss. All three of Helen's kids were good, but

DH did whatever he was supposed to do and was so affectionate that the ever-stoic Helen softened around him, and laughed more easily.

"You made your mother happy. She lit up when you were near."

DH reached across the table and held his aunt's hands. "I think you and I might miss Mommy the most."

Sonya shook her head, unable to speak.

"Dad is having a hard time, but he won't admit it. Whenever anyone says anything about Mommy, it's like he's gone. He's sitting there but just looks…anguished. I don't know the right word—" DH unfolded the napkin on his lap.

"Is he okay otherwise? How's his health?"

"Mido cooks for him and makes sure he takes his vitamins. He works so hard still. Never complains. He looks healthy, but we all worry about him."

"He managed the salon so well that we were able to expand."

DH could feel his BlackBerry buzzing, but he ignored it. He spent every waking minute at the firm, and he never got to see his aunt alone.

"Aunt, you're now the landlord. No more rent payments for Rose Salon."

"I've never owned my own building before."

"Congratulations," DH said. "It's a solid piece of commercial property. Not cheap, though. Everything is really expensive these days. I think even our little house in Cypress has doubled in value."

"I hope your bosses appreciate you," she said, sitting up straighter. "Your aunt has money, so I want to make sure you charge me your full fee and get credit. You're a wonderful business lawyer."

A frown crossed DH's bright face like a shadow. "I am a good lawyer, but my firm doesn't take me seriously. In a few months, I'm a fourth-year associate, and I don't think I'll ever make partner."

"When do lawyers get considered to make partner?" she asked.

"It depends on the firm. At mine, usually eighth or ninth for corporate. I was told that it used to be seventh, but every year, they keep pushing the goalposts. I can wait, but my problem is that I won't inherit any business from any of my partners, and it's nearly impossible to get these giant fee-generating clients on my own. I'm put on all the deals because I do the work that the other associates don't want to do, but all the partners I work for are worker bees and none of them are rainmakers. I should be out there hustling for the big kill, but all I do is other people's scut work."

"So what will you do?" Sonya asked, having a hard time believing that DH wouldn't be adored at his firm the way he was everywhere else. "Is there a future there?"

"It's up or out if I don't make partner, and I can tell that as much as my partners like me, none of them are going to give me their business outright. I'm everyone's boy but no one's boy. I need to be adopted. I need a serious backer, and I don't have that at Willings & Crane. If I don't make partner on my eighth or ninth year, then I'm just clogging up the system. I should probably find another firm."

❧

Back at the office, DH had several pink message slips for missed internal calls. His BlackBerry had been buzzing the entire time during lunch, but he had tried to put it out of his mind. The managing partner, Jack Pockett, wanted him to swing by his office.

DH knew it was about bonuses. At Willings & Crane, the partners gave out associate bonuses in late January. In 2005, he had billed 2,700 hours, so he was expecting something decent. His supervising partner, Eddie Veler, had tried to manage his expectations. "Profits per partner this year weren't great, DH. I know you worked your tail off."

Jack looked up from his desk when DH walked in. They both wore navy suits, but his had a faint windowpane pattern.

"Koh."

"Hey, Jack."

"Tough news. I think you heard from Veler."

"Managing expectations, right?"

"Koh. You are one smart cookie."

"So how bad is it?"

"Not good: $15,000."

"Oh," was all DH could say.

"I'm sorry," Jack said. "You look disappointed. It was the highest bonus of your class."

"I billed twenty-seven hundred hours. That is not a normal number. I was in this building easily over three thousand. I did nothing else last year except work."

DH studied the view of Beverly Hills behind Jack's desk. They were on the twelfth floor, and he could see tall buildings on the other side of the boulevard and, in the distance, palm trees, several blocks parallel to them.

He wished the numbers were different. DH had been counting on something closer to $40,000, so he could pay off his school debts and help out more at home. There was never any need to be rude to anyone, but DH was exhausted and in no mood to be polite. He felt like walking out.

Jack tented his fingers, elbows on his desk, and sighed briefly. "You've worked very hard, I realize. The firm appreciates your efforts. We had a decent year, but we thought we should limit our bonuses and salt some away for the future in case the economic picture changes. It's better for us to put money away rather than have to cut—"

DH stood up abruptly, getting ready to leave. This was the speech nearly all the lawyers heard even when the firm was making crazy amounts of money.

Jack raised his right hand to stop him from going.

"We really value you, DH."

"Jack, let me ask you something. Do you think I can make partner here?"

Jack didn't reply.

"Oh. I see."

"DH, I can't answer a question like that. You're very young still. It could be another five or six years before you could be up for partner."

"Wait, another five or six? I thought it would be four or five. Can't you tell from my work quality now if I have a shot?"

"We do not want you to leave. You're a valuable member of the corporate department of Willings & Crane, and we know you have options, DH."

"I'm confused. I just asked a simple question. Do I have a shot? I didn't say you had to put it in writing. Do I have a shot at making partner?"

"Hard to say."

DH inhaled, then exhaled. He tried to clear his head.

Jack folded his arms and looked down at his desk blotter. DH knew that it was partners like him who prevented associates like DH from getting ahead. Because his billable rate was so high and he had too few clients of his own, he had been made into a kind of administrator. Managing partner sounded like an important job, but at Willings & Crane, it was the job that no one really wanted.

The firm was going to bet that DH would stay another five or six years, but unless there was a major boom, his corporate partners couldn't justify another partner for a while. If anything, they'd want to bring in some lateral hires from a peer firm with clients of their own.

"I know you mean well," DH said. "Thank you for talking with me."

"Hey, man, don't leave like that," Jack said. "You want to have a drink? I can call the wife and kids and tell them that I'll be late."

DH shook his head, thinking that even the offer to have a drink wasn't a real offer. Had he said yes, he would have been the bad guy taking a husband and father away from his family.

"I'm good, Jack. Thanks," DH said, and walked out. He looked over his messages and realized that he didn't care.

❧

As soon as he entered Peter's kitchen, DH removed his necktie and stuffed it into his jacket pocket. He sank into the beige armchair by the patio doors. Mido was setting the table. Peter took out containers from the freezer and put one in the microwave to defrost. He filled a stockpot with water and set it on the large burner.

"Spaghetti and meatballs make everything better," Peter said. When DH had called him earlier with the bonus numbers, Peter had told him to just come over.

"Man, you okay?" Peter asked.

DH had his head in his hands, his fingers clasping his thick black hair.

"I got fucked. Again," DH said. "Fuckers fucked me. Why did I trust those assholes? I did nothing but work, work, and more fucking work. I got the shittiest bonus last year, too. My friends in the same kind of firms made three times what I made. But it's not the bonus that pisses me off—"

"You still have a job, right?" Mido said, wanting to sound positive, but, seeing his face, realized she had said the wrong thing.

"Yes, I have a fucking job, and yes, I make a good salary, and yes, I am grateful to be employed. However, I'm pretty sure that I will never make partner at this firm. I have the right to have big fucking dreams just like the White guys whose deals I manage, contracts I negotiate and draft, and—fuck, fuck, fuck."

"How do you know you won't make partner? That's not for a while, right?" Mido asked.

"I asked. I asked if I had a shot. The bastard wouldn't even answer. He said, 'Hard to say.' Fuck, fuckers."

Peter walked over to DH and mussed up his hair.

"I'm sorry, kid," he said in Korean. Although they had always been in the same grade, Peter was almost a year older.

"Fuck, fuck, fuck." DH laid his head on the back of the armchair.

Mido looked at Peter, who frowned. Neither knew what to say.

"You want to quit? I'm sure you can get another job," Mido asked, wondering if he would.

"I'm going to start looking tomorrow," DH said. He looked at Mido. "You think our lives would have been different if we never left?"

"Where?" Mido asked. "We lived in a lot of places."

"We were born in the States. What would have happened if we stayed in the States and didn't move around so much?"

Peter handed DH a bottle of beer. "I've lived in Seoul, London, Massachusetts, New York, Connecticut, and now California. I like it here. I like my life. I don't want to go back."

"Maybe I should be you, then," DH said. "I'll marry a nice Korean girl and return to the motherland. If I were you, I'd go back and live in Korea and join the business."

"What?" Mido said.

"Kidding," DH said.

Peter turned down the flame on the boiling water.

"Be my guest. My mother has always liked you," Peter said. "I am never doing that."

"How about this? Is it possible that had we stayed in Korea and not gone to Andover and Yale, I might have made partner at a firm and that you would have been appreciated for being a great songwriter? It's harder here for Asian guys—to make it in business and entertainment."

Peter considered this. "I get what you're saying."

"I work for five White guys, I do so much of their work, and they would make me do more if it were possible. Sometimes I catch their mistakes. I know I'm a really good lawyer."

"You're not wrong," Peter said, "but I'm just not that political. I can't make everything about race because it's too depressing. I know you worked your ass off, but would it have made you feel better if the partner told you that you had a shot when you really don't? The economy is weird. Law firm structures aren't sustainable. You said so yourself. The law firm has to be pyramid shaped with more associates forming the base. Isn't that what you told me? There can't be that many partners, right? That's not to say they're not assholes or that racism is not an issue."

When DH opened his mouth to protest, Peter said, "Koh, hold up, man.

I'm on your side. It's just that we can't prove anything. I don't know if it's about race or greed. It's probably about money."

"Nope."

"Can you wait them out?" Mido asked.

"Doubtful."

"Why?"

"Too top-heavy," DH said. "And I think they don't think I'm partner material. I can't prove it. It's just so different than when I was playing soccer. Things were so much clearer. I was an MVP on my team. My teammates voted me captain. The only thing that is clear is that my work must be fucking fantastic because all the partners want me to be staffed on their deals."

Peter sat down at the dining table.

"I'm sorry, man. I'm sure you know a lot more about this than we do."

"I'm going to get another job."

Mido sat down opposite Peter. "Great. Where?"

"I'm going to start looking in Korea. I know a headhunter who's scouting for American lawyers in a massive firm based in Seoul."

"Seriously?" Peter widened his eyes.

"Well, I'm going to look."

"Can you practice there?" Mido asked.

"I can't practice Korean law, but I can practice American law. There are two Korean firms who want to grow their US legal teams. Maybe I can make partner there. I'll need to bring in business, but maybe I can get more business in Korea than I would here."

"Wow," Mido said, never having thought that DH would be the one to return.

"The partner thing will come. I don't know anyone more competitive than you," Peter said.

❧

After DH drove back to his apartment, Mido and Peter cleaned up the kitchen.

"Would it have been better for me, too?" Mido asked.

"To be in Korea? No," Peter said. "Korea can be tough on women. Ask my mother."

Mido poured herself a glass of water. Peter's mother was coming to visit in a few weeks, and she was nervous about meeting her for the first time.

"I wonder if it would have been easier for me elsewhere. I mean, it's not bad here. It's really good in lots of ways." She didn't want to complain.

"You mean Sydney or Seoul?" Peter handed her a pot to dry. "School is cheaper in both places, and you would have finished your degree. You probably would never have worked in a hagwon. You might have married that guy Tek."

Mido shook her head. Tek was working at a new firm. He'd sent her an announcement about his new office, and she wrote him a note congratulating him. He wrote back. He hadn't yet married, he said, claiming work had taken over everything. Still preparing to become a barrister, he said. Yun told her that he must be still thinking of her since he'd written back right away.

"Can DH get a legal job with a Korean firm based in Seoul?"

"Yeah, he could get hired, but I think he's right. He'll have to bring in business to make partner."

"How would he get business?"

"I can ask my mother. Do you want me to ask?"

"I don't want DH to go back."

"Same," Peter said.

"But I never want him to feel slighted," she said.

"Even if he makes partner in Korea, they'll pay less than here, I think," Peter said.

"I think he would make a good partner. Not that I know what makes a partner good," Mido admitted, laughing. "I mean, he's always working on big deals, and he works round the clock. In our family, it was always Bo who was the smart one out of the three of us, and DH was the athlete, so it's funny to me that he went to all those Ivy League schools and became a corporate lawyer so young. I wonder if it's because DH was our mother's favorite."

"Your brother is a disciplined athlete. You have no idea how much work he can endure. Yes, he's smart, but more than that, he has incredible habits and self-control. Even tonight, he had half a bottle of beer. He got mad, but he also ate his dinner and returned to the office. He's planning something. Man, I could never put up with those people."

Peter wiped down the counter with a clean cloth.

"I should get home," Mido said.

He picked up his car keys.

5
Securitization

Shin served as the CEO of their insurance agency; however, Danbi owned and controlled Sweet Rain Realty, her real estate company. In her wallet, Danbi had two business cards, one as the president of Shin & Jung Insurance Agency and the other as CEO of Sweet Rain.

Flipping houses was easy. George tipped her off to excellent undervalued properties in Santa Ana, Anaheim, and Garden Grove. He taught her the 70 percent rule, so she never lost money after repairs. Through him, the mortgage lenders, and the real estate brokers, Danbi assembled a team of subcontractors, suppliers, and contractors to improve the fixer-uppers and sell the houses at a profit. Every buyer, even those without a job, seemed to get a mortgage.

Danbi created a checklist and revised it after each sale. After closing on a property, she'd put in a new boiler, repair the HVAC system, and update the kitchen and bathrooms within a few months. Sometimes she replaced the windows because that raised the price so dramatically. Always, she gave the houses a fresh coat of cream-colored paint and made sure to landscape properly. Iceberg roses or poppies that looked like fried eggs might set her back $150 but raised the curb appeal by about $1,000. It was a no-brainer: Add flowers. Sweet Rain Realty sold good-looking houses—ones that immigrant wives wanted to buy—and there were always lenders willing to make deals with any buyer.

In fifteen months, she flipped six houses, often doubling her money. For now, she had two fixer-uppers lined up to replace the one she was certain to sell. The hard-money lenders wanted to work with her, and sometimes she pitted one against the others to shave off a point. George called her a good student.

Whenever she had a question, George was happy to meet her. They had a standing date on Saturday afternoons when Anna went to her hagwons for math, piano, and golf. When there were flare-ups with her properties, he would find time for her during the week and even on Sundays after church. She had a second BlackBerry for her real estate business.

George wanted to see her at least twice a week. He kept nude Polaroids of her in his desk and texted her dozens of times a day. They had phone sex on the days they didn't see each other. When his wife, Sobin, made a point of snubbing her at church meetings, Danbi redoubled her attention toward him, aroused by George's single-minded devotion.

The colder George's wife was to her, the hotter Danbi grew toward George. When she bought costly lingerie, she didn't think only of George; she thought also of how Sobin could never wear a baby-pink silk brassiere and thong, and the thought alone of defeating an older woman cruelly animated her.

If there was a rubric for what constituted a desirable woman, Danbi was determined to outperform George's wife in every category. Sometimes it occurred to Danbi that if only Sobin had been a little nicer, she wouldn't have targeted George out of vengeance. Envy and rage toward a haughty, well-off wife had inspired Danbi to seduce him and ruin his marriage.

Like most men, George wanted to rescue women, and it was easy for Danbi to appear helpless on demand. Taehun Shin could not help her with real estate. He was busy growing the insurance business and did not seem to mind Danbi's foray into real estate. "The business is doing fine," she'd tell him. "I'm not losing money."

Occasionally she dipped into the customers' premiums, meant to be sent to the insurance carrier, since there was often a month or two of leeway. Always, Danbi returned the money and paid the premiums on behalf of the customers, so there was no real harm.

Shin didn't understand why her company was only in Danbi's name. "If Sweet Rain Realty was owned jointly, and if something happened to you, your wife and sons can try to claim their share," she reasoned. "Everything I have is yours. You know that. And I want to make this company successful so I have something to leave Anna."

❧

On Saturday, after the sitter took Anna to her hagwons, Danbi met George at the Hilton. Before lunch, they bathed and made love. He kissed her when he was done. George left her on the bed, put on a robe, and opened the room service menu.

"You should consider selling the Garden Grove houses," he told her. "I think it's a good time."

"That's crazy. I should wait a few months. I already have two offers on Magnolia Street, and if I push out the kitchen on the bigger one, I can get so much more. Don't you want a very rich girlfriend?"

"I don't think I was ever after your money," he said, putting aside the menu. He towered over her and grabbed her ass, and Danbi squirmed flirtatiously.

"You're terrible."

"I was after your heart. I am in love with you, Danbi Jung. Let's run away."

She kissed him to make him shut up. More and more often, he talked about love. Danbi found it amusing that men thought women wanted love, when they were far more interested in the practical realities of life. This arrangement was ideal for her. She enjoyed having two men. Each served a different need. If she had more time, she would have taken another lover if he was useful enough to her.

"I was on a call with some analysts, and they're talking bubble. My company just sold several holdings in Irvine at a good price."

"You should have sold one to me."

She opened his robe and drew his hips closer.

He laughed.

"I like your ambition, pretty lady," he said. "I can sell a few of your properties for you. There are some buyers that I know who would—"

She reached for him, and George closed his eyes and held his breath.

He wondered if the sex would be this powerful if they lived together. In college, with his first girlfriend, he was able to have sex more than once a day. His personal record was three times in twenty-four hours.

If he saw Danbi every day, would she be able to make him feel like a college sophomore? If his wife left him or passed away, he'd force her to leave Shin. He would even raise Anna, who was only in the second grade. A kid that young could handle a stepparent, he figured. She seemed like a good kid.

As Danbi continued to dote on him and impress him with her business acumen, George grew more critical of his wife. At home, small things about her grated on him, things he'd never noticed before.

Regularly his wife boasted about herself, taking credit for what she did at the kids' schools, their church, and charity events. When her friends called on the phone, she soothed them, but when she got off, she ridiculed their little problems. The cackle of her laughter and the loudness of her voice annoyed him. They were only two years apart in age, and she didn't take care of her figure. Whenever she saw someone in a restaurant or even on television who'd had work done, she'd judge them severely, reciting the list of their procedures.

"Eyes, nose, chin, lips, and boobs. That's so not her chin. Disgusting. Doesn't she know that she could die from unnecessary surgery?"

However, when their daughters wanted to get double eyelid surgery, she had allowed it, saying it was different because that procedure was safe. Bigger eyes were prettier, she thought. George wouldn't have minded if Sobin wanted to get any procedures. The world was judgmental, and he didn't know why people couldn't avail themselves of improvements.

Once, in bed, Danbi had sat up and picked up the hotel pen on the nightstand and tried to tuck it underneath her right breast, and the pen had rolled off her rib cage.

"Why did you do that?" he asked.

"When the boob holds the pen, I'm getting my breasts lifted."

"What?"

"You need a plan to preserve your assets."

She was only thirty-seven but looked far younger. When they went on trips as a couple, he could see how men wanted her. Even after having a child, she could still wear a string bikini. His wife had raised four kids well, but she had not done other things. Danbi owned an insurance agency and had learned how to flip houses. He could not help comparing them.

There were times when George could not remember why he had married Sobin. On holidays when the kids were home, George told himself that having an intact family was important. However, as the kids grew more independent, he wondered what it would be like to live in an empty house with his wife. Danbi made him feel young, sexual, and powerful. She adored him and needed his counsel. When he didn't see her, he looked forward to her texts and had to be careful because he couldn't get caught carrying both phones.

Danbi massaged him, and he grew more excited. Very gently, Danbi pulled back, still keeping her hands on his erection. She was teasing him, making him wait.

"The two houses in Garden Grove are worth over a million. I'm going to flip them this year." She sat up uncovered, looking proud.

"Yes, but you owe almost $600,000 on them," he said, trying to mount her, but she held him off, smiling. "You should sell the one on Magnolia Street that's pretty much done."

"I don't want to. Make me."

George laughed, more aroused by her petulance.

"Rates may kick up soon, and I don't know if you'll be able to keep up the payments. I already loaned you fifty, and I can't spot you much longer without being noticed—"

"I know I'm running out of cash, but we can get more. Can't we? I can pay it back as soon as I sell the two, but it makes more sense to wait a few more months. I feel it. I just know the market will get even hotter."

"I don't have access to that kind of cash. Your payments are almost $10,000 a month now, not including the cost of the improvements."

She embraced him and moaned quietly in his ear.

"Everything is getting expensive," he persisted. "I read another report on securitization, and things could always take a turn. That's why I unloaded some of our buildings."

"I don't want to sell now," she said. "Why should I leave several hundred thousand dollars on the table? I'm just starting."

She was running her fingers down his chest, nipping at his earlobe. He moaned and tried to make his point. "If rates go up, your payments will go up. You don't have any cash coming in. You are speculating right now, and you don't want to lose the properties in case—"

"You wouldn't let me lose."

George stood up and closed his robe. He tried to look stern.

"We've been through this, Danbi. I loaned you all my personal cash, and last time, we borrowed from the building fund to help with the rehab costs. You need a buffer. Mitigate your risks."

"We paid the church back."

"Well, no. I paid the church back, then—"

"It's been paid back. I do the same thing with the premiums. It's not a big deal."

"Bear Creek," he said. Her eyes flashed with interest.

"Will you get it?"

"If the Bear Creek deal works out, I might be able to save you one for an inside price. That one, you don't even have to do anything except find the buyer. You need to keep some cash reserves instead of constantly buying. What will you do if we get found out? Will you take care of me?"

"I will take care of you right now," she said, raising her eyebrows.

On paper, his company was richer than ever, but even he felt overleveraged. His father-in-law wanted to be prudent and had insisted on selling some of their holdings. George had always kept a modest personal slush fund, but he had burned through it paying for hotels, and recently, when Danbi wanted to buy her most expensive house to flip, he had loaned her the last of it. When she wanted the second property, he had borrowed from the church building fund without anyone finding out. He was now using his salary to pay for these rooms and trips, which wasn't difficult, but her cash requests were getting harder to hide. Now and then, he thought of buying a love nest for them, but knowing Danbi's requirements, he'd have to raise a lot more money.

He sat down on the sofa and looked sober.

"Come back to me," she said. "Or do I have to come get you?"

"What are your payments now? I was just guessing before."

"Almost $15,000 a month with the HOA fees and taxes, not including my contractors. I owe the contractors some more." She didn't want to admit that the contractors needed an additional $40,000 for the foundation because they had hit utility lines and enormous rocks while excavating. Already she had pulled the maximum cash advances on all of her credit cards. "The last time you told me to sell, I held, and I was right. Wasn't I?"

Two months prior, George had advised her to sell the properties in Santa Ana when she had a cash shortfall, but she had held on another month and made an additional $200,000. But immediately, Danbi had set her sights on even more expensive properties to flip, leaving her with no spare cash. She kept running out of money, even though her properties grew more valuable.

"The market can't always keep going up."

"I have to trust my gut. It will go up. The bigger kitchen is going to get me another $200,000. I just know it."

George smiled but didn't say anything.

"How can I let them go?" she asked. The house on Magnolia Street was far nicer than the ones she had flipped before. She also had her eye on a fixer-upper in Anaheim with great bones.

"Can you borrow some more premium money from your agency?" he asked.

Danbi nodded. Routinely she borrowed $5,000 or $10,000 from the business account, which held customers' insurance premium payments. Shin didn't like her doing this.

"You can sell the Garden Grove houses and buy others later when there's a dip. You should have more of a cash cushion. Also, you're taking all your profits and getting more expensive places—"

"The bankers don't mind. The lenders are fighting to lend me more money—"

"You can give yourself some breathing room."

"That last lead you brought me I missed out on because there was that bidding war."

"It's not a big deal, baby. You just haven't lost enough leads, so you think that was the last one. There will be more. I promise."

"Give me more. More," she said, climbing out of bed to get him.

❧

George wasn't wrong. The rates went up, and her interest and principal payments increased. Danbi withdrew $60,000 from the premium account of the insurance agency to make up the difference and to pay the contractors. Shin noticed it and got upset.

"You can't do that. We hold those premiums in custody for the clients who give us cash and checks. That's not our money. You need to put that money back."

"Don't you have more money?" she asked.

"No. You know exactly how much we have. Our personal joint account has been almost zero since you started getting the properties, and whatever we have goes to our overhead. We are stretched. I was thinking of firing our landscaper to save cash. We need to reduce our expenses. Anna's school tuition is coming up, and she goes to three hagwons at $2,000 a month. I almost bounced a check last week."

Danbi did her best to look contrite and tried to make herself cry.

"I'm doing all this for Anna," she said. "Why are you getting mad at me? If you were divorced, I wouldn't be so worried all the time about having to take care of my daughter."

Shin went to the den, and she followed him to make him feel better. When he was done and in the shower, Danbi sent a message to George on their BlackBerry.

"After church?"

In an instant, as if he'd been waiting for her message, he replied, "Yes."

After the eleven o'clock service, when others were having lunch, they would be able to see each other in the office where the Finance Committee usually met, which had a lock on the door.

6

Value

Despite the long flight, Renee emerged from customs looking as if she'd just been to a spa, her dark hair sleek and her unlined face well rested, having slept almost eight hours. Alert and pleased to be out of the airport, Renee focused on her only child.

"It was freezing in Seoul," she said, staring out the windshield. The Southern California weather never failed to astonish her. "It's January, and I don't have to wear a winter coat. Should I move here? Would you like that?"

"Sure," Peter said. "What would you do, though?" His mother wasn't serious, not that he would've minded.

"I could work on my golf game and fix you dinner."

Peter smiled. "I get home very late, and you'd be bored in a week."

"Do you have to go back to work today?" she asked.

"I'm good for the rest of the day."

"Wonderful. Let's go to the grocery store. Call your friends. Invite them to dinner."

Renee removed her dark sunglasses as they entered Zion Market. "Palm trees, sunshine, and all the conveniences of Seoul. So this is why you never come home, and your aging mother has to come all this way to see you."

"Aging? You're not even sixty." Peter pulled out a shopping cart, and Renee dropped her tote into the basket.

"Umma doesn't look sixty, right?" Renee flexed her left biceps, not waiting for a reply. A trainer came to her home gym twice a week, and she'd been lifting weights. Her lithe form was stronger than it had been in years. "Son, tell me how you are. I want to know everything."

"I have a girlfriend."

"Oh?" Renee looked concerned. She had met Cesca briefly, and though she was beautiful and charismatic, things had not gone well. "What does she do?"

"She's a tutor at the hagwon."

Renee smiled, relieved. She directed them toward the meat section.

"Not an actor, then."

"No."

"Is she nice? What's she like?"

"You'll like Mido. She's great."

"She's Korean?"

He nodded. She knew she had to wait until her son wanted to talk more about his girlfriend.

"How long are you staying this time?" he asked, changing the subject.

"Three days. Then I head to New York. I was hoping you might come with me to the East Coast. We can go skating at Rockefeller Center. Remember when—"

"I have work, Umma."

"Right," she said, inhaling deeply. "How is that going?"

"I like running the new hagwon."

"Really?" Renee considered her child's face. He did seem much happier than the last time she had seen him. It had been almost a year since her previous visit, which had been cut short because of her work. His face looked relaxed and tan. "Tell me all about the hagwon."

"The kids are good, and they're improving so much. I find it satisfying to see their progress. Weird. I never thought I'd teach math."

Renee smiled, thinking the same. Being a mother had surprised her. When he was born, she'd had so many dreams for him, and all of them seemed absurd to her now. His father had wanted him to be a judge or a professor, and she had wanted him to be an athlete because he loved soccer so much.

After her divorce, Peter had become even more private and withdrawn. It wasn't until he ran away in England that she'd realized that none of her dreams for him mattered. She had withdrawn him from the school in Wimbledon. At Andover, he had flourished. Renee thought her son had achieved some sort of equilibrium, until Peter left Yale and moved to California to be with that actress. And when Cesca threw him over for another guy, Peter had taken it hard, refusing to leave his apartment or go to school. When Peter started working at Exodus and transferred to Pomona, absolutely nothing mattered to her except for his well-being.

When her ex-husband got upset with his decision to leave Yale, she told him off. "It's people like you who make their children crazy."

"Pomona is good, but he'll have better options if he finishes Yale," Peter's father said. "It has more name value."

"He'll have better options if he makes these decisions by himself. You don't understand him. You don't even know him," she said.

"You don't know how life works."

"Fine. Our son still talks to me, though," she said.

❧

As they put the groceries in the trunk, Renee looked up at the blue sky. "This sunshine!"

"You should move here," Peter said, though that would never happen. His mother adored living in Seoul.

"Maybe I should, just to be close to you."

"I'd be happy with that." Peter meant this. He'd always gotten along with his mother.

They drove toward the house, and Renee had to stop herself from commenting again on the weather. Did Californians ever tire of it? "How's the music going? Any new songs?"

"I'm still writing, but I don't know. My boss Lion and I play gigs now and then at this restaurant, and we have a good local following. But I'm never going to—you know, make it here. In the States. My father was right. I see that now."

Renee didn't say anything. Her son had a remarkable voice, and often, when she watched *Music Camp* or *Music Band* at home, she knew her ex-husband had been correct. If Peter had stayed in Korea, she would have been able to make introductions to television studios and record companies, and once he got his chance, the fans would have probably loved him: He had the same kind of charisma and singing style that was popular on those hit shows. No one could become a star just from having contacts, but in Korea, he would have had a chance.

"You don't want to come back home?" she asked.

"To Seoul? Oh, no. I like it here."

"I miss you," she said. "Your mother"—Renee tapped her chest—"would like to see you all the time."

Peter smiled, having heard this ever since he left Seoul when he was a child. It was an exceptional privilege to study abroad, and both his parents had done the same, but Peter hadn't been sure if he was suited for it. Whenever he was in Korea, he felt observed and judged. Here he could just be Peter.

"I know you are an adult. I'd leave you alone in Seoul. Just once a week," she promised with a smile. "Saturday brunch at my house."

"We talk several times a week," Peter said as he pulled into the driveway.

"We send text messages several times a week," she corrected him. "We might talk on the phone once a week for maybe five minutes? Not enough. Not enough for this mother."

"You know who wants to go back?" Peter asked.

Renee narrowed her eyes, trying to guess.

"DH. He's interviewing with a big firm in Seoul that's looking for corporate associates from the States."

"Really?" She looked thoughtful, handing him a bag of groceries from the trunk. "No problem. I'll call our general counsel. They use all the best firms in Seoul."

"Yeah? I know you don't usually like doing that sort of thing."

"Anything for DH. He's your best friend, and I'm sure he's a good lawyer. Korea needs more kids like him to come back. All these young people keep leaving." Renee shook her head, repeating what her friends and colleagues were saying back home. She felt old-fashioned for echoing the sentiment, but what would happen to Korea if all the young people left? Why weren't there enough opportunities for the next generation? She didn't want well-off families like hers to be removed from the realities of ordinary people. If her grandfather and grandmother hadn't been so brave and industrious, she wouldn't have had it so easy.

"Can I tell him that you'll make a call?"

"No, don't do that. Make him come to dinner tonight."

"I'll see if he can get out of work."

"I'm going to get him a job," she announced. "And invite the girlfriend," she added.

"My girlfriend?" Peter pointed to himself.

"Yes, and if DH has one, then her, too. Invite everyone. I bought enough food for a dozen people."

"Mido is DH's younger sister."

"Oh, right!" Renee slapped her thigh. "The one who put him through law school. You told me about his younger sister, but I've never met her. And I've only spoken to Bo on the phone. Can he come to dinner?"

"I don't know. Everyone might be busy. It's very last minute."

"I want to see Mido's parents, too." Renee stopped, remembering that DH's mother had passed away. "Helen. She was such a nice woman. I remember her from graduation. How is DH's father doing? Is he okay?"

"He manages a nail salon. With Lion's wife's mother."

"Oh?"

"It's nice. DH's aunt owns it."

"Invite them, too."

Peter looked at his watch. It wasn't even one o'clock.

❧

He called everyone. *My mom is here, and she's cooking. She wants you to come to dinner.*

Renee said to be flexible about the arrival time, but dinner would be served at 7:30 p.m. The guys said yes. Yun, heavy in her third trimester, begged off. In the evenings, she was too sleepy to stay out, but she insisted that Lion go. John and Nari were working late, and Sonya, who was still visiting from Seoul, was at the shop with them.

Renee got to work, marinating bulgogi meat and preparing two kinds of stew before she started on a cake, which took the longest. While she cooked, she asked Peter to put on recordings of his latest songs.

When the bell rang, the guest Peter expected to arrive last came first.

"DH!" Renee shouted, and opened her arms.

"Renee Ajumma!" DH yelled back, bolting into the house like a child. He ran to hug her. He'd known her since he was a boy and felt closer to her than to his aunt, who was a wonderful person but not nearly as fun as Renee Ajumma, who knew music from every era and old American films and had a surprisingly broad and deep knowledge of cars. Moreover, Renee knew more about baseball and soccer than any man and understood the finer points of boxing, tennis, golf, squash, archery, and rowing. She could remember the details of nearly every Olympics in her lifetime.

In Renee's home office, her shelves were stocked with prized sports paraphernalia, gifts from professional players and team owners. She was the only girl in the third generation of a family with a major tire conglomerate, which was now publicly traded. Because of her excellent manners and English skills, the leaders of her family's company had liked to have her attend important meetings with foreign dignitaries and key overseas chief executives because she could talk to men about cars and sports—safe topics, and she never said the wrong thing. Lovely and elegant, and always appropriate, despite her divorce, she was treated like the family jewel. None of the daughters-in-law, even the ones from the more prestigious Korean families, could compare with Renee.

Of course, everyone hoped that Peter, Renee's only son, would join the company. He wouldn't be considered the successor, because each of Renee's three brothers had several children, and there were four cousins from her uncle's side. Nevertheless, the company would make room for Peter high up in the organizational chart if he returned.

DH put on an apron and started helping Renee.

An hour later, Lion and Mido arrived together, and as usual, Mido held back, remaining quiet. Renee didn't miss this. Bo called to apologize because he couldn't make it after all.

As the sheet cake cooled, Renee enlisted Mido to make the frosting, handing her the confectioners' sugar, cream cheese, and butter.

"Peter told me about all the wonderful things you've done for your family," Renee said to Mido in her British English. "I admire you."

Mido shook her head to deflect the compliment and continued to mix the ingredients.

"You look a great deal like your mother, who I liked so much. We met at DH's graduation."

Only a few people ever remarked on that. The resemblance was striking around the jawline.

"Peter said you're an extraordinary teacher, able to reach the most difficult pupils."

Mido felt shy, unable to speak to this worldly person, who seemed to envelop everyone in the room with her charisma and warmth.

"I know we'll be good friends," Renee said. "My mother never cooked. I doubt she knew where the kitchen was," she said, laughing. "I always loved being in the kitchen, so I learned how to make everything from our family cook. Korean food is healthy, and whenever I'm away and don't eat it regularly, I don't feel well. That's why I hired Mrs. Ma for Peter. Her cooking is very good, don't you think?"

Mido had never met anyone like Renee. This felt like talking to a well-off

Western woman rather than any of her mother's friends or relatives. Renee was open about her privileged background. Peter was much more reserved.

"Do you like to cook?" Renee asked her.

"I do, but I don't have a lot of time. Once a week, I prepare three large meals and pack them up in smaller containers. I freeze a lot of dinners," Mido said.

"When I cook, it feels like a holiday. When Peter lived at home, I didn't cook every day. The cook did, but I'd make his favorite dishes at least once a week, and always his birthday cake, a chocolate sheet cake with cream cheese frosting. I've seen him eat a whole one throughout the day."

"When is Peter's birthday? He won't tell me."

"Tomorrow!" Renee said. "That's why I came. Oh, Peter," she sighed, looking in his direction. He was laughing with Lion and DH.

"I had no idea."

"He doesn't like anyone to make a fuss."

Both women looked in his direction. Mido said, "I didn't even know how old he was until DH told me. His birthday is tomorrow? Wow."

Renee smiled, remembering the icy January morning when her labor pains began. Then, almost a full day later, she became a mother.

"I see your frosting is almost done."

Mido looked down at the bowl of creamy white frosting.

Renee slathered a dollop of frosting on the cake and began to spread it evenly.

"No one in the family likes chocolate cake except for Peter and me. They always say it's too sweet, but I don't think so." Renee smiled brightly.

Her excitement was infectious, and Mido smiled back. Her mother had cooked nearly every day but never baked. Birthday cake had been store-bought, and if they had dessert, it was fresh fruit. But her mother had loved cake, too.

As she watched Renee bustling about the kitchen, Mido felt like she understood Peter a little better. He wasn't just a guy who was good at math and singing; he was Renee's cherished son.

7

American Hagwon

Renee promised not to get in the way, and she didn't.

In Peter's large lecture class, she sat in the back of the room and took notes. After class, she insisted on paying for two of Fortress's proprietary study guides, and while Peter taught his seminars, where her presence would be noticed, Renee solved practice problems in the teachers' lounge. The other tutors didn't know what to make of the chic woman in the thin black turtleneck, brown leather pencil skirt, and narrow calf boots.

Valerie, an SAT tutor who worked on the weekends, stopped by Mido's office. The skinny graduate student in a green hoodie and jeans fiddled with the straps of her gray knapsack while sipping coffee from a paper cup.

"The lady in the leather skirt. New tutor?"

"Peter's mother," Mido said.

Once told, Valerie could see the resemblance: the large, deep-set eyes, thick dark hair, and creamy complexion. Peter dressed so simply that it was hard to imagine such a rich-looking mother.

"Why is she doing practice tests?" Valerie asked.

"Good question." Mido threw her hands up.

In the afternoon, Lion stopped by Fortress. Renee had now settled in Peter and Lion's shared office and was doing reading comprehension passages.

"Thank you for the amazing dinner last night. I haven't eaten so well in a long time," Lion said.

"Does your wife cook?" Renee asked, her left hand resting on the open practice test, her right holding a pencil.

"Oh, yes, Yun is an excellent cook. Like her mother. She enjoyed the slice of cake I brought back."

Renee smiled. "Mido mentioned that Yun's family helped her family a great deal."

"I think they helped each other." Lion gathered the documents he needed from his desk.

"I was told that Mido has not finished college. Is that normal for hagwon work? In Korea, one cannot tutor at a hagwon like this one without a college degree," Renee said.

"Mido is a special case. To be frank, we would not have hired her to be a tutor initially. She's my wife's childhood friend. When we opened our first hagwon, we hired her to help us out with administrative things, then gradually we noticed that she was really good with young kids at Exodus—that's our center in Cypress."

Renee nodded.

"She studied on her own and took practice SATs, and one day, she registered for it and got a perfect score on the first try. I suppose it shouldn't surprise me because she was at the University of Sydney. Like Peter, she's strong in both English and math. Normally I hire only college graduates or people with advanced degrees—teachers, graduate students, and people like Peter who come from creative fields. We started her out with a small high school class in verbal, and the kids' results improved dramatically. Then when we started college counseling, her brother DH thought she'd be good with the personal essay sections of the applications. So now she counsels kids for college applications and tutors SAT verbal."

"And I suppose she's good at tutoring?" Renee glanced at the study guide.

"Her students routinely improve a hundred or even two hundred points, which is very hard to do. She gets them to do the work of critical reading and memorizing all those words. Her students have the best scores at Fortress. She could teach more sections if she wanted."

"What's her secret?"

Lion furrowed his brow. He knew she was digging for more information about her son's girlfriend.

"Hard to say."

"Try," Renee prompted.

"She cares about them. I've come to believe that kids can't learn unless they feel that you care about them. Mido spends more time on each student than what's required. She writes them notes and gives each of them different things to read based on their personality and interests. The kids talk to her."

"Ah, so the kids listen to her."

"No. The kids talk to her, and she listens to them."

Renee thought about that. Even the night before she had seen how carefully Mido paid attention to everyone.

"Does she need to finish college?"

"Not to have this job, as far as I'm concerned."

"I see. I wish the students in Korea had a teacher like her," Renee said.

"Well, our students are Korean," Lion said. "They're mostly American citizens but almost all are ethnically Korean."

"I mean, the students in Korea. Not the Korean American ones here."

"What do you mean?" Lion asked.

"Many students in Korea are anxious. They work all the time and hardly have time to breathe, let alone sleep. My friends' children in international schools are under so much pressure. You should open a hagwon in Seoul. You could make millions."

Lion frowned. "I don't think so."

"Why not? I can back you. You could have Fortress Seoul."

"My kids need us here."

"You can make more money there, especially with high school students."

He looked down at his sneakers covered in dirt from a morning run. Yun had once mentioned opening another location in Orange County, but he felt terrible about how unfair it was that some kids could afford to have great tutors like Peter and Mido, while others could never have them. Fortress was not the most expensive hagwon in Irvine, but it wasn't cheap, either.

It had never been Lion's goal to get rich through teaching. He'd taken it up in order to support his music and avoid being a burden to his family. Somehow he'd become a famous hagwon owner and a part-time local musician. He played several times a week, but he knew he'd never tour to promote the Zekes. Every day he thought of the prospect of the baby, and it thrilled him to think of having a family with Yun. What he had once yearned for had changed, and surprisingly, making his music second, third, or even fourth in his life didn't bother him as much as he would have thought when he was younger.

"How much do the Fortress tutors make?" Renee asked.

Lion wasn't sure. Yun knew the figures better than he did.

"Full-time, starting base salary is $65,000, but Peter and Mido make more. They do a lot of administrative work and college consulting, which is more lucrative. As of last year, Peter and Mido get a percentage of the net profits of Fortress. However, they know that the profits from Fortress also subsidize Exodus, which has a poorer population of newer immigrants. We can keep the fees at Exodus low because Fortress earns so much more."

"You could charge more, then?" Renee appeared puzzled.

"I created Fortress because several parents asked me to open something like this for high school students in Irvine. Yun thought it would be a financial success, but I hadn't realized how well-off the people are in Irvine and Newport Beach. And now we depend on Fortress. Without its success, we'd have to change the fee structure of Exodus." Lion didn't mind talking about the business model. Often he wondered if what he was doing made sense to anyone else.

Peter had told his mother that Lion was a noble character like Robin Hood, wanting to take from the rich and give to the poor, but she hadn't understood what he meant until now. Lion's sincerity was evident, almost to the point of naivete.

"Aren't you concerned about Korea?"

"What do you mean?"

"The children of Korea are suffering. From too much pressure. The middle- and upper-middle-class families want their kids to study abroad because there are limited spots in the top Korean schools, and in a global economy, candidates who have exposure to the West do better in the job market. If you opened a great hagwon in Seoul for Korean students who want to study in America, then maybe you can send more Korean kids to the US. There are so many incredible schools here, but most of the Koreans only know the Ivies. You can tell them about the other schools. Then more Koreans would have a chance to study here."

"Is that a good thing? For more Korean kids to go to the US?" Lion didn't know the answer himself. "Also, wouldn't I just be helping more rich kids get into the highly selective schools beyond Harvard, Yale, and Princeton? International students usually don't get financial aid, so we'd only be helping students who already have all the resources. If we helped a student who didn't have resources, then what do we do when he can't pay the full tuition where he's accepted?" Lion shook his head.

"If you opened a Fortress in Seoul, then the money you raise there could help you expand Exodus in Cypress. Then you can help more poor kids here. Or you can open an Exodus in Seoul, too. What do you think?

You can do both. I bet if you opened a college consulting hagwon in Seoul, then the profits from that company would fund at least another fifty kids at Exodus or maybe more.

"In fact, I can guarantee that with just a little word of mouth, you can get a hundred students in Seoul to apply immediately."

"We already have students who fly from Korea just to work with Mido, which is so expensive. I mean, she's great, but—"

"I have buildings in Daechi-dong and Apgujeong. You can have two floors in the same one as Eagle Academy, a hagwon Peter attended."

"Why would you do that?"

"Because I was able to study in England and America. It changed my life. I always thought it would be great to create my own school which was more globally focused, but this could be a way to keep costs down since I'll donate the space, and I can help with the visas and start-up capitalization."

Lion didn't say anything. He was thinking.

"You could help poor kids here or in Seoul with the profits." Renee studied Lion's face. She knew people made deals if the offer aligned with their motivation. Lion wanted to be fair in an unfair world. Her grandfather had cared deeply about educating his children and the nation. It had been a dream of his to build excellent schools. Renee wanted to work with Lion, feeling certain that her brothers would help out through the company's foundation.

"Think about it," Renee said.

♣

She left for New York on Tuesday morning.

Peter hadn't been alone with Mido while his mother was staying with him. After work, she came over for dinner.

"I see you at work, but it's nicer when you're here," he said. "I think you should move in."

Mido shook her head, still smiling. "What? No. I don't think so." Her reply was to be expected. She still didn't sleep over.

"Was it good to see your mom?"

"Yeah. Hey, my mother has this crazy plan. Did Lion tell you?"

Peter opened the refrigerator and scanned its contents.

"No, what is it?"

"She wants us to save Korean children."

"Oh, is that all?"

"She wants Lion to open a Fortress and eventually an Exodus in Seoul. The same model, and we'd work there. She's willing to back it for two years even if it doesn't show a profit. I think the family foundation would support it. She just said not to worry."

Mido sat down near the window.

"How many students?"

"You're serious? You'd do it?" Peter pulled out glass containers from the freezer and set a pot of soup over the range to heat. He checked the rice cooker, which was full of steamed white rice with barley and mixed beans.

"If we could recruit good teachers and provide housing and excellent pay, then we could create a new kind of hagwon," she said. "Where would it be?"

"She has a few buildings in Gangnam which we can use. Apparently there's space in buildings in Apgujeong and Daechi-dong," he said.

"My aunt lives in Apgujeong," Mido said. "Can we have nice dorms for the tutors?"

"I guess." He shrugged. "My cousin owns hotels, and some of them are higher-end *gositel*s. I can't imagine we'd need that many rooms. My mother has always wanted to start a school. That's why she backed Eagle Academy. She charges below market rent to the owner, Tom Song, partly because he's her old friend, but also because she thinks Koreans should be exposed to Western education. It would be easier to open a new kind of hagwon than start another international school."

Mido snapped open the tops of the side dish containers and set them on the table. Peter ladled soup into bowls.

"If Bo stays here with my father, then I could try it."

"You can't teach the students there because you don't have a college degree, but you can train the tutors and manage the company, I guess?" Peter ate half of a pickled egg as he started to puzzle out what had seemed like an impossible idea until Mido took it seriously.

"Maybe if we did this, we can help more kids. Give out scholarships and lower the fees. We can train tutors to focus on customized learning. There are lots of college graduates and teachers who want to work in Korea." Mido grew more excited at the idea of taking Fortress to Korea. She felt like calling Yun to discuss it with her.

"I like it here. Don't you?" Peter looked worried.

"Yes, I do. We wouldn't go there forever."

"Don't kids need us here?"

"Yes, of course, but I think I'd like to try this. Maybe we can do something different, and somehow be more fair. I mean, unless you don't want to do it. I wouldn't do it without you," she said.

Mido never forgot her primary school in Seoul, the callousness of Mr. Na and the kindness of Mrs. Lim, the endless amounts of school homework and hagwon exercises. She had disliked the class ranking and corporal punishment. Eagle Academy had made it possible for her to catch up to her peers. She had never forgotten Sean Teacher: his handwritten notes of encouragement, how he sang "Danny Boy," and their occasional field trips to museums and parks. Of course, everything had been better because of Yun. She had learned so many things during that brief period in Seoul. Her classes in Sydney were far easier because she'd kept up with the strong students in Korea. As a grown-up, Mido wanted to know more, and it sounded exciting to go back but this time as someone who could help.

"Mido," Peter said, looking up at the ceiling thoughtfully, then facing her. "So you won't move in with me, but you'd be willing to go to Seoul to open an American hagwon. I can't imagine a country that needs private tutors less than Korea. There are thousands and thousands of hagwons there. A lot of them are really great ones. Korea is doing just fine without us."

"Yes, but theirs aren't like ours. We could bring them what we've learned here, and we can learn there what we don't know here. Maybe they don't need us, but I want to try. It could be helpful."

Peter leaned his head against his hand and considered everything the others had said—first his mother, then Lion, and now Mido. He didn't know if this was a great idea, but it wasn't a terrible one.

8
Repatriation

Seoul
July 2006

Renee made calls, and soon both DH and Mido found themselves in Seoul. Of course, Peter came, too.

In March, the law firm Kim & Gong hired DH. He quit Willings & Crane the morning after the offer came in writing. He walked into his managing partner's office and said, "I don't see a future here. I'm going to Seoul. Thanks, man." The partners tried to talk him out of it, but DH was unmoved.

Sonya helped him lease a large one-bedroom apartment in Yongsan, a few train stops from his offices in Jongno. He started his new job in April.

In May, Tom Song, the owner of Eagle Academy, reached out to Lion and floated the idea of a joint venture to create Fortress Seoul. To create the pilot program, Tom's former students Peter and Mido went to Seoul in June.

Although Renee lived in a large house in Hannam-dong, Peter did not want to live with his mother. She found him a three-bedroom unit in Complex 1 at the Apgujeong Hyundai Apartments, where Sonya's family also lived. He wanted Mido to stay with him, but Mido chose to move in with her brother DH.

Their aunt Sonya had returned to Seoul. Inexplicably to nearly everyone, she was now living alone in a newer building in the same large complex as the rest of her family, a five-minute walk from the Muns' primary residences. When Sonya offered Mido a spare bedroom, she declined her aunt politely. "I haven't lived with DH since he left for Andover, and Dad wanted me to check on him. Ever since Mom's gone, DH calls him less often."

From adolescence, the three Koh children had lived apart. DH was the first one to leave home for boarding school in Massachusetts. When Mido lived in Sydney after their father was rehired but effectively demoted at HRI, Bo remained in Seoul to study for the Suneung. In California, Mido lived with Bo and their parents, but DH lived alone in New York for law school, then in Los Angeles for work.

After Helen passed away, Bo had become even more serious, focused on getting his PhD in six years. While Mido was in Seoul, he went home to Cypress every weekend to be with his father.

People often remarked on how rarely the three Koh siblings fought, how well they got along. The reasons were simple. They didn't live with each other, and as a family, they had been through enough trials. And most importantly, Helen had taught her children: *You are responsible for your siblings. They should be your strongest allies.* Sonya and Kenny had been Helen's refuge and balm in a hostile world. She wanted this for her own children, too.

Mido hadn't been able to live with her brothers for very long, because they were studying in different countries, and now she wanted to live with DH, the only one who still made jokes.

He wouldn't accept rent from her, so she did the housekeeping. The day she arrived in Seoul, DH was at work. He'd left a key for her. Soon enough, she learned that he was always at work, and even when he went out, it was also for his job. When he came home, she was asleep, and when she was awake, he was asleep.

From the first day, she scrubbed his bathroom, washed loads of laundry, and stocked his kitchen with food and beverages beyond the half-empty case of ramyeon, water, and beer she had first found. She bought him a vacuum cleaner, pots, and pans.

Two days after she arrived, while she was making toast and coffee, he stumbled into the kitchen and wordlessly took the mug of coffee from her hands.

"Hey—"

"Rent," he said, taking a sip. Even exhausted, DH had a beautiful smile.

Dark circles shadowed his large dark eyes, and he looked paler than she'd ever seen him. He had lost weight and appeared less like his usual athletic self.

"You okay?" she asked, pouring herself another cup.

He dropped his head on her shoulder.

"Don't go back to Cypress."

"I never see you, though."

She frowned at what he was wearing. He had fallen asleep in his dress shirt and boxer shorts. Mido picked up a tissue.

"Close your eyes," she said, and he obeyed, allowing her to wipe away the sleep near his tear ducts.

"Thank you," he said, sounding like a child.

"Well, at least you took off your socks. You know, the first day I did the laundry—"

"Yes, thank you for that—"

"No, no, it's fine. It was funny because I found all these black balled-up socks on your bedroom floor, and every time I had an even number, I thought I'd found all the mates, but then another one would appear in some random corner of the room." Mido had marveled at the disparate locations of all the balled-up socks. "How many pairs of black socks do you own anyway?"

"I don't know. I don't do laundry, and it's so cheap to buy them here."

"Wow. Just wow." She shook her head.

"Oh, don't be like that. I don't even have time to sleep. I'm not used to all this drinking, either. I have no idea how people can drink so much. The women can put away so much soju—"

"Is it bad?"

"Actually, I really like it here. I'm not crazy about all the after-hours stuff, but the work is interesting, and I'm learning a lot. My Korean is getting so much better. I might live here."

"Forever?"

"Yeah, maybe. Everyone is always offering to introduce me to their daughter, sister, friend—"

Mido raised her eyebrows, not that she was surprised.

It had never been difficult for DH to meet women, but here, he felt like a prized stud bull. It didn't hurt that Renee Cha, the director of the THT Corporation, backed him, ensuring that he'd make partner as long as his work held up.

"Are you going to find a wife here?" Mido buttered a triangle of toast and handed it to her brother, and DH swallowed it in two bites.

"Do we have eggs?" he asked, ignoring her question.

Mido opened the refrigerator and pulled out a carton.

"Do you have time to eat?" she asked. "You've lost weight."

DH rubbed his hands together theatrically. "I want six fried eggs and a pound of bacon. Fatten me up, please."

Mido rolled her eyes and started cooking.

He sat down near the small round dining table.

"I'm not getting married right away. I'm kind of picky. Besides, I need to prove myself here. It's only been three months, and I want to make sure that I do a good job. I can't let Peter's mom down."

When the bacon was done, she used some of the fat to fry the eggs. DH ate two more slices of toast with butter and jam. Mido felt happy cooking as her brother chattered away.

"I think I could make partner here, or at least go back to the States with a lot of really cool experiences. I was doing good M&A work in Los Angeles, but here the transactions are at a whole other level because there's so much I don't know."

DH picked up a pair of chopsticks and selected a crispy piece of bacon from the pan.

"It's too hot," she warned.

Over the sink, he blew on it dramatically and crammed the entire piece into his mouth.

"Bo is still dating Priscilla, right?" he said, chewing. "He's older, so he should get married first."

"Birth order? You really have become more Korean," she said, setting his plate in front of him. She dropped more bread into the toaster.

"My first home-cooked meal in Seoul," he said, looking grateful, and dug in.

"You can't leave," DH said, admiring his suddenly well-organized apartment. On the counter was a basket of bananas, apples, and tangerines; in the open cupboard, he spotted his favorite cereal, crackers, tinned fish, and jars of crunchy peanut butter and grape jelly; and in the refrigerator, Mido had stocked regular and chocolate milk, eggs, tofu, bacon, and Pyrex containers of side dishes. The bathroom was cleaner than in its move-in condition. "Mommy would want it this way," he said, smiling.

"You're kind of a beast."

"Not true," DH said. "Almost every day, a stranger tells me that I am exceptionally nice-looking. I had no idea how appealing I was until I moved to Seoul. Just last week, I was on the train, and a woman who works for an ad agency scouted me to model."

Mido's two thumbs touched and her index fingers pointed upward to make the letter *W*. "Whatever." Her hagwon students made this sign to dismiss people who annoyed them.

"I threw away your shower curtain liner. I tried using the disinfectant spray in your bathroom cabinet, but it did nothing." Mido made a face of disgust. "Have you always lived like this? I guess at Andover and Yale, someone else probably cleaned the dorm bathrooms, but when you went to law school in New York, I hope you weren't this gross."

He smiled sweetly, and Mido imagined even their normally serious mother unable to keep from smiling back at him. Seeing his face made her miss their mother.

"I'm sorry, Mido. Your brother has filthy habits. I apologize," he said, hanging his head repentantly. "I work even harder here than I did in LA."

"So no sign of a girlfriend yet?"

"Nope." DH put down his chopsticks. "Hey, are you and Peter going to get married?" DH asked. Ever since he learned that she was dating Peter, he had been expecting an announcement.

With a new sponge, Mido swept up the toast crumbs from the counter. DH could tell that she was deliberately not answering him.

"Is he at least being nice?"

"Of course he is."

"He'd better be," DH said, playfully making a fist.

"What are you looking for in a girlfriend or wife?" It had never occurred to her before to ask. "Every woman you've ever dated has been good-looking." Mido had only met two briefly in Los Angeles and seen photographs of some of the others. "I noticed that all of them have long hair and are curvy."

DH grinned. "Guilty."

Mido waited for him to continue. He was thinking, having learned even more about women from living in Seoul.

"But I also need good conversation. I want to be with a woman who is smart. And ambitious. She also has to be nice."

Over the years, DH had dated many women. However, except for the beautiful Christina Suh, his first serious girlfriend at Yale, who had broken up with him to date a graduate student, DH hadn't been in a long-term relationship with anyone. Conscious of money and loans, and always forecasting before taking action, DH had intended to make partner in Los Angeles first, then find someone to marry, but he had changed course by moving to Korea.

If DH wanted a wife, of course, he could find one. However, he wanted to be madly in love when he was financially prepared for a wife and children. Having grown up watching his mother work all the time, DH wanted to be well-off enough that if his wife didn't want to work, she wouldn't have to. As soon as he paid off his law school loans, he planned to take care of his father and pay for Mido's education; he intended to make partner at this law firm or return to the States and find a large firm that would value his experience in Korea. At twenty-eight, DH felt in no rush to get married. Privately he figured Mido would be the first of all of them to marry.

Since he'd arrived in Korea, it seemed like a day hadn't passed without someone wanting to introduce him to a marriageable woman. He declined most offers, but now and then, when he couldn't refuse, he found himself sitting in a hotel lobby coffee shop, talking to a single woman from a good family who was interested in marrying an American Ivy League–educated lawyer. Naturally, the dates were awkward but tolerable. Sleeping with any of them was out of the question, because sex would imply a seriousness that DH did not yet feel.

Thus far, of all the arranged dates, he had found two women appealing, bright, and interesting: One was a surgeon and the other a sociology professor. Neither of them seemed concerned with his housekeeping, or child-rearing, though he knew that eventually those things would matter because he could do neither well. They could hire a housekeeper, but someone would have to take care of the children if they had any. It was hard to think that far ahead, so he didn't pursue either woman. DH could imagine marrying a Korean woman, but it occurred to him that it would be easier if she were also American.

Neither the surgeon nor the professor was anything like his mother, aunt, or sister—willing to sacrifice almost everything for her family. The women seemed like brilliant students, which attracted him, but he wondered if they would like him if he hadn't been educated at Andover, Yale, and Columbia Law School; they both brought up his educational résumé several times during the brief dates. Without any self-consciousness, the surgeon had said, "I could never be with someone who didn't graduate from an Ivy League college."

DH thought that was weird, but he had to admit that he wouldn't marry a woman unless she was also gorgeous and hot in bed, which might be far more superficial than his educational history.

The other thing that disturbed him about living in Seoul was how often his colleagues went to room salons. In his three months, he'd been asked to go to them more than a dozen times. DH didn't like to drink, and he had no wish to sleep with a prostitute, which made things awkward when he routinely refused the invitations. On the rare occasion when he went to the room salon, he had to learn to be careful with the hostesses.

After a few glasses of wine, one beautiful young woman, an aspiring actor, had offered to go upstairs to the attached hotel for a fee. When DH declined, the men seemed more surprised than the woman, who moved on to one of his colleagues, who was more than happy to follow her.

DH enjoyed talking to women, because he liked talking and the women seemed interesting. Two young hostesses had told him that they were working there to send their siblings to school, and he'd been moved by them, because it had reminded him of how Mido had worked at the hagwon to pay his and Bo's tuition.

Later, when DH relayed these stories to a fellow lawyer, a wealthy Korean who, like him, had been educated in the States, the lawyer was stern: "Don't get played, man."

The sad stories weren't always true. "The girls want to make easy money pouring drinks or work on their backs servicing the johns, then nail the idiots for bigger payouts. Watch out if they start messaging you with 'Oppa, buy me this or buy me that.' In fact, don't give them your number unless you like them, and no matter what, never believe their sob stories. You can't believe how many foreigners fall for that shit. In fact, never give them your number."

DH passed his clean plate to Mido.

"Thank you for breakfast. It was outstanding. You are the greatest. Peter doesn't deserve you."

Mido laughed.

"I should just live with Peter. His place is amazing," DH said.

"Yes, Peter's place is also very clean."

"He has help," DH retorted. "Not that I begrudge him. I owe that dude everything."

Peter had a different life from them. He was generous and worked harder than anyone, but when it came to domestic matters, his family money removed ordinary friction from daily life.

"How do you like it here?" DH asked.

Mido looked at him. "Seoul?"

"No, this apartment. Should I get something bigger? I could have gotten something else, but I was trying to save money."

"It's nice," Mido said, thinking that she'd hurt his feelings. "This is way nicer than our first place in Cypress. Thank you for letting me stay with you."

"Are you really not going to stay at Peter's?" DH asked.

"He asked me to, but I have to be careful. Apparently the press tracks Peter's personal life, and even Fortress Seoul is getting media attention. Dad wouldn't like reading about me in the papers—"

"The papers? They would report on you dating Peter?"

"That's what Peter said."

"Besides, you're going to marry him, right?"

Mido made a face and didn't say anything.

"I didn't realize what a big deal his family was until I started working at the firm. His family has a lot of money. Crazy amounts."

Mido shrugged. "It has nothing to do with me. I don't want to marry him."

"What?"

"We're not getting married."

"Ever?"

"Nope."

DH frowned, not having expected this, but knew better than to press it. Mido would clam up if she didn't want to talk about something. He was curious about the media thing.

"You think if you sleep at his place, the press will find out?"

"They could."

"But Dad can't possibly think that you're a virgin."

Mido shrugged. "He has never asked, and I will never tell."

Their father would not sanction living with a man without marrying him, and it did not seem likely that they'd get married anytime soon, or ever. Peter never brought up the subject, and Mido no longer knew how she felt about marriage. She liked being with him. Next to Yun, he was her closest friend. They loved each other; however, marriage meant something different to each of them. For Peter, marriage was a burden that would change everything.

"Dad's never going to check if you're sleeping over at Peter's."

"I know, but I don't want to lie to him."

"So I'm kind of a beast and you're kind of a liar." DH laughed, and Mido put the dishes and pan in the sink.

Renee had advised Peter that unless he and Mido were engaged, they needed to be careful. The director of an educational center would be judged for spending the night with a woman, especially a coworker. Every major newspaper had a reporter dedicated to the THT Corporation and the owner's family members. Peter had managed to stay out of the press by living overseas. The public was curious about the only child of the only daughter of the THT family, and the tabloids served their curiosity.

"Who cares what everyone thinks?" Peter had argued only a few days ago about Mido's refusal to sleep over. Yet Mido felt Peter's mother was right to advise caution. The longer she stayed here, the more she could see why Peter had refused to come back.

9
Whale

Orange County
April 2007

"You told me to sell. But you were wrong. I could've made more," Danbi said. "I should've stuck to my instincts. You owe me. Pay up."

George didn't say anything. He stroked her hair, wanting to calm her. She was bringing up the Magnolia Street house again.

"I'm still upset with you. I listened to you even though I felt that if I waited, I would've made more. The buyer flipped it two months later. I could've made that $200,000, which would really help me right now."

Squaring her shoulders, Danbi pushed out her chest and pouted as she watched him unbutton the front of her white dress. He let her keep talking. She leaned closer to him and blew lightly into his ear. He pushed her away gently, then bent down to remove her underwear. He stood up to face her.

Her front exposed, Danbi placed her arms around George's neck, and he lifted her up and backed her into the wall.

"Did you talk to the developer at Bear Creek?" she asked, licking his earlobe. "Can you get me that model house for 2.5? Vice-Chairman Han said he'd buy it for 3.5. He's coming to the States next month."

George closed his eyes and rocked against her, and Danbi swore at him quietly, telling him to hurry, to make her come, which excited him more. As he moved faster, Danbi jerked away and smiled.

He grabbed her hand, but she freed herself and laughed like a young girl, knowing that he liked her teasing.

In front of the curtained hotel window, Danbi slid out of her dress, then her blush-colored brassiere. She got on her knees and put her hands on his hips. Danbi looked up at him, wide-eyed, mouth parted slightly.

"Tell me. Did you talk to the man at Bear Creek? I have a million from the lender, and I have $450,000 for this deal. You said you can get me the rest. I'll pay you back the day after the closing."

Danbi started working on him, and as he grew more excited, she pulled away, then moved toward the bed, where she'd left her black leather pumps. She slipped on her shoes and stood at the foot of the bed, her hands covering her breasts. George liked it when she broke up the lovemaking into segments, forcing him to follow her lead.

"Where am I going to get $1,050,000?" George asked, smiling.

"From the building fund. No one will notice. You're in charge."

"$1.05 million is different than $100,000," George said. Twice, as the head of the Real Estate and Building Committee at Gospel Presbyterian Church, George had taken money out for Danbi's acquisitions, then returned the funds. Ever careful, he'd adjusted the records and prepared invoices just in case. The disbursements and repayments were not questioned. There was no money missing from the building fund, which held $6.7 million for the land purchase and construction of the new learning center. No one bothered to review the trail of funds.

"We'll return it right away," she said, bending over the bed and looking at him over her shoulder. "It's a bridge loan. I'll tithe just like last time. I promise. I promise."

George stood behind her, placing his hands on her rear end.

"The church will make ten percent," she said.

"It's too big a risk, Danbi. I know you can do this later—"

"I listened to you about Magnolia Street. You owe me this money," she said, kissing him lightly on the mouth. "How will I ever make enough to leave him if you don't help me with this one? This is the whale I want to catch. Vice-Chairman Han swore he'd buy it for 3.5."

Danbi knelt before him, but George hoisted her up and turned her around so he could finish.

❧

Bear Creek was the latest premier development in Irvine. The lots were often less than half an acre, but the gorgeous houses were enormous, often seven to ten thousand square feet, with every possible amenity. Already wealthy buyers from Seoul, Beijing, Hong Kong, and Taipei had expressed interest, and though things were slowing down in the region for the less expensive homes, foreign buyers shored up the luxury developments.

Huey Carlin, the developer, had promised one unit to George at $2.5 million. Carlin owed George a favor for an important easement, and selling a place to George at the inside price was like making a deposit of goodwill.

George had kept the Bear Creek unit for Danbi. He could have used it for his company, but he knew it would make her happy if she could flip her first whale.

❧

Less than two months later, on a sunny afternoon in Irvine, Bonhwa Han, the vice-chairman of HRG, showed up to the model house at Bear Creek as he had promised.

Educated in Seoul with a brief stint in Boston for business school, Han was one of the eleven grandchildren of the founder of HRG. As he approached early retirement, he was looking forward to spending more time in Southern California, where his sons were in school. They were interested in living in Irvine, and his wife thought it made sense to buy another house there.

Han knew Danbi from HRG. After the IMF Crisis, Danbi had boldly approached him in his office for advice about investments, and several times, they had met in hotel rooms. He had taken her out on a boat ride and to secluded parks on dates. He liked the smart girl more than hostesses, because she was adventurous. Later, she introduced him to another girl, then disappeared, saying something about family matters. Han had been surprised to learn that Danbi had moved to California with Taehun Shin, a former director of HRI.

Recently, when she reached out to him by email to get advice on interest rates and currency exchange, he'd mentioned wanting to move to California. "My sons go to UC Irvine," he'd said, and she didn't tell him that she knew this already from her cousin's wife, Bina, who followed news about Vice-Chairman Han's wife's family. Danbi knew that the older son had a Cyworld account, and the younger boy was on MySpace. "I could use a house in Orange County."

Danbi told him that she'd just bought a perfect place for herself but would be happy to sell it to him since she wasn't in a rush to move in, then sent him photographs of the Bear Creek property. Quickly they agreed on a price and set a date for a reunion.

When he rang the doorbell of the model house, Danbi let him in.

"It's been a while," he said to Danbi. "You look very beautiful."

Danbi smiled. She wore a new salmon-colored suit for the occasion. Once, when they'd made love in a men's bathroom stall, she'd worn a similar-colored bra and panty set beneath her clothes, and he had remarked how much he liked that color. His wife wore only white undergarments.

"How long has it been? Since—"

She laughed, covering her mouth with her left hand with its large diamond engagement ring. She didn't tell him how long it had been, not wanting to date herself, but they both knew it had been almost a decade.

"I was surprised when you said you wanted to buy a house here," Danbi said, though she had predicted as much with astonishing accuracy and had reached out to him knowing that he would have ready cash for such a property.

"It's so perfect that I had to buy it, and I would have kept it for myself, but if you get it, then we'll still be neighbors," she said. "I think I should remain in my house a little longer."

"Where do you live?"

"Woodbridge. It's also Irvine, a little north of here."

Han put his hand lightly on her jacket sleeve. He could feel her thin bones beneath the silk tweed fabric.

"I had no idea that you were becoming such a big shot," he said, admiring her diamond ring and gold watch. "I'm glad our reunion worked out today."

"Five bedrooms, five full bathrooms and two half baths," she said, her voice echoing in the unfurnished house.

The vice-chairman walked around the living room, his hands behind his back, admiring the pale wood flooring.

"I know you didn't want to close today, but I called the lawyer, and because it's a cash deal, we can do it as early as tomorrow if your schedule allows. I know how busy you are."

Han said nothing and continued to appraise the house, which was just like the photographs Danbi had sent. In many ways, it seemed larger and more spacious. They both wore their shoes, and he felt like removing them, so he did.

Danbi gasped lightly and touched her breastbone, and he looked at her hand.

"I don't know if it's clean. I mean, it's clean, of course, but there might be dust."

Han wore black dress socks. He shrugged like he didn't care.

"I haven't had a chance to get it mopped. Of course, when you and your family want to move in, I can certainly arrange all that for you. Find you someone to—"

He ignored her and opened every door on the first floor, then opened the door, painted a cobalt blue, near the kitchen. Below two shallow steps was a white-tiled laundry room with two sets of washing machines and dryers. Before he arrived, Danbi had turned on the lights in every room and sprayed lavender scent in the bathrooms. Han peered into the laundry room and spacious butler's pantry but didn't go in.

"$3.5 million," he said. "It's a lot."

"It's a very good price. Everyone wants this development. The best people will be buying here," she said.

Han approached the central staircase and climbed the steps. He checked the bedrooms closest to the upstairs landing, then went to the largest, which had a stunning view of the mountains.

Danbi stood by the door as Han gazed at the mountains. George had said that they had to close this week and return the money to the church. No one suspected anything, but he didn't like this delay. She'd promised to pay any missing interest and tithe from the profits.

"You can't fuck him," he'd said, and she'd said there was nothing like that in her relationship with the vice-chairman. George said he trusted no man with her, and she'd kept a straight face.

"Vice-Chairman Han," she said quietly. "Can you just imagine the sunrises and sunsets? You can have your morning coffee on the terrace outside the bedroom." Many years ago, he had wanted to do it on a balcony of a five-star hotel, so she did.

Han smiled at her. He had not forgotten the balcony, either.

"Do you have time for dinner?"

"Of course," she said. "I brought the sales contract since we've already agreed on the terms. The lawyer said that we could expedite the closing as early as maybe two and a half weeks. Three tops. That's when you'll return from your business in New York?"

"You wore the color I like," he said. "How clever of you to remember. I haven't forgotten anything."

Danbi opened the paper folder to show him the contracts. "We can get them notarized in town. I know several—" He sat on the window ledge, his arms folded across his chest, not saying a word, and she understood what he wanted. They were all the same, and she tried to figure out the order of what she would have to do now. She didn't want to do it on the terrace. "What did you want for dinner?" she asked. "I can make a reservation. There are so many wonderful restaurants near here."

Han turned to check the view. No one could see them inside the house, but he liked all the large windows.

"You hurt my feelings when you left without saying goodbye. I was under the impression that you introduced me to your friend because you were getting ready to move for your family. I had no idea that you were with that Shin Taehun. Wasn't he your boss's boss?" Han said at last. "And he had a wife and kids in New Jersey. He's my age."

Danbi smiled. This time she said nothing.

"Why did you call me?" he asked. "Did you miss me?"

She nodded.

"Come here. What are you wearing beneath your jacket?" he asked.

She closed the door behind her even though there was no one else in the house, and only she had the keys.

He opened the door to the terrace, and she followed.

❧

He wanted to get sushi, so she took him to Saya's, and after they ordered, he told her to cut the price.

"I can't do that," she said. "I bought it close to 3.5."

"It's too much," he said, drinking his brown tea. When he had the choice, Han didn't like to drink alcohol. Drinking too much was a weakness, and in general, he loathed drunkenness. "Change the contract. Otherwise I'm not buying it."

Danbi bit the inside of her lip. He had promised 3.5. The contracts were still in her purse. It was too late in the evening to get them notarized.

"Will you see your sons while you're here?"

He nodded yes and gestured to the server for more tea.

"Where are you staying?"

"At the Marriott."

She and George had been there many times. The front desk people knew her by face.

"Can you stay with me tonight?" he asked her.

"I have to go home. I have a daughter."

Han smiled. "How old?"

"Nine. I should be home now."

"With Shin Taehun?" he said, sounding a little jealous.

"With my daughter."

"Did he divorce his wife?"

Danbi shook her head no.

"But the ring." He gestured at it with his chin. "I thought both of us were married now. Fair game. If I buy the house, then you and I could see each other more often. I come through the West Coast a few times a year, and—"

She laughed.

"You didn't buy it close to 3.5. You bought at the inside price of 2.5. And Shin Taehun is not divorced. His wife grew up with mine. Do you know the most important part of buying something?"

Han straightened his lacquered chopsticks on their curved metal rest and looked up.

"Due diligence," he said.

Danbi picked up her teacup and steadied her breathing.

"I want the house. You can sell it to me for 2.95 and still walk away with a generous profit for less than two months' work, I imagine. We don't have brokers, so I'm saving us a fee. I'm a rich man, but not a stupid one. The house is wonderful, though." Han smiled generously, recollecting how breathtaking she'd looked on the terrace, the sun hanging low. Danbi had only improved with age.

Danbi touched her lower lip briefly, then wiped away the wine-colored lipstick from her fingertips with her napkin.

"I'd better go, Vice-Chairman Han."

"What? The food hasn't arrived."

"I thought you were a friend who could keep a promise. This is disappointing." She picked up her handbag. Danbi couldn't imagine sitting at the table a second longer.

Now he recalled all her funny games. He was prepared to play them for as long as she wanted, but money, well, that was different. He had given her money before, and she had mistaken his grace and caprice for ignorance. Years ago, she had lied to him about why she had to leave him, replacing herself with a substitute; however, he had noted the difference.

While she was seeing him, Danbi had been with another man, and eventually she'd left for America with him. She had wounded Han because he had cared for her. His wealthy father had taught him noblesse oblige for those deserving. Han had always liked giving big handouts to the less fortunate women he bedded. However, with Danbi, he no longer felt as generous. No one wants to be made a fool. There were many houses he could buy, and he felt no urgency. As soon as he saw the prepared contracts, he had known she needed to sell right away.

The rules never changed: Cash was king, and he had plenty of it. Surely he had taught her this when she had come to him for lessons.

Han didn't stir from his seat.

"Well, I will stay for dinner. I'm hungry. I enjoyed seeing you today," he said. "I'll head to New York in two days and return in a few weeks. I'll call you. Would you like that?"

Danbi walked out of the restaurant. She had played it wrong. If she told George, he would surely tell her to accept Han's price immediately.

For two and a half weeks, Danbi waited for Han to phone her, but he did not, and when she finally reached him, he apologized because he'd needed to head back to Seoul early for business reasons. "Next time I come to California, I'll let you know," he said, saying nothing about the house. The next day she phoned him again, and he was in his office in Seoul. "I'm hearing that prices will fall. I can wait. I'm in no rush, and you'll only grow lovelier."

Two days after their last call, the elders of the Finance Committee met with the elders of the building committee to discuss the missing amount from the building fund. The pastors had no choice but to call the police, who arrested George first. The authorities caught up with Danbi at LAX with her passport and $10,000 in cash.

10
Return

São Paolo, Brazil

The taxi driver dropped her off on Rua José Paulino. Nari stood outside the clothing and fabric store and stared at her husband through the plate glass. Seated on a barstool behind the counter, Joonho was reading a newspaper.

He was thinner and browner than she remembered. His reading glasses were perched on his sharp nose. When he was a boy, the children had called him Hawk because of his prominent nose and his broad shoulders. Gray and white patches streaked his thick black hair. She felt compelled to tell him to dye it, and Nari covered her mouth with her left hand, chiding herself for criticizing him in her thoughts. She was afraid to go inside.

The busy street was filled with clothing stores, manufacturers, and clusters of pedestrians in motion. With all the Korean signage, Bom Retiro felt more like downtown Seoul than anywhere in Orange County. All around her, there were Koreans moving about and colorful words in hangul on storefronts, and though Nari hardly knew any Portuguese, she felt like she could get by on the languages she already knew. Lion had taught her how to say "thank you," "help," and "please": *obrigada, ajuda,* and *por favor.*

Joonho didn't look up from his focused reading, and Nari pulled out a mirrored compact from her zippered nylon tote bag and checked her lipstick. Her forehead was mostly unlined, but the crow's-feet had deepened and spread toward her hairline. Before she got on the plane to Brazil, she'd had her hair cut, colored, and styled, hoping to look younger.

Nari pushed the glass door open, and a bell tinkled. Once he saw her, his mouth opened slightly, his feet still fixed to the floor.

"Nari."

She glanced around the store. He seemed to be alone. A faint musty odor of fabric and dust mingled with the smell of an unfamiliar lime aftershave. Joonho had always preferred citrusy scents.

Six mannequins were dressed in bright-colored evening gowns, and behind them were enormous bolts of jewel-toned fabrics. Rolls of measuring tape, pairs of scissors, and pincushions covered an oak worktable near the front counter, where Joonho stood.

"Let's go," Nari said.

"What?" Joonho remained dazed by her appearance, as if she were a ghost.

"I came to bring you home," she said, trying to keep her voice from breaking.

"How did you get here?"

"I took two planes."

Remembering himself, he picked up a barstool with a red leather cushion and brought it closer to her.

"Are you happy to see me?"

He nodded. "Why are you here?"

"You have a grandson."

"What?" Joonho put his hand over his heart.

"Yun had a baby, and I thought you should come home now. Michael is the most beautiful child in the whole world. Even more beautiful than our daughter."

"When did you get here?"

"Late last night."

He couldn't believe that his wife could travel all this way by herself.

"I put my things in the hotel room and took a nap. Lion found a very nice hotel for me. He was so worried about me coming." Nari didn't mention how she'd quarreled with Yun for two months about traveling to Brazil by herself. As soon as she received her American passport, she had pleaded with Yun and Lion about making the trip. "Do you have any coffee for me?"

Joonho rushed to an alcove behind a curtain. Nari could hear a spoon clinking against the mugs. He brought her the coffee.

"It tastes like Taster's," she said. "Why did I think that coffee would be different here?"

Joonho laughed. He didn't know what kind he drank, having bought the large red box at the mart down the street. Sometimes he forgot where he was. Seven days a week, he worked, and he never left the Korean neighborhood. He moved in a closed circuit of his studio apartment, the clothing store, and the mart. Once in a while, he and his cousin Max ate at a Korean restaurant on Rua Prates.

Joonho pulled his stool over to sit near her, but they did not touch. The married couple spoke to each other with the curiosity and politeness of two people on a blind date. He felt as nervous as when he'd first confessed his feelings for her in high school.

"Will you come home with me? Can you leave right away?" she asked.

"I haven't made back my fortune."

"Is this store yours?"

"It's my store, but I owe the manufacturers a lot for the cloth. Paying the tailors is expensive. I didn't know the margins would be this bad. All these clothing stores"—Joonho gestured to the businesses on the street—"we're just killing each other. The prices are so low."

Nari said nothing, knowing how bad her husband was at negotiating. His former partner, the one who'd stolen from them, had been the one who understood how to make money. Joonho was the one who knew how to work.

"I just didn't want to work in food anymore."

"My boss said there's a job for you," she said, referring to Sonya. "It's not food related."

He tilted his head attentively, wanting to go home, but still ashamed.

"We're opening a second nail salon and need another manager. You'd be doing the same job as Mido's father. My boss said that if you came back, you could have the position. She promised me. Elder Sonya Cho is an honest woman. She's Helen Cho's older sister. I wrote to you that she passed away."

Joonho bowed his head slightly in recognition.

"As a manager, I earn more than I did when I was running Shrimp Castle. I brought money with me. To pay off any of your debts. Will you come home?" Nari said again. She tucked in her lower lip, her eyes fearful that he might say no.

Joonho clasped his calloused hands. He wanted to hold her in his arms but didn't think he had the right to do that.

"Is Yun angry with me? Did she tell you not to tell me about the baby?" he asked, already knowing the answer. His daughter never called. On occasion, when he heard from Nari, she'd mention that Yun and Lion were fine and living well, but there was never any news from his daughter. Even a brief message from her in one of Nari's letters would have given him hope. "I guess I ruined her life. And yours."

Nari reached across the coffee tray and put his left hand in hers. He still wore his platinum wedding band.

"Every day, I was hoping that you'd come home. That you would walk through the doors of the nail salon and tell me that you're back for good."

He clenched his jaw, his eyes downcast.

"But then you didn't come. And when little Michael was born, he looked so much like you. Just like your baby pictures. When he was born, he had so much dark hair. Like a silky black mop above the sleepy face of an angel."

Nari dug into her tote bag and pulled out a small blue album filled with photographs of him and Yun.

"You missed his *baek-il*, but you can still make his first birthday party. Remember how I lost that pregnancy before Yun was born? The doctor said it was a boy. Our Yun has a son, and she wants to have three or four kids. Isn't that amazing?" Nari said, crying.

Joonho looked down, feeling the warmth of his wife's tiny hands, her nails a brilliant red. She looked so pretty in her pink linen dress, and he wanted to tell her but felt afraid.

"Where are you staying?"

"At the Luz Plaza. Near the park."

"Yes, that's a good one," he said.

Nari put her hands on his leathery face and felt the scruff of his beard.

"Look at all your freckles," she said, laughing. "I missed you so much."

Joonho couldn't speak.

"You didn't come for me, so I came for you."

He couldn't look at her face.

"I don't care if you don't have a cent. You took good care of me, and I should have said that, when we were having a hard time. If you don't want to work in the nail salon, you don't have to. I don't mind working. I like it."

"No, I want to work. I will work. I am glad you came here."

He wanted to tell her that he was grateful. All he had ever wanted was to go home.

"Are you hungry?" he asked.

"Yes. You should buy me breakfast."

"I should."

"*Yobo*, I don't want to get on those planes by myself. It was so scary. You should take me home," she said, looking at him imploringly. "Please."

Joonho nodded.

❧

When Lion and Yun made the announcement about Fortress Seoul in their email newsletter, over six hundred students applied for their pilot program for Korean students who wanted to attend college in the United States. In the first year, they had room for fifty students. Renee and Lion agreed that forty students would pay a reasonable, market-rate tuition, and ten students would receive a full scholarship, but no one was allowed to discuss their financial status, and, if anyone did, the offending student would face expulsion. Since nearly all international students paid full-freight tuition at American colleges, Renee and her company pledged to provide four-year private scholarships for the ten students.

Through assessments, Lion established a floor for high-aptitude students, and then, from that pool, he chose students by lottery. Standardize, then randomize. In addition to the hagwon tuition payments and pledge of college tuition for ten scholarship students, Renee's family provided Fortress Seoul with office space, dorm rooms, and airfare for the overseas tutors. Lion and Yun would figure out the math to make the numbers work so that the pilot program wouldn't lose money. Tom Song from Eagle Academy had always wanted to try something like this, but it would have been too expensive for him to do by himself.

From the beginning, Tom guessed why Renee had cooked up this scheme. When she came by his office in Daechi-dong, he asked her outright.

"Are you doing this so you can bring Peter back to Korea?" he asked.

"Yes," she said.

"It's an awful lot to go through to—"

"Also, I saw what happened when DH got a scholarship. You made that happen," she said. "It was your brilliant idea."

Tom scratched his head. Creating that scholarship for DH had been one of the strangest things he had ever been asked to do, but even he had to admit that it had been worth the subterfuge and white lies. As an international student of middle-class, white-collar parents, DH would never have received financial aid, and his parents would not have accepted such a generous gift from their son's friend's mother. Their pride wouldn't have allowed it.

"DH is a special case."

"Peter was better off having DH with him at school. Actually, both boys needed each other. Even when Peter was in California, DH's family took such good care of him, and they didn't know for the longest time about DH's scholarship. I think Peter got the better end of the bargain," Renee said.

"It was a lot of money," Tom said. "Not many people would have just paid for a stranger's kid. There's no one like you, Renee."

"I'm not wonderful. I have a lot of money. I told you that my grandfather and grandmother didn't go to college. Grandfather finished high school, but he wanted to be a pharmacist. Instead, he sold used tires, then learned how to manufacture them. He became rich because his timing worked out. He always wanted all of us to be educated and to help Korea."

It was true. Renee wanted her son, Peter, to move back to Seoul; however, she felt bad for the children here who worked unceasingly and their parents who had no idea how to make their kids competitive globally. Everyone just told the kids to do more work.

In high school, she had played tennis seriously. As an athlete, she knew work, talent, and luck were important, but smart coaching was essential, too. In her mind, there had to be another way for these kids to get a global education and bring back beneficial ideas to Korea. Her grandparents had loved the people of their country, and her saintly grandmother, who was almost a Buddhist nun after her husband died—just short of shaving her head—had always told her five children that one must share one's good fortune with those who had less.

Renee couldn't change things for everyone, but if she could affect the education of fifty children, while getting her own son to come back, then it was worth spending a fraction of her wealth on this hagwon experiment.

Soon enough, everyone had to admit it. Within just one academic year, Fortress Seoul had made a difference.

❧

Fortress Seoul occupied two floors of an office building in Daechi-dong, where there were many other hagwons. There were two executive offices, one teachers' lounge, three classrooms, and two spacious meeting areas. Within walking distance, there were six small suites in a long-term residential hotel reserved for three tutors, one college consultant, and the office managers—all from the United States. When Lion came to visit during the first month, Peter insisted that he stay with him. He also wanted to check in on Ginny, now a rising sophomore at UCLA, who was rethinking her premed track and had taken a year off from school to work as an assistant office manager to Mido. It had been her idea to follow Mido and Lion to work at Fortress Seoul to make money and spend time with her family. Her father had opened a restaurant supply export business in Busan, and Ginny's family finances had improved somewhat, but her grandmother now needed more care.

❧

Even after the fifty students were selected, there were numerous appeals to accept more applicants. Peter was getting better at saying no, and thankfully, Tom's petite, unassuming wife, Clara Song, was a master at turning people down. The number of parents who visited the office with boxes of ginseng, orchids, and fabric-wrapped gifts from luxury department stores diminished rapidly when they realized that no one at Fortress was allowed to accept any gifts or money.

Peter had taken the smaller of the two offices, enclosed by glass walls, because everyone tended to gather in the one that Mido and Ginny shared.

Needing to expand their team, they hired another American college consultant, who had a terrific reputation for being able to reach kids. Reg Sherman had been working at an international school in Seoul, and at the end of his term of employment, he decided to join Fortress. It was Mido's job to sort out his employment agreement and immigration issues, so she went to talk to their lawyers in Jongno.

In the imposing lobby of the law firm, the receptionist asked her to wait using formal language and with great deference, which surprised Mido. The last time she had been in Seoul, she was in middle school. Inside she still felt like a child, but now she was an adult, and somehow, through Renee's relationships, Fortress Seoul had become a client of this large and impressive law firm.

On the coffee table, there was a wide assortment of English-language and Korean newspapers, and Mido picked up a copy of the *International Herald Tribune*. Her father had told her that several families at church had recently lost their homes, unable to make their mortgage payments, which had gone up with rising interest rates. Each month Bo, DH, and Mido sent their father money to help with the mortgage, taxes, and expenses, so he was okay. He had a fixed rate, so his monthly payments hadn't changed.

As Mido scanned an article about subprime mortgages and foreclosures in California, she heard footsteps approaching.

"Mido?"

She heard his Australian accent. Tek stood in front of her, staring down with his familiar warm smile. He wore an expensive-looking gray suit and black leather Oxfords. Tek had always cared about his appearance. He seemed taller than she remembered. He looked wonderful.

She didn't know what to say.

"My first love is sitting in this lobby reading a newspaper," he said in Korean, laughing.

"Your accent has improved," Mido said, standing up.

"No, don't get up. Sit, sit."

Tek sat beside her on the leather sofa.

"Why are you here?" he asked.

"I'm here to see Linda Hur. She's an employment lawyer."

"Oh, I don't know her."

"Wait. Why are you here?" Mido asked.

"I'm here for work. One of our clients has a thorny issue with a Korean company, and it was easier to bring me in at this stage." Tek chuckled. "The other lawyer on this matter is a mate from the debate world who's now based in Seoul. We're trying to avoid an expensive contract renegotiation."

He smiled at Mido, just happy to be near her.

"Anyway, I'm talking too much. Gosh, it's terrific to see you. You look fantastic. I like your hair long." He pointed to her face. "It's very pretty."

"Oh, Tek. How strange it is to see you. I mean—"

"Wait, I tell you that you're pretty, and you tell me that it's strange to see me." Tek smiled. "Hey, what are you doing for lunch after? How long is your meeting? I can cancel my next appointment if you're free." He paused and checked his watch. "We could get dinner at this great place down the street. You used to be crazy about soondubu, right? Oh, hang on."

He picked up her left hand and inspected it, making Mido laugh out loud.

"You're not married, right? I'm not married yet. You broke my heart, so I hold you entirely responsible."

It was the same old Tek—open, funny, and full of hope. Being with him felt familiar and comfortable, and though she wasn't doing anything wrong, suddenly it occurred to her that perhaps this was not a good idea.

"How long are you in Seoul?" he asked.

"You've asked me a lot of questions," Mido observed.

"I know. I want to know everything. I've missed you. I'm not mad at you anymore. That's all. Can I just say that?"

A tall Korean woman, her severe face chalky white from foundation and lips stained a dark pink, appeared. She wore a brown wool skirt suit and low-heeled shoes.

"Hello, I'm Linda Hur. You must be Ms. Koh." Linda shook her hand, then glanced at Tek. "Are you together?"

Tek laughed. "We used to be. Right?" He turned to her and smiled mischievously.

Mido shook her head and pushed him away lightly.

"Don't mind me. I'm a lawyer from Sydney. I was just visiting your colleague Jonathan Yoo, and I ran into a dear old friend." Tek smiled. He held up his hand with the confidence of someone who always knew what to say. "Linda, could you just give us a minute?"

The lawyer retreated to the reception desk.

"Dinner tonight? I'm at the Grand Hyatt. How's six?"

She couldn't refuse. Tek would never accept no for an answer.

"Okay."

"The hotel lobby, then. Oh, here." He handed her his card. "My mobile number is there. So much to talk about."

She smiled, having been swept up in his enthusiasm and warmth. He wasn't angry at her.

❧

DH could not believe it.

"Are you going to tell Peter?" he whispered into the phone receiver.

"Of course. I already did."

"What did he say?"

"He said, 'Have a good time.' "

"Seriously?"

"He's not the jealous type."

"You're wrong, little sister. Everyone is the jealous type. Peter is a cool customer, but he's human," DH said. "Hang on, how did he look?"

"Great, but it's not like that."

"Wow. Didn't he want to marry you? Wait, is he married? He must be married."

"Nope. He picked up my hand to check if I was, then told me he's not."

"He wants you back. Men are simple."

"He said he's not angry at me."

"Yup, he wants you back."

"No, he wants to catch up, and I'm with Peter now."

"If you get back together with Tek, then you'll move back to Australia. Dad is better now, and you're done with your indentured servitude. But gosh, Fortress Seoul is a goner. Poor Peter. But he hasn't made an offer, and I do want my sister to get what she wants." DH glanced out his office window. He wished he could tell Peter to get his act together. "I guess you'll get married first of the three of us. Just as I thought."

"You're out of your mind. I'm not getting back together with Tek. And why do you assume marriage is even what I want? We're just having soondubu."

When they got off the phone, Mido felt less certain than she had sounded with her brother. She should've said no to dinner, but that would've been rude. Also, she was curious about how Tek was doing. They'd been so close for so long; wasn't it natural to want to know more about his life?

When she'd returned from the law firm and seen Peter, she'd mentioned seeing Tek in the lobby. Peter had not seemed bothered by it. In a normal tone of voice, he'd said, "Have a good time," then gone back to his office to review study materials.

11
Trust

They reached a settlement, and the Chairman put the agreement in writing.

Sonya would live in Seoul in the same complex and remain in California no longer than twelve weeks a year. She would never divorce Yong-gil, even after the Chairman died. The boys would inherit the business, and Sonya would have the controlling shares for her lifetime. The Chairman bought her a three-bedroom apartment in the newest building, a few minutes' walk from his residence. Each morning, she went to her former apartment and checked on the household.

It was summer, and the family had a Western-style breakfast: eggs, sautéed mushrooms and tomatoes, yogurt, and toast. Afterward, Yong-gil and their sons left for work as if nothing had changed. Her sons believed that Sonya had decided to move out because she was going through a change in her life. Menopause made women peculiar, she'd told them, and this was her solution.

The Chairman looked forward to the mornings when he could be alone with her.

"I'm going to California next month."

He said nothing, not needing to remind her that it could only be for a month.

"I've made all the arrangements with the housekeeper and your secretary, so you won't be inconvenienced."

"You look lovely in that dress."

Sonya wore a camel-colored cardigan over a dark-beige shift and nude stockings. As usual, she wore her wedding band, and, this morning, no other jewelry except for small brown pearls in her ears.

"Do you have a lot of work?" he asked.

After breakfast, she would remain in her home office and study the same packet of documents that the Chairman had reviewed the previous day. Except for where she slept, little had changed in the main residence. Even her bedroom remained the same, left unoccupied in case she wanted to come back, puzzling the staff, who knew she lived openly in the building across from theirs.

"I was going to look over the acquisition papers. What did you think of the deal?"

"The numbers make sense. It's easier to buy this realty company rather than building a new business in Hongdae."

They enjoyed talking about work. The Chairman believed that she was as smart as his nephew, who had gone to business school. He wondered what would have happened if she had remained at the company and not married his nephew. Would he have promoted her? He often imagined the different scenarios. How could he have known that his wife would die and that the only woman he wanted would be Yong-gil's wife?

The Chairman smoothed her hair, and Sonya pulled back. She looked in the direction of the kitchen. The cook and housekeeper were absorbed in eating their breakfast.

"Please don't." Sonya got up, and the Chairman followed her to her office and closed the door.

Once or twice a week, he tried to wear her down. Sonya refused to give in, but she could not imagine leaving the family home altogether. She loved him, and he knew this.

"I wish you wouldn't go to California," he said. "I know we have an agreement, but it is so hard when you are gone."

Sonya said nothing. When she was in the States, she thought of him even more than usual. She worried about his meals and health more than she did about her sons. They talked on the phone daily, which was also part of their agreement.

"I can't come here anymore if you insist—"

He moved closer to her, and she turned to the office door and opened it wide. There was no one in the hallway.

"If you keep doing this," she said to him firmly, "I'll have to do my work somewhere else."

The Chairman closed his eyes, preparing himself for the same speech she usually gave. He intended to persuade her. He believed that she would choose to return to their main residence. Her moving out could not possibly be permanent.

"I can get an office at the company. It makes more sense than to work from here."

The Chairman grimaced, familiar with this oft-repeated statement, which stung like a threat.

"I'll just stay in the room and let you read. I have my own reading to do."

Sonya acquiesced. She wanted him to stay with her. When he was near, she felt less anxious, and he felt the same.

After dinner, she returned to her apartment to bathe and sleep. In the morning, she would return. This arrangement had to be enough.

❧

Mido met Tek in the Grand Hyatt hotel lobby.

They got into a cab, and when Tek gave the directions to the driver in Korean, Mido marveled at his fluency. He seemed more confident than when she'd last seen him in Los Angeles.

"I never thought I'd run into you here," she said.

"Why? I'm Korean, too."

"Well, yes, and you seem at ease."

"I love Seoul."

"Really? Have you spent much time here?"

"Two of our large clients have important business relationships in Korea, so now and then my firm sends me over. Guess what? I'm still on track."

"To becoming a barrister?"

"Did you ever doubt it?" Tek grinned. It had always been his long-term plan to work at a firm and build commercial expertise so when he became a barrister, he would have ready referral business.

"When you're a barrister, you'll get to argue in court, right?" she asked.

"Yes. But sometimes we can work things out before going to court. I can fight you, or we can try to get on."

The way he said this made her think that Tek had said it before.

"Do you like it here?" he asked.

"Yes," Mido said.

"Seoul is a shorter flight, compared to the States. Everyone is nice to me here. Even my parents think that Seoul has gotten much better since they left. They've started coming back a lot."

"Wow." Mido blinked. It had been a little less than a year since she'd arrived, and though she felt comfortable here, she could not have imagined that Tek would like it so well.

"So Mido, why are you here?"

"We opened a hagwon. For college admissions. Kind of like the one we had in Irvine."

Tek looked puzzled. "There are a lot of those here already, no?"

"Yes," she answered, remembering how he felt about her work.

❧

Tek had made reservations at a galbi place where he knew everyone. The manager guided them to a wood-paneled private room, past the enormous public dining area swarming with fast-moving servers carrying large circular trays laden with marinated meats and side dishes.

"This is nice," Mido said of the well-appointed room with the rectangular grill table and four chairs for just the two of them. The server closed the door discreetly as he left.

"I'm trying to impress you. Are you impressed?"

She smiled, her eyes crinkling.

"Are you with that guy now?" Tek asked abruptly.

"Who? Peter?"

"The son of the THT heir."

"Yes, we're together. And I didn't know that about him for a long time."

"I didn't say you did."

"You looked him up," Mido said quietly, as she studied the menu. The prices were high. Tek used to prefer simpler things. Anzac cookies alone would delight him. This dinner would cost several hundred dollars. His clothes, shoes, and even this restaurant. Everything reeked of money.

"Why haven't you married him?"

"You don't waste any time."

"I'm an excellent lawyer," Tek said. "Have you forgotten?"

"No."

"I was thinking this afternoon that maybe we were meant to meet here. It's like neutral territory, or a kind of homecoming for people like us."

She looked up from the leather-bound menu, trying to see where he was going with this.

"I could never live in California, and you didn't want to live in Australia. But maybe we can be together here."

"I'm with Peter."

Tek appeared thoughtful. "I've known you longer than most people in my life."

Mido closed the menu and stared at him.

"Tek."

"Koh Mido, my first love." He laughed ruefully, saying this part in Korean as if he were reciting a moment in his autobiography. "I know, I know. You're with Peter."

Mido smiled and let him order their dinner. When they finished eating, she told him that she had to get back. He ordered a taxi for them and dropped her off at her brother's.

"I leave tomorrow morning for Sydney. Now that I have your number, I'll send you a message now and then. Not too often. I'm glad we're back in touch."

Tek held out his hand for her to shake, and she shook it before getting out of the car.

❧

When Mido opened the door to the apartment, DH and Peter were on the living room sofa watching a Pohang Steelers game, remnants of takeout on the coffee table in front of them.

"Oh, you're back," DH said, not turning his eyes away from the screen. "How's Tek?"

"Fine." She removed her shoes. Peter waved at her.

"How's the game?" she asked, gathering the empty containers. She piled them onto a tray and took them to the kitchen counter. When she returned, Peter was watching the game intently. He didn't say anything.

Mido looked at DH, and he raised his eyebrows conspiratorially.

"I'm going to wash up," he said. "Early-morning meetings. You stay and watch the game," DH said to Peter.

Mido sat down. "How was your night?"

"Good."

Peter smiled at her and appeared measured. He wasn't the sort to show his hand.

"You two usually watch games at your place."

"DH invited me over."

"Are you upset with me?" she asked.

"I'm not." Peter faced her and looked into her eyes like he was trying to see what was on her mind.

"He leaves tomorrow. For Sydney. Tek just wants to be friends."

"Men don't do that."

Mido had heard this before, but she didn't believe it. Lion was both her boss and Yun's husband, and he was her friend, too. Her brothers had female friends. The dinner had been lighthearted and fun. Tek had been flirtatious, and she'd enjoyed the attention, but she would never take it any further than that. If Peter didn't want her to be friends with him, then she wouldn't see him.

"Does it bother you?"

"No," Peter said.

Mido said nothing and watched a pizza commercial. The second half of the game started, but Peter turned to her.

"I came to Korea because of you. Because you wanted to try this hagwon idea. Because I thought we were going to help kids. It's a utopian mission, right? Our great educational experiment. We have a lot to do. I better get back home. Do you want to come back with me? We can't stay here."

"Tomorrow night."

Peter left without turning off the game.

❧

As Mido washed the glasses in the sink, DH came out of his room.

"I changed my mind. Tek is not the one. If he was, then you'd be with him."

"Wow," Mido said.

"Don't mess this up with Peter. He's the best guy in the world. I know he's got some hang-ups about marriage, but people like us don't understand what it's like to come from that kind of family."

"Their family is not better than ours."

"No, but they're different."

"So I'm learning."

"I guess Tek is still interested," DH said, sounding concerned.

Mido didn't say anything. She put the beer cans in the bin.

"I hope nothing bad happens between you and Peter," DH said, shaking his head.

"Why, because it'll hurt your relationship with his family's company? That's not going to happen," she said.

"That's harsh," DH said, wounded by her incisiveness. "But come to think of it, I guess if you pull the plug on Peter, then his mom won't like it, either. And I love Renee. Please don't hurt Renee."

"First you don't want me to hurt Peter, and now you're protecting Renee. Huh. I thought you were my brother."

"Don't listen to me. My imagination is running wild. This is what makes me a great corporate lawyer. I can foresee all sorts of problems."

"You're the second person tonight who's told me that he's a good lawyer. That can't be normal. Listen, there's nothing to worry about. More importantly, you should be on my side."

"I would step in front of a truck for you, and I trust you implicitly."

"I'm not going to hurt anyone. I may never see Tek again. It was weird running into him today, and I wasn't sure how to decline his dinner invitation."

"Peter was knocked out by it."

Mido stopped cleaning. Peter was her best friend, and it was true what he'd said earlier. He wouldn't have come back to Seoul, the city he didn't want to live in, unless she'd insisted that Fortress Seoul was a good idea. He had trusted her, and she had done something wrong.

"He said that it was okay for us to be friends."

"Dummy. You can't be friends with Tek. He's still single, right? He wanted to marry you. Dudes don't do that. Men are not friends with women. They wait around until you change your mind."

"Is there a manual I never got?"

"He has something to prove, and now that you're with Peter, an important person in Korea, Tek is going to pull out all the stops."

Mido stared at him like he was crazy.

"Okay. Where did he take you to dinner?"

"Palace Gate?" She was pretty sure that was the name.

"That's the most expensive galbi place in Korea." DH said this with the certainty of having won an argument.

Mido poured herself a glass of water and went to the sofa. It surprised her to think that DH would worry, or that Peter wouldn't trust her.

DH sat and put his arm around her shoulder.

"Now let's think about something else entirely, because I have big news," he said.

"What?"

"Bo called."

"Is Dad okay?"

"It's not about me. Or you."

"Spit it out, DH!" Mido was too tired for DH's games.

"Danbi Jung and George Hong were arrested."

"*Ajeossi*'s wife? I mean Mr. Shin."

"Yeah, well, sort of wife," DH said, shaking his head.

"George Hong? Isn't he an elder? Dad's on some committee with him, right?"

"They're all elders. Fucking bonkers."

"What did they do?"

"Turns out Danbi and George took money from the church building fund, and Danbi embezzled premiums from their insurance clients. George confessed to the whole thing."

"That's crazy. So why did Bo call you? Just to tell you this?" It wasn't like their brother to gossip.

"Mr. Shin's lawyer wanted to speak with Dad. Dad called Bo, and Bo called me, because I'm the consigliere."

"Huh?"

"I'm the general counsel. The family lawyer?"

Mido was confused. "Didn't Mr. Shin and that woman hurt Dad's career? I mean, Dad lost his job after the IMF Crisis, but he would've been better situated if she hadn't falsely accused him. Mom only told me a little about it, and Aunt Sonya just said that we should never ever deal with Danbi Jung. Not even say hi. Yun told me that she and Lion couldn't buy insurance from them."

Mido paused for a drink of water.

"Mom said she could forgive anyone who hurt her, but it was impossible to forgive anyone who hurt Dad," Mido said, remembering the time she'd asked her mother why their family avoided his oldest friend. "I think Dad had sort of forgiven him, but Mom disliked that woman till the very end."

"Can't imagine Mommy not forgiving someone," DH said.

"Hang on," Mido said, recalling something he'd said earlier. "And what did you mean, 'sort of wife'?"

"Turns out, Mary Ajumma and Ajeossi never got a divorce. And now she's out in California trying to help him."

"No way."

"Yeah. And Joey—"

"He's the oldest son, right?" Mido tried to remember him. It had been years since she last saw Mary Ajumma and her sons.

"Yeah. Joey and Luke are both lawyers. Anyway, Joey had to hire a white-collar lawyer for his dad in California. Ajeossi is so fucked."

12
Cleanup

When she saw Shin's number on the screen, Mary almost didn't pick up. She was about to head out to work, but she'd been meaning to speak with her husband about their eldest son's engagement. Joey didn't want his father at the wedding. As far as he and his younger brothers were concerned, their father might as well be dead. She held out hope that one day they'd forgive him.

Shin and his estranged wife spoke only a few times a year. He still sent Mary money each month, which helped with the mortgage and the high property taxes in Bergen County. She still worked at Sandoval's Flowers on East Ridgewood Avenue. At a moment's notice, Mary could put together a hundred boutonnieres for a prom or gorgeous wedding arrangements for the pickiest bride, or ferry a delivery across town when the driver got sick.

On the hall table, Mary put down her car keys and rested her stainless steel commuter mug filled with milky hot coffee. She wore a beige raincoat from her college days over a white button-up shirt, a quilted cotton work vest, and an A-line denim skirt. On her left shoulder, she carried a large canvas tote bag, which held her wallet and change purse, lip balm, a tissue packet, a ham and cheese sandwich she'd packed that morning, a thin cardigan, and the library books she'd return after work. As usual, she wore thin white socks beneath green garden clogs.

"I was wondering if the boys could help me find a good lawyer." Shin wasted no time with pleasantries.

"What?" Mary rested the tote bag by the brass umbrella stand.

"I need a lawyer who does white-collar criminal defense." From church and work, Shin knew several Korean lawyers, but he couldn't ask them. "I thought Joey and Luke might know which firms specialize in this out here."

"They don't do that kind of work," Mary said out of habit, repeating what her sons had advised their mother to say whenever people asked her for their help with immigration or family law. No one had ever sought help with criminal law. Joey was a securitization lawyer at Cleary Gottlieb, and Luke practiced bankruptcy litigation at Weil Gotshal.

"I could go to prison if they think I was involved. I need someone good. I didn't really understand what she was doing."

"What? What's going on? Why would you go to—" She couldn't say the word "prison."

"Danbi took money from the insurance account, and her boyfriend, George, took money from the church for her investment property. They said they were going to return it. I didn't know anything." Shin told her what he had just learned himself.

Still holding her phone, Mary sat down on the cold tile floor. There were no chairs in the foyer.

"Hello?" Shin said. "Hello?"

She felt like someone had shoved her to the ground and was holding her in place. At eye level with the shoe shelf, Mary stared at the neat row of Patrick's white sneakers and hospital clogs.

"Hello?" Shin repeated.

Suddenly it occurred to Mary that her husband's name might appear in the newspapers and that Joey's fiancée's parents might see it.

"Is this in the newspapers?"

"Yes," he said.

"I'll call you back."

In the evening, the boys came over and told her that she needed to divorce him immediately. In the morning, they made calls for their father and engaged Andy Kuo, a former prosecutor, who knew financial fraud well and specialized in white-collar work. Since George had implicated Danbi in his confession, they would be tried separately, Kuo said. Danbi, who had pleaded not guilty, was being detained without bail because she was a flight risk and had assaulted a deputy. Kuo would not represent Danbi, solely Shin. So far, Shin had not been charged with anything, but now, thanks to his sons, Shin had a lawyer.

The boys were thorough. Mary gave them the divorce agreement Shin had sent her before, and Joey asked a colleague who did family law to update the agreement. Luke booked Mary a flight and made reservations for a hotel in Irvine.

✤

Mary had never been anywhere in the United States except for New Jersey and New York. After Seoul, her entire world had been confined to these two states. Her boys had gone to college and law school in New York and New Jersey—the older two at NYU and Columbia, and her youngest at Rutgers. Their father had not been invited to any of the graduations. Shin had paid the college tuitions for all three of their sons and the mortgage for the house; for graduate schools, the boys took out loans.

When she reached his house, Mary parked her rented white Toyota in the circular driveway. The doors of the three-car garage were open, revealing a white Mercedes and a silver Porsche. She had not known that her husband was wealthy. He had sent her money regularly, never complaining about the amount. Had she known how he lived, she would have asked him for their sons' graduate school tuitions. The boys would have resisted, though.

The modern house was two stories high, and from the driveway, Mary could make out Italian sofas and large paintings on white walls behind the glass-fronted great room. Through the window, she saw a milky white chandelier set in the foyer ceiling above the pair of large oak doors.

Her husband opened the door.

His feet bare, Shin wore a white golf shirt and faded blue jeans. He hadn't shaved for days.

"Your hair," he said. Somehow, her long gray hair surprised him. He was trying to remember the last time he'd seen her. She used to dye it.

At sixty years old, Shin's hair was more salt and pepper than white, and still quite full. Danbi was thirty-nine, and she kept her straight black hair long, well below her shoulder blades.

Mary touched her head and looked down.

Seeing the hurt in her eyes, he felt stupid.

"I mean—"

"I stopped coloring it," she said.

"I appreciate you coming. All this way. I'm embarrassed. I didn't think this would be the first time seeing each other here. It's been so long. I am sorry. To you and the boys—"

Again, Mary touched her shoulder-length hair, which she wore in a low ponytail. She was fifty-nine years old. Her face was freckled, and faint lines crossed her pale brow and radiated around her brown eyes. She was still a beautiful woman and had never been vain. Over the years, she had lost interest in makeup and treatments. Recently, Joey's sweet fiancée, Gracie, had asked if she wanted an appointment at the salon with the bridal party, and Mary had remembered that there would be photographs. She still hadn't bought a dress.

Every cent had gone to her boys' education, their housing, and their food. Joey and Luke shared an apartment with two friends in the city to save money while repaying their law school loans. Patrick was in the nursing program at Rutgers. Joey and Luke wanted him to be a doctor, but Patrick preferred to make money sooner and avoid debt; he'd opted for Rutgers over the University of Pennsylvania and lived at home. When he was done with school, Mary planned to sell the house and buy a one-bedroom condo in Palisades Park. The property taxes were killing her budget.

❧

Shin leaned his back against the open door and closed his eyes. Mary stared at the wide marble door saddle and tried to keep from crying. Her father and mother had advised her not to marry him. They'd died without forgiving her.

"I don't know what else to say," Shin said.

"Can I come in?"

Shin shook his head, disgusted with himself for not having any sense. "I'm sorry," he said again, and brought her a pair of slippers.

In the living room, Mary didn't sit down. She pulled a manila envelope from her tote bag and took a deep breath.

"The boys told me that I have to divorce you. Right away. I need you to sign these papers. The lawyers just updated the forms you sent me that time. The house. You said I could have it."

Shin took the envelope but didn't open it.

Mary was a kind person and careful in the way she spoke. On the plane, she had prepared a script for their conversation, which included some news about the boys. She wasn't the sort of person who would abandon someone in crisis; she felt disloyal. Standing on the deep white pile carpet, she took in the elegance of the room, which looked like part of a millionaire's mansion on television.

"I have to get back to work. I am inconveniencing my employers," she said. "Mr. Sandoval is filling in for me, and he's older and gets tired. If you could just sign the agreement and the affidavit. Joey said we need to get them notarized. I'll take them back, and Joey said the lawyers will file—"

"Can you sit down?" he asked.

Mary sat on the ivory mohair-wool upholstered sectional in the exquisite living room, as nice as any she'd seen in the glossy magazines at her dentist's. Sand-colored rugs, an enormous gas-burning marble fireplace, a red-and-blue abstract wall-size painting hanging somehow on a thick wall of glass by the floating staircase. A thin carved wooden handrail led to the second floor. Huge panes of thick clear glass seemingly in every direction she looked.

Outside, through the living room window, she could make out the calm blue water of the Olympic-size communal swimming pool and rows of tennis courts for the residents of the development. Tall cypress trees lined the streets.

❧

"Let me get you coffee. Do you still drink your coffee with half a cup of hot milk?"

"I do. But I don't want coffee." Mary looked around the room. There were many framed photographs of his daughter, Anna, with Danbi. None of his sons, or her, not that she'd expected to see any.

"Is she here? Your daughter."

"She's at school."

"And your—"

"She's in jail. She tried to get bail but she couldn't." He could see Mary didn't want to know. "I don't care anymore, I guess."

"What? How can you say that?"

She had met Danbi once in Seoul at his office without understanding who she was. Later, there had been other opportunities to meet her, but Mary hadn't seen the point. There was a brief call where Mary hung up because she didn't know what to say. She'd met the others before Danbi—all pretty, sexy, and young. How could this one be any different? she'd figured, not expecting him to leave their marriage and sons.

"Danbi cheated with an elder from church. A younger man than me. Isn't that funny?" he said without smiling. "He stole money for her. He was married."

Mary frowned at the sordidness of it. Shin's house was pristine, not a thing out of place. Little Anna. Her sons had a half sister they had never met. She didn't want to think about her.

"The divorce agreement." She glanced at the envelope between them. "I need to go home."

"I asked you for a divorce and you always said no. Your religion wouldn't allow it," Shin said, sounding bitter. "And now you're in a hurry. Are you still Catholic?"

Mary tried to think of her sons. In her mind, they looked younger than they were now—more like three little boys than the grown men who gathered at her house for dinner every Sunday.

"Please." Mary stared at the envelope.

"I can lose everything I've worked for, and I don't know who will care for Anna."

Mary shook her head, understanding what he wanted.

"I cannot help you with Anna, too," she said. "You need to call a friend. I cannot be your friend."

"I've destroyed all the good in my life. I am sorry." Shin tried to take her hand, but Mary pulled away.

"I am garbage," he said.

She didn't know what to do.

"He might listen to you," Shin said suddenly. "You can call him. I need help."

"Who?"

"Koh Yohan. He lives here. I told you." He had tried to contact John several times, but he wouldn't answer.

Mary had missed Helen's funeral; she hadn't been able to afford the travel. She thought of the man who had always been so decent.

"He's an elder and everyone trusts him. He's on the important committees at church. John knows I'd never steal—"

Mary stared at her husband, his eyes desperate and sad.

"Can you ask him to speak with me?"

"I cannot."

"John would listen to you."

"Have you lost your mind? After what Jung Danbi did to him, I was so embarrassed. If his wife hadn't called me, I don't know if I could've ever faced her again. She was such a good person."

From the window, Mary's rental car looked like a cheap toy in the green sea of dark cypress trees and lush, well-cut grass. Over the years, at her church, poor men and women her age had died of different cancers, and sometimes Mary wondered if hard work alone could kill people.

"John would feel sorry for you," Shin said.

Mary couldn't believe what he was saying. What she had read in the newspapers about him and that woman, none of it made any sense. These were the sorts of things that happened to bad people. But her sons had explained that it was possible that their father could go to prison for embezzling insurance premiums even if he hadn't done it, because as the CEO, he should have known. He was lucky that the prosecutor hadn't chosen to charge him yet.

"I have no one left," he said. "I'll sign the agreement if you can get John to talk with me."

Every morning and night, Mary prayed to God to forgive him. She wanted to be free from the hatred, self-righteousness, and hardening of her heart. In her life, there were glorious beams of light—her church, her sons, and her work at the florist's. There'd been moments when she felt free of the humiliation, betrayal, and exhaustion. But in this living room with the soaring ceilings and lovely afternoon sunshine, the silver-framed images of that woman who was unquestionably more beautiful and their adorable child, evidence of their love—she wanted him to suffer. He was willing to hurt her again to save himself.

"I have no right to ask that good man to help you," Mary said.

"I need to talk with him. I have to know what's going on at church. He would know. No one else will tell me. I didn't do anything wrong," he said, and he watched her face crumple with disappointment because of course, he had done so many wrong things to her. "I mean, I didn't steal from my company or from the church. He knows me."

Mary wanted to be back at work, doing something with her hands. When she arranged flowers, she felt useful. A kind of tension was released from her shoulders.

She held out the envelope. "Are you going to sign this?"

"If you get him to talk with me, I'll sign. But please, please ask him. Our sons shouldn't have a father in prison. Imagine how that'll look if the boys ever want to get married."

Mary looked up and realized that she hadn't told him about Joey and

Gracie. The wedding was in six months. Gracie's parents had not connected that the Anaheim church scandal in the papers involved Joey's father. Of course, they would have to be told.

She knew he hadn't stolen any money. He was a terrible husband and father, but he had never been a man who was greedy for money. He had been lustful about sex and vain about his appearance, but he would never take a cent that didn't belong to him. The splendor of this house and the expensive cars were not like him, either, and Mary knew that all of this must have been what Danbi had wanted.

"Please ask for me. Please. I'll sign the agreement. I promise. You and the boys can throw me away. I won't bother you ever again. Please help me. Please save me this one time." Shin covered his mouth and wept. "I didn't take anyone's money. I'm the victim here. Who will care for Anna?"

Mary looked at him, then closed her eyes.

"We have to use your phone," he said. His number would show up on caller ID.

Mary took her mobile phone from her bag, and Shin dialed the number for Rose Salon. Nari answered.

"Hello," Mary said in Korean, and introduced herself as Helen's friend. She asked to speak with Koh Yohan.

13

Rosetta Stone

Year one of the fifty-student pilot program had been, perhaps, too successful. From word of mouth alone there were a staggering number of applicants for the following year's Fortress Seoul.

The five partners and managers met in the large conference room. They drank coffee and took notes. They were not the kind of people who were interested in congratulating themselves. Rather, they tried to figure out next steps. Tom and Clara Song, the owners of Eagle Academy, felt confident that they could double in size, but Peter and Mido weren't as certain. Lion, who had flown into Seoul alone the night before, listened carefully.

"I'd have to find more consultants and train them well," Peter said. "But I'd prefer to keep the size smaller. For another year, maybe."

"But we can help more kids," Tom countered. "Renee promised to find scholarships to send maybe even twenty kids to the United States if we double in size. This year we're sending ten."

Mido glanced at Lion, who refrained from talking. She couldn't tell if he was jet-lagged or thinking.

Tom, suffering from allergies, sneezed twice, and his wife, Clara, handed him a packet of tissues from her purse.

"We have enough applicants to double or even triple the number of students, but Peter is right. It all depends on the consultant-to-student ratio. Parents like that Fortress only does the application section, and the kids seem focused," Tom said, sniffling.

"We could keep it small and charge double," Clara said.

"Would that even work?" Lion asked, facing the owners of Eagle Academy. Yun was better at the pricing models, and he wished she had come with him. She was busy overseeing Exodus and Fortress and didn't want to leave the baby. "I don't know the market here very well. Could they even pay that?"

"We charge considerably less than most college consulting hagwons in Seoul. We can certainly increase our tuition, if only to reduce the number of applicants."

"That isn't why we came here," Mido said. "I thought we were going to be priced moderately and provide at least ten kids free tuition. If we're less expensive, we could expand the number of applicants and select the strongest students, right? Not just the ones who can pay more."

Lion was always trying to keep tuition prices down, and Yun had to remind him that they paid their tutors the highest rates in Orange County, so something had to give.

No resolution in sight, Clara raised her eyebrows and checked her phone before putting it away in her jacket pocket.

"I have to head back to Eagle," she said. "Three meetings with mother groups this afternoon. Everyone wants to take the summer session with Fortress, and I don't know how much longer I can hold them off. Please"—she folded her hands as if in prayer—"please just tell me the final numbers."

"I'll stay," Tom said to his wife, and Clara waved goodbye before leaving.

"Do you think we aren't charging enough?" Lion asked, and Tom laughed.

"Right now you're sort of running a charity, and it's interesting because you're getting better results than some of the best consulting hagwons here. We had eleven Ivy acceptances, one Stanford, two MIT, as well as the best state schools. Some of the kids who got into these schools surprised even me," Tom said. "The parents keep calling me to offer to take us out to dinner."

"Well, you know what that means," Peter said. He never let a parent buy him a meal because too often it came with an ask.

"They're mostly just trying to say thank you," Tom said, dismissing Peter's cynicism. "I'm just glad that Fortress Seoul is taking such good care of the kids. And you're doing an amazing job training the essay tutors," he said to Mido, who wasn't allowed to work with the students directly since she didn't have a college degree.

"I don't know how much longer we can stay here," Peter said.

Lion and Tom looked up.

Mido smiled at Peter, wanting to support him.

"The parents are making me crazy," Peter said. "There's no way I can handle twice the number. The kids are really bright, but they seem so freaked out. I feel like I spend half my time trying to remind them that this is not everything."

"But it feels like it is. To them," Tom said. "They've worked so hard for this moment. Believe it or not, you're removing much of the stress from their shoulders."

Mido sensed this was true. The students here wrote the tutors thank-you notes and brought them tiny jars of candies or stuffed animals. The cards mentioned how they felt better because they liked coming to Fortress to work on the applications and had someone to ask for help who didn't pressure them.

"Do you want to come home?" Lion asked Peter and Mido.

Before Peter had a chance to answer, Tom interrupted, "This hagwon might not work without you and Mido. Good teachers are incredibly rare."

The four of them decided to take a few days to think about a possible expansion. Tom left first, and Lion remained with Peter and Mido.

❧

While Lion spoke with Peter, Mido got a text.

Once or twice a month, she heard from Tek. She hadn't seen him since their dinner. Tek was dating someone, he said, which made Mido feel better about them being friends.

The message read: Heading to Seoul for work. Dinner tomorrow?

❧

Mido met him at a Japanese restaurant famous for its shabu-shabu. Tek was waiting at the table when she arrived.

"How's work?" Tek asked, sounding no different from when they were in college.

"It's busy. After I eat, I need to get back to the office. I have to review a lot of files."

"You're doomed."

"Hmm?"

"Your hours. Koreans work nonstop, and Americans never take any time off. You're both. If you had stayed in Australia, you'd have some balance in your life. When's the last time you went on holiday?" Tek asked, his Australian accent getting stronger.

Mido tried to think. After the family moved to California, she had never once taken a vacation. No one in her family had. Everyone worked. They had to.

"You have to take a holiday. All this work is not good for you. You're going to get sick."

"You work a lot," she observed, taking a sip of her tea.

"How long will you do this, Mido?" he asked.

"What?"

"This hagwon business. It's a nice, updated concept. Promotes more fairness. I get that. But you haven't finished uni. When does that come in?"

"It's funny. In LA, no one outside my family seemed to care whether or not I got my degree. At work, no one seems to care anymore. Here I get asked quite a lot. Not that it's stopped the business from succeeding."

"Koreans are so damn crazy about education and degrees," Tek said. "They're obsessed."

"That's not always a bad thing. I don't blame them. I mean, it's better than not caring very much about education. In the States, hardly any politician talks about reading, math, or science levels. It's like a taboo subject. Almost no one in America blinks if a child practices all the time for a sport, but it's somehow terrible if a child studies nonstop," she said. "I enjoy sports, but most kids won't become athletes. Nearly every kid could benefit from getting a sound education."

"You sound like a Korean parent," Tek said, laughing. "My mother used to tell me this when I wanted to keep playing badminton. I wasn't great, but I loved being on the team."

"That's good that you liked it and played," Mido said. "I don't mean it has to be one or the other."

"Well, at some point, you get serious and have to give up something to get something else," Tek said.

"Now who sounds like a Korean parent?" she said, smiling. "What is a Korean parent anyway? If you are Korean and have a kid, you're a Korean parent, and would you like someone to presume you're one way or the other? I've met so many Korean parents, and each one is different."

"I'm not having kids," Tek said. "I doubt it."

She was surprised. They had spoken about having children when they were together, and she didn't know what had brought this about.

"You might change your mind," she said. "Kids are great."

"Doesn't sound like it from my colleagues who have them. I am endlessly hearing about learning disabilities, or teenagers who are disobedient, or the expenses."

"Well, I like kids. The more I work with them, the more I like them."

Tek raised the temperature on the stove below the shabu-shabu pot.

"Koreans aren't having kids because of you," he said. He removed his jacket and rolled up his sleeves as if preparing to have an argument.

"What do you mean?"

"Hagwons cost too much. Everything costs too much, and if the kids don't turn out well, then parents get blamed. But all my counterparts here say they're sick and tired of the costs of education. Their number one complaint is hagwons. That's you."

"Is that why you invited me to dinner?" Mido asked. None of these arguments were new to her. It was true that every parent she had ever met complained about education costs and how it was impossible not to send a child to a hagwon, usually starting around kindergarten. "You wanted to lecture me about hagwons. You think I'm part of the problem."

"I think you should quit this absurd industry and finish your degree. Find your calling and do something else. You used to write plays." Tek said this last part more cautiously. He wanted to help her, but from her expression, he could tell that he'd hurt her feelings. "You were good at it. You were even considering acting. Remember?"

"You think I failed." Mido put down her teacup. She didn't want to get up and make things worse. No doubt he thought he was helping her, being a good friend. She wanted to see it from his side, but it was painful to be reminded of what she hadn't finished. "I didn't fail."

"I didn't mean to upset you." Tek rapped his forehead with his right fist like he was trying to discipline himself. "I just never went to a hagwon. My mother didn't believe in them. Neither did my father. They thought smart people didn't have to go. They bought me some test guides and said I'd be fine." He recalled just how clear his mother had been about his not needing a tutor or an exam prep course. *They're for anxious mothers who never went to elite schools*, she'd said, having gone to Korea University for her undergraduate degree, then earning an MSt at Oxford and a doctorate at Sydney.

"Mido, you're too smart to waste your life teaching a bunch of kids how to game a test or an application. It was a fine gig when you needed something for a stopgap and were taking care of your family, but now you're done."

Mido got up from her seat.

"Sit, Mido. Don't go. I'm sorry. I don't want to fight you about this."

She sat back down and exhaled.

"Tek, you went to private school in Sydney and had a mother and father who got advanced degrees abroad. You won a genetic lottery and live in a country where you were given every chance to succeed. I just don't think you should sit in judgment over the people here who don't have the same opportunities that you did. How dare you make generalizations about people you barely know? Just because you're ethnically Korean doesn't give you the right to speak about all Koreans. Your parents didn't raise you here."

Tek didn't know how to back down. It enraged him to think of her spending her life doing something that made no sense to him. "Koreans care too much about this shit, and it's wrong for you to participate in this culture of hypercompetition and status mania."

"Wow. So that's what you think of me."

"Not you, but how you're spending your life."

"What makes us better Koreans? What makes you so superior? Tek, you have no right."

"Are you still with that guy?"

"What?" Mido stared at him, wondering if he'd changed the subject to distract her.

"I broke up with that girl." Tek picked up his chopsticks, then put them down again. "She wasn't you."

The broth bubbled in the pot, and the meat and vegetables lay untouched.

Mido turned to the door and said nothing.

"I've loved you ever since we were kids. You can't possibly tell me that I have no right to tell you about what you were meant to do or who you were meant to be. I know how gifted you are."

"You think that being an actor or a playwright is somehow better than being a tutor or an education consultant. You're an elitist, Tek. I didn't know this about you. I help kids, and I'm trying to help them the best way I know how."

"You're only helping kids who can afford this shit," he said. "You're supporting this endless culture of striving and cutthroat competition in a nation that has an inferiority complex," he said, taking a deep breath to resume his argument, but Mido raised her hand.

"Tek. Most rich people here try to get their kid out of Korea by sending them abroad, but what about the poor or middle-class family who can't possibly afford to send their kid to college in the United States? You're going to look down on a middle-class parent for spending her last cent trying to help her kid learn English, when every corporate job here asks for your

TOEIC score? You can't be hired without a degree and top scores. It's not like America or Australia. Most parents don't want their kids to be factory workers, replaced by cheaper labor or machines. You know this."

Mido reached behind her chair for her bag and coat. "It's too easy to blame parents or feel superior to your simplistic ideas of Koreans. I thought you were smarter than that. It's not a compliment to me that you think I can be a playwright or an actor. I don't think that's a better job. It just sounds cooler to you than being a hagwon teacher."

"If you want to help kids so much, why don't you teach in a poor public school? We have them in Sydney, and I know you have them in America."

Tek could not stop himself. He had to prove her wrong, and Mido realized that she didn't want to fight him.

"Why do you get to question what I do?" she asked. "I never once told you to become a solicitor or barrister or anything."

"There's nothing wrong with becoming a lawyer. Anyone would be lucky to have my job." Tek stopped, seeing his own standards exposed. For him, there was something wrong with working at a hagwon. Yet he had protected insurance companies that chiseled their customers, denying payments for disputable claims. Why was that any better?

"I don't have to defend my life to you," she said.

"I just want the best for you."

Mido stood up.

"I have work to do. Thank you for dinner. Please don't call me anymore. I wish you well."

"Mido. I didn't mean for us to argue."

Tek asked for the bill and paid it, and when he reached the sidewalk, she was gone.

❧

When Mido returned to Fortress, most of the tutors were still at their desks in the main room. Peter sat in his office alone. A glass window divided their spaces, and he waved. Mido went to his office and put down her heavy tote bag on the armchair.

"You're back sooner than I thought you'd be," he said.

"Do you think we're wasting our lives?"

Peter laughed.

"What? No. I don't. But thank you for asking." He looked at her quizzically, not understanding why she seemed so upset.

"I think I need to get my degree."

"Here?"

"No. Back in California."

"Now? We've only been here for a year. Things are going well."

"I don't mean right this second," she said, not knowing exactly what she was trying to say.

"You should go back to college if you want. I know a great education consultant. She's considered the best in Orange County and now Seoul."

"Ha. I'll be twenty-nine in October," she said quietly.

"Hey, that's not old for college. But I thought we were going to take over the Korean hagwon market." Peter rubbed his hands like he was plotting something. "My family thinks we should get into the internet hagwon business. My uncle thinks that if we record the classes and go online, then we could scale up."

Mido made a face.

"Do you think I should get my degree?"

Peter looked thoughtful. "What's in your tote bag?"

She shrugged and picked up her bag.

"Two bottles of barley tea, lip gloss, hand lotion, sunglasses, and two books."

"What kind of books?"

Mido read out the titles: "*The Psychology of the Child* by Jean Piaget and Bärbel Inhelder and Erik Erikson's *Identity: Youth and Crisis.*"

"Oh, Lion." Peter rolled his eyes. "My dude never quits."

"He said they're really good. He said there are solid critiques of their ideas, but—"

Peter raised his hand as if to stop her. "But they are foundational to understanding how children learn. Lion tried to get me to read them, too. Unlike you, I flat-out refused. You don't have to, you know. It's not required."

"I know that. I just thought it might help me to become a better teacher. It's actually fascinating. Piaget argues that children learn in stages when they're developmentally ready, and I was thinking that matched my experiences at Exodus."

"Well, there's your answer."

"What answer?" Mido appeared confused.

"You miss school, and now you have a real reason to go back."

Mido held the old hardcover books in her hands and stared at them.

"Did you want to make an internet hagwon?" she asked him, not even understanding what that was exactly.

"Zero interest. No, negative interest. Someone smarter than me could do that. Probably should do that. Not me."

"What do you think Lion wants to do about Fortress Seoul?" she asked.

"He said we can decide. He misses the band. Personality-wise, maybe we're small-time hagwon operators."

Mido laughed. "Yeah, I miss hearing you guys sing." In the armchair, she pulled her knees to her chest and put her head down.

"Figures my uncle would come up with a way to monetize this even more." He tried to peek underneath her curtain of hair. "Hey, Mido. You home?"

Mido raised her head.

"Do we have to make a lot more money? Do we have to scale up?" she asked.

"No. We don't. It was just an idea from a rich family member. Rich people get rich because they have these moneymaking ideas. He said we could put out videos. Who knows how it would work when we focus so much on each student? I just thought you might like the idea because it could help more students who can't afford to live in Seoul."

Mido smiled at him.

"Peter, I want to have kids. Do you want to have any? I never asked you. I know you don't want to get married, but are you against kids?"

"I want kids. How many do you want?"

"I don't know. I liked being one of three."

"Let's have kids, then. You'd be good at being a mom."

Mido didn't know if that was true, but she was certain that she wanted to try being a mother. Even if Peter changed his mind, or if they broke up, she still wanted kids. School, relationships, and kids. There was supposed to be an order to things, and perhaps everything would be out of order for her, but the wishes remained, and the wishes were worth saving.

14
Friend

I was very sorry to hear about your wife," Mary said, holding the warm paper cup of milky instant coffee.

Not an hour went by when John didn't think of Helen. Everything made him miss her. A tree budding leaves. Mido's messages asking him if he'd eaten dinner. Bo's tapered hands. An unexpected parking spot. Every good thing to be had and hoped for reminded him of her. She was gone, but somehow she was with him. He wouldn't have understood this idea until he lost her—that she was alive in him.

His parents and older brother had died before John finished college. They were the kind of poor people few noticed. Until he died, his father had worked in a factory and was paid only when his boss had money. *Be early for work. Do your job so well that you are missed when absent. Never spend more than you have.* John lived by his father's teachings.

In the middle of the day, Mary and John were sitting in the Rose Salon employees' room behind a mirrored wall. This was where the workers ate their meals and took breaks. On the north wall were a two-door refrigerator, two microwaves, three hot water kettles, and an old television that was almost never turned on. Nari stocked a porcelain mixing bowl with chewing gum and mints so the nail technicians never had bad breath. All twenty-four of the gray metal employee lockers were in use, each one secured with a colored combination lock—blue, black, or red—a cube of privacy in a woman's working life.

From inside, anyone could see what was going on in the shop through the large two-way mirror that divided the back room from the front.

Recently Nari had changed the ceiling light fixtures to three small crystal chandeliers, and twice a week she arranged a red rose and baby's breath in the silver bud vase on every workstation, refusing to use fake flowers.

Mary caught John glancing at the digital clock in the old microwave.

"You must have been surprised to hear from me," she said.

John smiled at Shin's wife, feeling sorry for her. This could not have been her idea.

"Thank you for meeting me. I won't take long," she said, checking the mirrored wall. Neat rows of women labored, heads bowed over their customers' hands.

Mary knew women who worked at nail salons in Bergen County, and she felt grateful to have her job at the florist's, where she didn't have to touch strangers. A friend from church had told her that she liked the work except for having to make conversation because she was embarrassed about having an accent.

John picked up his coffee. Shin's wife was nervous, and he didn't want to rush her.

"I was glad to hear that Joey and Luke are now lawyers." He could remember the birth of each one.

Mary waved away the implied compliment. The boys had worked hard. She believed in God's provision but felt uncomfortable mentioning it for fear of sounding pious.

"How hard you must have worked to raise them."

"I can't take any credit." Mary hesitated. "Elder Koh."

John looked up.

"You're a person of faith, so I should say this. It wouldn't have been possible for me to raise my sons here without God."

"I understand."

Mary bit her short thumbnail.

"May I ask what brought you here?"

"My husband asked me to ask you to speak with him."

"Ah—" John was unsure how to respond.

"Would that be possible? I imagine you must have many good reasons not to."

"DH said that it was a criminal matter, so I should be careful. I didn't want to hurt the church."

"So you won't speak with him."

"What does he want?"

"I don't know," she said gravely.

"What will he do now?" John asked. "I imagine he has a lawyer."

"Joey and Luke got him someone. He wasn't arrested," she said. "But he's being investigated."

"For what?" John had heard from the minister and elders that George Hong had confessed to everything. Danbi had corroborated that Shin knew nothing.

"Something about conspiracy, premium diversion, and embezzlement. They're saying my husband must have known that she was taking money from the premium accounts."

John shook his head, considering.

"He says he had no idea. She had done this by herself. I guess for her real estate investments. I don't understand it very well."

"I read that she was buying houses and selling them for a profit. When buyers stopped making offers, I think she was stuck with an investment property with big loan payments."

"Yes, I read that, too, but I didn't understand why she was doing this. They seemed to be living so well."

John shrugged. He'd heard talk that Shin had debts for their house, business, and cars.

"Apparently it's also my husband's fault because as the CEO of the agency, he should have known."

Hearing the store doorbell chime, John turned reflexively to the mirrored glass. More customers came in and Nari greeted them. He turned back to Mary. "I don't understand how I can help."

John folded his hands and stared at the bottom of his coffee cup. He didn't remember finishing his drink, but it was all gone, and only a thin brown ring remained.

"Do you think that she'll go to prison?" Mary asked. Joey and Luke had explained that she could.

"DH thinks so. I don't know for how long exactly." John squirmed a bit in his chair. DH had said it was a special taking, and the penalties could be much higher than for a grand theft charge.

"It depends on the prosecutor and the judge," DH had told him. "And the deputy at the airport got hurt. So no bail, go straight to jail."

"I don't understand all of this. It's a terrible thing for our community," John said.

"I am sorry to bother you. My husband didn't think you would speak with him. Unless I asked you as a favor." She added, "I think he's ashamed."

John crossed his arms and looked down, unable to face her before saying, "But he wasn't ashamed to call you. I cannot imagine what you have had to endure. Your husband was my closest friend. He was like an older brother to me."

Mary was certain that Shin still believed that he and John would always be like brothers.

"I benefited from our relationship, but now, after all these years, I realize that I helped him, too. I did a great deal of work for him. In a way, it was fair when he took credit for my work, because he was in charge and took risks I didn't want to take, and after he got promoted, I'd usually get promoted, too. He let me travel overseas so my children could be educated abroad. I could never make enough money in Korea for the kind of life we had, and being an expatriate allowed us that. He took care of me, and I did the work. Then after that...that thing that happened with Jung Danbi in Korea, I started to understand more about who he really was. I shouldn't have fired her. It was unfair to fire her. I should have said no."

"My husband is a selfish man."

"He is weak, but so was I."

Mary shook her head, not understanding how he could blame himself.

"I've learned that weakness can be a dangerous thing," he said.

Mary splayed her fingers on the table. Her nails were cut short, and her knuckles had thickened. When she woke up in the mornings, her hands were often swollen.

"I asked my husband for a divorce. He had asked a number of times, but I'd always said no. I'm Catholic." Mary swallowed. "But Joey is getting married. I haven't even told my husband."

John's initial happiness at hearing her son's good news vanished as he appreciated how this mess could hurt him, too.

"The boys told me I had to cut ties right away. The newspapers." Anguished, Mary looked away. "And I can't be exposed to his liabilities, they said. I came to California so he would sign the divorce agreement." She pointed to her bag.

"I remember when Joey was born," John said. Mary had gone into labor unexpectedly when Shin and he were at a work dinner, and they had both left the restaurant and gone straight to the hospital.

"Joey asked me not to tell his father until the wedding is over. He's marrying another lawyer from a nice family. She's Korean but born here. Her mother works in Manhattan as an architect, and her father is a famous knee surgeon. Gracie goes to church and volunteers in the nursery every week. Joey is so blessed." Mary's face brightened, and for a moment, she looked beautiful again, like a woman without troubles, and John thought she deserved something good to happen to her.

"Congratulations," John said. "Please tell him congratulations for me. I wish him and Gracie happiness."

"Your children? How are they?"

"Bo is getting a PhD at UCLA, DH is working at a law firm in Seoul, and Mido is in Seoul opening a branch of a hagwon from California."

"A hagwon from America. In Seoul?"

John smiled and checked the mirrored wall to see if everything was okay at the store. The place was mostly full, with only a few empty chairs.

"No one is married yet," he said.

The kids being single didn't bother him the way it bothered others. Losing Helen had taught him that. His children were healthy and decent young people.

"I don't want anyone in the bride's family to know. But I know they have to be told. We'll tell Gracie and her parents, of course." Mary looked anguished. "If I could get the divorce right away, then maybe it won't hurt the boys as much. My husband said he'd sign the agreement if you—"

John didn't understand.

"I know Gracie will understand. She's such a dear girl. And my Joey. They don't deserve this awful thing." Mary folded her hands as if in prayer. "My husband said he'd sign if you would speak to him. If it wasn't for that, I wouldn't have come all this way and brought this shameful thing to your doorstep. Elder Koh, I am trying to get away from him and asking you to help. I am disgraced."

John shook his head. "It's he who is disgraced, not you."

"I'm asking myself how I can be so selfish," she said. "I'm a hypocrite. I am so sorry." The words tumbled out of her mouth. Mary hadn't planned on saying any of this.

John found the plastic box filled with napkins and disposable utensils left over from takeout meals. He pulled out some napkins and handed them to her. Mary wiped her eyes.

"I've known your husband for a lifetime. He would never steal money."

Mary couldn't speak.

"Where is he now?"

She pointed toward the parking lot.

John gestured to her bag.

"May I have the documents?"

She handed the manila envelope to him.

"Why don't you stay here for a bit? I'll be back after I speak with him."

John asked Nari to order Mary some lunch. He picked up a blue ballpoint pen from the reception desk and went to the parking lot alone. Shin got out of the car, and as he started to speak, John held up a hand.

"We're going to the bank. They have a notary."

♣

Ever punctual, at six o'clock, John arrived at Shin's house. Nari would close the salon without him. Shin invited him in and offered tea. Mary was gone.

"Did you take her to the airport?" John asked, checking his watch.

"No. She had to return the rental," Shin said. Joey had been able to change her return ticket, and Mary saw no reason to stay another night.

"I'm not supposed to be speaking with you," John said. "That's why I didn't return the calls."

"I understand," Shin said. "I appreciate you coming here."

John had never been to his house. Its grandeur astonished him, and Shin sensed what he was thinking.

"The bank owns the house, and now it's underwater." Shin let out a hollow laugh.

John didn't ask about the cars in the garage.

"Is there something you need? From me?"

"I have to go away for a few days. I was wondering if you could take Anna. If she could stay with your family. I thought maybe Mido could watch her."

"What? Mido is in Seoul."

"Anna is very easy. I have to take care of a few things, and I can't take her with me. It's already been so disruptive with Danbi being gone."

John was puzzled. He'd assumed that Shin wanted information about the church finances for the investigation, and DH had instructed him not to say anything.

"Where are you going?" John asked.

"I was going to try to raise some money. For the lawyers. I have a friend in New York who might be able to help. Anna goes to school from eight thirty to four, and now she has hagwon. I enrolled her in the one in Cypress, so you won't need to drive to Woodbridge."

"You don't have a babysitter or housekeeper?"

"Had to let them go. Money."

"How many days?"

"Four, maybe five. You're the only person I trust."

John covered his mouth. At home, it was only him most nights, and Bo came over on the weekends.

"I know it's short notice, and I'm very sorry to bother you. Danbi just ruined everything. Anna is such a good kid. Reminds me of your Mido."

"How old is Anna?"

"She turned nine in March," Shin said, smiling. From the side table, he picked up her framed third-grade portrait. She wore a white shirt and a navy blue pinafore. That morning, for picture day, Danbi had braided Anna's long hair and tied a blue velvet ribbon on the tail.

"Where is she?"

"Still at the hagwon. If you could pick her up for me, I'd really appreciate it."

John checked his watch. It was almost seven o'clock.

"Does she eat dinner there?"

Shin nodded, trusting that she must. He didn't know.

"I packed her suitcase already. It'll only be a few days. Please."

John inhaled deeply. Helen would have known what to say.

❧

On Saturday morning, John went to work, and Bo stayed home with Anna. He made her French toast with strawberries for breakfast.

"What would you like to do today?" he asked.

"I don't know." She stared down at her bare feet. Her mother said she had her father's wide feet. She had already washed her face and brushed her teeth without being reminded and dressed herself in a pink T-shirt and jeans.

"Did you want to watch television?"

"My mother doesn't let me do that. She said it will ruin my brain. When she was a girl, she never watched any."

"She's not entirely wrong. Do you like movies or video games?"

"I'm not allowed to play video games."

"I see." Bo smiled. "Well, I'm not very good at them anyway. My brother DH is amazing at all kinds of games. He's also an athlete."

"May I read the books in Mido's room?"

"Aren't they too old for you?"

"There are books for my age, too. I saw some." She wasn't sure if that was allowed, but the containers were open.

Anna walked toward Mido's room, and Bo followed her.

In the corner were a large open footlocker and a milk crate filled with some of their old books.

"Oh wow," Bo said. "You can definitely read them." He sat on the floor and rummaged through the piles.

The locker contained the Hardy Boys and the Nancy Drew Mystery Stories, and the smaller one had all seven volumes of the Chronicles of Narnia as well as *The Hobbit*, *The Fellowship of the Ring*, and *The Return of the King*. *The Two Towers* was missing. A big stack of Shakespeare plays was tied together with plastic twine. Bo knew his mother had put these aside, and Mido must not have been able to part with them.

"Is this what you want to do today?"

Anna smiled and reached for a Hardy Boys mystery.

"I like series books."

"I think there's over fifty of those, but we didn't have them all. We borrowed a bunch at the library. Those are the ones we got for birthday presents. We all read them."

"Do you ever go to the lakes?" she asked suddenly.

"Which lakes?"

"The ones in Woodbridge. Near my house."

"Oh, right, there are two of those. East, West?" Bo wasn't sure. "North or South? I've never been there. Isn't that funny? It's so close, too."

"North and South. My dad and I used to go sometimes. To look at the ducks and coots. You're not supposed to feed them or catch them."

"Coots?" Bo didn't know what that was. "Is that the fish?"

Anna laughed. "No! It's a bird. It's a dark-gray bird with a white beak and red eyes, and it looks like a duck, but it isn't a duck. They have skinny green feet that aren't webbed."

"Wow. Thank you for teaching me that," Bo said, and he meant it.

"Coots eat up the expensive shrubbery and poop a lot, and people in Woodbridge don't like them," she said. "Dad told me. People prefer the mallards. Mallards are wild ducks."

"Do you like the coots?"

"They're okay." She shrugged. "They can't help being coots."

Bo smiled. "Yeah. They can't help it."

Anna sat cross-legged and opened *The Secret of the Old Mill.*

"Do you want to go to one of the lakes today? I can take you."

Anna stared into space like she was thinking about it, then shook her head.

"I'm going to read now. Maybe later."

"Cool, I'll do my reading, too, then. I'll be over there." He pointed to the kitchen. "You can hang out with me if you want. There's a comfy armchair, which my brother calls the Throne. You can have it today, which makes you the ruler of the kingdom."

He left her in Mido's room with the door ajar and set up his books, legal pads, and laptop on the kitchen table where she could still see him. Within a few minutes, Anna brought her book and sat in the armchair not far from him.

✤

Anna was as sweet and mild-mannered as Shin had described. She stayed in Mido's room without complaint. After four days, the weather grew colder. When John looked through her suitcase for a sweater, he found the letters in the zippered section, one for Anna and another for John.

The police discovered Shin's body in the garage. He had never left for New York.

Bo took a week off from school to come home and help his father with Anna. Before the funeral, Shin's lawyer brought John a white bankers box with his name on it.

Shin had left him written instructions for the insurance agency and information relating to Anna—babysitter names and pediatrician contacts, immunization records, and her birth certificate. There was an old insurance policy on his life for $1 million with all four children as the beneficiaries. He'd left a letter for the boys and Mary.

"What did his letter for you say?" Bo asked his father.

"That his family was better off without him. He asked me to care for Anna. He apologized. He said thank you."

The letter to Anna was unsealed, and Bo advised that they read it just in case: "Be a good girl. Appa is so sorry and loves you very much."

Shin did not mention anything about the child's mother.

15
Liberation

The baby was taking a nap in the nursery, and Yun reviewed the projected financials in the den. Before Michael was born, she used to work from her office at Exodus on Saturdays and Sundays, but in the past year, she'd been working from home on weekends and Mondays.

After Peter and Mido left for Seoul, Lion hired a new director and account manager and a bookkeeper for both hagwons. They were extremely competent, but out of habit, Yun continued to check on all the jobs she used to do, no matter how many times Lion told her that she had to work less and rest more.

There was the familiar knock. Two raps against the wall, never the door. Her tall husband stood by the half-open door. Lion wore an Aretha Franklin T-shirt and faded blue jeans.

"Have you thought it through?" he asked.

"What if he leaves again?" Yun said.

"Well, if he does, he does."

Again they were discussing moving her parents into the two-bedroom apartment above the garage. Yun was relieved that her father had returned from Brazil, but she still felt awkward and mistrustful around him. They never discussed why he'd left or what had made him return.

"I don't mind if they live here," she said. "I just don't think I should ask them to move in."

Lion sat down on the love seat facing the television.

"Wife."

"Yes," she answered without looking up from her work. Yun circled figures she questioned with her blue marker.

"I think he's sorry," Lion said.

"I know, but he didn't say it." Yun refused to face Lion. If she saw her husband's tender expression, she would lose her resolve and feel sorry for her father. Both Nari and Lion had forgiven him, and Yun thought someone should hold up standards. "He's never going to say it."

"I'm not sure if men in his generation do stuff like that. I mean, there could be exceptions." Lion stared up at the ceiling like he was puzzling it out. He didn't like to make absolute statements. "It's hard to apologize, I guess," he said, and added, "So, do you want me to ask them?" Lion smiled at her. "I can. I'm happy to do it."

Finally she looked up at him from her papers, wondering how he could always be so patient and buoyant.

❧

By the time Nari and Joonho arrived with the takeout dinner from Mandu House, the baby was awake from his nap and playful. Joonho washed his hands and held Michael up in his arms. The baby squealed with joy. Near the dining table was a large white sheepskin rug covered with a fresh bath towel and Michael's favorite toys, and the grandfather and baby played on the floor.

Nari knew where everything was in her daughter's kitchen, and while Yun set the table, Nari heated up the chicken porridge for Michael. Lion took out drinks from the refrigerator.

"Shin Taehun died," Nari said.

"What?" Lion exclaimed, pausing in front of the open refrigerator door.

"When? How?" Yun stood still, a stack of plates, napkins, and chopsticks in her hands.

"Yesterday morning, the police found him. *Jasal.*"

Yun looked at her father. In one hand, he held a stuffed tiger, and in the other, a stuffed rabbit, mesmerizing the baby. When she was a child, he used to imitate all the animal sounds. Until now, she had forgotten this. Yun set down the dishes. The bags of food remained unopened.

"I thought he had a lawyer, and it wasn't his fault," Lion said. "Didn't you just see him? When he enrolled Anna?" he asked his wife.

"Oh, is that why he came to us?" Yun said. "She goes to school in Woodbridge, and there's a pretty good hagwon for her age in Irvine that's not far from their house, and I didn't get why he wouldn't enroll her there."

"He left Mido's father a letter," Nari said. "He asked him to take care of Anna. Can you believe that?"

Lion exhaled as if nothing could surprise him anymore. Joonho had heard all this earlier and continued to play with the baby.

Nari smiled at the baby and didn't want to say more. It was all too sad. Helen had never said anything bad about Taehun Shin and Danbi Jung, but she knew something had happened between the two couples. Helen had said that the men had been best friends. They had gone to college and served in KATUSA together.

The newspaper articles about Danbi Jung and George Hong and how much money they had stolen from Gospel Presbyterian were shocking enough. Now there was a terrible death, and the adults felt bad for the little girl. In light of another family's tragedy, Nari felt guilty for her good fortune, here with her daughter, son-in-law, and grandson and her husband who had returned home. Nari and Joonho might have lost their money and property, and now they worked for someone else's gain, but in their daughter's house, with their beautiful grandson gazing up at them, their old disappointments faded away.

Lion began to take the food containers from the bag.

"But Elder Shin was innocent," he said, repeating what the pastors and elders had discussed at the emergency session meeting. "Why would he do this?"

"His wife Mary flew in from New Jersey and asked for a divorce," Nari said. "I didn't know they weren't divorced already."

Nari picked up the baby and put him in the high chair, and the adults sat down.

Lion bowed his head to say grace, and they prayed for the lonely, the brokenhearted, and those without friends, work, or homes.

Michael tapped his little hands on the white plastic table attached to his chair, and Yun fed him spoonfuls of warm porridge. While she fed the baby, she ate dumplings. Whenever Michael reached for her food, she tore off tiny pieces of dumpling and chicken and put them on his tray, allowing him to feed himself.

"Look at how well he eats," Joonho said. "He's going to be big like his father."

"I think he looks like you," Nari said to her husband, and Joonho grinned. Everyone liked to be compared to Michael, who had a beautiful open face.

When there was a lull, Lion made his pitch to his in-laws.

"Yun and I would love it if you moved in with us. We have the two-bedroom apartment above the garage, which is bigger than your current apartment, or you could stay in the house. We have an extra bedroom here."

Joonho shook his head. "We don't want to be a bother. The apartment in Cypress is fine. The rent hasn't gone up much."

"No," Nari said firmly. "I want to live here. That way I can see Michael every day. The apartment above the garage is perfect. Besides, when Ginny comes home from Seoul, she can have everything stay the same in the house."

Quietly Yun fed the baby, who was now almost done with the porridge. Michael picked up the tiny pieces of shredded chicken and chewed, and the four adults looked as delighted as if he were performing a magic trick.

Joonho put his hand near Michael, and the baby grabbed his pinkie and laughed at his grandfather.

"I want to live here," Nari said again. "Are you sure we wouldn't be bothering you?" she asked Lion, who shook his head.

"We're healthy enough to take care of ourselves," Joonho assured them. "We know a young family needs their privacy."

"It wouldn't bother us," Yun said to her father. She smiled. "You could help me with Michael because he's going to have a little sister in five months. We will need your help."

With his free hand, Joonho covered his mouth to blink back tears. Nari shouted, "How can I be so blessed?" She wept. "Thank God, thank God, thank God," the young grandmother repeated.

❧

Her brother, Kenny, was visiting from Sydney, so Sonya invited Mido and DH over to her place. While they waited for DH, who was delayed at work, Sonya, Kenny, and Mido caught up, and Mido told her uncle about what was going on at home.

"Let me get this straight." Kenny turned to Mido. Surprised and slightly outraged, he sounded even more Australian. His accent grew more pronounced as his vowels lengthened and *r* sounds dropped. "That horrible woman, who falsely accused your father and destroyed his career, cheated on Shin with another married man, then embezzled money from their insurance company and church?"

Mido closed her eyes and nodded.

"Fuck me dead," Kenny said.

"Kenny." Sonya didn't approve of his cursing.

"And there's a kid?" he asked, undeterred by his older sister.

"Anna." Mido said the child's name.

Sonya, who'd heard most of this from Nari, sighed. She couldn't believe John was taking care of the child.

"Hang on. How can he take care of her? How old is she?" Kenny turned to Sonya in disbelief. "You know all this? Isn't he managing your salons?"

This time Sonya nodded, not wanting to make Mido uncomfortable.

"Dad feels badly for Anna. She's only nine," Mido said.

Sonya and Kenny could relate to this. They, too, had grown up like orphans. The doorbell rang and the housekeeper let DH in.

Kenny got up and hugged his nephew.

"You look very successful." Kenny had not seen him since his sister's funeral.

DH smiled. He wore a new blue suit and a French silk necktie Helen had bought for his law firm interviews years ago when he was a 1L.

"When are you coming to Sydney?" he asked. "Why are you working in Seoul? Are you going to get married soon? You a big shot now?"

"That's at least four questions," DH replied calmly. "I'd love to visit Sydney. I am not a big shot yet, but I'm working on it. I enjoy working here, and I might settle down in Seoul if I make partner." He smiled, pleased to have covered all the questions.

The housekeeper signaled, and Sonya led them to the dining room. Dinner was ready.

"How is Bo?" Kenny asked.

DH glanced at Mido, who spoke to him more regularly.

"He took a week off from school to help out with Anna. He's finishing up his requirements and teaching. I think there's clinical hours, exams, papers, and some licensing steps," she said.

DH looked at the food and glanced at his aunt to see if they could start eating. He was starving.

"My brother-in-law is now taking care of a dodgy mate's child whose backstabbing mother is in jail." Kenny looked worried. "Not sure why all the good people have to clean up the messes of the filthy sons of bitches—"

"Kenny."

"It's not like the kids don't know these words. They're adults." His wife,

Lily, was constantly telling him to clean up his language at home, even though their children swore better than he could when they wanted.

"When do you go back to school, Mido?" he asked.

Sonya looked up from the fish she was serving. Mido and DH put down their utensils. Everyone grew still.

"I want you to finish your degree," he said.

"She will," DH insisted.

"When?" Kenny asked. "How long will you be working at this hagwon? Your father's doing well enough now. Korea doesn't need another hagwon. You can come back to Sydney if you want to get your degree in education."

Mido accepted the plate of fish from her aunt.

Kenny rubbed his sunbrowned neck and stretched his shoulders. He pulled up the sleeves of his blue dress shirt. The leather watchband on his left wrist was frayed.

"Your mother loved you kids more than anything in the world," he said. "She wasn't the sort of mother who bragged, but you're all she thought of."

Mido wanted him to keep talking about her mother. DH was also paying close attention. He picked up his spoon and cocked his head like a puppy in the direction of his uncle.

"One day you'll have kids. I hope you do. Greatest part of my life. There's nothing I wouldn't do to support them. And your mother worked like a mule. She did it because she wanted to take care of you."

DH noticed that his uncle had the same nose as his mother, and the same gentle but firm way of speaking. He thought about the letters she'd sent him at school. Her handwriting sloped to the right, and when she wrote in English, her *i*'s were dotted high and to the right. In each brief letter, she reminded him to go to bed on time because sleep was important, told him that she believed in him and that he could commit his plans to the Lord. Always, there was a crisp $10 or $20 bill so he could buy pizza. "Mommy is always praying for you, my beloved son."

Kenny's eyes were wet.

"Oh, she talked about you all the time, DH. You know why she talked about you?"

Mido wondered if it was because he had done so well in sports and school.

"She said you made her laugh. You always made her laugh."

DH covered his mouth and began to sob.

Sonya patted his back. She almost never talked about Helen, but living alone in this apartment, she could not avoid her grief. The only person she wanted to talk to was Helen. She wanted to ask how she should live. Was this the right way? How do you live a wise life? How do you make decisions when there are so many uncertain outcomes? Helen might have understood why she had to move out. She couldn't divorce her husband or live with the Chairman like before. Her sister wouldn't have judged her or made her feel weak for continuing to love a man who wasn't her husband. She might have just sat with her.

"Did she talk about me?" Mido could not help asking.

"Oh, I think you might have been her favorite."

"No," Mido said. "DH was her favorite. Everyone knows that."

"I have four kids. The one I worry about the most, that one is my favorite. Doesn't make any sense until you think about it."

DH smiled. All his life, he had heard how much his mother loved him, and in that moment, he hoped his uncle was right.

"She worried about you the most. Especially when you were little. You were such a quiet little thing," Kenny said. "And she worried about you because you always took care of other people and didn't complain."

Mido stared at her uncle, her eyes shining, not knowing what to say. All her life she had been trying to be good, never to trouble her mother, but even that had caused her mother anguish.

"When your family moved to California and you started working at the hagwon and supporting your brothers"—Kenny paused—"she was so proud of you. But I know she wanted you to finish school. For you to have your own wishes. I know that." Kenny continued in spite of his tears. "She told me to make sure that you finished school. She was so worried—"

"Why was Mommy worried?" DH asked.

"Because you were so quiet," Sonya said to Mido. "But she wasn't concerned about that later. You learned how to talk, and you figured out how to teach kids. Did you know that your mother wanted to be a schoolteacher?"

DH shook his head. "Really?"

Kenny looked puzzled. "How did you not know that? My older sister Sonya was going to be a doctor, and my middle sister Helen was going to be a high school English teacher."

"You wanted to be a doctor?" Mido asked her aunt.

No one had touched their food. It was as if they were meeting each other for the first time.

"Yes, I wanted to be a doctor, but I couldn't afford to keep studying. So I got a job as a secretary, then married my husband and had the boys. Your mother wanted to be a teacher, but after she got married, she followed your father to New Jersey. The first job she got was at that department store in Paramus." Sonya remembered how excited Helen had been when she learned how much she'd earn. Her salary would go toward the children's educations, and her hours allowed her to be home when they returned from school.

"Did Mommy like her job?" DH asked, unloosening his necktie a little.

"She was good at her job. But it wasn't what she'd always wanted to do. I remember once, years ago, when you kids were little, right around New Year's Day, she called me crying from Paramus."

"Why?" Mido asked.

"A customer had blamed her for something she didn't do and wouldn't apologize after realizing the mistake. And that year, your mother didn't get a Christmas bonus even though she'd been promised one. She wanted to go back to school and get a degree to teach, but there was no time or money for that."

DH furrowed his brow, not knowing this story. He checked Mido's face. She was listening intently. Kenny leaned in. "So what did you tell her?"

"That a mother is a child's first teacher," Sonya said.

16

Information

The visiting area of the Santa Ana women's jail smelled like stale coffee, sweat, and disinfectant. Every now and then, John could hear a loud buzzer and the clang of a heavy metal gate opening and shutting.

Her back pin-straight, Danbi sat on the opposite side of the booth behind a thick pane of reinforced glass. She wore a white undershirt beneath her khaki shirt and pants; her dark hair was gathered with a rubber band. A few white strands sprouted like antennae from her side part. Her face bare except for lip balm, she looked younger and unfamiliar. Danbi held the handset lightly.

"Elder Koh, thank you for coming by," she said.

"I wanted to bring Anna, but the lawyer said—"

"I don't want her to know that I'm here."

John's wedding ring tapped against his handset. He never took it off. What would Helen say? he wondered in every difficult situation.

"Your daughter is a bright child. Losing her father was difficult for her. My son Bo is studying to be a child psychologist, and he thinks that maybe it would be good for Anna to see you."

"No. I don't want her to come here. And after"—she paused—"I might be in a worse place."

John understood her meaning. DH and Shin's lawyer had said this could go badly. The judge on her case was notoriously hard on women who committed felonies. Grand theft, special taking, conspiracy, embezzlement, and assault of an officer. Even without prior offenses and with full restitution, she would go to state prison for at least a year or two. A former prosecutor had told DH that the worst part wasn't the stealing, but the fact that the deputy chasing Danbi had fallen and broken her wrist and ankle.

"Your lawyer said your mother is alive. Did you want Anna to go to her?"

"No." Like an animal, Danbi tracked his eyes, trying to predict his next move. "And my cousin will not take her, either."

"Your cousin?"

"Frank Lim. And his wife, Bina. They're elders."

John knew of them from church but had never spoken to them.

"Frank is the son of my mother's sister." Her lawyer had reached out to Frank and Bina Lim about Anna. She'd thought Bina would take good care of Anna, but Frank said it was impossible. He had agreed to pay Danbi's legal bills and put commissary money into her books for the length of her detainment and prison term, and in return, she could never contact him or his family except through counsel. She could not return to Orange County to live. He'd made her sign a contract.

John didn't know what he should tell her about Anna, who'd been staying with him. Sometimes the child woke up in the middle of the night. When she cried, he sat with her and gave her a glass of water. At Shin's funeral, she'd overheard remarks about his death from adults and asked him and Bo to explain.

"Sometimes grown-ups drink too much and have accidents," John told the child. Every chance he could, Bo told Anna that her parents loved her. When she asked to see her mother, John followed Danbi's lawyer's instructions. "Your mother went to Korea for a job. She wants you to wait for her."

Danbi stared at John, her sad eyes imploring yet her chin jutted out slightly above her stiffened neck. She appeared both petulant and self-righteous.

"I've no right to ask you. But can you take her while I'm here?"

John focused on the visiting booth counter, a thick, pale slab of indeterminate building material.

"I spoke with Mary. Shin's wife," he said.

Danbi tried to look expressionless. She wished she'd worn makeup. Her skin felt papery all the time. The jail in Santa Ana was unbearable, and the other women there told her that state prison was far worse. Prison would give her more privileges, but she would be less safe. Every week in jail, she got three hours outside, but never all at once. The time she spent in jail would be deducted from any prison sentence. If only she hadn't pushed away the female deputy, who had tipped over like a bowling pin, then she might have gotten bail. "It was an accident," Danbi pleaded with the judge, but he did not believe her.

"Mary said she might be able to take her."

Danbi looked surprised.

John didn't mention that her sons weren't pleased about it, especially Patrick, the youngest. Mary felt awful about her ex-husband's death. "She just has to talk to her sons." The boys refused to attend the funeral, and Mary had come alone. Anna wouldn't leave Bo's side during the services.

"But then Anna wouldn't be in California, where you are," John said.

She kept quiet, trying to imagine what would happen if Anna lived with Shin's ex-wife. If the brothers liked her, then Anna would have a family.

Danbi blurted out, "If Mary says yes, then send her. Tell Anna that I had to stay in Korea and I can't have her live with me. I'll be back for her when things are better."

She didn't sound normal, John thought, but it wasn't as if he really knew her.

"I can't ask Mary to lie to the child," he said. "Mary isn't like that. Also, it can't be good for her to think that. Anna has already suffered the loss of her father." John tried to remember all the things Bo had explained that a bereaved child might be going through.

"What did you tell her? About her father?" Danbi said the words slowly.

"That it was an accident."

She exhaled quietly, relieved.

"It was an accident. He drank too much and made a bad decision. That wasn't really him," she said. "It's the truth."

John didn't know what else to say.

"If Anna lives in New Jersey with her brothers," Danbi said, "then she could forget about her father's death. This is the best I can do for her."

"Are you sure? Don't you want to see her?" John asked. Every other day, the child asked to see her mother.

Danbi clenched her fists, wanting to smash the glass with the heavy plastic handset.

"He shouldn't have done that," she said, not looking at John. "I thought he was stronger." Danbi turned to him. "I don't care if you believe me or not, but I did all this for them."

When their time was up, the guard took her away.

❧

When John returned to Rose Salon, it was only half full, and he went to his office to sit at his desk. He felt lightheaded and confused. When the phone rang, he picked up right away and smiled at hearing his daughter's voice.

"Did you eat?" he asked.

"Yes, Dad. Did you?" Mido asked. He sounded tired, and she could picture his windowless office in the back of the salon—the metal desk and chair, the single filing cabinet. "How are things with Anna? Is Bo able to get his schoolwork done?"

"I saw Anna's mother today."

"The jail? You went there?" Mido raised her voice slightly.

"Yes. It was fine enough. I felt sorry for her. And little Anna." From the open door, he could see Nari waving him over. Several customers had finished at the same time, and she needed help taking payment. "Is everything okay? With the hagwon?" he asked.

"Yes, the hagwon is doing well."

"I better go. Customers."

❧

Mido picked up the file for the next appointment on the schedule: another set of parents whose child hadn't been admitted to Fortress Seoul.

Professor Kim had gone to high school with Peter's father, and Professor Kim and his wife, Dr. Gu, wanted to make a special case for their youngest. Professor Kim, a scientist who'd received his PhD in the United States and taught at KAIST, had been a deputy minister in the previous administration. His cousin was the wife of a former president, and his sister was a prosecutor. When Renee rattled all this off to her, Mido let herself forget the details and just put them in the category of Very Important People.

Lately, every parent seemed to be some significant personage, or to know a high-status person. Peter said either no one was important or everyone was important. He didn't want to meet anyone whose grand pedigree preceded them.

Ginny, wearing one of the fashionable dresses she'd bought near Ewha, came into her office and handed her more folders. She had organized them in the order of requested appointments. Yun had taught Ginny how to run a hagwon so well that her competence allowed Mido to focus mostly on training the tutors. Peter joked that he'd rather work for Ginny than any other boss.

"All of these folks want meetings, too. Ideally today," Ginny said, shaking her head. Having spent most of her childhood at Exodus and after living with Yun and Lion, she could be as tough as any hagwon owner when it came to pushy parents.

"More parents? Today?" Mido frowned and opened the top folder in the pile.

"I tried to get rid of as many as possible, but they were very insistent."

Standing over Mido's shoulder, Ginny watched her skim the contents of the first folder.

Mido underlined the student's strengths with her blue pencil. There were no obvious weaknesses. The boy had wonderful grades and scores, had won international math competitions, and held an internship at a nanotechnology research lab at the California Institute of Technology. He knew how to code and build websites.

On the preferred list of schools, his parents had listed international choices: the usual Ivy League schools, Stanford, MIT, Caltech, Carnegie Mellon, and Cambridge. No doubt he would get something. Mido didn't think the child even needed Fortress Seoul.

"Impressive kid."

Peter had come in earlier and was sitting quietly on the office couch, his long legs crossed at the ankles. He was reviewing his own stack of folders.

"How are yours looking?" Mido asked.

Peter sat up straight, his face tense and arms crossed tightly.

"I wish you hadn't accepted the meeting with Professor Kim," he said.

"It will take only thirty minutes."

"Professor Kim is not my sort of person," he said. "I saw him at a family friend's wedding years ago, and no doubt he'll bring it up. Out of all the boring people I met that night, I remember him because he talked nonstop. He's going to tell us how important his people are. He argued that marriage was significant for breeding. Breeding. Like we're horses. That said, the wife is fairly normal." Peter laughed. "How in the world did I become the head of one of the hardest-to-get-into hagwons in Seoul? Life is fucking bizarre."

Ginny laughed and returned to her desk. "I'm going to Busan this weekend," she reminded them.

"Jealous," Peter said.

After the successful pilot year, they had received six hundred–plus applicants from over fourteen international schools in South Korea for the upcoming year. In the pilot year, they'd had about half that number from eight international schools.

The Eagle Academy/Fortress Seoul admissions committee, comprised of Tom and Clara Song, Peter, Mido, and three consultants, whittled down the 612 applicants to 180 high school juniors in the full-tuition paying group and twenty in the tuition-free group to make up two hundred EA/FS finalists.

Lion hand-numbered two hundred Ping-Pong balls—one for each finalist—with a permanent marker and put the balls into two containers—one small and one large.

In a rented school auditorium, EA/FS invited every finalist to witness the drawing, but no one could announce the results publicly.

In the first drawing, Lion blindfolded Peter's mother, Renee, and she chose ten tuition-free students from the twenty candidates, and on the second drawing, he blindfolded Tom and Clara, and they took turns selecting forty students out of the 180.

Each finalist was qualified; however, there was room for only fifty students. The results were random. No one was allowed to know who paid tuition and who did not. The committee established a standard floor for admissions based on the best grades, practice test scores, extracurricular activities, and draft essays, then randomized the final acceptances in public, so no one could complain about favoritism.

Lion had given interviews to two major newspapers, and two scholars had written editorials arguing against any kind of private college consulting for students even if 20 percent of them paid nothing. Three other scholars had written editorials arguing that since the system was deeply broken, some effort toward helping qualified poor students was better than nothing.

Tom Song, who'd now been a hagwon owner in Seoul for almost two decades, was quoted in one of the politically moderate newspapers saying, "Life is absolutely unfair; however, Koreans educated in America could help native Koreans navigate a complex American system."

Lion added in the same interview, "The EA/FS system is attempting to be less unfair in a category of unfair things." The published hagwon fees were below market rate and not onerous, so the articles had the unintended effect of making even more people seek out Eagle Academy/Fortress Seoul.

Professor Kim's son Sung was one of the 180 tuition-paying finalists; however, his Ping-Pong ball, number 87, was not selected, and consequently he would be unable to attend Fortress Seoul.

Ginny got up from her desk and stood close to Mido.

"They're here," she whispered dramatically, pointing to the glass-walled conference room where Professor Kim, his wife Dr. Gu, and Sung waited.

"They brought the kid? Why did they do that?" Peter shook his head.

Mido turned inconspicuously to check. The boy wore a navy flannel coat and a rep tie. Thick bangs almost covered his round eyes. He sat in the conference chair, staring up at the thin strip of molding between the ceiling and the wall.

"Poor bastard. Hasn't he been through enough?" Peter exhaled. He was wearing a black Arsenal jersey, jeans, and black canvas high-tops.

"Let me grab a jacket from my office. I don't want to hear about what I wore from my father."

"Oh, your mother called this morning," Ginny said. "I forgot."

"I know. She called again between my morning meetings."

"Oh?" Mido looked concerned.

"She's fine that we passed on them. We've passed on a lot of people in her orbit. I'm so fucking glad Lion made us do that public lottery with the Ping-Pong ball thing."

"I just wish parents could accept the ball's results," Ginny said.

"Seriously. Mom said the wife is nice and to be polite. To her anyway. The husband is hopeless," Peter said.

"I'll be nice. To both of them," Mido said, and Peter stuck out his tongue.

❧

When Peter and Mido walked into the room, the family stood up to bow. Peter and Mido bowed back and gestured for them to sit down. They smiled at the boy. Right away, Professor Kim summarized the contents of his son's file, stressing Sung's exceptional achievements. Peter continued to nod and smile. Mido was impressed by his calm demeanor.

"You see, it would actually be a feather in Fortress's cap to have him," the father said. "It's likely that he'll get into the very best universities in the world, and then you can include his acceptances in your results," he pointed out. "I know how these things work."

The mother smiled shyly, glancing now and then in the direction of their son, whose eyes were shaded by the curtain of his long dark bangs. She appeared gentle and concerned.

"Sung is a remarkable young man," Peter said. "I'm confident he'll get into a great school. There's no reason why he would not."

"Exactly, and your hagwon could take the credit for his acceptances. We're handing you an easy win," Professor Kim said in English.

The boy's hands were folded. He looked miserable, and Mido wanted to deliver him from this terrible awkwardness.

"Sung, we're very sorry that we don't have space. The good news is that you've already worked so hard, and frankly, I don't think you need us. I don't say that to just anyone." Mido smiled and looked carefully into his hooded eyes.

The mother smiled at her, appearing grateful.

"We understand it's more and more difficult to get into an American university now, especially schools like Harvard and Stanford, and we want to make sure that our Sung has everything he needs, especially when he has worked so hard already," the mother said. "We don't think the guidance counselor at his school understands the process nearly as well as you do."

"Both of you were present at the lottery, and unfortunately, we cannot change our admissions policy. All fifty students have been selected," Peter said. He didn't want to repeat Lion's "Standardize and Randomize" speech, which he had studied and felt ready to deliver.

"Our founder, Lion Han, returned to Orange County right after the drawing; however, you are welcome to contact him. We can set up that call for you if you like."

This was something he hated to do. Yet the Lion option was always there if Peter and Mido needed backup. Lion was good at this, somehow giving terrible news with grace and light. If they didn't want to talk to Lion, Tom Song could be much tougher. Worst-case scenario, his wife, Clara, would be available for cleanup.

"I was told that you grew up in Sydney. May I ask which school you went to?" Dr. Gu addressed Mido, wanting to find a personal connection. Often she knew someone who had gone to a school in Australia, because she had gotten a master's in public health in Sydney, and elite overseas Koreans could be a small group.

"I started at the University of Sydney, but I haven't finished my degree," Mido said.

"You finished it in the United States, then?" Professor Kim said.

"No. I don't have a college degree. I studied education for a year at Sydney, thinking that I might go into theater—"

Astonished, Sung spoke up. "You don't have a university degree?"

"No. I don't." Mido smiled.

"Oh!" the boy said, and laughed.

"See, you don't want to learn from a person like me," she said with a smile, hoping this might make his parents feel better about his not getting in.

Dr. Gu looked perplexed. "We were told that you teach the consultants. That you specialize in testing and essays."

"I think Mido might be one of the best in the world at what she does," Peter said. "Here she can't teach formally because she doesn't have a degree, but she is overseeing our program, and obviously the results speak for themselves."

"Are you going to finish your degree?" Sung asked her.

"Yes, I think I will."

"Won't you be too old for college?" Sung asked. His mother seemed chagrined, but Mido laughed.

"Yes, I will be older, but that's okay. I might even go after I have a child."

"Nice," Sung said, nodding. "Will you teach here? After you get your degree?"

"I don't know," Mido said, telling him the truth. It felt as if no one else were in the room except for the two of them. "I can do things out of order. And it's okay."

"What will you do then?" he asked.

"I'd probably do something like this but at a high school. Maybe become a guidance counselor, which I can't do now because I don't have the degrees. I guess I've been preparing."

The mother turned to her son. "Sung-joon-ah, can you wait in the lobby?" She pointed to the bench opposite the reception area.

The boy got up and bowed to Mido, then Peter, and left the room.

"He's a great kid," Peter said. "As Mido explained, we're sorry that we cannot work with him. I'm sure that this is our loss and not his. It just wouldn't be fair to make an exception."

Professor Kim said nothing, but it was clear that he was thinking; they could see an argument brewing. Then he said, raising his voice slightly, "How can you work here without a proper university degree? There are many university graduates with advanced degrees who worked hard to earn them who could do your job. It's unfair for you to pretend to be qualified. Shocking, actually."

He was enraged that he had bothered to take valuable time off from his work. He glanced at her with suspicion, then as quickly turned from her.

His wife asked, "Can you wait outside, too?"

To Peter and Mido's surprise, the man obeyed. Without saying goodbye, he pushed open the glass door and left.

"I am sorry about my husband. He's under enormous pressure. Everyone cares about where Sung gets into school, and my husband is determined that he get into the very top schools on the first try. Our oldest went to Princeton for a year, then transferred to Harvard. My husband would not relent because she was as qualified as the other children in Seoul who had been admitted to Harvard. Then our middle child got into MIT, so our youngest needs to do just as well as his sisters. Everyone is expecting the most from Sung, and he is suffering, I think. I was so taken by the fact that he asked you questions. He never does that."

Peter crossed his arms. "I'm sorry that we do not have space for him."

Dr. Gu reached into her handbag and withdrew an envelope.

Right away, both of them shook their heads and waved their hands no.

"Peter, I know you don't need this, but perhaps your colleague here might. There's no shame in getting paid for hard work. This is the exact amount of the tuition, and it would only be for you. Of course, we would pay the hagwon tuition, too. If there were more lessons needed, then surely—" Dr. Gu continued.

"Enough," Peter said, holding up his hands. They had been speaking in Korean, but suddenly he said this last word in English. "Enough," he repeated angrily.

He turned to Mido as if he was embarrassed that these people were somehow connected to him.

"*Jeokdanghi,*" he said to the mother, in a kind of pleading voice. "Be moderate. Please. This is all too much. It must not matter to this extent."

Peter's face colored, and he took a deep breath.

"I don't mean to be rude, but your son has done more than enough. It's like a disease, I think. This constant battle between greedy ambition versus moderation. Your son is incredible in terms of what's he's already accomplished, but we've seen too many kids like Sung, who think they have to keep trying. Jeokdanghi," he said. "Be moderate. Please."

The mother slid the fat envelope toward them, but Mido picked it up and reached over the table to return it to the woman's purse. Dr. Gu took it out again and put it on the table, her hand covering it.

"Also," Peter added, "Sung's father can feel pressure, but it's not okay for him to be disrespectful to Mido. I think your family should go now. That envelope." He looked up. "We don't do that here."

"My husband—"

"Sung's father obviously cares about education and his children. However, we cannot accept another student. Any president of Korea could ask us, but we'd still say no," Peter said, as if to dare her.

Dr. Gu sat, unmoving. At home, she and her husband had agreed that it was her job to give them the envelope.

Peter exhaled in exasperation. "Dr. Gu, Sung might not get into all those schools. Not because he doesn't deserve it, but because sometimes, it's not supposed to happen, and maybe it's better for him to learn that like everyone else. There is disappointment and sadness for even the hardest-working students. Maybe he has to learn how to adapt to that. Perhaps adapting to that disappointment is the lesson your child needs," Peter said.

"It's easy to say these careless things when you don't have children." Dr. Gu finally rose from her seat.

"I meant what I said to your son. I'm sorry we didn't get a chance to work with him, but thank you for thinking of us," she said.

Using both hands, Mido bowed lightly and returned the envelope to the boy's mother.

17
Repechage

Mido had slipped out of the office to pick up a guitar. On her way back, only two blocks away from Fortress Seoul, she spotted the boy sitting outside a convenience store.

"I like that canned coffee, too," she said to Sung.

"Oh, hello." He bowed reflexively. "Do you play?" Sung pointed to the guitar case.

"No. It's not mine," she said. The boy didn't look sad as much as lost, and she felt bad for him. "May I sit down?"

Sung nodded. He had taken off his blazer and necktie and rolled up his white shirtsleeves.

"Where do you want to go to school?" she asked.

"Somewhere far away."

"Can you take some time off? I mean, after you get in?"

"No." He smiled. "Nice idea, though. My sister asked me that, too, but, well, our father, you can just imagine."

Mido smiled. "He means well, I guess."

"Yes, they always do. They're not bad people." The boy sighed.

"You're very mature," she said.

"I have to be." He sipped his black coffee. "They tried to give you money, right?"

Mido didn't answer, and she stood up. "I'd better go. I just wanted to see if you're okay. You don't need the counseling. I just wanted to tell you that I read your file carefully, and you're really impressive. Whatever happens—"

"Please don't tell me that it doesn't matter where I go. That what matters is what I do there."

Mido frowned.

"Because it does matter," Sung insisted. "It matters to a lot of people."

Mido wondered if Peter, Lion, and she would ever change anyone's mind. "Many successful people in the world don't go to SNU or Harvard."

"Not so in Korea," he said. "Even I don't get many chances, and I have rich parents with connections. It's tough here even for people like me. Imagine how terrible it must be for people who don't have what I have. My friend Unji's mother is a hundred times worse than my father."

"Why?"

"Unji's family lost everything during IMF, her parents got divorced, and now she lives with her mother and grandparents, who pay for her school. If she doesn't get into an Ivy, I don't even know what will happen to her. I wish you could have taken her."

"Did she apply? To Fortress?"

"Of course. Didn't even make it as a finalist. But she wrote me a note on the day of the drawing to wish me luck." He shrugged. "Oh well. Life is full of disappointments, right? Ha ha. I'm learning how to adapt to them."

Mido felt awful.

"You know that your parents can't hire me because I don't have a degree."

"I know. My father is still angry about the meeting. He called you a fraud." Sung laughed.

"If you want, come by next Friday afternoon, and bring your friend Unji. I'll give you some guidance on your applications and make suggestions for the personal statements. I won't take a fee. I can't. Only for the afternoon, though, and you can't tell anyone. No one. Maybe three or four hours. Okay?" She handed him her card.

"Seriously?"

Mido placed her pointer finger across her lips so he'd understand it was a secret. She picked up the guitar case.

❧

Except for the light in Peter's office, the hagwon was dark when she returned. The counselors were gone for the night, and she tucked away the guitar case in the hall closet. She knocked on Peter's office door.

"I offered to help that kid Sung and his friend."

"What? You can't do that."

"I'm volunteering. Only the personal statements and some pointers for their applications. One afternoon. I'm not going to get paid. Fire me."

Peter looked at her sternly. "You softy."

"You're a weirdo," she said.

"You're a creep," he answered, laughing. Whenever they felt foolish about something, they broke up the lines from the Radiohead song. Sometimes he was the creep, and she was the weirdo.

"Can I ask you something? You won't get mad at me?" she said.

"Never."

"Why don't you play anymore?"

He took his time before answering.

"I think it's because I'm here. In Seoul, I feel like I have to be serious."

"But you like to play music. I think you need to. You're kind of crabby when you don't play."

"Crabby? Seriously?" He laughed.

"Hang on," she said, and walked briskly down the hall.

She returned with the guitar. "Here."

"What?" Peter's face broke into a grin. He cradled the guitar. "Hey, it's a Gibson ES-330! Is this from 1959?"

"That's what Mr. Gong, the store owner, said. I went to that big arcade in Jongno. Lion told me about it. He wants you to keep playing bass in the band, but you prefer to write music with a guitar, right? Mr. Gong said the Gibson's in great condition, and he put new strings on it. I bought the amp, too, but I couldn't carry all of it today. He said if you don't like it, I could get credit for something else."

"Why?" Peter looked up at her. "Why did you get this for me?"

"I miss hearing you sing and play. That's all."

"Is this like a wedding ring?" he asked.

"No." She laughed.

Peter looked disappointed, then brightened. He stared at the beautiful guitar and held it close to his chest.

"Hey, Peter, I think we should go back. We should hire more folks for here, but after this year. I want to go back to school."

"Yeah?" He waited for her to keep talking.

"If I go back now, I'll know better what I need to learn and for what reason. Before, when I was a first-year at uni, I was this blank slate. It was just expected that I go to college."

"That's true," Peter said, playing the first few bars of "Rosetta," a song he'd been working out for a long time.

"At Fortress, I've been teaching high school students how to take tests or how to fill out an application. The more I get to know these kids and parents, I feel like I'm getting to them too late. I made a bigger difference when I worked at Exodus and saw the little kids every day."

"What do you mean?"

"When I saw a kindergartner or third grader every day after school, I felt like I could see them becoming more confident and taught them to learn better. By the time we get these juniors and seniors, I feel like something is missing. I want to figure this out. There's more I need to learn. Do you know what I'm trying to say?"

"It's what Lion doesn't like about Fortress. The kids are stressed out, and the goals are wrong—they want to get in somewhere rather than get an education."

"Yes," Mido said. "And I want you to come back to California with me. I want to go home." Mido tried to read his expression. "You're not upset with me, right?"

"I've been waiting for you to say when."

❧

Mido called her father again to check in, but John didn't answer because he'd gone to Exodus to pick up Anna before heading home.

Seated in the carpeted waiting area, Anna was reading *The Silver Chair*, one of the old books she'd found in Mido's room. The third grader was no trouble at all. She dressed herself, did her homework, and never complained. At Exodus, Yun and Lion watched out for her. The child got on well with Bo and John. Gradually she appeared to be settling into her life in Cypress.

John didn't know how to tell her that she might be moving to New Jersey to live with Mary and Patrick. Bo thought that was the right decision, but he wondered if it might be wise to wait until the school year ended.

"Anna," John said, and the girl smiled.

"Hello, Uncle John," she said, calling him by the American name they'd agreed upon. Anna knew that John was her father's old friend. She knew no other relatives. She tucked in a piece of scrap paper as a placeholder and closed the book.

"Did you have a good day?" John took her by the hand.

In the car, Anna opened her book again.

"Uncle John," she called from the back seat, and he checked her reflection in the rearview mirror.

"Yes."

"Is it true that my mother is in jail?"

"Where did you hear that?"

"At the hagwon. Two girls told me. They go to our church. They said my mother stole money from the church and had a boyfriend. Is that why my father got drunk?"

John didn't answer her, and Anna looked out the car window.

The distance between Exodus and their house was less than five blocks. He parked the car, and when Anna came out of the car, he locked it.

"On Sunday, Bo bought us ice cream sandwiches. They were on sale, apparently. My daughter loved those when she was your age."

"I like them, too," Anna said. "I finished my homework already. At Exodus. May I read my book?"

"Don't you want any more dinner?" he asked.

"It was Bobby Kim's birthday, and his mother brought ten pizza pies for everyone. I had two slices," she said, then frowned, worried he might be upset with her. Danbi never allowed her to eat that much pizza.

"Do you want an ice cream?"

"Yes, please." Anna sat at the kitchen table with her book to read while she ate her dessert.

John pulled out some frozen dumplings and put them in the microwave to heat. Even after she finished her ice cream sandwich, Anna remained at the table reading while he ate his dinner. When he finished, he washed the dishes. Anna didn't budge from her seat.

"Bo will be home on Friday," John said. His son was able to get her to talk more, and he wondered if Anna would ask Bo about her mother being in jail. "Bo will be here before dinnertime."

Anna looked up from her book and smiled at the thought of Bo, who was always kind to her.

"I wish you could meet Mido and DH, too," John said. "You'd like them. DH is good at making jokes, and Mido is like you. Very thoughtful and gentle." He wanted to tell her about Helen—how lovely and wise she was—but couldn't imagine saying the words out loud, and he remembered that this child had lost a father so young.

"When Mido returns from Korea, will I have to move out of her room?" Anna asked.

John could see the fear in her deep-brown eyes.

"Do you like her room?"

She nodded solemnly.

"But I wouldn't want to bother her. It is her room."

John paused.

"Mido isn't like that. She wouldn't want you to give up the room." He couldn't bring himself to tell her about New Jersey.

Anna didn't return to her book but looked across the kitchen table, her eyes crinkled with worry.

"Do you like it here?" John asked her.

Anna turned to him and smiled. She nodded again.

"I would like to wait for my mother here. If that is okay with you and your family."

John looked at the child who sounded so grown-up.

"Yes, you can stay. As long as you like. We have many rooms."

"Do you think they'll like me?" The small round face looked anxious again.

"Mido and DH?" he asked.

"Yes," Anna said.

"Of course. How could they not?" John patted her back, wanting to comfort her.

Her eyes shining with relief, Anna returned to her reading, her mouth pursed in concentration.

At the table, John poured her a glass of water and placed it near her, and Anna drank it. Without a word, he picked up the stack of mail he'd brought in earlier and took out his newspapers. From the freezer, he got an ice cream for himself.

John sat beside his child and unfolded the newspaper.

Acknowledgments

This book took almost a decade to write and publish, so there are many people to acknowledge.

I want to thank my dear editor Reagan Arthur for her exquisite care and stewardship. I am indebted to my friend Ben Sevier for his steadiness and wisdom. I am thankful to the following members of my American publishing family: David Shelley, Cordelia Calvert, Emily Chen, Matthew Ballast, Beth de Guzman, Dana Li, Albert Tang, Taylor Navis, Mari C. Okuda, S. B. Kleinman, Rick Ball, Emily Baker, Jennifer Tordy, Elana Walters, Quinne Rogers, Allison Schuster, Maris Tasaka, Lauren Monaco, Laura Essex, Caroline Barbee, Melanie Schmidt, Mary Beth Thomas, Nicky Devaney, Constance Edmonds, Lara Ziccardi, Kitanna Hiromasa, Alexis Gilbert, Tricia Tamburr, and Jonathan Valuckas. I want to thank Michael Taeckens for his invaluable counsel and Electra Colevas for her gracious support.

I am grateful for my UK publishing family. I would like to express my profound admiration for my editor Kishani Widyaratna for her kindness and intelligence. I want to thank the following members of 4th Estate: David Roth-Ey, Patrick Hargadon, Liv Marsden, Aoife Inman, Essie Cousins, Paul Erdpresser, Isobel Gavaghan, Olivia Gaylor, Alex Gingell, Becca Heselton, Natasha Lanigan, Sarah Lewis, Molly Lo Re, Annie McCloskey, Jacqui Seagrove, and Ellen Woodley.

I count myself blessed to be represented by the incomparable Peter Straus and his colleagues at RCW: Nelka Bell, Sam Coates, Aanya Dave, David Dunn, Stephen Edwards, Sampurna Ganguly, Laurence Laluyaux, Lulu Rehman, Katharina Volckmer, and Emer Walsh.

I am grateful to Carolyn Conrad, Liza Montesano, Jeannie Suk Gersen, and Jacob Gersen for their brilliant counsel and friendship.

In the past ten years, I've had the great fortune of meeting the following young people who have served as my instructors as I learned how to write this book: I would like to thank Natalie Choo, Momo Takahashi, Edward

Kim, Sofia Patino-Duque, Emily Kim, Irene Kim, Eun Soo Lee, Gayoung Choi, Willa Cuthrell-Tuttleman, and Katherine Franco. Also, my thanks to Chloe Rhee, Kat Kim, Victoria M. J. Kim, and Benjamin Keyworth. Thank you for answering my queries, replying to my detailed emails and numerous texts, and guiding me through parts of Seoul, Orange County, London, and Sydney. Above all, thank you for your wit, insight, humor, and smart questions. You have inspired me at every step. I wanted this book to be worthy of all the lessons you have taught me.

To write this novel, I tried to understand the workings of the education systems of specific regions in the United States, Australia, England, Brazil, Canada, and South Korea as well as the culture, trade, jobs, commerce, insurance and real estate businesses, industries, manufacturing, neighborhoods, politics, economics, religion, class structure, music business, linguistic patterns, laws, and the lives of the diasporic people living in these countries. I had so many questions. There was so much I did not know. Beyond the critical scholarship and published writings, verification of details and practices required numerous interviews, meetings, and site visits. There were times I did not know how to keep going because each path forked to another road, a dark alley, and sometimes a narrower street. Along the journey, gracious folks, many of them strangers, kindly lit the way, gave me hope, and nourished me. I want to thank you.

Each of the following people gave generously of their hard-earned insights, valuable time, and unique points of view. They answered my questions patiently. I am indebted to the following individuals who have supported the research of this novel: Iris Ahn, Isaac Ahn, Eun Se Baik, Sharon Bromberg-Lim, Patrick Bubul, Allison Burroughs, Sean Y. Chae, David Chang, Judy Chang, Sophia Chang, Alex Chen, Arjun Chhabra, Hannah Pham Chieng, Jaeki Cho, Seungyeon Cho, Christina Choi, Ja Myung Choi, JungYoon Choi, Victoria Chon, Jane Chun, Elliot Chung, Lee Isaac Chung, Erin Davidge, Sean Deetlef, Vicky Deetlef, Christopher Faicco, Christopher Gaillard, Imogen Gardam, Elizabeth Gillies, Ilan Graf, Omar Gudino, Shinhee Han, Hrishikesh Hirway, Eve Cho Guillergan, Blake Hanley, Jonathan Hannah, Eleanor Hyun, Michelle Hung, James Hwang, Mihoko Iida, Diana Jang, Glory Jeon, Jiyun Jeon, Angie Jo, Kayla A. Jo, Nicole Kagan, Gene Kang, Hanseul Kang, Angel Kelly, Bobby Kim, David Kim, Elaine Kim, Eunice Kim, Eun Jung Kim, Hyunmie Amy Kim, Hyunsoo Kim, Jim Kim, Michael Kim, Miri Kim, Seongwon Kim, Simon Kim,

Tae Hoon Kim, Victoria J. Kim, Helen Kimm, Sean King, Jayne Kiwas, Anna Lau, Benjamin Law, B. K. Lee, C. J. Lee, David Lee, Hali Lee, Jay Lee, Jihan Lee, Marian Lee, Michelle Y. H. Lee, Lisa Lee, Paul Lee, Soeun Lee, Steve Lee, Wilson Lee, Beatrice Leung, Jesse Liebman, Zoe Le Marinel, Eric Lopez, Zoe Norton Lodge, Stephen MacArthur, Michael McCarthy, Michaela McGuire, Adam Mortara, Doyoung Na, Jane Oak, Asha Pai-Sethi, Kyoung Soo Paik, Erin Pak, Jennifer and Cliff Park, Ellia and JP Park, Jae Park, Jeannie Park, Jin Park, Jonghwan Park, Nathan Park, Patricia Park, Sunny Park, Susan Park, Tai Park, Steven Pollack, Michelle Rabsch, Richard Rhee, Wha Ja Rhee, Kirby Rock, Patti Saris, Jasper Schoff, Bom Shin, Jessica Shin, Susan Shin, Bruce Smith, Seungwon Sohn, Yeyoung Sohn, John Song, Leo Sorokin, Indira Talwani, Wengie, Dominic Wilcox, Howard Wise, Sam Wolfe, Jasmond Wong, Joyce Yang, Hyun He Yoo, Jess Yoo, HeeJung Yoon, and Kyung Yoon. There are others who are not listed here by their choice or by my error; I thank them profoundly for their contribution. I relied on scholarship, field research, and interviews; however, any errors of fact are my own.

I want to acknowledge the following individuals who participated in the Korean education diaspora interview project supported by the Radcliffe Institute for Advanced Study at Harvard University: Dyanne Ahn, Lina Bae, Sumin Chae, Sarah Chang, Chris Cheon, Milly Chi, Ashley Cho, Hyunoh Cho, Youngsun Cho, Albert Choi, Yoomin Choi, Michael Dejhtyar, Alex Gao, Senjuti Gayen, Hillary Hao, Timothy Im, Jason Huiheun Jung, EJ Kim, Geena Kim, Hyowon Kim, Jean Kim, Myeong Seo Kim, Sungho Kim, Vivekae Kim, Yejin Kim, Yelim Kim, Jaehui Ko, Brianni Jeemin Lee, Eileen Lee, Haein Lee, Isabel Seoyon Lee, Joseph Lee, Kangsan Lee, Suyeon Lee, Zion Lee, Michael Li, Susan Lin, Jessy Mei, Allison Park, Dennis Park, Helen Park, Sean Park, Seoyoon Park, Claire Spackman, Maria Tîrnovanu, Seungwook Won, Erika Yi.

When I could not get a teaching job or fathom the depth of research and writing required for this novel, I applied for two fellowships and miraculously received them in the same year. I am grateful to the Guggenheim Foundation and the Radcliffe Institute for Advanced Study at Harvard University for providing needed research funds for translators, books, site visits, and time. I could not have written this book without their significant support.

I could not have continued writing without the following people. I want to express my gratitude and admiration for Dionne Bennett, Elizabeth

Cuthrell, Robin Marantz Henig, Deva Hirsch, Bob Ouimette, Roxanne Fraser, Danny Hegglin, Genevieve Ko, Miwa Messer, Sunny Park, Erica Wagner, Miri Kim, Don and Patty Liu, Susan and Rob Shin, Miky Lee, Lois Perelson-Gross, Stewart Gross, Soo Mi Park, Richard Rhee, Ben Cosgrove, Myung Lee, Chris Mansfield, Sang Lee, Shelly Fisher Fishkin, Mina Kimes, Lisa Joy, Katie Phang, Juju Chang, Michael Luo, Donna and Neil Wilcox, Steven Barclay, Eliza Fischer, Tomiko Brown Nagin, Greg Harmon, Marc Nissen, Arthur Magun, Charis Meng, Shuk Shan Lee, Shawna Roachford, and Tanya Gross. Thank you for your work and friendship.

During the writing of this book, Kitty Burke, Yun Won Cho, Michael S. Kelly, Kashka Kubzdela, Leslie Larson, Gwen Robinson, Tatiana Schlossberg, and Billy Steinberg passed away. I will remember you.

All my love for Umma, Appa, Chris, and Sam: Thank you for your shining faith, courage, and love. Thank you for being my family. You inspire me.

M.J.L.